THE WAYFARERS

BY

STUART TOWER

The Lighthouse Press, Inc.
Deerfield Beach, Florida

The Lighthouse Press, Inc.
P.O. Box 910
Deerfield Beach, FL 33443
www.TheLighthousePress.com

The Wayfarers

Copyright © 2003 by Stuart Tower
www.TheWayfarersNovel.com
Cover Design by Jamon Walker of mythicstudio.com

This book may not be reproduced or distributed, in whole or in part, in
in print or by any other means without the written permission of the
author.

ISBN: 1-932211-02-0

This novel is a work of fiction. Any resemblance to actual events, locales,
companies, or persons living or dead is entirely coincidental. There are,
however, several factual events and historic figures featured throughout
the story. These are noted in the Chapter Notes found in the Appendix.

Library of Congress Cataloging-in-Publication data is available.

AUTHOR'S FOREWORD

There are compelling sagas that for one reason or another never see the light of day or the printed page. Others finally reach the telling stage but are subjugated to a paragraph where there should be chapter, or a chapter where there should be at the very least, a novel.

Doing the initial research for a history program I was in the process of designing I came across an old friend...the engaging, finely crafted book by Irving Howe, *World of Our Fathers*, which I had avidly read twenty-five years back. Rereading its pages I could only find a short, but comprehensive, reference to the elusive subject of my search... the story of Romania's Fusgeyers...the courageous, organized groups of determined men and women who went by foot across a hostile Europe, flying a decidedly unpopular Star of David flag, en route to America during the first decade of the 20th century. Indeed, theirs was a gallantly demonstrative march to freedom, boldly protesting the relentless government-sponsored trade boycotts which had caused abject impoverishment among whole segments of the downtrodden, disenfranchised population, and drawing world attention to the ubiquitous pogroms that had spilled over from Czarist Russia. Above all else, the endemically terminal hopelessness spoke volumes of their quest for a better tomorrow as part of a numerically far greater flight of emigrants from the vast eastern regions of the continent.

Having previously discovered a few oblique mentions of these Fusgeyers while making several visits to that shrouded corner of Eastern Europe during the height of the provocative, so-called "Cold War" and its aptly named "Iron Curtain", I must admit that the story grabbed hold of me and wouldn't let go. When I eventually conducted some slightly deeper archival research, it was as if the souls of these vociferously spirited protesters were imploring me to tell their story.

With such scant bibliographic choices available, I decided early on to write a fictionalized version of the Fusgeyer *raison d'etre*. To do so, I have objectively and liberally incorporated the history, geography, actual events and factual characters of the times. I can only hope that a century later I have succeeded in doing the Fusgeyers proud.

I humbly and respectfully present to you...

The Wayfarers.

Stuart Tower
Los Angeles,
California
2003

TABLE OF CONTENTS

Pre-Publication Comments
for
The Wayfarers

*In today's electronic society, plain old-fashioned, capti-
vating story-telling is rare. In The Wayfarers, Stuart Tower
has done just that!*

Steven Spielberg, Filmmaker

*I've been fascinated by ancestor emigration stories that
blend history with fiction since my days of study in the
Iowa Writers' Workshop. In The Wayfarers, his third title,
Stuart Tower has written his best-to-date! This historically-
accurate, emotionally heart-wrenching story tempers pathos
with humor. It gets you page-turning at once, keeps you
doing so till the last!*

Robert Stein, Colonel,USAF(Ret.),
Author of the best-selling *Black Samaritan*
and *Vengeance Equation*

*In the Wayfarers, Stuart Tower gives a fascinating
insight into the lives of men and women who made a remarkable journey. Their experiences, and the obstacles
they overcome, are instructive for every generation and
their heroism particularly resonates in our age.*

Rabbi David Baron
Author of *Moses on Management*

*Stuart Tower's The Wayfarers, transports us on an
incredible journey of the human spirit that transcends race,
religion and geography. Tower's genius is our passport to a
unique, transforming literary experience.*

Dr. Eli Schochet, Professor,
University of Judaism, Los Angeles, CA
Past-President, Rabbinical
Assembly of America, Western States
Region

The Holocaust haunts memory. How it does so can change the world. These themes have found eloquent expression in Stu Tower's poetic writing. Now, giving voice to poignant echoes of the even more distant past, The Wayfarers provides insight that we ignore at our own peril.

Professor John K. Roth,
Pitzer Professor of Philosophy,
Chair, Department of
Philosophy and Religious
Studies, Claremont McKenna College

ৡৣৡ

AUTHOR INFORMATION

Stuart Tower is a writer, lecturer, educator and world traveler, residing in Southern California.

Stuart Tower's other publishing credits include:

Withered Roots, published by Isaac Nathan Publishing, Los Angeles, CA, 1994.
Hear O Israel, published by Paideia House Publishers, New York, NY, 1983.

Visit www.BN.com, www.Amazon.com and www.Abe.com - Keyword: Title or Stuart F. Tower, for comments and reviews of his previously published work.

THE WAYFARERS

BY

STUART TOWER

ৼৡৼ

Life is temporary....freedom is forever !

To those who have broken from tyranny,
marching to a better tomorrow,
since time began

Prologue

St. Petersburg, March 13, 1881

Signs of spring had arrived much earlier than Alexander could remember. Perhaps it was merely a slight lulling respite before the inevitable March storms crippled Mother Russia once again. The massive snowfalls of the previous months, hammered by ten consecutive days of severe rainfall, had been reduced to thousands of rivulets all around the sprawling city known as the Venice of the North. St. Petersburg appeared its most brilliant that afternoon, with a strong, broad ray of sunlight bouncing off St. Isaac's golden dome.

Alexander breathed in deeply and closed the window, wincing at the sharpness of the cold air. Despite the sunshine, there was more than a hint of winter-past and winter-future in that briefest of breaths. He had a full Sunday schedule ahead, beginning with a boring, obligatory review of the palace guard on the muddy parade grounds on the north side of the armory.

He wouldn't be bored for long. Following the review was an agenda item that Alexander had been eagerly looking forward to. He would be signing into law some partial reforms to the election process—an act that would have been unheard of during his late father's regime.

For the past thirty years Alexander had been initiating reforms to appease the proletariat, particularly regarding the free election of local officials.

This, he thought wishfully, *will silence those fanatical bastards. Maybe they'll even consider a moratorium on those horrible bombings they've perpetrated these last few stressful years.* Alexander knew all too well that he, indeed, was the prime target. The exceptionally bold palace dining room bombing just a year ago was a near miss for him, and had resulted in the deaths of eleven guests and servants. These "Will of the People" fanatics were everywhere one turned!

By noon the agenda was clear, and Alexander was feeling quite good about himself and the new reforms. Good enough to venture out, to take an afternoon ride into the heart of the city. "Will of the People," *narodnaya volya*, be damned!

The carriage, a steel-reinforced gift from Napoleon III, and four attendants were waiting by a side entrance as Alexander walked over to the head of the horse guards, Colonel Malenko. The ramrod-stiff officer snapped smartly to sitting attention in the saddle, his eyes straight ahead.

"Colonel, I would like to pass through Nevski Prospekt and circle round by way of Catherine's Embankment alongside the canal on today's outing. Many of our people will be out and about on a lovely day like this, after all that dreadful rain. I'd like them to know that their Guardian is alive and well and cares so deeply about their welfare."

"Yes, Sire, we shall do that, Sire!"

And with that, the Czar of all the Russias stepped briskly into his plush carriage as one of the attendants signaled the footman to proceed.

The Colonel barked out orders, keeping his frisky white steed in line. Six red-uniformed horse guards preceded the carriage. Even with the currents of unrest that permeated the capital these days, there didn't appear to be justification for a larger contingent, or even a rear guard, for that matter.

It was a decision that proved to be a disastrous error of omission of the highest magnitude.

The explosion was heard back in the palace, where a premonition-driven Princess Yurevskaya, Alexander's former mistress and controversial wife, ran out onto the parade grounds. Just then, one of the horse guards dispatched by Malenko arrived, and with one brief look at the grief covering the young man's face, she collapsed in a heap of satin, velvet, and crinoline.

Czar Alexander II, for all of his demonstrated democratic ideals, for all of his power to mollify the rabble-rousers, for all of his gestures of goodwill toward the downtrodden, the poor, the minorities, was careening toward his death—blown to proverbial smithereens. The tightly wrapped miniature sticks of dynamite, expertly compressed into a metal container, had been literally tossed between his legs by one of the terminally disenchanted.

Life in Mother Russia, the Pale of Settlement, and its surrounding nations would quickly become a long-playing drama of terror, unspeakable deeds, and genocidal massacre. On this bloody day the tenuous future of those who would bear the full wrath of vengeance was changed forever.

And so begins our story ...

The Jews? One-third will convert.
One-third will die of starvation and disease.
One-third will flee.

Konstantin Pobedonostsev,
Procurator of the Holy Synod,
Russian Orthodox Church,
(responding to the "Jewish question" posed by
Alexander III)

BOOK ONE

THE QUEST

1

QUINCY

1904

I like the dreams of the future better than the history of the past...
Thomas Jefferson

Sixteen kilometers. What they call, uh, ten miles? Is that so difficult? She wants me to wait until this after-noon for pre-arranged transportation, like some little old man? Just point the way, lady. I walked from Birlad to Bremerhaven. I can walk to, what is it— Kvinzee— in three hours, easy, if I don't lose my way...

Seventeen-year-old Sholem Leib Friedman, all that he owned in the large pack on his back, was thinking of his meeting with the woman from the Hebrew Immigrant Aid Society. He had met with her after passing the physical ex-amination and after the immigration officers allowed him to walk through the gates at East Boston's entry station.

The New York-based relief agency was cautious; they had just opened the new Boston HIAS office, and they did not want "their people" to end up homeless, hungry, or— worse—in jail. No! She had wanted to make certain that her latest charge would find the Grossman House on Washing-ton Street in Quincy and show up for work in the shipyard that following Monday.

Everything had been carefully arranged with the Fore River Ship and Engine Company to hire any HIAS-sponsored immigrants as long as there continued to be a need for laborers. This unwritten contract had been faithfully observed for more than two years now, and more than one hundred able-bodied Jewish newcomers from Russia, Romania, and Austria-Hungary now worked in the yard. Not one had been fired, and the foremen generally praised their work ethic. This paved the way for Sholem, Nuchim, the comedians, the four cantors, and those others who would follow.

Cousins who had come to Boston in 1901 met Itzy Gelman and Mayer Kelemer at the entry station, and they were spending the weekend with family. Boston relatives also welcomed Nuchim Krasnigor, Menachem Katz, Mayer Bernstein, Velvel Niedl and Yitzhok Myerz. Sholem expected that they would all join him at the Grossman House in Quincy, where he was heading, by Sunday evening.

This Thursday morning, September 9, 1904, was perhaps the saddest day of Sholem's young and eventful life. Saying his farewells to Mordecai, Sendehr, Mendel, Esther, Rivka, Zed-Zed, Simmy, and all of the others to whom he'd become so close over the past months, tugged relentlessly at his heart. They had been through so much, and for so long. The sadness had begun the last two days at sea, when they could feel the journey's end coming and nostalgia for adventures past set in during the conversations about the future. Of the fifty-five Fusgeyers on board, only the eight going to Quincy, and Yaakov Nachman and Heshy Rosen who were headed for Montreal, would not be going on to New York when the *Cincinnatus* once again set sail that evening.

Later in the day, Sholem's very best friend and point team comrade, Yaakov, would be on his way to Canada, where he and homesick Heshy both had family. After taking the little jitney boat from the entry station, Sholem had walked with them to the railroad depot near the Italian North End of Boston and shared a tear-filled goodbye with Yaakov, vowing that they would meet again someday.

Now, on the last and loneliest leg of his long, adventurous journey—Birlad to Bremerhaven to Boston to "Kvinzee" (Quincy), April 1, 1904, to September 9, 1904—the wiry lad pushed onward on a bright and sunny Indian Summer day.

This is an enormously ugly city, thought Sholem as he picked up his pace along a busy boulevard. *Nothing at all like the beauty of Budapest, or Vienna, Prague, Berlin ...* The worldly young man who had just been to these bastions of European culture and civic pride was disappointed by a city filled with eyesore tenements and clothes hanging out of every window. His first view of an American metropolis was certainly not an appealing one.

Ironically, just a few blocks to his right, was the magnificence of the patrician city: Beacon Hill, Commonwealth Avenue, the beautiful Commons and the Back Bay, a golden-domed State House. One of the world's great seats of learning, Harvard University, was across the pristine Charles River in Cambridge.

One day in the very near future, Sholem would see the Boston that had become, over the past hundred years, one of America's most classically European and cultured landmarks. But today, on his walk, he would first cross the teeming Italian North End, then skirt the rough-and-tumble streets of South Boston, home to thousands of Irish immigrant families, many in their second or third generation. The HIAS lady had warned him of the danger lurking in this area, which he pompously ignored. The few gangs of young people that he noticed hanging about the countless pubs didn't bother him; not after what he had been through. He and Yaakov, picked by the cadre to be the point team, always in the vanguard, had learned quickly the hard way that the best defense against trouble is always to walk forward in a determined stride with shoulders squared, head held high, and eyes straight on.

Sholem thought to himself, while he looked at the Irish-American teenagers lollygagging around on the filthy streets, about the long-served reconnaissance duty that he had shared with Yaakov on their journey across Europe, a duty that other Fusgeyers did not relish. Mendel Buchman, the teacher, had remarked, "No wonder they volunteer! They're the fastest walkers and the fastest runners. When in doubt, they'll walk, then they'll run, and we'll never see them again!" Mendel knew that this was not to be taken seriously. He had also observed that each of the Fusgeyers could take a joke as well as anyone.

By noon Sholem estimated that he had walked about halfway from the railroad station. That would make it eight kilometers, *or about five miles*, he remembered to practice the conversion, and he decided to eat the packet of food supplied by HIAS. He had earlier filled the canteen that had seen him all across Europe, and he hadn't touched a drop until now. He had two small tomatoes, a cold potato, and a slab of meat between two heavy pieces of black rye. The HIAS lady had assured him that the food was kosher even before he had asked.

Their private rations onboard ship had outlasted the voyage to Boston, with enough left for the rest to take with them on the short sail to New York. The Fusgeyers were very proud that most of them had not broken the dietary laws, neither during the 2,500-kilometer trek, nor on board the *Cincinnatus*. Here in America, they would be on their own.

Approaching Quincy now, the scene unfolding for Sholem became increasingly more pleasant as it became more rural. The tenement structures gave way to small cottages, green lawns, flowers, stately elms, and an occasional very large, well-maintained house.

So this was Quincy! He had practiced the pronunciation since hearing it from the HIAS people: it was "Kwinzee," not "Kvinzee." The English that he had learned from Mendel would soon be put to good use. The HIAS staff had spoken only Yiddish to him, and he hadn't been able to talk to anyone since then. *How are you? I am plizzed to mit you. Denk you. My name is Sholem Friedman. Vere is di toilet? I am ongry. Plizz. I have come from Romania. How moch monyeh does dett cost? Vun, two, tree, four, fife, six, sayven, eight, nine, tzen, A, B, C, D, E, F, G.* He repeated the English to himself, harking back to those many nights by the campfire and onboard ship when Mendel had taught them as much English as they could absorb. Sholem and Maidele had become the most proficient, especially in pronouncing the difficult English words. Yiddish flowed, Romanian rolled, but English plodded as if on square wheels.

Sholem was impressed with the detailed directions handed to him by the HIAS lady. Once he had convinced her that he could walk to Quincy, she had spelled out in Yiddish and English on a yellow piece of paper exactly where he would see each landmark as he made his way. For example, he would pass by a tall building with an extended tower: *The Old Custom House ... check!* He would then pass along a paved street, one of the few signposted: *Atlantic Avenue ... check!* After about a mile, he would come to a building with a large sign announcing its presence: *American Sugar Refining Company... check!*

In Southie—the affectionate nickname for the Irish ghetto of South Boston—he would see a pub: *Runty O'Callahan's Bar... check!* After crossing a bridge over the Neponset River, there would be a church on his right with its name emblazoned on a sign: *Sacred Heart ... check!* Next he would come to the beginning of the historic city of Quincy and he would know this because he would see a blue and white arrow signpost: *Quincy* and *Hancock Street... check!* He would also pass a sign pointing to Newport Avenue, advertising *Bassett Machine Works, Automobile Repairers... check!*

Sholem knew the word "automobile" and had seen dozens of these strange machines in the larger European cities. But just on this short walk today he had counted more of them than he had ever seen in Budapest, Vienna, Prague, and Berlin combined! *This America will someday have more of these than horses*, he mused.

Now, walking along the electric-trolley tracks, Sholem had just four more checkpoints to cross. As he walked toward the center of the city, he would see the First Parish Church. The HIAS interviewer had proudly told him that two American presidents, both born in Quincy, were entombed with their wives in this church.

Across the way, there would be another sign: *Quincy. Population, 23,899. Founded, 1630.* At that point he was to turn to the left, passing the Thomas Crane Public Library, and follow unpaved Washington Street (past Elm, Lowe, and James Streets) until he saw *Grossman House* painted on a sign stuck into the lawn of a large, gray, three-story wooden structure at the corner of Stewart Street.

The informative HIAS interviewer had mentioned that Leib Grossman, who owned the house, was also an immigrant, from Russia, and he was a very successful peddler of a wide variety of merchandise. He had come to Quincy in the early 1880s and he and his large family lived in another part of town, having bought this house near the shipyard especially for the purpose of serving as the HIAS halfway house. The HIAS organization, she said, was most grateful for this magnanimous gesture.

This would be Sholem's home until he could settle into another. He was expected to leave as soon as he was able to pay for his own lodgings, to make room for the other newcomers who would be coming to work in the Quincy shipyard.

Reading the English words on the yellow sheet gave Sholem a gentle satisfaction. With each step the smile he wore became more prominent. He knew that his long, arduous yet exciting odyssey across the continent of Europe and across the breadth of the Atlantic Ocean was coming to an end, and he was now just a few kilometers from his new "home." A new adventure, perhaps ultimately even more exciting, was about to begin.

He was a thoroughly satisfied and very confident young man. Shaking his head as he walked on full of purpose now, Sholem realized that he was quite ready to forget the last six months: the preparations, the endless walking, the long ocean voyage. He only wanted to think about what

America had in store for him. Where would he end up? Who would he someday marry? Where would he live, how would he prosper, and where would he be when he finally sent for his family? Somewhat ruefully, he let himself think of his family and the life he had just left behind him. He missed his mother, his father, his brother, his sisters, his aunts, his uncles, cousins, grandparents, and Rabbi Nachman— he sorely missed them all. He missed the *shul* (synagogue), the town square, the smell of the open fields and forests, his many friends, and even his peasant neighbors. He missed Birlad. He missed Romania. He would never forget the impoverishment, the relentless government-sponsored anti-Semitism, the boycotts, the deadly pogrom mentality spilling over from Russia ...but still he missed Romania, he did.

However Sholem Friedman possessed an unusual quality. He had the mindset to make the most of what was to come, and the least of what had gone. For the rest of his long life he would always prefer to talk about tomorrow, the future, and rarely could he ever be coaxed to recall, to recount, to reminisce about yesterday. It was not for him to wallow in nostalgia. This was a unique trait, and Sholem Leib Friedman was, if nothing else at this moment, a unique human being.

Beside Atlantic waters, with their
waves of blue, stands historic, noble
Quincy, glorious to view.

Quincy Patriot Ledger, 1941

2

BEVERLY HILLS

2000

A man is a bundle of relations, a knot of roots,
whose flower and fruitage is the world ...
Ralph Waldo Emerson, Essay: First Series. *History* 1841

Nathan Friedman sat fidgeting in front of his computer screen.

I operated a successful business; I have built hundreds of buildings, including my own home. I supported my wife and children, gave them a comfortable life, and sent the kids to college. I did it all without a computer. I went sixty-eight years before my life gets fa-misht *with dot.com, AOL, Windows, machro, shmackro... What in the hell am I doing spending my evenings—for two years now— in front of this machine?*

He knew the answer to his question very well. He was on a quest to find out all he could about his late father's boyhood in Romania and susequent immigration to America nearly 100 years back, and nothing could have dragged him from the exploration of his roots.

Nathan had been immersed in research: genealogical and historical research. Maps, books, stories, referrals, bibliographies, photos, the whole *mishigus*. He had been a regu-

12

lar at Barnes & Noble and the public library for the past two years as well. His father, he believed, had trekked through Europe on the way to America, and Nathan was planning to follow his careful research back again, all the way to Romania. *Almost ready, almost ready!* he told himself now.

It had all begun eighteen years ago this month, on the fifth day of seven (*shiva*), Nathan had found himself alone on the patio after the *minyan* had left, having a one-way conversation with a forever-silent father.

Pop, I'm going to find your story. The story you would never tell me, or Mom, or Morris, or Ruth. What do you mean, you walked out of Romania? When did you walk out of Romania? Why did you walk out of Romania? Where did you go? And why the hell did you have to die on me, just when we had begun to talk with each other, not at each other!

"Nathan, you're still online? Do you realize it's after midnight?"

Rachel stood, hands on hips, in the arched doorway to the den—or, as Nathan now called it, The Computer Room. His wife was not really what one would think of as a menacing figure, and certainly anything but a nagging partner, contrary to her present posturing. If anything, nearly fifty years of an incredibly satisfying union had brought the Friedmans closer than ever.

At an elegantly young sixty-five, Rachel's dark hair had just begun to gray a bit. Time to consider the coloring processes, she had admitted to Annie last week. For the first five years of their marriage, she had worked side-by-side with her peripatetic builder-husband, putting her Berkeley education to use; organizing the crowded office space, working out schedules, doing the materials purchasing, the billing, the inventories. With a sly twinkle in her eyes, she would tell everyone that her degree in English Lit really had prepared her for these tasks. Then came baby Herbert, and she wouldn't return to her work until the parenting of all three children was in the waning stage.

By now Nathan had had enough of the screen. He logged

off gratefully and proclaimed, "Rachel, I think I finally have everything I need! I'm going to call tomorrow and order the tickets!"

"You're sure you want to go on this *mashiganah* mission? What if you run into nothing but dead ends?" Rachel asked.

Standing, stretching and walking over to embrace his wife, Nathan answered her question with one of his own. "Why can't I talk you into coming along? You'll love it, hon. It'll be worth it just to see Birlad, the countryside...to see Romania!"

"You know I can't, with all that's going on—helping Annie, my sister's surgery ... but you know how relieved I am that you're going to ask Herb and Eric to go with you. Are you going to tell them soon?"

Nathan didn't need reminding. The following Sunday, the time came for Nathan to ask his son and grandson to accompany him.

Nathan and Rachel asked Herb, Lisa, and the children over for brunch. Somewhere between Rachel's famous omelets and the decaf, after being silent much of the meal or exchanging mere pleasantries, Herb spoke up. "Dad, you must finally be getting used to retirement. You only popped into the office once last week. That's a record so far!"

"You must miss me terribly," replied Nathan with a mocking grin.

"No," Herb said, grinning back at his father, "but Marty does. He used to be able to beat you in an argument once in a while, you know. Not that I'm calling you a pushover or anything, but he doesn't win too many of them with me. Sally and Fawn miss you, too, Dad. Thanks to Mom's help, Sally has the files in great shape. And Fawn still charms the socks off everyone."

Herb stopped, not knowing what else to say, and seeing that his father, though amused, was not going to ask him anything about the family business he had left behind him. Lisa, his "best daughter-in-law" (as he never tired of saying to anyone who would listen), saved Nathan from a response. "So, Nathan, Rachel has been keeping me up on your big project. Are you really going to Romania this year?"

"Sooner than you think. In fact, next month, after school is out."

"What does school have to do with it?"

It was time, Nathan thought, and he leaned over to the buffet, picked up an envelope waved it around at everyone, and stood up to make his announcement "In this envelope are three plane tickets to Romania...I'm going to borrow your two men to ride shotgun with me, Lisa!"

"What are you talking about, Dad?"

"Herb, I'm asking you two guys to come with me! To Romania! To Birlad!"

"Are you kidding me, Grandpa?" The tall, dark, and gangly sixteen-year-old Eric—affectionately known, only to Nathan, as "Rico"—stopped in the midst of cutting himself yet another slab of Miss Grace's Luscious Lemon Cake, while Herb could only stammer, "What? When? I can't!"

"Yes you can. I need you guys, Herb. Look at the tickets. We leave the day school is out, and we'll be back ten days later."

"Eric, you can't go—you're supposed to be a counselor at my tennis camp this summer!" pouted twelve-year-old Cayla.

"No problem, Cayla, my sweet. He'll be back the week before camp begins," Nathan assured his granddaughter.

"Dad, you're really determined to solve the riddles your father left, aren't you? When we first talked about this, what was it, two years ago, I didn't dream it would become such a ... well, such an obsession with you. Mom tells me you're glued to the computer these days."

"I've done all I can as far as research will take it. Now we've got to go to the source—to Birlad. Trust me, Herb. It'll be a great experience!

"Don't be like me, son. If it weren't for Mom, I would never have left the business, even for a short trip or two. She's the one who's made me break away, and often, as you know. Being away, with all those trips, going all over the world....

"Believe me, Herbert, the business didn't lose a contract, not one." Nathan leaned forward. "Marty's been a very solid associate for over thirty years. Rely on him more and more, Herb. He can do it. He never once failed me."

Pushing his dessert aside, Nathan beckoned his potential travel companions to follow him into his den to look at the results of all his work. For Rico to follow Nathan knew he would have to bypass the family room and an NBA playoff game—the Lakers were fighting to stay alive against the Miami Heat. The kid was a reserve swingman on the BHHS hoop squad. Yet Nathan hoped that the idea of spending ten days in far-off Romania would intrigue Rico enough to walk right on by the game. He did.

"Mom told me about your research, Grandpa. I think that's cool. Do you really think you can find the answers you're looking for?"

"I certainly hope so."

"How?"

"How what?"

"How are you going to find out about Grandpa Sholem's immigration to America?"

"Eric," Herb warned, "I'm sure Grandpa will have a chance to answer all of your questions, assuming we go with him—"

"Herb, he wants an answer now. It's okay. Rico, the red file over there," Nathan pointed to a stack of color-coded files next to his printer, "is for the geography of Eastern Romania. It's all there: physical and topographical maps, Michelin highway maps...the people at the map store know me by name now!"

He went on after letting his grandson paw through the maps, devouring what he saw there. "Anyway, that blue file there behind the red one has all of the immigration details I could find. See, here's the ship's manifest out of Bremerhaven, Germany. 'The Lloyd Line ship, S.S. *Cincinnatus*, on August 15, 1904, arriving in East Boston, on September 8th.' Grandpa Sholem's name is clearly inscribed there, too." The three generations of Friedmans bent together to study the copy of the old document, and read the details of their elder Friedman.

> Sholem Friedman, age 17.
> Hometown: Birlad, Romania.
> Hebrew nationality.
> The equivalent of $25 in German
> money on his person.

"Why did they list him as having Hebrew nationality? Why not Jewish?" Herb asked.

"In Romania, according to Abram Sachar's *History of the Jews* and also Irving Howe's *World of Our Fathers*, and in many other references, the government of the time refused to recognize its Jews as citizens, nor did they accept 'Jewish' as a nationality. Only 'Hebrew' was acceptable. The czar's government in Russia treated its Jews as nonentities, too. Jewish life all over Eastern Europe at the turn of the century, boys," Nathan explained, "was full of impoverishment, treachery, starvation, and death and destruction.

"That's precisely why Grandpa Sholem and so many millions left for the promise of a better life in the West... England, Canada, America, even France and Germany, Australia, South Africa. Those who were influenced by the new Zionist movement ended up in Palestine, a God-forsaken place with mosquito-infested swamps and hostile neighbors who violently objected to a Jewish presence."

"Hostile neighbors? So what else is new, Dad?"

"Right. Things don't change much in a hundred years, Herb. Now Rico, take a look at this yellow file. Not much in it yet. It represents what I've been able to find about Jewish life in today's Romania. The people at 6505 Wilshire, that's our Jewish Federation Council, steered me to a list of the towns and cities where there's an official Jewish community. See here— Birlad. Fewer than forty families left, but here's the most important thing. The rabbi is still there, even though most of his congregants emigrated to Israel and America after the country's Chief Rabbi, Moshe Rosen, passed on two years ago."

He took a deep breath. "From these statistics, it seems there are fewer than 15,000 Jews in all of Romania, half the number there were even during Ceausescu's violent regime." Herb raised his eyebrows. Nathan continued, "But according to my information, the rabbi's in his late eighties, maybe ninety, and he succeeded his father who had to have been the main Birlader Rabbi when Grandpa Sholem was about to leave town in 1904. That's the answer I'm hoping for—that's *got* to be it.

"Rabbi Yossi Nachman is the only link with the past. Imagine it, guys! My father just may have walked all the way across the continent—1000, 1200, 1500 miles—to Bremerhaven, for God's sake! Nachman has got to know the answers. The how, the why, the when ... His father must have known, and he had to have passed it on."

"What makes you so sure, Dad? Maybe Nachman's father was the silent type! Grandpa Sholem sure was."

"Good question, Herb. Judaic history is bound by both written and oral tradition, and the keepers have typically been the teachers, the rabbis, the students, the Talmudists, and the historians. Grandpa Sholem was none of these. Most of the men of that era would not fit into any of those categories. But the elder Birlader Rabbi, let's hope and pray, was a teacher, a talker. My idea that he told his son this history, even if my own father never told me about it.

"This is the idea that has kept me moving toward the decision to travel to Birlad, to his roots, to *my* roots, yes, and to your roots, too. From Birlad to Beverly Hills in two generations! By way of Quincy, of course!"

"Makes sense to me, Dad."

Eric nodded in agreement. "Yeah. But how can you discuss anything with Rabbi Nachman in Romanian, Grandpa? Does he speak English?"

"I don't know, but Yiddish is very much alive and well in Romania. My Yiddish is rusty, but I'll get by. After a few hours with Nachman, I'll be okay, I'm sure!"

For the next hour, Nathan answered question after question: *Where will we be staying? What's the food like? Are we going to rent a car? How long a flight is it? Should we learn some Romanian phrases? Do we need shots? Do they like Americans, or do they hate us? What is Bucharest like? Is there a place to stay in Birlad? How far is it from Bucharest, Grandpa? Have you made any reservations, Dad? Can I wear jeans, Grandpa? Tee shirts? Do I need a tie, a suit? Let's look at the map again. I want to get really familiar with it!*

Nathan was exhausted, but enjoyed every minute of it, and was vastly relieved to see that Herb and Rico were interested; moreover, that they seemed already as hooked as he was! "Such enthusiasm!" he commented aloud. "Boy, did I pick the right team!"

Satisfied for now, Eric was the first to leave the room, making a beeline for the TV in the family room to catch the last quarter of the game.

Lisa came in to join Herb and Nathan to see how her father-in-law's recruiting session had gone, and Nathan could hear Cayla helping Grandma put the kitchen back in order.

On their nightly walk down Palm to Santa Monica Boulevard, along the park trail to Beverly Drive, it was Rachel who did most of the talking for a change. Nathan was enveloped in an aura of deep satisfaction. The afternoon kickoff session with his boys had gone well, far beyond his expectations. They were not only full of anticipation, they had also asked all the right questions, the questions he had hoped they would ask—intelligent, provocative, practical, and serious. And it had been such joy to have such a discussion with them at last!

For the first time Nathan truly felt that he would get to carry out his search mission. He was now about to go beyond the study, the research, the speculation, and into the great unknown. In three weeks, on June 6th, he and his boys would be flying toward Romania, back in time to 1904, back to their roots.

Nathan eschewed spending time at the computer during the weeks that followed. He spoke with Herb every day, sometimes two or three times. He visited the office once and spoke to Marty; his confidence factor seemed as strong as ever, thank God. Eric called every evening with cascades of questions, some Nathan answered, some rhetorical, and even a nonsensical one or two.

Nathan particularly enjoyed his phone call to the Chabad rabbi in Bucharest, Rabbi Chomsky, which had been suggested by Rabbi Cunin, Chabad's West Coast director. The friendly Chomsky promised he would contact Rabbi Nachman in Birlad and tell him of Nathan's forthcoming visit. Nathan had a phone number for Rabbi Nachman, and had tried on three occasions to reach him, but suffered severe static connections each time. *Third world?*

Getting visas at the Romanian consulate proved to be a frustrating experience. He took Herb and Eric's passports along with his own, and, after waiting in the cramped outer office at 11768 Wilshire for over an hour, he was ready to write a check for $105 to cover all three visa stamps and get out of there.

Wrong! The young clerk informed him that payment had to be made in cash. Nathan did not have enough cash to cover it, but he had noticed an ATM in the lobby and hurried to it. When he walked back up to the window to complete the transaction, the man at the counter told him he had to wait his turn all over again—behind the six people in line.

Forty minutes later, the same clerk, one Constantin Calescu, according to the brass name plate in front of him, asked how long the Friedman family expected to stay in Romania. Nathan responded, "ten days," and Romanian's answer was quick and brusque: "There is no need for visas for less than a one-month stay."

Without leaving America, Nathan was introduced to the anachronistic, socialistic bureaucracy known as Romania.

By Memorial Day weekend, Nathan could announce to Rachel that everything was done except the packing. Eric had decided that if he could spend two months in Israel the summer before with only a backpack, then he could easily do ten days in Romania with a slightly oversized daypack. Herb, on the other hand, was a notorious over-packer and had to be constantly pestered by his persuasive wife to cut back on everything so he could fit into one rollaway. *Three sports coats for Romania? Utterly absurd.*

* * *

When anticipating an adventurous journey, the departure date seems like it will never arrive, but it always does. On the sixth day of June, in the first year of the 21st century, Nathan Friedman, his son Herbert, and grandson Eric left California *en route* to their eventual destination—Birlad, in Eastern Romania.

3

ROMANIA

2000

Hullyvoood, Hullyvoood! Jeck Nikelsman! Tom Kroootz! L.A.
Leckers! Sheck Oneal! Koobey Brientz! CNN!
"Romanian Road Block Warrior"

The Romanian countryside is beautifully forested. The most charming, rustic-looking wooden cottages with brightly painted shutters dot the landscape, and even in June, wisps of white smoke waft upward from each chimney. Driving northeast on Highway E-85 from the center of Bucharest (Bucureshti), where the Friedmans had spent an uneventful jet-lagged night at a nondescript, but comfortable hotel on Calea Victoriei, the city's main avenue, the scene changed dramatically to a very rural one. Farmhouses, rolling, cultivated fields, livestock, tractors, aging trucks and busses, military vehicles, and the ubiquitous horse-drawn wagons began to appear everywhere just a few miles outside the city.

The Fiat Brava, an especially popular rental car throughout Europe, handled well as Herb drove on the undulating, unevenly paved highway, Eric sat navigating with map-on-knees, and a happy, tired Nathan smiled broadly in the back seat.

"*Oy! Romania, Romania, Romania, Romania*—" Nathan, without a warning to his heirs, chanted suddenly, and then hummed an accompanying melody. "Hell, I can't even remember any other words, except *Romania, Romania, Roma-*

nia, Romania. Pop and his cronies used to sing it at weddings, Bar Mitzvahs, and family gatherings. I wonder if anyone in Birlad still knows it?"

Looking at the passing scenes, especially the horse-and-wagon outfits, Herb said, "Can you believe it? We're in the twenty-first and they're still in the nineteenth!"

"Nineteenth what?"

"Century, Eric. The nineteenth century!"

"Oh! You got that right, Dad! I've noticed it, too."

The E-85 (a designated "European International Highway," which is supposed to raise the level of maintenance slightly above that of the pot-holed national roads), is one of the country's major north-south routes. "Just think of the San Diego Freeway—the '405'...no divider, two lanes, no shoulder, with cows crossing every few miles," quipped Nathan.

However inaccurate the portrayal of the road surfaces had been in them, the Friedmans were about to see that the guidebooks were right about one thing—the "RRBs,"the Romanian Road Blocks, were everywhere. And now, less than twenty miles out of the city, they approached their first military encounter. The deep green 1950s truck in the middle of the E-85 bore Romanian Army symbols and four soldiers—two straddled the center strip and two more lounged inside the vehicle. The "usual suspects" were queued up just ahead of the Fiat. Two civilian trucks of even earlier vintage, pre-dating three wheezing and snorting private heaps, waited for the innocuous interrogation to reach them. The southbound traffic, permitted to continue, slowly edged around the blockade.

The temperature had increased rather rapidly in the last hour, and Eric stripped to his Lakers T-shirt. Once the others moved forward and were dismissed on their way, two soldiers warily approached the Fiat. The pot-bellied one poked his hatless head through Herb's open window. Officers had made this same gesture at Nathan in Morocco, Turkey, and Chile and he had come to realize that it was merely a power game, one in many ways no different than those played every day in the high-rise office buildings along Wilshire and in Century City. Only the uniforms are different— olive drab replaced the slick Armani power suits. Eric and Herb, though, were a bit surprised to see the head pop suddenly through the window.

Resting his Kalashnikoff automatic rifle ominously on the doorframe, which turned Herb to pure alabaster, the chubby GI asked, *"Buna ziua, vorbesc Romaneshti?"*

Receiving only a puzzled look he said more sternly, *"Passaportul varog!"*

Catching the word "passport," Herb handed his over, and Eric and Nathan's followed. The soldier studied all three documents, and as he did so a horrible thought crossed Nathan's mind. *Please don't tell me we need VISAS! No way, Comrade! How did we breeze through passport control at the airport yesterday, otherwise? Is this going to be a diabolical game?*

Handing the passports to the other soldier, who looked old enough to be one of Nathan's tennis pals, the chubby one reached inside the car and took the keys from the ignition, saying. *"Scuzatsi ma!"*

Eric, remembering his words and phrases, translated "excuse me" under his breath for Herb and Nathan. Meanwhile, the corpulent one walked back to the trunk, unlocked and opened it, and once satisfied that there was no contraband or *Playboy* Magazines (highly coveted since Ceausescu's pseudo-Puritanical government had come into power) inside he came back to take the passports from his partner. Handing them back to Herb he said—with a smile— *"Americanets! Vorbitz engleza?"*

Realizing there didn't appear to be a problem, Herb breathed easier, smiling back as Eric proudly pointed to his Lakers shirt and blurted out, *"Da, da, Americans!"*

The younger road block "warrior," grinning broadly, shouted: *"Da, da, Bayberly Heels!"* pointing to Herb's passport. *"Hullyvoood, Hullyvoood! Jeck Nikelsman! Tom Kroootz! Leckers, Sheck Oneal, Koobey Brientz, Beel Clinton, CNN... Da! Da! Va multzumescfoarte mult! La revedere. La revedere*

Americanets!" And he gestured them on. Even his dour sidekick smiled as they passed by.

Nathan, Herb, and Eric, in the best of humor now with their relief, laughed at the scene, and waved a fond goodbye to the soldiers in the truck.

"Hey, Grandpa, I don't know about the nineteenth century—they knew Nicholson, Cruise, and hey, even Shaq! How do you figure?"

"Rico, me boy, even here in Romania Ted Turner's presence can be felt...CNN...the NBA...Hullyvooood! But you can expect a few more RRBs, according to the guidebooks. Hope Hullyvoood, Bayberly Heels, and the Leckers can breeze us through again!"

"But why these RRBs, Grandpa?"

"Well, we have to remember that this country has gone through some tough times. Nicolaei Ceausescu, who was overthrown and shot to death ten years ago, left the country in one of the worst states of impoverishment in its history—starvation in many regions, paralyzing paranoia... Now they've begun to experiment with a form of controlled socialism. They continue to suspect foreigners, particularly those from the West—and most especially Americans—of trying to plant the seeds for yet another revolution. Quite preposterous, in my opinion."

"I continue to be impressed with the enormous amount of research you've done, Dad."

" The Internet has been helpful, and the BH Library is very well stacked in its history section."

"Yay for the Internet! It sure does wonders for my term papers, Grandpa!"

"I swear, you kids don't know what the inside of a library is anymore. At the BH, all I see are adults. Say, Mr. Rand McNally, keep your father on the right road. I haven't seen a sign in miles."

"Okay—wait a minute...yeah, stay on E-85, which is also National #2.... Everyone, watch for signs that say Rimnicu Sarat or Focshani...Once we pass through Focshani, we'll be cutting off at Highway 24 to Tecuci...let's see...and that's only about fifty miles from Birlad. No, wait, thirty! I keep forgetting they use kilometers. Thanks for reminding me when we left Bucharest."

"Herb, watch the gas gauge. There's a shortage here. They've never recouped from the Arab embargo back in the '70s—Remember those gas lines? Yes well, keep it at no less than half a tank ... We've passed plenty of stations so far, but that's no guarantee that they have the product."

"Okay, Captain! I'm getting ready for some lunch. How about you guys?"

"Anytime, Dad. Maybe we can get some of those *savarinas* we had for dessert at the hotel last night. Wow, they were great!" Eric's eyes twinkled as he thought of the rum-soaked sweetcakes, a popular item on the menu of Romania's finest restaurants, as well as on the "iffy" street vendor's carts.

"I don't know if you two noticed, but we haven't passed anything that even remotely resembles a restaurant on the highway, and they seem to be well hidden in the towns. Not a Nate and Al's, or even a Taco Bell or a Denny's, that's for sure. I'd settle for one of Pink's Hot Dog's!" Nathan's smile convinced Eric that he was kidding. In all of his travels, Nathan had made it a point never to visit an American franchise establishment. Not even the reindeer burgers in Helsinki McDonalds, or the Kuala Lumpur KFC that offered satay of spicy something-or-other had enticed him.

"Looks like some signs ahead ... Slow a bit, Herb."

"Hey, Rimnicu Sarat, 10 kilometers...6 miles...Focshani, 50 kilometers...30 miles. Great! We can eat there. These are the first signs we've seen since the RRB. Jeez, they don't believe in letting you know where you are or where you're going in this country!"

"Part of the plan, Rico—they've got to keep you Bayberly-Heels-types in check. During my research, a young attorney friend who had come here to adopt a Romanian baby told me that every rental car is tracked throughout the country. He had learned this from a Marine sergeant at the U.S. Embassy in Bucharest.

"When we were stopped at that RRB, I'm sure they reported our license number to some central location. When we stop for lunch, someone at the restaurant will be doing his or her job by following us to wherever we park and reporting the license number in the same way. Whatever we find for a hotel tonight will do the same, and so on, and so on. A central computer receives input from gas stations, restaurants, lodgings, national parks, churches, and museums on the whereabouts of all rental cars. During Ceausescu's time, foreigners always received hotels' corner rooms, which were permanently bugged."

Eric was stunned. "This is right out of *X-Files* or James Bond. Do you think it really happens this way, Grandpa?"

Nathan answered him. "Xenophobia drives men to do strange things. Sometimes evil. Often despicable. Yes, even in our own country, Rico."

"Xenophobia?"

"The fear of foreigners, of anything strange or different. I told you that for most of the last 120 years, Romania has shut itself off from the Western world in varying degrees. Even our Jews here have this fear of strangers, Jewish or not. Gary Jacobs, the attorney I mentioned, said that when he and his wife decided to have lunch at the kosher dining hall in Bucharest, just to make contact with the Jewish community, the place was full of students, older people, a broad cross-section of the Jews of the city. For some reason, food was plentiful there, while elsewhere it was scarce.

"At any rate, everyone in the hall ignored them completely. They couldn't make eye contact with anyone, even the students in the crowd wouldn't meet their eyes. The *mashgiach*, the *kashruth* inspector who managed the establishment, responsible for strict adherence to the Biblical dietary laws, sat them in an isolated corner.

"In a friendly way the *mashgiach* explained in a mixture of Yiddish and severely broken English, 'Yinglish' we call it, that he seats all foreigners this way, Israelis and Americans, mostly. He said that he was merely respecting the fear that his locals felt toward them.

"Do you understand, Rico? Trepidation was part of their lives and the lives of the generations preceding them. Grandpa Sholem had a little of this left in him until the day he died, at ninety-three! May he rest in peace."

Nathan dabbed at his eyes, muttering something about the smog in Romania, before starting again. "Looks like we're coming into the big city of Focshani, boys. Follow all signs that say 'Centrum,' Herb. Might as well go into the center of town to park and find some food."

Focshani appeared to be quite compact and relatively clean. The traffic, particularly the horse-drawn wagons and black-smoke-spewing buses, was thick enough to indicate some activity. Indeed, it was market day, which was centered in the expansive town square. Rico spotted a diagonal parking space, and Herb quickly pulled into it.

As they wove their way through the colorful market stalls laden with fruits, vegetables, and items in jars, cans, baskets, boxes, and bags, Nathan thought that the old-style street market presented a glimpse of yesterday's Romania.

Herb used his pocketful of *lei* to buy some good-looking apples to keep in the car, Eric opted for purplish plums, and Nathan , being more practical and practiced, bagged a handful of figs. All for later. First, the travelers had to find some real food.

The ever-observant Eric walked ahead, drinking up the local color, and so he was the first to spot the inconspicuous *Restaurantul* sign down a narrow, cobbled street just off a corner of the square. A dilapidated, stand-alone wooden structure, with a cracked front window held together by some black tape, greeted the hungry travelers. Yet it appeared to be the most popular place in town; the market crowd filed in and out of the front door, which had last seen a fresh coat of paint in, perhaps the '70s, or '60s. Nathan speculated that maybe there wasn't any other choice. *Rachel would have settled for the fruit*, he thought with a warm grin.

Dressed in a skin-tight black skirt and red silk cleavage-baring blouse, a pretty hostess-waitress showed them to a table in the back of the smoke-filled room, and after bringing them three dog-eared menus, went off to greet some new arrivals.

"Things are sure looking better in Romania-Romania-Romania!" said Eric with a grin. "That is one hot gypsy mama!"

Looking through the thick menu, unable to translate anything, Nathan took a pocket language guide out of his jacket.

When Hot Gypsy Mama returned, smiling broadly, she surmised that there was a failure to communicate. "*Marea Britanie? Deutsche? Francia?*" she asked, trying to determine where they were from.

Eric, leaning closer to her confided, "*Americanets, USA, California, Hollywood...*"

"*Americanets! Da, da...nu vorbesc engleza! Vorbitzi romaneshte? Nu?*"

Seeing that this one-way conversation was going nowhere fast, Hot Gypsy Mama handed her pencil and a slip of paper to Eric, pointing to the menu, saying: "*Scrietzi, va rog! Indicatzi-mi-mi, va rog!*"

Nathan nodded his head to her, and said to the others, "I get it. Let's look over the menu and write down what we want. I'll look up the 'Ordering in a Restaurant' section of my handy-dandy little language guide."

Nathan almost immediately found something on the menu that also appeared in his guidebook: "*rasol Moldovenesc cu hrean*"—chicken in a sour cream and horseradish sauce. Rather than write it down, he got Herb and Eric to agree that they'd have the same, and he pointed to it on the menu. Hot Gypsy Mama vigorously shook her head sideways, saying "*Nu, nu!*" Nathan flipped the page, saw something else that matched his guidebook, and again she shook her head negatively. This time, she took his menu, pointed to one item on the fourth or fifth page and then to another on the last page, smiled, and said: "*Da, da*"

"Grandpa, is she saying they only have those two things, whatever they might be?"

"I'm afraid so, Rico. Once again, boys, welcome to the real world of Romania, Romania, Romania."

The Friedmans gave Hot Gypsy Mama the O.K. to bring *que sera, que sera,* and the language ordeal over, for now. A few minutes later, she came back with a steaming bowl of *mamaliga,* corn mush, which was the national dish, along with a surprisingly tasty chicken noodle casserole. But the best was yet to come. She brought three delicious-looking *savarinas* for dessert, along with some Turkish coffees. All agreed—not a bad lunch. No doubt, Focshani's best-kept secret!

The bill equaled a paltry six dollars in *lei,* and Nathan left an extra large tip, even knowing that tipping is not a common practice. As they left, Hot Gypsy Mama gave each of them a hearty hug, saying, *"La revedere, la revedere Americanets!"*

Herb drove off, heading north on the E-85, Eric watched for the National 24 cutoff toward Tecuci, and Nathan closed his eyes in the back seat, jet-lag taking over for a bit. He didn't sleep; doubts started coming forth.

What a crazy country this is! What in the world do I expect to find? Will the Birlader Rabbi know anything of value? Anything of interest to me? I hope Rabbi Chomsky contacted him. How the hell can we go back to 1904, nearly a century ago? What kind of a sentimental old fool am I? Why am I throwing away six, seven thousand dollars to drag my boys over here? For what? To indulge in my mashiganah *quest? Rachel has got to think I'm nuts. God, I miss her. She would have loved that restaurant scene...*

"Grandpa—there it is—the first Birlad sign. Ten kilometers. Just another six miles."

As they approached the outskirts along the Birlad River, running quite full even in June, Nathan's doubts dissipated."Oh, my God! Can you believe it! Here he lived, here he went to *cheder,* here he went to *shul,* here he played, and romped, and sang, and laughed, and cried—can you believe it? I can't believe it. Oh, my God, my God ... I'm here, Pop! Yes, we're all here, Pop! In Romania! In Birlad!"

4

BIRLAD

2000

*My grandfather, a fabulous storyteller, knew how to captivate
an audience. He would say: "Listen attentively, and above all,
remember that true tales are meant to be transmitted—to keep
them to oneself is to betray them."*
Elie Wiesel, *Souls on Fire*

The seventy-year-old-man with the soul and spring to
his step of a thirty-year-old, who had been humming and
singing and joking since leaving Bucharest that morning,
was now quite visibly overcome as they entered the town of
Birlad. The one pressing thought that had been in his mind
since beginning his research and planning weighed heavily
on him: *Was Rabbi Nachman the key to Pop's secrets? Will
he remember anything that the elder Rabbi Nachman, his father, had passed on about Pop? Will it, otherwise, be worth-
while just to see Birlad? Walk the town, perhaps see some
evidence of Pop's life here, and meet with some of those who
might have some vague memories of stories their parents or
grandparents told? After all, this would be about the best
most anyone could hope to achieve while chasing down their
roots all over this part of Europe, so devastated by two World
Wars and the Holocaust, and these post-war decades of old-
fashioned totalitarianism, under the transparent guise of communism.*

He knew that a mere 125,000 identifiable Jews remained

in all of Eastern Europe, excluding those who lived in the former Soviet Union. In Romania, mass immigration to Israel prior to and during Ceausescu's repressive regime had further depleted the number from over 400,000 to as little as 15,000 scattered in sixty organized communities and nearly a hundred more towns and villages with only a handful of families. Rabbi Nachman was still active, and so Nathan had assumed that Birlad would likely qualify as one of the sixty viable units of Romanian Jewry.

These statistics, these thoughts, these questions, these fears were rocking Nathan's brain: left side, right side, and all around the perimeter—when Eric broke in, saying brightly, "Okay, Grandpa, we're parking in the town square...here's your Birlad. Where to now?"

Stirred, Nathan just had to know. "Rico, tell me, Number One Grandson, have you enjoyed the day? Being in so foreign a country?"

"Are you kidding, Grandpa? It's been a real kick for me. Beats Palm Springs, Hawaii, or Cabo—and all those sunny places. Don't know any kids who've been here or anywhere close! Hey, it's really interesting...different! That's why I liked being in Israel last summer, too."

This was more than enough for Nathan, for the time being. The kid sounded genuinely enthusiastic, and Herb seemed to be responding well also.

"That's good enough for me, Rico," replied Nathan. " Now, let's go rabbi-hunting!"

Three very determined men—seventeen, forty-four, and the septuagenarian grandpa, all tanned and dressed in a wide range of California casual June-wear—from a Lakers T-shirt to muted sport shirt to jacket 'n jeans—left the rented Fiat in the very quiet, nearly uninhabited town square. The Friedmans stood out in marked contrast to the hustle and bustle of Focshani.

A burly, black-bearded man in a little kiosk, selling cigarettes and pipe tobacco, pointed to a narrow lane in response to Nathan's rehearsed question: "*Unde esta sinagoga, Rabbi Nachman?*" Briskly walking toward the *shul*, all three laughingly speculated on how a man the size of an NFL linebacker could fit into that kiosk every day. Halfway down the lane, they saw the rather imposing ramshackle wooden building bearing a faded *Mogen Dovid*. The oversized doors of the synagogue were locked! Nathan had not gotten this far just to be locked out now, and so he walked into the narrow alley alongside the structure to another door, with a heavy metal *mezuzzah* and a brass door-knocker, which Nathan knew must lead to the Rabbi's domicile. After one rap, his stomach leaped when he heard a strong voice from within say: "*Intratzi, intratzi varog!*"

Nathan opened the paint-deprived door, ushering Eric and Herb in front of him, and there they beheld a bear of a man with a flowing white beard. If he had had a guitar in hand, he would have been Theo Bikel personified. Rabbi Yossi Nachman, pleased at the sight of the three American visitors he had been expecting, warmly greeted each with a hug, saying—in Yiddish, of course—"You must be my dear Nathan Friedman. And these two handsome men are your son and grandson, no? Welcome! Welcome! Chomsky wrote to me a note explaining your visit. A real pleasure for me. To have guests is a beautiful *mitzvah* for me, but from America, yet...aha, aha...that is a wonder. Welcome to each of you, and especially to you, young man. Young Jews we don't often see! You all speak Yiddish, I suppose?"

Gesturing for them to sit in the comfortable chairs and on a well-worn sofa, Rabbi Nachman looked toward Nathan first for an answer. "Thank you, thank you, Rabbi. So very nice to meet you," replied Nathan, giving his rusty Yiddish its first workout. "I'm afraid only I speak the *mamaloshen*, not so very good as you can see. My son Herbert here knows a little, from his mother and me, and from my parents when they were alive. My grandson Eric, is a typical *Americaneh*, no Yiddish!"

Rabbi Nachman flashed an understanding smile and nodded. "So, I'm told your father, may he rest in peace, was a Birlader. True?"

"Yes. He left here in 1904. Born in Birlad in 1887. His

name was Sholem Leib Friedman, son of Moishe and Sora..."

The Rabbi interrupted. "Sholem Friedman. I know that name. My father always talked about his brother Yaakov who went to America, to Canada ...yes, yes, in 1904. Yaakov walked with Sholem Friedman, the grain merchant's eldest son."

Nathan sat wide-eyed on the edge of the velvet sofa. "Of course, Rabbi! My grandfather was a grain dealer. Bought rye and barley from the local farmers and sold it by the wagonload to the granaries in ...what was it... yes, Bereshti, I believe. My father worked with him before leaving for America. Rabbi, my dear Rabbi Nachman, your Uncle Yaakov was likely my father's good friend! They must have left Romania together."

It was halting and difficult to piece this all together in Yiddish, but the words were beginning to flow. All of Nathan's fears and doubts had slipped away. The story he came to hear appeared to him to be forthcoming. Nathan silently and hopefully prayed, *Please God, let the Rabbi give the longest speech of his life. I promise to listen to his every word! Amen!*

"Sounds like you're getting somewhere. What's going on, Dad?" Herb asked, leaning forward in his chair to the patient host, but not understanding more than a word here and there.

Nathan excused himself to the Rabbi and proceeded to synopsize the conversation for Herb and Eric in as few words as possible before turning again toward the patient Rabbi.

"What ever happened to your uncle?"

"Uncle Yaakov lived in Montreal, Canada. He fought with a Canadian unit attached to the British Army in France and was killed, sadly, in 1918. One week before the war ended. I was only six years old, but I still remember to this day when my father received word. My grandparents never got over it. They had not seen him from the day he left Birlad, though his frequent letters were always read to the whole family."

"Yes. Yes. I recall my mother, may she rest in peace,

telling me that Pop lost a friend in the so-called Great War. She told me that they had come to America together and had hoped to reunite in Montreal or in Quincy where Pop had lived. They could have been fighting the same battles in France because Pop was in the American army at the same time. What a terrible shame."

"Ay, yi, yi! What they went through together just to get to America, to leave Romania and get out of Europe. An amazing story. An amazing story."

Nathan thought, *It's time for the story to come out—I can feel it.*

"That is why I have come to Birlad, Rabbi. My father never talked much about leaving Birlad for America. Just that he and some friends had decided to leave because of the deplorable conditions. I could never get him to talk details. No details. Never. Only once he off-handedly mentioned 'walking.' What did he mean, Rabbi?"

Rabbi Nachman, almost shouting in his deep baritone voice, "The Fusgeyers, Naftali (using Nathan's *Yiddishe nomen*), the Fusgeyers! My father's favorite story. In fact, the favorite for all Birladers, all Eastern Romanian Yidden, past and present. The Fusgeyers. The Birlader Fusgeyers.

"When I was in *cheder*, after the Great War, this was a revered part of our studies, along with the Torah. We traced their routes on the maps, and we knew all of their names. It was like a holy ritual. The Fusgeyers, blessed be their remembrance. The oral tradition of Birlad for most of the last century. Even when I was a grown man with children of my own—eight of them, bless their lives—I re-told the Fusgeyer stories. Now, with all of my grandchildren and great-grandchildren, all in Eretz Yisroel, whenever I visit or they come see me, they ask me to tell the story, again and again. Even now, my dear wife left Sunday to visit with them, and you can be sure that she will be asked to tell a Fusgeyer story at some point during her stayover in Israel. My brother in Bucureshti is very ill so I remained to spend some time with him, but I am sure that my dear Raisel will be just fine telling the story on her own—she has heard it a hundred times!"

Nathan had been listening intently, hanging on every word, and pursing his lips so as not to interrupt, while Herb and Eric were beginning to fidget, waiting for the next synopsis. Nathan wished he could tell the Rabbi that he was "mesmerized" by his story already, but he could not think of an appropriate Yiddish term. He was having trouble finding the Yiddish for simpler, more common words, although it was getting easier with each minute; in fact, as the Rabbi continued to speak, Nathan began translating his words softly to Herb and Eric, interrupting now and again to ask the Rabbi questions.

"What exactly do you mean—Fusgeyer? I know that my father and Yaakov walked. But how far? Where, when, why? Yes, why? Please tell me everything you know!"

"Yes, yes, in due time, Naftali. It's a very long story. But first, a glass of my tea from Israel for everyone. You need some refreshment. You've come a long way from Bucureshti." He walked off into the tiny kitchen to boil up some water, and from there he asked: "So, where will you stay? At the Unirea? It's the only decent place in Birlad. Clean. Nice owners. They like foreigners, even Yidden, though we rarely get any of either here."

"Yes, we noticed it when we walked through the square. Looks fine."

"Heard you mention the name of that hotel we saw, Grandpa. Ask the rabbi if they have TV, CNN...love to catch the NBA playoff results and some Dodger scores."

"Eric, I'll bet they don't. And let's not stem the flow right now. Your grandpa's mission is looking pretty solid. Right, Dad?"

"Yes! So far, so good. I'm having a hard time understanding everything and making sense when I speak, but it's improving. Imagine, the Rabbi's uncle was your Grandpa Sholem's best friend! They actually left Birlad together. Now with this Fusgeyer story; it's almost too much! " He walked into the kitchen. "*Nu*, Rabbi, need any help?"

Nathan brought an ornate, antique silver tray, which

held a shiny tea pot, small glasses encased in silver holders, lump sugar, and a plate of pastries, back into the room. "Let's enjoy, then we will talk, and talk, and talk! Believe me, Naftali, we will talk!" assured the Rabbi. Nathan's impatience left him when this was punctuated by a well-placed wink from Birlad's Bikel.

"Wow! *Savarinas* again!" observed Eric happily.

Catching the word, Rabbi Nachman responded, "You don't think my wife would leave me without my favorite pastries. Even enough to take for my brother's family. I'm so happy, young man, that you already like what I like!" Nathan translated, and Eric responded with a big grin and a thumbs-up gesture, his mouth already full of the treat. The Birlader Rabbi returned the smile.

"Naftali, you will have a difficult time finding kosher food here in Eastern Romania. We manage, and for many years after the war we had a kosher dining room for those who wanted it. But since our population has severely dwindled, to thirty-six people now, it's everyone for himself. Some go to Piatra Neamts, others to Bacau or Iashi, pronounced "Yash," mind you, for meat. Shmuel Feldman still raises chickens and has been our *shochet* for many years. I go to Bucureshti every other month for meetings with the Rabbinic Council, and that's when we do our shopping. The meat, we keep in Shmuel's freezer."

"Rabbi, I'm afraid we're not so kosher. No problem."

"Yes, yes. I understand. *Americaner Yidden.* Rabbi Chomsky told me that it was possible you would not require kosher. He told me in the letter that only a small number in America keep kosher homes. Here, in Birlad, everyone is kosher, and all observe *Shabbat.* Some of the younger folks didn't, but they're all in Israel now.

Once everyone had downed two *savarinas* with very strong glasses of Israeli tea, which the Rabbi explained was really Turkish tea exported to Israel, Nathan was more than ready for the Rabbi to continue with the story. "You can tell Mrs. Nachman that her *savarinas* are the best in Romania. So now, the Fusgeyers, please, the Fusgeyers. Tell me all about them."

Then Nathan turned to Herb, speaking to him in English. "Herb, I think you and Eric should go to that hotel, check in—two rooms—unpack. Then you can scout the town. Take the Birlad folder from my carry-on and there will be some descriptive data on where I think Grandpa Sholem's house may be standing as yet.

"Rabbi," he switched back to his struggling Yiddish, "is the Friedman house still here?"

"I'm afraid not, Naftali. During the First War there were skirmishes in and around Birlad, and many houses were burnt to the ground. I think your father's family moved to Odessa during the war, where your grandmother had family."

"Yes, yes. They lived in Odessa before immigrating to Quincy in 1919, just in time for my father's wedding. They both died before I was born. The rest of the family all finally emigrated in the '20s, during the Red and White Civil War, and they've scattered all over the United States. I was able to get some information from one of my cousins in Detroit. But no mention, ever, of the Fusgeyers. Sholem Friedman was the only one to leave that way, it seems."

Translating for the boys, Nathan said, "You can be sure I'll tell you the whole story this evening. It'll be easier on the Rabbi without my interruptions for translating."

Herb and Eric bid a fond goodbye, hugs and handshakes, and the Rabbi's insistence that they take a few *savarinas* along with them to the hotel was well received by the younger Friedman.

"So, now Rabbi, tell me the story. This is a big day in my life. To be able to retrace my father's footsteps. My mother's story was so clear and easy to understand. She came to America as a baby in 1895, from Ignatovka, near Kiev, direct to Rotterdam by train with her parents and older sisters, and on to New York, and then to Boston where they had family. We have photographs, well-documented facts. But, my father...it's as if he flew on a magic carpet, nonstop, Birlad to Boston!"

The Rabbi, laughing: "Trace his footsteps, indeed. When you hear the story of the Fusgeyers there will be many footsteps to trace—perhaps well over 2,000 kilometers worth!"

"You're saying that they walked more than 2,000 kilometers—what is that, 1,200 miles?"

"Closer to 2,500 I've always been told."

"1,500 miles! Did they walk in small groups, large groups, alone, or...?"

"Now you're getting ahead of me, Naftali, dear man."

"Sorry, Rabbi. I promise I'll just listen. Please go on."

The Rabbi let out a long, plaintive sigh and began anew.

"No, Sholem and Yaakov did not walk alone. Absolutely not! And not with just a small group of friends. They walked across Europe in a highly organized group of the most courageous, impetuous, slightly mad but quite intelligent young people. Only a few, if any, over thirty years of age, and about sixty in all, including, in Sholem's Fusgeyer group, six women—young girls. These *kindelach* were not satisfied with just leaving for America or wherever. No, they insisted on making a statement for all of Romania, for all of Europe, for the whole world to see and hear. Just as the previous Birlader and other Fusgeyers had done, and the future groups would also do.

"They would march to America, so to speak, with flags flying. A Romanian flag and the new Zionist flag with a blue *Mogen Dovid*, drums beating and bugles blasting. A statement—a protest we would call it today. Against the planned pauperization of the Jewish communities in Poland, in Russia, in the Balkans, in the Baltic. Against the citizenship restrictions, against all anti-Jewish laws in every one of these countries, against the very effective boycotts of Jewish businesses, Jewish tradesmen. And, of course, against the rash of pogroms over the previous twenty years, from 1881 onward.

"You must remember from your study of history that when Czar Alexander II was blown to bits in 1881, it was blamed on the Jews. There followed from that day to this, pogroms as certain as the falling snow—as regular as the rain—as unforgiving as the hottest sun. Everywhere in this part of Europe, throughout Russia, Bukovina, Bessarabia; and in Iashi a bloody pogrom occurred in 1899. Oddly, it was frowned upon by the Romanian government, which was trying so hard to gain favor with the West, but, nevertheless, carried out by the local police.

"The year before Sholem and Yaakov left, Easter 1903, the most infamous of all of these genocidal tragedies took place in Kishinev. Most notable not because so many were hacked to death—the forty-nine killed actually being far from the most murdered at one time—but because for the first time, the world's newspapers paid attention and reported it. It was front-page news. Rallies were held in America, in France, in Germany, in England. Famous writers, statesmen, rabbis, ministers, and priests spoke out against the perpetrators.

"Even your president, Theodore Roosevelt, made a statement lashing out against the pogrom. But the one person who possibly did more than anyone to bring the notorious massacre to the world's attention was Chaim Nachman Bialik. You know of him, of course. Yes. He was the great Hebrew-language poet we all learned of during our school days. He was living in Odessa at the time, and he went to Kishinev right after the pogrom, witnessed the aftermath, and wrote *In the City of Slaughter*. My father could recite the entire long poem in Hebrew and in the Yiddish translation. When I was in *cheder*, he was also the *lehrer*, the teacher, and try as we might, none of the children could come close to matching him. Every time he recited, tears would flow from his eyes. When he did this for adults, everyone in the room would cry.

"All of these events and dramas sparked waves of mass migration. When the *Protocols of the Elders of Zion* were brought to light after the turn of the century, although they were conclusively branded as forgeries, a new round of pogroms and violent insults to Jewish existence started off the new century with death and destruction. After all, if these papers spoke so eloquently and convincingly of a Jewish plan for world domination, we must stop it at its core, reasoned the anti-Semites, the Jew-baiters, the usual rabble-rousers, the unemployed, the ruffians-for-hire..."

Nathan interrupted. "You know, Rabbi, the *Protocols* are still referred to by fascistic groups everywhere. Of course you must know that Hitler read them when he was a young man, prior to joining the German army in 1915, but did you know that later, when serving a jail sentence and writing *Mein Kampf,* he used the false theories to formulate his more bizarre ideas? Also, you probably have heard that Henry Ford—yes, the world famous auto maker—firmly believed in this so-called 'Jewish conspiracy,' and wrote *The International Jew*, along with constant rantings in his Michigan newspaper to chilling effect."

"Nothing seems to change over the centuries, Naftali. Our Jews are forever the enemy— the world's most popular scapegoat. The forgeries served as one more of the many blows to any chance for Jewish civil rights to be recognized in Eastern Europe. As if the Romanian government needed any more reasons for their actions."

The Rabbi poured another glass of tea for himself and Nathan, and, as was the custom, took a lump of sugar between his teeth, sipping the strong tea through it to fully enjoy the bittersweet flavor. After Nathan saw the Rabbi do this for the second time, he remembered that his *zaydeh,* his mother's father, always did the same. Yes, his Uncle Chaim, too. Pop was not a tea drinker. Despite the heaviness of the past hour, he grinned at the fond remembrances. Nostalgia can be as sweet as that lump of sugar between the Rabbi's teeth.

During this tea break, Nathan peppered Nachman with questions. He estimated that he may have lost twenty to thirty percent of the information, only because of the language problem, but he was able to piece it together effectively before the Rabbi was ready to proceed. Nathan was deeply impressed with the immense sense of factual history possessed by this sensitive, highly intelligent, worldly patriarch—a storyteller of the highest order. This was going far beyond what Nathan had even hoped for. *Beshert,* thought Nathan, *this was destined to be.*

Only one regret crossed his mind. If only he could have taken him back to Birlad to meet with Nachman many years ago, maybe Pop would have opened up the floodgates with his own recollections. Now, he would have to count on the Rabbi to tell the whole story, based on reports, letters, family histories, the great oral tradition so eminently carried on by the Rabbi's father and many other Birladers through time. *Not a bad substitute, though,* he thought.

"Rabbi Nachman, may I thank you again for what you're doing for me, for the time you're affording me?"

"Nonsense, my dear man, what else has an old man to do in Birlad these days? We don't even have a daily *minyan* anymore. I'm ashamed to say that we rarely get a *Shabbos minyan.* Luckily, for Rosh Hashonah and Yom Kippur, some of the outlying communities, so sparsely populated by a Jew here, and a Jew there, help us at least usher in the New Year properly. I know what you're going to ask, Naftali. No, we still do not count the women. And since I am the last Birlader Rabbi, with certainly no need for a successor, the men will not give in. One of my sons is a rabbi in Petach Tikvah for many years. He has always asked me to come and share the pulpit, not only for the High Holidays, but for Raisel and me to come to live. I cannot do that, Naftali. Not as long as there is a Jew in Birlad. Not as long as this *shul* still stands. Do you understand my feelings, Naftali?"

"Yes, of course, and I understand from Rabbi Chomsky that your subsistence is supplemented by the Rabbinic Council?"

"Thanks to the actions of my dear departed friend and colleague, Rabbi Moishe Rosen, may he rest in peace. Moishe was the Chief Rabbi, as you probably know, for nearly fifty years. When I graduated from the Rabbinical School in Budapest in 1938, we competed for a pulpit in Falticheni. He won, I lost. Instead I went to a *shul* in Iashi until my father became ill in 1950, and I returned to take over here. We had a very sizeable congregation then.

"The war years? Don't ask, Naftali. Iashi suffered terribly. Many were transported to misery, starvation, and death in Trans-dniestra. I was allowed to stay, as proof that Fascist Romania, even under Nazi influence, respected the clergy. Diabolical as it seems, they did this with many communities. However, Moishe Rosen and I kept in touch through those very difficult times and continued our friendship in the tumultuous postwar years. He went on to do heroic things, in my opinion, though he has been much maligned by many, even since his passing a few years back.

"A controversial figure? Yes, yes. Always. But a man of great vision and quiet courage? Yes, again yes. Why are there so few Jews left in Romania today? Because of Moishe's supreme efforts over the years—as a member of the Grand National Assembly of The Socialist Republic of Romania— the gates have almost always been wide open for those who wish to emigrate for a better life in Israel or elsewhere.

"Who can blame them for leaving? Not I. All of my own children have gone, as you know. But, Naftali, even more important, for those of us who have remained, he had been a true guardian angel from heaven above. Kosher kitchens, ritual baths, Talmud Torah schools, and homes for the aged and for the infirmed throughout the land. Even under Ceausescu, Moishe carried out his programs, sometimes with the full support of the government, including subsidies, no less. Oh, there are those who continue to denigrate his contributions, saying he was a dupe, a puppet of a totalitarian state led by a megalomaniacal monster. Naftali, I, for one, do not agree with any of that unfounded trash. I miss him at our Bucureshti meetings. I truly miss him."

"Well spoken, if I follow. You've used many words that I cannot translate. But back to our Fusgeyers and their walk." Nathan noticed that the Rabbi had closed his eyes perhaps to stem the tears welling up behind them. He continued.

"Obviously there were many thousands who walked to the ports, before 1904 and since. In fact, I recently read the biography of a famous Hollywood American who, at the age of seventeen, like Yaakov and my father, walked alone from

Warsaw to Hamburg, sailed to London, walked to Birming-
ham where he worked with an uncle, then walked to
Liverpool. He eventually sailed to Halifax, Nova Scotia, in
Canada; continued walking to Saint John, New Brunswick,
also Canada; and shortly thereafter, plodded in the snow to
New York City in the middle of winter. Yes, he was Shmuel
Gelbfisch—Samuel Goldfish, later known as Samuel
Goldwyn, a major *macher* in the history of the film indus-
try."

Not getting much of a response from the Rabbi, who
was still pensively sipping the tea, Nathan realized that he
was trying to coax the Birlader into restating the motivating factors for the long, arduous walk— and why it was so
different from all other migratory events. He decided to be
more direct, even as he realized that the Birlad Rabbi was
not able to relate to the Hollywood reference.

"Rabbi, please bear with me. There were, no doubt,
Swedes who had to walk to Goteborg or Malmo from wherever they lived, seeking to sail for America, and Minnesota,
the Dakotas, and many other states today have large populations of Scandinavian immigrants and generations of their
descendants. Some Norwegians must have walked to Bergen
and Oslo. Finns to Helsinki and Turku. Russians to Odessa
and St. Petersburg. Even Romanians to your Black Sea ports,
if they wished to do so. Remember, Rabbi, the very poor
Irish escaped the disastrous potato famine of the mid-nineteenth century, walking to Cork, and then sailing to Boston
or New York. Italians to Naples, Livorno or Genoa. French
to Marseilles or Le Havre. The Greeks, to Piraeus or to
Salonika. Turks to Izmir or Istanbul. I can go on and on,
but I want to get on with the Fusgeyers' story. Yes, I know
that in most of these cases the distance was not so vast and
they walked only because they were too poor to spend additional monies beyond the steerage fare. For those who could,
getting to the ports was never an insurmountable problem.
Bribes, lodgings, food, and various modes of transportation
could be paid for..."

"Aha! There's an important difference, Naftali! Our

Fusgeyers could have done that. That is, go to a closer port, like Odessa or Trieste. Even Constantza and Istanbul were possibilities, although passage from any of these ports was prohibitively more expensive than sailing out of the North Sea ports, and it meant a much longer voyage. But, listen closely, please. That is NOT the point. DEFINITELY NOT the point. Not their reasoning, not their *raison d'être*."

Nathan knew he had done his job well. The Rabbi, continued now with newfound vigor, gleaming eyes, and best of all, he was on the track Nathan hoped he would pursue! Rabbi Nachman finished his tea, put it down on the small table beside him with finality, and got on with the story.

"As I've said earlier, these children, these youngsters, were NOT going to leave as so many had in the '80s and '90s. They would not go *shah shtill*, slipping across borders quietly in the night. No, my dear Naftali! They would, as the other Fusgeyers had done, march ALL the way across the mass of Europe. No short-cuts. 2,500 very difficult and dangerous, hostile kilometers. Remember, Yaakov and Sholem were with the fourth Fusgeyer group to leave Birlad. From 1899 on, following the Iashi pogrom, other groups had left from Iashi itself, from Bacau, from Vaslui and Galatz, from Moineshti and, of course, Bucureshti and a few other Romanian towns. My father even heard of Fusgeyers leaving from Russia and Poland. Not all made it. Some groups fell into disarray before they reached the ports. Some Fusgeyers returned home. Some lost most of their people to the lure of the cities along the way. But our Birladers knew what they were doing and just how they were going to do it. And what they were doing, as it was with the other three groups from Birlad before them, was what they believed the only way to escape the hopeless morass that was Romania."

The venerable teacher and scholar, with eyes closed and voice rising, continued. "They were going with bravado, heads held high, marching—yes, marching—to the west like soldiers. Soldiers with weapons far more powerful than mere guns or cannons—their words, their flags! Sodiers with a noble purpose. To Hamburg, to Bremerhaven, to Rotterdam, to Antwerp. They had a statement to make, a job to do. God bless their memory! They were going to America. To another world. *Di Goldeneh Medina.* The Golden Land! America! America!"

Rabbi Nachman cleared his throat, lowered his pitch from its feverish peak to a more confidential tone, and began to tell what would eventually become the whole story as he knew it...

BOOK TWO

෧ஜ

"....OUT OF THE LAND OF EGYPT...."

5

BIRLAD

1904

*What do you suppose will satisfy the soul except to walk
free...*
Walt Whitman, *"Laws for Creation"*

"Faster, faster, he's gaining! Come on feet, fly!" muttered wafer-thin Sholem Friedman running like the wind
twenty paces ahead of the slightly heavier, shorter Yaakov
Nachman. These two seventeen-year-olds were beating up
the dusty path to town. A common sight in and around
Birlad, this swift pair, racing one another, racing the clock,
racing to *cheder*, racing to *shul*, racing home, and racing
away from home. Always running, rarely slowing down.
Where do they get all that energy, the Birladers wondered
each time they saw the boys breeze past them.

Gasping for breath when he reached the town square
pump, Sholem was first again. He grabbed the community
tin cup, rinsed it out, and pumped it full. Cold, clear water
from the deep well quenched his thirst. The second-placer
arrived and waited patiently, drawing in lungfuls of air, for
his swig.

"Sholem, running barefoot gives you an advantage every time."

"So who tells you that you have to run with those funny
shoes?"

"My mother, that's who! She helped me buy them in Focshani, and the store owner told me that competition runners in Greece wear them for racing." Pride would not allow Yaakov to mention that the "help" was money sorely needed for matters far more basic.

"Hasn't made a difference for you, Yak." Sholem's smirk was as wide as his narrow face. "I'm going home to eat supper and get my shoes. See you at the *shul.* Six o'clock. Don't forget."

"How could I?"

Indeed.

* * *

The Birlader *shul.* Known simply as just that, the Birlader *shul.* Nothing more. Nothing less. They say that a century ago, when the Turks ruled, there was a name, something like *Templul Mare*, the Great *Sinagoga*, or perhaps *Sinagoga Mare*. But never in anyone's memory did any name adorn the two-story wooden structure. So for as far back as anyone could remember, the Birlader *shul* was the Birlader *shul*, or just "the *shul*." Even Jews in some of the villages in the more remote parts of the district would say, "I'm going to the *shul*," and everyone assumed it was the Birlader *shul*, and not one of the shop-front *shtieblach* scattered around the town. Where else?

The *shul* was not at all an imposing structure like many of those all over the Europe of 1904. Even in downtrodden Romania, somehow money could be raised to erect the beautiful, ornate synagogues of Bucureshti, the few magnificent edifices to be found in Iashi. But like an old and comfortable shoe, the Jews of Birlad loved their warm and cozy *shul.* Occasionally, they would see photographs or sketches of the *Neue* (New) *shul* of Berlin or the Great Synagogue of Budapest or the Moorish dome on the Florence Synagogue, or in person they would visit the huge Choral Temple in Bucureshti. And these loyalists always seemed to agree: "Who needs it?"

THE WAYFARERS

At all hours of the day and night something would be going on at the *shul*. The men met and talked and argued about politics, the future, and the plight of Jews elsewhere. Somewhere, somehow, someone had it worse. Women met and sat upstairs even when there was nothing going on in the sanctuary, knowing their place, and not wishing to disturb the sanctity of the ancient *shul*.

In 1877, Benjamin Franklin Peixotto, an American newspaper editor and past president of B'nai Brith, who had been appointed U.S. Consul General to Romania the prior year came for a visit. Wishing to investigate the deplorable Jewish conditions that already were officially and widely denounced by most Western powers, he toured the Eastern Provinces and elected to spend Sabbath at the Birlader *shul*. Needless to say, this had become one of the single most notable events in its otherwise unremarkable past, and it was always the story that the Birladers related when asked about their town.

The interior was plain. The beadle, Leml Leventer, had polished the *shul* benches to the highest gloss for the past forty years. Leml, now in his mid-seventies, still loved to test out the gloss by sliding his posterior down one bench after another when he was sure no one else was about. The fact is, everyone was always tempted to do the "*tuchus* slide," especially the young, and they did!

The ark was nothing special. The eternal light, a simple design; the torahs, all covered with the same minimally embroidered deep purple fabric; and the *bimah*, the pulpit in the center of the sanctuary, was barely large enough to hold a rabbi, the lay cantor, and one or two elders at the same time.

The current rabbi, Eliahu Yehuda Nachman, who had just taken the pulpit in January after Rabbi Holtzer retired to live with his son in Odessa, was a local young man of twenty-four who had studied at the *yeshiva* in Kiev. His family had always claimed that they were direct descendants of the revered genius Rabbi of eighteenth century Vilna, and young Eliahu's *yeshiva* teachers found his scholarship to be extraordinary. The Birladers felt honored that he had chosen to return to his hometown to begin his career in the rabbinate. Could they have foreseen the future, they would have found a Nachman on the *bimah* throughout the difficult century ahead.

That night, when Yaakov and Sholem would join the others there at six o'clock on the 20th of March, 1904, the Birlader *shul* was about to formally recognize the fourth in a series of events that had begun at the turn of this new century. The Birlader Fusgeyers, fourth contingent, were there for what would be their final official meeting before their journey began. Emotions throughout the community had been slowly building to a peak from all the planning, the preparations, the haggling, the breast-beating, the "*oy vays*," the constant push-pull between parents reluctant to let go and their children who planted one foot already in America. Reluctant? In many cases, mamas and papas held a negative stand. Thinking that they would never see their offspring again, they weren't about to let go easily. Cajoling, threatening, wailing ... this was the order of the day. But these Fusgeyers —part of an organized group of sixty—had a mission, a purpose, and they were impossible to dissuade. The parents of those who had preceded these Fusgeyers in 1900, 1901, and 1903 and who remained as yet in Birlad worked to persuade this new set of bereft parents. Letters and journals, they told them, and even occasional bank drafts tended to fill the void. *Remember*, the deserted parents counseled, *our children are thriving in America and have spread the word of Romania to the world!*

In most cases the words had been encouraging—steady jobs, glowing reports of life in the *goldeneh medina*, the golden land. Unlike Fusgeyer groups from other towns, even in the rare situations of severe melancholy in the form of homesickness, not one had returned or even spoken of returning to Birlad. Since 1900, eleven families had gone on to join their Fusgeyers in America. There would be more, especially since there was no end to severe repression in sight, even with the continuous pressures applied by Western nations. The hatred of anything Jewish was so tightly woven into Romanian culture that any unraveling seemed quite impossibly remote.

As the Fusgeyers-to-be filed into the *shul*, it was no challenge to recognize the one young man who would lead the expedition. Mordecai was not the tallest, the strongest looking, the most handsome, the one with the wisest countenance, or the best dressed. But there was an aura about him. No need to demand silence. A hush blanketed the sanctuary as he stood up on the *bimah*. When he began to speak, charisma soaked his every word.

"*Kindelach*, my dear comrades, I have the news we have been waiting to share with you all tonight, thank God. A letter arrived yesterday from Berlin. The Labor Alliance has been able to book a block of passage for us on the Lloyd Line vessel *Cincinnatus*, steaming to Boston from Bremerhaven on August 15th, scheduled to arrive on September 8th, and going on to New York the following day!"

The cheering and back-slapping went on for a full minute. Mordecai Anieloff stood on the *bimah* grinning while his cadre, standing alongside, joined in the expected response—hugging, kissing one another on both cheeks, waving at the Fusgeyers on the shiny benches below and in the balcony above. Young Rabbi Nachman's reaction was far more sober. He sat in the very back of the *shul*, almost unnoticed by the celebrating attendees. He had been invited by Mordecai to join in, and for the first time a rabbi was among a meeting of the Birlad Fusgeyers. Mutually, they had felt it was inappropriate before this. Only Fusgeyers had been welcome at these sessions, primarily to avoid potential parental conflict.

Mordecai continued, once the *shul* quieted again, and everyone could see that the gravity of the task ahead lay in his face. "All that we have been preparing for is about to come to pass. According to our calculations and plans, we must leave in ten days in order to give ourselves ample time to reach Bremerhaven at least two weeks or more in advance of our sailing date. As our Scheduling Committee has reported, we have to consider various contingencies—weather problems, expected river crossing and border crossing delays, and God knows what. There is also the matter of being quarantined at the port."

"A question, Mordecai." Yaakov Nachman, the rabbi's younger brother, standing in the first row with his arm raised, spoke. "Was it not agreed that we wouldn't have to leave until after Pesach, which won't begin until the 17th of April?"

"I know, I know, Yaakov. But the schedulers had to make a decision. Do we miss Pesach at home and arrive in America before Rosh Hashonah, or vice versa? The decision was theirs, and we all agreed a long time ago that committee decisions had to be the final word. We didn't want to present everything to the general body for fear that we would forever be bogged down in the process. More or less, in that respect we've been following the lead of the 1900 contingent, just as the other two did."

"It was also a matter of ship and space availability according to the Labor Alliance people," added chair of the schedulers Zacharya Zelman, or "Zed-Zed," as everyone called him. There was, oddly enough, no further objection to the departure date. It hurt. It had been painful enough to think that this Pesach would be the last one spent with their families, and now it was not to be. Pesach on the road somewhere was not very appealing. Then again, Rosh Hashonah and Yom Kippur on the high seas was not a joyous option.

"Mordecai, after you told me the news this morning I thought about it all day. A practical idea came to me this evening that should please everyone. May I present it?" Rabbi Nachman's booming voice from the back of the *shul* came as a surprise to the six young ladies sitting in the women's balcony, since they couldn't see the last four or five rows of benches from their vantage point. These six were among the Fusgeyers-to-be, and the only females, yet they were not the first female Fusgeyers: Two had gone with the 1901 contingent, and three went with the 1903 group. Not everyone was happy that girls were going along, and in increasing numbers, least of all, the parents. But the girls themselves were delighted, and had cheered with the others, and Maidele Kaufman had celebrated by tossing some wrapped candies to the boys below, just as was the custom during an *auf-riffen* when the gallery pelted the bridegroom-to-be. The girls now strained forward for a glimpse of the Rabbi beneath them.

"Please, Rabbi, go on," responded Mordecai, hand-gesturing for him to speak.

"When you showed me your route map this morning, I happened to notice that your scheduled stop, coinciding with the first seder night, is to be in the vicinity of Sighet, in Maramuresh. With your permission, I will immediately write a letter to my former *yeshiva* classmate who happens to be assisting the rabbi of the town's largest *shul*. I'm sure he will be able to arrange for places for everyone to participate in a *seder*. Remember, to have a stranger at one's table for Pesach is a *mitzvah* of the highest order."

"I'm sure we would all welcome that, Rabbi. Please do so." A chorus of "Thank yous" followed from the assembly. Yaakov, in particular, flashed a warm smile back toward his older brother. He was enormously proud of Eli's accomplishments to date, even though he categorically rejected his parents' constant urging for him to attend the *yeshiva* in Kiev and follow his sibling into the rabbinate.

"We all have much to do over the next week-and-a-half. I would like each committee chair to give me a very brief report before we adjourn so that you can break the news to your families. I know that many of you have been experiencing a most difficult time of it since we formed our contingent so many months ago. But now that the departure date is a reality, I would be happy to speak personally with any parents—as if that will do any good." Mordecai gave a stifled laugh, knowing all too well that it was a poignantly sensitive issue in most Birlad households.

The first chair to give his final report was Zed-Zed, who went over the schedule, day by day. Birlad to Bremerhaven and on to Boston and New York, and the many, many stops in between. Dates, stopovers, flexibility, changes, the need for everyone to write up the same for their families to keep on hand. Zed-Zed was the only Fusgeyer who owned a watch, which he kept always on his person in his pocket. He left the chain hanging from the pocket and yanked it out whenever he wished to see the time or rewind the watch. And this happened often, so often that it was probably the primary reason he had been selected to this chair, and it was also a source of amusement for his fellow Fusgeyers. To keep the contingent on a schedule was important, but Mordecai periodically impressed upon Zed-Zed the importance also of flexibility over rigidity.

"Thank you, thank you, Zacharya. You have done a fine job as our time conscience and will continue to do so right on through our journey. When we finally part in America, I cannot imagine how are we all going to get up in time, eat on time, sleep on time, get to our work on time, meet our girl friends on time."

Mordecai's remarks elicited a ripple of laughter from the contingent, yet everyone knew just how essential Zed-Zed's timekeeping had been—and would continue to be. In the long days ahead, they would come to appreciate him even more.

Simmy Fiedleman was well suited to function as a "food *shnorrer.*" Both of his parents were considered to be the best bakers in the entire district; their bakery was noted as far away as Bucureshti in one direction and Iashi to the north. Even with the boycotts, they had been able to sustain the business by selling only to the Jewish population. They had been among the luckier ones. By leaving, Simmy could not take over the business as planned, however—a heartbreak for the Fiedelmans, whose older son had already gone with the first contingent four years ago.

Simmy's report, told with splashes of the rustic, off-color humor for which he was known, periodically raising the eyebrows of Rabbi Nachman, caused a gasp or two in the gallery as well as from a few of the others. He gave the final instructions about what each one should and should not bring along—the "should not" as important as the "should" in this case. Perishables, food that could go rancid or could become a cause for poisoning in any way, were a concern, and Simmy's admonishments were well-received by all. He detailed his elaborate *shnorring* plans—foraging pretexts that could be perpetrated upon unsuspecting communities and farmsteads, both Jewish and not, all along the way. Simmy claimed that his knowledge of such *chutzpah* came to him by observing some of the more successful beggars, of whom there were far too many throughout Romania, Russia, and the rest of Eastern Europe these days. These bedraggled Yiddish souls, some vagabonds, some locals, were dubbed *luftmenschen*, "those who make a living from the air," a rather descriptive phrase that told it all.

From his experience in the bakery, and also out and about delivering freshly baked breads from time to time, Simmy had the opportunity to chat with all of the town's *luftmenschen* and to watch them in action. Strangely enough, most were not classified as *shnorrers*—most had families— but they were recipients of daily charity, usually without even asking. The Fiedelmans freely handed out odds and ends of bread and pastry, particularly at day's end, and leftovers the next day. The tailors often gave out a stray pair of pants or a shirt, a coat, or a vest. The cobbler donated shoes that were beyond repair. The butcher gave away a *shtick* of salami, or a piece of *kishke*. The Jews of Birlad took care of their own, and an occasional stranger, without giving it a second thought, as did their co-religionists throughout the world. The great 13th century philosopher, Rabbi Moses ben Maimon (Maimonides), who wrote and spoke so endearingly of the glory of charity, would have been proud of these Birlader *Yidden*.

"All in all, Simmy, your report is sound, and I don't foresee any insurmountable problems with food and its storage. In the cities, the Jewish community organizations along our planned route have already been most cordial to the other three contingents. As we mentioned before, I wrote introductory letters to all of them. Even the smaller towns and villages have welcomed Fusgeyers before. We shall sustain ourselves very well, *kindelach. Daigeh nisht!* No need to worry!"

Thanking Simmy, Mordecai dismissed the chair and his committee of three, which included Pessel, one of those who had been listening so intently from the gallery. Pessel Vinocur, at eighteen, had been the homemaker for her widowed father and six siblings for over a year. Her sister Faigeleh, only sixteen, was to take over while Pessel attempted to carry out her ambitious plan to earn enough money to send for her entire family once she got to America. Pessel, of raven black hair and piercing brown eyes, was an exceptionally determined young lady. Her proud papa, Moishe, told everyone this constantly, and they knew it to be true.

Zed-Zed pulled out his trusty timepiece, pointed to it, and whispered to Mordecai. Nearly two hours had passed already. He wanted to adjourn as soon as possible, and so for the next half-hour the chairs were coaxed to make their presentations to the point and without embellishment.

Menachem Berman's Diplomatic Committee quickly outlined updates on their efforts, which would allow them to serve effectively as liaisons between the contingent and local functionaries, other officials, the military, and the police. A sensitive and critical responsibility not to be minimized in any way, as each of the other Fusgeyer groups duly noted in their journals.

The Medical Committee—headed by the local pharmacist's apprentice who had come to be known as "Doctor Hippocrates," nee Gershon Maibaum, and assisted by "Nurse Florence Nightingale," Maidele (nee Mirka Kaufman, "Maidele" being a diminutive signifying "little girl" that had stuck with her since birth)—was more than ready, at least for the beginning of the journey. They had bandages, antiseptics, powders, and a variety of medicines that would even make big city hospitals envious, thanks largely due to Gershon's mentor.

The kindness and generosity of Iancu Muresan, a respected pharmacist who openly decried the severe despotism and accompanying anti-Semitic acts practiced by his countrymen, had become a legend in the Jewish community. A devout practitioner of Romanian Orthodoxy, he was known to openly chastise Father Mihai for remarks supporting the boycotts. Because of this, among his own his popularity had declined precipitously, but among the Yidden, however, he was nothing less than a folk hero. When Muresan had taken on Gershon Maibaum as an apprentice two years ago his friend, Doctor Dinu Gheorghiu, who had himself taken on a Jewish assistant, Simcha Greenberger, had warned him of reprecussions. Simcha had been unceremoniously barred from finishing his medical studies in Bucureshti, but a sympathetic professor had sent him to the over-worked Gheorghiu.

Muresan had filled Gershon's pouch with large quantities of medical necessities and lectured both Gershon and Maidele on the dos and don'ts of emergency medicine. This was ably supplemented from time to time by "Doctor" Simcha who Gershon suspected was smitten a bit with the pretty little Maidele, she of the adorable *shicksie* nose. Yes, Gershon resented this and was privately very happy that Simcha wasn't to be a Fusgeyer. He rather liked that nose. Those eyes. That shapely figure. The sensuous lips. Gershon was in love. And to think that he, at first, had resisted having a "fainting female" assistant!

Mordecai appreciated the brevity of the Medical Committee's two-minute summation, as did the nervous timekeeper. Both gave nods of thanks to the nurse-doctor team.

Rivka Demkin, the only female chair, assisted by Itzy Gelman and Mayer Kelemer, had been warning all of the assemblage for months that everyone—and she always stressed *everyone*—would be expected to participate in the Entertainment Committee activities. Mordecai and those who understood the vital morale-building impact of such a committee respected her respectful command that entertaining be taken, well, seriously. In fact, one of the last year's Fusgeyers, in a letter from Baltimore, had sent on a message that entertainment on such a pressure-filled trip was essential, and he had mailed a plan for its implementation along with this note.

Rivka, Itzy, and Mayer had carried it even further. As a vehicle for fund-raising along the way, they would present a stage play in Yiddish language while on the road. Mendele Mocher Seforim's novel *Dos Vinshfingerl*, The Wishing Ring, which was a microcosmic insight into Jewish life in Eastern Europe, was the unanimous choice for adaptation. Frequent comedy skits and individual performances of singing, dancing, poetry recitations, as well as accordion, violin, trumpet, and coronet instrumentals were also scheduled for the long walk ahead.

Twenty-one-year-old Rivka would herself lead the way. For the past six years she had been known for her Purim costumes as a gypsy dancer. With each year that went by, her costumes had become more and more colorful, and her dancing more sophisticated—and more provocative! Her acquaintance with Zorka Romanescu, from the oxymoronic "permanent gypsy" encampment in the forest just outside town, had taught her much of the gypsy ways, and of their soulful music, dancing and dress. She had even harbored a desire to join the camp at one time, but, as a Jewess, this could only be the fantasy that it was. Besides, it wouldn't help her family one bit.

Since coming to Birlad to live with a widowed aunt, having left her poverty-stricken parents, twin sisters, and three brothers in Galatz, Rivka had been able to send them only meager amounts of money from her less than lucrative sewing business. Lately her parents had been talking about sending the twins to a "home" in Bucureshti if things did not somehow improve. But "improvement" in 1904 Romania was the unattainable. Rivka kept the trials of her family firmly in mind while she gave her report.

Rivka's assistants, Itzy Gelman and Mayer Kelemer, were, beyond a doubt, the funniest comic duo in all of Jewish Birlad, and were also widely known in Piatra, Focshani, Vaslui, and Iashi as well! Itzy was the *mashiganah* one and Mayer, the straight man, though their roles were completely interchangeable at times. Roars of laughter greeted their impromptu skits, and each Fusgeyer eagerly awaited their campfire antics. No one could evade their razor-sharp mockeries. Not even the Rabbi, nor the *shul* elders, the infirmed, the young and the old, and especially the *goyim*. Their completely irreverent rendition of Father Mihai's rabble-rousing, anti-Yid sermons gave sore ribs to all who would listen. Historically, there was never a targeted despot who could escape unscathed from derisive Jewish humor. The friendly chemist-pharmacist, Iancu Muresan, was, arguably, Itzy and Mayer's best fan, although so many others could lay a rightful claim to this title. Amidst the giggles that always accompanied the comic twins, even in as serious a moment as this was, the Entertainment Committee bowed and walked off the stage.

Mordecai wisely waited before calling on the next committee. Satisfied that the chuckles had died down, he gestured to Branko Horvitch. Branko, the oldest Fusgeyer at twenty-nine, and the only one who did not have a Yiddish or Hebrew name, had been conscripted into the Hapsburg army at seventeen. The Fusgeyers would now look to their eldest brother who was charged with the critical, sure-to-be-tested defense responsibility.

An orphan living and working in exotic Sarajevo, instead of fleeing the country clandestinely as so many others had done when summoned, Branko had opted to serve. The Hapsburgs ruled the Austro-Hungarian Empire fairly democratically, and their dominion stretched throughout most of Central Europe, as far south as the northernmost reaches of the fading Ottoman-occupied territory. Branko had spent his early childhood in the Ukrainian provinces of Czarist Russia, and his parents had been slaughtered during one of Alexander III's vengeful, ubiquitous pogroms in 1881. Six years old at the time, Branko had been hidden in a closet, only to come out to find his parents and two sisters' bodies in the wake of a bloody massacre.

From that traumatic event to the advent of his conscription, filthy orphanages, escapes, hunger, and wanderings had afflicted the embittered Branko. From six until he was thirteen he had been, for the most part, a pitiful urchin of the streets. For a short time he had lived with an aunt in Odessa, after which he served as a galley-helper on a small vessel, eventually winding up in Slavic Bosnia working as a farrier's helper.

Having been honorably separated from the Emperor's military after serving with distinction for twelve well-traveled years, Branko now found himself in Birlad as head of the Fusgeyer's Defense Committee. As Mordecai listened to Branko's report, he wondered: *How could this have come to pass? Not without a series of* beshert *coincidences.*

The 1903 Fusgeyers had engaged in the usual confrontations with various military forces in Romania, of course, but also in Austro-Hungarian and German territory. Branko's unit had met up with the Birladers in Hungary and had given them a difficult time. Interrogating the leader, Shimon Katz, Sergeant Horvitch gradually became guardedly sympathetic to a fellow Jew with such a noble purpose. He actually began to view Katz as a Moses leading the Children of Israel to the Promised Land, America. The thought of emigrating had entered Branko's mind, in and out several times recently. Listening to Shimon, he was soon deeply under the spell. Although he could not afford to say so at that time, he decided then and there he would join Birlad's next contingent. Single-mindedly, he headed directly to Eastern Romania in November, the day after his discharge. Mordecai had heard the ex-soldier's story, welcomed the volunteer with open arms, and thoughtfully found him some temporary employment with Leml Leventer's brother, Avrum the blacksmith.

Branko had tested Mordecai's patience many times, however. In fact, the other members of his committee, the three feisty Golub brothers, Yankel, Yoni and Yossi, also disagreed with some of his methods and suggestions for defense. Others, too, quietly resented the brashness of the older ex-soldier. Branko's twelve years in one of the most aggressive military units in Europe did nothing to temper his behavior. He was quite accustomed to, and an advocate of, force—wherever and whenever it seemed even the most remote of possibilities. But Mordecai, along with the other past contingent commanders, preached a non-violent, peaceful approach that included a tacit "no visible arms of any kind" policy that enabled the Diplomatic Committee to exercise tact and diplomacy in every situation. The Defense Committee was only put in charge at the last possible moment of a confrontational situation.

Branko's persuasive nature had only recently secured Mordecai's agreement that while arms would not be brandished, it would be up to each individual whether or not to carry completely concealed weapons in the supply wagon or on his person. Anyway, most of the Fusgeyers did not have access to anything more threatening than a woodcutter's axe, a blacksmith's hammer, or a pocketknife. A few contingent members had approached Branko asking for permission to secrete certain bullet-propelling weapons, and he had answered them in the affirmative, still keeping honest to the policy that Mordecai had accepted. Privately, Mordecai, as well as some of the more mature compeers, was grateful for Branko's enlistment.

Branko finished his report and stepped down. Mordecai thanked him solemnly, and called on his navigator next. In order to travel thousands of kilometers by foot to a definite destination, maps are among the most necessary tools. Yet, they were hard to come by. Sendehr *der Shreiber*, the scribe, had known this at the start, and consequently he took two trips to Iashi to buy some maps in a Romanian bookstore, adding these to the sketches sent back by the other contingents. Then Sendehr Efraim labored for many hours to compile readable documents covering the entire stretch. He poured over these every day and every night. He measured, he pinpointed and scaled, he memorized and theorized, he analyzed, and then he revised. He knew every river, lake, town, village, and mountain from Birlad to Bremerhaven. He was a walking atlas.

These activities were no surprise to those who knew Sendehr well, and Rabbi Nachman was perhaps the man most proud of Sendehr's accomplishments. More or less a loner, at nineteen Sendehr was still doing odd jobs around town, not wishing to do anything that would interfere with his writing or his love for history, geography, and literature. Jews had long been barred from the rather superficial schools of Romania, and so Sendehr and the others had received their formal education in the *cheders*. Luckily, Rabbi Holtzer had recognized that there would have to be some secular studies beyond Hebrew and Torah in his *cheder*, and he set about to provide this for them. Many rabbis were not as educated in the ways of the world as Holtzer was. The boys of Birlad had benefited measurably, and it showed. When Rabbi Nachman took the reins, the results of this approach became even more evident.

Sendehr read everything available, in both Romanian and Yiddish. His favorite was Sholom Aleichem, the great storyteller. He also read Seforim, Gordin and Peretz, and Mihai Eminescu, the popular Romanian folk-poet, until he read one of his many anti-Semitic outbursts that blatantly spoke of long, hook-nosed foreigners as a "foul and filthy brood." But Romanian literary circles honored Eminescu as Romania's greatest poet, nonetheless.

When Sendehr's writing skills in both languages were developing rapidly, Eli Nachman offered to serve as his sounding board, though Sendehr was long beyond *cheder* age. He was particularly impressed with a piece the boy had written on the Kishinev pogrom. With Sendehr's permission, he had sent it on to the *Iashi Yiddishe Shtimme*, and the editor had printed it alongside segments of Bialik's *In the City of Slaughter*, as the one-year anniversary of that mindless massacre approached. Sendehr's piece was a parody in a tongue-in-cheek style that blasted Czar Nicolai's cowardly endorsements of the widespread Russian pogrom mentality, which showed no signs of ending, regardless of mounting world opinion.

THE WAYFARERS

THE COWARDLY BEAR
(Der Behr, Der Pakhdin)

Come forth ye hulking Russian bear!
ye must bare your claws and teeth
to rip apart the hook-nosed *Zhid*
who has come to murder us a-bed

Ye bravest of all the behemoths
must tramp the streets of Kishinev
before the thieving usurers
send us all to meet our doom

They, the ones of ancient garb,
are threats to life and limb -
smite him, o heroic bear
before he drinks a baby's blood

Dispatch them all with mighty blows,
elders, mothers and the yet unborn
and the children, yea, the children,
those diabolical issues of Zion

What? Only forty-nine dead?
Could you not claim many more?
O Czarist bear, you now must wait,
to slay the *Zhid* another day.

Sendehr Efraim
Birlad, 1904
(translated from the Yiddish)

Sendehr rarely used his last name, only his first and middle. But to everyone, even to his parents and family, he was affectionately known as *Der Shreiber*. In addition to his important mapping responsibilities, Sendehr would be writing the journal. Mordecai recognized, when he sat down with the others to formulate the committees, that written documentation of their journey would preserve their story, help to propagate their mission, and serve as an instructor's manual to those Fusgeyers who would follow. While no one served on either of his committees except for himself, Sendehr appointed certain Fusgeyers to act as "reporters" for the daily journal. Nothing was to be missed. His talent with the pen, with the written word, would assure this. The journal would prove to be, by far, the most comprehensive word-picture of any of the Fusgeyer expeditions, before or since.

By now, the attendees were getting a bit restless, even though the committee heads presented their reports at shortened intervals. Amidst requests for a break, Mordecai assured everyone that by nine o'clock they would be on their way to their homes. Finance and Education would give their finals, and the last meeting of the Fusgeyers, Contingent Number Four, would be adjourned until departure time, nine o'clock in the morning on the first day of April, 1904.

Although mundane to most of those assembled, Nuchim Krasnigor's Finance Committee held, nevertheless, another crucial key to their mission. His experience as a bookkeeper for a small granary near Birlad more than qualified him to handle the numerous financial matters associated with the trek. Nuchim's family had come to Birlad when he was four, having fled from a village near Zhitomir in the Ukraine during the '80s, when Alexander III was lashing out at Jews everywhere within his vast domain. The family settled in Birlad, hoping that Romania would be a safe haven. By degrees, they were right. In Russia there was abject poverty and the constant threat of violent death. In Romania there was relentless impoverishment and only occasional violence, but as a granary worker the elder Krasnigor was able to find work and support his family of six.

When as a teenager Nuchim showed proficiency with figures, the practical granary owner, a local Romanian, put him to work doing the books. That had been seven years ago, and Nicolae Sfintu Gheorghe still bragged to his cronies of his brilliant Jew bookkeeper, the so-called *buna evrey* (good Jew). When Nuchim announced his intentions to leave for America, the disappointed Sfintu Gheorghe exacted a promise that he would train another *buna evrey* for the job. In three weeks time, Nuchim was satisfied that the rather lazy, but literate and intelligent *bon vivant luftmensch*, Chayim Kessel, was ready for the granary. He could add a column of numbers error-free, distinguish between the right side and the left side of the ledger, and he had the *chutzpah* to speak his severely broken Romanian whenever his new boss looked in on these on-the-job training sessions. Nuchim was visibly nervous, fearing that if all didn't go well after he left, his innocent and unsuspecting father would suffer the consequences. A reasonable fear that was not altogether unfounded: "Good Jew" could very easily become "dirty Jew" in the blink of an eye. Laborers like the elder Krasnigor could easily be found all over Birlad. This much-proven, harsh truism would haunt Nuchim every inch of the journey, and beyond it as well.

The economic order of Birlad's population, which approached 20,000 and included the never-to-be-citizen Jews who numbered approximately 4000 and the non-human gypsies whose camp fluctuated between 200 and 250, was a microcosm of *fin-de-siecle* Eastern Europe. Small home factories were common everywhere—shoemaking, furniture making, machine works, brick works, lumber mills, wine bottling plants, granaries—each run by the master and his family. The larger, more profitable ones were always ready to hire a few hands for production and distribution, sometimes temporary, sometimes more permanent. Only a few of these were Jewish-owned enterprises. The vast majority of them were not. However, the Jewish workers consistently proved their mettle at the brick works, the bottling plants, and the granaries that were scattered among the outlying farms. They were the most desirable hires even though most would not work on their Sabbath. But their overall reliability far surpassed that of the peripatetic *roma*, as the gypsies were called, and of the itinerant or local Romanian alcoholics. Alcoholism was a continuing, rampantly endemic problem, but few, if any, of the Jewish workers imbibed to any remarkable excess. The bosses knew this very well.

Among the surviving Jewish-owned businesses were a modest hostelry, a six-stool saloon-eatery, three bakeries, a half-dozen minuscule tailor shops, three cobblers, two butchers, two blacksmiths, a glass-blower's shop, two green-grocers, a millinery, and a haberdashery. All were hard hit by the perennial, dramatically devastating boycotts and could only rely upon their Jewish customers. Sadly, several had failed in the past year.

Unlike Nuchim who, at twenty-three, had been work-ing for a Romanian steadily at one job since he was sixteen, about half of the Fusgeyers either worked with their fami-lies or in their father's trade or did odd jobs around town. The other half, frustratingly, were usually unemployed or, worse, unemployable, unable to find income-producing work in a town already filled with jobless Romanians. Ample rea-son alone for wanting to exit this deepening abyss of futil-ity.

Nuchim's brief report was most encouraging. A draft from the Central Bank of Romania's Iashi office covering the balance due to the Jewish Labor Alliance in Berlin had been, finally, hand-delivered to the Krasnigor house by Yankel Golub. Yankel had been dispatched to Iashi by train to hand over the case full of currency to the Iashi represen-tative of the Alliance, who, in turn, walked into the bank to arrange for the draft. No, no. Yankel did not make the trip alone. Of course not. As planned, Branko, *der groisseh soldat,* the big soldier, with his Austrian army-issue Luger pistol hidden in his right boot, accompanied Yankel and did not take his eyes off the black case for one second.

The rugged Branko Horvitch cut a dominating figure. To say that his brigand-like dress and demeanor were a bit unsettling to both the bank's stuffy managing director and the rather meek, prissy, *pince-nez* bespectacled Alliance man, would be to understate it. Adding Yankel, *der shtarkeh bulvan,* to the equation, made for a most interesting afternoon. One that would be talked about for weeks in some of the best circles of Jewish Iashi, as well as in the daily *minyans* at the famed, golden-domed 17th century Great Synagogue. The *"Banditten foon Birlad,"* as they were humorously called, became known to all of Iashi.

Mordecai and Nuchim summed up the fiscal arrangements. They had made clear from the outset that once foundational monies had been raised the Fusgeyers would have to contribute the difference. Although they would raise other expense money during the journey, it could not be counted on as their only source. When the plans were publicly announced at *shul* during Rosh Hashonah, one of the elders on the *bimah,* Reb Moishe Mandlebaum, nudged the fundraising off to a rousing start with his substantial sum. Past Fusgeyer contingents had all received the same from him.

Reb Mandelbaum was, sadly, the one and only Birlader who could qualify as "comfortable," due largely to his exceptionally prudent business acumen, unusual foresight, and abundant *mazel.* In addition, ten families were willing to sacrifice, indeed, and pledged to provide whatever the final assessment would be for their own Fusgeyer. These families included the bakery Fieldelmans, Sholem Friedman's father the grain merchant, and the Golubs for all three of their sons. Not to say that any of these families didn't argue most vociferously against their offspring's *mashiganah* emigration ideas, however.

Additionally, the Jewish Labor Alliance headquarters in Berlin was quick to exercise its usual bargaining power with the shipping lines, amounting to a twenty-percent reduction in steerage fares. This assistance was followed by a stunning surprise in the shape of a sizeable stipend-per-person from the B'nai Brith Organization, a Jewish society founded in 1843 with headquarters in Washington. Apparently, the 1903 contingent leader, Shimon Katz, had joined a lodge in New York City and found that, in honor of the national past president, the aforementioned Benjamin Peixotto, this fast-growing, world-wide organization had introduced a program providing assistance for any organized group emigrating from Romania to the United States. Shimon quickly made the proper application for the 1904 contingent and forwarded the necessary papers to Mordecai, which were returned and approved. A bank draft was then sent to the Alliance people in Berlin and credited to the Birlad account.

What did all this amount to? What did it really mean to the Fusgeyers? Typical steerage passage at the time was equivalent to $40 (U.S.). The twenty-percent Alliance discount and the B'nai Brith's "Peixotto gift" reduced to a much more manageable amount the cost per Fusgeyer. In 1904 Romania, a Jewish family with an income of more than $100 (U.S.) annually was rare indeed.

Originally, seventy-two had enlisted between July and December, but nine subsequently dropped out, primarily due to parental pressure, and there was also one case of severe bronchial difficulties. The numerous training hikes had caused some anxiety for those in poorer physical shape, but that only served to increase personal pride and the determination to adhere to a more frequent, individualized conditioning process. Fusgeyers— alone and in small groups of three or four—could be seen tramping the paths around Birlad's surrounding forests, fields and hills, even through the cold winter months. In the snow, and in the rain as well, no one had to be prodded. No one even had to be asked. Self-motivation could not be stronger. They just did it!

What proved to be the last of the drop-outs before departure had just occurred that morning. Pinchas Zaslovsky and Ruvain Mushnick had decided to accept an offer they could not refuse. Their uncle had gone to Perth, Australia, in '02 to join an already large family group. Pinchas and Ruvain were offered full passage from Constantza to Istanbul to Perth, through the Suez Canal, with board and room for one year in exchange for helping Uncle Tevye build a thirty-room hostelry overlooking the Indian Ocean. Both sets of parents were quite relieved by this, since they had been planning to join Tevye, older brother to both the mothers.

No one, least of all Mordecai, could blame them for their choice, even at the last minute. Ideals, even the strongest and most noble, are sometimes subjugated to practicality. During the next ten days, nearly all of the Fusgeyers personally wished them *mazel.*

For a people known throughout the ages for study and learning and argumentative discourse, Talmudic, Biblical, and otherwise, is it any wonder that an Education Committee would be of prime import? In fact, this committee chairman was the first and easiest to appoint. Who else but Mendel Buchman? *Der Lehrer,* the teacher, the maestro. Mendel was born in Birlad the same year Benjamin Peixotto had made his historic visit, in 1877. Thirteen years later, a devastating cholera epidemic had stricken the entire Moldavia region, and tragically both of his parents and one older sister had perished. Mendel's mother Sophia had been a Jewess from Salonika, and Mendel, his younger sister, and his brother were sent to live with their grandparents in that Greek-Ottoman port city.

The Pareia family was well-to-do food importers, and Mendel, having already learned both the Greek and Turkish languages, was sent to an exclusive school founded by an Oxford graduate, where English was taught as the primary language. He had mastered English as quickly as he had learned the other tongues. By the age of eighteen, in addition to his Yiddish and Romanian, he was reasonably fluent in Greek, Turkish, and English, and had some familiarity with German as well.

The Headmaster-founder, Professor Endicott Montgomery-Lloyd, had recommended Mendel for Oxford, but his grandparents were reluctant to send him abroad. Instead, he attended a two-year teacher-training institute in Athens, excelling in everything he studied. For the next five years, Mendel taught there. During one of his visits to the Pareias, his grandfather showed him a letter received from a cousin who still lived in Birlad saying that Rabbi Holtzer was looking for help in the *cheder,* particularly for the secular subjects he felt so strongly about. Furthermore, this cousin had said he would tell the Rabbi about Mendel—with his permission, of course.

Events happened fast after that. Mendel, after so many years in the Gentile world, harbored a desire to teach Jewish youth, so he sent a letter, with his impeccable credentials, to Rabbi Holtzer and was promptly hired to start after the holidays in 1902. The salary was to be half that of the institute in Athens, but the rewards in helping Rabbi Holtzer introduce the lads of Birlad to some of the more worldly subjects would be most satisfying. This became exceptionally evident, with the boys taking to Mendel's personality immediately.

As a bonus, Rabbi Holtzer served as a *shadchan*, introducing the affable, bright bachelor to his beautiful niece, Esther Holtzer. Both had decided independent of one another to join the very next Fusgeyer group the day the 1903 contingent marched out of Birlad. Esther had recently been jilted by a homely *yeshiva bocher* from Iashi in an "arrangement" doomed from the start. She knew very well that she couldn't go through with it and was joyously relieved when he "fled" to another *yeshiva* in Czernovitz. The Rabbi's sister and her husband were quite mortified by the whole event, but happily accepted Mendel when he entered the besmirched picture.

Besides, thought Mendel, reflecting on how he had come to this point in his life, and looking up at his beloved in the gallery before he began, *that ravishing blonde-haired maiden would have made a terrible rebbitzen. Goodbye Athens, hello Birlad!*

Mendel Buchman's report merely reviewed the curriculum he had been designing for the trip. No one would be exempt from the daily English lessons, but the American history and geography lectures would be electives for those who wished to sit in. At the *cheder*, in Rabbi Holtzer's classes and, more recently, with Rabbi Nachman, only European history and geography had been studied. In practice, Mendel had done the bulk of the teaching. Eli Nachman had been, of course, upset about losing Mendel, but would, himself, go on teaching these subjects. It would probably have been extremely rare to find another *cheder* in all of Romania, or even within Russia, that placed such emphasis on the secular. In many circles it would have been considered just short of blasphemy.

The meeting officially adjourned at 9:03 p.m., by Zed-Zed's pocket-watch. Out in the street, the good fellowship that permeated all of these meetings during the past year was sharply evident. Arms around one another, the singing of refrains of various Yiddish and Hebrew melodies, Mendel and Esther tried to lead a respectable version of "God Save the Queen" from his school days, which Mendel had painstakingly taught to the willing Esther. His better English students from the informal lessons he had been giving joined in, and all had a good parting laugh—Rabbi Nachman laughed hardest and longest of all. England's Queen Victoria, who had passed on in 1901, would have been proud of the effort, indeed.

Ten days. Just ten days more. Ten days of last minute hurrying and scurrying, scattering and chattering, *oy-vay*ing and disobeying, of heaving sighs and painful good-byes. Ten days of inward fears and outward tears and vice versa. Ten days to farewell. For most, forever.

§

Nathan had spent the whole night unable to sleep, tossing and turning, pacing the hotel room, and looking at the rooftops of Birlad from his window. Rabbi Yossi Nachman had spoken non-stop, as if in a trance, and Nathan had hung onto every word, every phrase. He was thankful that Herb and Rico were asleep in the next room, but at breakfast he would have to repeat the whole story to them. *Pop, a runner? They'll sure get a kick out of that one! Who knew?* Nathan could hardly wait for his morning meeting with the good Rabbi.

6

GOODBYE BIRLAD, FOREVER

There are times when passion is stronger than reason.

Rabbi Eliahu Yehuda Nachman

Plans eventually reach a stage when at last they must be carried out, and on April 1, 1904, that day had come. It was almost as if the sun, well hidden for almost the entire month of March—one of the bleakest months in memory— had decided to honor the Fusgeyers's departure. It shone brightly and gave off the first real warmth of the year. The slightest evidence of buds on the plane trees and acacias and chestnuts, although still microscopic, held promise. Even the birds were in full chorus, many having returned from the fall migrations that had brought them back from the warmer climes of Greece and the island-dotted Aegean after a few weeks' stopover in the Danube delta.

It seemed that all of Jewish Birlad had converged on the town square to see the flower of Birlad youth off to America. Fathers, mothers, sisters, brothers, aunts, uncles, *zeydehs* and *bubbehs*, friends and acquaintances. Uncharacteristically, even the Romanian bosses who employed Jewish workers forgave their tardiness on this one occasion. Three ensembles of Yiddish street musicians, *klezmorim*—clarinets wailing, drums beating, accordions wheezing, fiddlers fiddling—took up three corners of the square, each group favored by loyal followers who surrounded them. The Fusgeyers had already entered the *shul*, followed by their closest kin, still obeying the traditional

73

separation rules—women upstairs, men downstairs. God forbid that the custom be broken on this, of all days! It would be as catastrophic as getting an evil eye from a toothless hag.

Rabbi Eliahu Yehuda Nachman, descended from the Vilna *Gaon*, the venerable genius, no less, knowing that Mordecai (and, especially, Zed-Zed) wanted to leave before nine o'clock, pulled his watch from his pocket, then stepped to the lectern. And after two of the elders demanded some measure of decorum, pounding on their prayer books for emphasis, Eli Nachman solemnly began.

"My dear friends and neighbors, it is such a beautiful morning that *ribono shel olam*, God in heaven, has bestowed upon us ... and upon your dear children." He glanced at the somber Mordecai sitting on the *bimah*, the dais, between the two elders.

"May all their days be full of sunshine and light as they begin this journey of a lifetime. Though I'm sure that they are prepared for the usual Romanian spring—wet! Especially as they climb over the Carpathian passes."

A short wave of nervous laughter momentarily drowned out the barely audible weeping, and Eli proceeded with a lighter delivery, smiling again at Mordecai.

"It seems like yesterday when you and I were in *cheder* together, dear friend. I remember the day of your Bar Mitzvah. You stumbled badly over one of the blessings, but Reb Moishe, here, whispered it, and you repeated verbatim. Remember? I don't think anyone even knew it happened ... until now!"

Another wave of laughter, and Eli knew that he had been able to temper, at least temporarily, the breast-beating sighs in the sanctuary. Having no children of his own yet, it was not easy for the newly betrothed Rabbi, who was younger than a few of the Fusgeyers, to feel the pain of a parent about to see a child off to *der andehr velt*, another world... and God knows what!

"*Oy, oy, vay iz mir*, woe is me! Now you are going to the other world, and you're taking so many with you, these beautiful sons of Birlad, and even six of our sweetest daughters.

But, Mordecai, dear old friend, I, for one, understand this journey, thanks to our many discussions and my talks with Sendehr, Branko, Menachem Berman, the Golub boys, and, of course, Reb Mendel who is leaving me with two dozen of the most complicated teaching outlines, which I'm still trying to decipher!" More reluctant laughter came.

"Once I learn that Russia is east, Lithuania is north, Vienna is west and Greece is south, then I'll be ready!"

Amid the chuckles, Eli felt that he'd lightened the emotions enough, but the serious matter at hand must be addressed, too.

"Mothers and fathers, loved ones to all our Fusgeyers, beginning tomorrow, I assure each and every one of you that *pride* will take over *sorrow*, *meaning* will reign over *emptiness*, *passion* will become stronger than *reason*. You will all embrace an understanding of the power wielded by your young ones. More power than the mightiest armies of Europe! More courage than the bravest of the brave! They are telling the world—yes, the entire world—that conditions here in Romania are totally unacceptable. Inhumane. Deplorable. As the American Secretary of State recently wrote to King Carol and the other signatories of the Berlin Treaty, this treatment is an international wrong. An international wrong, no less! And your children, as their preceding Fusgeyer groups did, are marching out of here, across the surface of Europe, demonstrating to the world that if they cannot enjoy a reasonably secure future here, then they will go elsewhere—to America—to Australia! There will continue to be a drain of the young, the youth of Europe, of Romania. As many of you now know, there is no stopping this avalanche. God bless our Fusgeyers, and God bless you who have given us our Fusgeyers! *Omayn!* Amen!"

Rabbi Eli Nachman paused and looked out over the packed congregation, wanting to make eye contact with every Fusgeyer, every family, at this dramatic moment. He did, for what seemed like a full minute, and then went on in a modulated tone.

"Those of you who were here for this morning's prayer, *minyan*—and I am pleased that so many of you did join us earlier—know that there is a special traveler's prayer, which we recited then. Now that all families are present, please join me in giving a proper send-off. Fusgeyers, please stand and repeat after me:

> May it be thy will, O Lord my God and God of my fathers, to conduct me in peace, to direct my steps in peace, to uphold me in peace, and to lead me in life, joy and peace unto the haven of my desire. O deliver me from every enemy, ambush and hurt by the way, and from all afflictions that visit and trouble the world. Send a blessing upon the work of my hands. Let me obtain grace, loving kindness and mercy in thine eyes and in the eyes of all who behold me. Hearken to the voice of my supplications; for thou art a God who hearkenest unto prayer and supplication. Blessed art thou, O Lord, who hearkenest unto prayer ... *Omayn!*

The *omayn* resounded in the house of prayer louder than it ever had before, and louder still was the sound of the *shofar*, ram's horn, when everyone rushed out the door to break the twenty-four hour Yom Kippur fast.

"Dear friends, before we leave to walk through the square and onto the bridge to say our goodbyes, I have one very special announcement to make. It is a *vunderlech* surprise that Mordecai and I have kept secret for more than a month. On the bridge there will be a *simcha*, a joyous event, this morning! Yes, a wedding!"

All eyes turned to Mendel and upstairs, in the gallery, to blushing, blonde Esther. Who else? It would have to be them. And they were right; no one had really thought that those two would march off to America without saying the vows. Shouts of *mazel tov* rang throughout the *shul*. Everyone converged on Mendel, slapping his back, shaking his hand, kissing his cheeks, while the womenfolk did the same with Esther, only a bit more gently. Eli Nachman was so thankful for this most perfect finale. The gladness of *simcha* upstaged the sadness of separation.

Meanwhile, the young Rabbi thought it appropriate to begin the singing of the closing hymn, *ayn calohaynu*, while the entire congregation moved out the exits. Zed-Zed was overjoyed at the frugality of the entire event. Just 8:47. *Now this is a rabbi like no other*, he thought.

Out in the people-blanketed streets, it was impossible to move very fast. But each Fusgeyer had an assignment to carry out—another one of the many well-rehearsed plans—to make the transition from sitting in the *shul* to forming a marching unit. The wedding ceremony would not disturb this maneuver; if anything, it would give everyone a little more time to get everything in place.

Reb Margolis, who had since gone on to the outpost of Key West, in Florida, where for some unknown reason a large group of Romanian Jews had settled around 1900, would have approved of this fine day. It fit his prescribed and proven morale-enhancing pattern perfectly. The leader of the first Birlad contingent, Shlomoh Margolis, had written in his notes to Rabbi Holtzer that this one moment was of critical importance to Fusgeyer morale, particularly during the first week.

The spirit, the "pomp and circumstance," the music, the bugles blasting, the adrenaline pumping, everyone's head held high, shoulders and arms swinging, the unified cadence, the crossing of the bridge. Shlomoh, who had returned once to assist a previous group, felt strongly that the positive emotions of this departure would ease the pain of those left behind, and relieve the Fusgeyers of some of the inevitable homesickness, malaise, and remorse, and offset the moroseness caused by long, hard days trekking overland and the tiresome days that would follow onboard ship. He would prove to be absolutely correct!

Weaving through the hordes, the cart *shlepper* had the most difficult time. The two-wheeled supply wagon had been parked outside the *shul* under the guard of a one-eyed but trustworthy unemployed oaf, Fetteh Levine. The decision had been made to not leave it over the bridge where it would have been too tempting for gangs of unemployed locals.

The *shleppers*, a pulling crew of six, had to wheel it through town and across to the far side of the bridge before the wedding ceremony began. Heshy Rosen, Pini Kantorowitz, Mottke Grunwald, Yoni Golub, Itzy Gelman and Ruvie Shapira, three on each of the extended arms, pulled the extra-heavy load of canvas tent halves, poles, and sundry goods. Sholem and Yaakov lead the way and tried to disperse the ever-growing multitudes as they did so.

These two were exempt from any of the heavier work assignments, having been semi-permanently assigned to the risky and possibly hazardous job of "point team," a centuries-old military term for soldiers positioned well in advance of the main body to scout out and report back any potential problems. Such problems included anything from swollen rivers, washed-out bridges, chasmal road-ruts, unwelcome marauders, and unfriendly villages to unfenced-in bulls. Sholem and Yaakov were the two swiftest youngsters in all of Jewish Birlad; there probably wasn't a Romanian in town that could outrun either of them. The local Yid-bashing bully, Alexandru Davidul, had tried it once and had never talked about it since. After all, thirty-lengths isn't even close!

After a few detours, the cart was quickly rolled over the bridge, followed by its erstwhile donor, Avrum Leventer, the brawny blacksmith. His ex-as-of-today employee, Branko Horvitch, had been highly commended by Mordecai for soliciting this most vital gift from his boss. No, heavens no, no one would ever consider accusing *der soldat* of even the slightest hint of coercion! Why, the generous Reb Leventer had even outfitted the rig with over-sized wheels, re-enforced spokes, and extra wide steel strapping. No matter, therefore, that the wagon's original owner, a Romanian farmer from nearby Balabaneshti, had ordered the retrofitting but had run out of money to pay for it. *Three warnings, then it's mine,* was Reb Leventer's bill-collecting policy, even for the few Romanians who defiantly broke the boycott. The sixty-six-year-old smithy could usually out-hammer, out-shoe, and out-work his three gentile competitors any day of the week. And, with Branko at his side, it was no contest at all. Now, however, he would have to find another *shtarkeh,* a strong one.

Meanwhile, by nine o'clock the two streets leading to the town's only bridge over the Birlad River were clogged with Fusgeyers, their clinging families, hundreds of well-wishers, the *klezmorim* and their followers, and a very angry Captain Polinou.

Astride his huge pure-white Arabian, the short, fat town magistrate made a comic figure. But he was a very powerful and potentially sinister individual, whose presence was never a laughing matter. There was no doubt in any Birlader Jew's mind about that. Polinou was the one local who truly relished carrying out King Carol's anti-semetic programs when he was "just following orders." Today was his favorite exercise: a day he had witnessed three other times since the new millennium began. Only on the High Holidays would there be this many *evrei,* Jews, milling about.

Since his arrival he had been bellowing out his orders in his deep baritone voice, trying to clear Calea Carolu, which led from the *shul* on Strada Kirov on past the town *piatsa.* His only help was an army sergeant from the ten-man constabulary who hated crowds of any kind and who therefore kept disappearing for ten minutes at a time. The bottleneck of townspeople trying to get their wagons through the tight streets was creating shortened tempers and razor-sharp barbs tossed indiscriminately at the nearest cluster of Jews. Polinou was reaching his imagined Armageddon—a showdown between the Romanian overlord and the bedraggled Jew—much sooner than he had on any of the other departure days. His horse whinnied while he turned to face the crowd.

"What are you goddam Jews trying to do? You know there's an ordinance prohibiting these sorts of gatherings! It's a demonstration! That's what I call it, you swinish Hebes! Disperse, you sons of Abraham! Everyone, disperse at once! Who wants to spend a week in jail? Eh? Who? C'mon, break it up! Break it up! Disperse, *Mumzerim!* (Jew-bastards!!) Goddamn you all!"

His riding crop was held high overhead, positioned to come down hard on some of the more elderly trying to give the white horse a wide berth. His colorful vernacular, salted with the many foul Yiddish expressions he had learned over the years, pierced the air and seemed to carry all the way to the bridge. In fact, he was heading straight for the bridge, determined to keep it open for all wagon traffic, wedding or no wedding. Jews going to America be damned! A veritable donnybrook was in store for the unsuspecting Fusgeyers.

Just then, the Prince of the Jews, in the unassuming person of one Reb Moishe Mandelbaum, impeccably dressed in his elder's go-to-*shul* uniform—including a semi-stove-pipe silk hat—entered the nearly chaotic scene. He immediately saw where he was needed. Standing next to the riding-crop side of the blustering Captain Polinou, he spoke in a gentle tone.

"Come, now, honorable Captain,"—in perfect Romanian—"you must certainly know that the Children of Israel are leaving today. All of these people are merely trying to wish them well and say their goodbyes. I'm sure there are those of you who are saying your good riddances ... Heh! Heh! ... Disperse? You know, Captain, dear, my people have been dispersed for eighteen, nineteen hundred years! Where can you disperse us to now? ... Heh! Heh! ... But I'm sure you can pretend that they are gathering in groups of no more than twelve. Then we would be abiding by your good King Carol's law. You know the one, dear Captain: 'Groups of more than twelve non-citizens shall be dealt with harshly by the magistrates,' and so on..."

With his guttural sounds at least three octaves higher—nearly an alto now—the slightly calmer Polinou peered down at the elder.

"Mandelbaum, please don't interfere with my duties, and don't you dare try one of your insulting bribes on me! The last time—was it June last year? Remember? You gave me three fat pullets, a new tunic—bright blue and gold— one of your wife's noodle pudding, and three loaves of her so-called Channah's Famous *mandelbroit*."

Now his voice dropped to a near whisper. "Times have changed, my little almond-bread-*mandelbroit*-Mandelbaum. It will cost you six chickens. Not pullets! Layers... Do you hear me, Mandelbaum? Your best layers. I love fresh eggs every morning! A-a-a-a-and, a new black leather holster for my pistol. Your Jew leathermaker—what's his name? Eh? Goldschen? Toldschen? Holdschen? He makes the best leather goods in the district. Don't tell him it's for me. No! You know... that boycott *mishigus,* nonsense! Oh, and don't forget, some more of Channah's Famous *mandelbroit!*"

"*Oy-oy-oy! Vay iz mir!* Captain Polinou, your Honor. You drive a very hard bargain. You'll be taking my very best layers from the best of my chicken farms."

"Tch! tch! tch! Here's a filthy-rich Yid who owns three town stores, is it? An orchard, two farms, a vineyard, and, what—four, five henhouses? You, of all the *Yidden,* can afford a gift every now and then. Or maybe we should investigate just how you were able to accumulate such properties. Eh, old man?"

"And the holster you want, too? You do not understand how Reb Wolschen will overcharge me! All right, all right ... I'll deliver the layers tomorrow before the Sabbath begins, yes. The *mandelbroit,* maybe by Monday if my Channah has the ingredients on hand. The holster, *oy vay,* I don't know how fast Wolschen works on such a thing, but I'll pay him a little extra—just for you, dear Captain."

"For some crazy reason, I like you, Mandelbaum. I like you. Maybe it's because we understand each other. I trust you. Don't ask me why. Just be at my house tomorrow afternoon with the layers. Not at the jail. Not at the constabulary barracks. My house. Understand? And not a blessed word out of you. This is always just between us *goniffs*."

Occasional exposure to a second language does not the expert make, as Polinou did not seem to know that *goniff* means "thief."

With these parting orders, the satisfied, rotund captain rode off away from the bridge. Moishe Mandelbaum again had done his thing and, again, it had worked!

Just then, as the wagons continued to creep through the dissipating crowds in an effort to cross the bridge, a loud, unfamiliar noise scared Elder Mandelbaum and the grateful folks surrounding their hero. Lo and behold, here came one of those new-fangled horseless carriages!

The proud owner squeezed the contraption's bulb-shaped trumpet. *Honk!* It was someone everyone knew about—Leonas Lupescu, from Bereshti, the owner of the largest granary in all Moldavia. Watching him maneuver down muddy Calea Carolu, Mandelbaum thought, *Soon we will have those monsters snorting all over Birlad, from what I have heard. Hmmm... Seems to me there's a lot of money to be made, somehow, involving those strange-looking machines...*

That good man would look into it very soon and very seriously. And eventually, very successfully.

It was known simply as the Birlad Bridge. The name of a Romanian patriot, or Romanian Orthodox metropolitan, or writer, or poet or king, prince, baron or count did not grace the simple old wooden structure arching over the river. The full span was perhaps ten horse lengths. Its width was barely enough for wagon trains to pass each other heading in opposite directions at the same time. Since the river water deepened by the run-offs, jumping and diving from the railings was a popular summer pastime for Birlad's youth, Jew and Gentile alike. That day, the bridge provided a final one-way passage for sixty Birlad non-citizens: the Fusgeyers, Contingent Number Four.

Once the Rabbi and the four *chuppah* holders, wedding canopy carriers, arrived at the bridge, the groom appeared dressed in his traveling clothes—gabardine khakis, low brown-laced boots, military-type canvas leggings, warm blue flannel shirt. To finish off his practical ensemble, for the formality of the occasion he had borrowed the Rabbi's high holiday silk top hat. Mendel Buchman took the honors of being the Birlader bridegroom with the most eccentric cos-. tume ever assembled.

Esther came along wearing her own fashion statement. This beautiful, light-skinned, Nordic-looking bride, *calleh*, took her place next to Mendel appearing quite similar to that of the groom, except that she donned the bridal head-dress. Rivka and Maidele helped her with a white mesh veil, and they placed some early-spring daisies strategically in her blonde hair-bun.

Rigidly positioned at the far end of the bridge, next to the loaded cart, was the official departure-day photographer, the only Jew in town with his own camera equipment. Lazar Freyer was a phenomenon in his own right. He prayed daily at the conveniently-located tailor's *shtiebel*, one of the nine storefront or home prayer sites in and around the town, most of them artisan or petty-trader-oriented. The ultra-orthodox regulars frowned upon Lazar's glorification of the human image to the extent that not one of them permitted himself to talk with him.

By 1900, the photo frenzy had encompassed the entire world, and many less-than-orthodox Jews were also drawn to it. The new couple would have a sepia-tone remembrance of this momentous day, thanks to Reb Freyer's proven expertise. His group photographs of the previous contingents proudly adorned the foyer of the *shul*. No, not his *shtiebel*, but the Birlader *shul*, the *sinagoga*, where Eli Nachman's Biblical interpretations were a bit more liberal.

Zed-Zed paced back and forth, purposefully taking exaggerated looks at his pocket watch while catching the Rabbi's eye, and certainly the wedding ceremony that followed was perhaps the shortest on record in the entire Diaspora! The ceremony—the seven-time walkaround, obligatory prayers, exchanging of vows, wine-drinking, traditional glass-breaking, lifting of the bride's veil, and, of course, the kiss; followed by an explosion of three well-rehearsed ensembles playing three different lively tunes, *freilachs*—ended with hundreds of onlookers clapping and shouting *siman tov un mazel tov un*— a good sign for good luck—and took up only four hundred and twenty ticks on Zed-Zed's watch. Esther's mother had hardly time enough to cry, while her father seemed stunned by it all. Mendel's sister, who had taken the train from Salonika to Sofia, Sofia to Bucureshti, Bucureshti to Birlad over the course of four long days, hugged and kissed her new sister-in-law, kissed and hugged her darling brother, all in a daze.

Final goodbyes had to come fast. The Fusgeyers were ready to walk across the bridge for the last time. Velvel Palastrant with his heavily dented trumpet, and Asher Leibovich with his drum slung over his right shoulder, set the cadence. They were followed closely by the Udler brothers, Bezalel and Zacharya; the older carrying the Romanian flag of blue, yellow and red vertical bars, the younger proudly lifting a Star of David flag, blue on a white background, with two blue horizontal bars.

Rivka's busy little fingers had created a copy of the handsome flag introduced by Theodor Herzl at the First World Zionist Congress of 1897. The founder of political Zionism himself had contributed to its final design. The Romanian flag, the genuine article, had been donated by a Constabulary corporal who couldn't believe that these Jews would actually carry the state symbol. He had given it to Mandelbaum one day as sort of a dare.

Yet flying this flag—an act of supreme *chutzpah*—was not incidental whimsy. It was purely political, with a score of ambiguities involved. Mordecai had thought about it long and hard before acquiescing to this idea suggested by Mendel and Branko. He finally came to realize that it could be a distinctly positive political move. Bezalel, the older Udler boy, had to be strongly convinced, however, before halfheartedly agreeing to carry it in full view of family and friends.

Just behind the flags came the cart and its *shleppers*, followed by a visibly emotional Mordecai Anieloff, the charismatic leader. The year of planning and hassling, jostling and hustling, *shnorring* and cajoling, humoring and babying, disciplining and commending was nearly over... and it was happening. The time had come at last to validate, discard, adapt and adopt, revise, again, and again, day after day, night after night. His long line of duties and responsibilities would not come to an end until the ship had docked in America. Then, for the rest of his days on Earth, he would never forget even one moment of this monumental undertaking. Nor would any of the others.

The rest of the troop bunched in behind the vanguard, turning to flick another wave, to blow another kiss, to give yet another wave of the hat, and to shout to just one more loved one. Straggling behind the procession as sort of temporary—very temporary—rear-guard were thirty or forty or more Birlad Jewish children and even a few of their truant Romanian friends, as well as a small group of rag-clad *roma* children. Eight-year-olds, ten-year-olds, elevens, twelves... all were getting a feel for what it would be like to march clear across the European continent toward America. Within a kilometer or two, they would be dropping off, to go back to their normal, everyday lives.

Before long, just past the lush Vasile dairy farm, the cart dropped to the rear as planned, and the slowly relaxing troop burst into the Fusgeyer song so well known by all Birladers:

"*Gayt yidlach in der vayter velt ... in Amerika vet ir ferdinen gelt.*"

"Go, young Jews, into the distant world ... in America you will earn a living."

* * *

Sholem and Yaakov, already manning the point about three hundred meters ahead of the spectacle, stopped when they heard the fading strains of the song drifting through the April air. Without a word between them, they took their last look across the river, at the distant rooftops and onion domes of their birthplace. They wept. Unashamedly.

7

THE TREK BEGINS

If a man does not keep pace with his companions,
perhaps it is because he hears a different drummer. Let him
step to the music he hears however measured or far away
Henry David Thoreau, *Walden*, 1857

Zed-Zed and Sendehr had quite some time ago agreed that the destination of the Fusgeyers's first day would be a coordinate approximately forty kilometers from Birlad, in a northwesterly direction on the Bacau Road. The small Mirescu farmstead was familiar to Sholem since he had ridden there to pick up a wagonload of barley just before winter had set in. Normally, Moishe Friedman would not come out this far for a customer, nor would he send Sholem so far away.

This trip had been a favor to Ion Cuza, an old Romanian grain merchant. Cuza was suffering from an attack of pleurisy, and. although he had no trust in any of his other competitors, he believed the Jew Friedman would not dare cheat him. He was right. Moishe kept his side of the hard bargain and handed Cuza fifty percent of the proceeds as soon as Sholem had returned from delivering the barley to the mill. Cuza knew full well that Moishe was feeling the effects of the boycott and, to make up for lost customers, he would not refuse to help anyone, especially just before winter arrived.

Vlad Mirescu, a raw-boned young man, stood by the hog pen when he heard his name called from the curve in the road below the cultivated field to the east. He was not at all surprised to see two figures walking up the path toward him. His brother had been out to the farm the week before and had mentioned that the Jews would be coming by. Vlad knew that they would stop here as the Birladers had done three times before.

The first of many bivouacs for these crazy Yids. Shaking his head with the thought, he felt he was the bigger man, to be playing host to these fools just as Romania had gotten rid of them forever. *Why don't they leave by the thousands,* he muttered to himself wryly. Little did he know that thousands were, in fact, leaving Romania since all he ever saw, personally, were the Fusgeyers.

"Say there, Farmer Mirescu, remember me? Sholem Friedman, the grain man."

"The last time I saw you, you loaded enough of my barley to break an axle. Heard old Cuza croaked. Your old man going to take over?"

"This is Yaakov Nachman. The others will be coming along soon—they're only a few minutes behind... *My* father pick up *your* harvest? No, unless you don't care about the boycott."

"You gave me a damned good price. He's got my business if he wants it. Money is all that matters to me. My wife is going to have our first-born next month. Extra mouth to feed. When my brother visits again next week, I'll tell him to see your father. He'd better not cheat me on the goddamn price."

"Thank you, kind sir! Where can we camp tonight where we won't cause you any problems? And we promise to clean up in the morning. It's a religious thing with us."

"Well, the others all used the flat meadow beyond those acacias. You can stink up our privy if you want. The others did. Took a week to sweeten it up. It's that food you people eat! Yech!"

Yaakov laughed heartily. "At least we don't eat your

hogs. Thank you, Vlad. Nice to meet you. We'll move down to direct our troops." With that, the point team backtracked to the road, where everyone was just gathering.

On this first day, the ranks had held surprisingly firm. The drummer kept cadence from the beginning. The trumpeter had yet to get his second wind, but the ebullient send-off certainly carried over all the way. Mordecai expected, just as Shlomoh Margolis had pointed out, that the extra push would last for as much as a week. Maybe as far as Sighet's Pesach *seders*. Even to Satu-Mare/Szatmar. Or beyond. *That would be most welcome*, thought Mordecai, who was deeply impressed by the camaraderie displayed on this first day—the girls marching together, holding hands and singing every tune they knew; Esther and Mendel walking lovey-dovey, hand-in-hand as newlyweds should; and Fusgeyers walking with friends, cousins, or brothers, but also switching over to others frequently. No one, it seemed, walked alone. *This troop will make it to the North Sea*, their leader believed it with his whole heart.

Before dark, those who opted for tent coverage selected their canvas halves from the cart, along with pegs, poles and rope. There were ten halves with which to make lean-tos to provide adequate shelter for four people each, and there were three sewn-together halves which would cover up to eight comfortably. Typically, unless there was a perceived threat of rain or spring snow, a goodly number of the contingent would opt to sleep under the stars using whatever type bed-blanket roll they had.

"The blacksmith wagon," as it was called with a wink of the eye aimed at Branko, had more than enough room in its extra deep bed to hold all of the canvas. It also contained certain food and water supplies, the "Doctor Hippocrates" pouches, and even the small cache of weapons wrapped in oil cloth—so expertly secreted in its womb by *der groisseh soldat,* the so-called big soldier, Branko, and certain unnamed co-conspirators. Hefting the wagon would build many a muscle during the next four months. Mordecai and Zed-Zed worked out an acceptable schedule where one would only have *shlepper* duty every eight days, not counting the "exempts."

Who were these exempts? The six females, each of whom would be more than "pulling their load" with other duties; the point team; even though they would be periodically relieved from their risky assignment; the good "doctor;" Zed-Zed; Sendehr; and Mordecai. The latter four would be readily available as supernumeraries to fill in for someone injured or ill. No one would ever complain beyond a half-hearted campfire gripe. Of this, Mordecai Anieloff was certain.

The evening meal consisted of as broad a variety imaginable. *Yiddishe mamas* had packed to overflowing knapsacks and food pouches before the group left. Dried meats were a favorite because of their staying power and stackable size. Simmy Fieldelman, "the food czar," followed the lead of past contingents: he had stocked three burlap bags full of these leathery but nourishing repasts. The load of lard-free hardtack would be quite easy to refill in many town groceries. The meats would be purchased only where there were kosher stores. Simmy, Sendehr, and Zed-Zed had pored over the past journals sent to Rabbi Holtzer and kept by Rabbi Nachman in a locked *shul* closet. Sendehr recorded all of this information on the two back pages of his leather-bound book so that Simmy would know exactly where supplies could be replenished along the way. He listed every Jewish home, *shul*, and store that had welcomed the other contingents, and Zed-Zed's committee scheduled stopovers coinciding with each daily leg weeks ago accordingly.

As for *kashruth*, it had been decided that Simmy would do everything possible to maintain these ancient dietary laws throughout the journey for those who wanted it, which was the majority. Everyone, kosher or not, was responsible for buying their own food above and beyond that which the Finance Committee's pool of food money could provide. The few who did not require strictly kosher would, of course, have the easier time of it, especially in the many decidedly non-Jewish districts. Privately, even the non-observant decided they would usually go along with the majority as a matter of respect for unity. It was also easier to share and share alike. Mordecai appreciated their decision deeply and he and the others recognized it as part of the "all-for-one, one-for-all" attitude the group was assuming. Interestingly enough, all three prior journals reported the same experience to some degree.

Other observances, such as daily prayer at sun-up, *tefillin*-wrapping, phylacteries, and *mincha-maarev* prayers late afternoon and evening were left to individual choice. Quick and noticeably shortened Sabbath services were to be conducted at sundown Friday and early Saturday morning before taking to the road. There certainly wasn't a shortage of Fusgeyers who could and would lead these services, including the layman's layman, Mendel Buchman. That first night in the open air, some of the better self-appointed would-be cantors, *chazzanim*, such as Menachem Katz, Mayer Bernstein and Velvel Niedl, loved the natural acoustics of their voices carrying over the treetops and beyond. The *Shema* had never sounded so melodious. So much so, that everyone would have agreed that God had heard this highest of affirmations.

A side note in Sendehr's daily journal (surely to the dismay of any Birladers who might read the weekly synopsis he would be sending to Rabbi Nachman) read:

> *Tonight I witnessed an interesting happening. At mincha-maarev, Rivka, Pessel, Chaike, Esther, Maidele, and Tsipporah proudly slipped among the men and openly prayed. They all wore head coverings and, in fact, Esther stood shoulder-to-shoulder with Mendel, and Maidele boldly held Gershon's hand. Perhaps this is merely a first-night phenomenon, but not one man objected, although some moved silently to the far side of the campfire. As far as I could determine, no one complained to Mordecai or to the "perpetrators" afterward. There was no sign of thunder or lightning and no booming voice shouting "Tor-nit, this is prohibited." Obviously, this has set a precedent for the remainder of the journey. Is this so terribly wrong?*

As an afterthought, the scribe wrote: *PREEVAHT, for your eyes only, Rabbi.*

The campfire glowed brilliantly, and after everyone had eaten their fill, several Fusgeyers offered to gather firewood, and soon a series of smaller fires blazed cheerfully in front of each pitched shelter. Doctor Hippocrates and his nurse reported to Mordecai no one, absolutely no one, in the troop had asked for anything of any kind from the medical pouches.

No one expected the journey to go on this way for very long, but taking it one day at a time, this first one was happily uneventful. Morale was at a peak, the stars were brightly shining, and there was no rain or inclemency in sight. Sweet and bitter scents of tobacco smoke wafted through the air. Many Fusgeyers enjoyed toking on pipes, rolled cigarettes, and miniature cigars filled with Turkish tobacco, but also an unusual number of them were non-smokers.

Sholem and Yaakov, for example, eschewed anything that would violate their respiratory systems and ultimately hamper their running abilities. Yaakov had read recently an article in the *Iashi Yiddishe Shtimme* daily about the negative effects of smoking. Evidently, some maverick doctor at the University of Berlin Medical School had come up with what he referred to as "incontrovertible proof of the inherent dangers of tobacco smoke." The men of the *shul* hearing of the theory, dubbed the doctor a Deutsche-quack, *"a nar mit a loch in kopp,"* a fool with a hole in his head, and *"an anti-semit."* So much for science.

After most had turned in, Sendehr, Zed-Zed, and Mordecai, under the same shelter, conferred over the maps and schedules. This was to be a nightly occurrence. Sometimes, far into the night, when specific problems needed attention the trio invited other committee heads under their canvas when the situation pertained to their jurisdiction.

Soon, their erstwhile hosts, Farmer Mirescu and his

very pregnant wife, Nadia, joined them.

"So you like our beautiful meadow for your first night away from home," commented Vlad Mirescu, exhaling a curlicue of smoke from the cigarette Zed-Zed had offered him. "Ahhh! Turkish tobacco. My favorite. Expensive. How do you Jews get the money for these things? I have to settle for that cheap, smelly, local—how you say— *dreck.*"

"Why complain, Mirescu? You have a lot that we can never have in this country," Sendehr asked him in his quiet, steady way.

"What do you mean, sir?" Nadia chimed in with a slight confrontational tone. "Life is very hard on the farm. Even I work all day, with a baby in my belly."

Mordecai set aside his deep pipe and spoke calmly.

"What Sendehr, here, means is simply just that. You own a farm. It's yours. You and Vlad are fully recognized citizens of this country. You can vote in any national or local election authorized by the parliament. Government officials, petty or major do not harass you. Unruly mobs do not scare you. No one will dare to pull your father's beard. The granaries or the grain merchants will never boycott your barley-rye-wheat crops. Your beautiful onion-domed churches in Motusheni or Puleshti or Birlad or wherever you pray on Sundays are sacrosanct. No one will break the windows or scrawl obscenities or crosses on the walls."

Nadia Mirescu stood aghast while Vlad stared squinty-eyed at Mordecai. They did not know what to say or how to react to this young man who spoke to them so plainly and on their level. Rather than have them suffer the pain of silence, Mordecai continued, not wishing to further embarrass his hosts.

"Yes, dear Nadia and Vlad. You know very well that Jewish life in Romania has become unbearable. You've seen groups of sixty, seventy, eighty young Jews leave the country. Leave their families and friends, their loved ones, behind. Perhaps never to see them again. Why in God's name would they be leaving if all of this were not true? Commonplace, at that! Even out here in the countryside you interact with the small communities surrounding you. You hear talk about everything I mentioned. There are no secrets when it comes to Romania's hatred for its Jews. If it were to be otherwise, most of these people, your age, my age, would be home in their own beds tonight."

Mordecai's use of the Romanian language was nothing short of eloquent, and in the end he dropped his tone and finished softly and without rancor.

The Mirescus, while harboring their own antithetical ideas of what Mordecai had tried so hard to explain, politely, sheepishly, bid their goodnights. Zed-Zed made sure to give Vlad a package of the Turkish tobacco he coveted, and a handshake before he could leave them.

As the couple turned to walk back toward the farm-house, Sendehr humbly added, "Thank you, again, for allowing us on your land." His grin was uncomfortable but true.

"Don't forget! Clean up before you leave," the young landowner shot back, getting in the last words, at least.

The next day's route was expected to be an easy one, taking them as far as a pine forest just beyond Bacau. Sendehr noted that a friendly family of beekeepers lived in a stone hut at the edge of the wood and had graciously provided jars of honey for Shlomoh Margolis's 1901 contingent. Good news for the many tea drinkers! Several of the group with family or friends in Bacau chose to spend the night in a warm house, and then to re-join them the next morning at the 7:00 a.m. start time.

* * *

No one in the entire camp noticed the silhouettes of two figures carrying a tent-half off into the adjoining fruit orchard.

Der Lehrer and his *Queen Esther* were not going to be picking apples on their wedding night.

8

PRISLOP PASS

I hold that man should strive to his uppermost for his life's set prize.

Sir Ernest Shackleford, *Antarctic Explorer*

Sholem and Yaakov were more or less appointed as permanent "point." And for the first week, since leaving home, they had handled the assignment when no one else had volunteered for it, and Mordecai had not selected anyone to take their places. They both seemed to thrive on it. Walking three hundred to five hundred meters ahead gave them a feel for the open road. Unencumbered, they felt that they were the lucky firsts of their comrades to see and experience everything they would eventually encounter. The first to see each lake, each river, each village, a town here, a farm there. The first to see each wondrous beauty of nature, minutes ahead of everyone else. The first to leap across a mud-hole, the first to feel the spray of a waterfall, and to see the deer, the cows, bulls, horses, a stranger approaching. The first to greet each *lantsman*, a fellow Jew, a *mezuzzah* on a doorpost, a *shul*, a church. But what they had just seen this morning, coming around a bend of the full-flowing Bistritsa River, was something they had hoped they would not see that day—Prislop Pass, off in the distance, in the very heart of the rugged Carpathians...covered with snow.

When Sendehr Efraim reached them, he spread out his Romanian Army maps, and corrected the point team. It was not Prislop Pass they had spotted. That mountain was in a dead-westerly direction and they were looking southwest. The peak that they could see had to be *Pasul* Tihuta, which was closer to them, and at an elevation of 1200 meters. If the Carpathians were blanketed at that height, *Pasul* Prislop, which was 1400 meters, would certainly be covered as well. Worse, the heavy, dark clouds over Tihuta were moving in a northerly direction toward Prislop.

Snow this time of year in the Carpathians was not at all unusual. However, the heavy rains of mid-March in past years had caused the residual snow to melt sooner than its regular thaw period. The same happened for more than a week-and-a-half this past March, but evidently a new storm had swept through this far north very recently. None of the other groups had left this early in the spring, and their journals had no mention of anything more than a slight dusting of snow on Prislop. Now, Fusgeyer contingent #4 faced a potentially treacherous climb over the pass, which they were scheduled to reach in two days.

When they had passed through Piatra the day before, word of their approach had spread through ahead of them to the large, hustling, bustling community of one of the Moldavian Region's leading concentration of Jews. As a result, the greeting they received was quite a bit more pronounced than at Bacau. The sight of the Romanian and Zionist flags and the sounds of the drum and the trumpet had brought out a small group of teenaged *cheder* students. Standing together in front of one of the numerous full-scale synagogues, they shouted, "Go to Palestine! Join the people at Rosh Pina! You belong in Palestine! Why are you going to America?" Their *lehrer* had come out to apologize to Mordecai, explaining that there was a strong Zionist connection in that city, and sixty former residents of Piatra were among the Romanian Jews at Rosh Pinah, one of a growing number of agricultural settlements in the Galilee.

Mordecai and the others understood that this outburst would probably recur in other towns along the way wherever there happened to be this yet-quite-rare vociferous Zionist sentiment.

Mordecai knew that although Birlad had only a flurry of such activity, the movement had grown noticeably since last year's most recent World Zionist Congress. Still, the vast majority of Eastern European Jews did not seem to subscribe to Theodor Herzl's unrelenting zeal in any significant numbers.

Sendehr Efraim found in his studies of history with Rabbi Holtzer and in his voracious reading that Herzl had brought his brand of aggressive Zionism to the forefront with his renowned 1896 essay *Der Judenstaat*, the idea of a Jewish State in Palestine. The idea of a sovereign domain for Jews had already proven to be the outline for all subsequent Zionist political thinking. Sendehr, who at one time began to consider Palestine as an alternate choice to America, also found that as a national movement, the idea dated back only to the beginnings of the nineteenth century. However, as a national concept it was as old as the Babylonian Exile of 586 B.C.E., when a longing for the homeland had consumed the distraught exiles. He was particularly awed by the words of the Psalmist who took the vow.

If I forget thee. O Jerusalem,
Let my right hand forget her cunning.
Let my tongue cleave to the roof of my mouth,
If I remember thee not;
If I set not Jerusalem
Above my chiefest joy.

Psalms, 137:5-6

Sendehr had also learned of the "Lovers of Zion" (*chovevei tziyon*) movement, which was the precursor of the WZO. It began as a pamphlet written by one Leo Pinsker in 1882, *Auto-Emancipation*, after he had personally witnessed and survived an Odessa pogrom the year before. Pinsker's ideas became the platform for the organization, which by 1892 had established fifty chapters worldwide, mostly in Russia and Poland, but also in the United States, Canada, and in the towns of Iashi and Piatra. Twenty-five thousand settlers from Russia, Poland, and Romania populated the *Chovevei Tziyon* settlements in Palestine from 1892-1903. Three Birlader families emigrated in 1899—against the warning of friends and other relatives—two more in 1901 and two the past year.

Their letters spoke of the harsh and frustrating conditions, the hostility of the Turkish authorities, the constant fear and reality of Arab attacks and depredations, the malaria and dysentery, the less-than-fertile soil and the inhospitable climate. But most disturbing were the consistent comments about the old established *Chassidic* and other ultra-orthodox communities. The farmers and the pious were at bitter odds with each other. The 20,000 pietists who had come to Palestine to devote themselves to prayer and Torah study—to hasten the coming of the elusive *Mashiach* and the Jewish Redemption—felt immediately threatened by the rationalistic newcomers, orthodox or not. "Besides," wrote one of the correspondents, "they unfairly think that we will eventually siphon off some of the charitable contributions they collect from the Diaspora, on which many of them exist. They look upon us as competitors for the already thinning donations, and as deterrents to the 'coming.'"

This kind of firsthand news tended to put off any consideration Sendehr, and quite a few of the other Fusgeyers, gave to the idea of Palestine as a refuge. The thought of life in America, also from firsthand reports—numerous letters from the other groups—had intrigued and heavily influenced the sixty trekkers. Sendehr and Mendel spent many hours, since the latter's arrival as the *lehrer*, in deep discussion of Jewish history and the state of Jewish affairs today, especially Palestine versus America. Rabbi Nachman was also well versed in these topics, and the three of them sat for hours in his tiny office, nearly every Sunday morning, from January until the day before departure.

At any rate, Mordecai and the cadre understood that these children of Piatra were not the last group to try to influence the Fusgeyers' course. Rabbi Nachman had often warned Mordecai that there would be many such push-pulls along the way: Budapest, Vienna, Prague, Berlin, England, France, and yes, even Argentina and Australia, would steal their way onto the menu.

The actual border between the Austro-Hungarian Empire and Romania began just beyond the Bistritsa, to its west. But although they split up and looked everywhere, Yaakov and Sholem were unable to find a sign for the Hungarian military border post, or the Romanian garrison, for that matter. Their campsite in the once Romanian, now Hungarian, town of Vatra Dornei was next to the Jewish cemetery. There were very few Jews, an unused *shul*, and not much of any organization there, according to the prior reports.

Sholem and Yaakov sought out a man named *Freilacher* Bereleh, Berel the Cheerful One, when they arrived in town just ahead of the main group, as usual. They found him with his wife, sharing a simple supper in their modest one-room cottage near the cemetery. Excusing his impoverished accommodations, Berel greeted them, and in just under two minutes, he raced through the story of Vatra Dornei and its Jews. An extremely literal boycott, local terrorism, two mysterious disappearances, rapidly increasing emigration, his own grown children walking off to Hapsburg Budapest, and—poof!—the virtual erasure of a community that could trace its origins back to the seventeenth century was complete. More importantly, the district magistrate paid no attention to the growing incidents of identifiable local hooliganism whenever it concerned the deeply diminished Jewish population.

When the point team had relayed this sad, but altogether too familiar story to Mordecai, he and his cadre decided, for the first time, to assign the Defense Committee to overnight vigilance. The three Golub boys and Branko would stand guard in four two-hour shifts beginning at 10 p.m., marked, of course, by Zed-Zed's timepiece. As a further precaution, Mordecai, following his strict non-confrontational policy, ordered the *mincha-maarev* singing and all conversation to be kept at a low volume. The campfire was also to be downscaled. The pine grove next to the unkempt headstone-filled grounds suited these purposes well. It was likely that this *modus operandi*, partially followed by the other groups, would set the pattern for most of the journey ahead.

The twenty-four-year-old leader never seemed to raise his voice. Not even in anger, of which he was quite capable. Yet he had the uncanny ability to tame some of the more rambunctious ones, especially the few under-sixteens and even some older troublemakers. Mordecai's droopy black mustache sometimes made it appear that he was frowning, but there was a perpetual gleam in his dark eyes that negated a negative countenance. And why would this young widower have any reason to be happy when everyone knew what had befallen him in the autumn of '02? Losing a wife and child, a boy, in the throes of a breech delivery gone awry was as devastating as a loved one's death can be. He mourned quietly through the *shiva* period, and within six months he had thrown himself headlong into planning for the next Fusgeyer contingent.

His father-in-law and mentor, Fischl Berman, the leading glass blower in all of Moldavian Romania, had hoped all along that Mordecai would be taken by the charms of his exotically beautiful daughter, Gittel, and when it had happened, he was the happiest man, yes, again, in all of Moldavian Romania. To compound the tragedy of his daughter's death and the simultaneous loss of what would have been his first grandchild, Fischl was now losing the man who was to take over his work as a *gluhz bluhzer*. Not only that, Mordecai was taking his son Menachem along. Fischl knew, however, that Menachem suffered the loss of his younger sister terribly, and that he thoroughly disliked the glass-blowing trade. Marching to America was truly God-sent for him, as it was for Mordecai.

Doctor Hippocrates made a brief announcement after evening services concerning the necessity to continue frequent bathing in the streams, lakes, and ponds. Even though the temperature had taken a distinct downturn as they neared the eastern slope of the Carpathians, personal hygiene was an important issue to be periodically addressed. His assistant, Maidele, had no compunction whatsoever in discussing these topics with male or female, and was quick to chastise slackers—privately and tactfully, of course.

Sanitation and cleanliness were a key a part of Jewish life even under the most humiliating conditions. Historically, the Jew religiously followed Biblical instruction on every mode of sanitary consideration. Many rabbis and scholars were quick to point out that this strict adherence to the Bible caused the Jewish population to increase at twice the rate of the non-Jewish population in the last decades of the nineteenth century. Numerous theories linking hygiene to longevity propounded by an army of social historians began with one important, indisputable, statistical fact: Among the general population, the death rate of infants had decreased from 50% to 40% from the beginning to the end of the century. Meanwhile, among Jews, it had steadily dipped from 40 to just under 25 percentage. Both the higher rate of population increase, and the corresponding lower rate of infant mortality was, according to numerous sociological studies of the period, the direct outcome of the ancient Jewish traditions of charity, the ubiquitous voluntary associations whose special task was to minister to the sick and indigent, the devoted care lavished upon the children, and the general infrequency of alcoholism and venereal disease.

Additionally, the care and cleaning of the campsite was a topic dear to Maidele's heart, and Gershon's as well. The troop's reputation was at stake here, as the "doctor" and "nurse" reminded everyone. Like it or not, these young men and women were thrust into the role of representing a people who would, in turn, be judged by their action or inaction.

General "policing" of the area before leaving in the mornings was a constant.

Each Fusgeyer was totally responsible for his or her own pick-ups, and the tent halves were to be returned to the cart before the morning meal, neatly folded, with pins and ropes stored within the fabric. Basic sanitation rules required slit-trenches to be dug—one for the males and one for the females—immediately after stopping for the night. They were to be secreted insofar as possible, behind trees or large rocks. To make matters easy to record, the cart *shleppers* each day would also be assigned this duty. The next day's *shleppers* drew the duty of refilling and tamping down the trenches just prior to departure time later that morning. Not the most pleasant of assignments, but a necessary one regardless. Nose-mouth-covering kerchiefs were at a premium, of course.

Previous journals proved that each contingent paid attention to the sanitation question, but with watchdogs like Doctor Hippocrates and his lovely Nurse Nightingale, it would seem that this 1904 entry would no doubt raise the standards. As for personal cleanliness, in actuality Gershon and Maidele had little trouble convincing the Fusgeyers to wash behind their ears and the more unmentionable parts of the body, surface and crevice both.

Laundering was yet another consideration for each individual. Cotton undergarments, which had been popularized in the century just past, were believed to increase worldwide overall life expectancy. Previously, heavy woolens, worn all winter, which in some locales lasted six months of the year, had provided a breeding ground for a variety of parasite-borne diseases. This was especially true in the peasant populations of Eastern Europe who were slow to join the cotton-users. For the Jew, since so many Jewish clothing peddlers roamed the districts, making the transition was a natural thing to do. Most of the Fusgeyers wore the newer long cottons and therefore found that doing one's laundry at dusk and drying near the small fire at night proved to be one effective practice, although near-outrageous creativity in this and most anything else, abounded. The expected grumbling and joking accompanied this emphasis on hygiene and cleanliness, but Gershon and Maidele predicted correctly that this would disappear before too long.

The next morning, mealtime, which followed the daily prayer session, brought a shocking surprise for all. At precisely 6:30 on this chilly day, with a brilliant sun just on the rise, bouncing into the camp with his happy demeanor, one *Freilacher* Bereleh upended the burlap sack he carried gingerly and over a hundred fresh eggs spilled out of it. With a quick *"Ess! Ess! Kindelach! Fuhrt gesunt!"* he bounced out as he had come.

Where did he get them? How did he get them? Everyone, in an astonished state, wondered aloud. Speculation ran wild as imaginations soared. He was a magician! He was a thief! He was a sorcerer! He was devil's apprentice! He was not human...he was a *golem!* His wife was really a gypsy! But everyone, who had no aversion to eggs, enjoyed one or two. Some fried them in the little pans that they carried in their sacks. Others boiled them in a little *fendl.* A few of the more daring ate them raw, washing them down with their morning tea. A glorious way to start the day! A conversation enhancement, to say the very least. Sendehr's journal would glow with a vivid description of this morning and its elfish folk hero.

As they were about ready to walk out of Vatra Dornei, Mordecai made a suggestion in an off-hand, rather mild manner, which resulted in a dozen volunteers taking a few minutes to clear, with their bare hands, the adjacent burial grounds of weeds, trash, and the like. That was the least they could do for The Cheerful One, who, as it turned out, had told Sholem and Yaakov that he was the only local who tried to take care of the ancient cemetery. As they filed down the road, they saw him standing, with his wife, on a little hillock behind his humble home, waving goodbye. They would not soon, if ever, forget him.

After this auspicious start, the day deteriorated rather quickly. By the time they reached the village of Iacobeni, at the crossroad to Cimpulung-Moldovenesc, the sun dropped behind fast-increasing storm clouds. The views of *Pasul Prislop* in the distance, which had been pure white to match its surrounding Carpathian range, faded altogether.

The point team began to notice that the telegraph poles, which had been prevalent between Birlad and Bacau, and again on the trek to Piatra, were no longer visible. They surmised that neither telegraph nor telephone service went any further northwest than Vatra Dornei, and they were quite right. Just an observation, mind you. The Fusgeyers weren't accustomed to using telephones, anyway; only a few could be found throughout Birlad. Among the Jews, aside from Moishe Mandelbaum, there were a slow-growing number of "community-use instruments" scattered about: at the hostelry, the saloon, Fishl Berman's glass-blowing shop, the Golub house, Avrum Leventer's stable, and in a few other shops and meeting spots. The town had long ago established a telegraph-cable counter inside the postal office, but in reality parts of Hungary, Romania, and neighboring Bulgaria were among the last regions of Europe to enter the modern age of communications. And they were excruciatingly and stubbornly slow about it.

Sholem and Yaakov also noticed a marked reduction in the number of farmers' wagons on the deep-rutted road. They reasoned that they were fast running out of cultivated land as they headed north-by-northwest into the higher elevations of the rugged Carpathian chain. The gnawing chill increased every minute, and both were happy they had pulled out their homemade mufflers, one green, one blue, after the noon meal break.

During the many planning sessions, weather had come up often as a topic of discussion. Branko, who had ridden in a wagon over the mountain range while en route to Birlad from his army separation at Miskolc in Hungary, had warned them of the possibility of early spring cool days and severely cold nights as they crossed the Carpathians. They agreed that they would probably experience a noticeable warming trend while proceeding down the western slopes into Transylvania (*Erdely*, the Hungarian name for the vast region...a sore point in Romanian-Austro-Hungarian relations) and continuing onto the broad Hungarian plains. From then on they could look forward to typical late spring weather, much like Birlad's. Or, as Itzy Gelman added, "*Umgevyntlekh oder gevyntlek...*unless there was unusual weather about! This would not be unusual. Usually."

The grade upward to the crest of the pass began at the very small hamlet of Cirlibaba. It was here that they would spend the night and prepare for their snow-trek. A deep depression in the foothills surrounding the community—consisting of one church and an array of woodcutter's huts—made for good protection against the wind, which started to kick up along the riverbanks. Sholem and Yaakov waited to get the approval of Mordecai and the others, but in the meantime, they sat down on a craggy outcrop just off the side of the road, peering down into the heavily wooded depression.

Still no sign of any border posts even though they were well inside the lines by now.

"Yak, I actually argued with my mother when she insisted that I take this muffler. I thought, springtime, no need of it."

"I paid attention to what Branko said about the Carpathians. Convinced me! I think with the snow up there, we'll probably end up wrapping our feet with our scarves," replied Yaakov, and just then he saw the group coming slowly up the rise in the road.

The talk that night, as they huddled around the fires, focused on only one subject—the next day: *What will it be like on the pass? Is there any shelter up there? How far do we have to walk before we head downhill? Where in God's name are the border points? We must not fly the Romanian flag any longer. How is everyone's food supply? Anyone ailing? Be sure to fill your drinking vessels in the river tonight or tomorrow morning. Wear your heaviest socks. Two pair, if you can fit into your shoes. No one pulls the cart for more than one hour. Zed-Zed will monitor the time. We will rotate six-man shifts every hour.*

Sendehr and Mordecai assured everyone, once more, that this would probably be the only exceptionally difficult terrain they must face. Once down on the Great Plain of Hungary there would be nothing comparable to Prislop. Mordecai bade goodnight to everyone with one final thought: "With everyone cooperating and working together, the pass will be surmountable."

In their shelter later, before turning in for the night, Zed-Zed confirmed his original schedule: One day to reach the summit. One day to get to more level ground. Stay up on the pass tomorrow night, about twenty kilometers. Reach the mountain village of Borsha for the next night, about twenty more kilometers. Then, it would be all downhill.

Sendehr agreed with these calculations, based on his very detailed army maps, which showed a base near Borsha. But both admitted that snow, heavier than just a dusting, could delay things. At any rate, they should, barring the unforeseen, reach Sighet for Pesach. That was still a goal not to be missed. Mordecai quietly listened to his experts, as he was wont to do, puffing on his oversized pipe filled with aromatic Turkish stuffings.

* * *

Sendehr, writing by the light of a dying fire, synopsized the journal entries for each day on pads of paper he had brought along. This was different than the previous years, when the scribe would send pages right out of the journal every few weeks. Sendehr knew that he wanted the original journal in his possession when he arrived at his destination. On this seventh night, Sendehr finished compiling his first weekly report. He would have to wait until they reached a postal station to mail it, and, according to his maps, the next one could be Borsha. At the end of his journal entry for this day, which encompassed the time from waking-up through Mordecai's final words to the Fusgeyers, Sendehr wrote the following:

> *Sitting by the fire tonight, I've never been prouder of any people in my life. I'm referring to the other fifty-nine Fusgeyers. To this point, they've demonstrated a powerful will to complete what they've started. The cooperation, the congeniality, the willingness to help one another, both the common sense and sense of humor, the adherence to discipline and rules, the sharing and the caring—it all overwhelms me. I know Mordecai feels the same and he periodically makes it known to the group. The morale is high as a direct result of this, the send-off we received, and the dry weather. Tomorrow, we face our first real challenge and I'm certain we will overcome it as sure as there is snow on Pasul Prislop.*

> *Mordecai is privately concerned with the border crossing, wherever it may be, as I am, mainly due to what Branko has told us of his former comrades' penchant for giving Jews a difficult time up to and including violence. They can't be any worse than our lovely Romanian Army, however. After all, our main reason for going this particular route, even though it's a longer one, is because of the near-disaster that befell the 1901 Fusgeyers when they were delayed for ten days near Moineshti. A Romanian platoon threatened to jail them all if they did not disperse and go home. They eventually had to take this same northern route, where presumably the army is still much more thinly-deployed. We pray so. So far we haven't seen any sign of either army. It's eerie. Traveling to Ciuc, on a straight line, according to my maps and the roads followed by the 1900 group, to Klausenberg (Cluj) and Debrecen would have been much more direct and level—and no Prislop to contend with. But if we really have avoided the Romanians, then it's been certainly worth the detour this far.*

> *For the time being, Mendel has postponed his English classes until we conquer Prislop. Rivka has made the final selection for her cast of Dos Vinshfingerl. Her goal is to begin serious rehearsals again after the pass, and I will have one of the parts. Yes, I am her final selec-*

tion! I like my part, and I play opposite Rivka.

Sendehr Efraim, Fusgeyer Contingent #4
En route, Cirlibaba, Moldavia
(I think we are in Hungary, but no sign as yet)
April 7, 1904 (2 Nisan, 5664)

The sun had not make an appearance by the time Sholem and Yaakov had left the next morning—with the group, as usual, three-to-five hundred meters behind. It was by far the coldest morning since leaving home. A wagonload of woodcutters, each with a large, shiny axe on his lap, passed the point team and turned off onto a logging road without showing the least bit of recognition. Shortly afterwards, another wagon, presumably coming down from the pass, carrying two drivers and an older woman sitting on a pile of bags, stopped when Sholem waved them down.

"How is the weather up there, comrades?" he asked the drivers.

"If you like snow and ice, it's near-perfect for you, children," blurted the toothless woman with the black babushka. Her men laughed uproariously and bolted ahead without saying anything more.

"Not at all bad, Sholem. This means that the wagon was able to get through the snow and left a track for us to follow. And if the wagon tramped down some of the snow, the cart *shlepping* won't be quite so difficult, either. I was hoping someone would be coming through," the optimistic Yak offered in response.

In less than an hour, everyone was feeling the steady upgrade, and even in the low-hanging gray clouds, obliterating any distances, sheer white began to bleed through. Snow awaited the Fusgeyers. Not much doubt about that in anyone's mind.

The pace noticeably slowed when the wagon road went through its first "horseshoe bend"—all uphill and growing steeper by each step, and, just around the bend, was the first sight of snow. The biting wind worsened along with each step, particularly where there wasn't any tree-break. Unfortunately, these barriers were becoming much sparser, and the sixty walkers were wrapped in every conceivable style of clothing, with a singular objective—warmth.

Zed-Zed and Sendehr, jointly pacing the kilometers, with the latter constantly unrolling the one army map covering the Northwestern Frontier and its meticulous detail of Prislop and vicinity, estimated that by high noon they would have covered only ten kilometers.

The third group of *shleppers* was ready to turn the cart over to the fourth, when Mordecai called for a halt. The already accumulated snow was now close to a half-meter deep, and the wagon tracks were becoming icier by the minute. At that moment, almost as if planned, flurries, followed by thicker flakes, began to fall steadily, blown horizontally by the swirling wind, making the lighting of fires nearly impossible.

Most made do with bites of dried meat, some hardtack, or a stray piece of very stale *challah* from a Piatra bakery. No tea. Nothing hot to warm the gullet. Despite a word from Dr. Hippocrates to drink plenty of water from their canteens to prevent dehydration, few took to his admonition. Instead, groups of three, four, or more gathered, used some kindling from the cart, and, with anybody's matches, tried to get a fire lit and going. After a short while, all standing groups succeeded and were able to coax a few minutes of warmth.

That's when Mordecai decided to take a count. Something did not feel right to him. ...Fifty-six, fifty-seven, fifty-eight. Fifty-eight! Two were nowhere to be seen. Leib Kalisher and his cousin Kalman Fuchs were missing, they quickly determined. Pessel and Chaike had seen them last, lagging behind where the big bend in the road began the steep rise. Immediately, Mordecai appointed Branko and Yossi Golub to search down the hill.

"Everyone stay where you are. Two are enough. We'll not leave without them. Don't worry," spoke the leader calmly. Traveling together, staying together and arriving together, after all, was the basic premise to which all the Fusgeyers had subscribed from the very beginning: a coordinated, well-planned, mutually-cooperative, interpersonal, equal effort. It was to be this way or not at all. Every person, entity, or organization met along the way would sense this spirit immediately upon meeting this group if the mission were to be carried out to its logical, effective conclusion. It would be this way if their message were to reach the journalists, those fellow Jews in more comfortable positions, or perhaps a king, a president, or a political figure, or if their march were to lighten the life of even one Romanian or Russian Jew. It would be this way if the mission were to make a profound impact at all.

"Thank you God. *Omayn*," a relieved Pessel uttered when the *groisseh bochers* returned within twenty minutes with Leib and an obviously shaken Kalman in tow. The latter had developed a sudden cramping, followed by gut-wrenching heaving, and Leib had stayed with him, but trying to call out to the rear echelons was in vain because of the howling wind.

Gershon immediately went to the pouches for a digestive powder, which both Doctor Simcha and pharmacist Muresan prescribed for such cramps. Without delay, Kalman swallowed it down with a swig of cold water. It didn't appear to be anything other than a bad stomachache. There probably wasn't a soul in camp who didn't' privately pray that it was nothing worse than that. Even the youngest and most carefree knew that in an isolated region, far from any doctor or hospital, fatalities could result from something minor if left untreated, or treated by guesswork.

This universal reality was in no way casting even the slightest aspersion toward the conscientious Doctor Hippocrates, but the dangers of ailment afflicting the trekkers was a constant worry for Mordecai—as it would be for any caring leader. Meanwhile, the snow continued and had quickly obliterated the wagon tracks, and he was faced with a decision: to stay or go on.

Zed-Zed wanted to push onward for at least three more hours to stay close to his schedule. "Unreasonable," firmly stated Sendehr. Branko stood with Zed-Zed, but Mordecai sided with Sendehr, and at random, ten others were asked their opinions.

While each presented persuasive arguments, Sholem and Yaakov returned from an independent reconnaissance mission, which had taken them about a kilometer up the road. They returned reporting that lack of visibility and faded tracks further on made it foolhardy to continue until morning. Once again, the sensible won over the impractical.

Simmy began distributing the protective canvas-halves from the cart. Selected teams went out to gather pine tree branches, for firewood, that they had spotted for the last two kilometers coming up the hill.

Mordecai and his cadre wanted to keep everyone moving for the next few hours to ward off any frostbite. Most essential, they warned, was that no one would be allowed to sit or lay down, no matter how exhausted they felt. In these bare hills, scarce bits of wood buried under so much snow, fires had to be kept small and used by more people than usual. The supply of matches, thank God, was adequate but would have to be replenished in the next week. With a bit of luck and some foresight, Simmy had been able to find and purchase only one box in Piatra, and it was now added gratefully to individual supplies of smaller boxes. The smokers never seemed to be matchless.

After *mincha-maarev*, darkness fell like a black blanket. Only the main campfire was left slightly ablaze and there was still plenty of newfound pine to place back into the cart for morning fires. None of the Fusgeyers had ever slept in the open in such freezing cold, engulfed by snow ... still falling. Certainly those who prayed that evening slipped in a beseeching word or two concerning the weather, and were later quick to add a delayed *omayn* when the snow not only let up, but it began to turn into a steady rain. Realistically, this could pose hard going in slushy snow for the morning, or it could just as easily spell the last snow until next winter...in America.

The sight of a camp filled with little white "snow is-lands" amid the mud of rain-melted snow greeted Mordecai when he arose before the light of dawn. Now it would be mud to battle. But somehow, this didn't seem to phase any-one when they each surveyed the landscape upon rising, due to the welcome warming that accompanied the rain during the night and early morning hours.

The uniform-of-the-day was, without exception, wet clothing, since nothing had dried out under the canvas during the night. After a morning meal, Sholem and Yaakov got to the Prislop summit and were greeted by a giant mudslide that came down from the adjacent hillside, cover-ing the entire wagon trail. They sighed and looked down upon a veritable quagmire of huge proportions that would take more than praying and a foolproof bit of strategizing to overcome.

When the others arrived, a hasty meeting was held be-tween cadre personnel and the leader. The initial problem concerned getting the cart through the barrier, but this was readily solved by lifting the vehicle, load and all, and carry-ing it over the ten-meter pile. It took twenty of the huskiest and strongest to do it—six on each side, four in back, and another four on the extended arms.

A roar from the onlookers went up when they succeeded. The walk to the North Sea could continue! Mordecai was beaming broadly as Fusgeyer morale climbed to new heights. Resiliency proved to be a most formidable trait in these de-termined young people.

Starting downhill at last, with Pietrasu Peak off to the south standing snow-topped at 2300 meters, the Fusgeyers sloshed through the slush and mud like children with the first snowfall. The singing, which had been absent for a few days, picked up in earnest as they felt themselves heading down the last long stretch before reaching level ground. Velvel Palastrant was itching to blow on his trumpet, but a wary Sendehr shushed him, knowing that a border post had to be looming up soon, according to his maps, but they had been wrong already—the same maps had shown them back in Vatra Dornei, where they never did appear.

Up ahead, two wagonloads of field workers were heading up the hill, and Sholem warned them of the mudslide. In turn, the driver of the lead wagon spoke, in Romanian, of a border post lying just ahead, at the mountain village of Borsha. He also knew why the Romanian side of the lines back in Vatra Dornei had been unmanned.

"Too little traffic to warrant the manning of a station. Ran out of budget for soldier pay and left the borders in that vicinity wide open. How do you like that, Jew-boys? Your lucky day, especially with the Hungarians moving their station back here to Borsha." The man then offered a more sobering thought, warning them of the rather surly Hungarian commander who showed his hatred for the local folks, Romanians, Jew or gypsy.

Branko would have his opportunity to prove his worth at this juncture. Sholem and Yaakov knew this very well, as did Mordecai, Sendehr, Zed-Zed, and every last one of the Fusgeyers. None the least, *der groisseh soldat*, Ex-sergeant Branko Horvitch, of the 19th Infantry Regiment, Hapsburg Honor Corps, "retired," knew he had work to do.

Borsha stood quite alone on the north bank of the River Visheu. The Birladers crossed over an unsteady, narrow bridge into the village itself, where a small array of shops provided for the Hungarian garrison and the few hundred people living in relative isolation here on the western slope of the Carpathians. Mordecai decided not to allow for a stop here, but to take on the border post immediately.

The mud-covered young Jews slogged on through the two-hundred-meter buffer zone between the quiet town and the garrison's barracks. Ever-shifting borders, wars, peace treaties, talks and more talks, broken negotiations, repaired relations, and then through the same cycles again and again, had made for a constant political tug-o-war over this territory for the last century.

The guards usually turned aside for the Jews who wished to leave Romania and transit through Austro-Hungarian lands. Policy throughout these regions was so intensely anti-Jewish that if the migrants could prove they weren't planning to stay, by showing letters of transit, ship passage documents, or the like, they were allowed to pass through all the same. *Good riddance, scum.* Not without some old-fashioned harassment, of course. Isolated border guards had to relieve the boredom somehow.

Surly would soon prove to be an adequate description of the monocle-wearing Captain Ferenc Sandor. Mordecai instructed Menachem Berman, head of the Diplomatic Committee, in his first test, and Sendehr Efraim, to flank *der groisseh soldat* as he went to the barracks office. He had decided earlier not to send the more vocally volatile Golub boys. This was to be done while everyone waited in the buffer zone until further instructions. No singing. No trumpet. No drum. Just wait, quietly.

Branko had on his person all of the necessary "proof-papers" that Mordecai handed him and would be able to speak in Hungarian, though most Hungarians living or stationed in Transylvania also spoke passable Romanian. Language would not be an issue at this time. His personal papers that showed his army release and signed references to the fact that he served with honor and distinction would prove to be more important than the generally required papers. Yes, the old soldier had a certain amount of pride that showed no signs of diminishing now.

Dexterously flipping his monocle between the fingers of his left hand, Captain Sandor asked Branko to sit down on the cushioned high-back chair, while gesturing for Menachem and Sendehr to sit on the hard bench in the corner. Both chose not to, preferring to stand on each side of their *groisseh soldat.* The stiff captain was still a bit taken aback at the snappy, heel-clicking salute he had received when Branko entered the room. As a knee-jerk reaction, he returned it, for a moment ignoring the fact that Branko was in mud-splattered civilian clothing. Having taken a rather cursory glance at Branko's packet of papers, group and personal, Sandor took his monocle and placed it back in its niche, squeezed by his squint in an annoying manner, and stared for a full minute at the big man seated in the red velvet chair.

"So-o-o, my dear man, you are representing that gaggle of geese standing across the field. Who are they? Who are you? And what the hell do you want from the Magyars of St. Izstvan? So you served in the Hapsburg Corps, soldier? You know we do not bow to anything Austrian, *Ausgleich* or Dual Monarchy nonsense be damned to hell."

Menachem broke in at this point to say politely, and with good intention, "Sir, we are only seeking a right of transit. We don't expect to be in Hungary for any more time than it takes to walk through Sighet, Satu-Mare, ah-h, I mean Szatmar, Debrecen..."

"See here, boy, I am not one of your Romanian-speaking lackeys. I understand little of what you say. Unless you can speak in my revered, ancient language, keep your Jew mouth shut," snapped Sandor, his spit spraying the unperturbed Branko.

The tone had been set, and Branko, holding up a hand to both Menachem and Sendehr, softly continued in a flawless Hungarian dialect: "Sir, we are just sixty people, walking across Europe to Bremerhaven; and from there, as you can see by our confirmed passage letter written in four languages, including yours, we will set off to America." Astutely, the Labor Alliance people had known enough to write the confirmation letter in German, Yiddish, Romanian and Hungarian.

Standing tall with folded arms, peering through his comic-opera monocle at the seated Branko, the captain hissed, "You know, and I know, that you Jews are soft. No other military among you, probably. And you think you're going to walk through my beautiful land? The Great Plains, the *nagyyfold*, will chew you up and spit you out! If not, the roving bandits will slice you all to ribbons before you ever get to see the sight of Budapest."

This taunting was so transparent to Branko and his honor guard that they each sensed the need for silence. To respond would place them directly into the lion's mouth. *We can take all you want to give. Just give us our transit visa and we'll be on our way.* These were the paramount thoughts buzzing through three of the brains in that little room.

"Your bloody brothers have made quite a mark for themselves in Budapest. They are forever trying to control our government, and the newspapers, and the theater with their great wealth. You see how tolerant our government is? We are not the uncivilized animals that one finds in Bucureshti or Saint Petersburg or among the Ottomans. No, no! Unlike the others, we welcomed the Jew into our midst. We granted them political equality while the Russkies and your filthy Romanians kept the Jews in rags and slaughtered them like sheep...and still do. Am I right? Even when I was due for promotion and transfer to Budapest, a goddamn Jew junior-officer was picked over me. Yes, even in the military Jews are welcomed. The Austrians love their Jews, don't they Horvitch?"

This alabaster white martinet was slowly turning beet red, and Branko, knowing that an incurably rabid, anti-Semitic Hungarian officer held the Fusgeyers' future in his sweaty palms, chanced his reply. "Yes, Captain, I met with nothing but friendship in my service to Austria...and Hungary, too, I might add. I went on, perhaps, ten joint-effort assignments, from Praha to Brody, from Vienna to Zagreb, from Temesvar to Sarajevo. I served an entire year with your famous Hortobagy Cavalry Unit."

At this juncture, he took a deep breath, exhaled, and carefully continued. "Honored Captain, we have to be in Sighet by the 16th, for religious purposes. We will quickly get out of your sight if you'll just sign a group transit visa for at least sixty days. We mean no harm to anyone. Just passing through the great and noble Magyar kingdom."

"What religious purposes, may I ask? Are you referring to your Passover?" Branko nodded, and Captain Ferenc Sandor continued, now with a smile: "Watch out for those Sighet Jews. They're the weird ones, y'know. They'll have you drinking some innocent child's blood and they'll call it wine. Or, as I've heard, they'll use the blood to bake those crackers. Yech! You Jews are still swinging from the trees."

With these cavalier bravados, Branko knew he had won, and at that moment, he watched as the captain went to his desk, took a pen, dipped it into the inkbottle, and started to fill in a printed form. It was a standard ten-week visa, good until June 22nd. Victory!

All the martinets, the Captain Ferenc Sandors of the world, could go through their well-practiced delaying tactics and their little mind games trying to provoke arguments or angry responses, but it began to appear that nothing or no one was going to stop this locomotive with its full head of steam.

9

PESACH–SIGHET

May all who are in need come and celebrate with us!
Haggadah, The Story of Passover

Even with his small lettering, Sendehr's description of the day took up three whole pages. At this rate, he'd need another journal by the time they got to Vienna, or Prague. So much had happened, culminating with the border incident, that he wrote without stopping for the better part of an hour. Two days later, he also wrote a few more paragraphs for the synopsis he planned to mail in Sighet and added a private message for Rabbi Nachman.

> *After meeting Captain Sandor, I harbored the notion that maybe there are worse enemies than the Romanians. Can we be hated everywhere? Why would there be such feelings in Hungary where, as Sandor admitted, Jews have been given citizenship and equal rights? If what he says is the least bit true, the Jews of Hungary have made and are still making important contributions to many phases of Magyar life. Could it possibly be that this very fact fuels an even more widespread animosity? There are times when I wish I had stayed at home and tried to live with what I had. And it's only been two weeks.*

THE WAYFARERS

A sweet Pesach, Rabbi, to the Nachman family.
Yaakov is feeling very well, mentally an physically,
and sends his love, as I do mine.

Sendehr Efraim, Fusgeyer Contingent #4
En route,Cuhea, Transylvanian Hungary
April 13, 1904 (8 Nisan, 5664)

Zed-Zed's timepiece would have to be turned back three centuries to match the picturesque villages leading to Sighet, along the River Tisza. Unlike the towns and villages in Moldavia, these places had vehemently resisted any innovations of the new century or the two prior to it. The women in their colorful dress, the men in clothing never before seen by the Fusgeyers, stopped whatever they were doing in their brightly painted homes with multi-colored shutter designs, or in the fields, to watch this strange group of young people march on by.

This occurred in each of the villages—Cuhea, Ieud, Rozavlea—and just before they reached Sighet, the pretty hamlet of Vadu Izei. Oddly enough, the villagers were friendly, chatting in Romanian with anyone who would stop. More than a few came out with offerings of fresh eggs, massive jars of pickled tomatoes, cauliflower, cucumbers, crab apples, and a variety of preserves. Everything from the last growing season.

The visibly budding trees in the surrounding orchards were weeks away from yielding anything ripe enough for picking; but the fertile-looking fields of rich, black earth were plowed and ready for spring planting. Simmy Fiedelman, "the food czar," was in a heaven of his own, stocking up on food supplies. Reb Krasnigor allotted Simmy enough from the "bank" to purchase beyond what some of the overly generous peasants so freely donated.

In Ieud, the Fusgeyers took a particular liking to three families cultivating the apple and pear trees, also selling eggs. A perfect place for an overdue break among the trees, and Zed-Zed so ordered as much. Within seconds, Rivka and her entire cast of would-be thespians gathered under a pear tree and proceeded to serenade the Ieudians with the Romanian version of the Yiddishe love ballad, *"Margaritekelech,"* a song of the little daisies blooming in spring, which was to be included in the play. Velvel Palastrant's trumpet accompaniment was as sweet as Gabriel's horn, during which Rivka's impromptu gypsy belly dance, *sans* the bare midriff, was the *pièce-de-resistance,* stunning all the onlookers—most of all Sendehr, whom she lured into playing the dance partner, in her most charmingly provocative way.

A grand time was had by all. Certainly this merriment was the most fun these serious wayfarers had enjoyed in too long a time. The Ieudians loved every minute of it, and it visibly saddened them to see the group continue on its way. They could still be seen waving when the first bend in the road came up. No doubt, it had been the most enjoyment they, too, had experienced in a long time.

Having camped in a sweet-smelling hay field outside of Vadu Izei, as soon as he awoke, Mordecai asked Sholem and Yaakov to walk faster than usual into Sighet. Sendehr estimated that it was a mere eight kilometers away according to his maps and the calculations that he and Zed-Zed had made months ago. Zed-Zed was delighted that his schedule was being met thus far. "Sighet on the 16th, and here we are!" he reported to Sendehr.

Once in Sighet, Mordecai asked the point team to find the *shul* where Rabbi Nachman's *yeshiva* colleague served as the assistant rabbi. He deduced that it would have to be the largest in town because an assistant was certainly a luxury that only those larger town or city synagogues could afford.

Mordecai was pleased that the Fusgeyers would be able to enjoy an extended rest since the first seder would not be held until the next evening, and they would not have to leave until the morning after the second seder. Hot, home-prepared food, sweet wine, and some welcome fellowship in celebrating Pesach would serve as a powerful impetus for the long march still ahead of them. The thought of being part of this small exodus while citing a much larger one three thousand years before would most certainly bring some deep, personal meaning for all the Birlader Fusgeyers.

The two speedsters, leaving behind their packs, covered the distance in slightly more than an hour. Yaakov even wore his Greek "racers" for the first time since leaving Birlad, so the two had a series of friendly little dash-races between telegraph poles, which had now begun to appear again. As usual, Sholem won handily each time, racers or no racers. And he won while wearing his dilapidated high-top boots, not barefoot!

They stopped to eat some olives and a piece of stale bread just at the spot where an old sign, in Romanian, proclaimed that they were about to enter Sighetul. The "ul" was painted out, and the remaining Sighet became "Sziget," replaced by some petty Magyar official who must have felt he had done his part to complete the virtual Magyarization of Hungary's Romanian minority in Transylvania. Another sign, in Hungarian, pointed to the cutoff toward Satu-Mare, which was heavily encumbered by its Magyar name: Szatmarnemetsi. Such confusion was only an insignificant part of the price paid throughout the ever-expanding and sometimes-contracting Dual Monarchy—The Austro-Hungarian Empire. This had been ongoing for more than a century, and was best symbolized by the official Hungarian bank notes—printed in eight languages on one side, and only Hungarian on the other. Magyarization rules!

Sighet/Sziget, a much larger version of the Tisza Valley villages they had passed through for the past few days, appeared cleaner, laid out in a modified grid fashion. The main streets were broader than those in Birlad, and the early morning activity more pronounced. The clean-shaven Sholem Friedman and the mustachioed Yaakov Nachman didn't particularly stand out as strangers in this town of twenty thousand, including upwards of seven thousand Jews.

They went directly to a Jewish shop, signified by the Hebrew lettering in the window: *Lehrbaum, der schneider-maven,* and were directed by the "expert tailor" to the main *shul.* After a short walk across the bridge over the meandering River Tisza, they caught sight of the domed Great Synagogue, adjacent to its extensive, well-kept cemetery. Much like Birlad, Sighet maintained two smaller places of worship and numerous *shtiebelach* in and around the compact town.

The day was cool and sunny as the Fusgeyers marched into town, trumpet and drum beating out a cadence for their feet to follow. The Romanian flag had been placed in the bottom of the cart just before the Borsha border post, and Rivka along with two of the tailors in the group had begun to plan the making of a Hungarian replacement. Discretion was most definitely the better part of valor under these circumstances. But the *Mogen Dovid* flag was being held proudly by its bearer, Zacharya Udler. It had been washed in the Tisza a few nights earlier and now appeared sparkling white to the gathering group of onlookers. The growing crowd shouted "Welcome, Fusgeyers" in Yiddish, and a group of giggling schoolgirls tossed some of the first flowers of spring, yellow *margaritekelech,* onto the marchers. Obviously, Rabbi Nachman's colleague had been busy passing the word of their pending arrival.

There, standing on a corner of the bridge, were Sholem, Yaakov, and a young man in the black garb of the rabbinate. Mordecai dispersed the troop and walked over to them. After proper introductions, which included some of the cadre standing by, the Rabbi, Yaakov Kurtzman, explained the schedule to Mordecai.

"It is so very good to have you all with us for Pesach. It seems that everyone wanted to host a few Fusgeyers, and so I've asked all volunteers to be at the *shul* for *mincha-maarev* in order to introduce and assign everyone."

"Excellent, Rabbi Kurtzman. We'll be there. I've told everyone to explore the town and meet at the *shul* at sundown. Will there be any problem leaving our cart on the *shul* grounds?"

"No, Mordecai, in fact you'll see that we have a very large sanctuary and an attached meeting room where any of you are welcome to sleep. Although, all of the hosts are offering lodging as well as the seder. How does a warm meal, and a warm bed appeal to your senses, eh?"

"*Boruch Hashem,* praised be the Lord, *Omayn!*" An echoing "*omayn*" came loudly from Zed-Zed, Sendehr, Sholem, Yaakov, and Simmy in unison and with great passion. After more than two weeks afoot, this stop would revitalize everyone for certain!

Preparing for the Passover was tantamount to thorough springtime cleaning, and on that first day in town, the Fusgeyers came across one last-minute, familiar scene after another: families beating carpets, washing all of the Pesach glasses and dinnerware and silverware, airing out the house and the bedding, and scouring the stoves. Some of the Jewish eateries in the town were closing for the entire eight days of the holiday, while others were also going through the cleaning processes so that they could offer strictly *pesachdickeh* meals after two seder nights.

Passover was an especially difficult time for those Fusgeyers who were a bit more melancholy in being away from home at holiday time than for some of the others. For the eight young men who had left wives and children behind, it was sure to be an especially lonely and empty Pesach. Also, there were five sets of brothers and the three Golubs, and so many homes in Birlad would have more than one empty place at the seder table that following evening. But the good people of Sighet would do everything possible to nurture the children of Birlad as if they, too, were family. And, indeed, they were.

Mordecai, Mendel and Esther, and Yaakov Nachman had their seders with Rabbi Kurtzman at the home of Shimon Pomerantz, titular head of the community. An ardent Zionist who had attended the 1903 Congress in Switzerland, Pomerantz showed a sincere appreciation for the Fusgeyer objectives, but politely insisted that they were headed in

122

the wrong direction. Palestine, after all, was to the south-east.

"I know you hear of the troubles our settlers are having in our Promised Land, but do you think it's any better in America? From what I know, your *goldeneh medina* is a veritable cauldron of anti-Semitism—anti-immigration of any kind, for that matter. And that hotheaded president of theirs, fighting with his own businessmen and industrialists, rattling his saber all over the world! Hmph! Won't any of your people reconsider? I can arrange free transportation for anyone, from either Constantsa or Balchik."

This was his job, his belief, and he felt it was also his duty to convince any Jew that Palestine must be, should be, his or her eventual destination for complete salvation. Palestine would someday be a Jewish State, and all would return to their holy Promised Land to live in peace forevermore. From this stance, he would not waver. Not that he was in any rush to make *aliyah* for himself or his family. He once carefully broached the idea to his married daughter, the one with his handsome twin ten-year-old grandsons, who forbade him ever to mention it in her children's presence again. Grandma saw to that.

A good portion of the first seder consisted of the reading of the *Haggadah*, the story of Passover, and its four standard questions, *der vier kashes*, and of course the fifth question posed by the host, "Why not Palestine?" The affable and able Gittel Pomerantz successfully shushed her over-eager husband on a few occasions. Alas, he soon came to the final realization that there was not even one potential *aliyah* at his table that night.

Without any official boycotts of Jewish business, and with full voting rights, full citizenship, and a growing economy throughout the massive empire, the life of the Jew in Sighet, as witnessed by these young Birladers, was far superior to the one they had just left behind or had ever before seen. Mendel Buchman later compared it favorably with the years he had spent in comfortably cordial Salonika and Athens. Granted, there was a steady flow of anti-Jewish sentiment in the Hapsburg Empire, either as a political ideology or of the hateful Captain Sandor variety, however, conditions were generally better than those found in the Pale or Romania.

All in all, there were sixteen host families, each with three or four Birladers at their seder tables. Sendehr, Zed-Zed, and Sholem Friedman were sent to a family accommodating twenty-two participants for the seders. The Viesls, whose family had lived in Sighet since coming from Krakow in the latter part of the seventeenth century, were most gracious hosts with an interesting and most eclectic array of guests, family, and friends. The meal, the singing, the friendliness were all sheer delight to the three eastern visitors. "I have never seen so much roast chicken at one sitting!" Sholem, the point man, remarked while all others laughed with him.

Times were indeed good for Sighet—or Sziget or Maramarosh Sziget or Sighetul Maramuresh—the mere name of the place lost in the over-riding messages during this celebration of freedom: deliverance from a pharaoh or a czar or a king, or a despot of any variety.

Eliezer Viesl wrote feature articles for the *Budapest Weekly Jewish Times* and was working on a novel of Jewish life in Transylvania. Sendehr hoped that he could talk with him. This opportunity came about after the seder, when all of the men gathered in the front room to quiz the Fusgeyers on their journey thus far. When it came to light that Sendehr was keeping a journal, Reb Viesl asked if he could take a look at it the next morning after *shul.* This pleased the budding writer no end. Morning couldn't come quickly enough.

After brief Pesach services, attended by most of the Fusgeyers, Viesl invited Sendehr to bring the journal back with him to his home. Over a cup of tea and some delicious honey cake, the host carefully read each page of the growing tome-to-be, covering seventeen days thus far. Sendehr patiently sipped his tea and scanned some of Reb Viesl's newspaper articles as the older man read intently.

"I like this, Sendehr. Your writing style is quite elegant.

Meticulously well-detailed. Are you going to write in English when you get to America? There are only a few Yiddish magazines, journals and newspapers from what I hear."

"Mendel Buchman, our *lehrer*, has been teaching me some fundamentals for the past six months. He's totally fluent, and he's been holding English classes every evening. Compulsory for everyone. He insists on it, and he's very persuasive. Then again, every one of us is also eager to learn...Reb Viesl, perhaps you can tell me what you're writing these days, besides the novel? I'd be most interested to know."

The host paused, then smiled. "As one journalist to another, in confidence, please. I went to Munkach last week. It's less than a day by wagon. Someone wrote a response to one of my columns in the *Budapest Weekly* last month and asked if I would be willing to interview a fascinating woman living incognito in Munkach. I agreed. Well, after this unnamed correspondent readied everything, I found myself sitting in a bare room with this rather striking woman in her early forties.

"Sendehr, you've heard, of course, of Alexander II's assassination in 1881 that set off the two decades of horror perpetrated against our people in the Pale," he paused as Sendehr nodded. "And of course, you Jews of Moldavian Romania have suffered as well, merely by the resulting contagion. Well, the woman I interviewed has been in hiding since then because she was a cell member of the People's Will terrorists, the *narodnaya volya*, and one of the six Jews involved.

"I can give you her name because she now wants the world to know of her deep remorse. Chasia Zitovitz. When she revealed her name to me I was quite stunned, because I remembered that she was listed as missing, a likely fugitive, in every newspaper throughout the region during the blood-stained '80s. Of the twenty-seven responsible for planning and execution of the attack, she is one of the few presumed to be alive today. One of the original cell members, the bomb thrower—Ignacy Hryniewicki—died as a result of the blast, and five others were captured that afternoon. They were unceremoniously hung three weeks later.

"Chasia and twenty others went into hiding. Some were subsequently apprehended. Over the years she managed to wend her way into Austro-Hungarian territory where she met and married a teacher in Munkach, and has lived there since. With only six of the original members known to be Yidden, Chasia included, this was more than enough for them to have to absorb the full blame, eh?"

"But, why such remorse, Reb Viesl?"

"Why? She has carried with her for all these years a deep-seated feeling of guilt that the ensuing rampage of pogroms, wanton killing of Jews, the boycotts, the anti-Jewish legislation—were incited by her deeds and those of her group. Now, she and her husband, childless, have left for Africa, to Cape Town, to join her only sister who lives there. But she wants to ask for forgiveness from the Jews of Eastern Europe. She wants to somehow atone for what she perceives to be her mortal sin. She wants the interview to appear only in Jewish newspapers or magazines and has granted me exclusive rights for the paper that prints most of my feature work, *The Budapest Weekly*, both the Hungarian and the Yiddish editions." He paused, then asked: "*Nu*, tell me, my young colleague, what is your opinion of all of this?"

Very proud that he had just been referred to as Viesl's colleague, but in no way intimidated by the veteran journalist the much younger man had been carefully weighing everything he had heard, and now confidently responded: "Rubbish! Nonsense! In no way do I condone murder or her part in it! To feel that she has the blood of her people on her hands is stretching guilt beyond reason. Alexander III needed no excuse to blame the minorities of Russia for his father's death, especially the *Zhid*. Czar Nicolai has voraciously continued this reckless policy for no reason other than sheer, inherent hatred of the enemy within. The Jew. Romania's stated policy of non-citizenship, non-recognition of its poverty-ridden Jews and all of the grief that accompanies it paints the Jew as the perennial villain.

"No, Chasia Zitovitz as an idealist, a young revolutionary, may have contributed to the assassination of Alexander, only changing things from unbelievably bad to worse. I see it as a change that was on its way, regardless. The assassination may only have expedited it somewhat. She is, perhaps, guilty of being an accessory to the murder of another human, but beyond that? I see no need for her continued remorsefulness."

A visibly stunned Viesl, overwhelmed by Sendehr's answer, gathered his thoughts: *A remarkably worldly answer from a provincial, small town yingele. A mere boy, he is! He appears so shy when one meets him for the first time. I would never have guessed that he had more than a cheder boy's grasp of the Yiddish language. He uses words that very few of our better-educated townspeople would feel comfortable with. And his rationale? Now, I'm curious beyond curious.*

"Tell me, Sendehr. Where did you get such knowledge of recent history? Your use of our Yiddish language, as I've already seen in your beautifully written journal, is on a highly educated level. Now you have just delivered an exceptionally profound and well-constructed judgment. A university student would have a difficult time bettering it. Bravo, Sendehr Efraim, bravo!"

This response was in keeping with Viesl's academic nature. He was modestly proud of the fact that he had been an invited guest numerous times, lecturing to Hungarian Literature classes at the university in Budapest and also at the predominantly Protestant university in closer Debrecen. No less than a major triumph for a Jewish writer from Sziget/ Sighet. Being a Jewish journalist in the Hungary of the late nineteenth and early twentieth centuries was not at all rare. It was estimated that as many as forty percent of the journalists were Jewish, as well as fully fifty percent of the realm's doctors and fifty-five percent of its merchants.

This was clearly not Romania or Russia. Emperor Franz Joseph, the dual monarch who had installed himself as both emperor of Austria and king of Hungary, wanted desperately to build the Empire into a force to be reckoned with. All minority prejudices aside, for the most part. It could not be said that continuing anti-Semitic agitation was not present in the form of blood-libel accusations, periodic anti-Jewish riots, and the unshakable, seething jealousy among the working and peasant classes.

"Thank you for your kindness, Reb Viesl. I look forward to reading your new novel. Will I be able to buy it in America?"

"Not to worry. We certainly will correspond, and I'll send you the novel and anything else I think you'll be interested in."

After another few hours of lighter discussion, they bid a fond goodbye to one another, both wondering if this initial meeting had been merely the beginning of a long and mutually rewarding association.

That night, after the second most enjoyable seder at the Viesls, Sendehr went back to the *shul* meeting hall where some of the Fusgeyers staying there were already sleeping. Writing by the light of a lone bulb, "the electric sun" as it was called when electricity first came to the smaller towns of Hungary and Romania, Sendehr finished the journal entries for the day and penned another private note to Eli Nachman:

Dear Rabbi:

I know now, without any doubts, that I will be a writer, a journalist, a man with a pen. Just from my brief, penetrating discussions during the past two days with this Sighet writer, I have been greatly impressed with his technique, his vast knowledge, his intellect, and his superb skill with the written word. He was very complimentary of my journal-writing, but I know he was probably just being a cordial host. He did seem quite sincere, though. Don't worry, I know that I have a lot to learn, and learning to write well in English will be a formidable challenge. I won't neglect my Yiddish writing, and of that you can be sure. Rabbi, please remember the name Eliezer Viesl. I am certain that his eloquence will someday touch readers everywhere, perhaps Jew and Gentile alike.

Sendehr Efraim, Sighet, Transylvania, Hungary, April 18, 1904 (13 Nissan, 5664)

§

"So, Rabbi, I get it now. Your dear father was able to follow the Fusgeyers every step of the way. Even though *der shreiber's* journal went to America with him, the weekly synopses and private notes must have been quite extensive and descriptive."

"Naftali, unfortunately, some of what I'm telling you is from the memory of a man grown very old. You see, as I told you yesterday, I've been able to piece together all of the threads of the Fusgeyer garment, but some threads are thinner than other more reliable yarns. They sent many letters home to Birlad after their arrival in America. Sendehr was, by far, the most prolific. But Mendel, Mordecai, Pessel, Nuchim, your father, and Yaakov—they all corresponded regularly with family, friends, and my father. Many of the others did the same. Thank God, my father was a saver of every piece of paper. However, I am sorry to say that he gave me some packets of the correspondences to safeguard during the second war, and I failed. You see, he and my mother were also able to survive the Iron Guard and the Nazis because here in Birlad they gathered Jews from all over the district and made a closed ghetto. Including the very spot we're sitting in now, oh yes, yes indeed. The Iron

Guard commander magnanimously felt that at least one of the three rabbis at that time should be the spokesman for his flock, and my father was chosen for this role."

Nathan shook his head, incredulous at this part of the history he had not known. The Rabbi continued. "By the time they had decided to completely liquidate Birlad, by sending its Jews to the camps of disease and starvation, a most certain death in Trans-dniestria where so many had already gone, the Red Army had recoiled from its defensive position in far off Stalingrad. It was racing westward across the scorched earth of Mother Russia, while a stunned German army went into full retreat. Accordingly, military priorities shifted dramatically, and Birlad was spared. Meanwhile, Pechora, which was to be their announced destination in Trans-dniestria, was one of the treacherous refugee camps where very few Romanian Jews survived the war."

"And the papers?"

"I had them all locked in a box which I kept in my personal book closet in my Iashi *shul.* As I told you yesterday, Iashi was again the scene of a horrible pogrom, orchestrated by a potent combination of Romanian army regulars, Iron Guardsmen and the local police. Historians have since determined that it was the first of the war's larger massacres. You must understand that the Iashi prefecture had nearly fifty thousand Jews in 1941, with over one hundred *shtiebels* and synagogues." Nathan nodded again.

"Well, in Bucureshti," Rabbi Nachman went on, "Chief Rabbi Saffran was feverishly working to protect the heavy Jewish population all along the Pruth River, the Russian border that the Nazi and Romanian troops had penetrated in June 1941. Nazi Germany was by then officially at war with its former Soviet ally, and we all feared that in the end, the loser would be the Jew. As the world knows, we were frightfully correct."

Rabbi Yossi Nachman took a long sip of tea from a cooling glass, adjusted his glasses, and let out a deep, mournful sigh. Nathan let a moment of silence go by before questioning him. "Where were you at the time? How did you survive all this?"

The storyteller, giving immediate credit to the "grace of God almighty," continued.

"As one of the youngest rabbis in the city, it was decided by the Guard commander that I, along with three others, should serve on the Jewish Council in place of five of the older rabbis. This gesture was partially due to the fact that we each spoke fluent Romanian along with Yiddish, while many of Iashi's Jews only spoke Yiddish and some of the Moldovan Russian dialect. Only twelve of the city's synagogues remained open, including mine. I was able to conduct services every day, but people stayed away. *Minyans* were sparse. The rumors that Polish synagogues had been set afire with entire congregations inside petrified everyone. Of course, later, we found that these were not just rumors.

"But, anyway, the fierce and deadly pogrom actually lasted nearly two weeks. It is hard to believe that such an egregious crime against humanity was triggered out of frustration alone. Yes, frustration on the part of the Romanian troops and their less-than-human guardsmen. They were supposed to go into battle across the Pruth, but the Nazi advance was so effective that the Iron Guard regiments had met no opposition. Some of the units, ordered to return to Iashi, were thoroughly geared up for a war. Frustrated by the lack of a confrontation, they decided to take it out on Iashi's Jews. In fact, it is well-documented that they broke into the Salachna Synagogue and simulated fire on their own troops, later conveniently blaming this attack on the Iashi Jews. Can you imagine, Naftali?" Nathan could only stare, waiting for more.

"The next day, we on the council were summoned to the office of the commandant, Stavresco, who had already called for a roundup of every Jew within a one-kilometer radius of the Salachna *shul*. Thank God, to this day, that my wife and two little children had gone to Birlad to relative safety to visit our parents.

"Remember, at this point, June 1941, Birlad was far

enough from the Russian front to be unimportant to the Romanian armies and its Iron Guard units. But in Iashi, the gloating commandant had us stand on the balcony of his office to witness our people being herded into Prefecture Square. Shooting started immediately, at random. All possible exits were guarded by machine-gun emplacements..."

Rabbi Nachman, overcome by this rekindling of such nightmarish memories, excused himself for a moment, took a handkerchief to his eyes, and despite a plea from Nathan to adjourn until tomorrow, he waved the concern off and went on. The quaver in his voice, however, would not stop.

"After an hour or so, the thousands still standing were marched to the rail yards where they were packed into boxcars. One of my colleagues counted thirty-two sealed cars in the very long train. The actual number of people or cars has never been determined, but the usual accepted number, if it matters, and it certainly doesn't, was approximately five thousand—with only days to live and suffer. No food, no water, packed tightly, one hundred fifty in each car, in midsummer heat.

"We later found out that this was a 'train-to-nowhere', and in fact it stayed where it was in the yards for two days. Then it slowly steamed to Tirgu Frumos where the contents of a number of cars were dumped on the tracks, while the local council, who were summoned by the guards, looked on in horror.

"Only a handful of the deportees were alive. Suffocation was the main cause of death at this stage, and dehydration, and eventually starvation hunted those still alive, killing them in a matter of days as the death-train meandered to and fro, then finally back to Iashi. The bodies of the dead were left in the cars for two more days. These were mostly men, but hundreds of naive women and children, thinking at the outset that their husbands and fathers were being deported somewhere safer than Iashi, had pushed onto the freight cars to join them. Each Iron Guardsman had simply and happily accommodated them with a helpful hoist into the death car. In two weeks' time, fourteen thousand of Iashi's Jewish community had been murdered.

"Dear God, Rabbi! That has to be one of the most ghastly holocaust stories I have ever heard." Yossi Nachman nodded slowly and went on.

"Yes. Yes. I signed a petition asking for some semblance of mercy for our community from the Iron Guard commandant. He answered by sending a squad to my *shul*. When they arrived, they ransacked it, burnt the torahs, and started a bonfire in the courtyard. And, Naftali, the answer to your question—they threw the wooden chest that contained my father's Fusgeyer papers into the flames. One of my foolish congregants risked his own life by grabbing it from the fire after much of its contents were singed, some beyond recognition. Those I could save at that point, I did."

"But, even with that fire loss, it seems that you, your father, and so many other Birladers have carried on this relentlessly superb oral tradition. The letters and other papers—the Sendehr synopses, and so on—had already served a purpose. Aside from the historical document perspective, that is. After all, I have been the recipient of this fascinating re-telling these past three days, and for this I am eternally grateful and respectful."

"Not enough, Naftali, not enough. You must take this story back to America with you. You must continue to share it with others. The story of your dear father and the Fusgeyers. It begs to be told again and again, to each succeeding generation as we have done here in Birlad. I hope you will. No! I know you will, my dear friend."

That night, as Nathan repeated the highlights of the day to Herb and Eric, he decided he needed a short break from these emotion-packed sessions. He found it hard to believe that he had only spent three days with Rabbi Nachman. With the weekend approaching and a departure date set for the following Friday, they would at least have a few days to see some of the sights referred to in Sendehr's synopses: where the Vlad Mirescu hog farm might have been, Bacau, Piatra, Vatra Dornei, Prislop Pass, Borsha, and

Sighet. Yes, they'd follow some of the footsteps of Sholem Leib Friedman...by automobile. An Italian automobile in Romania, at that.

En route, they would also take in the magnificent Bicaz Gorges and Lacu Roshu, the Red Lake, as well as the ancient churches in Humor, Moldovitsa, and Voronets, with their world-renowned frescoes covering both outside and inside. The boys were more than ready for this, and even laughingly referred to the "RRBs" which they were sure to encounter along the way.

"Hullyvoood! Tom Krootz! Leckers! Jeck Nikelsman! Sheck Oneal," sang out Eric "Rico" Friedman, great-grand of the swiftest runner in old Birlad!

BOOK THREE

✺

ENCOUNTERS

10

ENCOUNTERS: ROAD TO BUDAPEST

*Go! Go to wherever you are going! America? Good! There are no
Jews in America. Only heathens, savages,* vilde banditten *like
yourselves. Go! Go!*
The Szatmar Rebbe, 1904

The three-day stay in Sighet was more than just a morale injection; the physical strides of the marchers were
more powerful and deliberate now. The singing was more
frequent, as was the laughter, the joking, practical or otherwise, and the occasional horseplay. Could it be that their
first protracted rest, which had brought them hot, delicious seder food in comfortable surroundings and copious
additions to their food stores, had also given them spiritual
buoyancy?

Yes, and now numerous packages of matzos, bags of
honey cake, sponge cake, coconut macaroon cookies, preserves, dried fruits, almonds and smoked meats, and even
a supply of sweet grape wine—which was especially made
for Pesach in the famous vineyards of Tokaj, 150 kilometers to the west—jiggled noisily in the overloaded cart. All
of the foregoing were, of course, *pesachdickeh*, strictly kosher for Pesach, and food and drink staples that would see
the Fusgeyers through the remaining six days of the holiday. The gracious people of the town with many names
had outdone themselves. They would not be soon forgotten by a most appreciative group of Fusgeyers, as Sendehr

noted in his journal. All of this good food, and joy, fellow-ship and love was about to be sorely tempered.

A few days later, while approaching Szatmarnemetsi, known simply as Szatmar, but also as Satu-Mare by the Romanian minority of Transylvania, Sholem and Yaakov, as they walked their usual distance ahead, were overtaken and stopped by two men riding a two-horse wagon that came up from behind them. Both men were heavily bearded and wore the clothes of ultra-orthodox *chassidim*: the fur-trimmed hat, the breeches, the white stockings. Men dressed in such costuming was not an unusual sight for the Birladers, since similarly dressed *chassidim* were found throughout Romania, in all parts of the Austro-Hungarian Empire and the vast Czar-decreed region of Russia to which Jews were restricted since the Napoleonic Wars. For more than a century, this territory that stretched from the Baltic Sea to the Black Sea was known as the Pale of Settlement, or simply the Pale, and also included the eastern provinces of a divided Poland.

"*Boruch Hashem, sholom aleichem. Nu boychicks*, are you with the group of young walkers we just passed?"

"*Sholom aleichem*," Sholem repeated and nodded.

The taller of the two men continued, "You're going to Szatmar, yes? Since it is going to be near the start of the Sabbath by the time you get there, you are welcome to pray at our *shul*. We have room for all of you. *Sholom aleichem, Boruch Hashem!*"

After giving simple directions to their *shul*, the men rode off.

Polite enough. Understandable to Sholem and Yaakov, and also when relayed to Mordecai. A nice gesture on the part of these ultra-orthodox *chassidim*. When they stopped for a rest about ten kilometers from Szatmar Sholem and Yaakov passed the invitation on to everyone, saying that, of course, anyone who wished to welcome the Sabbath Queen at the *chassid szinagoga* could do so. There were six other synagogues in Szatmar, which matched Sighet in its Jew-ish population. In fact, the same sect had a *shul* in Sighet, though Rabbi Kurtzman had mentioned that he and some of the other rabbis were presently at odds with the local *chassidim* over certain Talmudic interpretations concerning *kashruth*. At this point these young travelers from the east had no reason to think that they would have any trouble from the *chassidim*.

Szatmar, on the western edges of Transylvania, or Erdely, was like Sighet in every respect: Romanian and Hungarian were in equal use and the Magyarization process was quite complete. Signs were all in Hungarian, with a few in German to placate the large German minority in the Maramarosh/Maramuresh region. Only a few of the signs were in Romanian at all. Yiddish was the language of trade, commerce, and general conversation among the Jews. The Szatmar *chassidim*, according to Rabbi Kurtzman and Shimon Pomerantz back in Sighet, were the most rabid anti-Zionists among all *chassidic* sects. Additionally, they were widely known to be the most intransigent in dealing with anyone not meeting their extreme dictates and ultra-orthodox mores.

Beginning in the early eighteenth century with the teachings of Israel Baal Shem Tov, the Master of the Good Name, the *Chassidic* movement caught fire throughout Central and Eastern Europe, and especially in the Pale. It defied the consistent treacheries heaped upon the Jewish masses, and commanded its followers to return to the teachings, but this time with a newborn fervor. The classless, stateless, and starving creatures took *chassidism* on as a weapon, a way to surmount the mundane existence. The Baal Shem Tov was a messenger from God sent to give light to their darkness, to give hope to their despair, and to give the soul manna and nectar.

Chassidic dynasties began to appear everywhere. Cities and towns from Warsaw to Minsk and Pinsk, from Vilna to Kiev, and from the smaller towns of Lubavitch in the Pale to Berditchev, from Sighet to Szatmar—all of these and many more boasted of a major *Chassidic* movement during the eighteenth and nineteenth centuries. Its founding rebbe, his ensuing lineage, and their disciples—truly dynamic, resourceful men with fiery souls—headed each dynasty. The "rebbe," a term of loyal endearment, was not necessarily ordained, but was often the object of awe and veneration from his followers, which sometimes grew into stories of sheer mystical ability.

"All the king's men," the pogroms, the harsh imprisonment, the hopelessness, could do nothing to prevent the new wave of excitement brought on by the revitalization of millions of the downtrodden. Not that this phenomenal grassroots ground swell didn't meet with resistance and relentless opposition within the ranks of its co-religionists; it did quite to the contrary.

Historically, this doctrinal gap ranged from the narrow to the unbridgeable. Everywhere, rabbinic authorities and scholars condemned the Baal Shem and his disciples. Rabbi Elijah ben Shlomo best typified the *mitnagdim*, those fierce opponents in the rabbinate majority. The Vilna *Gaon* (1720-1797) went so far that in 1768 he pronounced a virtual ban on *chassidism* and conferred the solemn formula of *charem* on the teachings of the late Baal Shem Tov (d.1760). Five years later, this foremost religious authority of the times ordered the seizing and burning of all *chassidic* writings, and he went on to forbid interfaith marriage or any contact with the heretics and their followers.

More than a hundred years had passed from then until now. Yet the *chassidim* of Szatmar had changed little in their ideas, their objectives, their world views, their lifestyle. Of all the dynasties of the two centuries past, *Chassidism* was the only one that had not moved from its original purpose. On the contrary, the tradition had solidified, grown, and prospered in this northeastern corner of Transylvania, Hungarian Erdely.

Entering this realm, the holiest of the holiest, the Children of Birlad in all their innocence with a powerful purpose of their very own, decided to pitch camp on the verdant banks of the River Szamos. The weather that had come down from Sighet had been dry and mostly comfortable, without a rain cloud in sight since Prislop Pass. Getting on toward the end of April, sundown had been getting later day by day. Now with the Sabbath arriving, the position of their camp allowed those who wished to participate in the short *erev Shabbos* service to take their pick from the cluster of synagogues around the main square and the road leading to the river's edge.

Some of the Fusgeyers had family in Szatmar and opted to spend the evening with them, inviting a few of the others along. Others went off in small groups to walk the town or drop in on one or another of the houses of worship. Unfortunately, whereas Jews the world over usually dress in their finer clothes to greet the Sabbath Queen, the finest clothes the light-traveling Birladers had for seders in Sighet, and now for Sabbath in Szatmar, were considered to be decidedly unorthodox. Nevertheless, the *shul-geyers*, numbering more than half of the sixty, had no qualms about lending their sweet voices to their congregation of choice.

Branko and Yossi Golub volunteered to stay behind to guard the cart and everyone's packs scattered about under the tent-halves. Others simply lounged around the campsite resting, napping, reading one of Mendel's or their own books; chatting; talking about home, their loved ones, and mostly about America. *What will it really be like, in America? Eh?*

Sholem and Yaakov found the Szatmar *chassidishe shul* and were followed by Mendel and Esther, Rivka, Sendehr, Tsippy, Chaike, Pessel, Simmy Fiedelman, Yoni Golub, Menachem Berman, Menachem Katz, Mayer Bernstein, Velvel Niedl, and Yitzhok Myerz. They sent a strong representation, since they had received a personal invitation, and none of them had ever been to a *chassidishe shul*, not even to the little Bratzlaver *shtiebel* in Birlad. Since there was no balcony, a *mechitza* was in place in the sanctuary, behind which the Fusgeyer girls would be expected to sit. There were no other women present; many parts of the service were repeated during the Sabbath eve meal at home, and the women would be busy with domestic preparations.

The busy beadle made sure everyone had a prayer book, although the fifty or more Szatmar *chassidim* seemed to know everything from memory, and indeed, even a few of the Fusgeyers could match them. The singing—ah, yes, the tremulous chanting—went on with a flourish unlike anything the visitors had ever heard. They were enjoying the ambience immensely. The periodic roof-raising singing of the "three cantors" drowned out the congregational voices, causing some sidelong glances from the beadle and others. The service ended within a half-hour. Shouts of *a guten Shabbos* rang out, and the Rebbe seemed to vanish from the *bimah*. The beadle reminded the Fusgeyers that prayers would begin at seven in the morning, and the two *chassidim* who met Sholem and Yaakov on the road into town came over to wish them all a *guten Shabbos*, and then nothing more was said. As was the case in all but the growing number of Neolog, Reform, Movement synagogues in Hungary and Austria, Friday evening was usually an abbreviated service because the Sabbath meal, accompanied by more praying and singing, awaited them at home. In actuality, Friday evening in the synagogue with a *minyan* present was treated only slightly differently from the weekday *mincha-maarev* services. The *chassidim* usually followed this approach, although there were different emphases within the various sects.

Saturday morning would be the same as any other for the Fusgeyers. It had been decided months ago, primarily by consensus but with the concurrence of Zed-Zed and the Schedule Committee, that morning prayers would, of course, include a fast Sabbath service in camp. Then, off to the march as any other day. However, if they were in or very near a town with a Jewish community and a *shul*, anyone wishing to do so could spend the Sabbath morning at the *shul*. Accordingly, the group would then leave later in the morning, closer to noon, in order to get in a goodly portion of their goal for the day, and any straggling *shul*-goers could catch up if their particular services were not finished by then. Szatmar was to be the first place where this plan would be actually put to the test.

The "cantors," having had a brief but fulfilling songfest at the Szatmar *chassidishe shul*, opted to go back there in the morning, with their "trainee" Yitzhok Myerz in tow. Sholem and Yaakov had to take up the point as usual and could not afford to be late because they were busy attending services. No one chose to go to any of the other synagogues, but Heshy Rosen, Gershon, and Maidele were going to be at Heshy's cousin's home and would meet everyone at noon on the west side of town on the road to Debrecen. So far, so good.

Mordecai and Zed-Zed, satisfied that the clean-up crew had left a tidy-looking river bank, started the march into and then out of town at precisely noontime. Stopping by the *shul*, Sendehr ran in to nudge the cantors, but the service had apparently just ended. At that moment, the Szatmar *tzadik* was about to come out the front door, followed by his usual long entourage, superseding Menachem, Mayer, Velvel and Yitzhok—the melodic voices of Birlad.

Rebbe Shmuel Bentziyon Gelbfeder, he of the long flowing white beard, stopped abruptly when he saw the foot soldiers of the Birlader Fusgeyer Contingent standing at ease on the street, four abreast, dressed in their rather *shmatah*-like, rag-tag travel togs. The Zionist *Mogen Dovid* flag flew unfurled proudly. The Rebbe's entourage, like a pack of bodyguards, crowded around him awaiting the words that he was certain to bellow forth. And bellow forth he did! Like the roar of a wounded rhinoceros!

"Please tell me, O Lord my God! What do I see in my path? Do I see a herd of disrespectful heathens? Or are you peasant *goyim* in tattered rags? Worse yet, do I see young wayward people, children of Jewish families, also disrespectful, dishonoring the good Sabbath? And what, pray tell me, is that abominable flag you are so brazenly flying on the Lord's day? That one with the blue *Mogen Dovid!*"

This speech-while-standing-on-the-steps was delivered in rapid-fire rhythm, its shock value difficult to overestimate. The smoke rising from his ears and his piercing dark eyes may have been imagined, but to the Birladers, they were very real. Stunned and speechless, , all eyes shifted to Mordecai. He of the cool, even temper. He, diplomacy and tact personified. He, the leader in every sense. *What will he say? What will he do? What can he do?*

The silence that filled the warm air was deafening. It went on for what seemed like minutes, but it lasted only seconds. Mordecai walked up the stairs, book-ended by Sendehr and Zed-Zed, and followed by Menachem Berman. Branko leaned against the cart and watched every movement. The others stood frozen in place.

"*A guten Shabbos, meine tyreh Rebbe, a sehr guten Shabbos!* Is there some way we have offended your good person? Your *shul?* Our symbol of Judaism? Your God? My God? Please tell me, dear Rebbe. Perhaps I can rectify it."

With a voice that, perhaps, could have been God calling to Moses from Mount Sinai, or maybe the audacious Levi-Yitzhak of Berditchev and his famous argument with God, during the course of which he chastised him for lack of support, Rebbe Shmuel Bentziyon Gelbfeder snorted fire again:

"You, the young leader, I presume, are insulting me with your defiant *chutzpah!* We know who you are. Fusgeyers, I believe you call yourselves with all the disgusting romantic notion of a Sholem Aleichem or a Mendele Seforim. I was told a group of walkers just passed through here last year. But, it was not on the Sabbath! They just walked through without any fanfare, and a good riddance to them, and soon to you."

"I pray, sir, please identify our sins and I will be happy to explain or, at least, beg your forgiveness. For is it not of our faith to forgive, to atone?" Mordecai barely got these words in before the Rebbe started up again.

"For a leader, you are a *nar*, a fool. First you march by my *shul* in filthy clothing on the Sabbath. Then you brazenly fly the flag of those *vilde* Zionists. Herzl and his maniacs! Who do they think they are? Pre-empting the *mashiach!* In doing so, they, and you, are burning our six-pointed symbol *in dred erein, in gehenna!* Just asking for a state in Eretz Yisroel has incurred the wrath of every real Jew in the world and also the *goyim un anti-Semitten.*

"Listen to me, young man, even more important than everything I have said, you are desecrating the holy Sabbath in a most sinful manner. You are walking through my town, wheeling that overloaded wagon, *shlepping* it by manual labor. You are Jewish by birth, perhaps, and heathens by practice. God will punish you long before you reach whatever your destination happens to be."

Mordecai, never a reluctant discussant, could not repress the growing feeling that to carry this on any further would serve no purpose. If anything, the vitriol spewing from the Rebbe was deep into the runaway process of escalation. Furthermore, Mordecai's patriarchal posture as the protector of his large flock deterred him from wanting to risk the chance of a schism developing. He also realized that there might well be some Fusgeyers, the more religious factions, who agreed to some degree with the Rebbe. No, probably not on the Zionist issue, but very possibly on the Sabbatarian issue.

One of the finer points of Biblical interpretation was seeping toward the forefront here, and it might become necessary to resort to the old Talmudic practice of *pilpul,* the dialectic art of splitting hairs over a complex subject. *Well, it was certainly a candidate for a campfire exercise in rationale,* Mordecai thought, not noticing that he was running out of time to respond effectively to the Rebbe.

He had started down the steps, stopping nose-to-nose with Mordecai. Wildly waving one of the bony arms that protruded from his wide kaftan sleeves, his voice lowered to a strange hiss, and he took up where he left off.

"You went to a *cheder,* no? You presumably studied Torah with one of your ill-trained, heretical so-called rabbis, no? Well, Reb Commandant, perhaps you will remember the references to keeping the *Shabbos,* beginning with Exodus, chapter twenty, the Fourth Commandment:

> Remember the Sabbath day, to keep it
> holy. Six days shalt thou labor and do all
> thy work; but the seventh day is a Sabbath
> unto the Lord thy God, in it thou shalt not
> do any manner of work, thou nor thy son,
> nor thy daughter, nor thy man-servant,
> nor thy maid-servant, nor thy cattle, nor
> thy stranger that is within thy gates; for
> in six days the Lord made heaven and
> earth, the sea and all that in them is, and
> rested on the seventh day; wherefore the
> Lord blessed the Sabbath day and hal-
> lowed it.

"May I remind you, young sir, that traveling is considered a forbidden labor, whether by foot, by horse, by wagon,
or by train. *Shlepping* that cart is prohibited labor. You
people are traveling, you're *shlepping*, and you are, *in every
way*, desecrating the Sabbath. You may think you can do
so anywhere you choose, but not in the vicinity of my *shul*,
my congregation! Do you have any idea how serious and
despicable the breaking of the Sabbath is considered to be?
Obviously, you do not know. *Oy, oy, oy!* You and your rabbis are bankrupt, deaf and blind! Let me refer you to the
Book of Numbers, chapter fifteen:

> ...And while the children of Israel were in
> the wilderness they found a man gathering
> wood upon the Sabbath day. And those who
> found him gathering wood brought him
> unto Moses and Aaron, and unto all the
> congregation. And they placed him in
> custody, because it had not been declared
> what should be done to him. And the Lord
> said unto Moses: The man shall surely be
> put to death; all the congregation shall
> stone him with stones outside the camp.
> And all the congregation stoned him with
> stones, and he died, as the Lord com-
> manded Moses.

"You don't seem to comprehend the Hebrew from the Torah. I will translate for all of you *goyim*, verbatim." And he proceeded to do so in a classical sing-song Yiddish, continuing to wave his arms about as he spoke, his entourage swaying back and forth trance-like, *daven*-ing, praying.

When the Rebbe finished his Yiddish rendition he dismissed everyone with a final wave of the arms, giving Mordecai no chance for rebuttal, for questions, for dispute, or even for agreement. Nothing. Just some rapid-fire parting remarks as his followers made a pathway down the stairs and onto the street for him to follow.

"Go! Go to wherever you are going! America? Good! There are no Jews in America. Only heathens, savages, *vilde banditten* like yourselves. Go! Go!"

In seconds, the Szatmar *chassidic* Rebbe disappeared into a certain self-protective oblivion as the dumbfounded troop stood in utter silence. Mordecai broke the spell with a forced smile, and spoke to the shocked Fusgeyers who surrounded him.

"*Nu, a guten Shabbos, vilde banditten!* Zed-Zed's schedule is heading for ruin. Let's show the good people of Szatmar who we are! Look alive now, boys and girls, *meine klayneh banditten.* Let's move smartly! We have ground to cover this afternoon. I know that some of you possibly agree with the Rebbe, to an extent, regarding the sanctification of the Sabbath. Perhaps a good old-fashioned *pilpul* will be in order this evening." There were several nods, assuring Mordecai that it was quite right to address this sensitive subject.

With flags still flying overhead, but tactfully without trumpet or drum sounds, they marched out of town toward the road to Debrecen. Having neatly folded away the Romanian flag, Rivka had sewn together, out of some material her sweet hostess in Sighet had been able to hunt up, a makeshift replica of the red, white, and green Hungarian banner. It looked just fine to the naked eye and would certainly serve the purpose, as they were now deep into the Hungarian territory of the Austro-Hungarian Empire, with insufferable, inevitable Captain Sandor types to deal with. With a pen and his black ink, Sendehr was able to sketch the Hapsburg Family emblem into the upper-left corner, which also looked authentic from afar. No doubt about it, they were flying a "kosher" Magyar flag, these ever-resourceful wayfarers.

Menachem Berman, the cautious one, had also pointed out to Rivka that it would be wise to sew together the left-over material to represent the official Empire horizontal bars of red-white-red. Although Branko assured everyone that the Emperor's home-based Hungarian troops were predominantly in control of everything east of the Danube and known to be strongly nationalistic in sentiment and unabashedly anti-Empire, it was always possible that they might encounter units of Franz-Josef loyalists. Resourceful? Yes, indeed they were.

Just before sundown they were able to make it to the suggested encampment site in an idyllic, early-blossoming birch forest. Having stocked up on their water supplies in Szatmar and at a farmer's well en route, the lack of a stream was of no consequence here. Firewood was in abundance. The days and nights had been exceptionally kind bringing only good weather since the mountain passes, although heavy clouds now appeared far to the western horizon.

The much-anticipated discussion, preceding Mendel's English instruction, was about to begin. Everyone, including the six young women, was given an opportunity to voice an opinion or two. And voice them they did. The ancient art of *pilpul*, practiced primarily in the rabbinical schools of Europe, the *yeshivas*, was also introduced in the *cheders*, especially if the local rabbi was an able practitioner and proponent of the sheer power and redeeming value of hair-splitting. Such had been the case in Birlad for Rabbi Holtzer, followed by Rabbi Nachman, and to some extent by the *lehrer* for more secular studies. In fact, Mendel Buchman had brought a new meaning to the application of these polemical exercises to the youngsters of Birlad each time he posed a provocative question to them.

...Should a Jew charge interest for a loan to a family member?

...Should Romania eliminate its monarchal form of government?

...Will the motor-driven vehicle replace the horse-and-wagon?

...Is it kosher to drink wine from the vineyard of a *goy*?

...Is it acceptable to use a telephone on the Sabbath?

...To where should Jews emigrate? America? Palestine? Germany? England? Australia? South Africa?

From the time Rabbi Holtzer came to Birlad in 1857, every *cheder* pupil had participated in some form of *pilpul*. Of course, Rabbi Nachman continued this practice and most of those who were gathered around the campfire, in this lovely birch wood, were experienced in these give-and-take arguments. Only the very youngest had little practice, and had just recently been in Mendel's classes for the first time, but his pride shone through when three of his former pupils contributed seriously and intelligently.

There was only one question on the agenda on this night: "Should we or should we not walk on the Sabbath?"

At the outset, it was explained that "walking" here meant the usual daily kilometers, cart-*shlepping*, sanitation-ditch digging and so on.

...The Szatmar Rebbe made a good point. We are only Jews if we follow all ten of the commandments literally.

...But only walking on the Sabbath does not break the Fourth Commandment.

...The old Rebbe represents an ossified segment of the Jewish community of Europe, and today he's nothing but an anachronism that time will evaporate.

...Yes, but his interpretation of the Law cannot be dis puted here.

...But his long beard and *payotim*, the ridiculous garb, his clinging to rigors and customs, all of this and more segregates the Jew from the *goy*, but even more from the other Jews in the world. He despises us. That's not being a man of God!

...Yes, but his kind tells us that every step we take to ward the modern Jew is the path to certain corrup- tion.

...They are in such a minority, yet they unofficially ex communicate the rest of us.

...What is wrong with walking on the Sabbath? I don't understand.

...It constitutes travel, and travel is prohibited accord- ing to the Rebbe.

...Maybe *shlepping* the cart is the real problem.

...Yes, but how do we get around that one, my friend?

...Setting religion and commandments and the Szatmar zealot aside, maybe we should consider this dilemma from a more practical point of view.

...What do you mean by that? Explain.

For two hours these and many more statements, argu- ments, rebuttals, re-phrasings, and conflicting philosophies filled the cool air. Only when the good Doctor Hippocrates, the even-tempered Gershon Maibaum, introduced the last point—"setting religion and commandments and the *chassidim* aside"—into the discussion did the end come into view.

He went on to expand his statement to a hushed audience. "If Zed-Zed agrees that we won't be thrown too far off schedule, maybe we should strongly consider a day of rest. The three days spent in Sighet served as an obvious tonic for each of us. Why? Because we were all well-rested for the first time since leaving home two weeks before. I could see it in your faces, your strides, your smiles, and your singing. Physically, mentally, spiritually, I for one, feel that a day of rest, yes, on the Sabbath, would do much more good than harm."

Just like that, the *pilpul* unwound like a balloon running out of air. The more religious Fusgeyers who had argued that the Rebbe had made a powerful point, albeit that he tended toward the inflammatory, were quite ready to accept Gershon's proposal from any level: religious, physical, metaphysical, or practical. And surprisingly, even those on the far end of the scale who did not want to capitulate because of newly confirmed animosity toward the rabid, extremist sects recognized, at least, the value of rest. Plain and simple. One day of complete rest. Ah, yes, how sweet that could be for aching bones, sore feet, sweaty clothes, breaking backs, *shleppers'* forearms.

Zed-Zed had long ago built into the schedule more than adequate contingency time. After a very quick conference with Mordecai and Sendehr, with his spread-out maps, he gave his affirmative opinion to the delight of all factions. The cheering was deafening!

It was getting late, and Mendel decided to cancel his class. Enough education had been dispensed, he wisely concluded. After all, participating in this democratic process was an unmatched and broadening experience, and this session had accomplished more than that. The cohesiveness for which leaders always strive had reached its apex here on the edge of Hungary's Great Plain, the expansive *Nagyyafold.*

The three days of uneventful walking took the wayfaring Birladers from the birch forest to the largest city they had seen to date, Debrecen, where the terrain changed abruptly from rolling green hills to flatland and grassland. Sendehr's maps, especially the Romanian army map that included all of Transylvanian Hungary and enough of the Great Plain, made new analysis of the course an easy task. The elevations all the way to Budapest varied by minimal meters, hardly posing any climbing problems for these hardy veterans of the Carpathians and its Prislop Pass, which was now only a recent memory, but which would be great fodder for future story-telling to children and grandchildren.

A heavy April rain one day east of Debrecen had luckily not resulted in a mud mire. It was one of the few roads that had evidently been hard-packed with a mixture of gravel and larger stones, causing a sharp, annoying friction sound from the metal-encircled wheels of the cart. The rain had shown no sign of letting up during the last ten kilometers into Debrecen, and the soaked-to-the-skin trekkers looked forward to some kind of shelter.

The barrenness they met after leaving the birch trees made them wonder if they'd ever see a grove again. This question was soon answered as they trudged through the outlying areas of the city, where they were greeted by park-like stretches and every conceivable kind of bush, tree, early spring flower and lush grass. Nowhere had they seen such beautifully kept cottages, each with its own cultivated bed of colorful flora; and such clean streets with many cement sidewalks; and as soon as they entered the main core of the city, cobblestone streets unfolded in every direction. Only those who had been to Iashi and Bucureshti, or in Mendel's case, his years at the British schools in Salonika and Athens, and of course Branko, who traveled all over Europe, were the least bit familiar with a city like this.

It was mid-week, and a visit to the first *shul* they came across, one with magnificent twin towers and a golden dome nestled in between, was the very one that had been cited by one of the other journal keepers. The beadle, a man named

Dovidl, welcomed Sholem and Yaakov, and when the main body arrived he directed the wayfarers to a large barn adjacent to the property belonging to a a member of the congregation. Not a moment too soon, either; the rain increased in volume ten-fold. Dovidl informed the group that *mincha-maarev* would begin in less than an hour.

To everyone's delight, there was no livestock, but only heaps of aromatic, dry hay strewn about the wooden, high-ceilinged structure. This was going to be their inn for the night, and it was only the second time that most of them would have had a roof over their heads since the April 1st departure. The comedians, Itzy Gelman and Mayer Kelemer, wasted no time in rattling off a series of hilarious "*Yezeleh-in-the-manger*" jokes, reminding their captive audience that "should three wise men appear at the barn door, please let them in. Remember, they'll probably be bearing gifts!" Dovidl heard the bursts of laughter, and must have wondered how these wet, tired walkers could maintain any semblance of humor. Then again, he had never met the famous Birlad duo of Gelman and Kelemer.

After sundown services, attended by some of the party while others just enjoyed relaxing on their beds of hay, Mendel and Esther came out from their hidden little hay-nest behind one of the few partitions, stalls once used by cows or horses. Mendel announced that English class would start after everyone had eaten their evening meal, and Zed-Zed locked his suggestion in, giving the class a commencement time of seven o'clock. At the appointed time, everyone gathered around Mendel, sitting on the hay in concentric half-circles.

Mendel had parts of six English-language books with him and used these as guides to familiarize his students with the sounds of the language and word usage. The progress made during this initial stage of the journey amazed everyone and pleased Mendel no end. He had three Bret Harte short stories which he had found at a Salonika bookseller's; James Fennimore Cooper's *The Last of the Mohicans* and *Leatherstocking*; dog-eared parts of Mark

Twain's *Tom Sawyer* and *Huckleberry Finn*; and excerpts from Jonathan Swift's *Gulliver's Travels*, all of which were remnants from Mendel's days at the British school.

The students particularly liked Swift's satirical philosophies, especially the part where Gulliver discovers the two factions of Lilliputians: the Big-enders and the Little-enders, referring to which end of an egg they preferred to open first. *Did this call for pilpul?*

The fastest learners thus far were Sholem Friedman and Maidele, although there were a few others not far behind. Sholem could quote certain passages from Bret Harte's "The Outcasts of Poker Flat," the saddest of Harte's California Gold Rush era offerings, and bring tears to the eyes of those who understood even some of the words. The ending was a particular source of accomplishment for Sholem as he exercised every manner of dramatic elocution in proclaiming:

> *Beneat dis tree lies die bawdy of John Oakhurst who strock a strick of bed lock on die twenty-terd of Novembehr ett-teen feefty und hended in hees checks on di savent Detsembehr, ett-teen-feefty. und polseless und kolt, mit un derreengehr by hees side und a boolett in hees hott, beneat di snow lay he who vas at vunce di strongast und yet die veakest of di outkests foon Pocker Flett.*

Mendel always led the applause as the others followed amidst a tear here and there. Yes, they understood that a hero had died performing a heroic act. Maidele loved the character of Becky Thatcher and would also quote from some of her lines, while Gershon tried very hard to learn some of young Tom Sawyer's words. But every last one of the group could count to a hundred in passable English, and not one would ever refuse to read from the books. Each earned the highest grade for effort and enthusiasm. This contingent would never be lost in the streets of Boston or New York, or wherever else they might end up. They would be able to make themselves understood to a point, and no one would ever be too embarrassed to try—and try again.

By far the most humorous incident during these daily lessons had taken place back in Vatra Dornei when Mendel began reading from a well-frayed copy of the *The Last of the Mohicans*, stopping after every few words to explain their meanings. This being the beginning of the journey, his goal was simply to familiarize his students with the sounds. Of course, this called for the tedious back-and-forth translation between Yiddish and English and provided an opportunity for occasional word-play fun.

Yankel Golub, the eldest of his brood, spoke up. "That's what I'm going to do in America!" Everyone looked on quizzically as he continued, "I will be a British soldier and wear a fine-looking red cut-a-way coat."

Mendel responded in a paternal manner saying, "But Yankele, there are no British soldiers remaining in the United States. Perhaps Canada, but not in New York or Boston."

"So, *nu*, Mendele, is this good or bad for the Yidden?" asked a dead-serious Yankel.

The roar of laughter exploded and sporadically returned all evening long.

The overnight comfort in the hay barn was seen as a sign from *der himl*, heavens above, among the more God-fearing. As they strapped on their phylacteries during morning prayers, the thanks to God for this wonderful shelter from the heavy rains resounded throughout the barn. A number of the Fusgeyers went next door for the service, and they seemed to impress the early morning *minyan* of Debreceners with the fact that they paid so much attention to the rituals.

A rotund, yellow-bearded man in an embroidered kaftan happened to be standing next to Simmy Fiedelman, and he was in the process of taking off his forehead phylactery when he asked if the Fusgeyers accepted donations. The astonished "food czar" gulped a time or two but recovered quickly enough to vigorously nod his head in the affirmative.

Usually, it was entirely the other way around. Strangers praying in a *shul* were expected to leave a small token of their gratitude for the upkeep of the *shul* or for the *cheder* fund or for the rabbi's *kiddush schnapps* or the rebbitzen's charitable projects for the local poor. This kindly benefactor, one Benyumin Kremnitzer, shoved a large bill of local currency into Simmy's tunic pocket as Nuchim Krasnigor and Heshy Rosen looked on in utter bewilderment. Nuchim, seeing his "fund" swell so unexpectedly, joined in the profuse *shayneh danks*. Later when he and Simmy would discover exactly how much the denomination was worth, they would be even more amazed and thankful.

"You will please see that this money is used for the benefit of everyone. I think what you are doing is a blessing. You young people are the future, and I am told that the future for you begins in America. May God travel all the way with you! My brother is already a *macher* in Philadelphia, so maybe I will follow one day soon. *L'shana haba'ah b'America!*" These were the honorable Hungarian's parting remarks.

Mordecai had learned in the *shul* the night before that the growing city of Debrecen was unique among Hungarian and Romanian cities: it was the center of Hungarian Protestantism. Actually, the majority of its citizens were Protestant Calvinists and this had been true for more than three hundred years, back to the Reformation. Its Great Church was the largest Protestant church in all of Hungary.

This was all very new to the Birladers. They had been brought up under the long shadow cast by Romanian Orthodoxy with which they always equated all of Christianity, although their ancestors of two generations past had learned more than they ever wanted to know about Allah and Islam from the Ottomans who ruled the region. In this atmosphere surrounding Debrecen, the Jew, who was allowed residency only since the 1840s, prospered and was treated as close to an equal as anywhere in the entire eastern half of Europe.

Easter Sunday had come and gone, and it was comforting to know that there was no Father Mihai lurking about.

Even marching to that birch forest on the holiday, no one had sensed the need for extra vigilance in this part of Hungary. In fact, all of the Fusgeyers agreed that it had been the most tension-free Easter anyone could remember, privately praying that it had been a time of lessened violence and vandalism back home in Birlad.

Taking full advantage of a break in the rain and seeing that the sun was showing signs of filtering through the clouds, the march through the heart of the Jewish quarter of Debrecen was as uplifting as any other. Word had spread that the Fusgeyers had spent the night in the hay barn next to the great *shul*, and many shopkeepers lined the main street even before they opened up for business. One of the butchers tossed six cured-meat loaves into the cart as it passed by him. The *shleppers* cheered him, and an overjoyed Itzy Gelman went over to give the beefy, unsuspecting redhead a hug, accompanied by a trumpet blast from Velvel Palastrant and a spirited drum roll from Asher Leibovich.

As they passed by Szigistaub's Bakery, a young girl worker, perhaps the owner's daughter, with pigtails flying rushed over to the cart and laid five rounded loaves of pumpernickel and rye breads and a large overflowing bag of pastries into it. The onlookers were beaming from ear to ear, and this time Rivka did the embracing honors. Menachem Berman, ever the proper one, not wishing to offend any of these very hospitable natives, held back a frisky Mayer Kelemer who was on his way to upstage the stage-lady. (These irreverent jokesters had to be closely monitored at all times! Add the food czar to this watch-list...)

By the time they had left the center of the city behind, a sack of fresh eggs, some of the first fruits and vegetables of spring, jugs of well water, a large can of milk from the dairyman—who Sendehr dubbed "Tevye" for his love of Sholem Aleichem's story of the same name—and a load of assorted foodstuffs all found their way onto the now top-heavy cart. Although the *shleppers* were as happy as anyone for the generous cornucopia, they also prayed for their shift to be completed sooner then scheduled with the weight of their burden now doubled. This had become *takeh*, a *shlep* that surpassed even the Sighet haul.

Sendehr's original route through the Great Plains was changed somewhat after he and Zed-Zed conferred with a young traveling farm-tool salesman during the *minyan* that morning. He convinced them that a more direct route through the heart of the Hortobagy (Horto-bahzh), a grassy prairie covering over 100,000 hectares and easily the most typical part of the plains terrain, would be the more practical way to go. In that region villages, many of which held small Jewish populations, were widely scattered. The bigger cities on the main road from Debrecen to Budapest such as Szolnok and Cegled were fast becoming heavily industrialized, and the resulting freight wagon jams were a frustrating nuisance. One of the concerns was that the cart would not fare well under such conditions, especially as it was now so over-laden with Debrecen's kindness.

The friendly peddler, one Ruvain Veiner from Transylvanian Temesvar/Timoshoara, and his two-horse wagon had been delayed for hours several times. He also warned of unruly anti-Hapsburg activity that continually took place in these cities full of citizens who would not take kindly to sixty Jews carrying the Zionist flag, let alone a flag with the Franz-Josef emblem.

Mordecai had also noticed for the past few days that wagon traffic was getting much thicker on these main Hungarian roads. He agreed fully with Veiner's suggestion, and they proceeded to the cutoff road that would eventually lead them to the famous nine-arched bridge over the Hortobagy River. Even though this was not the route followed or recommended by the other contingents, Mordecai and his cadre agreed to the change of plan, and Zed-Zed determined that the schedule would not suffer in any way.

Branko Horvitch was now in very familiar territory. He silently disagreed with the decision to walk through the Hortobagy. On military duty, serving with the joint Austro-Hungarian Hortobagy Calvary Regiment, he had patrolled these parts for nearly a year. Keeping the peace between violently anti-Hapsburg *csikosh,* wild "cowboys" who rode wilder horses, and the peaceful new settlers coming in from both the northern and southern territories as well as Transylvania to the east, was a duty difficult enough. Watching your back once they knew you were a transfer from the Emperor's Honor Guard was much harder. Yes, the area was sparsely populated, and had no wagon jams to contend with, friendly villagers, oceans of undulating grassland, a stunning array of purple, yellow, and white wildflowers dotting the flat landscape, plenty of water, and fertile, highly arable land. All of this tended to mask the seeds of unrest planted by the *csikosh,* the outspoken anti-immigrant cattle-ranch owners, and their growing support among these very villagers, Jews included, who dared not openly oppose them. Ultimately, their strong feelings were directed to the man for whom they held responsible for this unacceptable inflow of immigrant trash.

Emperor Franz Josef, in his desire to populate the more sparsely settled districts of the Hortobagy—in fact the entire Great Plain territory in general—had instituted far-reaching programs of re-settlement. The land-tenancy enticements for the Slovak dirt poor of Galicia and Ruthenia, certain of the German and Romanian minorities of Transylvania, and the southern Slavs in Empire-controlled Slovenia, Croatia, and Serbia presented too good an opportunity to ignore.

But *der groisseh soldat* kept his thoughts quiet for two compelling reasons. Firstly, he did not want to alarm the Fusgeyers for what could very possibly be unwarranted paranoia on his part since they would simply be marching through with no intention to stay. The transit visa with Captain Sandor's curlicue signature would be proof enough, and might effectively keep any of the *csikosh* at bay. Also, he knew that his honorable release papers and smooth, unaccented Hungarian would help the wayfarers deal with military interference—or any confrontation.

There was another reason for his silence, though; to which he would never admit, not even privately. Branko Horvitch, the twenty-nine-year-old veteran who had already lived a lifetime—which is supposed to begin with birth, not as his did, with the horrors of death—rather enjoyed the challenge of imminent danger. He was enormously confident in his abilities to defend these youngsters, to outwit any real and perceived enemies, and he would welcome the chance to prove it. In the Hortobagy, he felt this opportunity might readily present itself. He was inwardly ashamed of this dangerous cavalier attitude and had long ago promised himself that he would never let it override reason and common sense.

In truth, one more rather emotional reason that he did not object to the new turn of events was that one of his favorite places in all of Hungary was along this road. Just on the other side of the two-hundred-year-old nine-arched bridge they would be crossing in just a few days was the splendiferous Nagycsarda (The Great Inn). Built in 1699, a renowned "watering-hole" frequented by the nobility and upper classes of the Empire who primarily came to hunt, it held many a fond memory for the *soldat*. It was here that the lonely soldier had spent many off-duty evenings sipping sweet *Tokaj* and occasionally squeezing his meager subsistence allowance enough so that he could afford a sumptuous meal. The food was hardly kosher, but this was of no matter to the largely unobservant Horvitch. The *gulyash*, the *rantott leves*, piping hot soups followed by the steak-onions-paprika-potatoes dish of *serpenyosh rostelyosh* far surpassed any of his bland military rations, especially on a cold, wind-swept wintry day. The Inn's dark local brew served as an unmatchable thirst-quencher on a hot, dry midsummer's day after a long, hard ride across the grassy *puszta*. Truly a destination for all seasons.

And although the inn had brought Branko these creature comforts, it also reminded him of the sweetest and at the same time the most bitter remembrance of all. Her name was Margit Vasary. Margit was a voluptuous, dark-eyed pastry-baker's helper at the inn, and the first real love of Branko's adventurous life. She was barely eighteen when she smiled flirtatiously at the handsome young man who cut a most romantic figure in the colorful red and blue horse-soldier's uniform of the elite Hortobagy Cavalry. Their periodic rendezvous in her tiny room at the back end of the kitchen developed into a serious two-sided affair before long, but it was also leaping headlong toward a tragically sad end.

As a not quite naive teenager, Margit became vaguely suspicious of the obvious lower-anatomical defect represented by Branko's circumcision, his "covenant with God" performed as prescribed on the eighth day following his birth in the Russian Ukraine. Branko's response to her playful questions was always off-handed, sarcastically humorous. He just didn't think his birth religion was germane to their relationship in any way. He was quite wrong.

She persisted and one day indiscreetly asked one of his comrades, an Austrian half-Jew, if Branko was indeed *zhido*. He told her the truth. Reluctantly.

The answer was devastating to Margit, although not altogether unexpected. She was petrified of the reactions of her parents and her older brothers, all of whom lived in or near the town of Hortobagy. One of her brother's closest friends worked in the kitchen. They were all good Hungarians. They were all intensely Catholic. They were all hard-line nationalists. They were all unequivocally opposed to any foreign elements—and they each especially despised those who crucified their Lord and Savior.

The bitter ending came swiftly and painfully for both lovers. Margit later married a hard-drinking, abusive *csiko* twice her age.

* * *

Encamped deep into the grasslands near a cluster of small villages, the Fusgeyers thoroughly enjoyed the first Sabbath day of rest. Rivka and her cast of nine scene-stealers spent the beautiful afternoon in rehearsal. Zed-Zed, Yaakov, and Sholem read haltingly to each other from Harte's poignant stories, Mendel dropping by every now and then to help. Others read, chatted, slept, ambled through the high grass, and strolled into the two nearby villages—always looking to the west. Pondering. *What awaits us beyond that undulating green grass horizon? What will we encounter along the way, in Budapest, in Vienna, in Prague, Dresden, Berlin, Hamburg, Bremerhaven, Boston, New York? What, dear God, what?*

11

ENCOUNTERS: BUDAPEST

Senatus populusque Judaeorum
Vladimir Ze'ev Jabotinsky, Jewish Patriot, 1880-1940

Sendehr Efraim *der shreiber* was a resourceful young man, though not quite the *shnorrer* as Simmy, the unmatchable food czar. In Debrecen, Sendehr had sidled up to Dovidl the Beadle and asked if he could take a bottle of ink and some pen nibs from the *cheder* supplies. How could Dovidl refuse a *geyer*, a a marcher for a cause—for emancipation, for America? He didn't. Sendehr had already used the small bottle he had taken along that Nuchim had "borrowed" from his granary job. Nibs get clogged, especially with the constant use of a prolific *shreiber.* Smudging graphite pencils simply wouldn't do for journal-writing. In the meantime, Branko was able to beg an Empire map, circa 1890, from the Hortobagy town constabulary, which would complement Sendehr's Romanian Army map that ran off the page at the Hortobagy River. (Sendehr's cache of maps for the Empire and for Germany was pre-Berlin Treaty, and he relished the idea of possessing those with up-to-date border definitions, name changes, and the like.) The congenial constable appreciated the two bottles of Tokaj that Branko gave him, which one of the Golub boys had slipped under his oilskin duster from the *schnapps* table at morning prayers in the luxurious Debrecen *shul.* It was critically important to obtain good maps and writing materials for the journal; such justification and rationalization, deftly interwoven, were not at all lacking among certain *geyers*!

Sendehr found himself writing more frequent personal messages to Eli Nachman. Understandably so. He had observed so much in sixteen hours every day for a month that now, closing in on Budapest, merely writing in the journal was not quite enough. He needed to flesh out the bare-bones observations he made in the informational journal, and he did so by giving some space to his deeper inner thoughts in the letters to the Rabbi—not to be read to congregants and Fusgeyer parents at Sabbath services, in most cases. Rabbi Eliahu Yehuda Nachman, a man with wisdom far beyond his tender age of twenty-four, understood this need and looked forward to each installment of this phase of Sendehr's reporting, such as the following.

> *Dear Rabbi,*
> *Our encounter with the Szatmar Rebbe, as you know from my last synopsis mailed from Debrecen, left a sour impression on me. I don't wish to speak for everyone on this matter. Even though we came to the agreement to sit out the Sabbath, and we all thoroughly enjoy and look forward to our one day of complete rest, the thing that bothers me most is the manner in which the Rebbe presented his argument—no, rather his demands. I have observed, sadly, that during the last week that a small number of our people have slacked off from morning and evening prayers and I'm even suspicious that a few have slid from the kashruth pledge we made. I am certain that this is, in a way, a rebellion against the dogmatic and unsettling harangue issued by the Rebbe. I don't know what we will find in the bigger cities—Budapest, Vienna, Prague, Dresden, Berlin—and I cannot begin to imagine what Judaism is like in America. This much is obvious— Rebbe Gelbfeder did the reputation of supreme, extreme orthodoxy no earthly or heavenly good in Szatmar on that recent, infamously memorable Sabbath day.*

THE WAYFARERS

*In other matters, Branko privately told me of his
concerns in crossing the Hortobagy Region of the Great
Plains of Eastern Hungary, but today even he admitted
that he was pleasantly surprised at the relatively
problem-free transit thus far. I say "relatively" because
we did encounter some rather unsavory riders (csikosh)
on two different occasions. Leaving the town of
Hortobagy, we crossed the famed nine-arch bridge over
the Hortobagy River, which was swollen from the last
few heavy rains. There, six of the wildest-looking
horsemen we have seen waved their long-barreled
pistols at us, which they had leveled at poor Sholem
and Yaakov a good five minutes before we arrived at the
spot. Branko spoke to the biggest man and he explained
who we were and where we were going, and had
Mordecai show them the transit visa in Captain
Sandor's handwriting. It satisfied them, but they had to
fire a series of volleys into the air, to sort of prove their
toughness and their manhood. Off they went, showing
off some derring-do riding skills, which we all rather
enjoyed. In fact, they got a rousing cheer from the Birlad
boys, and the girls, too, I might add!*

*This prepared us for the next group of horsemen we
encountered a few days ago just before entering the
town of Tiszafured alongside the same River Tisza that
we crossed in Sighet, although here it was much wider.
An archaic, sagging bridge was under repair and a gang
of csikosh was charging exorbitant fees to take "mama's
Jew-boys and Jewess bitches" across on their barge.
Nuchim and Mordecai negotiated with them, with the
help of Branko's translation skills, but when they again
brandished a veritable arsenal of weaponry we paid
their fee reluctantly and went across—but only after two
of the Golubs had to hold back the mashiganah third
who wanted to wrest control of the barge. As the
accompanying taunting insults flew freely, we all had to
grit our teeth and swallow hard. Magyar banditten!
Mendel uses English words, American names to describe*

them..."cowboys," "highway robbers," "Jesse James,"
"desperados," and "raiders." As Mordecai later said,
paying a few extra coins-of-the-realm to avoid further grief
was well worth it! Agreed!

Obviously, I won't include this much detail in my
next synopsis, which I hope to mail from Jaszbereny,
the next town of any size. I see no need to upset anyone
over these minor incidents. Although they were tense,
believe me, may nothing ahead be any worse! Omayn!
Zwei mohl Omayn!

One other thing, Rabbi. I know that many of our
Fusgeyers are writing letters and mailing them in the
postal stations en route. I also know that a few are
probably expressing homesickness. Please tell any
parents that may share their worries with you that they
can be assured that everyone is healthy, eating
properly, getting a goodly amount of rest, and in
general, thriving day by day. Outwardly, no one seems
to be remorseful enough to the extent of returning, if
given a choice at the moment. Indeed, each of us does
have this choice. The overall resolve of this remarkable
group has not diminished. Mordecai is a leader like no
other and every last one of us will follow him to
America. Of that, I am certain.

> My best wishes to you,
> I am, Sendehr Efraim,
> Jaszapati, Hungary,
> April 30, 1904 (25 Nisan, 5664)

Note: Rehearsals for the play are progressing very
well. We plan to stage it as soon as we can arrange for
a theater, a shul, or a meeting-hall in large cities like
Budapest, or Vienna. I love acting my part. Rivka thinks
I should consider Yiddish theater in New York. I think
she is just being polite, but she is a brilliant director and
actress. She takes me into her confidence more and more.
That, I like!

THE WAYFARERS

*Something else, Rabbi. When we passed by the
magnificent structure called The Great Inn, near the town
of Hortobagy, Branko went to sit on a bald hillock about
100 meters to the north. He motioned us on, and I
watched him sitting there until he was out of our sight.
He sat still and alone for at least thirty minutes. He
rejoined us as we were finishing our mid-day meal and
he seemed extraordinarily melancholy. Unusual, out of
character for him. I can only imagine that the place
brought back some memories of the days when he was
stationed in the vicinity. I suppose certain memories,
good or bad, can do that to a person.*

For some time now, Mordecai had been harboring trepidation concerning Budapest. It would be the largest city, by
far, that most Fusgeyers had ever been in. Branko had been
everywhere in this part of the continent; Mendel had spent
many years in Salonika; and he and Nuchim had been to
Bucureshti. Some had visited Iashi. For the rest of the group,
however, Birlad and its encircling, immediate environs had
been their limit of travel. Budapest was a major metropolis
in the vast Austro-Hungarian Empire, with a growing reputation for leadership in the arts, in commerce, in trade, in
education, in architecture, and in city-planning—even a
subway system had opened in 1896, the first on the continent. Now, these innocent *kindelach* were about to be exposed to all of the elements of big city life. *Is it good or bad
for my Yidden?* Taking a leaf from Yankel Golub's well-worn
book, he laughed wryly to himself as he walked along the
road with the others from Sulysop to the capital.

1904 Budapest offered all the advantages of Paris, Berlin, Amsterdam, London, or New York. The advancement of
civilization brings undesirable elements as well; as a city
grows, so do its problems. Budapest was no exception to
this. Perhaps this was the basis for Mordecai's worrisome
thoughts, well founded or not.

The schedule called for the Wayfarers to spend three
days in Budapest, arriving on a Friday afternoon and leav-

ing on Monday morning. Zed-Zed saw no need to shorten this. The last contingent had been permitted to use the huge courtyard of the Great Synagogue on Dohany *utca* in which to bivouac, and the assumption was to do the same.

The road led through the sprawling city park and spilled onto a broad boulevard, under which ran the first completed line of the transportation marvel—the wondrous underground rail system. Here the marchers caused quite a stir as they gawked at the long rows of neo-Renaissance buildings with their ornate facades.

Motorcars, along with a steady stream of wagons and carriages passing by kept them from walking on the cobblestone street. Seeing and hearing so much traffic chugging up and down the avenue shocked most of the group, as they had only seen the Lupescu machine for the first time on the day they left Birlad. These were somewhat larger and many decibels noisier and the country cousins bunched up away from them as best they could on the narrow cement sidewalks. A nearby uniformed police officer observing them barked out some orders, which no one understood, but which was effective enough to scatter them down some of the side streets.

Meanwhile, the cart rolled merrily along, pulled by its *shleppers,* as if nothing had happened. Luckily, everyone rendezvoused at the next main intersection, which was the newly finished Grand Boulevard of Budapest: the beautifully designed, busy *Nagykorut.* Yaakov Nachman and the others watched their usually calm and poised leader frantically waving his arms about trying to settle everyone down and get their attention at the same time. "Welcome to the big city, *boychiks un maidelach!* Gather up, gather up! Over here!" Mordecai cried.

Yaakov had been sent to guide the group to the *shul* courtyard where Sholem and Branko awaited their arrival. Knowing the city as he did from numerous previous visits and understanding the rare Magyar language, Branko was invaluable at this point. It was, in a way, a triumph for the big soldier to come back to the Empire charged with the responsibility to help in leading these young Jews to fabled America. The short walk down the remainder of the impressive, tree-lined, flower-filled boulevard took them to the magnificent State Opera House, only a few hundred meters from the even more striking grandeur that was Budapest's Great Synagogue, *Nagyzsinagoga*. The sight of the red brick, ceramic-trimmed behemoth of a building, topped by the ubiquitous twin towers they had noticed in many other Hungarian synagogues, large and small alike, was enough to bring them to an immediate halt, just to stare. Lipot Baumhorn, the noted local architect who had designed nearly thirty nineteenth-century synagogues throughout Hungary, often said that he wished he could take credit for this one. It was, however, the product of a Moorish-style design by a Viennese, Ludwig von Forster, completed in 1859 and it was considered to be one of the largest houses of worship in the world. Certainly in Europe.

"Wait until you see the inside," Sholem told the group, "It has four balconies. Can you believe it?"

"Mordecai, you can fit three Birlads in it," quipped Branko.

"No, no, *soldat,* the beadle just told us that three thousand people can be seated here. With our four thousand Yidden, too many would have to stand to pray," the quick-thinking Sholem replied. This was enough to break the circle of awe, and chuckling soon rippled through the group.

The beadle, a charming pixie who introduced himself as Reb Teitelman, came over to join the conversation, and in a mix of Hungarian and Germanic Yiddish he welcomed everyone. Reb Teitelman next added proudly that the famous Hungarian composer, Franz Liszt, and the Frenchman, George Camille Saint-Saens, had both played some of their compositions here on the enormous organ containing no fewer than five thousand pipes. He went back to the massive main doors and, throwing them open, invited all to take a look inside.

"*Nu, nu,* did you ever see anything like this, eh?"

He was accustomed evidently to dealing with visiting Jews from all over Europe who wanted to look over this phenomenon. Hundreds of photographs had been taken over the years, and pictures of the Great Synagogue, interior and exterior, could be found from Odessa to Bucharest, from Warsaw to Paris, Berlin to London, and in many American cities. Even the Birlad *shul* had a picture postal card tacked up in the *cheder*. After the brief tour, he summoned everyone out through the side exit and showed them to their quarters in the courtyard and the adjoining *cheder* rooms. He had hosted the past year's group and asked if anyone had heard from them—"How do they like America?"—and left, reminding them of the time when Sabbath was to begin. Later each week now, of course, with the sun setting now close to eight o'clock. He winked at them as he was about to walk back into the sanctuary and added proudly: "We have a sumptuous *Oneg Shabbat* every Friday. *Strudels,* cakes, cookies, probably some *kugel* and *tsimus*. I hope you'll be hungry enough, eh?"

Yes, this was going to be like a vacation, all right. There was even enough space in the *cheder* classrooms to hold everyone, so the tent-halves didn't have to be unpacked. Since they held regularly scheduled classes on Sunday morning the beadle requested that bedrolls, knapsacks, and the like should be neatly stacked in a corner of each room. To find such pleasures had to be an act of compassion from above. *Boruch Hashem! Omayn!*

Rivka decided not to use Budapest as the debut site for her play. Too overwhelming. Perhaps a smaller town, like Gyor or Pozsony, would be better. This modified plan would work out especially well if they arrived on Friday night and put on the play Saturday night, after *havdalah.* The change of venue suited Sendehr just fine. He didn't think he was quite ready anyway. Itzy and Mayer seemed to know their parts perfectly. Mottke Grunwald and Tsippy Eshman were struggling, but Chaike Traubman, Pessel Vinocur, and Esther Buchman had smaller roles and could have been ready this weekend. Nuchim had twice impressed upon

Rivka the critical need to stage the play in order to replenish the dwindling "bank," but after watching a few scenes, he, too, agreed that a few more days of these rehearsals couldn't hurt.

Kalman Fuchs and his little concertina, which was far more squeaky than sweet, and the trumpeter with his dented horn, accompanied by the drummer boy, would provide the background music and were beginning to sound much better. Their renditions of old and newer folk tunes like "*Oifn Pripitchok*," "*Rozhinkes mit Mandeln*," "*Margaritekelech*," and an arrangement of *klezmer* tunes had been well-received around the campfires in recent days.

The Golub Brothers *kosatzke*, the vigorous Russian high-flying dance, drew cheers at the talent nights, which consisted of everything from hilarious skits a la Gelman and Kelemer, to singing, dancing, instrumentals, poetry recitations, and a mini-recital from the "three cantors"— whose eager "trainee" had not yet been invited to be the fourth.

Rivka insisted on everyone participating at one time or another, and to date only a few of the terminally shy had escaped. Mordecai gave these activities his full support and had recently started one evening with a rapid-fire, five-minute, seriocomic presentation of "What We Will Each Be Doing One Year From Now," leaving absolutely no one out.

Now that the Fusgeyers had arrived in Budapest, and would be heading in a northwesterly direction toward Vienna, Prague, and Berlin, they were forced to address the language barrier. Their use of Romanian ended rather abruptly in the Great Plains of Eastern Hungary, and Yiddish now was beginning to have its problems, too; the further west they marched. Branko's Hungarian and German were more than just adequate, and so in this respect contingent #4 was far more fortunate than the other groups, none of which had passable fluency in any other languages in their ranks.

The German language, which would soon become all-important for the remainder of the overland journey, produced a strain of "Germanic Yiddish," which the Wayfarers imagined they could use for general purposes—and they did not expect to engage in too many deep conversations, anyway. The Yiddish of the Fusgeyer, including that of both Branko and Mendel Buchman who learned their other languages while teenagers and young adults, was the classical jargon of their forefathers, developed over six or seven centuries, much of which was spent in exiled wanderings. Wherever they lived, they soon learned to speak the vernacular of the land, but since ancient times they used the characters of the Hebrew alphabet when writing in any language. They had done the same thing with Persian, Greek, Latin, Arabic, Spanish (Ladino), Italian, French, and German. It was from the latter that Yiddish sprang into wide use.

It had its beginnings in the Rhine Valley, covering both Western Germany and Eastern France, as far back as the eleventh and twelfth centuries. A series of expulsions from France had resulted in eastward migrations, adding to the growing size of the settled Jewish communities in Germany. Only the fragmentation of the German baronial territories made it nearly impossible to issue any nationwide blanket dispersal of its Jews as had occurred in England, Spain and France.

Had the Jews been able to live and thrive in France—Yiddish might have developed with a French rather than a Germanic base. But the five murderous Crusades en route to the "Holy Land" marched through the well-entrenched Jewish communities along the Rhine from 1096 through the thirteenth century, resulting in widespread killing and destruction. The Black Death plague of 1348-1349 followed, and surviving Jews by the tens of thousands fled ever-eastward, their very lives hanging in the balance: to Bavaria, Bohemia, Moravia, Slovakia, Austria, Hungary, and finally to the Polish provinces and into Russia. Their language went with them, and as they integrated with the few Slavonic Jews of the region in the centuries that followed, Yiddish became the *mamaloshen.*

Philologists studying the historiography of the language up to the time of the mass migrations of the 1880s and 1890s varied little in their fractional breakdown of the component elements: seventy percent German, twenty percent Hebrew and Aramaic, and ten percent Russian, Polish, Ukrainian, Slovakian, Romanian, and a smattering of other borrowed, localized words.

The Budapest Yidden would be the first outright "foreign" brethren that the Birlader Fusgeyers would encounter. Those in Transylvania and Eastern Hungary had retained much of the *Yiddishkeit*, including the language and religious customs that the Fusgeyers had all been raised and schooled with, although certain Germanic-Austrian and Magyar influences were present.

But the Budapest Jew of 1904 was from an altogether different element: a big city. The Budapest Jew came from two or three generations of steadily increasing assimilation, tacit acceptance into social circles heretofore prohibited, and actual elevation into the stratosphere of Hungarian nobility. This, Sendehr Efraim had learned from his Pesach discussions with Reb Viesl in Sighet. Yes, three hundred and fifty families, Jewish or "once Jewish," claiming titles ranging from Lord and Lady to Baron and Baroness—and even including members of the Hungarian Parliament, like Ignac Hirschler, Chairman of the Neolog (Reform) congregation in Pest, as well as other Neolog leaders such as Zsigmond Schossgerger, Zsigmond Kornfeld and Karoly Svab.

Jews had been a major and welcome driving force behind Hungary's industrial boom of the latter half of the nineteenth century, building vast commercial and industrial empires in railway construction, flour-milling, cement, sugar-refining, textiles, and porcelain. Most of these capitalist elite Jews and many of the middle-class turned swiftly and happily to Neolog Judaism, which, without the constraints of the old orthodoxy, they found much more palatable.

The Magyars typically felt this *Zhido* invasion to be an

encroachment forced upon the Old Guard by the controlling Hapsburg family. The more anti-Semitic Hungarian would often say, "when the emperor in Vienna vomits another *Zhid*, the stench reaches our Parliament building on the Danube." Nevertheless, the assimilative juggernaut rolled onward and upward. In fact, Hungarian Jews began in earnest to take Magyar names while discarding their Hebrew and Yiddish names—something rarely done among the Jewish masses in Poland, Russia, or Romania. But in Hungary there was liberal use of Istvan, Zoltan, Ferenc, Endre, Imre, Erzabet, Marta, and even Maria and Theresa.

Aside from the country Jews, mostly of Galician and Slovak origin, and the *Chassidic* sects peppered here and there, who used it regularly, the Yiddish language began losing ground, especially in Budapest during the middle and latter part of the past century and the first few years of the new century. If a man wanted full acceptance in Budapest then he must speak Hungarian only, and follow their customs—and for the many who first switched to Neolog Judaism, the next logical step was official religious conversion. Sadly but assuredly, the baptismal font increasingly became a gathering place for Budapest's finest Jews. Not nearly in the numbers Germany was producing, but, nevertheless, significantly so.

This, then, was the Budapest of 1904—the Budapest that the more naive Fusgeyer would find daunting, perhaps upsetting, and certainly strange. Those few who had the opportunity to listen to Sendehr's comments after his Viesl meetings were more or less prepared for this phenomenon; the others would observe it in the flesh during their three-day visit.

Mordecai, in one of his frequent pensive moments, did not expect to lose anyone to the lure of this beautiful city. He proved to be right. Nor did he expect to lose anyone here for any other reason. He proved to be wrong.

The restful weekend was shaping up to be most pleasurable for those attending the synagogue. At the outset, the president of the enormous congregation, Imre

Steinman, welcomed the Fusgeyers, asking them to stand to be recognized. This was a noble gesture of hospitality on his part, and then, more importantly, he added a few most complimentary remarks, making reference to an article by Eliezer Viesl in the current *Budapest Weekly Jewish News*, which featured the Birladers. Sendehr's face lit up like a *Chanukah menorah* all aglow! Neither he nor any of the others could wait until they could read the piece, copies of which, the president mentioned, were available in the adjoining reception hall.

Immediately following the very animated, participatory *erev Shabbat*, the much-anticipated *Oneg Shabbat* was everything the beadle had advertised. A veritable banquet that far surpassed the herring, *challah*, and plum brandy offerings at the Birlad *shul*: fruits, dried and fresh; *kugel*, *strudel*, and *tsimus*; cakes of every variety; indigenous *Hungarishe* pastries; and the *piece de resistance*—the delicious miniature pancake, *palacsinta*, filled with walnuts, jams, raisins and chocolate.

"*A moychel fur di boychel,*" exclaimed a smiling Chaike, pigtails flying from under her kerchief as she darted back to the *cheder* rooms to invite any stragglers—that is, those who didn't opt to see the wonders of the town in lieu of services. No one to be seen, just empty rooms.

The few hundred attendees mingling in the large adjoining room made it quite evident that a more extensive Sabbath-eve ceremony was in favor here in Budapest, at least in this Great Synagogue. It was treated like an event rather than a quick rendition that made everyone eager to leave. Fusgeyers stood in small groups scanning copies of the newspaper, *kvelling* over Branko's interpretation of Viesl's flowery description of their mission. Most of the congregation had not met the other contingents, none of whom had stopped in Budapest during a Sabbath weekend, so this was turning into a novel experience for them. Not one of them, dressed in up-to-date finery, seemed to be the least bit disturbed by the raggedy appearance of these daring youths. "All the way from Romania?" was repeated time after time by the admiring Budapestians.

Branko, who Mordecai had asked to be on hand for any necessary translating, flitted around the room trying to serve this need. However, a goodly number of the congregants, including Steinman the president and Rabbi Shmuel Schulhofer, conversed comfortably in Yiddish with the Fusgeyers. Steinman had already cornered Sendehr and was insisting on all the details of the journey. "You must be *der shreiber* who Viesl refers to in the article. Your leader, over there, pointed you out." Sendehr, blushing a bit and munching on a mouth-watering slab of noodle *kugel*, did the best he could to answer in a few sentences the president's questions that dealt with more than five weeks and more than eight-hundred kilometers of travel.

Before the crowd began filing out of the room, a most remarkable offer came from an Endre Koffler, owner of a shoe factory across the Danube in the Buda Hills. Standing next to the Rabbi, he announced his personal invitation for the Fusgeyers to call at his establishment between noon and three on Sunday to be fitted by his weekend foreman to good, solid, high-top walkers. Quickly, he added diplomatically that there were smaller sizes that, although not made for women, would probably fit them.

This was met with a mixture of disbelief and sheer joy, followed by a broad chorus of "thank yous" and applause emanating from every corner of the cavern-like hall. Koffler gave the directions to Branko and Mordecai, both of whom personally thanked him for his great generosity. Rabbi Schulhofer stood by basking in the pride of a father whose son had given *tzedakah* without being asked. This magnanimous gesture did not at all surprise him, because Endre Koffler was known for years throughout the community as the consummate philanthropic Jewish businessman. But for many of the Fusgeyers, this kindness had come at a most critical time: soles, old to begin the journey with, had either worn out or were full of holes patched haphazardly with every conceivable type of material. Only a very few were fortunate enough to have owned and brought a spare pair of shoes along.

"Anieloff, sir, I wonder if I might have a parting word with you?" asked a young gentleman with a neatly trimmed steel-gray Vandyke.

"Yes, but of course," replied the very happy Mordecai, as the last of his contingent left the room.

"Allow me to introduce myself, sir. I am Claude-Pierre Farber, and I represent the late Baron Maurice De Hirsch's organization, the J.C.A." Farber's clipped Yiddish had a distinct French hue to it, although Mordecai did not detect it as such.

"And that is?"

"Oh, sorry, the J.C.A. is the Jewish Colonization Association, headquartered in Paris. Baron De Hirsch, who passed on in 1896, established it for the sole purpose of rescuing our fellow Jews from the eastern lands, the Pale of Settlement, and re-settling them on broad expanses of farm and ranch land he was able to purchase in the Western hemisphere."

"I see. Well, as you may know from the announcements tonight, we are going by foot to Bremerhaven, then on to America."

"A most amazing and fascinating story, indeed, Anieloff. I read the article in the *News*. I have heard of other Fusgeyer groups over the past few years, and I wish you a good journey and good fortune in America. Perhaps you will be at the synagogue tomorrow morning? I am going to speak from the pulpit just before Torah-reading, to present a report on my organization's work...not that we expect any migratory explosion from beautiful Budapest, heh, heh, heh!"

Mordecai broke into a broad smile knowing this to be a glaringly obvious truth.

"I have just returned from a tour of the Ukraine and Bessarabia where I spoke to overflowing audiences in Odessa, Kishinev, Staro Konstantinov, Kiev, Zhitomir, and Shepetovka. Good God, man, our people have suffered for so many years! We offer them free transportation, the chance to work good fertile land, and it all falls on deaf ears. If and when they do emigrate, it'll be to the slums of New York like the million who left in the last two decades. From the abject poverty of the *shtetl* to the filthy tenements of the American cities."

"I am, myself, going to New York. A few are going to Boston and Montreal, but it's New York for the rest of us—to start with. Where we'll end up, God knows."

"Argentina, my good young man, Argentina! Have you heard of the Argentine? Do you know anything about this *Gan Eden*? This land of green *pampas*, handsome mountains, healthy, beautiful people. Very European, as a matter of fact."

"I've seen maps. I know that Spanish is the language, and that it's in South America. Very little else."

"Please be sure to hear my presentation tomorrow. I hope you will all be there. Good night. *A guten Shabbos.*" With this, the expensively suited Claude-Pierre Farber bowed slightly, replaced *yarmulke* with black bowler, and exited.

Mordecai stood puzzled for a moment by Farber's remarks. *Argentina? Farm land? Grazing land? Tenements?* Most of this did not make sense, mainly because of Yiddish/English terms he had never heard before. *It will probably be cleared up when I listen to the report in the morning,* he thought.

"Mordecai! Mordecai! There you are! We're going to do it! We're going to put it on! Sunday evening!"

An excited Rivka Demkin grabbed Mordecai's arms as he was about to enter one of the *cheder* rooms where he had left his blanket-bed roll.

"The play? I thought you weren't ready?"

"No, no. Yes, I mean no—we'll just have to be ready."

"What she means, Mordecai, is that one of the fancy *shul* ladies convinced her to do it Sunday," said a much calmer Sendehr, disappointed that he might have to work fast to memorize some of his stickier lines.

"Here, come sit at this desk, take a deep breath, and tell me the whole story, Rivkeleh. Oh, Sendehr, has everyone returned from wherever they went tonight?"

"Yes, everyone. But quite a few just left to walk down to the Danube and along the promenade, which we heard, is well-lit and very beautiful at night. Rivka and I were on our way. Maybe you'll come, too."

"Yes, perhaps, but let me hear the news first"

"During the *Oneg Shabbat* one of the lovely ladies, an Eva Goldener, asked me if we intended to stage our play while in Budapest. She had read about it in Reb Viesl's article, which referred to it as one of our money-raising projects. When I told her that we would probably wait until Gyor or Pozsony, she pleaded with me—and promised that she would get us a capacity audience, all prepared to donate to our group. As for the Yiddish, she claimed that although many do not use the language very much these days, nearly everyone remembers enough from their childhood, from their grandparents, to have at least a basic understanding. I just could not say 'no' to the dear lady, whose Yiddish was quite understandable. During services tomorrow an announcement will be made, and with telephones very much in use in this city, she promised she would have a calling committee at work. And—oh yes—they will charge an entrance fee and all of the proceeds come directly to us! Can you imagine? For that—yes, we'll be ready even if we have to rehearse all night long!"

"*Oy, vay iz mir, vay iz mir!*" Sendehr Efraim held his face with both hands.

"Rivkeleh, you made a very good decision. I am very proud of you. It will be just fine, and your cast will give a beautiful performance. Even 'Sendehr Shakespeare' here! As you know, the money is very important—not knowing any of the unforeseen expenses we may meet, and our 'bank' has diminished appreciably. You've done a wonderful turn, my dear!" Mordecai kissed Rivka on both cheeks.

"*Nu, kinder*, what are you waiting for, the romantic Danube awaits you! I'm going to get a good sleep. Good night and *guten Shabbos*! And remember, if you'll be doing last-minute rehearsing on Sunday, I'll arrange for you and the cast to be quickly accommodated at the shoe factory, noon time. You certainly don't want to miss out on that gift from heaven above!"

When Zed-Zed came into the room, Mordecai quietly told him the Baron De Hirsch Argentina story. The perceptive keeper-of-the-schedule reacted as Mordecai had expected, and asked if the leader was concerned that any Fusgeyer would think seriously about the offer.

"In my heart, I don't believe so, Zed-Zed. But my head says that a few could possibly be vulnerable to the idea of a life on the open grasslands, *pampas* as this Farber called it. We won't stand in anybody's way, but we should not encourage it, either. I would dearly hate to see a rash decision made. Being stranded without any friends around you can be a devastating experience. Regardless, we will continue to press on. I, for one, am more anxious than ever to see what life in America is all about. First hand! No *bubbeh meisehs*, no secondhand stories. Firsthand! With my own eyes!"

"And I, too, Mordecai. Although, I don't think I will spend too much time with my Uncle Chaim. Remember I told you he lives on the East Side of New York, works in a hat factory, has three children—and they all live in one room. In a letter last year, he promised my parents that he could get me a good job working next to him. Somehow, that does not in any way appeal to me."

"As I told that Farber fellow this evening, none of us knows just where we'll end up. It is a cause for a certain amount of anxiety with most of our group, and that's precisely why I gave that sort of off-handed presentation a few weeks ago—to diffuse the anxiety and tone down the whole matter—to put the entire question into an acceptable perspective. You'll find your place, Zed-Zed; of that I have little doubt. We all will, eventually. I heard or read somewhere that America is called 'the land of opportunity.' Sounds very good to me. I'm ready. Good night and *guten Shabbos*, dear friend."

Mordecai did not fall asleep quickly. He never did. Like a protective parent, he waited until the sound of the last

Fusgeyer shuffling through the courtyard could be heard through the open windows of the classroom. He then wondered a bit how Rivka and Sendehr had enjoyed the walk along the river's promenade. He broke into his patented broad grin at that thought and finally dozed off, thinking what a grand day it had been for the children of Birlad, buffeted by the sights and sounds of the sophistication that was turn-of-the-century Budapest.

Claude-Pierre turned out to be a masterful lecturer— No, an orator. An orator who kept the largest audience he had ever faced spellbound for nearly an hour. This was twice the time that the synagogue's program chairman had allotted him, yet no one made any move to cut him short. The entire ground floor was filled, as were two of the balconies of women-folk. All of the Fusgeyers were in attendance, at Mordecai's strong suggestion, including Rivka's nervous thespians, foregoing a morning rehearsal session she had tried to plan at the last minute. During the Torah-reading which preceded Claude-Pierre, Mordecai, Sendehr, Zed-Zed, and Mendel were given *aliyahs*—which, again, was perceived as yet another in this series of *haimishe* gestures on the part of Jewish Budapest.

The first part of Farber's dramatic presentation brought tears to the eyes of many in the congregation. His vivid descriptions of the horrendously inhumane conditions in and around the Pale painted a multi-colored word-picture that seemed to bounce off the prisms in the huge crystal chandeliers. Not that they had not heard similar reports, complete with recent photographs, from the rash of Jewish charitable organizations that saw Budapest as a prime target for their fund-raising. He finished this phase of his lecture by emphatically stating that this was a problem begging for a solution, and it was the sacred duty of worldwide Jewry to become involved.

The silver-tongued Parisian had a way of stating this that made each pair of listening ears and watching eyes feel that Farber was speaking as an honored guest at a cozy dinner in their own dining room, or over brandy and cigars in their drawing room. He got to them. Each and every one. But now that he had so eloquently posed the well-known problem, he went in for the *coup de grace*. If he were a *toreador* in a Spanish bullring, it would be his final thrust of the sword between the weakened *toro's* eyes. The crowd pleaser. The euphonic *olé*! The solution!

Claude-Pierre's solution was the rather simplistic one so widely announced and funded by his illustrious mentor, the 1891 founder of the JCA. As was his father before him, Baron Maurice De Hirsch was a billionaire French Jew, one of the richest men in the world and a renowned philanthropist of the highest regard and reputation. But most of all, he was a thinking, feeling human being—a *mensch*—with a worldly vision and a not-to-be-denied desire to become personally involved with each project.

The central idea behind his establishment of the JCA (actually referred to by Yiddish-speaking communities as the ICA—the "I" representing the common pronunciation of "Yiddishe" as "Iddishe") was to take the Pale's Jewish population and resettle them. Not in the cities of Western Europe or America; not in Paris, London, Berlin, New York, Philadelphia, or Boston,; not in the city slums, the overcrowded, unsanitary tenements, nor in the notorious sweatshops. Quite on the contrary.

The Baron promoted this one salient theory: he envisaged a mass emigration of the Jews from Eastern Europe to rural areas, to farmland, to grazing land. In this way, the Jew could escape the anti-Semitism so endemic to the villages, towns and cities within the Pale; he wanted something better for those who had the courage to strive for it.

De Hirsch had already purchased vast tracts of land in such diverse locations as Woodbine, New Jersey, and in Connecticut, Pennsylvania, upstate New York, and Western Canada's Manitoba and Saskatchewan—where the tiny, struggling cooperative of "Hirsch" had honored the Baron's name. Most of the relocation attempts had languished, then completely faded.

The attempt to relocate the immigrants to rural areas

in order to protect them from the ravages of the big American city was nothing new. During the 1880s, the Am Olam (Eternal People) organization sent new immigrants to such remote places as Sicily Island, Louisiana, where a Mississippi River flood destroyed all of their equipment, in their effort to set up farm cooperatives. Another cooperative in Eastern Arkansas suffered malaria and yellow fever, quickly disbanded, and returned to New York after twenty settlers had perished. Still others failed in Cremieux, South Dakota, and New Odessa, Oregon—the latter having lasted a record five years before final abandonment. Most survivors of these experiments returned to the East Coast cities; some, in disgust, sailed back to Europe.

Along with these massive colonization attempts, the JCA also had established trade schools throughout Europe, and in 1896 one of De Hirsch's board members and shareholders, the eminent Baron Edmund De Rothschild, joined him in providing desperately needed financial aid for certain floundering colonies in Palestine. Unfortunately, the management company they selected to operate these sites failed miserably, coming under frequent attacks for their ineptness.

None of this was known to Mordecai or any of his Birladers. Perhaps some of the more worldly congregants had read or heard of these failed JCA experiments, but here in 1904, in Budapest, one of Europe's most charming and wealthy cities, Claude-Pierre mentioned none of these things; and rightly so. Instead, he dwelt heavily upon the moderate successes of the JCA in Argentina and on recently purchased land in Brazil, at Rio Grande do Sul, where the colony of "Bessarabia" (most of the new settlers came from that region in Southern Russia) had been established earlier in the year.

Tantamount to Gabriel blowing his horn, the speaker ended with a well-calculated flourish, recounting the adventurous history of Jewish colonization in the Argentine hinterlands where Baron De Hirsch had purchased 100,000 hectares even before forming the JCA. The colony of

Moisesville—also named for the Baron, using the Spanish equivalent for Maurice/Moshe—continued to thrive, according to Claude-Pierre, and additional colonies had also been established during the past decade in the provinces of Santa Fe, Entre Ríos, and La Pampa. The settlers received all the necessary equipment, training, credit lines, and a network of schools for their children. What more could one ask?

He implored the leaders of the Budapest community to encourage their vast business and government contacts throughout the Austro-Hungarian Empire, Russia, and Romania to seek out and convince potential Jewish émigrés to contact the JCA's newly opened Budapest offices for information. By so doing they would be offered ship transportation from Trieste and Marseilles to Buenos Aires, where representatives would meet them. Anyone with family in the East was encouraged to do the same. He did not mention the United States, Canada, or Palestine, of course.

The speaker's featured topic of the day was Argentina, where JCA colonies were thriving, with plenty of room for more settlers. Precisely why Claude-Pierre had left Mordecai with that suggestive thought: *Argentina.*

The *kiddush* repast following *musaf* was not quite up to the *erev Shabbos* spread, but it served as a rich substitute for the typically lean Fusgeyer noontime meal. Besides, there were ample opportunities for pocket-stuffing. Most of this was pre-empted by the ever-magical Simmy *der schnorrer,* who had already wheedled from the beadle all of the leftovers from the *shul* pantry. Perhaps the perishables would either go stale or become inedible by the middle of the week, but, oh, what delicious refreshments they would make while following the pretty *Dunakanyar,* the Danube bend, on Monday as it wound from Budapest to Esztergom/Gran!

It was at the *kiddush* repast that the first hint of Fusgeyer defection sprouted. Standing next to a smiling Claude-Pierre Farber and engaging in animated conversation with him, three "interested parties seeking answers" were jealously herded further into a corner by the JCA recruiter. Mordecai, Zed-Zed, and Sendehr, each watching from a different vantage point in the large hall, each speculated, inwardly, independently, on the outcome of this scene. Perhaps they were only expressing mild interest. On the other hand, it could very well be "serious contemplation," "sincere investigation," or simply "fact-finding" or even the ultimate, "final fact-finding, preceding final decision-making."

What are they doing in that corner with Farber, for ten minutes already? When Farber talks, our boys do nothing but nod. What in the name of ribono shel olam *does that indicate other than full acceptance, total capitulation? They're actually going to Argentina? Argentine farmers? Argentine "cowboys"—what is it, "gauchos?"* These were the thoughts racing through the tangled brain waves of the two cadre and their esteemed leader. If they had shared these thoughts, each would have agreed that Farber could probably convince a Romanian *schicker* to give up drinking. He was that good.

The Singerman lads, Berel and Dovid, who everyone mistakenly thought to be twins, and the long-bearded Yehuda Gelman, Itzy's cousin, finally came back to the *kiddush* table spread, the latter holding in his hand what appeared to be a playing card. They approached Mordecai, who was engaged in a conversation with four of the younger *shul* women, who had probably heard that he was a widower.

"Pardon us, Mordecai. Can we have a few minutes with you, please?"

Mordecai excused himself from the circle of women, put his arm around Yehuda, the Singermans trailing a length behind them, and whispered, "*Nu* Yuda, how did you like the speech this morning?"

"Mordecai, the Singermans and I are considering the possibility of going to Argentina. You know that the three of us worked together for Reb Mandelbaum on the chicken farms. Berel and Dovid have become experts over these years, and they can coax even the laziest layer to give an extra push. Out pops the egg. A miracle. What do you think,

Mordecai? None of us really wants the city life that Farber described."

The group of four stopped now that they had distanced themselves from the others. Mordecai spoke first. "Yuda, and Bereleh, and Dovidl, my dear friends. It is not what *I* think or feel or do that's important now. This has to be *your* decision. It is for each of you alone to make. I know nothing about Argentina, but in America, I do know that we have friends, Birladers, and many different types of opportunities, I hear. Even on the farms, as well."

Berel leaned forward, saying, "Mordecai, Claude-Pierre tells us that the one thing they are missing in their Argentine colonies are experienced chicken hands. He feels that we can have a place of our own. Just chickens. I can send for my Sora and little Chaya. They will love the country life. I don't want my Chaya to grow up in a, what is it called, 'taynamunt'."

Dovid added, "You say we can work on a farm in America. But how can we be sure? This is certain, Mordecai. They'll pay for transportation. For Berel's family, too. Claude-Pierre also says that there are many available Jewish *maidelach* in Argentina for bachelors. Everybody in the colonies speaks Yiddish. We won't even have to learn Spanish."

Mordecai took all of this in, and as he did so he realized that it might be impossible to salvage them.

"How soon do you have to make your decision, boys?"

"The next boat for South America leaves Trieste in two weeks, and twenty Russians are already waiting there. We have to agree to go by Monday, so we can take the Budapest-Trieste train, and the JCA will provide lodgings until the boat sails. I wish you would tell us your opinion, Mordecai," pleaded an anxious, fidgeting Berel.

"Bereleh, I am committed to take the Fusgeyers to America. I will do that. I wish I could convince you to come along the rest of the way, but it appears that you've made your decision otherwise already. If this is true, I will announce it this afternoon and you can be sure everyone will wish you the best fortune, and they will sincerely mean

every word of it. That, of course, will include me. As you
may or may not know, each of the prior Birlad contingents
dropped a few members for various reasons. Not many.
Maybe three or four here and there. Some decided to stay
with relatives along the way. A few others returned to Birlad
before reaching the port. Remember Moishe Perelman and
Leml Vereniker? In fact, one of the Iashi groups two years
ago disintegrated completely. Only a handful stayed together
and actually went on to America. Most went home. Their
reasons? I don't know. I do know there was a fair amount of
some contagious sickness, and some cases of severe homesickness, too. Also, rumor has it that there was constant
bickering and a lack of overall cohesiveness. We have had
none of that, and at the least sign, I absolutely will not
tolerate it. You know that. Contrarily, we have had—and
will have—a one hundred percent cooperative effort. Your
leaving will not hurt the mission, although we will miss
you. And, I mean that, dear friends, from the very bottom of
my heart."

No one spoke. Berel and Dovid stared at each other;
Yuda stared at his shoes. All three awaited a final word
from Mordecai, if there was to be one. He did not disappoint.

"*Khaverim*, when I visit Argentina I will want someplace
to stay, and eggs for breakfast!"

This surprising remark from the unflappable one
brought a chuckle and a smile to the three chicken-shep-
herds. The spring-coil tension was reduced to a limp *lokshen.*

"Look, what I'm saying, boys, is although I, as your
leader, would dearly love for us to arrive in America in full
complement, I cannot foresee all the counter-influences we
may meet en route. And Claude-Pierre, if anything, is a most
formidable and persuasive gentleman."

The difficult conversation was about to end with those
words, but Yehuda was quick to add that they would take
the rest of the weekend to make a final decision. Mordecai
nodded with a paternal, knowing smile. He hoped that this
would mean that everything would turn out fine, no mat-

ter what was decided, *vos vet zayn, vet zayn.*

While Rivka assiduously rehearsed her nervous cast throughout the remainder of the Sabbath, the others had a grand time exploring the Queen City of the Danube.

Branko led those who wished to accompany him on a merry ride on the subway trains. Of this group, only Branko and Yankel Golub had ever been on a train before. Some rode three or four stops, got off, reversed direction and did this rotating exercise, without needing to expend another coin, until they tired of it. They were excited when another Jewish passenger told them that New York was soon to open a subway with even more kilometers of track than Budapest's system. Meanwhile, the more Sabbath-observant were waiting until sundown, when they would follow the same procedure, guided by the newest underground veteran, the now worldly Yankel.

Above ground, the Fusgeyers did not tire of admiring the motor-driven carriages that they saw in abundance on every street in town. One friendly couple—the driver wore a light canvas "duster" and strange goggles that were topped by a leather headpiece—offered Branko, Yossi, and Yoni Golub a ride back to the *shul.* Still others spent the day pleasantly wandering the tree-filled parks and broad boulevards, walking in and out of the many shops along the way, peering at the artistic window displays, and wondering all the while whether New York would be as beautiful and clean. To a degree, disappointment awaited them.

Sholem and Yaakov, true to form, decided that a race over the famous *Lanchid,* known as the "chain bridge," was in order. City bridges proved ideal for this pastime. Even with one of his soon-to-be-replaced shoes in irreparable condition, the speedy Friedman outdistanced he of the Greek "racers" across and back. The long, British-designed expanse, inaugurated in 1849, had become known all over Europe. It was also the first bridge to connect Buda and Pest (Pesht) when they were separate cities, prior to the 1873 consolidation.

Looking out over the river, Sholem and Yaakov speculated whether they would see any comparable spans over rivers in America. Sadly reminded that they would part with one another on the other side of the Atlantic, Sholem quipped: "Yak, are you sure you want to go to Montreal? How will I ever find anybody else I can always beat??" And with that barb, Sholem raced away, his mangled sole flapping, while the second-best runner in Budapest that Saturday afternoon stood arms akimbo for a second, then gave chase—fruitlessly, as always.

Along Dohany *utca*, neighboring Dob *utca*, and Sip *utca* the countless Jewish-owned stores came very much alive at sundown. Restaurants, small cafes, clothing, jewelry, shoe and hardware stores, bakeries, groceries, butchers—the streets full of the noisiest hawkers imaginable—drew all of the Fusgeyers, including the exhausted thespians. The hard-driving director had made a decision to let them rest until tomorrow afternoon's final run-through. She and her cast felt that they were now ready, come what may!

It seemed as though the entire Budapest Jewish community had taken to the streets at the same time. They had. According to Zed-Zed, sundown was scheduled for 7:37, and by eight o'clock one couldn't find a table at the restaurants or cafes. Many of the shops were filled with people standing shoulder-to-shoulder.

But the biggest attraction in the entire Pest area of the city, by far, was found at the busy intersection of Dohany and Erzabet Korut. Long lines had formed all day long, and before the evening was over, every Fusgeyer would also have attended this magical event, this phenomenon, this veritable bombardment of the senses— the moving picture!

Budapest's first showing of this new art had begun just a few years year ago, as all of the continent clamored to join the world-wide craze which had quickly grown from a novelty to a bonafide industry in less than a decade.

At the 200-seat *Duna Szinhaz*, the Fusgeyers watched wide-eyed as a train engine roared around a bend. The image was projected on an oversized white sheet, and someone in the orchestra pit played a pipe organ, emulating the locomotive's toot. When the train bore down on the audience, accompanied by the crescendo blasts of the organ, only the thoroughly jaded could refrain from wincing and flinching. The theater emptied out every thirty or forty few minutes, and the Birladers couldn't stop talking about what they had seen for days to come.

They all looked ahead longingly to the next showing, whether it would be Pozsony, Vienna, or Prague. Meanwhile, unbeknownst to them, back in Birlad a Bucureshti entrepreneur offered to set up this wonderment there. It would come complete with one of Thomas Edison's projectors and three different reels of film, one of which was a newly acquired copy of "The Great Train Robbery"—far more thrilling and much longer than the speeding engine film that mesmerized the Birladers in Budapest. What they also didn't realize was that all American cities, especially New York, were by then inundated with little hole-in-the-wall nickel-a-showing storefronts—"nickelodeons"—where many a workingman squandered a portion from his meager pay envelope. Of course, by this time in America the nickel show had skyrocketed to a quarter in the better emporia.

But this is a toy, a passing fancy. It will never replace the live stage play, thought millions of first-time viewers in every part of the world. The Fusgeyers believed this, too, as did all of those preparing to see Rivka's version of Mendele Mocher Seforim's *Dos Vinshfingerl* the following evening. Actors and actresses, very much alive, costumed, telling a story, playing with emotions; and background music, again, alive. This was the theater of life itself, not a mere floating image on a white sheet. God, no!

Sixty pairs of factory-fresh shoes adorned the coarsely callused feet of sixty happy Fusgeyers as they filed into the large reception hall of the Great Synagogue. Movable chairs had been placed in rows, and the slightly elevated speaker's platform was transformed into an adequate makeshift stage. They were under strict orders not to take a chair until all of the paying clientele were seated. By curtain time, if there had been a curtain, every one of the three hundred chairs was filled by an elegantly dressed man or woman. Along the back wall and the two side walls, the Fusgeyers and a handful of latecomers stood. Some of the seated gentlemen, recognizing that there were women standing, graciously gave up their seats. The Fusgeyer *femmes*, waiting for their respective turns to go on stage, since there wasn't any backstage, were also recipients of this genteel gesture.

A bejeweled Eva Goldener and her committee collected money at the door, with Nuchim Krasnigor standing close at hand, smiling as he contemplated the proceeds, which would significantly swell the Fusgeyer cooperative "bank." The sconces along the walls and a series of smaller lamps hanging from the high ceiling had all been converted to electric power during the past decade, as was the massive chandelier in the adjoining main sanctuary. Moreover, the entire complex had been wired at no charge, thanks to the generosity of Budapest's largest bulb manufacturer who served for many years as a member of the congregational board. The one lamp over the platform was of low wattage, but it served to set the mood very effectively when all of the other lights were off.

Rivka had coached her cast to speak slightly louder and a beat slower than usual in order to accommodate those who were not fully fluent in Yiddish or had neither spoken nor heard it in a long time.

The story of the wishing-ring, *Dos Vinshfingerl*, embodied the daily life of Hershele, Sendehr's role, living from birth until maturity in the hopelessly subjugated ghetto'ed-town of Kabtzansk, "pauper-town." The play displayed more or less a microcosm of all East European Jewish life of the times, delineating the entire physical and spiritual life of the community, its day-to-day activities, its trials and tribulations, specific problems, ethical folkways, religious values and practices.

The story was, arguably, one of the more painfully realistic ones of the era. People who lived in the Pale, Congress Poland or Romania could easily identify with Kabtzansk. But more importantly, the story afforded these

Hungarians who lived in relative luxury a vivid picture of the much harder life that their fellow Jews to the east lived. Rivka, with the help of the comedy pair of Gelman and Kelemer took a slice of poetic license in transforming Seforim's printed page into a workable stage play, and interjected a bit of humor here and there to lighten up the heavy subject occasionally. Itzy as the affable *luftmensch,* a character full of pathos and seasoned with his brand of dry-wry humor, was just one example of such comedy.

The timing of each one of the script's lines was impeccable, and the appreciative audience delighted in every minute of the presentation. Tears flowed at the right moments, laughter came when unexpected, and the applause was thunderous at the end of the one-act gem. Rivka and her proud cast bowed profusely and greedily quaffed every drop of adulation that flowed, especially when they were singled out during the refreshment hour, which had been beautifully arranged by Eva Goldener and her volunteers. The praises came from all quarters, including a popular young local playwright who seemed to enjoy the offering, language difficulties notwithstanding. The exhausted storytellers now looked ahead eagerly to their next engagement. Rivka was elated, and even Sendehr wished they could have performed a second act!

This highly successful staging provided a fitting end to a most rewarding stopover, crowned sweetly by Nuchim's bank bag bursting at its seams. The next day—on the road once again. *Oy! Es iz shver zu zayn a Fusgeyer Yid!*

Sendehr had great difficulty falling asleep; his adrenaline flowed over the dam in torrents. Imagine, he only had to be prompted once by Maidele, and as the play went on his confidence grew exponentially. To be sure, the acting bug had bitten, and with Rivka he was smitten! *Oy, vay iz mir!*

He arose from his bedroll, took his pen, ink bottle, and writing paper, and tip-toed among the snores, lifting the latch of the classroom door silently to go outside into the mild night. The moon was full, and its glow gave enough light so that Sendehr could sit on one of the benches in the courtyard to write.

>*Dear Rabbi:*
>
>*Tomorrow, actually in a few hours, we leave Budapest after a most wonderful stay, as you will see from my synopsis, which I will mail during the week, as usual. The play was excellent and with over three hundred in attendance our coffers are over-flowing.*
>
>*I am reasonably certain, however, that we will be losing three of our group tomorrow. I'll provide the details in the synopsis, as I see no reason this cannot be shared with the congregation. The Singerman brothers and Itzy Gelman's cousin Yehuda, are leaving, and are off to Argentina, no less. I feel the move will suit them all very well, and they seem to be happy about the prospect. In the morning they will reveal their final decisions. They have to leave for Trieste to rendezvous with a Buenos Aires-bound ship. I somehow feel that this won't be the last of our losses, but I pray that I am wrong. But the rest of us will forge onward, never losing sight of our purpose.*
>
>*And that is being accomplished each step of the way. Again, the synopsis will tell all, but the big news is that Eliezer Viesl's exceptionally complimentary article (in Hungarian), which I'm including with this letter, could be posted in at least six additional newspapers. To translate, see Doctor Simcha who speaks Hungarian quite well. Tonight, I had the distinct pleasure of meeting Elie's editor, Alexander Kordan, of the Budapest Weekly Jewish News. He's from an old local family, accepted on all levels of Budapest society, yet he doesn't shy away from even the most controversial subjects. He informed us proudly that the Yiddishe version of Elie's Hungarian-language article was to be shared with the Iashi Yiddishe Shtimme, the Galatz Voch, and the Bucureshti Shofar, so you will soon*

see it reprinted in Romania. Of course, Viesl was careful not to mention Birlad or any of our names. No need to ask for trouble. But of far more value for our purposes, he told me that he corresponds regularly with a fiery publisher of an upstart newspaper in New York, and has good contact with the editors at the London Jewish Chronicle, the Parisian Israelite and the Berlin Yiddishe Vort. He's certain that Elie's article will soon appear in all of these in the appropriate language.

Rabbi, this even surpassed the euphoria of the play! Our word is getting out, even much more so than any of the previous Fusgeyer groups, I believe. Mordecai and I privately rejoice at this realization and we profusely thanked Kordan. By the way he is called "Sander," which he claims is a common short name for people named Alexander. Perhaps that is from where "Sendehr" is derived, also. Do you know?

Your dear brother is thriving on this little walk of ours. He appears happy and healthy and is full of enthusiasm, all of which is quite contagious to the people around him. He and Sholem carry out their adventurous "point" duties with relish. I don't think Yak will stop competing with Sholem until he someday out-races him! Unfortunately, they will separate when we arrive in America. I pray they will meet again and race once more.

In signing off, I'll briefly mention that after the play Rivka referred to me as her "leading man." Geee-valt! How I loved that, Rabbi!

> Sendehr Efraim,
> Budapest, Hungary, 2:00 a.m.,
> May 9, 1904 (4 Iyar, 5664

12

ENCOUNTERS: ROAD TO VIENNA

Willows bathing in the sun,
swaying gently in the breeze.
Will it be like this in America?
Sendehr Efraim, *The Sojourner*

For the good citizens of Hungary's fairest city, scurrying, helter-skelter, to their stores and offices that Monday morning, the sight of smartly marching youth, four abreast, in perfect military columnar fashion, flying two flags, six pulling a heavily-laden cart, a drum rum-tumming and on occasion, a trumpet blasting staccato notes up and down the scale, generated two questions: Who are these Jews? Where are they going? Those in carriages, horse-less and horse-drawn, strollers, policemen, residents, were all puzzled. The man up front, with the droopy black mustache must be their leader, they mused, and begged a third question: Why is he smiling so broadly?

Sholem and Yaakov in the vanguard as usual, had already crossed the *Lanchid* and walked briskly alongside the Danube, water gently lapping at the embankments. They soon passed the Endre Koffler shoe factory just beyond the Royal Palace on Buda's Castle Hill, looked down on their still-shiny brogans, and silently gave thanks for these sorely needed gifts. Not a day too soon, at least for Sholem. He vowed to remember this gracious act of generosity for the rest of his days.

They looked back and were emotionally impressed with the colorful picture of their comrades crossing the bridge over the *Duna*, the Danube. Sholem mentioned to his reconnaissance partner that this very same river snaked its way to the south into Serbia, then eastward, where its deep gorges formed the border between Romania and Bulgaria before swinging onward to Galatz, Tulcea, its multi-fingered delta, and finally emptying into the Black Sea. He had traced it on Sendehr's map one day. Yaakov asked where its source was located and all Sholem could answer was "off the map, somewhere in the west." Good enough.

The plan was to follow the great waterway into what was called The Danube Bend, *Dunakanyar* in the language of the Magyars. Sendehr's Hungarian charts showed it twisting to the west at the town of Esztergom (Gran was its Austrian designation), after passing Szentendre and Visegrad, and then it could be followed all the way to Vienna and beyond. Having such a long, clear guideline for the first time since following the Bistritsa in Romania was enormously helpful to this advance party.

Sendehr, Zed-Zed and Mordecai had shared the same thought when they were confirming schedule and direction the evening before. Home, Birlad, was far away now and faded further away with each step they took. Then again, each of these deliberate strides was taking them closer and closer to their new home. New life. New world.

Yes, of course Mordecai was smiling as he set the pace! His sagging black mustachio was nearly raised to a horizontal plane while his lips curved heavenward. He had much to feel good about. The success of the stage play. The needed cash it brought in. The shoes. Oh, they do feel great! The Viesl article. The potential that it might appear in so many other newspapers, and was bound to make an impact if it should do so. The wonder of the moving image on a white sheet. The subway. The many motorcars. The marvels of this new century! And above all of this, which most certainly would qualify as *dayenu, dayenu*: the consummate hospitality from the people of the Great Synagogue. So many blessings in so short a time. *Boruch Hashem. Boruch Hashem. Omayn. Omayn!*

But, ribono shel olam, he asked under his breath, *why is it that so much joy has to be tempered with a dose of sadness?* Saying farewell to the Singerman brothers and Yehuda Gelman had not been easy. For anyone. Their decision to leave the group to go to Argentina had come as no surprise to Mordecai. Not one of the group failed to embrace each of the three when the announcement was made at the morning meal. Mordecai was very pleased with this spontaneous reaction of camaraderie. All wished them *mazel* as they made their way to Claude-Pierre's JCA office...the first steps toward their new lives on the Argentinean *pampas. Zayt gezunt, khaverim!*

Mordecai expected losses. Each of the other contingents from Birlad and many other Romanian towns had experienced them. All much more significant in number than these three. He was privately relieved that there were no others succumbing to the lure of farm living in South America.

Walking alongside and just behind the leader was the capable cadre of committee heads; all aglow in similarly satisfied states. Taking up the rear even the *shleppers* showed a purposeful gait, although the towpath along the river was sandy in parts, making for a more back-straining pull. Every now and then, a team of draft-horses, roped to an offshore barge full of Budapest-produced materials for the upriver towns, made it necessary for these human competitors to detour into the deeper silt. The *oy, vays* could be heard by all.

Rivka, still showing the pride of a lioness ruling her domain, could think only of the well-received premiere performance of the "Fusgeyer Players." Her biggest moment in the aftermath had come when she was introduced to one of the bright, young shining playwrights of the Hungarian stage scene. Unfortunately, the completely assimilated Ferenc Molnar could understand only small portions of the Yiddish, but his hosts, major supporters of Budapest theater, had been capable of feeding him enough key lines during the performance. The 25-year-old, highly popular social-humorist was complimented Rivka, her cast, and her stage direction enthusiastically. A bonafide dramatist, no less, had capped-off their triumphant evening! A good review by a stuffy London critic could mean no more.

Zed-Zed's schedule had not been significantly compromised at any time since April 1st. For this he was as self-satisfied as any other cadre felt. Unbeknownst to all but Sendehr and Mordecai, the meticulous timekeeper had carefully built in a series of "extra days," cushions to be used as needed. He had thoughtfully reserved a day here and a day there for rest, illness (God forbid!), severely inclement weather, detainment, or for whatever reason. In addition to these days, he had added twelve more if needed. In other words, their arrivals in Berlin, then in Hamburg and finally in Bremerhaven were right on schedule for the period between July 10th to August 1st. The extra days would provide, at the very least, two weeks to get everything in order, and from what Zed-Zed had learned from all of the prior information, the mass of paperwork technicalities and medical examinations could be overwhelming. Then there was the unavoidable matter of required quarantine. The Sabbath rest was easily accommodated with this kind of comfortable planning, and there was not a Fusgeyer who did not appreciate this.

Mendel and Esther never tired of holding hands as they marched, and conversed in English as often as they could making sure that the "students" could hear as much of the language on a daily basis. Esther's usage had improved almost as much as Sholem's, who at this point, could proudly synopsize one of Harte's stories, or Twain's, and relate it to the group in English without too many halts. Mendel was happy with the effort everyone was making. Even some of the more reluctant ones could, by now, speak enough words and commonly used phrases to slide by in America. At least until they were able to build on it, day by day, and develop their sentence structure, vocabulary and pronunciation. This would happen, Mendel proudly and sincerely believed.

On most every evening at least half would remain voluntarily after the English class for history and geography instruction. Mendel had prepared a curriculum that covered the highlights of United States history. Key presidential figures included Washington, the Adamses, Jefferson, Monroe, Jackson, Lincoln, and the current Teddy Roosevelt. The two defining wars they studied were the Revolution and the Civil War. Slavery was discussed, as was the Manifest Destiny and territory expansion. To understand the legal issues in their adoptive country, lessons were held on the make-up of the legislative and judicial branches, how laws were made and repealed, and, most of all, what this meant to the new immigrant...the Fusgeyer.

Mendel had found a map of the United States, circa 1900, in Salonika three years back, which he had redrawn and enlarged on a piece of paper, including a recalculated scale. This showed the outline of the forty-five states, and the territories of Oklahoma, New Mexico, Arizona, Alaska and Hawaii as well. He had penciled-in state names, the major cities of the country, and its rivers and mountain ranges. This was borrowed almost every evening. Three and four at a time would pore over the makeshift map, quizzing one another, using the scale to judge distances with Sendehr's eager help, speculating on where they would like to live.

Mottke Grunwald, for example, loved the sound of "Idaho", and enjoyed repeating it periodically. Pessel Vinocur was drawn to "Michigan." "Sounds like *mishigus*, but if I'm a *Birlader*, then living in Michigan I'd become a *Michiganer*," she would laugh. Asher, the drummer-boy, was partial to "Texas," especially after hearing Mendel talk about the Battle of the Alamo. Yankel Golub loved to think of himself as an Indian in Indiana, where they all must live, of course. The Gelman-Kelemer jesters liked "Connecticut" so much they had to put it into a ribald poem, pronouncing it "Connecticutz" to rhyme with a popular scatological Yiddish word. How else could they make these six young ladies titter and blush? For shy little Tsipporah, they composed a song in Yiddish and English, which she adored. "*Oy*, Tsippy from Mississippi," or "*Oy, Tsippaleh foon Mississippaleh.*" Mendel knew that the more fun they derived as they got accustomed to the new names the better they would feel about pronouncing them when it came time to do so.

For Yaakov and Heshy Rosen's benefit, Mendel also included Montreal and the Saint Lawrence River, mainly to show their proximity to New York. More than anything else, the students were impressed by the long coastline from Maine to Florida, and around the Gulf of Mexico to Texas...and if that weren't enough, the west coast and the Pacific Ocean, from Washington to California. Only Branko, who had been stationed on the Adriatic near Dubrovnik/ Ragusa for a few months, Mendel who had lived on the Aegean in Salonika, and the very few who had either been to Odessa or Constantsa on the Black Sea, had ever seen any ocean. But, as Mendel pointed out, in a few months time they would be getting all the ocean they could handle...and then some.

Menachem Berman, thankfully, had very little involvement up to now, a fact that translated into "no problems" of earth-shaking dimensions. Aside from the border-crossing tensions with the almost-forgotten Captain Sandor, the river-crossing episode with the "highway robbers", and isolated, relatively painless confrontations with a few minor uniform-wearers, diplomacy and its tools had not been necessary. This in no way lulled Menachem into a false sense of security. On the contrary.

During the O*neg Shabbat* Menachem had a long discussion with the only Jewish member of the Budapest City Council, a Ferenc Haltai, who had his eyes on the mayoralty, which would later come to pass. Haltai, a nephew of the Budapest-born Zionist Theodor Herzl, warned of a potential hazard in Vienna, which had become the focal point of Europe's mass trans-migratory era. It was in this capital of culture where the known anti-Semitic mayor, Karl Lueger, was making loud noises about "all these damned dregs from the east, Czar Nicolai's sewage, cluttering up the alleys of the *Judegasse*." According to the well-informed Haltai, Burgermeister Lueger had been threatening to close off the entire city to "immigrant trash," and had actually done so on three occasions since taking office in 1895. Crossing the border into Austria could become an issue these days. Xenophobia at its very worst was evidently alive and kicking in that part of the Empire.

Branko and his Defense Committee, as their assignment required, were perpetually "on alert." Mordecai and all of the Fusgeyers depended on this; however, only in an extreme emergency would they be required to act aggressively. Menachem was always worried about the cache of weapons secreted in the cart. Back at the river-crossing, the incident with the Golub boys prompted Mordecai and Menachem to insist that no one would again be allowed to carry any weapons on his person, with the possible exception of *der soldat* under certain prescribed circumstances. All must be placed in pre-assigned positions within the cart. To their knowledge, this critical order was being obeyed.

The *eppes essen* food czar, marching along with the medical team of Hippocrates and Nightingale, was having a far easier time than he ever imagined. This was largely due to the generosity of every Jewish community en route...from "Freilacher" Bereleh, the egg man of Vatra Dornei, to the kind folks of Sighet, the shop owners of Debrecen, the villagers of the Great Plains and the Hortobagy, and most recently, the Jews of Budapest. His "stores" were spilling over, and if this luck continued, any weight loss, including his own— which he could afford—would be due to the exercise of the trek, not to lack of food intake.

Doctor Hippocrates and Nurse Florence Nightingale also had reason to be thankful. Not one major medical emergency had occurred, *kayn eyn-oreh zol nit zayn*. Not that the dreaded "evil eye" was anywhere to be seen, but this team treated every little cut and bruise, upset stomach, headache, blister, ankle sprain, and the like immediately upon being notified or recognized in order to ward off something that could become more serious. The preventive approach by these exceptionally conscientious caregivers had received an appreciable assist by generous pharmacists and a few doctors along the way.

Doctor Chaim Hirschfeld, whom the group met when he crossed paths with them while traveling on horseback to visit his patients in a cluster of small towns, was particularly helpful with advice and supplies. These included tinctures, salves, powders, tonics and bandages, some of which he had coerced gently from an indebted Romanian colleague in the nearby Transylvanian town of Carei. This kindness added immeasurably to the fortunate head start so graciously afforded by the pharmacist Iancu Muresan back in Birlad. Gershon and Maidele promised the good doctor they would correspond with him from the United States. "Better yet, a picture postal card of that Statue of Liberty, please," the circuit-riding practitioner requested.

Nuchim Krasnigor's Finance Committee was doing exceptionally well, thank you. In fact, Ruvie Shapira, who handled the ledger under Nuchim's very close supervision, had already filled up a full page with "incoming monies". The donations received in Sighet, Debrecen, and Budapest; the original gift from Reb Mandelbaum, and a few lesser contributions from other Birladers; the handsome stipend from B'nai Brith U.S.A.; and the windfall from the 300 tickets sold for the play would be more than enough to see everyone through to the port at Bremerhaven. The money was secretly distributed among five cadre for safekeeping, and kept out of sight. Only Nuchim himself carried enough for daily purchases. In case of any robbery the plan called for Nuchim to sacrifice the cash he was carrying in order to deflect a more intensified search by the perpetrators. As for local currency, Nuchim was able to cash in all of the Romanian *lei* for the currency acceptable anywhere within the Empire. He was planning to exchange that money for German *marks* when they reached Dresden. United States of America greenback dollars would be made available at the port according to reports from the other Birlad contingents.

Mordecai, at this moment, en route from Budapest to Vienna, could be assured that the current state of Birlader Fusgeyer Contingent # 4 was one to be maintained. Not to be fixed. Not to be changed. *Please, dear God in heaven, just maintain us. Dayenu!* prayed the wise and cautious shepherd, leading his trusting flock toward the rest of their lives. But for the moment, this euphoria would have to be set aside.

In a very short time, mid-morning, approaching the vast Roman ruins on the Szentendre road, the sight of a wild-running Yaakov Nachman coming toward them took everyone by surprise. Out of breath, he could barely issue forth with, "Hurry, hurry, soldiers...Sholem!"

Ordering everyone else to stay put Mordecai didn't have to say a word to Branko, Sendehr, Zed-Zed and Menachem. They fell in right behind him as they double-timed in a trot behind Yaakov who strained for every intake of air. It seemed to each of them to take forever, but they finally approached what appeared to be a widespread gypsy encampment amid the extensive ruins of the ancient Roman city, Aquincum. Imre Steinman, the Budapestian *shul* president, had briefly mentioned this as a point of historic interest when Sendehr was explaining the Danube-hugging route they had planned.

The scene that greeted Mordecai and his lieutenants bordered on the bizarre. Six tall, uniformed horsemen, sabers drawn by three, long-barreled pistols brandished by the others, surrounding ten frightened *rom*, all men. In the midst of this pandemoniac cacophony, Hungarian, Romany, Romanian, and Yiddish blended together like a veritable Tower of Babel. Sholem, defiantly and standing protectively next to the eldest-looking *rom* who was bleeding profusely from a saber slash on his forearm, was yelling in a mixture of Romanian-Yiddish and newly-acquired English, something that sounded like, "I not geepsy, *ich bin* a *Romanische, Romaneshti*, no geepsy, ondershtend me, *vershtesht?*"

When the commander, resplendent in plumed headgear with fifty kilos of gold braid spilling down from his epaulets to his hips, spotted the Birladers, he nudged his shiny black steed over to them and in Hungarian asked, "Who is the leader of this motley bunch?"

Mordecai stepped forward, closely shadowed by Branko who pointed to him and responded in perfect Magyar dialect, "Mordecai Anieloff, here, is our commanding officer, sir," punctuated by a crispy-smart salute, automatically returned as a knee-jerk reaction by the unknowing horseman, just as Branko had received on a few other occasions.

"And who in holy hell are you, big man?"

"Sergeant Branko Horvitch, retired, His Excellency's Honor Guard, sir!"

"Oh, a Franz Josef lackey, eh? Had enough of military life, did you! Well, what part of all this is any of your business, may I ask?"

"That man, over there, with the small green pack on his back, is one of our people. He's definitely not one of the gypsies, as he's been saying, sir."

"You don't say, soldier boy! Well, we are in the process of impounding all these confounded gypsy bastards wherever we can find them. We want them back in Russia or Romania, even Austria. There is no longer any welcome for these scavenging parasites here. Maybe old Franz wants to invite them for dinner at the Imperial Palace in Vienna. But in Hungary? No, by God! This Magyar part of his megalomaniac's dream has no use for anything Austrian or anything heathen. Mark my words, soldier, we're heading for an independent Hungary sooner than fat-boy thinks."

He paused, leaned down from his horse, and peered into Branko and Mordecai's eyes, slowly rolling his next words over his lips, "I take it you're one of these Jew-mobs on your way out of Europe, eh? I've encountered more goddamn Christ-killers out of the east than I ever cared to see. Slovaks, Romanians, Russians. All Jews. You seem to love this *Duna* road. As long as you're on your way out of this God-fearing land I'm happy as hell to watch your kosher asses scuffling along this route heading west. Far west. Follow Columbus over the ocean, I pray!" And with this spat-out tirade, he trotted back to his quarry.

"God, I hope we have this situation in hand, Branko." Mordecai watched in horror as one of the soldiers jabbed his saber under Sholem's chin.

Just then, the Commander seemed about to order his men to release Sholem. But instead, the edgy saber-wielder had decided to make an example of Sholem for the other unruly detainees to witness, and with a quarter-twist his deftly-controlled maneuver took a tiny slice of Sholem's beardless chin, drawing a gush of pure Jewish blood.

Sholem gasped, as did his comrades, and they ran toward him, led by his racing teammate. Yaakov held Sholem as Sendehr and Zed-Zed applied pressure on the chin, hoping to stem the incessant spewing. Flasks at the ready, pouring a trickle of water every few seconds to keep the wound clean, and using whatever cloth they could find in their packs, they managed to slow the bleeding. Next they walked Sholem over to a spreading elm tree and propped him up against the trunk in the shade. Yaakov was sent running full speed to fetch Gershon and Maidele, who arrived white-faced in a few minutes, bearing a leather bag full of bandages, clean cloths and antiseptic salves. In a few seconds, Maidele pinched the wound with all of her strength, holding it shut, while Doctor Hippocrates demonstrated his worth, making an adhering butterfly-bandage and placing it across the wound to prevent it from re-opening.

Mordecai and Branko, meanwhile, keeping a wary eye on the base of the elm tree went through the usual mental gymnastics with the commander. Papers, the list of fifty-seven identification numbers and names, the Birlad magistrate's release form, Captain Sandor's transit document, the Alliance passenger-voucher lists, *ad nauseam.* Mordecai sighed with relief when the inquisitor recognized Sandor's name and identified the captain as one of his officer-school classmates. *Boruch Hashem!*

By this time the anxious contingent, having been told by Yaakov that Mordecai wanted them to come ahead, had gathered around Sholem and his doctoring pair. All worry melted somewhat when Sholem joked that Gershon had wanted to tighten a tourniquet around his neck to stop the bleeding. "After all," a more relaxed Sholem said, careful not to open his mouth too wide, "Gershon pointed out that my neck would be the nearest pressure point to the wound." Those close enough to hear this guffawed with great pleasure, knowing that the front-runner was out of any real danger. And the saucy Tsippy slipped in, "So, Doctor Hippocrates, it would be acceptable to choke your patient to death as long as it stops the bleeding, eh?" Again, hearty laughter, which seemed to be a bit disturbing to the commander who, incidentally, offered no remorse or apology for his over-zealous saber-trooper.

Satisfied that this group would be continuing westward to Austria, to Germany, and on to America, he bade them go on...but not without a last condescending remark. "Gutebye, *viszontlatashro, la revedere, auf wiedersehen, au revoir,* Jew-bastards !" With this he returned at a gallop to his brave *banditten,* who by now were thundering through the gypsy camp, kicking up cloud-sized billows of dust; knocking down tents; scattering clothes; and herding in the six rickety nomad wagons bursting with frightened men, sobbing women, screaming children, bawling babes-in-arms, and drawn by whinnying, bare-boned horses.

Where were these wanderers going? Probably across the river at some point, and then east, under perpetual guard, to Brody on the Russian frontier or somewhere in Bukovina on the Romanian border. From there, they would be dispersed unceremoniously into one country or the other, depending on the arguments from the unreceptive border troops who would not have any "welcome" signs hanging about. Truly, they were a people without a country. Unfortunately, this scene was more frequently being played out all over the region...not only with the gypsies, but also for those hapless Jews who could not prove they possessed the means to travel beyond the Empire's boundaries. Makeshift hell-holes and lean-to villages were beginning to spring up everywhere along the aforementioned borders, forming a "no man's land" of disgustingly indescribable conditions.

"Deportation to the east!" A chilling phrase that would continue to work its way deep into the bowels of the century ahead, echoed in the Fusgeyer heads as they watched the deportees' forced departure.

After being delayed for nearly three hours, and covering less than fifteen kilometers since they left the center of Budapest, Zed-Zed and Mordecai announced that this would be the overnight camp. "Enough thrills and spills for one day," shot back the ever-ready Itzy.

The first-century Roman ruins would provide a surrealistic milieu for the evening. Plenty of firewood, river water for washing, a little fishing for those who wished to cast for the evening meal, and a usable well just over the first rise, discovered by Branko and Yoni Golub who had just reconnoitered the area. Yoni had been visibly upset at missing all of the earlier action. " I'd like to have a turn at that slice-happy Magyar-*mumzer!* I'd wrap his saber around his neck until it looked like his lanyard," he had sputtered loudly enough for the entire contingent to hear. Branko had to grab him by the arm and walk him out on that scouting mission just to calm him down. His brothers were no cooler. *Good God, I've got to watch these three like a mother hen,* complained the Defense Minister to himself.

Sholem's bandages, in order to hold the underlying anchor-bandage in place, were wound under his chin and around his head four or five times. He looked like the start of some serious mummifying.

"King Tut visits Ancient Rome," laughed Mendel, explaining the legendary Egyptian king. On the serious side, during the initial change of bandages just before the evening meal, Gershon announced to the entire camp, "The bleeding has stopped to a slight ooze! Our runner will live! *Lang leben Sholem!* " The loud *huzzahs* could certainly have awakened the long-dead citizens of old Aquincum, heretofore resting so peacefully under Mother Earth for more than eighteen centuries.

Within the week, Sholem's wound required only a gauze bandage and appeared to be healing nicely. No doubt there would be permanent scarring, but he was perceptive enough to realize that it could have been worse. In fact, everyone was thankful that the entire episode didn't expand into the range of the unthinkable.

The heavily-trafficked river reached its 90-degree bend just beyond the town of Visegrad, putting the Fusgeyers on a westward course when, two days later, they walked into a setting sun. Once they reached Vienna, Sendehr's maps showed a more northwesterly direction to Prague, to Berlin, to Hamburg and on to Bremerhaven.

There was no doubt that the "telephone committee" ladies of Budapest whose efforts so successfully filled the hall for the play there, were once again busy on the increasingly-popular invention, contacting friends and relatives all along the Danube bend. The picturesque towns of the area...Szentendre, Visegrad, and Esztergom...were all on the alert for the Fusgeyers march-through. The townspeople greeted the walkers heartily, and Jewish shop owners contributed product much the way Debrecen did. During the stopover in ecclesiastical Esztergom—the former capital of ancient Hungary where its first king, Izstvan, was crowned—the community hosted a gala party at its Moorish-style *zheenagoga*, another of famed architect Lipot Baumhorn's masterful creations.

The women of the small community, prompted by their counterparts to the south, prepared an after-*maarev* spread of *latkes*, *kugels*, cakes, *palacsinta*, assorted delicacies of every variety for the visitors, and for the first time, the Birladers were not the only wayfaring strangers in town. Joining in, beside the *minyan*-goers, were twenty-two Pale refugees, three entire families...the Magovskys, the Grinbergs and the Pendelmans. More Yiddish was spoken that evening than at any time since the building was dedicated in 1888. Moishe Magovsky explained the predicament of the group to Sendehr and Mordecai in a story brimming with sadness.

They had left Ignatovka, near Kiev, for Brody, the Empire's border town, by train three months ago. At Brody, which was swollen far beyond its facilities to handle such steady increases of emigrants, they were stranded for three weeks and were urged to turn back by Jewish aid organizations. Funds had simply dried up and no further relief was forthcoming. The three families, whose patriarchs were first cousins, made a unanimous decision to start walking west with whatever supplies they could scrounge. Not much at that! At Kaschau/Kassa in Slovakia, the travelers contracted a strain of influenza and were isolated in a blacksmith's barn, where some local *shul* members helped to feed them on a daily basis. Well enough to leave once again, they were able to reach Balassagyarmat, to the north of Budapest. After a short stay, the Jewish community there provided them with wagon transportation to Esztergom, but they were stopped by a Hungarian patrol and because they had no clear transit papers they were made temporary wards of the Esztergom community. They were left with orders that they must show visible means of support within two weeks, or face deportation to Russia.

Sendehr and Mordecai learned from Reb Magovsky that thousands were halted in this way. They were either deported or had to find work or a sponsor immediately, and apply for a transit visa. Was traversing the face of a hostile Europe at this time fraught with difficulties? Yes. A resounding yes.

Neither young man was in the least prepared for what was about to happen next. The three heads of family, more or less cornering them just as they were about to leave for the campsite on the riverbank, wanted to present a proposal for them.

Reb Grinberg proceeded without invitation. "Our wives and children are all quite well now, and we are ready to proceed to Vienna and then to the ports, Hamburg or Bremerhaven. We would like to join you young people. We have some funds and will pay you whatever you require. Please. We cannot do it alone. And we cannot impose on these good people any longer."

Mordecai looked to Sendehr who shrugged his shoulders. Were these two at a loss for words? Hardly. The leader recovered, as he was expected to do.

"I understand your unfortunate predicament, gentlemen. Please believe me. I wish we could be of help, but I'm afraid what you ask is out of the question."

"We won't hold you back, Reb Anieloff. Our older children are of the same age as some of your Fusgeyers we saw tonight. The women can help, too. I am a carpenter, Moishe is a brick-mason, and Shimon was the best tailor in Ignatovka. You won't be sorry. I promise."

"All well and good, dear *khaverim*. But everything is not so simple, thanks to the severe hostility we face. Patrols are getting more commonplace every day, and as I told you earlier this evening, we had a very unsettling bit of harassment near Budapest on Monday. Actual blood spilling, sirs. But even more to the point, we have all of the necessary papers to get through to the ports: transit visas, proof of shipping arrangements, approved Romanian government papers. Everything. And from what I understand, you do not have the required documents, and are therefore vulnerable. I cannot chance a patrol stopping you and detaining us by association. It can be disastrous, as I'm sure you realize.

"We planned this undertaking diligently for the better part of a year, mind you. Three other Birlad contingents went before us and are in America today. I owe the deepest allegiances not only to my people out there, but to all of their families back home. I cannot, and will not, compromise my duty to those here now, nor will I sacrifice our mission. I am sincerely sorry, gentlemen. I can only hope that you understand our dilemma."

Seeing that Mordecai's reasoning was firm and that no amount of cajoling, counter-arguing or, yes, even begging, would budge him, Moishe Magovsky simply grabbed his hand and wished him luck. The others followed.

Mordecai and Sendehr walked to the tranquil riverside campsite in silence.

In his next personal note to Rabbi Nachman, Sendehr wrote:

Dear Rabbi,

I hope you have already received my synopsis, which I mailed from Budapest on Monday. I dropped it in one of the postal boxes that these bigger cities have in abundance. According to one of the postal posters that Branko read for me, they claim delivery anywhere in the Austro-Hungarian Empire within five days. I'm not sure how long it will take for this to reach you in Romania, however I received your very welcome letter that Rabbi Schulhofer held for me at the Great Synagogue. I read it to everyone this past week. Getting news from home is a marvelous morale stimulant. Keep them coming, please! The list of scheduled stopovers that you have is holding quite firm so you can mail accordingly. No major adjustments have had to be made as yet.

Less than hour after I stamped the envelope and dropped the synopsis into the postal box, a frightening incident took place. We encountered one of the Hungarian army patrols while they were rounding up gypsies. Sholem was cut by one of the soldiers who had mistaken him for one of them. First, let me assure you that he is just fine, sporting a small scar under his chin. Neither Yaakov nor anyone else was hurt in any way. I'll include the whole incident in my next synopsis, and I'm sure that if you decide to share everything with the congregation you'll prepare the Friedman family beforehand.

As I said, the patrols are thickening in this part of the Empire, but our papers are all in such perfect order we don't expect any insurmountable difficulties. The hatred of anything Jewish by these Magyars can match Captain Polinou and Father Mihai's loathing any day of the week. It's so nice to be popular wherever you may travel!

You will also read about the decision that Mordecai had to make this past week concerning a large group of

Russians who wanted to tag along with us. We felt badly turning them aside, but it was the only sensible thing to do. I pray that you will agree when you read the circumstances involved. It seems to pain Mordecai even now, and I must admit that I feel a periodic pang, too. In all, Rabbi Nachman, the migratory problems are becoming worse, and even lethal in many incidents.

Please don't encourage anyone to leave Birlad until and unless they've done the careful planning and necessary document preparation first. Otherwise, the deportations appear to be on a sharp increase. These Hungarian patrols don't need much of an excuse to turn people back to Russia or Romania. I've watched them closely. They revel in human tragedy. I don't mean to be that stiff-necked, but we have seen it up close. And it's ugly, Rabbi. Branko has made it clear that the Austrian army is quite the same in every respect. But we have every intention of continuing to fly the Mogen Dovid alongside the Hungarian flag. Rivka, at this very moment, is sewing together a piece of cloth that will eventually turn into the Hapsburg royal flag that we will fly in Austria, Moravia and Bohemia.

The riverside villages in this part of the country are quaint and friendly. Even some of the peasants have offered us bread, water and milk. One lovely older lady in Labatlan gave us a tray full of freshly baked cakes. She must have known some Jews, although none lived in her village, because she insisted that she used only butter and eggs, no lard, no lard, never lard! Not everyone partook, but I'm afraid that except for our most religious fringe we do tend to bend a bit; however, I assure you that kashruth is still the rule rather than the exception for most of us.

We plan to present the play again in Raab/Gyor, Pressburg/Pozsony or Wien/Vienna...geevalt...these dual names in Hapsburg territory can be most confusing! Just to make sure that we don't get complacent, Rivka runs us through a scene every night. I can't wait to perform it again. Rivka and I take a long walk every evening after

*Mendel's instruction. I look forward to it all day long. The
kilometers have never been so easy to cover.*

 Sendehr Efraim,
  near Komarn/Komarom, Hungary,
  May 16, 1904 (11 Iyar, 5664)

 *Note: Please tell my mother and father to write a
message in your next letter, like I did in my last letter to
you. I hope my family is well. Tell them I'm healthy and
happy. What more can any of us ask? By the way, as I
stated above, I will not forget to write in the next
synopsis of your little brother's valiant efforts during
the Sholem incident. You can be very proud of Yaakov. A
little piece I wrote a few weeks ago follows:*

THE SOJOURNER
(Der Dervaliker)

Raindrops - April's rain
soaking fertile fields
of the Emperor's vast domain -
geese - white goslings
mud-waddling down
the rut-filled road to town -
a grassland village
one step beyond
the endless plain -
a blanket of golden yellow
soon will cover this land -
birch trees - slender, white,
to become laden with leaf
willows, bathing in the sun,
swaying gently in the breeze.
Will it be like this in America?
Sendehr Efraim,
Hungary, 1904/5664
(translated from the Yiddish)

§

After returning from a most interesting weekend touring the north and west of Romania, which the three
Friedmans enjoyed thoroughly, Nathan decided to take a
Sunday evening walk through the small section of town
where most of the remaining Jewish families resided. Since
arriving in Birlad that past Tuesday he had spent three and
a half days and parts of two nights meeting with Rabbi
Nachman.

In review, a relaxed Nathan thought, *this last week has
been so very well spent. Draining, but well worth the 8,000-
mile journey. It was so good to get away this weekend with
the boys. Seeing Bacau, Piatra Neamts, Vatra Dornei and
Prislop Pass. My God, imagine Pop climbing over those hills
in a snowstorm! Contacting the remnants of the Jewish community in Sighet, Elie Wiesel's town! I've read all of his books.
Satu-Mare, where the great chassid confrontation had taken
place! The old cemeteries, the former synagogues now so
sadly transformed into public buildings, warehouses, and
apartments. The intriguing, picturesque countryside of
Transylvania...*

All of this enabled Nathan to clear his fact-filled, story-
filled mind, in preparation for the next week. *Rabbi Nachman
will be well rested by tomorrow morning, too, and should be
raring to go on with it.*

As he turned toward the hotel where Herb and Rico
would be ready to go out to dinner at the little mom and
pop cafe they had grown to like, Nathan spotted Berel
Usher, the president of the shrinking, once-bustling community. He had met him briefly at the *shul* a few days
back, and evidently he, too, was out for a *shpatzier*.

"Ah, Mister Friedman. How are you getting on with our
dear Rabbi?"

"A good evening, Reb Usher. I can not begin to tell you how absolutely fascinating and informative this last week has been. Rabbi Nachman is the best storyteller I have ever had the pleasure of knowing."

"We are the lucky ones; to have had him in our midst all these years. He and his father are the only Rabbis I have had. I missed you at our Sabbath *minyans*, Reb Friedman. We barely made it."

"I am truly sorry. I felt that while we're here I wanted to give my son and grandson a look at some of the country. We visited many of the places where my father and the Fusgeyers walked. A very emotional experience, to say the least."

"When I was still in *cheder*, the elder Rabbi Eliahu Nachman never missed a term without repeating the story, tracing their steps on old maps. To him, the Fusgeyers symbolized the old Romania. The Romania that, for the Yidden, was far more threatening than some of our recent regimes."

"I can understand that, Reb Usher. But, tell me, what does the future hold for your little community, for the Birlader Yidden?"

"A good question, with only a sad answer. Young people, as Nachman probably told you, no longer live here. Over the years they have gone to *Eretz Yisroel*, some to America, and a few even to Bucureshti and Iashi. There are also former Birladers living in Budapest, Berlin and Paris. These young men and women were born during or just after the war. What you have here today are the Berel Ushers and the Yossi Nachmans. What will happen? We will die, heh, heh! Some day, the Jew of Birlad will be history, in *Gan Eden* alongside the Fusgeyers."

"Why haven't you gone to Israel also? I understand that Rabbi Rosen kept the emigration gates open most of the time."

"A fair question, Reb Friedman. I can only answer for myself. This has been my home since birth. Our children and their families are all in Israel. We visit every year and they come here periodically. I am pensioned from my lifetime job as a bookkeeper for the prefecture where my wife worked as a clerk, but regardless; I have no intention of leaving, nor have I ever considered it. Here I stay, for better or for worse. Heh-heh. My parents were also born right here, along with one set of grandparents. I can trace a Birlader Usher back to the Ottoman days. At that time the family came from Odessa and settled here to begin operating a small granary. The granary stayed in my family until the strict boycotts and the severe legislation of 1902.

"According to my father and verified by the elder Nachman, the so-called 'Artisan Bill' that went into imme-diate effect was the final deathblow to all of Birlad's Jews, numbering nearly 5,000 at the turn of the century. The Ar-tisan Bill stated that in order to carry on any trade special authorization must be obtained from the local magistrates. But, now listen closely to this, Reb Friedman; 'strangers,'—we Jews, you see—could only get this authorization if they could produce foreign passport papers and proof that in their respective countries reciprocal rights are accorded to Romanians. Who were the "strangers?" The Jewish non-citizens, of course! How many of our people could comply with this strangling *dreck?* None! Absolutely no one!"

"So this law was in effect before the 1904 Fusgeyers left?"

"Yes, and no. Although the law came into being in 1902, many petty officials—the local magistrates—in this part of the country did not enforce it right away. After all, it was in their best interests to keep the Jew working, earning an income. How else would they ensure the steady flow of *unterkoyfn gelt*...the bribery money? The legislators in Bucureshti also understood this ingrown culture so very little coercion was used on the magistrates for the first two years. Later, more pressure was exerted and by the end of 1904 my father's family lost the granary during a period of three months when the law was finally put into full effect.

"By early 1905, as the elder Nachman had told me, not one Jewish artisan or tradesman could earn a living as such. Coincidentally, that time period also marked the peak of Jewish emigration from Romania, and within a few years the community dwindled to less than half of what it was. Life for those who stayed, including my entire family, was halved dramatically. Half the income. Half the food. Half the life from before. Most men took jobs at meager pay since the Romanians preferred Jewish workers, but knowing of their desperation they paid them half of what the Romanian earned. The granaries, the bottling plant, the brick yard, the wineries, the farms, all jumped at the chance to hire the former artisans and tradesmen, the tailors, the cobblers, the rope-makers, the umbrella-makers, the tavern-keepers, the bakers, the candle-makers, the butchers, the cafe owners. My father was only ten years old at the time and he went to work as a barrel washer at one of the wineries. Afterwards and to the day that he died, may he rest in peace, he never looked at another grape."

Nathan chuckled a little, and then said; "During my recent research I remember reading numerous references on the subject of anti-Jewish legislation in Romania, from 1880 onward. This Artisan Bill seemed to be the culmination of over twenty years of the most remarkable legislative persecution perpetrated by any government in history to that point in time. Of course, in the 1930s the Nuremberg Laws of Nazi Germany were not quite as subtle. More like a sledgehammer! Tell me, as a matter of interest, how did Moishe Mandelbaum fare during this final insult?"

"Oh, I see the Rabbi told you of this fascinating man. Heh-heh! He was one of Rabbi Eli's favorite people, too. My father told me that he bought Avrum Leventer's blacksmith barn just before the law went into effect. He pulled everything he possibly could out of his hat and used it to bribe the magistrate, a Captain Golinu, or Polinou, offering him a good part of his property just to keep the Jewish tradesmen in operation. But Bucureshti was by then watching the local magistrates very closely and Polinou would hear nothing of it. However, he agreed to let Mandelbaum keep the largest of his chicken sheds, and he could stay on at the blacksmith's barn...but he had to sign it over to the magistrate's brother-in-law to make it legal, for half of the profits. Of course, this move allowed Leventer and several others to keep working as employees, and within a year it became the first motorcar repair shop between Focshani and Iashi.

"My father remembered when Mandelbaum, just after the first war, became a dealer of French and Italian-made automobiles, expanded the barn into a showroom-repair garage, opened others in Vaslui and Focshani, paid off his "partner" after the magistrate died, and grew wealthy again. Never was there a more generous, kinder philanthropist in these parts. He hired twice as many Jews as the business warranted, practically single-handedly supported the *shul* and a few of the little *shtieblach*. He even put up most of the original funding for the old-age home which lasted in Birlad for over fifty years. He died a very old, fulfilled man when I was a child. May he rest in peace."

"Yes, *omayn* to that! Truly a man to remember and revere. Well, sir, I certainly am indebted to you for all of this information. Believe me, I know so much more of my father's home town than I ever dreamed I could know."

"Why don't you and your family join us for tea Tuesday afternoon, Naftali? Yes, yes, my wife makes a wonderful *savarina*, too. Nachman told me your grandson enjoys that delicious pastry! Say about four? We'll have the Rabbi come and a few other Birladers, too. How many do we still have, after all?"

"Thank you for the invitation, Reb Usher. If your wife's *savarinas* can match the *rebbitzens*, we'll be there. Good evening, dear sir. I certainly enjoyed our talk just standing on the street corner, leaning against this fence. Reminds me of my teenage days. Say, perhaps you and your wife can join us at Cafanea Popescu, over there. Excellent *saramura de peshte!* Wonderful *Feteasca* selections. I know it isn't..."

"Thank you, Reb Friedman, but we still maintain *kashruth*. My wife and my supper await me at this moment. Until Tuesday afternoon, then." And down the street went the pleasant man.

Now, this sure was an added bonus! thought a most appreciative Nathan.

That night he drew up a plan for Herb and Rico to drive down early Monday morning to the shore resorts near Constantsa for an overnight stay. This way he knew that Rico would have a chance to swim in the Black Sea. Good for "bragging rights" at Beverly Hills High.

At breakfast, the hotel manager suggested that the so-called "Mythology Belt" where the resorts were named for the country's Graeco-Roman past, would be ideal for a short visit. Broad sandy beaches, casinos, "good" hotels. The "good", of course, was questionable, but the names of Neptune, Jupiter, Saturn and Venus adorned four of these westernized ocean-side villages. "Sounds like Venice Beach goes Balkan!" Herb described, after reading the map. In addition, Constantsa boasted one of the best museums in the country...an open-air archaeological site in the town center, featuring storehouses, mosaic floors and shops from the fourth-century Roman occupation. Rico was nearly as interested in this as he was in the possibility of the European-style nudie beaches the hotel manager relished talking about. Or at least he said he was. Herb just wanted a Black Sea tan.

Just before they left Nathan issued his last warning about the "RRBs". During the weekend trip they had breezed through four of these with the usual comical bantering. "Don't get too cocky, boys!" he added as he waved goodbye.

Rabbi Nachman was very pleased to see Nathan at his door later that morning, and the first thing he talked about was the Fusgeyer visit to Budapest. They had left off on Friday with the highway robbery incident at Tiszafured, Hungary. Yossi Nachman showed Nathan some ancient-looking loose-leaf. He had taken the description of the beautiful weekend in Budapest from one of Sendehr's synopses, fully intact, as it had survived the flames when the Iron Guard in Iashi had thrown the Rabbi's wooden box filled with his father's papers into the fire. Nathan was happy to see that at least some of the weekly synopses and private notes were legible. But what followed shocked Nathan for a brief moment, and so he stood up rather suddenly, hands to forehead.

"My God, so that's how Pop got that scar! He might have been killed on the spot. My God, my God! Rabbi, the scar was just below the very front of the chin-bone. Visible, yes, but only as a straight, faded two-inch line. Doctor Hippocrates and Nurse Nightingale certainly did a most professional job of it. Lucky it wasn't an HMO. Pop would have been waiting treatment for a week. Heh! Sorry, Rabbi, inside joke." He explained briefly what had caused his amazement, holding his thumb and forefinger apart showed the size of the scar.

"When we were little I remember my sister Ruth asking him where he got that wound, and he facetiously said he had been in a sword fight with Robin Hood. My mother—who must have known the truth, I see now—laughed and added that Pop got the upper hand because any picture of Robin Hood shows him bearded. That was to hide all of the retaliatory slashes Pop got in. Wait till I tell my Rachel when I phone her tonight! And Morris and Ruth! Pop told the same story to my kids when they were young. Why couldn't he bring himself to tell the real facts?"

"Naftali, so many of that generation, as well as the Holocaust survivors of our generation, did not and do not want to burden young people with these heavy memories. *Shveig, nisht fur di kinder*, has been our guiding admonishment. I, myself, have told my own family very few details about the war, the Iashi pogrom, or the deportations. At least now, I understand, there is a Shoah Foundation established by your Steven Spielberg, gathering and recording massive amounts of information from survivors all over the world. A timely idea, since most of us are now in our seventies, eighties and older. They have offices all over Europe, and the Bucureshti staff is scheduled to visit Birlad one day soon. At our last Rabbi's conference they sent a speaker. The interview videotapes she showed us were exceptional.

Oy, oy. Some system, I tell you!"

"I've heard all about it, Rabbi. My sister is one of the Los Angeles interviewers. She tells me that over 50,000 have been taped worldwide so far. In addition to the large survivor population in Israel, I believe they are now concentrating on Russia, Poland, Romania and all the rest of the European countries, east and west as well. Spielberg introduced the project after he made *Schindler's List*, donating his personal profits from the film. $19,000,000! Have you heard of the book and the movie, Rabbi?"

"Yes, yes. It showed in Bucureshti for many months. My brother went to see it and was amazed at how the actors spoke Romanian on the screen. He had never seen this phenomenon before. He was most impressed with the movie since he barely survived the war himself, especially during the frequent Iron Guard actions. Did I tell you? No? He was the young editor of a weekly Jewish newspaper, and had to walk a very fine line. But in January '41 he stepped over that line when he printed posters placed all over the city condemning the excesses of the Guard, which had clashed with Marshal Antonescu in a bloody power struggle. As usual, *unsereh Yidden*, Bucureshti's Jews, were caught in the middle and it degenerated into a full-fledged pogrom. Numerous Jewish shops and synagogues were put to the torch and looted, and hundreds were murdered. You may have read of it, Naftali."

"Yes, in my research. Wasn't that the infamous nightmare where the bodies of many of the better-known victims were hung by the hooks used for cattle in the kosher slaughterhouse, as well as in the windows of each kosher butcher shop?"

Yossi Nachman nodded and began to weep, but continued. "Exactly. I knew some of the rabbis among the victims. It took them only a few days to arrest my dear little brother Shimon, and he was sent to a wretched forced labor camp near Ploeshti. He weighed as much as a sparrow when the Red Army liberated the camp. I saw him a few weeks later and honestly didn't recognize him." Seeing that the Rabbi was distraught, Nathan went to boil some water for tea.

Once a cup was set in front of him, he was able to continue. "Shimon witnessed the American air attacks on the vast Ploeshti oil fields adjacent to the camp and saw death coming swiftly for him each time a bomb exploded. For years he had trouble sleeping as he kept re-living the bombings. Not the beatings or the starvation rations, only the bombings for some reason."

"I can understand it. The concussions and the shock waves of bombs exploding that close can be devastatingly traumatic for years afterward. This affected thousands of combat veterans, and even survivors of the London blitz."

"So I've heard. Poor Shimon has been sickly all these years since the war. The doctors do not give him much time. I fear my visit this week may be the last time I'll see him alive." The Rabbi paused for a moment and continued. "Nu, my dear Reb Friedman, we're off course again. Let's go back to our Fusgeyers!"

"Yes, I'd like that, too; but by the way, Rabbi, here is something that just occurred to me. You mentioned that you were going to see Shimon this week. We'll be leaving for Bucharest and the airport early Friday morning. Can we take you?"

"Wonderful! I'm going to spend the Sabbath with Shimon. Reb Usher will fill in for me here. Then I can take the train back some day next week. Thank you. Thank you."

Before they adjourned for the day, Yossi Nachman was able to bring Nathan through to Esztergom and the incident of the three refugee families wanting to join in with the Fusgeyers. Both quickly agreed that as heart wrenching as it may have been, nearly one hundred years ago Mordecai had made the proper decision. Unquestionably.

* * *

Traveling down what passed for a major highway toward the Black Sea, Rico spotted a school with a basketball court, and two gangly teenagers playing a bit of one-on-one. Here in the land that had produced the 7-foot-3-inch NBA star, Gheorghe Muresan, these kids were much shorter...perhaps six-footers, give or take a couple of inches. Herb saw the wistful look in his son's eyes as he pointed out the scene.

"Well, what d'ya think, Dad? Are you up to it? Can we take 'em?"

Herb pulled over and winked at his eager son. "Let's go for it, Kobe!"

13

ENCOUNTERS: VIENNA

I would have to tell you about the flag and at that point you would have waxed sarcastic: A flag? A flag is nothing more than a rag on a stick. No, sir, a flag is more than that. With a flag you can lead people where you want to, even into the promised land. They will live and die for a flag. It is, in fact, the only thing for which the masses are prepared to die.

Theodor Herzl, 1895

Emperor Franz Josef ruled over an immense territory ranging from Brody on the Russian border to the east to Sarajevo in Bosnia to the south, Bohemia and the German border to the north, and the Swiss-German borders in the west. The seeds of unrest had been planted everywhere throughout the realm. Now the crop was ready for harvest.

The Polish Galicians, the Ruthenians, the Bohemians, the Moravians, the Slovaks, the Serbs, the Bosnians, the Magyars, the Transylvanian Romanians, all were enemies from within. Not one, it seems, wanted to remain any longer an indentured downstairs servant in the House of Hapsburg. Independence was the cry of the day, from one end of the vast Empire to the other. With unrest prevalent, a paralyzing paranoia set in at every border and border within border. The Austrian Imperial Army did not for one moment trust its Hungarian sub-allies, and vice-versa.

The Fusgeyers saw proof of this all along the way. They

encountered Austrian patrols in Raab/Gyor and near Pressburg/Pozsony, where only a few years back there would have been a preponderance of Magyar troops. The document checking had become more regular and at the same time more thorough and intense. At one point, in the heart of Gyor, Mordecai and the entourage that kept him company for such situations were held in the municipal building for four frustrating, nerve-wracking hours of grueling interrogation.

"So, you say you're going to Bremerhaven. You're sailing to the United States of America. Why are you flying that Jew-flag? That's an insult, you goddamn baby-bloodsuckers! Your papers show records for sixty people. Where are the missing three? You have passage booked for sixty and only fifty-seven are accounted for? Eh?

"What was that ignorant bootlicking Magyar thinking when he issued you this goddamn transit visa? Captain Ferenc Sandor. Hmmm. One of those infernal incompetent asses we have to cope with...

"Who gave you permission to sew in the Hapsburg emblem on your Hungarian flag? Sandor? What do you intend to fly in Austria? In Germany? Why do you people always think that laws do not apply to you? You think your goddamn high and mighty parchment scrolls are the only laws you have to obey?

"Who is paying for all of this? Some fat, rich *shmutzfinken* Jew? What organization is behind this illegal demonstration? One of those goddamn socialist mobs? It's clearly classified as a demonstration. That's treason, pure and simple, you bastards! You realize that, don't you? We can deport you pell-mell back into your Romanian dung heap. The Deutsches will thank us! What kind of troublemakers are you? What are you up to? Do you have any weapons? What are you carrying in that peasant cart out there?"

The rapid-fire inquisition went on without giving anyone a chance to respond. Finally Branko, who had listened calmly to the man's tirade, his hands clasped loosely behind his back, was prepared to stand firm and planned to deliver an innocuous, non-committal reply. He answered in pure German, which quickly and wisely, he knew, nullified any Yiddish response Mordecai had to be anxious to give.

"Colonel, sir, we certainly mean no harm to anyone. We are completely self-sufficient. As you can see, we are heading to the port of Bremerhaven. Three of our original group have gone on to Argentina, sailing from Trieste. Their names are Berel and Dovid Singerman, and Yehuda Gelman." He pointed to the paper he was holding.

"See, here, sir. We just hadn't removed their names from our documents. We do not carry weapons. No, sir! The cart holds merely our sheltering equipment and some foodstuffs, medical supplies, shovels and smaller tools, sirs."

In his waistband, concealed by his over-sized army-issue oilskin, Branko carried a revolver. He went for this dangerous bluff rather than to give the panel any excuse to detain them any longer–or worse yet, to search the wagon, or incarcerate or deport them.

He remembered clearly this line of questioning from his own days of serving the Emperor. The lesson had been the same, then and now. Always bury the suspect under a barrage of questions, innuendoes, lies, threats and insults. Be aggressive; put the other on the defensive at all times. These rules were right out of the Empire's soldier's manual, which he knew chapter and verse, beginning to end.

Branko had guessed correctly. His crisp confession was enough. While only partially the truth, it was direct and to the point, and it succeeded. No further search. No further questions. It was a gamble that could have just as easily turned into a disaster. Mordecai's tight skin, normally tanned from long months under the sun, had turned white. Zed-Zed, Menachem and Sendehr were each breathing heavily, pulses pounding at a runner's pace.

When they were finally released with nothing more than one last vitriolic tongue-lashing by the foul-mouthed, Jew-baiting, Austrian senior officer, Mordecai made the unilateral decision not to stay overnight in the city. It would be dark in less than an hour; and Rivka had decided days ago not to perform *Dos Vinshfingerl*, the "Wishing Ring," in Raab/Gyor where Yiddish would be far rarer than in Budapest. They would walk a few more kilometers and pitch camp, rather than chance a change of heart by the Austrian martinets.

Mordecai planned to proceed as scheduled from there, crossing the Danube into borderless Hungarian Slovakia for a Sabbath stop in Pozsony, the obligatory Hungarian name given to Slovak Bratislava, which was also saddled with the Germanic-Austrian name of Pressburg. The beleaguered Slovaks argued this demeaning issue with fire in their eyes. Mottke and Pincus Bercovici had an uncle living there, and it had always been the policy of Birlader Fusgeyers to schedule stopovers wherever possible for such family visits. Such a visit was only skipped if the town was too far off the route, and occasionally a Fusgeyer visited alone and then caught up at the next encampment.

The Sabbath weekend in the handsome old city with three names was quite pleasurable, on a smaller, quieter scale than the Budapest stop. Germanic-Yiddish was in common use here, and the play was successful. Nuchim, feeling every bit the impresario, welcomed the income derived from the visit into the "bank." Rivka could have given him a good argument on that, if only to burst his growing ego-bubble!

The real test came the following week, after re-crossing the Danube to reach Vienna. The challenge wasn't unexpected. They had heard but chose to ignore the rampant rumors of new restrictions on foreigners and strangers and instead planned a bold entrance into the famed city of beauty and music.

Jews had made major contributions in all fields during the latter half of the past century, and Mordecai and his cadre agreed that they would not want anyone to miss seeing Vienna. It would take more than a despotic, half-crazed mayor to deter them! All of the Birlad groups had written glowing reports of the magnificent Vienna/Wien. To make it even more inviting, there was a *Neolog* (Reform) seminary that welcomed emigrating groups to use its assembly rooms while visiting, space permitting, donations expected and accepted.

But Vienna, after all, would have to wait.

In direct defiance of the protests made by many leading citizens, Jewish and others, the rabid anti-immigrant, anti-Semitic, pan-Germanic mayor once again attempted to prohibit admittance to all "strangers." Franz Josef, who had not addressed this edict, was seen by all of Europe as giving tacit approval to Mayor Lueger's totalitarianism. This was his third such closing since taking the reins of office in 1895.

At all of the city entrances, barbed wire holding pens were hastily constructed, and immigrants, both individuals and groups, were corralled inside them until they were personally interviewed and determined to be acceptable. Otherwise, they were summarily rejected on the spot. The railroad stations in the northern precincts of the city and on the western limits were also used for this odious purpose.

The impenetrable ring of soldiery and city police, at a stratospheric expense to the taxpayer, turned back the vast majority of visitors with little or no explanation. The Fusgeyers, in what could have been construed as a counter-defiant act, were determined to crack the veneer. Oh, yes, they could have gone on toward Prague without missing a beat, but there was hardly a member who wasn't overjoyed at the decision to wait it out, flags flying in the breeze.

Perhaps what they did next went against Mordecai's steadfast non-confrontational policies, but he and the cadre unanimously decided that the core issue of their mission statement demanded that they to carry the protest into the heart of where it mattered most. Herr Lueger's 1904 Vienna was a prime candidate.

In a driving rain, they pitched their tent-halves within the perimeter of the holding pen in the outlying town of

Schwechat, to which they had been escorted by a troop of cavalry with pistols drawn. The entrance sign read, in German:

ALL ALIENS MUST SUBMIT PAPERS AND BE PREPARED FOR LENGTHY DELAYS. THOSE WITHOUT PAPERS IN PERFECT ORDER MUST GO ELSEWHERE. YOU ARE NOT WELCOME IN WIEN.

- Karl Lueger, Mayor

What determined "perfect order" would remain to be seen. Historically, at least for gypsies and Jews, perfection was completely unattainable.

Once again, the cadre team, with Branko as their interpreter, had entered the holy chapel of the unwanted. Here, there were no Austrian sub-officers, just two enlisted clerks and a much older colonel, a highly-decorated member of the elite Vienna Security Police, Immigration Battalion.

This time the questioning took less than twenty minutes, mainly due to the growing queue of other entry-seekers. The result was less than desired. *Wait. Just wait. We'll advise you tomorrow. Or the next day. Or the next.* It was a crude game, one that Lueger hoped would make the applicants eschew Vienna and go elsewhere.

Ironically, inside the city of Vienna, living and working at Bergasse 19, was a physician who could have quickly diagnosed these delaying tactics as a psychological mind game. That controversial doctor was one Sigmund Shlomo Freud, himself a Jew. He had been seeing patients at his home since his graduation from Vienna University Medical School in 1891, and worked at introducing a form of psychoanalysis that was on its way to becoming the most famous psychological theory of all time. Moreover, he was among the professional people, the teachers, doctors, lawyers, and especially Jews, for whom Lueger's acts were appalling. They had signed petitions, had audiences with Franz Josef, made impassioned speeches, and all to no avail.

Unfortunately, they were a distinct minority. By far,

the citizenry of Vienna supported Lueger's tactics. To this vast majority, the city was fast becoming a victim of urban decay. This was largely due to a clash of cultures and mores, but the finger of blame pointed directly at the immigrant.

Keep the scum out! Vienna for the Viennese!

Inedible food was made available at a price to all detainees. None of it was kosher, of course, and was offered at a cost that surpassed exorbitant. For the Fusgeyers, this posed no problem, as Simmy had replenished the supplies throughout the journey. The visit to Pozsony had been particularly rewarding to his incessant *shnorring.*

Later that night the group voted: stay or leave? The "stay" results were nearly unanimous, 55-2. Who were the two in the minority? Itzy G. and Mayer K., of course. The quipsters had even composed a hilarious ditty on the spot, singing in harmony: "we should march into the barracks, overpower the guards, continue on through the streets of Vienna, go directly to the Shoenbrunn Palace and dump the Emperor's chamber pot on his head. *Vayter, Franzeleh Yosseleh ken gehen in drerd arein!*" "Furthermore, Franz Josef can go to hell." As for Lueger, the closing couplet, "*an umglick oyf im,*" merely asked for an ugly incident to befall the *mumzer.*

The guards around the compound were shocked out of their boots to hear such hearty laughter coming from people under such deplorable conditions. Mordecai, as usual, appreciated this well-timed bit of humor and agreed. "Good suggestion, boys! Let's do it! I trust you will treat us to another poetic masterpiece when they drop the *goyishe* noose around your *Yiddishe kopp!*" More laughter. Hard to keep these Fusgeyers down.

In a more serious vein, Mendel was asked to cancel English class because of the rain; but the brain trust huddled in Mordecai's shelter for an abbreviated *pilpul,* the hair-splitting discourse.

...They're not going to keep us very long. This place is overcrowded already.

...Yes, but they could escort us back to Romania.

...Never. We are too large a group. Logistically impossible.

...For spite they could do it. It would only take two or three soldiers with guns.

...Our papers are in order. They'll let us go into the city tomorrow.

...Remember, we are free to go anywhere in Austria ex cept Vienna.

...We could probably have entered by coming in from another direction.

...Someone would certainly notice sixty marchers, and reported us.

...Too risky. Some Vaslui people were jailed for months during the last shutdown.

...Listen. We'll wait them out. The schedule is no prob lem. Right, Zed-Zed?

...We can afford a few days here, Mordecai.

...Are you keeping an eye on the Golubs, Branko? This is vital, you know.

...Right. And don't forget I don't want anyone speaking Yiddish to these Austrians. Not now. Let me talk only in German. It's a serious irritant to them, Mordecai. To their ears the difference is obvious.

...Understand. I appreciate your cutting me off before. Thank you, Branko.

...Why don't we sneak someone into town and ask for help from the Jewish Council?

...Again, too risky. Sholem and Yaakov saw a way around this place before we arrived under escort, but wisely decided against venturing any further. We cannot af ford anything that will give them a reason to hold us indefinitely.

...So, are we all agreed? Waiting is the only sensible policy at this time.

...Agreed.

When they adjourned after the briefest of meetings, the rain had ceased, and they replaced it with music and song. The group of gypsies, with little or no hope of crashing the barriers, already had a fiddle and accordion session going. The Fusgeyers rebuilt their campfire and began their own folk song and dance. Velvel's trumpet never sounded sweeter, Asher's muffled drum taps and Kalman's slightly improved concertina accompaniment, joining with the group of now four *chazzanim* and a lovely chorus of female sopranos, filled the sweet smelling post-rain night air. The "Fusgeyer Song," a poignant, melancholic lullaby composed by Avrum Loffelger from the first Birlad contingent ended the evening, easily evoking the usual tears.

> "Where did Father go, Mother dear?"
> "He went to find bread, to earn money.
> Sleep, my little one, sleep my child!
> Cold and gloomy is the house
> and long it is ere the morrow comes.
> He went to America, far,
> and other distant lands,
> work to find, work..."
> Silent is the child and pensive
> and then asks again:
> "Why so far away?
> Here, Mother, in this place,
> is there no bread for us?"

As much as it ripped through their hearts, the few Fusgeyer fathers always seemed to lead the singing when it came to this piece. Perhaps the singing helped stifle their tears. Or maybe it reminded them, once again, of their mission. As if anyone needed to be reminded on a night like this!

Patience paid off. Two days later, on a Thursday morning, the colonel informed them begrudgingly that they would be allowed formal entrance into the hallowed city. However, the admittance papers specified that they must leave by Monday noon, the 31st day of May. He sharply reminded them that their transit visa was good only until June 22nd, and they had better be out of Austrian territory by then or else they'd be in jail as illegal immigrants. He meant it. Branko asked no further questions after Mordecai pulled him gently by the arm, whispering with a smile, "Let's go. Quickly, Sergeant."

Vienna appeared to the Fusgeyers, at least on the surface, to be every bit as appealing as Budapest: the architecture, the broad boulevards, the bountiful shop windows, and the dress and gaiety of its throngs. This, then, was the famous window to the west, a more than subtle contrast to the drabness that afflicted much of the eastern expanse of the continent.

Immediately, they began to draw crowds who watched in assorted states of disbelief as they marched down the broad, pedestrian-filled Karntner Strasse, flags flying, past the elegantly classical Stadt Opera Haus. Sholem and Yaakov had already found the seminary buildings on the Fleischmarkt, past St. Stephen's Cathedral on Rotenturm Strasse, just as Sendehr's city map had indicated. The swift Sholem doubled back to lead the way for the others. This had been the usual mode of operation whenever entering the larger, more complex cities.

The fact that Sendehr was always thinking far ahead in such geographic directional matters helped immensely. While in Pozsony, realizing that his Hungarian map only included the parts of the Empire that abutted the old Austrian borders, he had found a bookstore with a good selection of maps covering all of the remainder of Austria, Moravia, Bohemia and into Germany as far as Hamburg. That would be quite enough for the rest of the journey. The city maps of Vienna, Prague, Dresden, Berlin and Hamburg were well defined and fully detailed. Sendehr was fulfilled. He had completed an important part of his job, and his mind was already racing ahead to consider maps of New York City.

Watching this demonstration from the door of the Hotel Sacher Cafe where he had just had his morning tea, a portly gentleman was stupefied as he stared at the Zionist flag rippling in the breeze. Doctor Max Nordau had never before seen this rare phenomenon of so large a group of young people flying the flag of his dreams. He followed them, falling in just behind the overburdened cart that was being pulled by sheer manpower. *Amazing*, he thought. At one of his favorite Viennese restaurants, the four-hundred-year-old *Griechen Beisl*, The Greek Vessel, on Fleishmarkt, he guessed where they were going and, sure enough, he followed them down the busy sidewalks at the edge of old Jew Street, *das Judegasse.*

At the seminary, Reform Judaism's answer to the *yeshivot,* the orthodox schools that had proliferated throughout Eastern Europe over the past few centuries, the Fusgeyers filed into the substantial edifice. Plain, no markings, just an inconspicuous silver *Mogen Dovid* straddled the entranceway's massive oak doors. Even the *mezuzzah,* the Biblical verses on the doorpost, was miniscule in proportion. The school's name was carved into a large stone surrounded by red bricks to the left of the front steps: The Rabbi Samson Wertheimer Seminary.

"Who is the leader of this magnificent Zionist parade?" thundered the man who had caught up with them at last, and who wore a white beard with an oversized handlebar mustache, a derby and a finely tailored plaid suit.

Yankel Golub, assigned to watch over the cart until he

was relieved answered the guttural Germanic-Yiddish. "You're talking to me? Please wait a minute and Mordecai Anieloff will be out here." With this, Yankel sent Chaike, who was fetching something from the cart, to get Mordecai or Branko. In a moment the former appeared.

"Yes, my dear sir, you wish to speak to me?" said Mordecai, already pleased with the way the day had been going and with the more-than-adequate lodging arrangements.

"Yes. Yes. Perhaps you can tell me why you're marching, where you're going, and the story behind the fact that you're flying the Zionist flag? I am deeply entrenched in that glorious movement and I'm most interested to know!"

"Of course, sir. Come inside, and I'll be pleased to answer your questions."

Inside of ten minutes Mordecai was able to tell the polished gentlemen everything he wanted to know. He seemed to understand Mordecai's Yiddish and asked no further questions until the leader finished the Fusgeyer story, flag and all. He had made it quite clear that America, not Palestine, was their destination.

"Yes, indeed, I have heard of you wayfarers, but yours is the first group I've met in person. Believe me, young man, to see that Zionist flag held proudly aloft got me shivering! You see, as I mentioned briefly, my whole life now is deeply immersed in the quest for a Jewish State. Since meeting the illustrious founder of the movement in '95, and again at the first Zionist Congress in Basle, Switzerland, two years later, every waking moment of every day and most nights has been overflowing with Zionism, Zionism and still more Zionism! Both he and I have dedicated the rest of our lives to this noble mission. I live in Paris and spend a good deal of my time in Berlin, but I'm visiting him here at the moment."

"I take it you refer to Herzl? Theodor Herzl?"

"Yes, of course. Who hasn't heard of Herzl? The Czar, the Pope, the British Parliament, the President and Congress of United States, the Kaiser of Germany, the King of

Italy, and, oh, yes, Sultan Abdul-Hamid of Turkey. He has touched the hearts and minds of them all! And yet there is still no Jewish State! They listen. They smile. Yet they do not act. Damn it to hell!"

He paused for a moment, twirling the tapered corners of his mustache, engaged in some deliberate thought. "Perhaps you will do both of us the honor of coming to tea at his home tomorrow afternoon. I'm sure Herr Herzl would be interested in meeting a young man of such foresight and courage, being one himself."

Slightly flushed by the compliment, Mordecai considered the invitation seriously.

To meet Herzl here in Vienna would be a fascinating opportunity, but I hesitate to expose any of the cadre, or even myself, to the legendary persuasiveness of a man who by all accounts is being driven to sheer madness and ill health chasing a dream. A wild scheme of a dream at that. But it should be important to experience, nevertheless. I'm confident we can handle it. We'll do it!

"Doctor Nordau, I'll be there, but I'd like to have two of my cadre along, if I may."

"Certainly, Reb Anieloff. Say, at three o'clock. Here, I'll write down the address. Haizingergasse 29. I look forward to seeing you again. I should mention that Herr Herzl is not at all well. He recently returned to Vienna from a round of executive committee meetings, and the doctors are very upset with him for not heeding their warnings to slow down. As a physician myself, I tend to agree. It's his heart, you know. Seems to be a weakness there. He won't let me examine him... afraid I'll side with the others and shut him down."

"Are you sure he'll be up to meeting us?"

"By all means. I would be derelict in my allegiance if I didn't give him the chance to talk with you. To meet Jewish youth who are escaping the dastardly repression of the eastern governments, on their own, so bravely, so organized, will be an elixir for Theodor. And flying his flag all the way from Romania yet! Oh, ho! No. No. That's too much to deny him."

"Are you sure he won't become too dangerously excited by trying to convince us we are headed in the wrong direction?" asked Mordecai.

Nordau laughed, got up and headed for the door. "I can't promise anything of that sort, Reb Anieloff. Good day. Enjoy your time in Vienna. Once you cut through the rabid anti-Semitism and its Haman of a mayor, it's really quite lovely, you know!"

Mordecai had to sit back down for a moment. Everything had happened so fast and the doctor's eloquent Germanized form of Yiddish had been hard to understand. Little did he know that he had just had a session with a word master and a master salesman, a respected and mesmerizing orator who had stood by Herzl's side during these very frustrating years, a man who was singularly responsible for keeping Herzl's spirit alive when all appeared lost. He was pleased that he had decided to accept the invitation to tea.

Surmising that the encounter with Herzl would somehow be a memorable one, he chose Sendehr Efraim as one of his companions for the next afternoon, knowing that he alone was capable of mentally registering everything said, and afterward would quickly record it in his journal for posterity's sake. The other was Mendel. A young man of worldliness and scholarship, Mendel knew more, perhaps, of Herzl's movement than any of the other cadre. Thinking that one more, say Branko or Menachem Berman, especially the former, might be overwhelming for his host, he stayed with just the two.

The Fusgeyers had an entire three days to explore the delights of Vienna. It was even more cosmopolitan in appearance and culture than Budapest. Just a few hundred meters from the seminary, Fleischmarkt turned into the *Judegasse*, Jew Street. This was the center of Leopoldstadt, the over-crowded Jewish Vienna, where the group could hear the Yiddish of the thousands of refugees from Poland and the more eastern stretches of the Pale. Add a liberal sprinkling of German, Polish, Russian, Romanian, Slovak,

Czech, a few Southern Slavic dialects, and the resulting lingo-babble could become indecipherable! Yet just by crossing back to Karntner Strasse, Saint Stephen's Cathedral and the Hotel Sacher, one could be immersed at once in a different world of cultured gentility.

They had been carefully forewarned to carry their personal identification papers with them at all times, and Rivka, Sendehr, Mendel and Esther did just that. On their Thursday afternoon stroll they soon found themselves passing the handsome opera house, followed by the imposing Imperial Palace and its wide lawns and colorful, flower-filled grounds. Others investigated the numerous shops and parks surrounding the broad, bustling streets. The nickelodeons and the electrified trams along Rotenturm Strasse lured more than just a few Fusgeyers, but some opted to stay at the seminary to spend a quiet afternoon and evening. The cart, in the meantime, had been securely stored in the carriage barn within the quadrangle of the building.

Finding Haizingergasse on Friday was by no means a simple task. It was in the midst of Leopoldstadt where the streets were wound tighter than intestines. Sendehr had his trusty city map along and finally, just before the appointed hour, the tea guests arrived at the humble Theodor Herzl apartment.

A housemaid opened the door and led the three guests into a sun-filled room overlooking the busy street. Dr. Nordau greeted them and had Mordecai introduce himself and the others to a frail-looking man seated on a lounge next to the window. The man who they knew must be Theodor Herzl lay there, covered with an afghan, his long, rich black beard contrasting with the orange and yellow knitted squares He looked so worn out; they would have been surprised to learn that Herzl was but forty-four years old.

"Please excuse me for not rising. So good of you to come! Max has told me of your mission. No less than a biblical Exodus revisited, I must say. I confess I read all about it in the *Wienner Neue Presse* last month. A very descriptive article by a writer for our counterpart paper in Budapest, the *Jewish Weekly*, Eliezer Viesl. I like his style. Said he met you all during Pesach in Hungary. I told Max to keep an eye out for you, not knowing when and if you would arrive in Vienna. As luck would have it, he caught up with you yesterday."

So it had not been an accidental meeting with Nordau, after all! Mordecai smiled across at the doctor who smiled in return and spoke up.

"One of Herr Herzl's former colleagues with the *Presse* was at the camp in Schwechat when you were released yesterday morning. He was there doing a piece on Lueger's anti-immigration policies. In fact, his carriage passed you on the road into Vienna and he rang me up at my hotel, announcing your estimated time of arrival. Admittedly, even though the Viesl article spoke of the flag, I was quite moved when I actually saw it flying so brazenly. Yes, Mordecai, it really did affect me, which prompted me to follow you to the seminary. Originally, we were going to send a messenger inviting you to tea. Am I forgiven for this surreptitious act?"

Mordecai said, jokingly, to Sendehr, "Be sure to include this confession when you write in our journal, and spell Doctor Nordau's Yiddish name properly."

"Simcha Mayer, Reb Efraim. Yes, Simcha Mayer. My father was a rabbi in Budapest, and I had a very disciplined *cheder* education, I'll say. We spoke Yiddish and Hungarian at home. I'm afraid my Yiddish has become a bit more formal since I left home and began traveling widely in Europe. I have been writing primarily in French and German since then, but speaking in public, particularly at the Zionist Congress with so many easterners in attendance, I depend on the *mamaloshen*. Perhaps that's why I understand you so well, Mordecai."

"I wish I could say the same, Reb Nordau. Germanic Yiddish and Birlader Yiddish fail to meet on occasion, as they did from time to time yesterday!"

In an aside to Mendel, in high-tone Oxonian English, Nordau followed with, "I understand that you also speak

English, sir. Mine is a bit rusty, but could certainly use a workout. Jump in with it at anytime, if you will. Herr Herzl understands it somewhat, too, but rarely admits it. Heh. Heh."

This congenial repartee warmed the air considerably, even to the point where the obviously uncomfortable Herzl joined in the laughter and conversation.

"No harm done, gentlemen. Seriously, my dear Fusgeyers, I'm sure you find my Yiddish much the same. Having traveled deep into Russia, I've had to make a concerted effort to speak in the vernacular, where the literary version merely falls on deaf ears in the town and villages."

"Yes, Reb Herzl, I wondered how you were able to communicate your plans for a Jewish State to the very people who would make up that state," responded the young Sendehr Efraim.

"Thank you, kind sir, for so conveniently opening up the subject which I want to discuss in detail with you three. But first let us partake of some tea and refreshments. All kosher from the wonderful bakery across the way. My shadowing physicians forbid the sweet cakes and Nordau here is a spy, I tell you. No *schnapps*, no *vienerschnitzel*, no cigars. In your honor, lads, I tell them all to jump into the Danube! You, most of all, Max. Good God, you're a neurologist. What do you know of my heart condition?"

Max shook his head in disgust and threw up his hands, surrendering.

While everyone partook in the tea and cakes, Herzl waited for the proper moment and continued.

"This is a rare opportunity for both Max and me. We've spouted off all of the virtues of having a Jewish state, preferably in Palestine. We've written, spoken, preached, argued, cajoled, compromised, debated and, yes, begged. But rarely have we done so to or with the young. Always to the town elders, the government elders, the monarchies, the czardoms, the sheikdoms, the parliaments. The old, damn it, never to the young like your good selves. Who are the delegates to our congresses? The old; established, well off, the professionals. No one under thirty, and most well over fifty." The sick man's eyes were blazing.

"Slow down a bit, Theodor. Please stay more calm."

"Haven't you left for the Danube yet, Max? To jump in? The truth is, my boys, I was overjoyed when I read and heard that you were heading this way with sixty young Romanian Jews, taking drastic action to leave the stagnancy and impoverishment, the violence and futility of the eastern lands! I am so pleased that you are going off as an organized group, to a better life somewhere, anywhere, in your case, to America. This, to me and to Max, and to every Zionist in this world, corroborates once and for all the screaming need for a Jewish State of our own. Your singular action says more than all the thousands of words Max and I have written, the books, the papers, the endless speeches, the tedious meetings, the incessant polemics, and the constant analyses.

"Mordecai, Sendehr, Reb Buchman, *you* are exactly what Zionism is all about! Do you understand? All of the hundreds of thousands of other Jewish emigrants during the past, difficult twenty years clearly have illustrated the desperate need for a place to call our home." He broke off for a moment, coughing. After a few seconds he was able to continue.

"But listen closely. Those Fusgeyers who preceded you since the new century began, and now, your group, magnifies the situation and the need ten thousand percent! Viesl's story of your mission should have appeared in every Jewish periodical in the world, as well as the leading secular newspapers and magazines. I only wish I had the power to distribute it so widely. Now, I must take a few minutes to regain my breathing properly. Forgive me, please."

Addressing Max Nordau while their host lay back for a needed rest, Mendel commented, "I, for one, am taken a bit by surprise at Reb Herzl's remarks. Quite. You both realize full well that we are emigrating from here to America, to the United States, where the vast majority of Eastern European Jews have settled since 1881. Oh, some have dropped off in England, or here in Vienna, Berlin, Paris, or in Budapest. We even had three of our contingent leave us to join the Baron De Hirsch colonies in Argentina. Others have found their way to Australia and we know of the settlements in Palestine. But, again, *America*, both the United States and Canada, have received most of our *Yidden*. Where in the world do we fit into your dream of a Jewish State in Palestine? It most certainly was a viable option for us, but we, as all of the other Fusgeyer groups had before us, unanimously opted for the far west, over the ocean to America. We simply see no alternative for us and for many of the families left behind."

Sitting up again, rest or no rest, Herzl spoke with a raspy, weakened voice.

"Allow me to answer, please, Max. You see, Reb Buchman, we can speak of stark idealism. My ideal has been, and perhaps will always be, a Jewish State in the land of our long-ago forefathers. The land of Avraham, Yitzhok and Yaakov. Of Dovid *Ha Melech*, Solomon, Moshe and Aaron. What more logical destination can there be? I have always asked myself. The Land of Zion. Hence, Zionists and Zionism. My ideal. My *Gan Eden*. But now, young men, I have reached an impasse with all of the powers that be, both within the movement and those surrounding us. Friends, foes, friendly foes, false and dangerous friends."

Painfully exhausted, Herzl went from his half-sitting position on the chaise to a completely reclining one. He let out a long sigh and the accompanying wheeze was audible to everyone in the small room. Even to the untrained eye and ear, this was obviously a brave man fighting two battles simultaneously. One for his ideal. One for his life. Tragically, he was losing both.

Nordau took up the story. "What my dear friend is alluding to is not so simple to explain, Mordecai, Sendehr, Mendel. But let me go back nearly ten years. It is 1895 and I was living in Paris. The Dreyfus Trial. A microcosmic example of all of the injustice that has been done to our people. You've heard of it? Yes? This brought out the worse of the anti-Semites. Every Jew-hater, mild or extreme, crawled out of the sewers of Paris. Captain Dreyfus, an honorable Jewish officer in the Republic's army, became the symbol of every Jew living in Jerusalem back when Reb Yeshua was sentenced to die by the Roman authorities. Nineteen hundred years ago! We're Christ-killers, all of us!"

He took a long breath, looked at the three young men sitting on the sagging divan, and glanced at his mentor before continuing. "At the time, Theodor was the Paris correspondent for the *Neue Presse*, working the abhorrent trial. He was there, in the courtyard, observing the final defamation of the so-called guilty traitor Dreyfus, his sword broken in two, his epaulets ripped off, being sent off in utter disgrace to Devil's Island in the Caribbean for a life of penal servitude. All of this was accompanied by an unruly mob crying 'death to the Jews,' carrying it over into the streets of Paris for days on end.

"Once again the anti-Semites were at work, even there in the very nation that was the first in Europe to provide full emancipation for its Jews! Once again they demonstrated their singular method of pouncing upon any act of wrongdoing, actual or alleged, real or imagined, laying the guilt on all Jews, everywhere. All of us! And it was there and then that Theodor had his epiphany.

"This brilliant and restless young man, assimilationist in every respect, witnessed what had befallen the Children of Israel at every turn for centuries, and it disturbed him beyond the point of mere distraction. We met for the first time... do you remember, Theodor?"

Checking to see if the body under the afghan had been napping, Nordau received a snappier response than expected.

"Of course I do, you old busybody, *yenteh*. I presented my pamphlet to you that following winter. You with the international reputation as a man of letters, *moi*, just an itinerant newspaper writer. Go on with it, Max. You're making

242

me look good for a change."

It pleased not only Nordau, but also all present, to see that Herzl was still very much alert and with his droll sense of humor intact. Sendehr guessed that not many people had seen this side of the man.

"*Der Judenstaat*, The Jewish State. I scanned the manuscript and truly became an ardent Zionist then and there. It was February of '96, Theodor. As I told you earlier, Mordecai, it became then and has been ever since my life's work. Our life's work. But as Reb Herzl has told you far more eloquently than I can, the mission is far from being accomplished. Still thousands of miles from your noble goal, you are light-years closer than we Zionists are to our elusive one. So you've had some border hassles, some unforeseen barriers as you've walked along? Believe me, one Zionist meeting, worldwide or local, throws up more formidable, unscalable mountains to climb. One long sought-after audience with an influential statesman or ruler can be more devastating and frustrating than the most virulent, anti-Semitic Austrian cavalry officer."

Mordecai stood up at this point, and asked, "What barriers, specifically, have you encountered? We would like to better understand your dilemma. Even though we're determined to reach America, I'm sure you seek the support of American Jewry. Maybe we are potential Zionists. Who knows? We three, of all the Fusgeyers, come here with an open mind. I know that Mendel is quite well versed in the history of the movement. Sendehr and I perhaps know less of it," contributed Mordecai, who up until now had been an intense listener only.

Herzl, again sitting up, interrupted before Nordau could answer him.

"Gentlemen, it is important to note, just in case you don't know, that Dreyfus had been purely innocent all along. This convoluted sham of plot and counterplot finally resulted in his release from Devil's Island and a full pardon. Now go on, Max. I just don't have the strength. Please forgive me."

"Would it be best if we were to leave now?" asked a concerned Mordecai.

"No. Absolutely not. I want to hear the rest of the story from Max, just to see where I've gone wrong, and the exciting part where he comes galloping to the rescue of world Jewry." Even Nordau joined the laughter that followed Herzl's remark.

Mordecai interjected, "As I pointed out, we are willing to hear the whole story and support your idea of a Jewish State in any way we can. But, that support will come only from us once we are in America, sirs."

"Fair enough," answered Nordau, "but perhaps both Theodor and I have not been honest enough with you. We have as yet to tell you the full reason why we sought you out and invited you here.

"To explain this to you, I'll have to go on with the brief history of the movement since Theodor saw to it that *Der Judenstaat* was widely distributed, just eight years ago. In historical fact, since the dispersion, Jews have yearned to return to the holy sights, to the Land of Zion, *Eretz Yisroel*. Over the centuries, some did just that, as individuals, families, and small groups. Primarily the very religious. The *chassids*, the Torah scholars. In the past century, organizations such as The Lovers of Zion promoted a return program, and in fact that organization tacitly merged with our movement at the outset.

"But in *Der Judenstaat*, Theodor establishes for the first time a political form of Zionism. A homeland for the Jew. With borders and rights guaranteed by the world powers. A nation with a government. Trading with other national entities. A proud nation of Jewish citizens stepping up to the conference table with all the others. This, my friends, is what makes our Zionist movement different than all of the other return movements."

Nordau paused for a moment to check on the closed-eyed Herzl, and then continued.

"You see, it was all well and good with the wary world when small colonies of Jews settled in Palestine in the ancient and recent past. But our Zionism calls for, no, it *demands* more than that. Much, much more than that. And therein lies the crux of the problem. The impasse. The heartache. Or, as our detractors say, the illusion. With all of the factions, and factions within factions, it's a wonder we've come this far. But in reality, we are still no closer to a Jewish State in Palestine. To sum up, one need only go back to last year's Congress in Switzerland to see what I mean. More or less a final blow for Theodor. For me. For all of us within the movement who strongly argue that any piece of land, anywhere, for our Jewish State, is better than no land at all.

"The Turks have played with us as unwanted children all these years. Up to and including extortion. Money in return for favors never granted. "Criminal" is the only word in my vocabulary that fits their actions. They know they are fast losing their grip on what's left of their Ottoman Empire, and that Palestine will soon fall into British hands.

"We've tried everything. The Brits are past masters of the promise. They even toyed with the idea of giving us the Sinai. Yet, still nothing firm as far as their plans for Palestine and our goal of a Jewish nation.

"Prior to our ' 03 Congress, Joseph Chamberlain, their Colonial Secretary, threw us little Hebrew pests a bone. A bone in the form of Uganda. Far off, equatorially hot, isolated Uganda, in the very heart of the 'Dark Continent'. Uganda would be ours to settle, with our own officials, a free hand in elections, fully autonomous except for the right of His Majesty's government to exercise general control. Not what we had striven for. Not the independent Jewish State, but perhaps the only option available at this time."

"Coming so soon after the Kishinev pogrom, Mendel added, "I can see where you and Reb Herzl were interested, even if only as an emergency measure. At least a place to which people could escape on an immediate basis. Perhaps not the ultimate answer to the conditions that prevail in the Pale, in Romania, Poland, but..."

Mendel's response was quickly met with a display of

recognition on the part of the prostrate Herzl who interrupted him mid-thought, surprising Nordau and the others who thought him to be slumbering.

"Precisely, dear lad. Bravo! That is exactly what my feelings were and still are. A port in the storm. A temporary haven. But the hardheaded Russian delegation accused me of betraying the Zionist cause, of being a dupe of British imperialism and of diverting the aims of our movement. I had to agree that this solution was not the Zion we wanted. That it was only a stopgap until we could garner more support morally and financially. But they wouldn't listen. They stormed out of the conference hall, even after a test vote gave the Uganda Proposal a majority. A rather Pyrrhic victory, I must add, because those dissidents who left and eventually held a special conference in Kharkov were easily the most influential. Headed by Menachem Mendel Ussishkin, they had always proclaimed that greater emphasis be placed on the continuing colonization of Palestine regardless of the futile political situation. Stressing the word futile."

"So where do things stand today?" Sendehr was frowning, puzzled.

Nordau took up the mantle while Herzl lay down once more, face grayer than it had been when they first arrived. Even a layman could see the very essence of life ebbing from his palsied body.

Before the conversation went on, Nordau asked the maid to bring Herzl's medicine tray, and he saw to it that his friend took everything he was due for before he had drifted to sleep. They adjourned into the cramped kitchen area so as not to wake him again.

"As you can see, the excitement, the strain, the acrimonious debates of the past August and its aftermath have taken their toll on him. Professionally, I must tell you, his health, his heart, has been on a rapid downhill cycle since then and I fear he has passed the point of no return. I plan to stay in Vienna for another week so I can at the very least assist with the massive amount of communication, letter writing and answering he's faced with.

"He had no choice but to engage in *realpolitik* and he finally acceded to Ussishkin's demands that Uganda be dropped and new emphasis placed on colonizing, praying for world opinion, fat pocketbooks and the good graces of Mother England to provide a permanent refuge. The recent executive committee session in Vienna solidified this thinking. That insufferable elitist Chamberlain was heard to mutter something about "these historically ungrateful Sons of Abraham" in his reaction to the tacit Uganda rejection. The Russian faction even had the audacity to rationalize their disapproval by telling a *London Times* reporter that since Uganda was not mentioned by name in the Bible, it would be against God's will to establish a Jewish homeland there. Can you imagine such irrelevant juvenile drivel?

"But that brings us back to you, our wayfaring lads of Romania. You are beginning to see the picture now that you are fully aware of the status of today's World Zionist Organization.

Nordau took a breath.

"We need money, lots of it, if we're to continue the difficulties of colonization in the hopes of something better materializing in the future. You know, when Theodor went on a *shnorring* mission to the Rothschilds and De Hirsches and other monied families of Europe, he was summarily refused. No, I shouldn't be so harsh. They were willing to provide for specifically earmarked colonies here and there in Palestine, emblazoned with their names, of course, and they did so, and are still giving. But none were willing to put their influence and full support behind the political nature of the cause. *The Jewish State*. Big money in the United States delivers a pittance in ratio to the pennies collected by the common man in his little blue *keren kayemeth*, Jewish National Fund box. Why? Same reason. When one is so far removed from the horrors of life and the threat of death in the Pale, it is difficult to be convinced of the urgency in needing a homeland under our terms.

"Herzl wants me to write a dramatic series about you

and your mission, and I would see that it is sent to every major secular newspaper in the world. My name, as a writer, has earned an international following, especially since the wide acceptance of my numerous books, which are generously classified as social criticism. In particular, *Conventional Lies of Our Civilization* and *Paradoxes*. Both extremely controversial, but also major contributions to my reputation in literary circles, deserved or undeserved. Heh, heh." His smile-driven wink was designed to indicate to his guests a certain degree of humility.

Mendel said, eagerly, "Aha! Aha! Haven't read either, but my professor in Salonika spoke well of them and included the English translations on our alternate reading list. Not until just now did I realize that you were that author, Doctor!"

"Thank you, Reb Buchman. Your professor was surely a man of great literary taste. At any rate, we must penetrate the *goyishe velt,* the gentile world, more effectively than we have thus far. The Jewish State idea has to be spread far and wide. For instance, can you imagine how many influential Karl Luegers, anti-Semitic mayors of large cities, heads of state, key players in world politics, would love for their Jews to leave, en masse, for Palestine? Good riddance, once and for all! Even though the *tsittering,* nervous, rabbi of this city thinks we're insane, Lueger is already putting his verbal support behind Zionism. He looks upon Herzl as his savior, if you'll excuse the pitiful pun! Sort of his personal pied piper. But of far greater value are those more moderate government officials who, out of a sense of justice, could be sold on our cause. The combined international influences can do nothing but help bring about our desired aims, in the long run at least."

Nordau's voice grew more intense. "I've already begun to outline the series of articles. It will feature the reasons why you deem it impractical to immigrate to the Holy Land in favor of America. Nothing there for you. No promise of anything but belligerent Arabs, intransigent Turks, and someday the stiff Brit, vulture-sized mosquitoes, malaria and dysentery. And these realities are easily the most compelling reasons why only a trickle of colonists have dotted the Palestinian landscape while millions have gone west. Like yourselves. But I am going to stress particularly the youth aspect. Here are the young, so sorely needed in any colonial venture, and they go west. Only west. Organized, determined, of a single mind. They go west. The youth of the Pale and Romania and Poland go west. Only west. Do you see? West to blend in and fully assimilate with God knows who or what. The process of dilution has become epidemic, especially in America.

"Where will it end? Without a Jewish State there is no long-range hope. Now please don't misunderstand. I'm not petitioning for you to turn your course around. I realize that would be an exercise in pure futility. But, I warn you! Theodor and I are going to use you to the fullest extent that we can. A classic case of the ends justifying the means. Your mission can help our mission. Do you see that now?"

Mordecai had listened hard, and when both Mendel and Sendehr looked over to him, deferring to his leadership for an answer, he spoke.

"Doctor Nordau, if it's permission you're seeking, there is certainly nothing we can do to stop you. If it's our approval you want, I see no harm in it. I trust you to write the truth. If by doing so, the World Zionist cause can be enhanced in any way, than I, for only one of fifty-seven say, get on with it, and God be with you every step of the way."

"Here! Here! *Boruch Hashem!* Blessed is the Lord!" chimed Mendel and Sendehr in unison.

"Thank you kindly. I must warn you that I move with alacrity. With my well-known Magyar *chutzpah* I have already arranged for a professional photographer to take group and individual pictures on Sunday morning when you're ready to leave Vienna. I'll need these to accompany the articles. Would that be acceptable?"

"By all means, sir. I would ask you to follow Viesl's lead, not mentioning Birlad by name. Just Romania. None of our last names, either. No need of them."

Mordecai seemed more animated than at any time during the afternoon, and began to convey his enthusiasm to the others.

"You understand, of course, that we get a great deal out of this, too. Viesl's article, as you've seen, highlights the goal of our mission as one to bring a focus on the unspeakable conditions, the reasons for our leaving Romania. Just as those escaping the Pale are doing. Only in our case it is, as you know, a more highly organized protest. A demonstration, as some of our nemeses have been quick to accuse us of. So dual objectives, hopefully, will be greatly served by your writing. You can be assured that your Zionist flag, after all a symbol that represents the diaspora Jew as well, will proudly wave from here to Bremerhaven."

"Indeed. And the ultimate beneficiaries, the eventual victors, shall be the Jewish people. Our people. Whether they stay behind or emigrate, east or west. Please, God! Oh, if our nation were already in existence, millions would consider it! Young people like your good selves would be marching to *Gan Eden*!"

The big man was quite overcome, and a stream of tears trickling down each cheek toward his white beard and mustache. Mordecai arose to embrace the broad-girthed Zionist stalwart, followed in rapid succession by Mendel and Sendehr.

"You will make a powerful leader of world Zionism, Doctor Nordau,'" observed Sendehr Efraim.

"Oh, no, no. Not on your life. I'm much too battle-weary. With the certainty of Theodor stepping down very soon, David Wolffsohn from Berlin is the likely successor. He is one of us, a most loyal lieutenant, but possibly better prepared to further compromise with the Russians. Did I mention that our followers are referred to as the Politicals, whereas theirs are the Practicals? That says it all! Reminds me of one of my dear late father's stories.

"It seems that the congregants of a little *shul* somewhere in the endless steppes of the Ukraine fell uncontrollably deep within a schism. The rabbi could do nothing to bring the two arguing factions together. One insisted that the congregation must stand during the recitation of the *shema,* while the other stood firm on the right to sit if they wished. This went on throughout the year—Yom Kippur, Rosh Hashonah, the Sabbath—culminating with each side refusing to talk to the other. Finally, the rabbi decided to bring the issue to a venerable ninety-five-year-old sage living in a forest cabin nearby.

"Representatives of each faction agreed to lay the problem at the feet of the wise old man. The first group told its side to the sage, restating that it's ancient Jewish custom to remain standing during the *shema,* and his answer was simply that it is not necessarily an accepted Jewish custom. The second group presented its argument, insisting that it is unquestionably Jewish custom to sit if you wish. Again, the sage quietly stated that to sit is not necessarily a Jewish custom. The ensuing invectives, and shouting, and screaming and breast-beating wildly went on, creating a deafening din. With a twinkle in his eye, the old master looked at the very disturbed rabbi and said, 'now that, that is Jewish custom!'"

A good laugh was very much in order at this juncture, and laugh they did.

Halting this joviality abruptly, the doctor continued. "Good God, friends, not to belabor these civil war issues among brethren, nor to glorify some of the insanity that threatens the entire Zionist movement, but after the in-fighting at the meetings in '03, when I returned to Paris, a young hot-headed Russian Zionist shot at me! Yes, with a gun! Real bullets! Can you believe it? Thank God his aim was as wild as he was when he shouted, 'Death to Nordau, the East African!' The radical *mumzer!* The Parisian police didn't even bother to search for him, figuring one Jew shooting at another wasn't worth the fuss. I decided not to press the issue, not needing that kind of further notoriety."

These last remarks served as a sobering end to the previous laughter, and the three invited guests sat in stunned silence.

Then, they knew, it was time to go. All four softly walked into Herzl's sitting room to find him standing by the window, gazing at the approaching dusk, afghan draped over his sloping shoulders. His frailty came through unmistakably, cradled by the rays of the fast-sinking sun.

"Gentlemen, I heard your laughter, and I take it that Max's proposition has met with your approval. Am I right, Max? Yes? Thank you. Thank you, my good young men. It will help us immeasurably. Of that you can be sure. I'm sorry I wasn't livelier company, but from the bottom of my very tired heart, I appreciate your coming to tea. I wish you nothing but success on your journey, and in America. Perhaps one of you will become a member of their esteemed Congress or Supreme Court someday, and you will support our Jewish State. Please God!"

At that point, just before the goodbyes, Theodor Herzl, the founder of a simple, one-track idea that would not, could not fade, reached into his pocket and pulled out three imprinted *shekels*, replicas of the ancient Hebrew coins.

He handed one to each of the young visitors, saying in a voice that was nearly a whisper, "When you're in America enjoying your new lives and the excitement of that grand and glorious experiment called the United States, carry these with you to remind you of our struggle and your part in it. And now goodbye, Mordecai, Sendehr, Mendel. In America, remember who you are, always. I myself forgot, once."

The final embraces were in silence, tears difficult to hold back, as Max Nordau showed the Fusgeyers to the door, where he, too, bade them goodbye but with the reminder that he would see them again on Sunday morning.

Privately, not one of the four expected the man whose noble dream had become a magnificent obsession to live much longer. Sadly, it seemed to all that this would soon come to pass.

This was not the time for discussion. It was solely a time for reflection, and each of the three found himself walking at a slow pace, immersed in a recapitulation of the intensely illuminating encounter. Now they knew exactly why they had been summoned, having independently agreed with the reasoning. Each also felt a certain pride and genuine appreciation that they had just witnessed something far more than a dreamer at the end of his life.

They had been part of something historic. Something that had the potential of changing the way the world thought about the Jew. Something that would shift balances, rewrite unfair laws, provide sustenance for the impoverished, manna for the famished, and hope for the hopeless.

Yes, above and beyond anything else, hope. Herzl's dream: hope, *ha tikvah.*

§

"Thirty-eight to twelve! Thirrrty-eight to twwwelvvve! I can't believe they creamed us, Dad. How many easy lay-ups did you blow?"

"About as many as the flat bricks you tossed from the top of the key, hot-shot," laughed the forty-plus poor-excuse-for-Larry Bird.

"Aw, that octopus Anton was all over me, Dad," retaliated the number eight man on the BHHS hoop team's rotation.

"Well, we had fun anyway, Kobe, pal. I won't mention it to anyone if you won't."

"Promise. I feel like we let down our whole country out there. Man, what a sky-hook Nico had. Anton must've hit ten shots from the perimeter!"

And so it went. The Friedman boys, as Nathan referred to these round ball junkies, rented some straw mats after changing into their bathing trunks, and spread out in the warm midday June sun. The shimmering, golden sands of

Eforie Sud on the calm Black Sea coast stretched on for miles.

"Say, I don't suppose you noticed that there's a critical shortage of tops for female bathing togs, sonny boy," the older guy with the aching knees chuckled.

"You mean the red-hot gypsy mamas parading up and down the beach? Nope, haven't seen a thing. No sir, not me!"

"Okay. Again, I won't say a thing if you don't, Rico."

Herb rarely called his son Rico. That was Nathan's personal nickname for Eric. Everyone thought it was just a natural diminutive for E-ric, using the "Ric" and adding the "o." Herb, though, knew better. Born and brought up in Quincy, near Boston and old Fenway Park, his dad was a typical frustrated but rabid Red Sox fan. Even with all of the runner-up finishes and rare pennants, and even after coming to California. Ted Williams was his favorite hero, of course. But later, after the Splendid Splinter hung up his spikes, Nathan took a liking to another Boston player, a spunky, hard-hitting infielder with the poetic Italianate name of Rico Petrocelli.

Hence the Rico tag. Eric was proud of being the only kid in Beverly Hills, or probably on the entire West Coast, upholding that honor. Baseball might not be his game, but Rico was his name!

After a dip in the warm water, not yet used to its tranquility compared with the rough surf of the Pacific, Rico lay down to dry off and thought about what had transpired in the less-than-a-week they had been in this country. It was beautiful, yet backward, mysterious, yet naturally wide-open.

"Dad, we've sure learned a lot about your Grandpa Sholem this past week."

"More than I thought possible. I really had my doubts on your grandfather finding out very much on this mission. But Nachman seems to be exceptionally well versed on the Fusgeyer story. Son, can you imagine that Sholem was your age when he started that trek? Doesn't that blow your mind?"

"Y'know, Dad, it's not the physical walk so much as the history surrounding it that's so amazing. Sholem and his friends had all the odds against them. Sort of like sixty young folks my age, a little older, tramping through Sioux or Apache country in 1875, unarmed for the most part, and no friendly cavalry to protect or rescue them. No John Wayne or even Ronald Reagan in yellow-striped blues riding at full speed, Winchesters blazing away."

"Hey, good analogy! Now that's putting the whole thing in perspective relative to something we've seen time and time again... me the originals, you on the TV re-runs!"

Herb was smiling

"When we get back to Birlad tomorrow I'm sure that Grandpa will have more to tell us. I'm so happy for him. I've never seen him so full of enthusiasm and excitement. It's something you and I can't fully comprehend. We know so much about our dads and moms. Not much of a mystery there! You know all about my childhood, my teens, college years, your mom...and I can trace both my parent's lives from birth to today. Just think, your kids and your grandchildren will have thousands of photos, videos, mementos of my life, mom's life, your grandparent's lives...and now with this incredible Romanian discovery, you'll have some great stories to tell!"

"I'll leave that to you, Dad. I can see you now, holding my kids on your knee and telling them all about the Fusgeyers, Sholem's running, Prislop Pass, Branko, Mordecai, Sendehr and the Romanian Road Blocks! I wonder how much you'll jazz it up."

"As if it needed any added color!"

On the shores of the Black Sea, father and son shared a smile at those last remarks. But the growing teen-ager had already packed away a heavy lunch in the small cafe in Nuntashi following the hard-fought loss, and he was already beginning to think about his next meal.

14

ENCOUNTERS: ROAD TO PRAGUE

Our whole history inclines us towards the democratic powers. Our renaissance is a logical link between us and the democracies of the west.
Thomas Garrigue Masaryk,President of the
new Czechoslovakia,Inaugural Address, 1918

Sendehr Efraim sported a red, slightly swollen knuckle from grasping his nib pen for so long. Writing daily in the journal and crafting a weekly synopsis for Rabbi Nachman caused this to happen. His resolve to include even the most minute detail was the major contributor. His agile mind fluttered through these details, sorted them out, shuffled them around, massaged them gently, and only much later poured them into his writing. For what had transpired during the seventy-two hours in Vienna, the entire process was treated to a vertiginous exercise. It would have appeared like this in his head in between sorts, shuffles, massages, before, finally, he could manufacture written words:

...the Herzl-Nordau meeting, again and
again...the long walk with Rivka... results of the
Herzl-Nordau meeting... sleeping in the hard pews
of the chapel in the seminary...well, at least a roof
over our heads, and it did rain a bit a few
times...only one water closet??...seminary faculty
and students very accommodating...so Simmy

struck it rich in the food stores of the seminary and in the Judegasse shops...no surprise...we'll eat like a pferd for the next week...or more... Mordecai's warning for everyone to carry papers and avoid the police...why in God's name didn't Dovid and Mottke pay attention?...the Herzl-Nordau meeting...how long will Herzl live?...looked sehr krank ... Nordau's articles can be valuable...I love holding Rivka's hands while we walk...the Herzl-Nordau meeting, again...a great learning experience...Mendel thinks Herzl's dream will someday come true...Mordecai strongly feels it will, too...even if it takes fifty years...I agree, but I believe it will take all of that...a half-century...too much opposition...from within and without...a grandiose idea whose time may some- day arrive...Lueger is probably overjoyed that fifty- seven Jews left his precious city this morning...loved those pastry shops on Judegasse...the taiglach, the rugelach, the honey lekach...the reports on the Seittenstettengasse shul were quite good...thank you everyone, for the description...glad that Rivka suggested that long walk...the electric lights of Vienna made Budapest look like a city in the dark...came across so many emigrants on the road today...some tailed along for a while, but no one can keep up our pace...the two families from Temesvar/Timoshoara seem to be in good shape...the man and wife with their two little ones from Botoshani have been on the road for three months already...my God...will they ever get to the ports?...seems like they have money for passage once they get there...I pray for them...I sometimes envy those with enough money to take the trains...but that's not our purpose...the Herzl- Nordau meeting, again and again...can't get it out of my head...the walk with Rivka, again and again...don't want to get it out of my head! I hope we will live close to one another in America...maybe *together? H-m-m....Branko and Mordecai had to go to the police headquarters to rescue Mottke and Dovid...if Heshy hadn't lagged behind to make eyes at a pretty girl, he would have been taken in, too...luckily he had the sense to dash back to the seminary to get Branko and Mordecai...they'd still be in custody...the photograph session this morning was good fun...Nordau must have had the photographer take fifty pictures...happy I was sitting next to Rivka...the way the photographer had us all sit on the grass in front of the church across from the seminary must have been the first time so many, if any, Jews sat on that lawn...oy, that Itzy Gelman...can't wait to see that picture someday...imagine, Itzy will be in it twice...yes, twice...just by running from one end to the other while the photographer slowly swiveled the camera box from left to right to fit in the whole group...hope Max will get a copy and send it to me after I send him an address...Rivka says Itzy and Mayer will end up on Broadway in New York...but they're going to Boston...is there a Broadway in Boston?...who should know!...wonder what the Singerman boys and Yehuda Gelman are doing today...must be sailing across the Atlantic to Buenos Aires already...that letter from Rabbi Nachman I picked up at the Postal Office was disturbing...a new tyrant of a magistrate...enforcing the boycott, talking about preventing all Jewish tradesmen from doing business...something about licenses...my father, what can he do?...my father, please God...I've got to send for them as soon as I can...sooner...I should share this with everyone...I can't...will just make them angry and sad...many of them get letters every now and then anyway, so soon everyone will know what's happening back home...it's just not good...not that it ever was...and many of them write home, too...ay, yi, yi, Rivka's hand was so soft and warm, her lips so full...tonight we will kiss again!...been told that some of the boys met a group of girls on the Judegasse last night...everyone's so quiet about it...no bragging yet...our "cantors" singing at the shul must have been great...being invited to sing with the choir...everyone who went couldn't stop talking about our boys...never saw or heard a choir in a shul before Budapest and Vienna...Mendel is going to teach us the pledge to the American flag tonight...interesting...never heard of such a thing...Nuchim thinks we'll have a very comfortable surplus of money when we get to Bremerhaven... Boruch Hashem! ...God, I can't get the Herzl meeting out of my mind...no place to store it...too much...too big...too powerful ...major consequences! ...Enough, enough, dear brain, I've got to rest!*

That morning, Sendehr and Zed-Zed went over the schedule and the maps covering Vienna to Prague. No unusual terrain to be concerned about. Straightforward. Sendehr estimated 350 kilometers, through Stockerau, Hollabrunn, Znaim/Znojmo, Teltsch/Telc, and Tabor. Zed-Zed's schedule called for a one-day stop in Znojmo for the Shavuos Festival, with plans to arrive in Prague for a Sabbath weekend ten days later. Unless, of course, the Austrian military planned to harass them along the way. This was always somewhere in everyone's mind, Branko's most of all. He knew their tactics all too well. His own role in the treatment of emigrating groups was one he wished to forget, but couldn't. He wondered, *how many good deeds would it take?*

After yet another crossing of the Danube by flat-bottom ferry, which would be their last, the grove of pines referred to in one of the earlier journals loomed close by. The setting, just a kilometer from the town of Stockerau, was magnificent. The smell of pine permeated the air, filling everyone's nostrils to their aromatic delight. The copious needles lay in thick mounds throughout the dense grove, just damp enough from the recent showers to negate any fire hazard potentiality. The nature of the low slung pine boughs made it necessary to keep any fires to a minimum. With the unseasonably warm weather, no one opted to start one on that balmy night, anyway.

Considering the sights, the sounds, the crowded streets, the good smells as well as the bad of Vienna now behind them, the wayfarers were sure that this idyllic place was surely their private Garden of Eden.

April showers marked the way into Moravian Znojmo, known also by its German name, Znaim, bringing out the brilliant green of the rolling hills. This was orchard and vineyard country, and the vines were midway to their September harvest fullest. Not quite ready for eating; otherwise the grape lovers among the Fusgeyers would have purple streaks all over their chins and fingers. Beards would bear stains enough to anger any patrolling vintner.

The very few Jews along the way, in Stockerau and Hollabrunn, quietly but admiringly greeted the troop and were generous in their handouts of fruit, preserves, milk and eggs. The advance scouts, Sholem and Yaakov, simply used the most common means of identifying the Jewish homes in the smaller towns and villages, in order to alert them that the Fusgeyers were on their way—*the mezuzzah*— *"and thou shalt write them upon the doorposts of thy house and upon thy gates."* (Deuteronomy vi, 4-9). There were plain, wooden receptacles and fancy metal ones, ornate and filigreed, with painted figurines. Every conceivable type of *shema*-holding piece could be found signifying "the Jewish home" all over the world. If a Jew had once lived in a house later occupied by a gentile family, the nail holes were usually still there, unless filled in and painted over.

Unfortunately during times of violence, the pogroms, or the earlier crusades, the *mezuzzah* served an untoward purpose, but for the Fusgeyers, it signaled that there were local sympathizers behind those doors who could be summoned to "rally 'round the flag"...a monumental, first time occasion for most of them. The sheer joy upon seeing the *Mogen Dovid* proudly held aloft made it a day everyone would always remember, and also a time to thank God.

Isolated Znojmo, where the sparse community, influenced by a small but steady stream of Polish-Jewish immigration, spoke an eastern Yiddish more familiar to the Birladers, was deeply into the spirit of this happy holiday. As was the custom, Jewish homes and the entrance to the synagogue were decorated with the branches of small trees. The Festival of Weeks, marking exactly fifty days, seven weeks from the time of Pesach, commemorated the wheat harvest. Here in the rich, agricultural Moravian highlands, the meaning of the festival was a practical one, and to a degree even the huge majority of non-Jews participated in it.

As was also true for the vineyards, the wheat fields weren't quite ready for the reaper, but the surrounding orchards were laden with apricots, apples, peaches, plums and pears. Baskets-full were seen in front of many homes, even on the town hall steps and in the gazebo of the central square. Simmy, for one, assumed that everything was there for the taking. And he took. And took again. After all, the young provider had scores of people to feed.

A number of greeters invited Mordecai to send one or two of his troop to stay in each of their houses overnight, and many took advantage of this kind gesture. The others pitched camp down the street from the *shul*, on an empty plot of ground bisected by a winding stream, forded by an ancient wooden footbridge.

Everyone chose to attend the small, overcrowded *shul*, both that evening and the next morning. To facilitate this, Nuchim had paid a tavern keeper whose inn was nearby the field to keep his eye on the cart. The rabbi, a young goatee-wearing Berliner, welcomed them and spoke kindly of their mission, mentioning to his congregants without being prompted that all donations, food and *groschen*, would be happily accepted. The "three cantors", now four, performed admirably, as always.

The Shavuos festival coincided with the Biblical date that Moses received the Proclamation of the Ten Command-ments, and during the morning service Mordecai was in-vited to say a few words from the *bimah.* He turned this honor over to Mendel, who spoke eloquently of the Jewish condition in Romania, underlining the *haimishe* treatment they had been receiving along the way, and singling out the good people of Znojmo and their rabbi.

All the visitors were later invited to the adjoining hall to partake of a *bisl zu essen* that the women of the *shul* had prepared last-minute in their honor. Smoked fish, pickled herring, pumpernickel bread, *strudel* and *lokshn kugel,* fruits, and the traditional Shavuos specialty; deliciously rich, creamy cheesecakes in all their seductive glory. The Znojmo *balabustehs* came through in grand style, and from the looks of their hefty menfolk, this enormous display of food was commonly prepared and presented at their own home tables.

Rabbi Gottesmann, humbly excusing his Deutsche-ac-cented Yiddish, thanked Mendel and the beaming "cantors" for their participation in his cantor-less *shul,* and ap-proached Mordecai who had just sampled a piece of one of the cheesecake delights. Two other travelers also present for the holiday stood with the Fusgeyer leader.

"Rabbi Gottesmann, this hospitality is unmatched by any of the many smaller communities we have visited. Thank you very much," came Mordecai's heartfelt thanks. "May I introduce some fellow walkers: Moishe Gelernter and Pinchas Rembaum from Czernowitz. They've been on the roads for about the same period of time as we have. Two months."

Moishe, the older of the two, shook hands with the rabbi, adding, "We are going across Bohemia, through Karlsbad, and on to Germany to Antwerp. Our uncle living there is purchasing passage for us to America. We, too, thank you for this wonderful welcome. We've just come from nearby Nikolsburg/Mikulov where we stayed with family for a few days, and since our papers are in proper order Mordecai has agreed to let us join with him until we part ways in Prague. Our cousins warned us of some ruffian hordes in the area just west of here. Do you know of them, Rabbi?"

"No, not that I've heard, gentlemen. However, these Fusgeyers have had a few anxious moments, I'm told; however, they've been able to stave off every peril. You are wise to travel part way with them. Friends, I must admit that here in the Moravian regions of Franz Josef's empire we have food in abundance and the officials treat us with some level of decency. They are not overly kind, but are at least fair on the surface. The most notable event from which we still feel occasional repercussions was the infamous and ugly blood-libel case up in Polna, north of here near Iglau. The Hilsner affair.

"A young Jewish shoemaker named Leopold Hilsner was charged with the murder of a nineteen-year-old local seamstress just before Pesach and Easter. His accusers also claimed that Hilsner had done the deed, with the help of the village's very small Jewish congregation, in order to drain the victim's blood to make the matzos. Heh, heh! Can you believe it? This same old nonsensical, horrendous story has been handed down through the centuries. I'm surprised you haven't heard of this case. Periodic rioting and unrest throughout this part of the continent soon followed the incident. Some journalists compared it to the Dreyfus affair. Seems to have died down a bit since the trial in 1900, although I just arrived here from Berlin in '02."

"Yes, our cousins talked about it last night. Evidently Mikulov was the scene of one such bloody riot while the trial was taking place in Brunn/Brno. The *shul* was defaced, all windows smashed, and numerous Jewish shops were looted and set afire. Cousin Tevye lost a horse and a wagon to the *mumzerim.* Thankfully, no one was killed."

"*Omayn!* Nothing violent here in Znojmo, but many towns in Bohemia, Moravia and Slovakia suffered, and a wave of this newly fueled anti-Semitism spilled over into Austria-proper and Hungary, into Galicia and Poland. Brno was under martial law during the entire trial, which swiftly resulted in the death penalty for Hilsner."

Mendel, who has been standing by, acknowledged, "I read about it in the *Iashi Yiddishe Shtimme*, which seemed to minimize it for fear of panicking the community, coming on the heels of their horrible '99 pogrom. You remember now, Mordecai?"

"Yes, yes. Of course. I hadn't realized that it had such a broad impact."

"It most certainly did, gentlemen," Gottesmann rejoined. "In fact, as we speak, one of the exceptionally fair-minded Czechs is deeply involved in appealing the case. Be on the watch for his name. Tomasha Masaryk. He came out loud and clear against this age-old superstition, the accusation of ritual murder. Believe me, he is a man risking his reputation, if not his life, by taking such a contrary position. Increasingly, there are those who privately talk of his charismatic greatness that could someday propel him into the world's spotlight...but listen to this interesting side fact. This rather foolhardy Masaryk recently traveled to Palestine to visit the Jewish settlements, and has since become very supportive of a future Jewish State. At the same time he has openly condemned anti-Semitism, in this part of the empire, at least. Can you believe it? The man can certainly stir the pot!"

"Who knows, maybe we'll find more of the same in America...anti-Semitism, blood libel, boycotts. Won't know for sure until we get there. Certainly hope not. What is the current situation in Germany, Rabbi?" asked Pinchas Rembaum.

"Good question. You will find when you cross into Germany that in spite of periodic revivals of overt anti-Semitism the Jew is more fully emancipated there than anywhere else on the continent. I see a great future for the German Jew in this century ahead. Reb Anieloff, be sure you see the magnificence of the New Synagogue, *Der Neue Shul*, in Berlin on Oranienburgerstrasse. It is a domed masterpiece that more than matches any of the grand cathedrals of Europe, including the Vatican."

"We'll do that, Rabbi Gottesmann. I believe it's on the same street as the Labor Alliance headquarters where we'll be staying, but the greeting and kindness you have given my people in your little *shul* means much more to us than the mere size of a larger edifice."

"*Boruch Hashem. Fuhrt sich gesunt,* all of you.*"

Breaking bivouac the following morning, the cart overflowing with foodstuffs once again, the Fusgeyers began to notice that the roads toward Prague were not nearly as heavily traveled as those between Vienna and Znojmo had been. Signposts were becoming rarer and Sendehr's maps had to be consulted often to prevent drifting too far off course.

Gelernter and Rembaum, the boys from Czernowitz, proved to be two very pleasant youngsters in their late teens, and the Fusgeyers took them in comfortably. In fact, Itzy had already tried to convince them to go to Bremerhaven with them. They couldn't do that, of course, with passage already awaiting them in Antwerp. Since Czernowitz was Austro-Hungarian territory they didn't even require a transit visa. Only their town magistrate's signature on their identification documents was necessary, and that would be enough to reach the German border where they would have to apply for papers to get them to Belgium.

They had an important document in their possession from the widely known and respected Alliance Israelite Universelle, a very powerful immigrant aid organization headquartered in Paris, which directed them to their transmigration offices in Frankfurt-am-Main. From there they would be helped with the papers to get them through to Antwerp. In effect, this document, recognized at all borders, was proof that they would not be a burden on any country. It served the same purpose as that of the Fusgeyers' Jewish Labor Alliance "proof-of-passage" papers.

At this time, at the height of the exploding "Romanian Exodus," Jewish aid agencies throughout Europe were stretched far beyond their means and "homeless camps" were proliferating in every corner of Romania. As Rabbi

Nachman's sobering letter to Sendehr pointed out, the severity behind the newly enforced tradesman restrictions resulted in thousands of Romanian Jews having no means of livelihood at all. It had happened so suddenly! This poorest of countries had become, in every sense, the land of the living dead. Even though Sendehr kept the latest letter confidential, the Vienna Postal Station had passed out more than a few family letters to the Birlad transients, each confirming the same heartbreaking news of the precipitous events at home. There wasn't a Fusgeyer who was not jolted into a renewed sense of urgency to get to America, and to begin earning money to be able to send for his loved ones as soon as possible.

Four days later—after they passed a restful Sabbath in a picture book glen a few kilometers west of Telc, followed by two days of moderately heavy rainfall—the group entered Sobeslau in much the same fashion followed throughout the journey. It had become an automatic drill familiar to every member of the troop, even though Branko perceptively realized that the Austrian military most definitely knew of their approximate location each day. He clearly remembered that organized groups of ten or more came under the heading of "close surveillance, border to border, without fail."

Whenever Sholem and Yaakov entered each town, hamlet, village or city, the rest of the group began to fill ranks and form up, but wait also for any stragglers. The flags were hoisted from their upright positions in the cart and handed down to the designated bearers-of-the-day. The "Trumpet *Bluzehr*" and the "Drummer Boy" took their instruments out of the cart, and a final signal came from either Mordecai or Branko. At this point, the formation lined up four abreast and marched. The stragglers who didn't make it in time for the march would catch up at some later point. Everyone knew each day approximately where the group would end up that night. No one had lost his or her way yet! All present and accounted for!

Every known epithet, taunt, insult, and cry of "dirty

Jews," "Christ killers" and the like were every bit as common on one hand as the warm terms of endearment coming from the mini-minority Jewish communities on the other. Every day produced its Jew-haters-and-baiters who bristled at the sight of the Star of David. But there was one other salient element to contend with in Czech-country: nationalism. Unbridled, vociferous, and in some locales, violently anti-Hapsburg.

The very same fighter for justice, Masaryk, once a member of the Austrian parliament, professor of philosophy at the university in Prague—or Praha as the nationalists insisted on calling their chief city—was the head of the most effective and uncontrollable nationalist movement in all of the Austro-Hungarian Empire. The broad realm was beginning to buckle under its own weight and he had become the most painful of the many thorns under Franz Josef's fingernails. Independence was a lifelong goal for this spellbinding orator, and the citizens of Bohemia and Moravia gathered daily to march squarely behind him. The mere mention of his name in Vienna brought chills to the family in power...clearly, he was a runaway stallion to be reckoned with.

All this meant that the well-intentioned purchase of an official, Hapsburg-emblematic Austrian flag that Rivka found in a Viennese used-goods shop, to replace the plain red-white-red, would best be put to rest. The Bohemian-Moravian highlands were not the place to show allegiance of any kind to Franz and family. Discretion over valor caused some thinking of the design for a German flag, and Sendehr asked the Berliner rabbi in Znojmo to describe it. Somewhere along the way, Rivka would keep an eye out for the proper material in black, yellow and red. This, of course, would be most necessary in Germany. Flying the host country's flag alongside the *Mogen Dovid* was an act of deference, political correctness and a show of protocol. In reality, it was an attempt to avoid trouble at all cost. Birlad contingents had done the same in the past, and numerous Romanian Fusgeyer groups copied it to a large degree. Tempering *chutzpah!*

Since it was just before noon when the Fusgeyers marched through the hilltop town of Sobeslau/Sobeslav, they stopped for a rest and a midday meal on the far north end, at a signpost that read "Tabor" and "Praha." As soon as the cart pulled up, with Fusgeyers scattered on both sides of the dusty road, the district's Austrian Cavalry trotted in for a visit. Long overdue, but expected...by Branko, at least.

These were some of the Empire's crack troopers, stationed throughout Bohemia to discourage any German attack from the north. Heavily deployed in the region due north of Praha, units were also based strategically in abundance in these highlands where a major stand would have to be made as a last line of defense for the homeland...Austria proper. The century just past saw numerous attempts by the Prussian militarists to gain a foothold in and around Praha, as the vital first step toward ultimate victory over the all-powerful House of Hapsburg.

"Who leads this filthy rabble?" Sholem directed the lead officer, who sat astride the snow white Lippizaner, toward Mordecai. Sholem had guessed right: it was still difficult for the Birladers to understand the high German that the more educated Austrians used. The similarities to Yiddish were far more numerous in the everyday German vernacular...the speech of the common folk.

"I assume you have all of the papers for my inspection." The officer addressed this to both Mordecai and Branko, who now stood together before him. Branko stepped forward as the plan dictated.

"Yes, my Captain, we have everything in order for your approval, sir!" Branko's usual snappy salute followed, but this time it failed. The saddle-sitting officer did not return it like many of the others had since the Borsha incident with Captain Sandor.

Mordecai handed up the packet of "proof" papers to the captain, who dutifully thumbed through them, and while looking directly at Branko and Mordecai with a twisted grin, proceeded to tear up the transit visa, letting the shreds flutter to the ground.

"I have just canceled your transit visa. As of yesterday, we no longer recognize such documents that are signed by the Hungarian army's officer corps."

Shaken, the usually cool Branko could only sputter. "B-b-but, sir, it does not expire until midnight on the 22nd of this month. It was accepted by the Vienna entry guards."

"You did not hear what I said, Jew. Transit visas signed by the Hungarians are no longer valid. They are worthless."

"How, then, do we get to the German border without that document, may I ask, most respectfully, your honor?"

By now, the tension had rippled through most of the Fusgeyers. Those who had seen the ugly act relayed it to those who had heard and even partially understood the brief conversation. The Czernowitz pair held fast, moderately secure that their documents were in acceptable order should they be singled out. In reality this was highly unlikely since the Austrians didn't bother at this juncture to count heads. The few stragglers who had not yet arrived and those already engaged in setting up camp would hear the unsettling news soon enough. Menachem Berman, Nuchim, Sendehr and Zed-Zed all crowded around their leader waiting for the answer to Branko's question.

"I would say, former Sergeant Horvitch, is it, then?... Yes, well, you must now depend on the goodness of my heart. And when it comes to stinking Jews, or thieving gypsies, or Czech rebel scum, there is very little goodness left. At this moment, you are traveling within my Emperor's domain illegally."

Obviously, the Captain had seen Branko's personal army papers, which he had slipped into the packet after the border crossing at Borsha: to no avail—yet. Time to use that to full advantage, although this horseman seemed a nasty, immovable object.

"As you have seen, my honorable superior, I have served the Emperor well, and..."

"Spare me. You may have been a soldier once, but you've

become nothing but a Jew without a country...at my mercy, I might add," interrupted the adversarial Austrian sharply.

"Y'know, Herr Horvitch, all I see around me are young Christ-killers who would make a valuable addition to the work gangs of convict road builders that we have placed between here and the' outposts of Kaiser Willi's *schweinhunds*."

"Sir, we are on our way out of Europe. We are Jews you will never have to cope with again. Romania was more than happy to get rid of us. Russia, Congress Poland? Same story. All anybody wants to do is to ship out their Jews. That's why you see so many of us going through your country by every mode of transportation. Some by wagon, others by train. We, sir, are walkers, mere wayfarers. It takes us a little longer, but we're going. We're leaving. Yes, sir, we are leaving. We just ask for enough time to reach the border."

"And I suppose you are willing to pay a head fee to do so?"

"I don't understand, sir?"

"You know perfectly well what I mean! These 'fees' bought you many a schooner of beer. I'll give you a temporary permit to reach the border at a fee of, let's say, three Austrian shillings for each Jewish lice-filled head. I would say that's more than fair, don't you agree, former Sergeant Horvitch?" He once again slowly drew out the word former... "And; oh, yes, that loaded wagon you have over there will be another ten. Let's make it an even two hundred for simplicity's sake...and let's make it quick. I'm losing the patience I never had."

Branko huddled with the cadre and Mordecai in a hastily called meeting, punctuated by Nuchim's '*oy, vay iz mir!*' Compared to the pittances paid in graft to some of the local militia in Hungary, or the gross overpayment made to the river crossing raftsmen-*banditten* in the Hortobagy, this was a monumental sum. It hurt...badly...a knife to the heart of what had the promise of being a financial surplus beyond even the most optimistic thinking. If any one had an alternative, it was left unsaid.

Nuchim had the two hundred on his person, while the major portion of the very substantial "bank" had been divided among some of the cadre and a few others in the troop. This was the security decoy measure Nuchim had devised at the outset. Under a most mild protest, with a shrug of his shoulders, he gave the shillings to Branko.

Before handing the money over to the enemy, Branko asked, with an innocent tone in his voice, "The permit, sir. How many days does it signify?"

"I have it here in my hands. It's a form already signed by the Chancellor-in-Charge of Security and I will now fill in the dates that will allow you exactly ten days to leave the Empire. June 18th according to my calculations. But, I warn all of you, as I said before, there are many roads to build and defense structures to be shored-up. I shall not hesitate to have you arrested on sight, one minute after noon on that day if you are anywhere this side of the border postings. We'll put you all to work so you can forget about your Amer-i-kah, Amer-i-kah for a good long time. Now give it to me!"

Shielding themselves from the clouds of dust that the galloping horsemen kicked up, knowing that this bribery was no more than a sham that would buy a night of revelry for the officer and his henchmen, there was no time to wallow in self-pity. Mordecai was well aware that he had to do everything possible to resurrect any breech in morale that may have resulted from this insulting assault. Standing on a large outcropping, he began the repair work.

"Gather 'round, please. Everyone. As some of you already know, we have been granted a ten-day permit, a temporary group visa, to travel through the remainder of Hapsburg territory. The threats that Captain *Paskudnyak* handed down are just that. Threats. There is no reason why we can't be deep into Germany before the 18th of this month, still having time to spend this Sabbath in Prague. Am I correct, ' Father Time'?" With this, Zed-Zed mounted the protruding tor.

"Yes, Mordecai. Even with one whole day in Prague, Sendehr and I had us arriving in Dresden by the 18th on the original schedule. From Prague to the border it is merely one hundred kilometers of slowly rising terrain. To add a more comfortable cushion, with the days getting longer we may yet decide to add a few hours of additional walking for a day or two."

This calculation gave the leader an opportunity to lighten up the dark day a bit.

"For those of you, and you know who you are, who *fressed un fressed* on those cheesecakes in Znojmo, your pants will soon fit again! Perhaps we should do a few extra hours walking every day, Zed-Zed. We need more of this outdoor exercise! Good for the fat *tuchus!*"

The hearty laughter and good-natured finger pointing that followed proved to be the best medicine Mordecai could administer. He judiciously decided to drop it right there. There was a good deal of ground to cover before nightfall.

§

Berel Usher had evidently planned the Tuesday afternoon tea for sometime. It was not at all just a spontaneous invitation that he had issued to Nathan that previous Sunday evening. In fact, should the truth be known, when Rabbi Nachman mentioned Nathan's pending arrival a month back, Berel had already set the date aside. In attendance were more than half of the Yidden of Birlad, anxious to meet the American family. *From Beverly Hills yet! Ay-yi-yi!*

Nathan was very happy that Herb and Rico arrived back in Birlad early enough so that they could join him for the festivities at the Usher home. It would have appeared a bit awkward had they not done so. Herb was red as a beet from exposure to the penetrating Black Sea sun, and Rico, dark to begin with, had added a few extra layers of deep tan. Both had freshened up, discarded the beach bum look and changed to slacks and sport shirts. The Friedman boys, all three of them, represented the United States of America in fine fashion. Good thing. The Birladers were all wearing their *yomtovdickeh* best. This, without a doubt, was a highlight event for each of them, including the dapper eighty-eight year old Rabbi with his Armani blue and red tie...a Chanukah gift from one of his children.

Dvorah Usher, a handsome lady of charm and good taste, simply out-did herself. Freshly-baked *savarinas* warmed plates in every corner of the compact living room. A beautiful silver tea setting, coffee urns and trays of pastry varieties, cut up fruits, chocolate candies and more punctuated the festive ambience.

Berel did all of the introductions and nearly all had something to say about the Fusgeyer tradition. Most spoke Yiddish, although a few seemed more comfortable with Romanian, and for these folks Berel served as a most competent translator.

"So, Reb Friedman, I had two great-uncles who were with your father in 1904. My grandfather used to show me their letters from America. He, himself, emigrated to 'Chi-caw-gah' in 1927 to be with two of his sons and their families. My father was the only one who didn't go. I often wished that he had. I'd be speaking your English now. Heh. Heh." This from an octogenarian named Iancu Levin who had long ago retired from his civil servant job in the Birlad prefecture office.

The conversations, language barriers falling down all over the room, emanated from everyone present. The Friedmans were center stage and loving it. Nathan couldn't help thinking how Rachel would enjoy this remarkable gathering, and he would certainly give her a full description when he made his nightly phone call later that evening.

Just a random conversation sampling:

"I watch your 'Kojak' every week. Some policeman he is. Better to watch than that *Moishe Kapoyr* 'Colombo'. He

gives me a headache with his new *mishigus* for every crime."
This was addressed to Rico and Herb, both of whom
launched into 'pidgin Yinglish' to comment on the great
amount of America's finest re-runs that clogged up Romanian TV. The man and his wife, obviously big fans of these
ancient products, proudly announced their all-time favorites: "Gunsmoke" and "Gilligan's Island".

"So how do you like our Birlad, Reb Friedman? A little
different now than it was during your father's time. My
grandfather, Shmulkeh Cohen, must've known him."

"Ceausescu wasn't that bad. He was mostly good, for
us Yidden at least. I think he was afraid of us. Why? Don't
ask."

"In Birlad, we were most fortunate. The Rabbi's father
watched out for us during the war. Not one person was
deported to Trans-dniestria. Thank God. Before they could
get rid of us, the Red Army was pushing the Nazi *mumzerim*
back to Berlin."

"Yes, Rabbi Nachman is quite right. Moishe Rosen
single-handedly gave dignity to all of the remaining Jews of
Romania. Without him, who knows what would have happened these last fifty years."

"Israel? My children, too, are there. What would I do
there? This is my home. I was born here, on the next street.
There is now a petrol station where the house was. And I
will die here and be buried in the cemetery on the hill as
you cross the bridge. My sons can come from Tel Aviv and
say *kaddish* over me...and if not, how will I know?"

"So my sister and her family live in 'Tookson'...in a
desert. Nothing but sunshine, she writes. Come to 'Azeronah'
she says, and you'll live another fifty years. Who needs it?
I've got to have snow in my backyard every winter. The shoveling keeps me young."

"Tell me about your drive to the north and the west,
Reb Friedman. I have been to Sighet. I was invited to join
Berel and Rabbi Nachman when Elie Wiesel visited one
time. Rabbi Rosen had asked rabbis from all over Romania
to be present when they dedicated the little museum in

the house where Wiesel was born. Some man! A speaker? *Ay,yi,yi!* The greatest."

"It's quite sad on the Sabbath and other holidays when maybe only thirty people are present. At other times we barely make a *minyan.* At one time, before the war, there were *shtieblach* all over town, too. Now, ten, twenty, maybe thirty voices pray and sing in a *shul* that used to fill to capacity when I was a child. Sad. Very sad...but, *nu, a zay geht dos.*"

"Such a handsome boy, your *aynekel.* Reb Friedman, listen, I have a granddaughter in Tiberias his age. *Nu,* maybe a *shiddach?*

"Berel, did you tell Reb Friedman that some other Americans were here a few years ago? From Maryland. The Margolises, Rita and Sol, if I recall. His grandfather Shlomoh was the Fusgeyer leader in 1901. Imagine! Lovely people."

"Why don't we leave for *Eretz Yisroel?* For America? Not so simple, my dear man. To uproot a man and his woman at our ages is *narishkayt.* Besides, don't cry over us. Romania today is not the terrible Romania of your grandfather's day. My wife and I have very comfortable pensions, government health programs, plenty of good doctors and hospitals...and we still have our *shul* with our Yossi Nachman."

The word-flow did not begin to wane until seven, when people started to leave after saying their good-byes and hugging Nathan and the boys with a familial love that had an unbroken chain of nearly six millennia of familiarity and warmth to it. Nathan felt as though he was embracing the children and grandchildren of his father's friends in the old Birlad of 1904...and that was the reality of it. Tears? What would be the purpose of such a satisfying evening without any? Where there were Yidden talking of the old days, it seems there would have to be a river of salty tears.

"Well, Nathan, I probably won't be seeing you before you leave on Friday. Yossi tells me that you're taking him to Bucureshti, so I'll be conducting Sabbath services this week. If he doesn't be more careful I'll take his job away. Don't breathe a word of this to him, but I still have trouble reading directly from the Torah." Berel Usher whispered the last remark, but just loud enough for the Rabbi to hear.

"Don't worry, Bereleh. I know. That's why I always have Iancu looking over your shoulder, so he can prompt you a little. And IF I had a contract for you to rip up, you would be doing me the biggest favor of my life, dear man."

With these parting laughs and the Californians' final thanks to the Ushers for such a memorable afternoon and evening, they walked down the street merrily toward the *shul* to escort Rabbi Nachman to his door. No need to drive the rental car this short way.

"Rabbi, I can't begin to tell you how we enjoyed this. Here we are talking all this time about the Fusgeyers, Birlad at the turn of the century, and now this gathering. It was, to me, like a certain closure. A completion of the circle. Birlad, 1904...Birlad, 2000."

"I agree, Naftali. Now I think you can also understand my reluctance to leave Romania. I just couldn't do that to these dear *menschen*. They all need me, and even more so, I need them." Nathan nodded comprehending the Rabbi's point more so now than he had been able to ascertain before. Yossi Nachman, grinning warmly, put his arms around the three *Amerikaners*. "Tomorrow, Naftali, tomorrow. I still have to get our Fusgeyers to Prague. To Berlin. To Bremerhaven. We have a lot of ground to cover!"

§

My dear Rabbi,

As you will see in my synopsis for this week, so much has happened. Mostly good. Some not so good. We'll be marching into Prague tomorrow around noon. Praha, they call it. We are under a bit of pressure now with only limited time to leave the Austro-Hungarian Empire, per order of one of their insufferable officers. I'm even sorry to hear that our old Captain Polinou has been ousted. By comparison to some of these banditten, *he is a princely* mensch. *Tell this to Reb Mandelbaum. He'll enjoy hearing it.*

Yesterday, we were walking through the unfenced grounds of Franz Ferdinand's Konopiste Castle, and we were stunned when one of the caretakers invited us to tour the beautiful old buildings. He said that the Jewish flag, as he called it, reminded him that his hero, Tomasha Masaryk, insisted that the Jews were Children of God and should be treated as such. I was praying that Itzy and Mayer wouldn't say something stupid in reaction to that statement. They didn't, thank God.

It seems that the Archduke and his family were taking the cures at the Karlsbad spa, and the place was empty. Although we have passed by and seen many such castles and palaces since leaving Birlad, this was the first time we have seen an interior. Breathtaking, to say the very least. The girls kept sighing every time they touched a drape, a tapestry, the linen, the porcelain, the vases. Animal-head hunting trophies everywhere. I think we could have fit the entire town of Birlad into it and have plenty of room to spare. Huge. I will write all of the details about this Masaryk in my synopsis, as I've already mentioned him a few times in the journal.

Quite unique after the constant hostility we have endured from the Hungarian and Austrian military...and others, I might add...townspeople, traveling merchants, farmers, tavern-keepers, shopkeepers and the like. It's something we have come to expect and always have, so when you hear of a Masaryk and then receive such a welcome from a caretaker, it's extraordinarily refreshing. If we think it will be much friendlier in America, perhaps our expectations are too unrealistic. I try not to think too much about it.

Perhaps Herzl is right. As you know, he is completely convinced that the only place where we can be free is in a state of our own. What is your opinion, Rabbi? You have the synopsis covering our Herzl meeting. When you and Mendel and I had those quiet sessions in your office you seemed to agree that America should be our destination; not once did you suggest Palestine. No, I'm not wavering, nor is anyone else, since the trio left to Argentina. Our single-minded will is as strong as ever, but we all think about these burning questions often.

I have not mentioned your letter, which I retrieved at the Vienna Postal Office nearly two weeks ago, to anyone...but they all know about the new restrictions through the letters some have received from home, and from the occasional Yiddishe Romanians we've passed on the road. It's hardly news any more. We're all deeply concerned for our families. I go to sleep worrying about it every night.

Is it possible that by the time we arrive in Berlin, Nordau's articles may have been printed around Europe? Maybe even America? It may be too much to hope for, but the resulting pressure could possibly affect an end to the tradesmen restrictions. We have heard that the Russians are having so many military problems with Japan, especially along their Pacific Coast, that the Pale has been relatively quiet this spring. No Easter pogroms. We are all hoping that this is true. Do you know?

Mendel's English lessons have considerably more meaning to all of us as each day goes by. I can read and pronounce quite well now, but understanding is another story. I sometimes wonder whether I will ever

*be able to write coherently in English. Rivka's
encouragement is my strength. She is fond of saying that
anything I strive for I will achieve. I'm beginning to believe
it, Rabbi. We kiss on the lips most every night. I feel I can
tell you this. We do nothing much more than that. But
that's all that happens. Please believe me, that's all. Oy,
vay iz mir! It's very difficult, Rabbi, very difficult.
Entshuldig mir for being so open, but being very close to
marriage yourself you must surely understand what I
mean.*

    *As always, please keep this letter confidential
between us. Thank you. Yaakov continues to be a most
valuable member of our contingent. He and Sholem,
always in the "front lines" for us.*

    *My best regards to everyone in Birlad. A special
greeting to my dear family.*

> *I am, yours truly,*
> *Sendehr Efraim,*
> *en route Praha, encamped about twenty kilometers
>   southeast.*
> *June 10, 1904 (7 Sivan, 5664)*

Note: I pledge allegiance to the flag of the United
States of America and to the Republic for which it
stands. One nation, with liberty and justice for all.

*I know you don't read very much English, but try
pronouncing the words. You should hear it when we all
recite together!* Oy vay! *Still a lot of hard travel ahead
and an ocean to cross, but already we're Americans!*
Lang leben *America!* Lang leben *President Theedoh
Rosenvelt!*

15

ENCOUNTERS: PRAGUE

Prague won't let go...this mother has claws.
Franz Kafka

The moon has told me no city is as beautiful as Prague.
Jan Neruda

Entering the outlying districts of Prague on what was by far the warmest day of the journey, Sholem and Yaakov were dressed lightly. These two and the others had begun to discard most of their heavy clothing, favoring just shirts, blouses and cotton singlets for the summer months. The accepted practice was to leave excess clothing somewhere, or carry it in one's bedroll or knapsack, but not to clog up the already overloaded cart with it. The prevailing positive attitude was... *I'll have a job and be able to afford some new heavy clothing in America in plenty of time for winter!*

Many a peasant left behind in their wake now sported a jacket, a sweater, a padded jerkin, a duster, itchy woolen britches or skirt as a souvenir of this great trek. The poorer looking the farmstead or rural cottage, the more likely that its residents would be the beneficiaries of discarded Fusgeyer outerwear. Some of the Jewish indigents in Vienna were also fortunate recipients, while most of the fellow Jews they met in Znojmo, Telc, Sobeslav and Tabor did not appear to be in need of this kind of help.

The first glimpses of this ancient, medieval-looking city enthralled Sholem and Yaakov.. They entered the city from the south because a washed out bridge near the east entrance prohibited them from going in straightaway. The spring floods seemed to have swollen the broad Moldau/Vltava beyond its limits, causing it to spill over its banks leading to some of its narrow tributaries and resulting in heavy damages throughout Central Bohemia. Sendehr had already told them not to cross any of the bridges over the Vltava until they reached the Karluv Most, the Charles Bridge, and so Sholem and Yaakov quick-stepped along its west bank. As soon as the others had caught up to them at the bridge the entire contingent would march across it into Stare Mesto (Old Town), then on into the very old ghetto, Jewish Town, Josefov. At this pace, they would arrive before noon at the Labor Alliance office in the Jewish Town Hall where two nights lodgings would be made available. These preparations had been prearranged in the correspondence between Mordecai and the Alliance. Their office in Vienna had arranged the comfortable seminary stay and had written about similar lodgings in Prague.

As the point team waited for the main body at the entrance to the Charles Bridge, two ancient towers guarded the way. The smaller one, named for the eighth-century Queen Judith of Bohemia, was open, and Yaakov ran up the circular staircase just in time to view the rest of the Fusgeyers coming up the river road. He greeted them with shouts and waves from the turrets of the popularly named Judith Tower. Sholem waited below for the form-up to begin before he and Yaakov could half-sprint over the pedestrian-filled bridge to wait in the Stare Mesto square.

As usual, the citizens were taken aback by the Fusgeyer parade. Only a few recognized the *Mogen Dovid* and none had any idea who these young, highly spirited, tanned people were or where they had come from. Velvel Palastrant had learned an uplifting, lilting Bohemian folk tune at a public band concert in Tabor, and played it sweetly on his trumpet as they were marching, much to the delight of the spectators on the bridge who sang the Czech words while clapping in time with the music.

Statues on both sides of the bridge represented everything from mythical kings and queens to the most shocking one of all: Jesus Christ on the cross in the middle of the span. However, it was not the sight of the bronzed Jesus figure that stopped the Fusgeyers in their tracks, but the gold-leafed Hebrew letters hanging across his chest:

KADOSH KADOSH KADOSH ADONAI TZVAOS
(Holy, Holy, Holy is the Lord of Hosts)

The words came from a prayer that even the least observant knew by heart, as it was uttered twice daily. Gathered around the statue, gawking, the group began to break up after Mordecai ordered everyone to disperse lest they cause a pedestrian traffic jam of mammoth proportions. In the meantime, Sendehr knelt down to read the plaque attached to the base of the statue, and here the story unfolded in all of its drama. Written in three languages—Czech, Latin and German—Branko knelt beside Sendehr to translate as Zed-Zed led everyone toward the far end of the bridge in order to eliminate the growing congestion.

"From what I can tell, nearly three hundred years ago—1609 it says here—one of our *Yiddlach* desecrated this statue in some way. As a collective punishment, the ghetto community had to pay to affix the *Kadosh* letters, and in gold, no less. A bit tarnished, I'd say, but a very expensive necklace adorns their savior's chest, indeed."

Walking to join the others, Sendehr remarked, "I just wonder how many lives were lost along with the payment, Branko."

Once they, too, had heard the story, the point team walked ahead to carry out their usual daily assignment.

"What kind of city is this Praha? *Yaisele* with *Kadosh* draped on his crucified body? What are we stepping into, Yak?" Sholem asked his equally puzzled comrade.

"I'm thinking, regardless of the words on the plaque,

that maybe it's a warning of some sort."

"No, I don't think anyone would go to such lengths. After all, the letters are actually part of the statue itself. Simply a three-hundred-year-old incident, I'd say."

"Naive. Naive, dear old friend. Remember Father Michai's brother, the artist? Stefan Coliescu? A real *mumzer!* All he ever did was paint those horrible crucifixion paintings, showing *unsereh Yidden* dancing around the dying body with grotesque smiles on their faces. If there's one Coliescu, there must be thousands all over Europe. Sculptors, too. Nineteen centuries and they can't even begin to forget or admit the real circumstances behind *Yaisele* on the cross. *Gevalt. Gevalt.*"

"Yak, you know as well as I do that emotions running so deep are not easily tempered. Rabbi Holtzer used to say that only education of the masses would someday bring an end to anti-Semitism, pogroms, boycotts and the whole miserable mess."

"*Alivai, alivai un omayn. Zwei mahl omayn!*"

"*Omayn. Omayn.*"

All the while during this conversation, Sholem had been looking out for the Stare Mesto square, and all of a sudden they were right in the middle of it. The garish pink of the baroque city hall, with its intricate mechanical clock taking up half the structure, was arguably the most colorful structure they had come across. The noonday crowds had thinned out, and now only the more affluent sat in the numerous outdoor cafes lining the cobblestone square. The instructions were to turn left and find Parizska Street, which would lead them to Jewish Town. Just beyond the cathedral stretched a lovely modern street with clean, broad sidewalks and handsome, attached structures...and then the awful din began.

The incessant clamor of large-scale construction work, smoke-filled air, and whirling, swirling dust pockets engulfed the senses of the two unsuspecting wayfarers. In front of them, metal and wooden fences blocked the street, large painted arrows pointed the way to a detour of sorts, and the confused point team came to a standstill. Without saying as much since communication was nearly impossible in the racket, they decided to wait at these haphazardly set barricades until Mordecai and some of the cadre arrived.

"*Nu*, what is this *balagan* all about?" Zed-Zed asked loudly.

"Maybe Yak and I should sneak through that opening in the fence and ask someone."

"Do it, Sholem. I'll join you two," Branko added, no doubt with Mordecai's nodded approval. As usual, his knowledge of German would be invaluable, especially here where it was heard as frequently as Czech was spoken.

What they encountered beyond the fence was demolition beyond anything they had ever seen. Buildings had been flattened. Wagons were loading up enormous amounts of debris and carrying it off to who-knows-where. Heavily sweating workmen by the hundreds wielded pickaxes and shovels and even air drills which Yaakov and Sholem had never seen before, but which were nothing new to Branko who had supervised prisoner road building gangs during his army career.

It appeared to the trio that seven or eight long city blocks were being demolished, and they could not see any new construction anywhere within this scene. At quick glance it seemed that only five or possibly six buildings remained standing. Branko spotted a man in uniform, presumably a local policeman, and approached him. Obviously the entire area was out-of-bounds for pedestrian, wagon or motor car traffic, and the wild gestures of the man armed with a long-barreled pistol clearly indicated that he was very unhappy with this blatant incursion.

"We're demolishing this old rat-trap of a Jew-ghetto," the gaudily uniformed one announced. "All that will be standing by next week will be that town hall of theirs over there, the old synagogue across the street from it, and a few other buildings leading to that forest of old broken stones they call a cemetery. Now, if you intend to visit that town hall, as you asked, you'll have to go round by way of Siroka and Bilkova Streets." He pointed the direction and walked away so there could be no further questions.

Branko didn't have to repeat anything to Sholem and Yaakov. They had gotten the gist, and now they picked their way back to the others Mordecai, however, wondered why the Vienna Alliance office mentioned nothing about this colossal upheaval, although it mattered little in the scheme of things for his Fusgeyers. By Sunday morning they would be on their way once again.

The short detour put them directly at the entrance to the Josefov Town Hall in Praha's venerable Jewish Town, a name given to the compact ghetto centuries before. The three-story building, painted in pink like its counterpart in the Stare Mesto square, offered a most unique clock with Hebrew letters on its face, which drew the gaping stares of the Birladers. The entire Alliance staff, standing in front of the entrance greeted them. Their chief officer, Herschel Schwartzmann, apologized for the noise and was quick to explain that everything happening was for the ultimate benefit of Praha's Jewish population. Evidently, the town fathers felt that such action was long overdue, and the former dwellers of what was described as substandard hovels in every respect were being absorbed comfortably in other Jewish districts of the city. This massive urban renewal project, which would grow nearly into a total rebuilding of the entire city, had begun in 1896 and would eventually benefit all citizens, according to Schwartzmann. In the meantime, as he cheerfully pointed out, progress meant inconvenience and certain annoyances, but so be it. He repeated that in the long run, it was *sehr gut fur di Yidden!*

"As for the buildings still standing—this town hall; the *Alte-Neue* shul next door, which is the oldest still in use in all the world—since 1270—except for a few periods of expulsion; the Pinkas *shul* next to the ancient cemetery; and the Klausen *shul*, the city has assured us that they have set aside funds to renovate where the city deems it is necessary to do so. We find it hard to believe that we are to be the recipients of such a magnanimous gesture, but I must tell you, Jewish life here has never been more peaceful, thank God." With these informative remarks the Alliance chief bade everyone enter.

The quarters on the third floor of the building were more than adequate, with two fully equipped bathrooms and cots for thirty. The others, of course, would make do with their bedrolls on the floor. In fact, Schwartzmann showed them the stairway to the roof, an access point to a night's sleep under the stars for those who chose to do so. Best of all, he invited them to partake of the *Shabbos* dinner being prepared in the community kitchen in the basement of the building. This, he told them, was a necessary service for the many in transition who awaited new lodgings in other parts of the city. Having had a letter from the Vienna office, Schwartzmann had correctly estimated their arrival and arranged an earlier private sitting for the guests from Romania.

They also learned that three nights before, eighty Romanian Fusgeyers from Bacau who had come by way of Czernowitz, Tarnow, and Brno had used these quarters. The Birladers remembered hearing of this larger contingent that had left three weeks before them when they themselves had traveled through Bacau. Evidently, the other group had since run into some difficulties that slowed them down considerably. Hearing this news, Mendel Paretsky spoke of his cousin Duvid Pascal, and his cousin's brother-in-law, Berel Eisenfeld, both of whom had been with the 1903 Bacau Fusgeyers, who wrote from Canada that it had taken them nearly six months to reach Hamburg. Pascal and Eisenfeld had recorded every conceivable type of minor and not-so-minor catastrophe that had befallen that particular Bacau group. Zed-Zed noted to himself that all things considered, they were doing just fine so far, and better yet, they were right on schedule! He muttered a near silent prayer on the spot. Observing this, Mendel and Mordecai did the same. It couldn't hurt.

By early that Friday afternoon, since the sun would be

late in setting, nearly everyone was out exploring medieval, intriguing Praha. They found it to be every bit as up-to-date as Budapest and Vienna, with all the attractions that the Birladers had enjoyed in the latter two—nickelodeons peppered throughout Wenceslas Square, trams everywhere, a rash of those pesky motor cars sputtering up and down each street, the latest fashions from Paris sashaying along those same streets, and even two very small kosher cafes that offered barely edible dumplings, dubbed "cannonballs" by those who sampled them. A few groups went back to the Charles Bridge to stroll from end to end and back again, looking over the paintings of a few starving artists and listening to the "buskers," the itinerant musicians found in every town and city in this part of Europe, as they went.

Sholem and Yaakov, egged on by some of the younger wayfarers, put on a two man race, from one end of the bridge to the other and back. Very few pedestrians were walking at the time, late afternoon, although the cheers could have been heard back in Stare Mesto. Knowing that they would probably do some running before the day was out, Yaakov had worn his trusty "racers," worn to a wafer thin sole by now. Sholem , as usual, whipped off his heavy socks and his sturdy Budapest walkers, and proceeded, barefoot, of course, to outdistance his frustrated foil once again. Wiry Avigdor Semelweiss, one of the fourteen-year-olds, was foolish enough to challenge Sholem, and instead Yaakov handily outraced him, as sort of a consolation prize. Sholem's grin could have cracked a window somewhere in Praha.

Rivka insisted that the beautiful blue and yellow parasol was far too expensive for Sendehr to buy from the vendor on the bridge. He paid no heed. She loved it.

"It will protect your beautiful skin from the American sun, Rivkeleh."

"Why? Is the sun in America stronger than here or in Birlad, love?"

"You're dark enough where the sun wouldn't splotch your face anyway. I just wanted you to have it as sort of a m-m-memento…of Praha…and, er, uh, m-m-me." The suddenly shy master of the written word couldn't look her in the eye as he stuttered.

"But, Sendehrel, you shouldn't be spending what few crowns you have. We still have a long way to go…"

"Yes, yes, Rivka *zeesa*, but remember, the streets are lined with gold in America…"

"A *bubbeh meiseh*, and you know it!"

Arm-in-arm they strolled down the bridge and decided to walk up the hill to the imposing Hradcany Castle, which overlooked the raging Vltava. The sun was not due to set for at least another two hours. Ahead, they spotted Esther and Mendel, who strode up the steeply inclined cobblestone lane toward the castle with Chaike, Tsippy, Maidele and the good Doctor Hippocrates.

"Shall we catch up with them?"

Pausing as if to answer, Sendehr smiled instead, and with a wink of the eye, slowly shook his head. Togetherness was an everyday necessity with the wayfarers. There was a time for camaraderie, for solidarity, to be with the others, but this wasn't it.

Closing the bright parasol, Rivka squeezed his arm just a bit tighter, and winked back, brushing her long black tresses against his shoulder…bathing Sendehr's heart in the warmth of so subtle a gesture.

After a simple but filling *shabbosdickeh* meal, those who opted to attend the ancient *Alte-Neue shul* across the alleyway found standing room only. The phenomenon of a rabbi in his ninety-second year, standing at the helm of the thirteenth-century *shul*, drew people from all over the city, even for the short *erev Shabbos* service. Add this to the rumor that Rabbi Moshe Blankfort had periodic clandestine visits from the famed Praha Golem, and even numerous *goyim* were tempted to attend. Maybe some did, at that. The very thought that this gentle man in the last stage of his eventful life knew something about the Golem that was beyond the thousands of words written on the mystical subject had intrigued Sendehr from the moment one of the kitchen staff mentioned it at dinner.

Rivka knew then and there that her leading man would be seeking out a meeting with the Rabbi at sometime during the next twenty-four hours. She was somewhat relieved, then, that she had decided to forego any performance of *Vinshfingerl* for Saturday evening. With sunset coming much later now, and a very early departure set for Sunday morning, she had made that decision earlier in the week.

Nuchim Krasnigor, the always thinking "Chancellor of the Exchequer," considered that the funds normally expected from the performances, based on those already presented, and realized that they could possibly be matched, maybe surpassed, if a Fusgeyer comrade would speak at each of five synagogues on *Shabbos* morning. Mordecai, Sendehr, Zed-Zed, Mendel, Menachem Berman, Branko, or even Simmy, if he could be trusted to keep a civil tongue could handle these brief fund-raising speeches. The two clowns, Itzy and Mayer, though? Forget it! Approaching Herschel Schwartzmann with the request, Nuchim announced simply that he and four others would do the honors. Rivka would have been outstanding with all of her stage presence, but a woman on the *bimah* would have been considered heresy of the highest magnitude.

The amiable Alliance chief agreed to visit each *shul* that evening to arrange the brief guest presentation for the next morning. He saw no reason why the request would be denied. All Czech Jews were reasonably fluent in a version of Germanic Yiddish so language would not be a major hurdle here. More importantly, with the increasing influence and affluence of the Czech Jew, a minor windfall was possible. Since the most observant congregants would not be carrying cash on their persons during the Sabbath, pledges were to be made aloud in *shul*, but the hard money would be brought to the town hall office after sundown. How this stand-up-and-pledge method cut down on any Sabbath reneging at synagogues throughout the world, Praha included, was an amazing phenomenon.

After the Austrian *paskudnyak* tore up the original transit pass and then robbed them, Nuchim began to look for ways to erase the deficit. Not that the two-hundred shilling fine broke the "bank," but it had made a significant dent. As a matter of fact, the musical show they had staged in Tabor, along with some local donations, brought in twice that amount. Velvel Palastrant and his ever-improving angelic trumpet, the lively accordion accompaniment to the "cantors" and to the folk singing of Rivka and her cast, more than pleased the Tabor townspeople who had been quick to join in the melodic fun.

The robbery had little or no affect on the food supply. Simmy kept the Birladers better fed than any group of trekkers anywhere. The annoyingly aggressive, coarse-speaking youngster had sheer *chutzpah.* As the comic duo often proclaimed, Simmy could convince a starving man to part with his last piece of bread...and no one was altogether sure that he hadn't done this from time to time. God forbid! The overriding question was, "Is America ready for Simmy Fiedleman?" That Sabbath evening, after dinner, Simmy was hard at work with his high-powered *shnorring.* The cart would be full again on Sunday, as always.

The storage of the cart and its invaluable stores were a problem for the wayfarers while they stayed over in Praha. Schwartzmann pointed out that prowlers were all over the citywide destruction/construction sites. It was not at all safe to leave the cart unmanned anywhere, but none of the building's doorways could accommodate it, either, so Branko had to post Fusgeyer guards throughout the stay...armed, it should be noted, with weapons secreted, of course. Mordecai would have it no other way, and it was assumed that "good soldier" Branko almost always followed these standing orders. The Golub trio? Doubtful. Highly doubtful!

At the *Alte-Neue shul,* Rabbi Blankfort, whose voice had become noticeably weaker since Pesach, according to his regulars, nevertheless welcomed the sizeable group of Fusgeyers in attendance warmly. He also spoke endearingly of a few similarly minded groups that had passed through Praha since the turn of the century. Of all the rabbis that the Birladers had encountered, Rabbi Blankfort appeared to be the most genuinely in favor of such missions. Only their own spiritual leader's support equaled his encouragement. Otherwise, there hadbeen a hint of reticence in the voices of the host clergy throughout the journey, thus far. Good men, they thought no doubt, but still of the *'sha! shtill! macht nisht kein tumul !'* school of Yiddish thought. Their messages seemed to translate into "stay, hope for the best and things will get better...someday...maybe... please, God!"

Rabbi Blankfort was not usually one who would speak on *erev Shabbos,* saving his labored remarks for the next day's sermon. But on this Friday evening, at the appropriate time between *aleinu* and the mourner's *kaddish,* the bent over, little man straightened up more than anyone could remember. The voice was stronger than it had been at anytime in recent memory. The usually half closed eyes were now wide open, hands holding firmly upon the sides of the lectern, and except for a slight, uncontrollable shaking of his right arm a great strength seemed to possess him. He paused for a full minute, swaying from side to side, raising the anxiety of all present until finally the high pitched words issued forth:

"Again it came to me. This very morning. Again it spoke to me through the voice of the Maharal, in the clearest language, of terrible things to come. Tomorrow I will tell you of these. *Guten Shabbos!*"

His watery blue eyes shed a stream of tears as he slumped back down into his plush, red upholstered highback chair, while the cantor quickly went on to lead the mourner's *kaddish.* The stunned worshippers trained their eyes on the *tallis*-wrapped Rabbi as they, in unison, mouthed the words *yisgadal, vyiskadash shmay rabah...*

Total silence followed the *kaddish.* The cantor, shaken by the Rabbi's brief, but resounding words, stooped over to see if the weakened man needed assistance in leaving the *bimah.* The regular worshippers, bolstered by thirty or so

Fusgeyers and a goodly number of other assorted guests, quietly filed out of the sanctuary, waiting until they reached the street before exploding in animated conversation. A puzzled, wrinkle-browed Sendehr, for one, was anxious to listen. Rivka had already heard some buzzing from the women who had sat with her in the warm and overly crowded female "annex," as they exited, through the main sanctuary. Along with Esther and Chaike they listened intently, as the mystery began to build for *Shabbos* morning. *What had Rabbi Blankfort meant?*

"This time *der alte iz farfallen,* he is ready to step down. The Golem! Did you hear? The Golem again. And this time with the Maharal's voice? Imagine!" This sputtering comment from one of the male congregants seemed to set the tone for the sidewalk tribunal which all but placed the venerable spiritual leader into terminal retirement, isolation, or out to pasture. When a rabbi his age persisted on visits from a fabled past, what is a congregation to do? This was the third time in the past month that he eagerly told of nocturnal, as well as broad daylight visits, from the supernatural, each time with a message that made no sense even to the most learned. The Biblical scholars. The talmudists. Not even the kabbalists. No one could even begin to interpret the old man's angst. Severe dementia had struck. Senility in its most potent form had engulfed the dear man. This brilliant analyst...this renowned scholar...this gentle, kind human being...this man who had earned the respect of the Jew and many of "the others" throughout all of Bohemia and Moravia for more than half a century, was fading fast. Some spoke of the rabbi's affliction with humor, most with kind concern, but all had reached a consensus on *erev Shabbos.*

"Rivka, I must speak with Rabbi Blankfort before we leave Praha," uttered a disturbed and determined Sendehr in response to what he was hearing.

"Why? For what purpose?"

"You cannot simply discard a man because he's had a vision. If you could do that then where in the world would I be? You know I'm always dreaming, and I've told you of the many visions I have experienced in my young life. Shall I be sent off to sit under a fig tree to wait for the *mashiach*, too?"

"Sweetheart, what do you hope to gain in a conversation with an obviously senile, and quite disturbed old man?"

"The wisdom is still there. Don't you see? I want to meet with him, probe his mind to see what might be of value. Some insight. Some advice. Some sage remarks. Anything. A man who has walked this earth for nearly a century has to have something to say. To throw him on the dung heap is to burn a library. Don't you agree? Don't you?"

"You make a point, Sendehrel. I can't argue. Go. Meet with him. It will have to be tomorrow, on *Shabbos*, so you won't be able to take notes. Remember, we'll be leaving very early Sunday morning. Perhaps you should try to see him now."

"You're right. Now. Tonight. It's still early enough."

With that, Sendehr gave Rivka a quick peck on the nose, rushed into the *shul*, and caught the cantor just as he was about to walk out of the rear entrance.

"Excuse me, sir. Where can I find the Rabbi? I want to see him about something urgent if I may."

"Hold on a minute, young man. You're one of the Fusgeyers, I see. You know that Rabbi Blankfort is quite exhausted and is already in his apartment across the alley. I would say he'll be asleep in a matter of minutes."

"But I just have to see him. I don't want to disturb his rest tomorrow afternoon. We're leaving Sunday, early. Please take me to him, cantor!"

Noting the extreme urgency in Sendehr's blazing dark eyes, the portly, pink-cheeked baritone shook his head, shrugged his shoulders, and then beckoned for Sendehr to follow him out the door and across the alley. At its dreary end sat the basement apartment next to the Alliance kitchen, where Rabbi Blankfort had been living since the *rebbitzen* had passed on in '95.

There was no light in the cramped quarters aside from

a flickering candle that had been lit before the sun set and was down to its last "three-fingers" worth. Although the building and the *shul* next door had been electrified for decades, the basement quarters had not been included. The cantor was ready to take his leave after the Rabbi had agreed to allow "a few minutes" for Sendehr, but hesitated.

Sendehr took a hard-backed chair and moved closer to the narrow bed where Rabbi Blankfort lay fully clothed. The evening was exceptionally warm for June, and the cantor asked if the Rabbi wanted to take some time to undress in the adjoining bedroom, and get into his nightshirt and robe.

"No, no, after this young man leaves will be time enough. Do you think I am already some one-hundred-year-old who has to go to sleep like a baby so early in the evening? Go home to your family, Zalman, and *guten Shabbos*...Now, my dear Fusgeyer, what shall we talk about?"

The nonagenarian master put Sendehr completely at ease, and he knew that now he would seize this rare opportunity with both hands and squeeze tightly.

"Dear Rabbi Blankfort, I was intrigued by your brief comments regarding your visit from the Golem. I just had to talk with you. I might add that I am a writer and the journal-keeper for my group of Fusgeyers."

"*Oy*, I love your Eastern Yiddish. Sendehr, is it? When I was at the *yeshiva* many of my colleagues were from Russia, Poland and Romania. I was constantly chastised for my use of the stiff Germanic form of our *mamaloshen* and ever since I find it easy to lapse into your dialect. It's quite comforting to me."

Sendehr thought, *this man is far from even a vague senility...he's an absolute treasure!* "Perhaps you can refresh me. During my *cheder* days I was introduced to the story of Rabbi Loew and the Golem...but nothing in depth."

"Ah, yes, but of course. It will be good for you to know something of the past before I relate to you the impact of my recent meetings with him, and Rabbi Loew, I might add."

Sendehr was a bit taken aback and tried not to register it, but the mention that the famed Yehuda Loew also appeared in Blankfort's vision sequences certainly made him incredulous once again. *Where in the world would this conversation go?* It was time to find out.

"Now I remember. It was Rabbi Loew who was given the name *Maharal.* Doesn't it mean something like 'most respected teacher'...or was that someone else?"

"Yes, yes. Very good, indeed! Our great Rabbi Yehudah Leib Loew, son of Bezalel, served the Jewish people of Bohemia, and especially the city of Praha, three hundred years ago, throughout the latter half of the sixteenth century and into the first decade of the seventeenth. Comparatively speaking, years of moderate comfort for all the Jews in this region, believe me."

Rabbi Blankfort had actually used the Hebrew calendar designations which Sendehr transposed in his mind to the corresponding numerology of the Christian era. This skill always delighted his friends and family.

The Rabbi continued after drinking a bit of water from the glass by his side.

"Before you leave, be sure to visit his grave in the old cemetery. Leave some *kvittlech.* I assure you they will be answered."

Sendehr remained sitting at the edge of the uncomfortable chair. *Go on, Rabbi,* he urged, mentally, *tell me about your visions!*

"So, my dear young man, what exactly is it you wish to talk about? My visions, I suppose? My visits from the Golem? The Maharal's voice? Tell me! I seem to have gotten a burst of energy. Do you see what talking with young, interesting people does for an old man? Even on *erev Shabbos."* As Sendehr watched him, transfixed now, he appeared to mutter 'thank you, thank you Maharal'...as if Rabbi Loew himself was responsible for his newfound strength. His eyes had brightened and his face was beaming under the beard.

A relieved and near ecstatic Sendehr blurted out, "Yes, yes, Rabbi! Your visions. Your visits from the Golem and the Maharal. Particularly this morning. What are these ter-

rible things you mentioned?" Silently he chastised himself
for sounding too anxious, but the Rabbi didn't seem in the
least perturbed, and responded to him with a smooth, whispering flow.

"So, Sendehr Efraim ben Moishe, you cannot wait until tomorrow, eh? Well, that's very perceptive of you. Why?
Because I have decided not to bring up the conversation
again, ever, even though tonight I promised to do so. No, I
will not. Absolutely not. But I will tell you everything for one
simple reason, which shall become quite clear as we go along.
Before I do, however, I want your solemn word that you will
not repeat this to anyone in my congregation. To your comrades, yes. But to no one else here in Praha. Do you understand, Sendehr?"

"Yes, of course, " replied the nineteen-year-old without
hesitation, quite surprised that Rabbi Blankfort remembered
his name, his second name and his father's name after only
hearing it once when Sendehr had introduced himself earlier. "You have my word on that."

"*Oy, vay,* where do I begin, my young friend? I'll assume that you know only the typical *cheder* stories about
the Golem: how it came to be, its short life, its purposeful
mission. Ah, but there were many Golems in the past and
there will likely be many more. The ancient idea of man
playing at being God and creating life is not peculiar to
Jewish tradition by any means. If you come across King
Dovid's Psalm 139/16 you'll see that it comes from mystical kabbalistic learning. It is where Dovid thanks God for
having wonderfully made him.

"As for the name, 'Golem' originates from an ancient
Hebrew word which is ascribed different meaning, but which
signifies mass, matter or lifeless being without spirit or intelligence. But our Praha Golem was purely a man of clay,
made by the Maharal for a distinct reason...to save the Jews
of Praha from yet another disaster like the one that had
befallen them two hundred years prior, when the ghetto
was all but totally destroyed. Thousands died. Thousands.
Olzay hashalom! "

The Rabbi moaned, his lips moving and eyes nearly closed. Some moments passed. Sendehr moved closer to see if he was asleep, and as he did the elder sat up slowly, propped a pillow behind himself, smiled a reassuring smile at the young man beside him and continued.

"No, *yingeleh,* I won't continue to bore you with the history of our Praha Golem. I will now get to what you want to hear. Have you ever heard of Nostradamus? Michel de Nostredame, his real name?"

Sendehr shook his head.

"No? Well, he was a Frenchman, in fact a Jewish man who converted to Catholicism. He was also a physician and most famous as an astronomer who made startling predictions. He was a contemporary of Rabbi Loew, and was alive at about the time that the Rabbi fashioned the Golem. Many of Nostradamus's prophecies have come to pass during the past few hundred years, as strange as they may have sounded to those who knew him. For example, he was correct that man would fly when this century began. Yes indeed—in America first, last year, and now in France, men fly in the air with a machine! Think of that Sendehrel! In Birlad you may not have received the news of this. Just as the genius had predicted boats would sail under the water by the middle of last century. It happened. It happened during the American war…their civil war…but listen closely, please.

"I firmly believe that the Maharal, through the monstrous Golem that he produced from the clay of the Vltava, had, no, *has* these amazing powers of exceptional foresight. *Oy, vay iz mir, vay iz mir!* I only wish I had not heard him speak these words! Why me, Lord God, why me?"

"Are they so terrible, Rabbi Blankfort? Catastrophic? The end of the world?"

"You will see, you will see. Patience, *yingeleh!* The Maharal, through the Golem, spoke only of the years ahead in this century, and they are to be worse than the plagues over Egypt. Much more horrible than the pogroms that have already befallen our people. *Folg mir!* More terrifying than the deathly crusades. The Black Death. Famine. Pestilence. Yes, Sendehr, the Maharal spoke to me only of death and destruction...the annihilation of *ahleh unsereh Yidden! In gantzen!* Throughout the length and breadth of Europe. *Oy, gevalt! Oy, geeeee-valt!*" Both hands went to his forehead as he rocked to and fro.

Sendehr wondered what to do to calm the venerable one, but before he could make a move the Rabbi grabbed hold of Sendehr's right arm, his whole body trembling, and whispered fervently:

"You must not tarry! Promise me! You and your Fusgeyers must go on to America! There, I think you will be safe. Go, please go! Send for your families just as quickly as you can, before it is too late! The century ahead will be a terrifying one. Perhaps the darkest and bloodiest since God made heaven and earth! *Vay iz mir! Oy, vay iz mir!*"

Sobbing uncontrollably, the distraught Moshe Blankfort slipped from Sendehr's arms and lay back on his pillow. Sendehr filled the glass of water from the pitcher on the table and motioned for him to take a sip, which he did. It seemed to calm him to the point where his labored breathing slowed down measurably.

"You must forgive me, dear boy, but perhaps you see now why I cannot deliver on my promise to tell my congregants of this. You must understand that these visits from the Golem and its maker have been going on for many years, and not until recently have I mentioned this phenomenon to my congregants or anyone here in Praha. Already, they have me in *yener velt*. There are those so-called elders who would consign me to a *kranken-shvester*, in the *mayshescaynem*. But I must stay in the pulpit! I have much to do, Sendehr, much to say. In good time, my dear one, even though I told you earlier that I would never bring this up again, perhaps I will, slowly, cautiously repeat the Maharal's words to the right people at the right time, while I am still of this earth. *Farshtayst?*"

Trying not to appear overly troubled by these astounding revelations, Sendehr merely slowly and deliberately nodded his head.

"Good. I already have your word to speak of this only with your own Fusgeyers? At least, of course, until you leave Praha. After that, on the contrary, speak to anyone you wish. Spread the word. Please. Tell the *ganzer velt.* But remember, you will be ridiculed, chastised, and perhaps shunned and even spat upon. People love to hear good news. Good things. Not the ugly. The tragic. The horrific. And it is always the messenger who bears the brunt of disbelief. So, Sendehr, exercise extreme caution in the telling of these things. Pick your place and the time, and above all, the recipient. You're a writer? Good. The printing press will be your ally. The entire Diaspora is your readership. May God always be watching over you."

"Rabbi Blankfort, why have you chosen to tell me this? You could have easily put me off and I would be none the wiser."

"Aha! I am using you, just as the Maharal has been using me. Remember, the Golem is merely the conduit. The channel. When you came here, what, two hours ago...God in heaven, it must be nearing ten o'clock...I fully intended to spend a few minutes and ignore any questions referring to my remarks made in *shul.* But then I thought 'here is a very bright youngster, a writer, a journalist. Perhaps I should tell him all, for everyone's eventual benefit. Also, he is a traveler and can spread the word, and try to move as many of our people out of Europe as possible.'... Yes, of course I am using you. I plead guilty to that charge! *Ahl chait, ahl chait!* Sue me, if you will!"

It was good to hear the Rabbi's high-pitched laugh at the end of such serious discourse, and Sendehr grabbed the opportunity to relax and chuckle a bit with him.

This was highly combustible, bizarre material, and he would have to sort it out, analyze it, and perhaps discuss it privately with Mendel or Mordecai before addressing it any further. If at all. That is exactly where it stood, and the wily, very old and brilliantly perceptive man of God must have seen a tinge of potentially terminal skepticism in

Sendehr's eyes.

"So, *nu*, now I shall go into a bit of detail before we part. You see, as I mentioned earlier, the Golem and the Maharal have actually been my frequent guests for more than twenty years now. You must wonder how this can be so, when they are from another time. Indulge me, please. Let me reconstruct the first visit.

"It was around Chanukah time, 5641...or about 1880. They told me that a very important person would be assassinated...and this would be very bad for the Jews, particularly those millions in the Pale of Settlement. Who? Alexander II, a fairly good friend of the Jews who had begun to promote and endorse certain civil and political reforms. This was very significant, and our leaders everywhere in Europe hailed him. *At last, a Russian czar who was unafraid to change things, to franchise the disenfranchised, thereby benefiting the Pale's minorities, of whom our Jews were by far the most numerous*, we thought. Did he have enemies? *Gevalt!* I should say so! There were probably hundreds of Russians ready and willing to do him in, from the man in the street to some of his top echelon. But here is the as-tounding thing. This visit came, yes, now I recall, on the last night of the holiday, when all eight candles and the *shamus* were lit.

"My wife and I had been at our eldest son's house to be with the *aineklech*. Our two youngest children were living in Vienna with their families at the time. On the way home I stopped to visit a sick congregant next door, while my wife went into our house. When I went back out on the street, there they were. I was shocked—right in front of me stood this lumbering, enormous Golem, four heads taller than the towering Maharal who, in fact, was called *der hoche* because of his own unusual stature, as well as because of the high esteem he enjoyed in the community. When the Maharal identified himself I could only look up into his eyes, awestruck, and when the Golem spoke with the Maharal's voice I had to brace myself against a lamppost...else I surely would have folded under."

The Rabbi paused, and uttered something excusing his wandering mind, saying that maybe he should be in that old age home after all...but after another drink of water and a suck of a pared lemon sitting in a plate by his side, he carried on.

"Now here is the extraordinary prediction I heard. *The Czar*, said the Maharal's voice through the Golem's lips, *will be murdered.* There had been many failed attempts during that past year so this statement by itself was not too far-fetched, but then he got much more specific. *He will be killed by a fatal hand bomb thrown by terrorists as he rides in his carriage alongside Saint Petersburg's Catherine Embankment on the thirteenth of March, 1881, the seventh of Adar, in our year, 5641.*"

"What! If I properly recall my history that is precisely what occurred! I cannot believe it."

"Believe it, my son, believe it with all your heart. Knowing that this would be highly ominous for the millions of Jews in the Pale, I frantically wrote letters to my colleagues in Kiev, Odessa, Minsk, Vilna. Most of them completely ignored me. A *bubbeh meiseh*, they thought. Only one, a *yeshiva* dean in Konotop, passed the information on to some of the very few key Jews at the universities. Absolutely nothing was ever responded to. The rest, I'm afraid we all know too well. For the next two decades, and even now, the furies of hell on earth were unleashed. Alexander III was a brutal heir, and now Nicolai is much worse. The Maharal and Golem came to me many times during those years, warning of a pogrom about to take place here and there, a ritual murder accusation here, a calamity there...all verified, but I had done nothing. I did not act in any way. I kept it all to myself. Afraid of rebuff and embarrassment? Yes. A coward not willing to place my reputation below the horror that would certainly, and did, occur. Proven time and again. Kishinev was predicted to the day. Iashi, too. Chilling, but very true. I died a little each time. My dear wife, may she rest in peace, died knowing the torture I was going through. No one else knew anything. But now I can't bear the dilemma any longer.

I vowed that the next visit would be treated differently. And now I am making sure that this latest visit is approached in a new way."

"Yes, of course, with me as the sole messenger, I suppose?" stated Sendehr, not knowing how to take this idea of responsibility. .

"No, no. I will also sound the alarm on my terms as I have agreed to do. Not tomorrow, but soon; and methodically, carefully. But, I am counting on you to do the same, Sendehr. Can't you see? It is absolutely *beshairt* that you came to me on this *erev Shabbos*. This holiest time of the week. You were sent to me...you, a young man on this great adventure of yours, on the road to a land of gold—to *America*. A Fusgeyer so eager to leave this continent, to leave with such a flourish, to leave protesting the deplorable treatment our people are undergoing in the Pale and in Romania, and even now, though more tacitly, throughout the Empire and into Germany. Is it any better in France, with the aftermath of the Dreyfus affair? I think not. Now the Maharal tells us it will get far worse everywhere in the years ahead."

"Well, since you've gone this far, he must have given you more detail about those events like he did when he told you how and when the assassination of Czar Alexander would occur. I want to hear specifics, Rabbi. Enough generalities."

Sendehr shocked himself with his newfound assertiveness. Not that he was fully agreeing to do as the master asked. Not just yet, anyway.

"I can only pray that the Maharal is, for once, totally wrong. That he overestimated, or misunderstood, Sendehr, or that his interpretations and analyses were skewed incorrectly, or misconstrued in some major way. *Oy, mein Gott*, I pray to you!"

Sendehr saw Blankfort's strength and energy fading again. He was much too fatigued to continue. He knew that he had pushed him too aggressively at this time of night. They agreed, much to the relief of the venerable one, to continue that next night, after *havdalah.* Sendehr simply had to see it all the way through to a logical end.

Sendehr, *der shreiber,* a boy fast growing into mature manhood with each passing day, would find that on this night, sleep would be impossible.

* * *

On the roof-top between the two gabled ends of the building, the balmy Sabbath evening brought out nearly half the entire troop of Fusgeyers, most of whom chose to sleep on their bedrolls under the stars. Most of the young men, Pessel, Chaike, and Tsippy were wearing their summer singlets, light cotton shirts or blouses, and the atmosphere was one of warm camaraderie. Laughter, and some gentle humming and singing, washed down the side of the ancient town hall and into the streets. When they greeted Sendehr, there was no talk of Rabbi Blankfort and his highly provocative words, or of Sendehr's whereabouts for the past few hours. He was certain that Rivka had said nothing about his meeting. Her knowing wink told him he was right, and he didn't think anyone had seen him enter the little apartment either. For this, he was very relieved. There would be plenty of time to discuss the matter later that next night or on Sunday.

When they were finally alone, off in the far corner of the roof, Rivka took Sendehr's face in her hands and whispered, "Whatever happened down there is weighing heavily upon your soul, my love."

Sendehr drew a deep sigh and paused for a moment. "I have to have time to think it through, Rivkaleh. It is more than earthshaking. It has me confused, bewildered and most of all, very humble, *ahneevesdik.*"

He proceeded, slowly, to start to tell Rivka everything, but she stopped him in the middle of a sentence before he could get past anything of significance.

"*Shah,* Sendehrel, I think it would be best if you continue to keep it to yourself, for now. I can see where it has affected you so emotionally. Think it through, weigh it, analyze it, tonight and tomorrow. Then on Sunday, or whenever you tell the others, Mordecai and Mendel and anyone else you choose to tell, we'll go over it together."

Sendehr paused, looked deep into Rivka's dark eyes, and finally felt less stressed and more relaxed then at anytime during the past few hours.

"Thank you, sweet one, thank you. Right again! I really don't want to talk about it now. I can't seem to sort it out smoothly enough to make any sense. I feel so drained of energy, yet I can't face going to sleep. Would you walk with me along the river? Come. It's still early." As he spoke, the clock with the Hebrew letters on the building's steeple struck half past the hour of ten.

The path along the still swollen Vltava was situated on a high embankment, safe from the overflow that had flooded low-lying riverfronts. Hradcany Castle across the river, on a hilltop, looked eerie in the half-moon light...a huge Noah's ark come to rest on Mount Ararat. The Hapsburg relations who had occupied the castle these many years had for some reason refused to extend the electric lighting to the outer rim of the castle walls. It would have been so much more appealing to the citizenry. A beautiful sight, in fact. It would have certainly complemented the well-lit lampposts along the Charles Bridge, *Karluv Most,* still at this time of night full of noisy pedestrians who were enjoying the musicians, magicians and mimes, and their continuous performances. Perhaps these unwelcome Austrian intruders feared drawing any more attention to themselves. Revolutionaries were everywhere these days, you know! The Czars, the Emperors, the Kings.... They would tell you that!

With the moonlight dancing over the rushing waters, and *shpatziering* couples cluttering up the pathway, Sendehr steered Rivka to one of the rickety wooden benches under the graceful weeping willow trees in abundance on both sides of the river, on Kampa Island and in the city parks. There was already a couple seated on the adjoining bench...a gaunt figure of a young man, perhaps early twenties, and a short, plump woman who looked somewhat younger. The man was rather over-dressed for such a warm summer's night in a tight-fitting gray suit with a crisp white shirt, a silken black cravat, and he held a shiny, black bowler on his lap. He answered Sendehr's Yiddish *gut ovnt* in a clip-toned guttural German: *guten abend, meine frau und herr.*

Introductions were made and for a few minutes both couples sat quietly, content to gaze at the bridge, the river and the castle. Rivka broke the silence, feeling that it would be good for Sendehr to become involved with some innocuous, casual conversation to distract him for now from his deep and bothersome self-communion.

"So you are visiting from Olmutz, Miss Lowy?"

"Please call me Feigeh. Yes. Franz and I are cousins. My father is his mother's brother and I love to visit Praha whenever I can. Franz and his sisters Valli, Elli and Ottla spend a week in our little town during grape harvest every September."

"Your Yiddish is very close to ours, I see. There are quite a few words that give me trouble with the Germanic pronunciations. Mr. Kafka—or may I call you Franz—you must have studied in a German language school," chipped in Sendehr, pleasing Rivka, who gave his sleeve a little tug of approval.

"Yes, I attended the German-language *gymnasium* here, and I have been studying literature for the past two years at the University of Prague. And you, sir, are from Romania, you said?"

In a matter of minutes, Franz Kafka and his cousin Feigeh were hearing the Fusgeyer story for the first time. In fact, Sendehr enjoyed the telling, as it did, indeed, help to soothe his churning mind. Rivka joined in and amazed both of the listeners with her exploits both as a female Fusgeyer and as stage play director, actor, writer and dancer.

The stoic young Kafka warmed up a degree or two and told of life in the Empire and in Praha, which he referred to solely as Prague, and of his studies and ambitions. He went so far as to complain about his domineering father, Hermann, who operated a wholesale haberdashery just a step away from the *Alte-Neue shul.* (Little wonder that his clothes were so neat, then!) With the chaotic destruction/construction going at such a pace, business had never been worse for him, resulting in a renewed streak of meanness that boded poorly for the Kafka household. The man, it seems, was not at all an observant Jew, but rather put forth his Czech nationalism whenever it was convenient. In fact, the younger Kafka admitted it saved the shop during the terrible anti-Jewish riots of the late '90s. As was the custom with unmarried young people at the time, Franz continued to live at home, seeking his tyrannical father's approbation in vain.

Feigeh described Olmutz, the dramatically beautiful Sternbeck Castle nearby, and the life of a Jewish girl growing up in a town where she was in such a marked minority. Sendehr and Rivka thought it sounded like Birlad, but with only 200 Jewish families in Olmutz—also known by the Czech name, Olomouc—the ratios between the many and the few were much further apart.

When Franz rose to leave with Feigeh, he bowed stiffly to Rivka and addressed the two Birladers, reverting to his formal style.

"Would you care to meet with us and one of my college mates tomorrow? He would enjoy meeting you, I'm sure, to hear firsthand of your remarkable venture."

"Yes, Franz. We'll be attending *shul* in the morning, but how would two o'clock be?" asked Sendehr with a nod of approval from Rivka.

"It sounds quite excellent. Perhaps we can all take a long walk upriver to Vysehrad. It's lovely there: castle ruins, gardens, riverviews and all. You Romanians enjoy going by foot it would seem!"

To this, Feigeh added, "How would you like me to prepare a dining basket from my aunt's over-bursting larder? She's the only one who insists on keeping the *kashruth,* at least in the house."

"We'd like that, wouldn't we Sendehr? These restful Sabbath days are a Godsend for us. It was such a pleasure meeting and talking with you both."

"Tomorrow at two, right here at this spot, then."

With a brief round of obligatory pleasantries, Herr Franz Kafka, known to only a few by the Czech name, Frantishek, and Cousin Feigeh Lowy, took their leave. His silhouette, no wider than a stiletto, topped by the bowler, looked quite bizarre.

Rivka and Sendehr sat for another hour, content with the quiet, romantic setting. They talked and giggled about how odd they must have looked to Franz and Feigeh, in their Fusgeyer road get-up, brogues and all.

"I have the feeling that Franz, as unhappy and disturbed as he appears, is actually quite brilliant. It will be interesting to meet who he has chosen as a friend at the university."

"He seemed to be genuinely fascinated by our story. Feigeh, too. Maybe he'll open up more on our hike tomorrow."

"Tomorrow! We'll have to be back before sundown. I want to be with the Rabbi precisely following *havdalah.* That would be sometime after nine with the sun setting so late."

"I hope it will be a brief session, my love. We're leaving at sunrise Sunday according to Zed-Zed."

"I have to get the details, Rivka, no matter how long it takes, but I don't think he can hold up for more than an hour or two after such a long Sabbath day. You know the longest day of the year is only a week off.

Sendehr's voice had a certain unstoppable determination to it, almost as if he had just made his decision to spread the "word" without even hearing it.

If nothing else, he had to take the prophecies seriously at this time. The Maharal had been correct too many times, according to Blankfort, unless this was all a figment of the aging one's imagination, his inner thoughts taking shape as reality in the external world and manifesting his belief system in public where it did not belong. There was only one course for Sendehr Efraim, guardian of the journal, *der shreiber*, to follow.

Sitting on the bench overlooking the Vltava, arm around Rivka's shoulder, he plunged into deep thought.

See it through, consider and reconsider the evidence, the implications, the potential repercussions...aha! Perhaps another pilpul would be in order...a discussion with my comrades...they will help me make the final decision. Is this story, this soothsaying, a window-on-the-future, something we should help disseminate, an alarm to be sounded? Or is it too bizarre, too otherworldly, too incredible...to be discarded, to be left with the old Rabbi? Abi gesunt zoll er zein.

Mordecai, Mendel, Zed-Zed, Nuchim, Branko...they certainly wouldn't let me make a fool of myself. It would reflect poorly on the entire troop...and much of Jewish Europe will dismiss our derring-do as pure, unadulterated folly? No, please God, no!

Sendehr tossed around on his flattened bedroll all through a fitful night, but he was content with the initial decision to hold off telling anyone else for the time being. For this, he was most grateful to Rivka, as she slept in the nearby corner of the rooftop, next to Pessel, Chaike and Tsippy. His forever-fertile mind was in perpetual motion, diving into a mixed bag of new thoughts. *How will the Rabbi go about reneging on his promise to tell all to the Sabbath congregation in the morning? Will he really open up to me, all the way, after havdalah? Or will he opt to break that promise, too? What was it about this Kafka chap that bordered on the enigmatic? The iconoclastic? Strange sort, eh? Ay,yi,yi, this Praha is literally bathing in the occult, awash in the theosophic, kabbalistic mysticism that is far beyond comprehension...the supernatural lurking in every ancient building, around every corner. No wonder the Golem was handmade here! Where else?*

16

ENCOUNTERS: THE GREAT ESCAPE

These are the times that try men's souls.
Thomas Paine, *The American Crisis* (1776)

The Sunday march out of Praha was something that all who were there would always remember—the Fusgeyers, the people of Jewish Praha, Josefov, and any other early-rising citizen of the city who happened to be in the vicinity.

Although the good and honorable Rabbi Moshe Blankfort shocked and disappointed his *Shabbos* congregation when he told them that he had decided not to share Rabbi Loew's sacred words with them (not just yet, "lest you persist in thinking that I am an old man given to increasing hallucinations"), he did leave them with some rather forceful commands.

This style of his recalled his younger days when he had been known to summarily admonish sinners, as did his Catholic and Lutheran colleagues. In those days, to the chagrin of his stiff-necked board, he had demonstrated an unpopular, contrary nature at times, and was far more literal and much less liberal in his Biblical interpretations and Talmudic discourses than now. Blankfort issued these commands from the pulpit just before the final benediction, in the Biblical commandment form of "thou shalt."

•Thou shalt honor our distinguished
guests from Romania.
•Thou shalt arise a little earlier than usual
on Sunday morning.
•Thou shalt gather in the torn-up streets of
our Jewish town, and onto the river embankment at precisely seven o'clock.
•Thou shalt bring out our community's
brass band in full regalia.
•Thou shalt afford our young Fusgeyer
heroes a farewell sendoff unlike anything
heretofore.

Verily, it all came to pass on a bright, sunny Sunday morning in June.

The cart, pulled along with increasing difficulty, was once again splitting at its seams, brimming over with food supplies that had been donated and *shnorred*, "borrowed." Simmy Fieldelman again did his job well, both over the table and slightly under it. "Hide your daughters and your *challahs*, ladies, Fiedelman prowls tonight!" joked Itzy and Mayer... and this was the sanitized version!

The Sabbath morning fundraising pleas were also suc- cessful. The generosity of the Praha Jews had gone far be- yond expectations. At the Pinkhas *shul*, Mordecai gave an impassioned history of the Fusgeyer movement from 1899 to the present, covering their trials and tribulations, suc- cesses and foibles, and also including some references to the lives of some Birladers after arriving in America. Pledges followed.

Menachem Berman mesmerized the small but wealthi- est congregation at the Meisel *shul* down the narrow street from the Jewish Town Hall, and it appeared that every fam- ily represented there had pledged to donate. Marcus Mordecai Meisel, mayor of the ghetto, had built the syna- gogue during the time of the Maharal. He had designed it to be his private prayer house, and it had been rebuilt three times since then. This 1840s version was the most ornate of all, and its congregation now kept it up and also came forth with sizable commitments to the Fusgeyers.

Nuchim, the engineer of these speaking events, told of some of the hardships along the trail in order to inculcate the attendees of the Klaus *shul*, the town's main reliquary for *objets d'Judaica*. With brief stories of Prislop Pass, the bandits in Hungary, and confrontations with the military everywhere, he built to a crescendo, ending in a true fund-seeking flourish, stressing the need for adequate monies to cover the remaining distance to Bremerhaven.

Zed-Zed was dispatched to the Spanish Synagogue, so called because of its Moorish architecture, the only place of worship constructed in the previous century. Unfortunately, the massive urban renewal project rendered this *shul* inaccessible for the better part of three years, and a temporary sanctuary had been set up in a warehouse loft on an adjoining street.

Nevertheless, Zed-Zed's presentation of the scheduling and logistical problems that his committee dealt with, peppered with bits of humor, was met with a substantial response of healthy pledges.

At each of these synagogues, the rabbis had received a quick midmorning visit from Blankfort's beadle, Hellmann, who went to the *bimah*, pulpit area, and politely whispered something into the resident rabbi's ear, then quickly proceeded on to the next. He was passing along Blankfort's simple request to his junior colleagues. "Please have everyone turn out for the farewell to our visiting Fusgeyers at seven tomorrow morning. Do not be conspicuous by your absence." Knowing their senior colleague was sometimes cantankerous, they expected cooperation to be no less than unanimous.

Meanwhile, at the Alte-Neue *shul*, Mendel had spoken with dramatic eloquence of the purposes of, the reasoning behind and the motivating factors for such an undertaking. If it had been proper to applaud on *Shabbos in shul*, he certainly would have received a standing ovation. At the very least, he had unknowingly given Rabbi Blankfort a tran-

sitory move to enter into his famed commandment posture, and of course the Rabbi embraced the opening with
gusto.

Not only did the hard money, kroner upon kroner, pour
into the Alliance office after sundown, but those who did
not pay their pledges then and there arrived Sunday morning, stuffing wads of kroner into the pockets of their designated speakers.

Nuchim did the math, and arrived at a total that, when
added to the cash on hand, placed the financial affairs of
the 1904 Birlader Fusgeyers in a recuperative position.
Mordecai himself led the cries of *Gott tsedanken*, closely
followed by a chorus of surrounding cadre, an *omayn, omayn*
from the Finance Chair, and a "pooh, pooh, pooh" in unison from the distaff side... yet another Eastern European
superstition, *einglaybenish*. No Italian opera could sound
any better than this spirited cantata.

The good Doctor Hippocrates was also the proud recipient of a most welcome gift from none other than Rabbi
Blankfort's personal physician, one Eliyosef Warmbrand.
Standing next to Gershon and Maidele at the closing Sabbath prayer, *havdalah*, Dr. Warmbrand was quite taken with
their stories about practicing medicine on the trek. Furthermore, although educated in English at St. Andrews
Medical College in Scotland, he had originally come from
Warsaw, and was conversant in Eastern Yiddish. Understanding their dialect well, he was astonished to hear
Gershon talk in technical medical terms usually associated
only with graduate physicians. Warmbrand referred to
Gershon thereafter as Doctor Maibaum, and to Maidele as
Nurse Kaufman. (That is, until he was corrected by the ever-
present Itzy the Busybody, who was standing nearby, glee-
fully spilling the Hippocrates and Nightingale truth.)

Following their conversation, Dr. Warmbrand asked
Gershon and Maidele to come to his home in the Mala Strana
district across the Charles Bridge, to meet his wife and child
and to share a light Saturday night supper. This they did,
enjoying the rare social evening immensely. Later, they

would not need to be told that the doctor was the finest diagnostician in the city and was also an exceptionally kind and gentle person. As they were about to return to their lodgings, the doctor took them into his home office.

As the couple looked around the office, finding it well equipped, the doctor proceeded to fill up his very own handsome black leather physician's satchel with every item one imagined to be found in a medical milieu saying, "You have a long way ahead of you. You may think you have enough supplies, but there is no such thing as having too much on hand. Believe me, I know this from my own experience." When Gershon hesitated to take the beautiful bag, the insouciant answer was simply, "Nonsense. My wife bought me a new one for my birthday, on the cabinet there, so use this in good health. That's what it's for, after all!"

On their way back over the Charles Bridge, Doctor Maibaum and Nurse Kaufman, repeatedly addressing each other with their newly anointed professional titles, could utter only one word over and over again in describing their benefactor, Eliyosef Warmbrand of Praha: *mensch!*—a fine human being!

* * *

The plan that Zed-Zed and Sendehr drew up, and had since modified out of necessity, called for the Fusgeyers to spend their first night out of Praha along the lower Moldau, or Vltava, as it was called proudly by all self-respecting Czech nationalists. This would be at the forty-kilometer mark, passing through Theriesenstadt/Terezin and Leitmeritz/ Litomerice the next day, and crossing the border into Germany by late afternoon on Tuesday, June 15th. This way, the group would still have enough time, by noon on the 18th, to show their newly-issued limited transit letters required at the border of the Austro-Hungarian Empire. The Emperor's designated hatchet man, Captain "*Paskudnyak*," "viper" that he was, had drawn his open hand across his throat, emphasizing that the transit letters termination date was indisputable. If they never saw him again, it would be much too soon.

Sendehr and Rivka did something unusual after the last of the Praha citizenry shouted their goodbyes. While the Josefov brass band in full uniform stood by the side of the road playing their final spirited marching music, and the remaining children waved their *Simchas Torah* paper *Mogen Dovid* flags, the inseparables fell in step with the point team in the vanguard on the well-graded crushed rock road.

Sholem and Yaakov had decided to walk closer to the river embankment where the rushing water had subsided just a few kilometers north of the city. It was here that Rivka nudged Sendehr to follow a bit behind the point so that they could converse in privacy.

"I assume you haven't said anything as yet. Is that why you wanted to be up here for the time being?"

"Rivka, as I said last night, the detail that the Rabbi described so meticulously horrified me. It did nothing less than cloud my already muddled mind. Maybe tonight we can look at everything rationally. I did tell Mordecai that I have something I want to discuss with him, and also Mendel."

"Good. Very good. After that I want to know more. Please."

"Yes, yes, *zeesa*, my sweet, of course."

Sendehr had already related some of the starker generalities to Rivka. No specifics yet. He had met with the Rabbi for two solid hours, after *havdalah*. Prior to that, during the afternoon hike to Vysehrad and the sumptuous picnic, even Kafka had asked if there was anything bothering him.

The enormous burden of carrying advanced knowledge of future misfortunes for European Jewry according to the Maharal's dire forecasts was trouble enough for even for a vigorous nineteen-year-old. Yes, even for Sendehr Efraim, *der shreiber*, the scribe, who not only walked from Birlad to Praha, but who also had found himself hopelessly, madly, wildly in love for the first time. Complications of every variety seemed to be encompassing his very being. More than once he had said to himself, *life was so much simpler in Birlad.*

At the upcoming crossroad, the boys from Czernowitz, Pinchas Rembaum and Moishe Gelernter, would be taking the Karlsbad/Karlovo Vary fork. They had formed attachments with a number of the Fusgeyers and the parting would be a sorrowful one; but with passage waiting for them in Antwerp, they had no sensible alternative. At the junction, some of the group vowed to meet them someday in America, but this was commonplace at such farewells, and rarely realized unless the immigrants ended up in the same sections of New York, Philadelphia, Chicago, Boston or wherever they ultimately settled.

These days, many emigrants meeting on the road to the ports, or on the trains and wagons, became companions out of logical necessity or proximity. Once in America, caught up in the hectic day-to-day competitive chase for lodgings, for jobs, or for education, and busy reconnecting with relatives and other compatriots, there would be precious little time or inclination to hunt up the whereabouts of someone they had met en route. This was a study in social reality, which everyone would learn sooner or later.

Pinchas and Moishe turned back to wave, time and again, receiving returning gestures each time until they finally were out of sight. *"Lang leben in America, khaverim,"* were the last words of good cheer that echoed through the summer-wheat and barley fields of Upper Bohemia. "Long life in America, friends." What better wish could there be?

No one bothered to set up tents on a warm night with no rain in sight. There was no need for much wood gathering, and the reserve water containers were fresh and full. The setting was as bucolic as any other they had found en route. A herd of dairy cows grazed in the lush green pasture, a small farmstead sat in the distance, the narrowing Vltava/Moldau was running calm at near normal depth, and the main roadway was yet in sight some three hundred meters to the west. They had covered forty uneventful kilometers since the rousing sendoff at seven, and Mordecai silently prayed for the remainder of the trek to be as peaceful.

Others may have done the same. One-on-one, to God in heaven!

Following supper, Mendel held his daily English class, stressing the most commonly used words when describing the landscape: mountainous, hilly, flat, wooded, swampy, muddy, rugged, sparse, populous, uninhabited, crowded, lush, arid, fruited. Yes, as in "above the fruited plain" from *America the Beautiful*, which the Birladers had learned weeks ago. The six sopranos and the "four cantors" could now give a stirring rendition of the praiseful hymn, accompanied so ably by trumpet, accordion and drums.

During his days at the British School, Mendel first came across the 1890s patriotic poem by Katharine Lee Bates, a professor at Wellesley College in Massachusetts. Two Americans, a man and wife from Maryland, both faculty members of the British school, had written some music for it. In their frequent periods of terminal homesickness the pair would sing the song, accompanying their voices with cello and piano playing. Mendel had taken a liking to it; he copied the words and remembered the music, changing it a bit before introducing it to his Fusgeyers as part of their English language indoctrination.

Altered more than just cosmetically, with Velvel the Trumpeter's help, if the truth were told, the pleasant melody by now somehow resembled a composite of the then popular Yiddish folk songs: *Mein Shteteleh Belz, Oyfn Pripachok, Rozhinkes Mit Mandeln,* and *Yidl Mit Di Fidl.* This was not in the least surprising—these were the most requested and favorite selections in the tireless trumpeter's campfire repertoire!

Mendel asked Sholem Friedman to use some of the descriptive landscape words in a sentence:

I vawk di moddy road troo rugged heels und come out on flet, dosty fields vere dere's no pipple, uninhevited, erid sure not losh.

316

Mendel led the applause, sporting a broad smile of satisfaction, having taught well.

The moment the class was dismissed, Mordecai beckoned to *der lehrer*, who came right over to his side.

"Sendehr wants to meet with the two of us. The two of us *only*. I haven't said anything to you, Mendel, but I've noticed something strange about Sendehr's behavior these past two days. I'm concerned. Let's find out what's going on."

His companion nodded in agreement. "Esther and I were with Rivka and Sendehr yesterday afternoon, along with some Praha people. He seemed especially pensive and reserved in his conversation. But, then again, he frequently is, so I thought nothing of it."

The three decided to sit on a rocky outcropping at river's edge just far enough away from the campsite to be out of earshot. Others knew enough to stay away, assuming there was some good reason behind their obvious need for privacy. When Rivka was asked what she knew, her response was one of rehearsed flippancy. "You know those three! As usual, they are bothering their little-boy heads over perceived problems that will probably never come to pass!" Her flirtatious smile, accented by her brighter-than-white teeth, insured that the questioner would not persist. Well, not with the same question, at least.

"You're saying that, in Blankfort's visions, the Golem's lips moved and the voice of Rabbi Loew came through? This would have to be the only way, because in all the stories I have ever heard, the Golem was completely mute," exclaimed an obviously skeptical Mendel following Sendehr's opening remarks. All three were careful to keep their voices down.

"Uncanny! You say the Maharal, according to Rabbi Blankfort correctly predicted the Czar's assassination in historical detail. Is this true?"

Hearing this remark, punctuated by the wry smile of a doubtful Mordecai, the still unperturbed Sendehr went on to describe several other predictions that were later proven to have happened accurately. There was no more to say about those that were already proven, identified as such by Blankfort, a great believer.

But now Sendehr had to launch directly into the crux, the core, dead center, yet-to-happen: the fate of European Jewry according to the Maharal. Or perhaps it really was Blankfort's educated vision of the future. Mendel and Mordecai, and Sendehr, of course, would have to decide for themselves. *Pilpul*? Perhaps. Sendehr did not embellish, color, taint or change in any way anything that Rabbi Blankfort had told him on Saturday night. He took out his crumpled notes and began to read in an eerily solemn monotone, slightly above a whisper.

For the next few minutes, only the sound of Sendehr speaking Blankfort's words permeated the dusk of an early summer's evening:

"...This century will be one of great disasters for our people throughout Europe.

...By the end of this year, the Czar Nicolai will vociferously blame the defeat of the Russian navy by the Japanese on the Jews of the Pale. Pogroms will immediately increase. Specifically, Odessa's surrounding 'Jewish villages' will suffer the most, while Sebastopol in the Crimea, Kherson, Makarov near Kiev, Zhitomir, Poltava, Kharkov, Kovno, Berdichev and Vilna will be the major targeted communities. Many thousands will die and thousands will be rendered homeless.

...A major ritual murder accusation will end up in a noted trial seven years hence, with all the expected repercussions.

...One of the Hapsburgs will be assassinated in 1914, exploding into a war involving all major and many secondary nations in Europe. America will be drawn in to help save France from the invading Germans. The Germans will roundly defeat the Czar's army on six occasions, retreating in mass chaos each time. Caught in the midst of this, the Jews of Poland and the Pale will suffer hundreds of thousands of deaths, many by stray artillery shells, others by starvation. The German invaders will be known as 'better for the Jews' than the Czar's armies. The frustrations of constant defeat will be brutally enacted on all civilians in their path.

...The aftermath of this bloody war will see a temporary reprieve for our *Yidden.*' Some of the newly-established independent nations will issue weak emancipation legislation for their minorities, inherited and native alike. On the other hand, these same countries will invoke severe boycotts and trading restrictions on their Jews during the 1920s and 1930s. Once again, overt anti-Semitism and abject impoverishment will be the bane of their existence.

...A new and horrifying Haman will arise in Germany at this time, just as his arch rival grows in power throughout the new Russia.

...In the 1930s Jews will be in even greater peril when this tyrannical German madman and his increasing followers legislate, put into actual law, policies that will lead to the eventual extermination of millions of Europe's Jews.

...A world once again at war by the end of that decade, where fifty million people will die, will result in rapid acceleration of the mass slaughter of Jews all over the continent by bizarre systems and methods never before employed. Much too ghastly to describe. When it becomes clearer to me, I shall return with the details. We have only one Hebrew word to describe what I so clearly envision: *shoah,* a firestorm, a whirlwind of destruction.

...There will be only a few safe havens for our people if they take heed of these warnings. They must plan now, posthaste, to emigrate to the west, as far west as possible. Even to another hemisphere – to North America, to South America, to Australia. Perhaps Palestine, where a new homeland will become a reality a few years after this monstrous conflagration ends.

...For the latter half of the century ahead, those who survive these plagues of death will enjoy a resurgence of the Jewish presence everywhere, in every phase of life's endeavors; but they must guard this apex diligently so as never to revert to the past. To this last remark I must say, you must say, *Omayn!* May it be God's will!"

With watery eyes, the messenger paused, then whispered, "Mordecai. Mendel. These are the words, the alleged words of the great Maharal, Rabbi Yehuda Leib Loew, through the lips of his Golem, almost verbatim, that Rabbi Blankfort passed on to me last night. He was crying uncontrollably, bitterly, when he finished. *Oys Shabbos*, thank God, so I was able to take these notes. He wants me, us, the Fusgeyers, to spread this message of doom and gloom to anyone who will listen. He wants us to sound the alarm. I can say no more."

All three sat in silence. It seemed that hours had gone by, but Mordecai spoke just as the darkness of night closed in tightly.

"This much we do know. Rabbi Blankfort is a very old man. For years, according to Schwartzmann the Alliance man, his mind has been showing a gradual decline. He is known to ramble during sermons and even in personal conversations. During Sabbath services yesterday he actually mistakenly sat in what is reputed to be the original chair of Rabbi Loew. Out of respect, it remains on the *bimah*, but no one had used it for three hundred years, until then. Mendel, Sendehr, you both must have seen this. These and other cold, hard facts do not allow for one to place much credence in what he says, especially something of such astounding magnitude, yet so incredible."

"It appears that we're in a *pilpul* mode. Shall we go on, friends?"

Mendel and Mordecai, in unison, nodded their heads in acceptance of Sendehr's challenge, and the words began to fly. Each statement met with reaction, counter-reaction, counter-counter-reaction, *ad infinitum.* They struggled often to keep from increasing their voices. As always, civility ruled throughout the *pilpul* and when the questions, answers, arguments, counter-arguments and new challenges finally were exhausted, the three respectful comrades put their arms around each other, admitting that they were in an impasse. More than an hour had passed.

"So we have agreed that we disagree, agreed?"

"No, Sendehr, I honestly feel that we have at least recognized the full extent of the dilemma. As for a solution, perhaps in time."

"But we must take some sort of a stand among the three of us," interrupted Mendel, the most aggressive and longest-winded participant.

"How can we ever hope to do that? We would each have to believe that Blankfort actually heard these words, and given that supposition, that he passed them along to Sendehr without twisting or embellishing them completely out of shape. Did Moshe *actually* talk with God on Mount Sinai? How about the burning bush? Was the Red Sea *actually* parted so that Moshe and his escaping flock could walk across it? Any thinking Jew has asked these questions seeking answers for millennia. How can we ever be reasonably sure of anything so remote, coming from one rabbi three centuries dead, and the other a victim of growing irrationality?"

"Aha! This being the case, how would you feel if we do not officially involve the group, but instead I will merely act as an unattached individual whenever telling the story to strangers? I can do so without endorsing it, without appearing alarmed by it, just repeating the predictions in such a way that the listener can be made to feel that he, too, has the choice of passing it off as nonsense, or passing it along as truth, *emes*, or just relaying it to others as a conversation piece. You two can do the same, of course. Good God, even in my young life, and yours, we constantly hear stories of predicted disasters of one kind or another which we shrug off or soon forget. Granted, nothing even closely approaching this."

Mendel nodded. "Why not? I don't see any harm in that. Do it if you wish as far as I'm concerned, Sendehr. Both Mordecai and I can do the same. As for the very remote possibility that there is any solid substance to all this, we can carefully pass the word, without undue alarm, to our group, and to anyone we meet from here to America, in the calm, casual manner you've suggested. In my estimation, there is not one Fusgeyer who doesn't plan to urge his loved ones to leave Romania as soon as humanly possible, Rabbi Blankfort's visions, or not, Rabbi Loew's predictions, or not, *shoah* or not!" He then got up to leave, feeling that all had been said that could be said and discussed at this point.

Mordecai yawned, and stretching, he rose to his feet next. "Let's table it for tonight," he said. "We have a lot to think about, and you can be assured that Mendel and I will share this burden with you, dear Sendehr. On the other hand, let's not forget for one moment that we still have a task to perform. We've got to safely bring fifty-seven Birladers from here to Bremerhaven to America!"

As if on cue, each put on his most sincere smile, as hard as it may have been, and went back to join the others, most of them already in dreamland. Sendehr hoped that Rivka was among the latter, yet he knew full well that she would be pacing among the pines, awaiting word. He was wrong. Rivka slept soundly, curled up in her bedroll on a mattress of pine needles and crushed cones.

In another in his series of letters to Rabbi Nachman marked *PREEVAHT*, the scribe related the entire incident from Friday night up to the meeting just ended, the *pilpul* and its results.

> *Dear Rabbi:*
>
> *I know that my weekly synopsis is not due for a few days yet, but I have news of such import that will not appear in the mere outline of our daily events...so I am sending you this very private letter. You will notice that a few items are certainly not of that category, but most of the following are. I'm so sure that you will fully agree.*

By the light of a lantern, Sendehr wrote, scratched out, rewrote. He covered the entire weekend's events with particular emphasis on Rabbi Loew's predictions, and included the final statements made by Mendel and Mordecai, and his own words. He was confident that Eli would send an answer to the Berlin Main Postal Office, marked "Hold for Addressee," as he had done in both Budapest and Vienna.

To change the morbid tone of his private letter, Sendehr decided to include some comments on his meeting with the young Franz Kafka, although he planned to briefly mention this in the weekly summary also.

> *We met a rather fascinating student, a Czech Jew with some provocative ideas. His name is Franz Kafka.*
>
> *This man is perhaps the thinnest adult I have ever seen. I can think of several Birlader mamas and bubbehs who would fatten him up in no time. Forgive me, that's not the point, Rabbi, of course. In our discussions, particularly on a long walk we took on Shabbos afternoon, Mendel, Esther, Rivka and I could scarcely contain ourselves from getting into name-calling and other childish pursuits with this pompous, highly opinionated, and rude yet extremely interesting local. His college mate, a man by the name of Max Brod, was slightly less direct but every bit as intellectual. I can honestly say that Mendel held his own quite well, and I'd like to think that I was able to contribute along with some welcome calming remarks from Esther and Rivka.*
>
> *For example, Kafka, who is not at all religious, and in fact almost completely non-observant, stated that bar mitzvah is "senseless dribble and a rite of passage no different than paganism," citing his own as a complete waste of time. Coming from a family of quasi-assimilationists, and disliking his own father, he went on to describe the leftovers of such dilution of Judaism as "insufficient scrap, a mere nothing, a joke, not even a joke."*
>
> · *I found this to be hypocritical coming from someone who seemed to favor the assimilationist bent, almost as if he were secretly hoping that his family could have*

retained more traditional Judaism. Yet he was also praiseful of the practice of Talmudic discussion and debate, and there seems to be more than just a morsel of Jewish sensibility in this thinking. Brod refers to this as Kafka's true self. I see him as a walking picture of dichotomy, so much so that he is a rabid proponent of both Zionism and Torah study. Only the trappings of religion does he violently object to.

But he also sees Jews as being the most obsessively chauvinistic people on the face of the earth (and I'm quoting him), forever wondering whether everything and anything bodes well or bad for the Jew...always asking whether that person is Jewish, or is she Jewish, or is the doctor Jewish, the policeman, the teacher, the politician, did he marry a Jew, did she, are Jews allowed here or there, at that school or this one...that the whole world is either Jewish or incidental. No in-between!

With statements like this, meant to shock and disturb, this Kafka chap can be insufferably abrasive and argumentative beyond reason. And I picked up all of this from just a few short hours in his company! He is somewhat of an enigma, yet he has flashes of humor and pleasantness.

Meanwhile, his friend Max refers to his writing as having the potential for greatness and, can you imagine, worldwide recognition. He even goes so far as to call his style 'Kafka-esque,' which I find to be exceptionally hubristic, premature, and immature, for that matter. On the other hand, none of us who met him can intelligently comment, having never seen any of his work. According to Brod, his work, which sounded as if it must be quite extensive, consists only of a few short stories and commentaries as a product of university assignments. But Mendel and I do agree that if his eventual writing cannot make sense of his presently convoluted thought processes, the world will never hear of him.

Keep an eye out for his name, anyway, Rabbi.
Respecting your interest in all things literary I thought
you would like to have these comments.

As for my own future, I suggested to Rivka after our
Kafka meetings that perhaps I am not contrary or
controversial enough to be a writer. Not yet anyway. She
agreed, especially with the 'not yet.' She is the power
behind my will!

I remain, your friend, and always your pupil,
Sendehr Efraim

Camped on the shores of the Vltava (Moldau), forty
kilometers north of Praha, twenty kilometers south of
Terezin, (Theresienstadt, to the German-speaking
majority) Sunday, June 13, 1904 (10 Sivan, 5664)

Note: Best wishes to all in Birlad. Give my love to
all my family, too. After visiting Rabbi Loew's grave in
the most unusual old Praha cemetery, I wrote this piece,
which I want to share with everyone.

THE STONE FOREST
(*Der Vald foon Shteyn*)

Seeking out this walled-in corner,
a maze-like forest of eroding stone,
this resting place from medieval time
forms an endless montage of *alef, bet* -
a layered landscape of tilting steles
recounting countless tribulations
a mass of *kvittlech*, notes to heaven,
resting on the Maharal's monument,
his Golem standing endless guard -
Praha, city fair, you have honored
history well, preserving this precious
legacy of hallowed ground.

Sendehr Efraim, Praha, 1904
(translated from the Yiddish)

Just before he fell asleep, Sendehr addressed an envelope to Eliezer Viesl in Sighet. He planned to fill it with a few carefully thought-out pages in the next few days. He felt strongly that if anyone in this world should be told about this Loew phenomenon, it was the master journalist of Hungary. Having written no more than the address on the envelope, Sendehr was already anxiously anticipating its return.

The camp was cocooned in silence. Only a few Fusgeyers were still awake, some smoking their pipes or tiny Czech cigars, others sipping tea made from the large pot of boiling water on the solitary fire, which was fast reducing to embers. It was a study in heavenly tranquility.

Rivka awoke just before dawn. Softly slinking over to Sendehr's bedroll, she whispered him awake, holding her fingers to his lips to stifle any sudden outcry.

"*Sendehrel meine,* I sat under the pines waiting for you last night. I must have fallen asleep; I was so frazzled and tired. What happened with Mordecai and Mendel? We can talk if we speak quietly or whisper like this. No one will be really awake for another hour, I'd say."

This was most definitely not the time nor the place Sendehr had wanted to discuss subjects of such serious portent. But he rationalized, asking himself the question once posed by the great Hillel the Elder, foremost of the ancient Talmudic sages, *if not now, when?* Would there ever be a "good" time?

He proceeded at first groggily, holding Rivka close by his prostrate body so he could whisper the details. He reached into his tunic pocket for the notes, and within just ten minutes was able to convey every word to his awestruck, wide-eyed, gasping Rivka. Her tears flowed while Sendehr attempted to soothe her by saying that nothing was chiseled in stone, that this could all be Blankfort's wild imagination, that we have decided how to deal with it rationally and sensibly. He went on to repeat the plan of action to which the triumvirate had agreed, and asked for her help in maintaining the calm, not drawing an inordinate amount of attention to the dilemma or to the words of Blankfort/Loew/ the Golem. She understood, and promised to handle it cautiously, as he had fully expected her to. There was nothing left to say at that moment.

For the first stage of the new day's trek the group decided not to fly the Empire's flag. Too many nationalist sympathizers in this part of Bohemia. No need to bring down their wrath unnecessarily. The *Mogen Dovid*, however, would still proudly fly in all its glory, *anti-Semitten* be damned. The honors went to Bezalel Udler, who hadn't pulled the duty since starting out on the road, when he had been assigned the Romanian flag. He had hated bearing this flag, especially as it was his brother Zacharya who carried the *Mogen Dovid*. He was pleased to oblige this one-week assignment.

Rivka had already prepared the black eagle German banner she had been able to get from Max Brod, Kafka's friend. Brod was a student nationalist-activist and had personally pilfered the yellow, red and black flag from a German-loving student, son of a Czech brewery owner. He felt it would serve a good purpose in helping the Fusgeyers pass safely through the historically and fiercely xenophobic, anti-Semitic Second Reich, which was not much different than the First, and likely displaying the same characteristics that any eventual Third would have.

Surprisingly, no one approached Mordecai, Mendel or Sendehr with any questions. Pessel and Chaike quietly asked Rivka if anything was wrong. Their polite indiscretion told to her that they thought it was a relationship problem between the lovers, and she let them go on thinking that. Esther walked with Mendel as if nothing had happened, and Rivka, in fact, wondered whether Mendel had said anything to his wife or not. It would not have been out of the young teacher's character to keep the secret to himself.

They were about to approach the quiet town of Melnik, following the last of the Vltava as it flowed into the broad River Labe (Elbe, to the German-speakers). It was here that Zed-Zed and Sendehr warned the point team to veer off to the left and stay on the west bank of the larger river that would guide them all the way to Dresden.

The main road was at least three kilometers off to the west at this point, which fit the walking plan perfectly. From this point onward to the border, discretion was the most sensible part of valor in order to avoid any confrontation with the military. As further insurance, they would have to skirt the fortress at Theresienstadt, knowing that it held the largest garrison of Franz Josef's troops between here and Germany. This was the most common intelligence data passed along to the Fusgeyers from many Praha Jews, including Rabbi Blankfort. In the days of research and preparation, Sendehr, Zed-Zed and Mordecai had also read about this fort, mentioned in some of the earlier journals and letters from their predecessor Birladers.

The small town of Theresienstadt/Terezin consisted of a large fortress with two-story barracks next to a smaller one containing a foreboding prison. These were built in 1780 to ward off Prussian attacks from the north, and named in honor of the Empress Maria Theresa.

The town was the fortress and the fortress was the town. Its residents were all in some way involved with the Austrian troops, either as tradesmen, laborers, kitchen help or provisioners. Every sign in town proclaimed "Theresienstadt" although the proud, younger Czechs insisted on "Terezin," except in the presence of the military, which was known to crack heads for such an affront.

The prison was usually filled to capacity, and its detainees served indeterminate sentences, thereby providing a steady supply of road building fodder. An army needed modern highways to move its artillery and supplies, especially with the advent of the motor car and truck. The impetuous young Prussian Kaiser was thought to be completely unpredictable and could attack from the north and west at any time. They called him "Crazy Willi," with more than a grain of truth in the expression.

This unjust imprisonment was hard labor at its worst; something that nationalistic leaders like Masaryk deplored and cited in every rallying cry. Franz Josef paid no heed, and his loyal royalists followed his lead. As everywhere else in the powder keg world of 1904, martinets jealously guarded the keys. Their chilling, facetious words, frequently bellowed at the labor force, were laid out in wrought iron over the prison's main entrance. *Arbeit Macht Frei*: Work Makes You Free. There was a guttural ring to it that gave the phrase a certain feel of permanence, as if generations of slave labor had heard it before, and many more would suffer with it ringing in their ears deep into the new century.

The normal midday break, during the heat of the day, was welcomed. In this weather, the conscientious doctor-nurse team made sure that everyone drank enough water to prevent dehydration. Only one such case had occurred, two weeks back, and the patient recovered quickly. Menachem Zilber was now the first to drink heartily at every opportunity, and to pester everyone else to do the same. Gershon and Maidel were delighted to have such a walking endorsement, annoying *nudzh* that Zilber was.

Strange! Sholem and Yaakov, marching three hundred meters ahead though still in sight, seemed to suddenly disappear around a twist in the riverside path. Usually, the single shrill whistle from Zed-Zed would be enough to make them realize that it was break time. After a few minutes, Branko decided to send Yankel Golub to scout it out and fetch them. Yankel, of the three brothers, seemed to relish this kind of duty He always answered the call to action with a "Yes, sir, Sergeant!" and a snappy salute that Branko felt silly in returning.

No sooner than Yankel turned around the bend than two burly Austrian soldiers appeared, rifles at the ready and marching in a double time cadence toward the already relaxing, scattered-about troop.

Branko and Mordecai, sensing unwanted trouble, ordered everyone to stay still and calm. "Don't make any sudden moves, keep your hands out in the open, visible at all times. Please. This might be serious, but do not show alarm."

Branko knew the drill, having been himself on the rifle-wielding side of this situation many times. Highly disciplined after all this time as a cohesive unit, every man and woman quickly complied. They showed no panic, but hearts beat in unison...thump, thump, thump...nearly audible to each other.

Within a minute the two uniformed *soldaten* had arrived, stopping a short distance in front of the now very concerned leaders. Branko saw that their safety levers were in the "off" position on both weapons. Still, he was of the "best defense is a good offense" school of soldiering, and was determined to speak first to take some modicum of control. He stood taller than anyone else, and with his legs spread apart and hands on hips he looked quite formidable. His long hair and moustache topped by a broad-brimmed black hat, a dirty tan cavalryman's duster-coat he wore in spite of the hot sun, and his well-worn Austrian army boots made him look like a brigand. This was checkmate defiance in the flesh and full dress!

"Good afternoon, *soldaten.* Sergeant Branko Horvitch, his Highnesses Honor Guard, Honorably Retired, at your service." In a booming voice, punctuated by a rigid salute and a heel clicking that could be heard in Vienna, *der groisseh soldat* was even somewhat impressed by his own bravado.

This disarming welcome momentarily paralyzed the adrenaline-pumped Franz Josef regulars until they regained their mission. The senior of the two, who wore two red chevrons on his blue sleeve, could only say one word through his clenched teeth, hand extended, "Papers."

"We are en route to Germany, and on to America. You will see by this transit letter that we have four days remaining in which to leave this beautiful Bohemia of yours." With this remark, Branko reached his hand toward Mordecai who produced the documents, to which Branko added his dog-eared army release papers, and handed the packet to the lance corporal.

"Aha! Captain Ullbricht, who countersigned this letter, is due to arrive today or tonight for an inspection tour of our road widening project. I'll just keep all of this to show him. I am sure that he'll be pleased to see that three of your Israelites have volunteered to help for the rest of the week. We've run short of tramps, drunks and sniveling petty thieves from our fortress prison. In fact, I think we'll take a few more of you! There's work to be done. We have goals to meet!"

He waved his cocked rifle first toward Bezalel Udler, who leaned on the pole holding the *Mogen Dovid* flag; and next to Menachem Berman standing beside to him; then to the oversized Mottkeleh Bercovici and his equally hefty cousin, Pini Kantorovitz; and on to a broad-shouldered Heshy Rosen; and finally to a stunned, disbelieving Itzy Gelman, who had slipped partially behind an acacia tree a moment too late. Aside from Bezalel and Menachem, the others were the strongest looking of the group. The soldiers intended to add more muscle to the convict work force.

"Step lively, volunteers, leave everything behind," snapped the other soldier, nervously waving his carbine.

All six obeyed after Branko gave them a short nod. Mordecai protested vehemently, but their protests met ignoring eyes and deaf ears, as the uniformed perpetrators shoved the six "volunteers" ahead of them and were quickly trotting back up the narrow, dusty roadway.

"Don't despair, comrades. We'll get you back very soon!" Mordecai meant for his parting words, shouted in Romanian, to give hope, but probably did little to erase the picture that was swiftly developing in each of the abductee's minds – that of of a ship leaving port without them.

Literally within minutes, Mordecai and Branko hastily drew up orders of the day with the silent, grim, full understanding and cooperation of the cadre. Then, with Mordecai standing by his side, Branko issued forth the orders with his usual brand of authority.

1. Sholem, Yaakov, Menachem, Yankel Golub and the others need to be extricated from their captor's grasp

before mid-afternoon, before Ullbricht arrives or receives word of our presence.

2. Sendehr, Yossi Golub, Rivka and Avi Semelweiss—step up here. Don't ask any questions yet.

3. Everyone listen closely. You will have just five minutes from this moment by Zed-Zed's trusty timepiece to prepare for immediate departure. Simmy is in charge of the cart and the *shleppers.* Yoni Golub, I know you want to help rescue your brother, but you're needed to go along with Simmy, to take Mottke's place on the *shlepping* crew. You'll have sole access to the remaining weapons, to be used only if *absolutely necessary.* Hear me? You people will precede everyone else when Zed-Zed gives the signal.

4. Sendehr's maps here show a fifty-square kilometer patch of pine forest beginning about ten kilometers due northwest of Leitmeritz/Litomerice. According to the 1903 reports, there will be a 30-40 meter tall water tower just before an apple orchard ends abruptly at the first line of trees. That will be our rendezvous point. Quickly, now, memorize the key points.

5. Four groups, more or less equally divided by the cadre will leave here at five-minute intervals, beginning in, ah, three minutes. Zed-Zed, mark time! Each group will use the bypass road about one kilometer behind us.

6. Nuchim, you will lead the first group. Pick ten people right now to take with you. Everyone should be ready to go. Mendel and Esther, take the second group. Velvel Palastrant, the third. Zed-Zed the last. Simmy, are you ready with the cart? Here's a quick map sketch Sendehr drew for you. Good. Go! All group leaders gather round to familiarize yourselves with Sendehr's maps. Just memorize the key points and road junctions. There are good road signs in this area, and we've given you both the German and Czech names for all locales so you won't be confused. The

water tower should be visible for several kilometers. Be sure to use it as your beacon.

7. Gershon and Maidele, you will go with Zed-Zed, but lag a bit behind him in the event that anyone needs medical help following the rescue. We hope to be no more than minutes behind you.

8. Groups one and two, you will continue following Simmy and the cart, avoiding Leitmeritz/Litomerice, until you come to a point just across the river from Theresienstadt/Terezin. You will then follow the only northerly country lane the rest of the way until it meets up with the river within sight of the orchard, water tower and forest edge.

9. Groups three and four, stay as parallel as possible, following another road marked on Sendehr's map which Zed-Zed will be carrying. Use the small villages of Lebcheven/Libochovany and Sebitz/Sebuzin as your landmarks, but remember: both also to be widely circumvented.

10. Spread out, do nothing to draw attention. If by chance military or police units appear, do not panic, but try to blend in with local villagers walking the same paths. If near a cluster of houses, disperse and meet again on the other side. Once in the orchard, be prepared to disappear into the thickness of the forest. Otherwise, wait for the rest of us and our rescued comrades to appear.

11. And by God's hand, we will!

With this, Mordecai gave out with a booming *omayn!* All followed suit. There were hugs for all still standing by, ready for Zed-Zed's interval signal to leave.

Everyone, particularly the group leaders, understood the orders and knew the gravity of the situation. Common sense was not at all in short supply with these Fusgeyers. *Yiddishe kopps* prevailed. Even Mayer Kelemer, worried about Itzy, hoping he would stifle himself and be careful with his loose words, was as deeply morose as anyone could remember. Not a laugh, not a gag, not a smile was forthcoming.

The remarkable precision with which the mass dispersal was being carried out at such short notice appeared to be a condition for which they had trained for years. Such was not the case, even though there had been casual talk of the possible need for such contingencies. Complacency would find no practitioners here.

By the time Zed-Zed's group was about to leave, bringing up the rear, the rescue team was ready to go. This was planned and ordered in all of thirty minutes, from the time Simmy and the cart left, up to this heart-pounding moment.

It had to work. There was no acceptable alternative and everyone understood this implicitly.

Branko and Golub would each carry fully-loaded, ten-inch-barrel, Romanian army-issue revolvers. These had been stored in the cart, though rarely brought out from under the piles of food and supplies since leaving home. Mordecai had extracted a promise from each that they would be concealed and not brandished or used except as a last resort, and only if critical to the mission. He knew that neither of them could be completely trusted to honor the agreement, Yossi Golub least of all, but Mordecai did not have the luxury of alternatives.

The three of them would form a flank team, remaining undercover, but close enough to witness the staged drama. If needed, they could be there in seconds. Branko was positive that there would be no more than three or four armed guards for a road working crew. He had pulled enough of this boring duty himself and was completely familiar with troop-sparing regulations when it concerned non-combatant operations.

Why was Mordecai personally taking part in the mission? Shouldn't he go on with the main body and leave this for Branko? No. No. The undisputed, singular leader of the 1904 Birlad Fusgeyers was not about to abdicate, to place this most dangerously confrontational of all incidents to befall the group in anyone else's hands. If anything taking place at this monumental, defining moment could go without saying, this most certainly was it.

Why was Avigdor "Avi" Semelweiss selected only minutes after Mordecai asked Rivka to come up with a scenario for rescue? This was destined to become self-evident to all once Rivka's drama began. Suffice it to say that Avi, besides being the third fastest runner, was a fourteen-year-old who was so short and thin that he appeared to be nine or ten. As for Rivka and Sendehr, the curtain was about to part. Let the cast take their places!

Rivka, resplendent in a makeshift gypsy dress, a *babushka* covering her dark tresses, long looped earrings drooping from each ear, and a hip swinging swagger, led the way. Looking like every woman of the night seen in Budapest, Vienna and Praha, she was flanked by Sendehr and Avi. Once Mordecai and his party safely blended into the trees on the riverside of the bend, they picked up the pace.

When they came around the bend, they were in full view of a thirty-odd man labor force, the drivers of two horse drawn wagons, and four soldiers. The only reaction came from the newly conscripted nine, and a rapid but barely discernable shake of Rivka's head stopped that in its tracks.

No one called out, no one gave a sign of recognition, and all nine continued with their assigned pick-axing or shoveling. As luck would have it, three of the soldiers were eating their midday meals, sitting together on a fallen log, their rifles stacked off to the side. The fourth, the one holding the Fusgeyers's papers, watched the work effort while leaning against a tree only a few meters from the hidden Branko, Mordecai and Yossi. The two supply wagon teamsters, likely unarmed, appeared to be napping under a pine tree more than a hundred meters up the road.

Rivka had played to audiences far more animated than this.

Sendehr was adorned in full makeup of dried and

brushed river mud, just on the off-chance that one of the soldiers might spot him, since he had been standing near Mordecai during their foray into the Fusgeyer camp. He wore his straw hat pulled down over his eyes and was acting the part of a blind man, using his walking stick to feel his way. Rivka held one of his arms, and she tried to control the wriggling Avi with her other arm.

The little one walked in a severely deformed manner, dribbled from the mouth disgustingly, wailed in an eerie, piercing tone, and flailed his little pencil thin arms and legs wildly, In this way he wrenched his way free from Rivka, only to have her grab his hand again and again. He kept up the wailing and flailing continuously from the moment they came into view. Wild blueberries mashed into his lips gave his mouth a cadaverous look. Avi was nothing short of superb.

As they approached the three soldiers, Rivka pulled the actors aside for a moment to let a passing wagon go through the morass of piled dirt and stone. No need for any additional witnesses. By this time, the three targets had stopped in mid-mouthful, unable to continue, waiting for the trio of misfit gypsy trash to pass through.

Avi, at Rivka's prompt, spittle all over his mouth and chin, went straight for the soldiers, causing one of them to drop his field kit full of sausages and potatoes. They yelled frantically for Rivka to "get your little crippled bastard out of here." Rivka complied, reeling in the still flailing and wailing banshee.

Coming center stage, Rivka, in melodic *roma* language, punctuated by broken Romanian and Germanic-Yiddish, begged their forgiveness, saying *"entschuldig mir, entschuldig mir, bitte, vobitzi, imu pare rau, bitte,"* and with these apologies she bowed profusely while decadently showing a bit of beautifully curved leg. Then, in a flamboyantly exaggerated motion, she drew from her knapsack the *piece de resistance*, a bottle of coveted Znojmo wine, known all over Central Europe simply as Moravian "Deep Purple."

Their eyes widened and jaws dropped when they saw

the label and the distinctive bottle, and the corporal grabbed for it. He quickly pulled the cork from the bottle with his teeth and guzzled. Passing it to his underlings, he yelled across the road to the lance corporal, "Adolf, come over and have a drink. It's the best!"

Branko certainly knows the Austrian military's gluttonous passion for anything alcoholic, thought Rivka.

The next minute seemed eternal to the intrepid dramatic cast, the anxiously waiting three-in-the-bush, and the disbelieving, dumbstruck captive nine watching everything unfold theatrically. When the sergeant abruptly doubled over, vomiting in cascades, followed in quick succession by the other three of Austria's finest, pandemonium broke loose. In a flash, Sendehr grabbed the stricken lance corporal's fallen rifle, as Branko leaped out of hiding, searching for and finding the papers in the man's shoulder pouch.

Simultaneously, Yossi made a dash for the three stacked weapons. The nine detainees recovered quickly from their surprise, and ran toward a beckoning Mordecai, into the pine grove, followed by the miraculously cured Avi, the painted "gypsy," and the suddenly sighted blind man. Meanwhile, the unarmed teamsters in the distance, wanting no part of this action, could be seen driving their wagons off in a cloud of dust.

A few of the puzzled prisoners tried to follow the Fusgeyers into the grove, but Branko, wielding one of the rifles, waved them off and motioned for them to head in the opposite direction. There was no place for excess baggage on this freedom train!

Once across the narrow bridge on the outskirts of Leitmeritz/Litomerice, the plan called for splitting into two parties. Branko took one, Mordecai the other, and each headed at a fast trot to the two parallel northbound roads that the earlier departing groups had followed. So far, so good! Much too early to celebrate; but once they did take a few seconds to thank God.

Omayn resounded in the fields of Bohemia.

Within the hour, an unexpected cloudburst added to

their definite advantage in eluding any eventual search parties. Mud-faced Sendehr whimsically thanked the late, great Rabbi Loew, for he saw his fine hand somewhere in all of this. Mordecai showed his agreement with a mischievous wink at Rivka's co-star.

Gershon and Maidele had followed their orders exactly, and had as such dropped quite far behind Zed-Zed. Branko's group soon caught up to them, and they received the happy news that Mordecai was close behind. They could see there was no need for medical assistance, and hugs and kisses were shared all around.

"Gershon, I don't know what you gave Rivka out of your new medicine bag, but it worked well beyond belief. You looking for patients? There are four violently *krank soldaten* back there who won't be sitting down to a good meal for weeks," gloated a proud and exhausted Branko.

"It really worked out?"

"Oh, yes, indeed. That wine we saved from Znojmo mixed very well. Rivka, imitate the sounds of retching Austrians!"

"I just took the bottle marked *Achtung* that you gave me and poured the whole thing into the wine bottle," offered a delighted Rivka, noticing Mordecai's group trudging up the hill, and relieved to see a rain-drenched Sendehr waving at her.

"The whole bottle! *Oy,vay iz mir!* My good God, Rivka! That was the most powerful emetic ever made. Dr. Warmbrand warned me to use it with great care. Just one spoonful would have effectively induced rapid vomiting in an elephant!"

"A fine doctor, you are, Gershon. You gave me no dosage directions!" With that, everyone within earshot howled with laughter, amid back-slapping all around.

By four o'clock the rendezvous and an ecstatic reunion took place at the base of the water tower. All fifty-seven Fusgeyers were accounted for, and ready for the next step in their escape from Austrian-occupied Bohemia. Those few who expected to rest in the wet pine forest that night did not register much surprise when Mordecai announced that a night dash to the border was in order.

They would have a light supper, rest until dark, and then proceed as directed to the German border. Not until then would they breathe easily. Even though no one appeared to be in the area of the forest, it was still important to keep the silence. This would be difficult, since all were so eager to sing and shout and dance that night. Little wonder, after a day that saw such a full range of emotions, but it would have to wait.

* * *

Captain Ullbricht was enraged.

Other than issuing orders, he didn't speak to anyone. *They must be stopped. They must pay.* These were the only two thoughts in his mind. The four victims, as deathly sick as they were, abed in the fort's hospital, received hard slaps across the face from the *paskudnyak* after he had ordered the sergeant and the lance corporal to rip off their stripes.

As Chief Road Improvement Officer for the Bohemian Protectorate, he had the unchecked power and responsibility to get the road building jobs done with dispatch. The Austro-Hungarian Empire was deep in the throes of modernizing its military in order to contend with the Germans, the French, the Russians and the British. Top priority had long ago been given to road construction and maintenance in order to move men and equipment rapidly and economically, for offensive or defensive purposes.

Every fort, large and small alike, between Praha and the German border had been telephoned or telegraphed to be on the constant alert for the criminals. Branko Horvitch and Mordecai Anieloff, the only names known, were deemed co-conspirators in the attempted murder of "four gallant Soldiers of the Empire."

Rivka was described as a "murderous gypsy prostitute, the third conspirator and perpetrator of the dastardly insane deed." Her "crippled bastard son" and "blind pimp" were named as "dangerous accessories to this brutal act."

The nine escapees were referred to as "duly conscripted workers in the Empire's labor force, currently at-large as deserters," with sentences of two years at hard labor pronounced upon each, listed as "unidentified Jew" *in absentia.* The rest of the Fusgeyers were referred to as a "ragged band of thieving Jew-Romanian vagabonds, lacking proper papers."

Like a cornered animal, Captain Ignatius Ullbricht gnashed his fangs, seeking the ultimate in revenge.

* * *

The quarter moon, obscured by lingering rain clouds, would provide little navigational assistance for this run to the border. Sendehr pored over his maps with special diligence. He had to be exact. There was absolutely no margin for error. He was fortunate that he had found such a recent, exquisitely detailed Austrian army topographical survey map along with an 1880 map of Bohemia. The army map clearly indicated the location of every military installation. Something to avoid, in this case!

After heated discussion, not *pilpul* style, the cadre decided against splitting into four separate groups again. They would work with intervals and point teams filling in predetermined positions. In this way, they would reach the German border all at once, rather than coping with delays that could occur with four groups traveling in the dark of night. The consummate question was where?

Just where should we, can we, cross the border? The manned Austrian stations were marked on the army map and one had to assume that they would be patrolling all night, on the lookout for the notorious Birlad *banditten.* It was Sendehr's responsibility to select a point on the face of the map where a safe crossing could be made. Obviously some isolated spot between the manned stations. He conferred with Zed-Zed as usual, and they agreed to stay far to the east of Aussig/Usti nad Labem where the largest army installation was located. This base translated into more manpower and more frequent search missions throughout the night.

It was logically and correctly assumed that word of their brazen breakout had fanned out all over Northern Bohemia. What they didn't know was the extent of the vengeance Ullbricht was attempting to exact. They had hit him hard where his ego was exposed, and most likely he would be joining the hot pursuit.

"Here, Zed, we've got to cross here. It's midway between stations at Cinovec, here, and just a short distance from Tetschen/Decin. No more than twenty kilometers. That should bring us into this German village, here, Breitnau, just over the border by sunrise." Sendehr marked each point with a big dot so all concerned could see it clearly during the final briefing.

Zed-Zed frowned. "All well and good. But how do we cross the Elbe without using this bridge, here, just south of Tetschen? You know for certain all bridges across the river will be watched."

Both of them pondered this dilemma for a few moments until Sendehr broke in with "Aha! Have you noticed that every town and village on the banks of the river has had its own public dock with three, four and more row boats tied up to it?"

"Are you suggesting, Admiral Sendehr Shmendehr, that we become the Birlad Navy?"

This plan and others were hashed over until the last light of day faded at nine o'clock. The sun had made a brief appearance as the rain clouds passed, and only a sliver of a moon would be lighting the way for the next eight or nine hours. With approximately twenty kilometers to the Tetschen bridge area and another twenty to the selected border point, they estimated no more than five kilometers per hour considering the pitch dark night travel ahead, and possible delays to evade detection.

They also resigned themselves to the very real possibility of having to leave the trusty cart behind. This would slow them down further, when much of the contents could be distributed and carried. No one looked forward to this, especially Simmy.

It had never been said that the road to America would be a smooth one, but nevertheless the Fusgeyers were once again into the trek, by the grace of God, to Germany, nonstop. *Please, God!*

* * *

Confronted at the first light of dawn by six uniforms, four rifles and two Luger revolvers leveled at them, the lead point team consisting of Sendehr, Sholem, Yaakov and Branko, wearily extended their tired arms into the air.

Branko, who could do nothing but break into a smile of deep satisfaction and joy, knew a German army uniform when he saw one. "Mission accomplished, lads," he whispered.

Branko had known all along that his former comrades would not be quite so diligent in attempting to apprehend them. He remembered distinctly that night patrols were rarely if ever deployed during peacetime. Night was traditionally a time for carousing and heavy drinking, not heavy duty. Platoon commanders were not anxious for a stray bullet in the back, and consequently they were turtle-slow in issuing such orders, Captain Ignatius Ullbricht and his confounded road building be damned!

That would explain the relative ease with which they were able to travel by night to get this far. The ever-alert ex-Sergeant Horvitch had not shared this fact with anyone, lest their guards be let down.

Even the cart escaped certain abandonment when Branko insisted that the narrow, sagging bridge below Tetschen/Decin would not be a problem to cross. A bit of stealthy reconnaissance proved him right. Not a soldier in sight. Not a soldier in sight all night!

At the Breitnau Barracks it took some of Branko's *chutzpah* to tell of the daring raid at the expense of the embarrassed Austrians. His story met with hearty guffaws from their neighboring enemies. When Mordecai showed the papers to the still-chuckling commander, proving their intentions, destination and prepaid ticketing, he was granted a ninety-day transit visa immediately. More than adequate, when the August 15th sailing date was only sixty days away!

The German government was obviously eager to send someone else's "Jewish problem" to America.

§

"I can't believe you're coming home tomorrow, sweetheart."

"These ten days have been a blur, hon. I still have an all-day session with Rabbi Nachman today, and we're driving him to Bucharest tomorrow."

"Herbert called Lisa about an hour ago. Six a.m. your time."

"He and Rico must have gone out for a jog, as usual. I'll see them at breakfast in a few minutes. Yesterday, they explored Birlad like two detectives, with the help of a local schoolteacher who speaks English well. He has a sister living in Pasadena."

"I'm so glad they're there with you. Lisa said they're really getting a lot out of this trip."

"I know they are. I think, if nothing else, it has certainly instilled a sense of history and genealogy in both of them. Especially Rico. Kid asks the damnedest, most provocative questions. Won't stop until he gets an answer. I like that."

Just two days to go. Maybe I should extend. Hope we can cover the rest of the story. I feel as though I'm my own father, and that tomorrow we'll be leaving on foot. To Budapest. To Prague. To Berlin. To Bremerhaven.

These were just a few of the thoughts of one Nathan Friedman, 7:00 a.m., June 15, 2000, Birlad, Romania.

17

ENCOUNTERS: ROAD TO BERLIN

...There I was, ready to build my body, my muscles, my stamina, when all of a sudden, out of nowhere, come my rescuers. Did I ask to be saved? Do I really want to walk the rest of the way to Bremerhaven when I could be in a cozy, warm jail with hot, trayfeh food and a giant leper for a cellmate? Thank you for nothing!

An ungrateful Itzy Gelman

It is written in the Talmud: "To save one life is as if to save the entire world." Even if it's Itzy Gelman's?

A response by Mayer Kelemer

Sendehr never missed a day of journal entries...even during the daring rescue. In another in the series of private letters to Eli Nachman, following his synopsis of the past week's enormously exciting events, he confided:

Rabbi, there is absolutely no one amongst us who has not thanked God for His gracious deliverance, privately or openly. When I think of all the things that could have gone amiss, I shudder and shake. I am certain that this is not a rare phenomenon within our group...especially those directly involved...not for a long time to come.

It has been steadily raining hard since Shabbos. We have not ventured forth from this abandoned, leaky old barn since yesterday morning. Everything is either damp or thoroughly wet; half of us are sneezing, the other half is coughing, and each one of us is bone-tired. Maybe this is God's way of saying we need some proper rest after the turbulent events that have propelled us through the last week. Zed-Zed and I suggested to Mordecai that because we are so well ahead of schedule we could afford an extra few days for this special shelter—Ribono shel olam, a solid roof would have been even better!

The people of Jewish Dresden are an enigma to us. They seem so cold and distant. For example, we staged our little play on Saturday night, and the attendance did not come close to that of similar sized communities. The applause was polite, but hardly what one would call enthusiastic. We realize that the language problem is more than a minor hindrance. The Viennese and the Czechs seemed more comfortable with the German-Yiddish mix than do the Germans we have thus far encountered. Branko and Mendel were constantly translating. Our Kalman Fuchs, whose father came to Birlad from Munich, was able to assist Branko on occasion, taking a bit of the pressure off him. He remarked how similar the German-Jewish aloofness was to his own father's personality—a comment from Kalman that surprised a number of us. I remember Branko, though, smiling and nodding his head knowingly at the time, calling into account his twelve years service with the Austrians.

At the Neolog synagogue where we performed Vinschfingerl we had a brief conversation with one congregant that made more sense with every new encounter we faced that weekend.

Gershon Weiss had emigrated from Radom, Poland, about ten years ago. He has a wife and seven children, and he was a maker of non-kosher sausages in a large factory. When the owner of the enterprise died the eldest son decided it was distasteful to have a Jew working there, so Weiss and his family immigrated to Dresden where his wife's uncle has a large meat processing business. The point he made that German Jews utterly despise Eastern Jews, the ostjuden, and the severe animosities he revealed that they showed them was both new and shocking to both Mordecai and me.

Oh, yes, we have seen rare occasions of this deprecatory attitude on this journey, as practiced by the chassidim of Szatmar and some individual Hungarian, Austrian, and to a lesser extent, Czech Jews in our encounters. But not to the bitter extent Reb Weiss woefully described. He claims that it is ingrained as deeply as German nationalism and abject anti-Semitism. We pray that he is overreacting, but only the next few weeks will tell. I'll keep you informed.

Rivka is disturbed to think about the reality of it. I'm not to that point yet, but I can empathize with her. I think she was mostly affected by the obvious snobbery, which, indeed, was far more pronounced in the synagogue during the play performance and on the streets and in the shops than any we have ever seen. Only a handful turned out on the road leading to town to welcome us even after Sholem and Yaakov spread the word by arriving first as they usually do. Obviously, the German Jew hawt zein eigeneh mishigas. As Itzy is quick to suggest, "Maybe we should have bought a shpritzer in that Viennese perfume shop and sprayed every one of us. Then again, it may also be our traveling finery that annoys them!"

One other incident is also troubling and, yes, embarrassing at the same time. I already reported this in the attached synopsis, but I prefer to go into detail herein.

Meeting those ten stragglers from the Galatz Fusgeyer brigade just before we entered Dresden was disconcerting to all of us, to say the least. "Stragglers" is probably not the right word to use for them; "Remnants" *would be more descriptive and appropriate. It was exceedingly sad to hear their story. I personally attribute the tragedy to their lack of unified leadership. Thanks to God, we have had solidarity in abundance since we formed the group last year. To think that they experienced constant divisiveness from the day they left home leaves us all incredulous. I shudder to think that without the example of Mordecai's leadership, and the cadre's strong sense of pride and duty, we could very possibly be facing a similar predicament. Nevertheless, we still have a long march ahead of us.*

They started out with nearly eighty. They called themselves "Students, Workers and Clerks of Galatz," and as they walked through the southern regions of Hungary by way of Temesvar/Timishoara, everything began to disintegrate. They were able to get that far only because a philanthropist in Bucureshti arranged passage proof through l'Alliance Israelite Universelle, and he provided the group with enough money for the purchase of passage if and when they arrived in Hamburg...in cash! This was a major mistake on his part, as you will see, Rabbi.

No one, absolutely no one, picked up the reins of leadership. They had to forage for food each day and had no advance planning, no route plans, and no maps. It's a miracle they somehow got through to Germany, bypassing Budapest, Vienna and Praha in favor of Bavaria. By the time they crossed the border at Passau on the Danube more than half the group had turned back, hoping to reach Galatz by their own efforts.

One day after crossing the German border, a very quiet man, a goniff who joined the group in Timishoara, stole all of the money from the pouch carried by one person. Yes, one person! They had not even thought of distributing the funds among six, seven or ten people, as we do. No precautions for any type of security was ever administered evidently...truly a most naive, in fact, ignorant group. It was most fortunate that they were able to avoid the Theresienstadt area where we had our own near-disaster. They would have all ended up working in the forced labor gangs for who knows how long!

With only twenty left on the roster, and no money to purchase passage if they should actually reach Hamburg, one of them, in markedly belated fashion, took charge. He decided that they should look for work in Dresden, Chemnitz or Leipzig, even though their transit visa had less than two weeks remaining. They had failed to find anything in any city, being summarily turned away in a very unpleasant manner by the Jewish communities, and another ten marchers scattered to the winds, heading for God knows where...and with none of the necessary papers in hand!

When we met the remaining ten, they were on their way to Praha to throw themselves on the mercy of the good people of Jewish Town. My guess is that they were probably able to get a transit visa from the Hapsburg border guards only because they were seen as most welcome additions for Ullbricht's construction projects. Mendel, Branko, Mordecai and I vehemently protested their irrational plan, strongly advising them to walk east through Poland and turn toward Romania through Czernowitz, clandestinely crossing the borders while praying for the good disposition of any military or local constabulary they met along the way. As an alternative, we urged them to consider heading back toward Berlin to look for help from either the Labor Alliance or the aforementioned Israelite Universelle. They didn't seem to want to listen.

Tragically, they'll more than likely be seeing the inside of Theresienstadt in a week or so. We all feel so saddened by this, but at least we gave them some food supplies and what little money Nuchim felt we could afford to spare.

Perhaps you can contact one of the rabbis in Galatz and tell him of this horrible dilemma. The leader who spoke for the tattered group was Chaim Mentzer, a dis-

traught and beaten lad who has tried his best. There, but for the grace of God...we are so very fortunate, Rabbi Nachman!

I look forward to receiving your letters when we arrive in Berlin.

I have also been writing to Elie Viesl frequently. His articles have been a boon to our effort, and we hope that soon Max Nordau's feature stories will enhance our mission. These two extremely influential and respected journalists can stimulate public opinion with just a few strokes of the pen. My dear King Carol, beware; sit up and take notice!

I am, your correspondent in Germany,Sendehr Efraim,waiting out the third day of summer rainstorms,just north of Dresden, nearing Grossenhain...Tuesday, June 22, 1904 (19 Sivan, 5664)

Here, in the recently unified nation that had given the world the lyrical poetry of Goethe, the orchestral compositions of Brahms, and the graceful fugues of Bach, the Wayfarers of Birlad forged ahead toward their goal.

"Prislop Pass in a violent snowstorm, the hazardous border crossings, Pesach in Sighet, the Szatmar Rebbe, the bandits of the Hortobagy, the glitter of Budapest, the saber-wielding incident at Szentendre, detention at Schwechat, the Herzl meeting, confrontation in Lower Bohemia, the Maharal's dire predictions, the great escape from certain catastrophe...all this in less than three months." Mendel Buchman recited this litany of Wayfarer history-in-the-making events proudly, as if he needed to convince himself and those who heard him that they had really accomplished such marvelous feats. In his own inimitable manner he periodically offered this recapitulation as a prelude to his elective history lectures.

Tonight he felt duly obligated to introduce those interested to the pendulous history of the Jew in Germany, having seen and heard the reactions to the less-than-enthusiastic greetings and tepid hospitality afforded by the Dresdner Yidden. Mendel had been an ardent reader of the precious few books written in the century just past concerning the Jewish condition in the various regions of Central and Eastern Europe. As for Germany, Moses Goldhammer's *Germany and the Jew* was something he avidly read in English while at school in Greece, and found it to be more than just a history. It was, by his account, a social commentary, a foreboding, and a sociological treatise well respected by many exegetic historians of the period. Montgomery-Lloyd, his professor at the school in Salonika, knowing of his interest in the subject, recommended Goldhammer along with Felix Rotmann's *Jewish Business and the German Economy: Partners or Foes?*

"Now that we are in Germany, with little to do but wait for the torrents to subside, I want to familiarize you with this chameleon of a country, in regard to *unsereh Yidden*." So began the Aristotelian scholar, as he tried to project his voice above the constant din of the driving rainstorm, cloudbursts and crackling lightning.

Although only about fifteen sat huddled around a wet mound of aromatic hay to listen to Mendel, his eloquence, as usual, was fit for any college lecture hall. As he had been doing more frequently lately, English words and phrases were intentionally slipped into Yiddish phrases. For example, *"nisht azay zufridden* are the cold Dresdner *Yidden"*—the cold Jews of Dresden are not very happy—to which Sholem quickly added, "On di udder hent, I tink dat many Joos *zein sehr zufridden* in dis Choiman *Gan Eden"*—I think that many Jews are very happy in this German Garden of Eden. Obviously, the Yiddish was needed for rhyming effect, if for no other reason, and the laughter was able to entice the additional attendance of a few who had stayed away fearing an ultra-intellectual pedagogic session was in store for them.

With a fat raindrop clinging stubbornly to the end of his long nose, Mendel went on to describe various cataclysmic events that had befallen Germany's Jews, beginning with the days following Martin Luther's rise to fame and The Holy Roman Empire in the sixteenth century. In Wittenberg, situated between Dresden and Berlin, the Augustinian monk took his stand. Luther refused to appear at the Vatican before Pope Leo X, who, in turn, excommunicated him. As for the perennial toothache in the jaw of any other religious movement—the Jew—Luther at first openly praised and later, far more vociferously, condemned.

> *The Jews are the best blood on earth; through them alone the Holy Ghost wished to give all books of Holy Scripture to the world; they are the children and we are the guests and the strangers.*

In denouncing the clergy for their brutal and senseless fulmination against the Jews, 1524.

> *If we would help them, so must we exercise, not the law of the Pope, but that of Christian love...show them a friendly spirit, permit them to live and to work, so that they have cause and means to be with us and amongst us...and if some remain obstinate, what of it? Not every one of us is a good Christian.*
>
> From his pamphlet *Jesus Was Born a Jew* published seven times in one year, 1526.

In his stinging pamphlet entitled *Concerning the Jews and their Lies*, written in 1543, Luther contradicted all of the aforementioned by accusing the Jews of everything from well poisoning to murdering Christian children. He called for the burning of the synagogues, the confiscation of Jewish wealth, and denounced Jewish physicians for poisoning their patients, concluding with the inflammatory inference:

> *I say to you, as a countryman, if the Jews refuse to be converted, we ought not suffer them or bear with them any longer.*

351

The newly courageous Protestant communities of that era in Germany listened. And they listened well. The obdurate monk-reformer had metamorphosed into a raving draconian, once again posing the incantatory conundrum that would be echoed through the centuries ahead; to be known simply as the "Jewish problem."

Mendel mentioned this Lutheran syndrome to set the stage for the more current events, particularly targeting the anti-*ostjuden* phenomenon that the Fusgeyers had begun to encounter.

"Unlike our *landsmen* in Birlad or in the Pale, the German—and yes, a goodly percentage of other Western European Jews—had seen the distinct advantages of assimilating into the prevailing surrounding cultures. Do you remember some of the Budapest thinking? Viennese? Praha? Just consider the German to be more so! They hoped during the numerous acts of emancipation following the French Revolution that they would someday no longer be seen as permanent outsiders, thereby gaining rights traditionally denied them. Today they still have that vision. They have since dropped the old garb, the 'exotic' behaviors, the pariah stigma, and especially the use of the Yiddish language. Talk to any German Jew today and he will insist on speaking pure German, not even the Germanic-Yiddish that was so prevalent in Praha and Vienna. They will go so far as to pretend not to understand a word we speak. They have made, and continue to make, a concerted effort to steer clear of any reminder of their 'barbaric' past. They cringe at the sight of any Jew who would be an embarrassment to them. Us? Of course! Especially you, Yoni!" quipped the *lehrer*, pointing to the youngest Golub who had a deep, puzzled look on his frowning face. He sat hunched up near an off-the-hinge barn door. Mendel knew very well that it was difficult for Yoni and some of the younger ones to grasp the finer meaning of how historic events had led to the Wayfarers' plight. But, he persisted in these lessons because he felt that apathy and ignorance had no place in their futures.

"So, *nu* Mendel, is it good or bad for the Yidden?"

Yankel's well calculated and familiar, personal shibboleth brought out the usual raucous laughter. Two rain-soaked locals in a wagon riding by on the muddy lane two hundred meters away couldn't begin to imagine what was going on in that dilapidated old barn, and they were much too wet to bother investigating the laughter coming from it.

As he concluded this most illuminating talk, Mendel was certain that most understood the dynamics of the German-Jewish condition. Mordecai, recalling a letter sent from one of the 1901 'geyers to Rabbi Holtzer that decried the demeaning nature of his tenement landlord, a second-generation German Jew who constantly and openly referred to his Romanian tenants as "*mamaliga* morons," wondered aloud if this was common in New York.

"Mordecai, statistics do not lie. The German refugees populating New York and other eastern American cities—Boston, Philadelphia, Newark, Baltimore—in the middle of last century, carried with them the very hostility I've been describing. The same condescending attitude that the *Poylisher* in Dresden related to you and Sendehr. Historically, it takes more than just one or two generations for this type of prejudice to dissipate.

"This is not in any way to infer that everything about the German Jew is undesirable. No. In America, he has been in the forefront of providing *ostjuden* refugees every variety of financial assistance and social program, from what I've been able to determine. His goal is to lift them up to his standards, while not getting his hands too dirty. In that way, he must feel that they, too, will assimilate to a greater degree and all will be roses and rose water for the new American Jew. A noble thought. Practical? We shall soon see for ourselves."

"*Ay, yi, yi,* what are we getting into?" frets a nearby Pessel Vinocur within earshot.

"*Daigeh nisht, shvesterel*...not to worry, little sister...when Birlad meets New York, everything will change!" responds the always-cocky Food Czar.

"What about Boston, Sim?" asks Comedian Number Two.

"That, Mister Laugh-man, is your problem!"

"You see, *boychicklach,* we should have all stayed in Theresienstadt!"

With that final retort from Comedian Number One, the formal part of the evening came to a fitting close.

The plan was to start off, rain or shine, the following morning. What was in store for them on the road to Berlin, and in the city itself, was to continue to be an intriguing mystery waiting to be solved. Only a good night's sleep was next on the agenda.

§

At breakfast, Nathan finally appeared to show signs of exhaustion from the last nine long days, possibly due to the intermittent sleep he experienced during the past few nights. He was more than pleased with the success of the visit, having been fortunate enough to find the one person in Romania, and likely in the entire world, who could tell the Fusgeyer story with authority and certain inalienable proofs. Nathan had even been able to trace the beginning steps of the trek, following them by automobile. Most importantly to him, though, was that his son and grandson were happily involved in the quest.

Nevertheless, there was something missing, and this had begun to disturb him. He couldn't put his finger directly on it, but he was convinced that it was merely a closure problem; still hazy, but he would have to sort it out before leaving Rabbi Nachman in Bucharest on Friday. Time was running out fast. Nathan even toyed with the idea of staying the weekend in Bucharest and flying back to L.A. on Monday, sending Herb and Rico back as scheduled and promised. But, for what purpose? To what end? The Rabbi would be busy visiting with his ailing brother, and what could he see or do in Bucharest that would provide the resolution he sought?

"So what have you boys scheduled for your last day in Birlad?"

"Don't laugh when I tell you what Eric talked me into last night."

"I'll tell Grandpa, Dad. We're going to freshen the white-wash on the Rabbi's house, paint the door, the doorway and windowsills. Blue trim. We'll make it look like new in no time. It needs it so badly; don't you think? The hardware store has a good selection of paints and brushes—we checked them out yesterday. We even recruited our 'guide' Petru to help. He's bringing us some old T-shirts and pants to wear, and..."

Eric's near stream-of-consciousness spilled out so rapidly that Nathan's cobwebs cleared.

"Great, Rico! What a wonderful idea. You're right, it sure as hell needs it. I was thinking of mentioning it to Berel Usher and now I won't have to. Proud of you guys! My boys!"

He put a firm grip on Herb's arms across the table, and in turn, on Rico's.

"I'll tell Rabbi Nachman before you get there. I'll also try to get his permission to take off the *mezuzzah*. Beats trying to paint around it."

With that, and one last cautious sip of the potent Turkish coffee to which he had somehow, somewhat, almost, but not quite gotten accustomed to, Nathan adopted a jaunty stride toward the Birlad *shul* and his storyteller nonpareil. He didn't care to dwell any further upon his "closure" dilemma, not wanting to risk blocking the copious interactive flow of these past nine extraordinary days.

Rabbi Nachman protested the spruce-up, but was inwardly delighted and very surprised by its announcement, and soon after he gave in and rounded up a few tools to assist Nathan in removing "the verses of Deuteronomy" from the doorpost of his home. This accomplished, the two inseparables took up their diurnal posts in the cramped sitting room, bathed by a bright splash of morning sunlight streaming through the window panes.

"Naftali, my dear friend, between this morning and our farewells tomorrow, I'm going to take you from central Germany to its port at Bremerhaven."

"My head is still swimming from that hair-raising rescue, Rabbi. I'm so pleased that you were able to piece together this stirring episode of their incredible story. I went over it with the Herb and Eric last night, and they were enthralled by the planning, the precision and the sheer *chutzpah* of it all. You can be sure it will be repeated and yes, embellished, many times back in California, as will the entire saga."

"As I've said, fortunately, Sendehr Efraim and Mordecai both kept in periodic touch with my father over the years, and parts of the Fusgeyer story were re-hashed many times. Uncle Yaakov's correspondence from Montreal, until he was killed in France, also adds a great deal to my recollection now. When this surviving packet of letters began to become frayed and showed some yellowing, my father copied many of them onto fresh paper in Yiddish, using a Hebrew-lettered typewriter, which I still have. When you place into the mix the few documents and letters I've been given from various Birlad families after my father passed on and I took over the pulpit, you can readily see how the archives have been painstakingly built and maintained. Also, we must not overlook the oral tradition which has always been part of Fusgeyer history...more so in Birlad than in any other Romanian town from which they had ventured forth. But as you have indicated, Naftali, by and large, most of the Fusgeyers in America talked little and wrote less about their experiences. Your own father, for example."

"Not only the Fusgeyers, Rabbi. I have found that it's common for immigrants to be very reluctant to talk of their transmigrational experiences in anything more than vague generalities. For some deep-seated psychological reason, they have wanted to, in effect, bury the past and only address their dreams of a bright future. We're very blessed to have had a Sendehr the Writer, a Mordecai the Leader, a Mendel the Teacher, and your Uncle Yaakov. They were the exceptions."

"*Omayn!* In fact, only a handful from any of the four Fusgeyer groups ever wrote much, if anything. Only a small number of families had come forth in all those years, and only three represented the 1904s, according to what my father had told me before he died. Naturally, many had immigrated themselves...to Palestine, then to Israel, to America...following their children in most cases. You've seen what remains out of a Jewish population that hovered near 4,000 as late as the 1920s."

"Sendehr's journal, Rabbi. I've never asked about it."

"Ah, yes, the original 1904 journal still exists. Indeed it does! When Sendehr passed on in 1972, I received a beautiful letter from his wife..."

"Rivka, I'll bet!"

"Who else? She was nearly ninety then, and very much alive and alert. She told me that they had moved from Manhattan to Boston in the 1940s when Sendehr became editor of a prestigious literary magazine in Cambridge, where they renewed contact with the Boston-area contingent of Fusgeyers. By then he had built a distinguished career as a renowned columnist for both Yiddish and English-language newspapers and magazines, and at one time had become the leading American voice for the emancipation of Romanian Jewry. After he retired in 1955, Sendehr became a prolific writer of historical novels, yet never included any reference to the Fusgeyer story. Rivka's letter explained that since they both felt that the subject was something they cherished so deeply, since it had shaped their lives so enduringly, it was far too personal to put into print.

"Oddly enough, during their several happy reunions with the Quincy and Boston Fusgeyers after a thirty-year lapse, very little was said about the old days in Birlad or about the trek itself. Everything seemed to focus on their lives since coming to America. Since this had also become their experience when meeting frequently with New York Birladers, Rivka rightly assumed that this was a conscious avoidance on everyone's part.

"Meanwhile, she had become a very popular playwright and stage director, also both in Yiddish and English, often enticing Sendehr to play a small role, which he dearly relished. They raised three children during all of these career-doings and I received word from their eldest son when Rivka died two years later."

Nathan was visibly moved by the Rabbi's description. "A beautiful story. I can't believe that my father failed to contact any of these old mates after moving to California. I think now it may be that when Yaakov was killed in the war he grew reluctant to re-establish any closeness with his former comrades. While he lived in Quincy it seems as though he may have. Who knows? But the journal, Rabbi. Where is it now?"

"Alexander, Sendehr and Rivka's son, had placed it in the archives of YIVO, The Jewish Research Institute in New York, where it remains today, as far as I can gather. According to him, the YIVO staff told him that only one other firsthand chronicle concerning Romanian Fusgeyers can be found in any public or private institution. It happens to be one man's autobiography called *Reminiscences of a Fusgeyer, From Romania to America*. A Jacob Finkelstein from the township of Hush(i) wrote the memoir based on his travels with the 1900 group from Birlad. The difference being that Finkelstein wrote this paper many years after the journey, from memory. Sendehr's journal is both first-hand and immediate, as we know. There were no other official journals intact that anyone knows of, kept by any of the groups either before or after Sendehr's. I'll give you Alexander's address in New York, of course. He sent me a note about ten years ago when he called on one of my sons during a trip to Israel. He would be close to my age now, if still alive...*alivai!*"

"I pray so. By all means, I will contact him as soon as I return."

"I'm sure you would like to hear what happened to the others. I saved this information for today, but we'll still have plenty of time to get you to Bremerhaven and then on to your America. Don't worry. I won't leave you stranded in Deutschland, of all places. Eh?"

"Mordecai, Mendel, Branko, and any of the others you can tell me about…"

"Let's start with Mordecai. Our Mordecai Anieloff evidently became a powerful and respected labor leader. My father told me that Mordecai worked in the garment factories and became progressively disillusioned with the prevailing conditions. Followers of the famous union man, former cigar maker Samuel Gompers, recruited him. They were impressed with his quiet, yet effective persuasiveness, and he soon became known as a leading proponent for improving safety conditions throughout a number of allied industries. At a Fusgeyers's affair in Brooklyn he was happy to see Pessel Vinocur, who was divorced from a very unhappy marriage that bore two children. Shortly afterward, Mordecai, who had never remarried after the tragic loss of his young wife in Birlad, wooed and wed Pessel in 1910. He worked for, what is it?…on his letterheads here…the American Federation of Labor, until his death in 1945.

"Zed-Zed learned to repair watches and had a shop in Brooklyn. I was very sorry to hear that he was badly gassed in the first war, and died just a few years later. I was a young boy of nine at the time, and I still remember how my father was shaken by this sadness, as was all of Birlad."

Nathan listened in awe and responded with the same mournful sadness, feeling that he knew each and every Fusgeyer personally after these nine days with Rabbi Nachman.

"Mendel Buchman. Once a scholar, always a scholar, as they say. After earning two graduate degrees at night, no less, he became a revered and much-honored professor at the City College of New York. He and Esther Holtzer had the first Fusgeyer baby in early 1905, and added seven more over the years. Whenever Mordecai was scheduled to give an important union speech he called on Mendel and Sendehr who became his personal ghostwriting team, if you will. The three remained the closest of friends, closely watching and analyzing world situations in connection with the Prague predictions. Whenever there was a match, my father could expect a long letter from one of them, usually Sendehr, shortly thereafter."

"I would have guessed it!" slipped in Nathan. "Please go on, Rabbi."

"Simmy Fiedelman, as to be expected, worked as a counterman in a delicatessen, whatever that means. He later was able to borrow enough money, through one of his patented *chutzpah* dealings, to buy the place. A letter from our Menachem Berman, who was one of his best customers, informed my father that Simmy retired to Florida in 1940 after selling the business. Menachem was a long-time salesman for one of Simmy's meat suppliers.

"Nuchim Krasnigor worked as a minor clerk in the bookkeeping department at that shipbuilding company in Kvinzee, and he was urged often by my father's open letters to the Kvinzee Fusgeyers, to attend night school in Boston. He finally did and he became a public accountant. Both he and his wife continually credited any of his later successes to my father for pushing him in the right direction. With all such letters my father beamed with pride, especially when passing the word to his congregants.

"You see I have all of this information in writing, and all sixty are mentioned here. Sendehr and Mendel, in particular, periodically sent updates on everyone...even the Argentinians and some of those few who left little or no trace. You'll have to have this translated, Naftali, but you may be able to make out a goodly portion of it. Thank God my dear father kept certain records safely secreted in Birlad. Otherwise, they would have been in the box that was partially burnt, and we would have had even less to go on."

At this point the painters had arrived and were quietly setting about to do their chores. Only the swish-swish sound of the brushes and the scratching sound of light sandpapering could be heard from within. The two seniors just sat back and smiled warmly, content that their participation was one of periodic inspection only.

"We'll save your brief commentary on the others for later today, especially where I'll have the full written report to take home with me. I'm not surprised to hear that Mordecai, Sendehr and Mendel stayed very close. They were some trio! Simmy? I suppose I could have predicted his life. I'll bet that *hondler* was wheeling and dealing right up to the end! But he sure carried out his job, and more, for his comrades! About him, a movie should be made."

"Did I mention, Naftali, that Simmy was the first to send for his entire family? The Fiedelman bakery was one of the very last of many Birlad businesses that the boycott eventually murdered. Yes, murdered...that's the only word for it, Naftali. The elder Fiedelmans worked in bakeries around New York, and when Simmy bought the delicatessen he was able to expand the bakery counter for them to operate. A *mitzvah!* The boy had a gracious heart under all that gruff veneer."

During morning tea break, Berel Usher dropped in to bid his goodbyes, and was astonished to see the flurry of activity going on. "It's unfortunate you're leaving tomorrow, Naftali. The whole *shul* can use a painting. My house, too!" he joshed.

This was the unexpected, ideal opening for Nathan to stuff a wad of *lei* bills into Berel's hand, and without waiting for the customary protest, he said, "Have it done, Berel. Have it done. It should look fresh for the holidays this fall. Call it a bit of California sunshine if you wish!" Nathan had already planned to call on Berel later that day to deliver this heartfelt donation.

"I cannot say enough. Thank you, thank you, Nathan Friedman. You know, by my calculations, Birlad probably gave the world about three hundred Fusgeyers. But from that core, three generations later there must be thousands of descendants. If you are an example of the offspring group, how lucky the rest of the world has been." With that, Berel

Usher, erstwhile president of the remnant community bear-hugged and kissed Nathan on both cheeks in true European tradition, as did the Rabbi as well.

Reb Usher's parting jibe: "Yossi, don't even think of telling Raisel that you painted the house by yourself! Have a nice visit in Bucureshti. With me in the pulpit, you won't have a job when you return!"

"*Gott tsedanken*, Bereleh!"

The hearty laughter echoed out the open freshly painted door and down the narrow alley to the square beyond, as the paint crew wondered what it was all about.

§

The agrarian plain stretched like a green-brown carpet before Sholem and Yaakov; the hot summer sun steam cleaning it, and dried the last of the road's wet spots from the furious three-day rainfall earlier that week. The main body lagged far behind the vanguard, and the overall pace slowed as the midday heat became blistering and relentless.

"There's a good spot for our noon stop, Yak." Zed-Zed's harsh whistle, which could have startled the dead in the small fenced burial ground next to the tall, steeple-topped church, had just pierced their ears. Yaakov followed the direction of Sholem's finger pointing and saw that behind the church was a thick grove of acacia trees that would provide a cool rest for the Birladers. He waved them forward with a sweep of his arms, and within a few minutes the entire company arrived, cart and all.

Since the church appeared to be empty, Bezalel Udler took the *Mogen Dovid* from Heshy Rosen, who had the honored duty that week, and placed it in all its glory into the flag-holding sconce next to the double front doors. The German Imperial Black Eagle—black, yellow and red flag of the Second Reich—borne by an uncaring Pini Kantorovitz, ended up unceremoniously propped against one of the trees. Bezalel, perennial prankster that he was, waxed proud as could be of his little coup, capping it off with a sly grin and the haughtiest wink of an eye. Itzy and Mayer loved it. Mordecai just shook his head, while Reb Berman, the tactful diplomat, shrugged his shoulders, palms held upward.

Thus far, since crossing the German border, they had endured many derisive remarks shouted at them as they had passed through Dresden and the smaller towns and villages, and occasionally when they had seen others on the lightly traveled road. Some farm boys, crusty old-timers on their wagons, an innkeeper or two, a constable, a traveling salesman in a horseless carriage, constant gaggles of school children, collectively and independently offered:

"*Achtung*, Jew bastards, we know where you're going! Just keep on going there! Faster! *Deutschland uber alles!*"

"Your ship's waiting, Christ killers! Take the Greeks and the gypsies with you!"

"No baby blood for you blood suckers to drink in this town! Move on. Move on!"

"Where's my gun? It's kill-a-Yid week! Your Jew-flag will look like Swiss cheese!"

"Go on to America, Jews. The Indians will scalp your bloody heads!"

"What are you? Polocks? Czechs? Bulgars? Turks? Romanians? What's the difference? You're all stinking Jews!"

And the ubiquitous: "Germany for Germans! Get out!"

The land of Goethe, Bach and Brahms? The new empire of virtue, culture, science and learning? The Second Reich of tolerance, compassion and opportunity?

"Even your Jews of Dresden, oblivious to the perpetual target on your *tuchuses*, moon and crow over your baroque gem, 'The Florence of the North'—once so dubbed by the same elite world travelers who could never decide just which was truly 'The Venice of the North': Belgium's Brugge with its extensive network of canals, or St. Petersburg with an equally impressive waterway system," wryly observed Mendel after a heated discussion on contemporary social issues with the young assistant rabbi of Dresden's Neolog synagogue. No doubt the usually even-tempered teacher's uncharacteristic reaction had been in no small way instigated by the supercilious twit and his repeated reference to "you people" this, and "you people" that.

"You people." Translation: "You dirt-poor, uneducated, embarrassing, low class, naive *ostjuden.*"

Mendel was certain that somehow this would not be the last time he or the others would hear the insulting "you people" from German and Jew alike while tramping German soil. What he didn't know, or perhaps was reluctant to dwell upon at length, was whether or not this would carry over to America. He privately dreaded the thought as much as the anticipation, as did many of the Fusgeyers. The mysterious unknown continued to lurk over the horizon.

Pastor Gustavus Hof knew an opportunity when he saw one. The sight of the *Mogen Dovid* flying from the sconce at his front door was a "calling" in his holy Lutheran mindset. Once over the initial shock, he calmly stepped down from his neatly fringed surrey, walked up the stairs, removed the flag and began to wave it slowly from side to side.

This was a surrealistic scene to behold for the young Jews of Birlad. Slowly, deliberately, they left the coolness of the grove and their noonday meals to "rally round their flag." The fast-thinking Menachem Berman, always politically aware, took along the German banner, and in response, waved it high, to and fro. Hardly causing a stalemate, the sharp-featured, alabaster-skinned, yellow-haired Teuton, in marked contrast to the tanned, dark-haired scraggly Semites, ceased his flag waving. Instead, he held the *Mogen Dovid* pole upright at his side and began to speak. Branko and Mendel immediately flanked Mordecai and Menachem in order to translate where necessary.

"So you are the Jews from the east that some of my

school children have told me about," he began, in all likelihood referring to those *mumzerim*, the little urchins who had issued forth such polite, loving remarks as they passed through their nearby village.

"I personally wish to welcome you to the Grace Lutheran Church in the Holy Name of our founder, the beloved Martin of Wittenberg. How far have you come, pray tell?"

"Romania. Birlad, Romania, Herr Pastor," answered Branko politely. When some of the younger boys heard "Birlad" and "Romania," they snatched at the reason to let out some hearty, noisy cheers, led by their heroic ringleader, Avi the actor ...who else?

"I presume you are one of the many groups and individuals we have seen over these last few years, walking to the ports, then on to America. We have no work for you in the new Germany, so we are indeed happy to see that you're just passing through. The Greeks, the Serbs, the Turks all come to stay, and take the bread right out of the mouths of good, God-fearing Germans—literally out of my parishioner's mouths. At least you *ostjuden* seem to know what's good for you."

After a quick translation assist from Branko, Mordecai reached into his jacket pocket and pulled out the transit visa, holding it high, in order to punctuate what he instructed Branko to say.

"We know of your kind and generous treatment of your own Jews here in your new Germany, past and present, good pastor. We wouldn't think of imposing on you and your church, and the dear people of Germany. Germany for Germans, that's our belief! And we shall continue to uphold it. We are on our way to America!"

Whether young Hof was seasoned enough to recognize the ancient art of Yiddish sarcasm, practiced with such finesse by the leader and his defense minister, was not at all obvious. Instead, he launched into the proselytizer's well-rehearsed, nineteen-centuries-old harangue. With such a large and seemingly attentive audience he would be remiss not to. But as soon as the words *Gott, Yaysuz*

Kreest, heilige, and a few other clues spouted forth, taken together with the glazed over look in the pastor's blue eyes and his repeated outstretched arm gestures toward heaven, the throng began to fade away. After all, there was still uneaten food to munch under the trees. As they retreated, they couldn't resist muttering *dreck, putz, anti-Semit, feygeleh, mumzer,* producing the faintest of grins on the faces of the cadre and Bezalel who remained behind, the latter, doggedly determined to retrieve the *Mogen Dovid* when the time came. It had become his sole responsibility and he knew it without being told.

The youngest to the oldest among them was all too familiar with this strategy to conversion; each one had witnessed such proselytizing from the time they could walk and talk. Father Mihai and his cohorts *hawt gehuckt* this *chinek* every week, falling on the deafest of ears in and around town. Mihai's followers delivered leaflets to every Jewish house and business during Easter Holy Week, offering every kind of inducement if they would only shed their Jewish ways and accept Jesus into their wretched lives. Branko suffered this litany throughout his long Hapsburg army career, and Mendel could hardly get through a week at the Brit school without being subjected to the drone. Even his beloved Professor Montgomery-Lloyd, on occasion, would politely suggest conversion in a more practical sense, as a ploy to opening up the doors to Oxford or Cambridge.

In summation, this exercise in utter futility had become an insufferable bore to these fifty-seven *Yidlach.* Yet they were about to find out that multitudes of their co-religionists in Germany, in their constant drive for full inclusion had taken that one extra step beyond mere assimilation. The baptisteries had become an increasingly popular venue for them during the century just past.

"I see that some of you people practice little in the way of civilized decorum. Here I stand offering you extreme salvation, a way to gain immediate membership into world society, a way in which your life in America can be a pleasant and fruitful one, and your rabble turns away from me.

I say, you people bring on your own troubles and..."

Mendel, seeing the bullfighter's red cape waving at him once again, could stand it no longer.

"Pardon me, Herr Pastor, I sincerely hope you can understand my rather weak, Yiddish-ized German. Sergeant Branko, here, will help me along. I beg you to listen closely, sir. I, for one, will not stand here and listen to your patently condescending babble. Do not, I repeat, do not use the term 'you people' in our presence, or in reference to any Jew or Greek or Turk or gypsy. It is most insulting, and you know it. Now, if you have anything further to say on a different subject, we may listen for a minute or two before our schedule demands that we move on. After all, that seems to be your ultimate goal, since your failure in uncovering any conversion candidates appears abundantly evident."

Branko translated Mendel's words literally, and a flush-faced Hof attempted a sputtering retort, but stopped in mid-consonant. At this pause, Bezalel rushed to the top step to recapture the *Mogen Dovid* from the weakened grip of Grace Lutheran's spiritual leader. The spectacle was over.

Would Mendel have delivered such a brazen scolding back at home? Certainly not. In Hungary? In Austria? In Czech Bohemia? Again, no. But within the confines of liberal Deutschland, where the twentieth-century Jew basked in the sunshine of his dichotomous existence—one of presumed emancipation and tolerance, tempered by classical, long-standing jealous hatred—Mendel felt a certain impunity. This was not to say that there wouldn't be some serious discussions with Reb Berman concerning the propriety of it all.

Only Reb Diplomacy and Branko stayed on for a brief minute, soothing the unnerved Hof. With the interpreter's assistance, Menachem added the parting words.

"With all due respect, Herr Pastor, I strongly recommend that in the future you try to win over converts one or two at a time. A noble try, sir, a noble effort, indeed. Saint Martin would be proud of you."

Branko and Berman placed brotherly arms around the

shaken cleric's cloaked shoulder as if trying to comfort a child in distress, bade farewell, and went off to join the already departing heathen sinners.

In terms purely mathematical, Jewish conversions to any Christian denomination were an insignificant fraction in 1904 Europe, although any official statistics were largely unavailable. On the other hand, most Christians accepted that Germany led all European countries in the conversion rate by a wide margin. When word reached the Rhine Valley during the fourteenth century that thousands of Jews had been murdered in Toledo and Seville simply for refusing to convert, only a minuscule number of Jews even considered conversion. There was nothing to gain. In contrast, the unification of the country toward the mid-nineteenth century once again made for an attractive argument by the proselytizing clergy. They had learned that to offer salvation through the acceptance of Jesus Christ as Lord and Savior was not quite enough to lure the more sophisticated German Jew. In its stead, the promise of ready acceptance into the social order proved to be the major motivating factor.

Among those succumbing to this permanent invitation were such notables as the poet Heinrich Heine, who represented himself as a religious freethinker as far back as 1825 by devoting himself to Jewish Enlightenment. Just imagine the irony of it all: coming so far into the light from the darkness of the ghetto that he had submitted to total conversion.

Eduard Ganz, the pioneer philosopher of law, found that his well publicized trip to the baptismal font allowed him a public career; albeit short-lived, with his early death at age forty-one. And, the continentally influential writer Karl Ludwig Boerne, after his much-publicized conversion, became a champion for human rights, assaulting the widespread bigotry of his generation with bold statements such as "German minds dwell on Alpine heights; but German hearts pant in damp marshes."

Many of the earliest leaders of this movement toward the outside world saw their own progeny go the so-called extra step. Moses Mendelssohn, the great philosopher, founded the German Jewish Enlightenment in the mid-eighteenth century when Jews were still being locked in the ghetto every night and needed special permits just to live in Berlin. His social-climbing, banker son Abraham thought he could spare his own children from social and other forms of anti-Jewish discrimination by baptizing them as Lutherans at birth. Felix, the important composer, even had a decidedly non-Jewish name tacked on by his father, to complete the cover-up. During his earlier years he was known as Felix Mendelssohn-Bartholdy, until as an adult he dropped it.

Mendel had also learned from Goldhammer's all-encompassing treatise that it was estimated as many as half the Jews of Berlin during the first half of the nineteenth century were converts, most to Lutheran Protestantism, and the rest to Catholicism.

Those who look for a reason for the rapid advance of a radically reformed Judaism during this period of universal assimilation in Germany can think of it as an expeditious antidote to stem the rising tide of apostasy. From their lofty perches, the fathers of the enlightenment, for the most part, did not anticipate the cascade of conversions, and one answer to this growing problem was to make the practice of Judaism less restrictive, more appealing to the younger generations. To a degree, it worked that way, but steady conversion continued into the twentieth century.

As he marched at the rear of the column, after leaving the shade trees at the Pastor's church, Mendel shared all of the foregoing with the hyper-inquisitive Sendehr, who lagged behind to speak with him.

"I have to admit, Mendel, that you've illuminated my mind with these answers to each and every one of my questions."

"Well, Reb *Shreiber*, a dull mind needs constant illumination," joked Mendel, in a sassy mood since his satisfying confrontation with the proselytizing pastor.

"I'm warning you, Reb *Lehrer*, this questioning will happen every time you decide to march alongside me. You'd be better off up there with Esther."

In any case, as Mendel had announced during that rainy day, this was the Germany the Fusgeyers were crossing. This represented both the ordinary German and Germany's Jewry that they would meet along the way, for better or for worse.

No one had any doubts that the accompanying comedians would capitalize on the happenings of the day, as they did, later that night. Encamped by the uninhabited shores of a pristine pond near Elsterwerda, engulfed by a brilliant sunset of myriad colors, Itzy and Mayer, most ably supported by the celebrated child actor, little Avi Semelweiss, vividly brought to life a heterogeneous host of historically fabled characters.

Mayer hilariously overplayed the venerable anatagonist Father Mihai; a morosely suicidal Pastor Gustavus Hof; the villainous Haman; a narcissistic Adam in the Garden of Eden; the vexatious *paskudnyak* Captain Ullbricht as a new convert to Judaism; and the oligarchic magistrate Captain Polinou and his personal nemesis, the wily Reb Mandelbaum of Birlad.

Avi became Jonah of Biblical fame and a fashion conscious Joseph of the many-colored coat. Both skits brought the mesmerized audience to fits of laughter.

Itzy Gelman, comic thespian extraordinaire, cavorted with great relish all around the campfire in a wide variety of roles: "Freilacher Bereleh"of Vatra Dornei; a wild- dancing Szatmar Rebbe; the heroic and beautiful Queen Esther; Jonah's Yiddish-talking whale; both Eve and the serpent; a lisping soprano Martin Luther; a stuttering Pope Leo X; and a pompous, controversial Pope Pius IX. The latter was also known as Pio Nono, who had a six-year-old Bolognese Jewish child, Edgardo Mortara, who he had kidnapped in 1858, and began raising him thereafter to become a priest. Pio Nono could also proudly lay claim to re-ghetto-izing the Jews of Rome as late as 1870, repeatedly referring to them as dogs: "too many of them, and we hear them howling in the streets." Itzy squeezed every last laugh out of the entire program.

Was all of this bordering on the blasphemous? The impiously irreverent? Obviously, yes, in certain circles, which shall remain nameless.

Rivka, Pessel and Maidele had hastily pulled together some magnificent props and partial costumes, including the fig leaf for Adam, white *yarmulkehs* for the Popes, a long grass wig for both the Queen and Eve, and so on, and on...Enough said! A rich imagination can deliciously fill in all of the dialogue and action.

Although some of these *shticks* were part of their classic repertoire back home, Itzy and Mayer cleverly improvised this "theater of the absurd" to become a boisterous, uproarious, and occasionally ribald work of performing art. The mirthful sounds and thunderous applause came in a constant stream from beginning to end...three hours nonstop, with *a capella* farragoes from the vastly improving "four cantors" during some of the longer costume changes. Truly a night to cherish and remember, and still laugh about, for many years to come.

Mordecai and Branko laughed beyond the point of tears and as hard and as long as anyone else. But the moment the show ended, the always-on-duty leader directed his ever-alert security chief to post a guard for the first time in many weeks.

§

Nathan Friedman was leaning forward at the edge of the overstuffed chair, completely and utterly stupefied. For the past half-hour he had listened to a description of Sendehr's meetings with Rabbi Blankfort in Praha, nearly one hundred years back. The Birlader Rabbi, never showing a hint of caducity, was careful not to omit a syllable in his deliberate delivery, reading directly from Sendehr's letters to the late elder Nachman.

"Dear God! Those predictions certainly did come to pass, as you and I well know!"

"As I said before I began, this is a most provocative subject. Precisely why I've saved it for today, even though it came about the Sabbath before the escape."

"This may well be the ultimate exercise in hindsight, for one thing. What in the world did your father think of this? I'm dying to know, Rabbi."

"We discussed it numerous times. It was closely guarded as an internal family matter. I know this may shock you further, but my father kept it very quiet, to a degree."

"To what degree, may I ask?" posed Nathan, both puzzled and incredulous.

"Of course, he discussed it at the time with certain elders of the *shul.* Of this, I am reasonably certain. That was his way. But to mention this to the community-at-large arbitrarily? No. He was never an alarmist by nature or by deed. His letter to Sendehr, a copy of which Alexander included in subsequent correspondence with me, exposes his true feelings on the matter. Here, let me read it to you. You'll see that it will anticipate most of your further questions on this matter."

> *Greetings to all:*
>
> *Sendehr, I hope this reaches you at the main Berlin Postal Office. As usual, Postmaster Nicolescu lettered the envelope for me, but with the prevailing tensions here in Birlad, maybe he sent it to Madagascar or India or China. Who knows?*
>
> *I read and re-read your notes numerous times. I have developed some very strong opinions on the whole matter, which I will share with you herein. Rabbi Blankfort is no doubt a man of great intellect, and probably just as great imagination. I, for one, do not see his visitations from the Maharal as anything but*

that...imagination, groisseh fantazyeh. *Yes, we all see people from the past in our dreams, and we converse with them, too. And they give us messages and greetings and warnings...and it stays with us for days and months, even years. The warnings usually unfulfilled. In this case, I firmly believe that the rabbi has used this dream, or dreams, to solidify his own thoughts of the future. If anything, this is the rule rather than the exception for any of us, and most particularly for a ninety-year-old, educated, venerated rabbinical leader of great stature. He has seen much, and been part of nearly a century of history, good and bad. Let me attempt to address each point from your letter.*

For example, to predict a pogrom these days is something a cheder *child could do. With regularity, no less. To say that the Jews will be blamed for Russia's defeat in their current war with Japan is also obvious. Any setbacks suffered by the czars for the past three hundred years have been eventually laid at the feet of the Zhid. That is, if, indeed, little Japan can beat the Russian Bear at his game. We all watch it closely, even though news is slow and sketchy, at best. The predicted target cities and towns have all at one time or another been victimized by pogroms. When I was at the yeshiva in Kiev there wasn't a town in the entire Pale that wasn't on constant alert. What more can they do now? They were powerless then, and still are today, and will be tomorrow, barring a certified miracle. The coming of the* mashiach *will do! Pouring paranoia upon already existing fear will do no earthly good, in my estimation. If we had some sort of acceptable sign or proof, perhaps, but we have none, Sendehr, and you know this as well as I do. Meanwhile,* unsereh Birlader Yidden, *with the boycott firmly in place and ironclad fists are keeping it there, and those barely existing in the Pale, where also tomorrow's bread is never a surety, would all dismiss this as* narishkeit. *Can you imagine the reactions of my father, yours, Mandelbaum, Berman, Leventer, if I pass this along? Oy, gevalt! They would have me put away!*

Thus far, then, prophecy is hardly the word to describe the Rabbi Blankfort's ruminations. You can be assured I will keep a wide open mind on all of this, even though it will be years, decades in fact, before the most horrifying predictions can be verified or denied. Hopefully, the latter, dear God!

As to the more imminent—the blood libel, for one— there have been and will no doubt continue to be ridiculous accusations of this sort. Here he actually signifies a year... 1911. We'll see in another seven years, but my question is, so what? What can we do to prevent this? Nothing aside from our continuing thrust toward full emancipation in the Pale, Romania and in fact, all regions of Europe. I'm afraid even that unlikely event would do nothing to obliterate anti-Semitism from this mashiganah velt. In fact, is this noble goal attainable at all? In Romania? In Poland? In Germany? In Russia? In Antarctica, among the penguins? At the risk of appearing incurably cynical, no!

As for the assassination of a Hapsburg in 1914, the entire family is a living, breathing, moving target for every bloodthirsty revolutionary from Brody to Praha and back. There will not be a surprised face in all of Central Europe if one of the young dukes or if the emperor himself is pierced by a bullet. Blankfort's message that a war involving all or most governments of Europe will begin immediately following this murder has been and will continue to be a commonly addressed discussion item in every capital on this troubled continent. Something to trigger such a disaster could very likely be the pernicious elimination of a Hapsburg, or a Romanov, or the King of England, or Kaiser Wilhelm or someone near and dear to any of those ruling families.

May I repeat, Sendehrel, I don't at all feel there is anything for anyone to be alarmed about. The comments about the Maharal accurately predicting the assassination of Alexander in 1881 is, again, a product of his vivid imagination, I'm sure. I can predict yesterday's weather just as accurately, as well, as can every human being in this shrinking world!

His repeated references to the Golem reminds me of the countless stories of the Praha Golem that we all heard when we were children. I recall Rabbi Holtzer scaring the living daylights out of my cheder class. In fact, Mordecai and I were in our second year and we proceeded to visit this fright upon the younger children on the way home that night, including three of whom are on the road with you right now. Mention this at one of your campfires and you'll see who responds. I was the grunting, speechless Golem, and Mordecai was my master. I choke with laughter when I remember the looks on the little cherub's faces. How inexcusably cruel we were! Remind Mordecai, please. Rabbi Holtzer and our parents roundly chastised both of us. My skepticism as to whether there ever was a Golem in Old Praha has never waned, I'm afraid. It cannot be called irreligious. There is nothing religious about the Golem story, in any way.

Now, before I mail this letter to you, I will address the last and most intriguing part of this non-prophesy, this dream, this ninety-year-old's window on world's events: the Haman figure appearing in Germany later in this century. Yes, indeed, I can easily conceive of today's Germany giving birth to a monster, to a Haman, if you will.

That culture's long record of overt anti-Semitism, suckled by all with their mother's milk, could spawn such an animal as described in the Rabbi's comments, whether attributed to his visions of the Maharal, or not. The reference to a world war, the monumental persecution of our people—a veritable 'shoah' as he says—and an independent state of our own in Palestine; all of this is possible—especially the latter with all of this Herzl activity going on, something that you and Mendel and Mordecai were privileged to see and hear firsthand in Vienna. I do believe that such a monumental achievement will take place in the future, possibly by mid-century. Only as the result of a 'shoah'? I pray not. Please God!

Sendehr, there is little more I can say about this Rabbi Blankfort's dreams. Yes, dreams, Sendehr. I promise to you, my dear friend, that I will keep all of this stored in the recesses of my brain as I observe the daily events taking place around us and around our fast-deflating globe. If and when any of these predicted events become fact, we will use up a few paragraphs in our continuing correspondence.

We at home are so extremely proud of all of you. Your dear father still plots every move on that old map you left with him, and he brings it to shul every time he has added anything to it with red ink. You've all been through some traumatic experiences and have come through handsomely. You have learned so much, and you have all grown in stature as a result. There are times when trial by fire can be rewarding and illuminating, if you will excuse my closing pun.

Be well, and may God continue to watch over your mission. Give my greetings to one and all, and a very special one to your Rivkeleh. Heh! Heh!

> I remain, your Rabbi,
> and especially your friend,
> Eli
> Birlad, June 20, 1904 (17 Sivan 5664)

"Oh, my! *Ay,yi, yi!* Excellent! Bravo! There isn't a doubt in my mind that I would have written the same letter at that given time. And you, Rabbi?"

"Most probably. However, there are other letters that have survived, and it is exceptionally interesting to see where my father experienced a growing sense of wonderment as each of the prophesies became stark reality."

"Wouldn't we all, for God's sake! But as an adult you lived through part of this with your father. What occurred between the two of you as each event unfolded?"

"Hmm...well, I knew of his ongoing correspondence with Sendehr when I was a schoolboy, and it was always a major event at our house. Many times, my father would have me read the letter aloud to the whole family who sat around the hearth listening. Sometimes we would discuss it for hours after supper. For many people in Birlad who had no children or other relatives in America, this was their only contact, and many times my father would read the letters to the congregants. They provided an adjunct to everyone's scope of knowledge. But I suppose you want to know what the '20s and '30s were like as world events catapulted head-long into an all-consuming conflagration, and my father and I frequently had to look knowingly into each others troubled eyes."

"Exactly."

"More directly, Naftali, you are asking why in the name of a merciful God were we not sounding the alarm, knowing of these dire predictions? And if it were at all possible to alert the Jews of Europe, who would listen?"

"Again, you understand my dilemma to the core."

"The point where all of the reasonable doubts my father had thrown up to Sendehr faded completely was in 1933, when Adolf Hitler, with a minority party, was elected to the Chancellery. I came home for Pesach from my rabbinical college in Budapest at that time, and I remember my father saying that he was petrified by this turn of events. Hitler as Chancellor now played directly into the prediction that a madman would quickly introduce and champion legislation that would eventually lead to the deaths of millions—first in Germany, then in all of Europe, and conceivably throughout the entire world. I shall never forget the look of impending doom on his face. Yes, this was the very point in time, twenty-nine years after receiving Sendehr's report from Praha. I remember him saying many times that either Rabbi

Blankfort was exceptionally clairvoyant, or he was the premier conjectural master in the history of the world. He even mused for a moment that the Maharal's fine hand—the same busy hand that fashioned the Golem—was behind all of this in some indecipherable manner. I don't recall that he ever repeated this improbability after 1933.

"By that year, though, numerous individuals and sociopolitical groups were 'crying wolf' as the saying goes. Think back for a moment. The mass exodus in the period following the 1881 assassination, the continuous rash of progoms and harsh legislation that followed, and the Iashi and the Kishinev massacres, all contributed directly to the emigration of some two-and-a-half to three million Yidden before the eve of World War I. The relatively unsettling times during and following that war resulted in much fewer of our surviving people leaving Romania, or from anywhere in Europe. By the '30s the new threat began to take shape. Notably, the Zionists, motivated by the pressing drive for recruits to Palestine following the Balfour Declaration of 1917, used the rise of the National Socialists in Germany—and similar fascistic groups here in Romania—the heavy boycotts in Poland, and nationalism growing like a wild fire as a self-serving alarm system. Most Romanians who left the country during those years opted for Palestine; some surreptitiously, most illegally, severe quotas notwithstanding.

"In the meantime, after Hitler's insidious Nuremberg Laws went into effect, certain loud voices reverberated in the countryside and cities of Eastern and Central Europe, screaming and pleading for the Jews to leave while they could, *if* they could. This weak and isolated effort multiplied dramatically when the Germans marched unopposed into Austria in March 1938, and later that year, in November, *Kristallnacht* shocked the Jewish world. But these cries were typically met with disbelief, apathy, and yes, pure ignorance of what was going on about them. There were rabbis who refused to let these alarmists step foot in their synagogues, let alone speak from their pulpits. There were recorded situations where Yidden insisted that the local magistrate expel these madmen from their precincts. Too few listened, too few heard, and far too many didn't want to hear. The rest is history. *Shoah.*"

"It's still, to this day, hard to imagine that with all of the indelible writing on the wall, so few took heed," agreed Nathan, knowing so well the appalling genocidal statistics that bore this out. He knew equally as well of the impossible extenuating circumstances, none the least of which was all-encompassing, cunningly planned, abject pauperism.

"As to warning and ultimate rescue, although I know there were others, there are only two persons who stand out in my mind to this day. One who carried out the most massive rescue operation with exceptional gallantry, and another who sounded the alarm, speaking all over the region, tirelessly and vociferously; the heroine Ruth Kluger and the didactic, though much-maligned, Vladimir Ze'ev Jabotinsky."

"I don't know of the first, Rabbi, but I certainly heard and read a great deal about Jabotinsky's exploits," responded Nathan.

"However, I can tell you much more about Ruthie's most valiant efforts, of which both my father and I were an intimate part. She fits into the 'escape' picture like no other. Her eventual book, *The Last Escape: the Launching of the Largest Secret Rescue Movement of All Time,* is one of the classic treatments on the subject.

"This, I most certainly want to hear."

"Sit back, Naftali, this is a captivating story. After those cascading acts of ignominy following Hitler's arrival on the world scene, a young Romanian Jewess who had been living in Palestine, appeared back in Bucureshti. Ruth Kluger. She was a secret representative of the Mossad, a Jewish illegal immigration organization, which, as you probably know, later became the Israeli Secret Service. For a time, just before the war began in earnest, Ruth served on Ben Gurion's staff, attending many last minute, clandestine "es-

cape" meetings held somewhere deep in the volcano before it erupted. Naftali, this *pitzeleh*, barely out of her teenage years, performed subtle and not-so-subtle acts of pure
heroism usually reserved for soldiers of fortune and cowboy frontiersmen like those your Hollywood films glorify.
She proceeded to wheedle her way into King Carol's best
graces, was actually given his protection at one time, arranged for escape routes through Slovakia, Hungary,
Bucovina, Galicia, all over this part of Europe, ending at
our ports where there would be adequate and somewhat
less-than-adequate transportation to Haifa in Palestine.

"When Hitler finally invaded Poland on September 1,
1939, Ruthie had already escorted hundreds of Polish refugees to those ports on the Black Sea—Constantza, Varna,
Balchik—wherever a ship could be anchored. Her logistical
planning and *schnorring* were the stuff of legend. Ship fuel,
food, medical supplies, clothing, blankets, discarded shoes—
everything necessary for a successful rescue mission. She
found volunteers from both the Jewish communities and
the Romanian seashore, never taking 'no' for an answer:
painters, rust-scraping laborers, electricians, welders, deck
hands—don't ask. A leaky, rusty derelict of a boat could be
made serviceable and livable; an old barn for temporary
living quarters, the same.

"She visited nearly every Jewish community between
Bucureshti and Bukovina, warning our people that the war
would one day engulf Romania. She stopped in Birlad where
she did not have to convince my father of the state of urgency. She was, of course, not allowed to speak from the
bimah, but when he repeated her message to his congregation, and also to a number of the *shtieblach*, he spoke for
her to the usual deaf ears. Only two Birlader families accepted her offer of a place on one of the refugee ships
bound for Palestine out of Balchik. My father sent her on
to me in Iashi..."

The Rabbi paused with a recognizably wistful look in
his eyes before continuing. "I must admit, I was captured
by her verve, her flashing smile, her movie star looks, her

manner of dress, her intellect. After all, Nafatali, I was a young, unattached *bocher* who was the perpetual target of every single woman in my congregation, and a few of the other synagogues, too. Not to mention, God forgive them, one or two of the married ladies. I was not to meet my Raiseleh until the next year..."

"It's O.K., it's fine. I understand, Rabbi. I completely understand, believe me," interrupted Nathan with a grin as wide as the Danube Delta.

"But, alas, as available as I was, Ruthie was quite involved with a young man from Botoshani, or Suceava, I don't exactly recall which. Getting over my initial heartbreak, I then decided I would help her wherever and whenever I could. I believed most strongly that anyone who could get out should do so posthaste.

"The Hitler-Stalin friendship pact was doomed to failure in my mind, eventually making it that much more difficult to emigrate, and the clock was ticking loudly. The escape window would close shut in the not-too-distant future and most of Europe's Yidden would be trapped. Yes, no doubt, the Blankfort predictions had become stark reality by then. My father and I would have admitted that our actions were thus guided, partially at least.

"For the next year our wondrous Ruthie worked feverishly to fully utilize the Black Sea ports. Her name became synonymous with ' hope.' As you may also know from your interest in history, there were some tragic events involved with this mass attempt to flee. Un-seaworthy ships sank at sea, and violent interference by unfriendly naval vessels handed them their miserable lot of detention, near-starvation, and death due to lack of medicines and medical help, and so on. In this context one must mention the *Struma* and the *Salvador*, two of the ancient vessels that never reached Haifa, both sinking with an enormous loss of life. The *Struma* in particular exploded and sank in the Bosporus Canal near Constantinople, under most suspicious conditions.

"Ruthie worked in concert with understaffed, underfunded agencies while arranging these extremely delicate negotiations for the purchase of both the vessels and the vital supplies. My help was limited by my congregational work, of course; but safe and secure way stations were important to the overall effort and I was able to arrange some in Iashi and surrounding towns. To the south, in the Birlad district, my father did the same. Even a handful of congregants, although sadly believing that nothing adverse could possibly happen to Romania, volunteered to help us in both Iashi and Birlad. As I said, Ruth Kluger was truly a woman of valor...a modern day Biblical Ruth."

"Remarkable story, Rabbi. I've got to know! What happened to Ruth during and after the war? Is she still living?"

"I'm overjoyed to say that she spent the war years relatively safe in Palestine. The Mossad spirited her out of Romania in June of '41 when Hitler finally jilted Comrade Stalin and invaded Mother Russia. She took on a Hebrew name, Ruth Aliav, and served with distinction in the Knesset for many years, receiving major commendations for her rescue record. Her name belongs alongside that of Raoul Wallenberg.

"There are today thousands of people all over the world who owe their very existence to Ruthie's untiring work in rescuing their parents or grandparents. Each time I visit my children in Israel, we meet for a *glesseleh tay* to talk over the old days. Yes, yes, Naftali, my Raiseleh joins with us..."

With dueling winks and hearty chuckles the septuagenarian and octogenarian, arm-in-arm, headed for the kitchen to brew up some of that potent Israeli-Turkish tea, but not before Yossi Nachman's well timed afterthought, "...uh, most of the time!"

§

Previously, only the 1903'ers had flown the *Mogen Dovid* throughout their entire journey. They reported several isolated incidents of nasty taunting in Hungary, Austria, Bohemia and Germany; none became dangerously confrontational, and they didn't make much of it in any correspondence.

Stone throwing, however, could develop into a serious matter, and this is exactly what befell the current assemblage en route to Berlin. The cart *shleppers* got the worst of it since they had fallen behind the main group while climbing a steep grade just after they had walked through the "Hansel and Gretel" town of Finsterwalde; full of window boxes, sharply gabled gingerbread cottages, cobblestone lanes, and sundry faux alpine trimmings. In one colorful Yiddish word: *umgepahtchkit.*

Branko was on edge as he observed the frequency and the tone of those Mendel referred to in English as "the mocking-birds." Since Dresden, taunting had become a daily occurrence, and with the increased intensity the *soldat* knew it was only a matter of time before it escalated into something more than jeering. His uncanny sixth sense went into high gear as they left Finsterwalde behind. He became concerned about the vulnerable cart when he saw that it had lagged behind so he began to backtrack. Too late.

The first stone was expertly thrown by a *pisher* no more than ten years old. This seemed to be the younger of the "mocking birds" or *klayneh mumzerim,* the Yiddish term of choice called upon by most of the Fusgeyers. These youngsters shouted insults while the rocks soared out of their hands. "Dirty Jew!" "Go home *Juden!*" and the usual assorted niceties were audible proof of the oft cited "mother's milk" source for the xenophobia and accompanying anti-Semitism, tightly woven into the very fabric of Teutonic character. And, in truth, more often than not the adult crowd would follow their children's example that they had set themselves and escalate the name calling and worse.

A veritable barrage of stones of all sizes, pieces of jagged coal, steaming turds of fresh horse manure and an array of unidentifiable objects showered on the Fusgeyers from behind trees, telephone/telegraph poles and fences. All six of the crew, whose hands and arms were engaged with the toil of *shlepping* the heavy cart, were too weary to fight back, even if it had been their orders to do so, which it had not. At first they were so stunned that they stood stock-still, and then dove under the cart so it wouldn't be left unguarded to the little predators.

The nearest cluster walking over the crest of the rise about a hundred meters away heard their yells for help. Already on his way back toward the cart, within less than half a minute, Branko, joined by Yossi and Yankel Golub, and seconds later by the senior cadre, swooped downhill to the beleaguered cart and crew. Leaping out from behind their hiding places, at least fifteen urchins scattered back into the town like field mice, with Branko and the Golubs in hot pursuit. Yoni had been on *shlep* duty, which was no doubt the only reason Branko had not assigned an additional rear guard that morning—not that it hadn't crossed his mind, given the events of the past week.

Only Velvel Niedl was hit by one of the flying missiles, drawing blood from his chin, and Doctor Hippocrates quickly pronounced as only a superficial wound. He instructed an out-of-breath, panting Nurse Nightingale to clean and dress the ugly wound thoroughly.

"Thank God. This all could have been much worse. We may have lost one of our four cantors," teased Maidele. Velvel, sanguinolent chin about to be scrubbed and painted with iodine by the adorable angel, managed his trademark toothy smile. The quartet would remain so.

Mordecai, relieved that the damage had been nearly entirely averted, issued his heavenly thanks before quickly continuing back into town with Menachem Berman, Mendel and Sendehr by his side, keeping their eyes on Branko and the Golubs as they gave chase to the "future felons of Finsterwalde."

Everything happened so fast that Mordecai could not

temper the situation. He would have regrouped and gone forward, not giving Branko permission to carry the incident any further. Now he had no choice but to support the action when he saw the security team capture three of the imps, holding each of them like a "piglet-to-market."

"*Oy vay!* What is our *soldat* going to do next? He's got to let them go. Let's just get out of this town, Mordecai."

"Menachem, he's coming this way. Let us all calm down and think rationally. It's vital that we do just that."

The squealing little brats, each firmly held by their captor, were frightened to the point of fast-flowing tears. The very sight of Branko and his "Golub troops" would have scared a scarecrow. They seemed to have a penchant for long black beards and mustaches, and severe black shirts and pants, even in this hot summer sun. The frightening sight of the periodic flash of weaponry tucked into each of their belts under their shirts—something absolutely forbidden by Mordecai, who wasn't about to toss this infraction into the fray now—made the children begin to scream.

Before any discussion as to what to do next could even begin, marching onto the scene in front of the town-council hall, *das rathaus,* came three young flaxen-haired, Rubenesque mothers, followed by half of the at-large stone throwers, and a balloon of a man with a heavily waxed handlebar mustache.

"As Past Burgermeister of this fair and peaceful town, I demand to know what is going on here." He pointed at Branko and the Golubs who stood holding three children under thick arms. Branko having given the Golubs orders not to let go under any circumstances, was surprisingly and tacitly supported by the nodding agreements of both Mordecai and Menachem.

In near perfect Deutsch, Branko answeredwith the anxious question. "My honorable Herr Burgermeister, good afternoon. Our walk through your perfectly charming hamlet was grossly marred by these youngsters and their compatriots who deigned to throw potentially lethal weapons at us. Now, dear fellow, we are peace-loving, God-fearing, God's chosen Jewish men and woman from far off Romania, transiting your beautiful hills and valleys on our way to a new life in America. We have legal papers if you wish to inspect them."

"That will not be necessary. I'm sure you've been checked and re-checked by our constabulary forces. Now please let the babies go, *mein herr,* and get on your way.

"When I saw you marching through town, I couldn't help thinking, *There go fifty or sixty good jobs in Berlin or Hamburg.*"

"Not to worry, *mein herr.* I assure you that we will be leaving from Bremerhaven." Branko pauses for a moment while his eyes darted around the quite empty *rathaus* square. Good. Secure. "But, we are strongly considering taking along these incorrigible little monsters with us to America." Again, a pause. "Or perhaps we'll just s-l-o-w-l-y drain their blood so we can bake the *matzos* to sustain us on the way. We often do that kind of thing, you know..."

The shrieks that issued forth after this threatening outburst from a Branko who had transformed from a pleasant smiling, gentle giant to a version of Count Vlad Dracula personified pierced the afternoon sky. The chorus of wailing mothers were wringing their hands and aprons in unison while the retired Burgermeister sputtered and fumed, and now at least ten horror-stricken children were bawling like they would never see their mamas again. Having understood enough of the conversation in German, Mordecai and Menachem could do nothing but bite their lips and grit their teeth. Mendel and Sendehr stood there wide-eyed.

With this desired reaction from the ordinary citizenry, Branko calmly and gently dropped his squirming, red-faced quarry, followed in order by Yankel and Yossi. As the three little ones ran tripping over one another, screaming to their mothers, while Branko, grinning broadly, tipped his broad black hat to each *haus frau,* with a leering wink, and then snapped to attention, smartly saluting a disbelieving ex-mayor. Turning on his booted heel, the *soldat* did a perfectly executed about-face, copied in turn by his well-trained staff as they fell in behind him, counting cadence as they marched back to the cart...*ein, zwei, drei, vier.* Mordecai and his cadre of three, fearing almost certain repercussions, could do nothing at this juncture, but follow their lead.

As they all walked over the top of the hill in a more relaxed step, cart now closely behind, Mordecai sidled up to his defense chief and half-whispered, "You know I cannot and will not endorse this behavior, 'Sergeant' Horvitch. You may have put us all in great jeopardy back there! We have a long way to go to Bremerhaven, and I'm certain that our newly gained dark reputation will follow us." And in a barely audible, full whisper, "Privately, old boy, I loved it! I positively loved it! We all did! But don't ever let it happen again. Do you hear, my former 'Sergeant,' from now on 'lowly Private Horvitch'?" They both tried very hard not to laugh over this purely symbolic demotion, but failed.

As the description of the incident was repeated verbatim for everyone, peals of laughter could be heard for the next few kilometers. But morale had reached its highest peak since post-escape. Itzy could only grumble that he should have been sent for, telling Mayer Kelemer in a loud voice what he would have said and done given the opportunity. Everyone in their immediate vicinity doubled-over with laughter.

There had been little or no traffic on the less than primary road to Berlin, and when the horseless carriage pulled up to a stop beside Branko and Mordecai, no one paid much attention. But the driver turned out to be none other than Herr ex-Burgermeister who proceeded to stand up next to the steering lever, hat in hand.

"Gentlemen, gentlemen. I did not want to let this day pass without offering my sincere apologies for the most despicable actions of our young people. Completely uncalled for, out of order and entirely embarrassing for the fine folk of Finsterwalde. To treat God's chosen, His Children of Israel, in this manner is inexcusable, and moreover, so un-Christian-like. Parents, teachers and officials of our town will not tolerate it. You can rest assured that each little devil will be punished accordingly, and will be given an abundance of extra assignments in bible school. May you find it in your hearts to forgive these transgressions, and may God watch over you on your voyage to America."

The petty politician placed his straw chapeau back on his perspiring bald head, and saluted Branko—who returned it with a snap—while everyone else looked on in utterly silent bedazzlement, having picked up enough Yiddish-sounding words to recognize the gist of this unexpected, yet profound contrition. Spontaneously, all broke out in a round of cheering aimed at the driver. A peaceful calm of great inner satisfaction embraced Branko and Mordecai warmly.

"Imagine that, Mayerel. A pro-Semite is alive and well in Deutschland," remarked Itzy, as they both stood there riveted in wonderment.

* * *

A few days following this bizarre afternoon, after Mordecai and Branko decided to avoid any further separations by tightening up the formation, Sholem and Yaakov had reduced their normal lead to less than two hundred meters.

"So, *nu*, Sholem, have you considered my invitation to live in Montreal?"

"Itzy and Mayer and all of the others with family in Boston have been trying to convince me to go with them instead of New York. Montreal? I think not, Yak. I don't feel it's for me."

"Why not? It is thought to be a beautiful city, the Paris of North America, situated on the banks of a large river..."

"*Frozen* river, Yak! Frozen!"

"You'll have plenty of cold in Boston or New York, too, Sholem! And besides, I need your running competition. Someday I'll beat you!"

"What? With snowshoes?"

And so it went, give and take, until they came upon the billboards popping up at the side of the road around a bend, just beyond a sign signifying Berlin: 32 km. The postings were huge and unusually colorful, compared to the few bland and ugly advertisements they had seen approaching other cities. Romania had a minimal number of these roadside encroachments, but they seemed to be popular throughout the Hapsburg Empire, proliferating even further in Germany.

Sendehr and Zed-Zed had chosen this exceptionally quiet road between Dresden and Berlin as part of their plan to avoid the major highways because of heavy wagon traffic, and especially with the growing number of motorcars and trucks everywhere. That would explain the surprise registered by the point team when they came upon not one, but three billboards standing in a row. They stood there trying to decipher the language and were only able to pick out a few key words, coupled with very graphic, multicolored pictures. When Branko arrived with the main body they converged while he read, translated where necessary and explained the content of the first.

WELCOME TO THE GREATEST SHOW EVER ASSEMBLED

Appearing for its sixth engagement in the great city of Berlin

*** The Wild West of Buffalo Bill Cody will

entertain you, thrill you, intrigue you

beyond your wildest imagination.

*** Come see the sweetheart of the prairie,

Annie Oakley, the unmatchable

THE WAYFARERS

sharpshooter, drill a bullet through an
Ace of Spades from fifty meters.
*** Watch in awe as savage and bloodthirsty
Indians attack the pioneers.
*** Cheer Buffalo Bill as he leads a cavalry
charge to fight them off.

All of this in three hours packed full of the most colorful
excitement showing in the civilized world today.

Kaiser Wilhem II Stadion
on Kurfurstendamm, 1-22 July, 1904

COWBOYS, INDIANS,
DAMSELS IN DISTRESS,
THE GREAT BUFFALO BILL

HURRY ! HURRY! HURRY!
PURCHASE YOUR TICKETS NOW!

Come one, come all!
Don't miss this Show to end all Shows!

Special acts on 4 July, honoring U.S.A.

Independence Day.

Gigantic fireworks display.

With this first slice of Americana, and the "Wild West" to boot—that symbol of wide open spaces where Americans lived adventurous and wonderful lives—fifty-seven pairs of eyes were glued to the advertisement. The board, at least four-men tall and as wide as six Captain Polinous or seven ex-Finsterwalde Burgermeisters, featured a full-colored sketch of the world famous buffalo hunter. His flowing white beard, white "ten-gallon" hat, arm around a rifle toting Annie Oakley, complete with deerskin fringed jerkin and long skirt, was a classic picture. Three bare-chested, dark-skinned, heavily feathered Indian warriors on horseback, lurked menacingly in the background.

The exciting buzzing and chattering wouldn't stop until Branko began reading from the second billboard, in front of which Rivka already stood with respectful eyes riveted on the face of Sarah Bernhardt, arguably the world's greatest actress of the time.

NOW PLAYING

Sarah Bernhardt, the pride of Europe, brings her

heralded **Theatre Sarah Bernhardt** to delight Berlin

audiences with Victor Hugo's "*Hernani*" (In French,

with abridged translations available for all) The role of

Dona Sol will be played by Bernhardt's protege,

Hermione Cartier. Miss Bernhardt will perform the
soliloquy from Racine's *Phaedra.*

Theater aficionados, do not miss this outstanding event!

3 July through 18 July

Theater Unter den Linden

"Sendehr, I've just got to see Miss Bernhardt! I've never seen a real play before."

"What, *Dos Vinshfingerl* isn't real, Rivkeleh?"

"I don't mean that, of course!" Rivka snapped, then softened, realizing that he was only teasing, and asked seriously, "Will you help me get to see her?"

"Of course. I don't know what it costs, but you'll see Bernhardt. *Daigeh nisht.*"

Rivka stood gazing at the picture on the billboard, then finally walked away, joining everyone listening to Branko describe the meaning of the third sign at the roadside. She was still beaming from ear to ear.

The last sign was simpler in design than the others, with large letters calling for attention. Everything was in five languages: German, Polish, Czech, Cyrillic-lettered Russian and Hebrew-lettered Yiddish. Omitted were Hungarian, Romanian, Greek, Turkish, Bulgarian and Slavic Serbian, but the intent of the message was crystal clear.

ACHTUNG ACHTUNG ACHTUNG

Do not under any circumstances enter Berlin unless:
1. You are a citizen of the Second Reich, with proper papers.
2. You have a bona fide current transit visa, properly endorsed.
3. You have steamship vouchers or certified letters signifying departure from Hamburg, Bremen, Bremerhaven or any North Sea or Atlantic port.
*** No gypsy trash will be allowed entrance into the city at any time. You are in Germany illegally and will be dealt withaccordingly. Municipal Police will stop everyone at all entrances to the city. Penalty for nonconformance to the above restrictions will be swift and severe.

Hermann Goeringer,
Reichmarshal
Brandenburg-Mecklenburg Regions

The board was fittingly plastered with crude graffitos announcing "Germany for Germans."

Nothing was said. No surprises. All papers were in order. Nothing to fear. As they started up the road, Itzy responded to Herr Goeringer's demands.

"*Gevalt!* We're about as welcome as Father Mihai at my Bar Mitzvah."

Another kilometer or two, and Yankel Golub had his usual moment.

"*Nu*, Mendel, this Boffaleh Beel...good or bad for the Jews?"

18

ENCOUNTERS: BERLIN-
A FOREBODING

Ich bin ein Berliner!
John F. Kennedy, 1963

Black boots, jackboots, shiny black jackboots,
marching on the streets of Imperial Berlin.

Sendehr Efraim, 1904

If the trek of the Fusgeyers in 1904 could be matched to a "Scale of Overall Reception," in degrees of warmest to coldest, it would appear thusly:

Romania, from Birlad to Borsha...warmer than expected from the Romanians, very warm from fellow Jews.

Splitting the Austro-Hungarian Empire into national regions, Hungary... would be classified as noticeably cool from the Hungarians, and warm from the Jews...although Budapest would be labeled as much warmer than expected from the Jewish community.

Austria... showed little warmth and would nudge into the cooling category from both Jew and non-Jew, but treatment from the Viennese seminary staff was comfortably warmer.

Czech Moravia...warm reception from the small Jewish communities, especially Znojmo, and more than a bit cooler from the local Moravians. Czech Bohemia... exceptionally warm from Praha's Jews and a few centigrades cooler, but not uncomfortably so, from the local Czechs.

> (It is important to note that the usual reception from the military, the city police, the district and town constabularies, and the local magistrates, ran from cold to Arctic freezing everywhere—from Birlad to Berlin—as the mountain of foregoing evidence clearly indicates.)

As for Germany, thus far the scale was frozen at the freezing point from the reception of both tribes...the genuine twenty-second-generation German, or the assimilationists who were in outright denial; the latter indignantly proclaiming that indeed they were not Jewish, *per se*, but rightfully members of the "Mosaic persuasion."

Hearing this phrase for the first time himself, Branko had a difficult time translating the German into under-standable Yiddish for the others, and ended up telling Mordecai that the two Dresden Neolog synagogue elders who had proudly issued this statement were *"Moishe Yidden."* From then on the label stuck, much to the cha-grin of the frequent recipients of this condescending Branko-ism, who bridled at this or any other coarse *ostjuden* jargon that they could not understand. They did seem to recognize, however, that they were the subjects of ridicule. While they stood befuddled, the Fusgeyers stifled their giggles each time someone spoke the descriptive phrase aloud. As was to be expected, the Gelman-Kelemer duo milked it for all they could...and then some!

Although the "arms length" treatment was painful, ob-taining the necessary transit documents from the border station officers in little Breitnau went relatively smoothly. It would turn out that Germany's three major steamship lines, a source of great national pride on all seven seas, had paved the way to a trouble free entry at all border crossings for any one holding legitimate vouchers for passage. Their combined influence was obviously tantamount to a directive from Kaiser Willi himself, who was equally intent on shipping everyone out as fast as he could. *Germany for Germans!*

The prospects for any reasonable warmth that could translate into a genuine interest in their mission lay within Berlin...the chances of finding it, unlikely. Nevertheless, there was a certain amount of guarded optimism in the air, especially among those who kept a wary eye out for sociopolitical indicators of any significance, positive or negative. They could, of course, always count on the consistent Yankel to ask his usual provocative question at the appropriate time...*is it good or bad for the Yidden?*

On this, their last encampment before Berlin, the contingent showed their restlessness more than ever before. It seems they could smell the North Sea, the port, the ship, and the broad Atlantic. Every conversation, during, before and after Mendel's nightly English lesson branched off the notion that this was the beginning of the final segments of their long trek. Mendel sensed this mainly because it had affected him in the same way, and the lesson concentrated on words and phrases for the port and the transatlantic crossing:

Captain. The crew. Galley. Bow. Stern. Aft. Alee. Portside. Lifeboat. Lifeboat drill. Gangplank. The Bridge is where the Captain steers the ship. The sailor climbs to the crow's nest. Sea Gulls. Pier. Dock. Seaport. Ocean Liner. Voyage. Horizon. Ocean swells. Rough seas. Toilet. I am seasick, I am going to vomit; get out of the way!

Asking for a volunteer to put some of the words into a few sentences, Mendel didn't have the slightest doubt as to who that person would be. Sholem proudly offered:

Ven de bott leafs de dock, vee know dat a hoshun

*voytch is gut fur seek pipuls. Eef you not awreddy
seek, you veel be ven de smokstek smoks un de*
keptin *steers de bott into de roff hoshun svells.*

Teacher Buchman beamed as broadly and proudly as
his star pupil when everyone applauded the masterful effort. Rivka jumped up to reward the blushing foot racer
with a kiss on his forehead. A giggly Maidele and a serious
Chaike followed her lead. *Nu, it pays to be a volunteer,* the
point man thought happily.

Mordecai, flanked by Zed-Zed and Sendehr, delivered
the surprise just after Mendel's class in the abandoned
warehouse they were fortunate enough to find.

"*Meine tyereh khaverim,*" he began, with the wide smile
that was his trademark, and which stood in contrast to his
usual no-nonsense approach to most everything, "how would
you like ten days in the grand city of Berlin?"

The disbelieving, then affirming, loud *huzzahs* and accompanying applause seemed like they would never end,
until Mordecai raised his hand as the recognized signal to
quiet down.

"Zed-Zed and Sendehr have consulted the map and the
schedule and have adjusted them both so that we may do
so. Zed-Zed," Mordecai motioned his schedule maven to
come forward.

"From the past reports we deduce that the ports, including Bremerhaven, are not exactly inviting places in
which to spend any more time than is absolutely necessary. They are typically dirty and overcrowded with refugees like ourselves, and of course none of us are favorites of
the locals or the *Moishe Yidden.* Heh-Heh! It appears that
we may face as much as a two-week quarantine when we
arrive in Bremerhaven, as each of the three Birlader groups
have noted.

"Therefore, by reaching Berlin tomorrow, and staying
through two Sabbaths in the reportedly comfortable Alliance dormitories that have been arranged for us, we can
still reach Bremerhaven with more than the two weeks to

spare before sailing on the 15th of August. Rather than a prolonged stay in Hamburg or any of the smaller towns en route, we judged that Berlin is the logical and preferred choice." Zed-Zed gestured to Sendehr to say a few words.

"Why is everyone smiling at me? Is it something Zed-Zed or Mordecai just said?" At this, the smiles morphed into laughter. Shaking his head, amused by his comrades' delight, Sendehr went on. "The excellent maps I found in Dresden show no topographical hardships ahead, and the rest of our way into Bremerhaven should prove unchallenging, barring the unforeseen, which we've seen far too often. Seriously, as you must know very well by now, we have no way of forecasting any potential trouble or delay, but as I've reported to our commander, I see no reason not to endorse an extended stay in Berlin, from where I stand, geographically speaking." The cheering and hugging resumed.

Fifty-seven well-seasoned trekkers from Romania would be entering the pride of the Second Reich the following day. The camaraderie, which had been diluted a few times since the "Great Escape," returned with unsurpassed vigor on the spot. The *schnapps* and bottles of golden *Deutsche bier* from Simmy's latest *schnorring* expedition, and what was left of that special Moravian vintage, emetic-free as it was, succeeded in breaking down the last vestiges of reserve. Not that there were any *shickorim* in camp, which in fact included a majority who eschewed the harder liquor in favor of the tea, the brew or the wine...especially the youngest members. Avi, showoff that he had become, liberally sampled the *schnapps* when he was sure that his young friends were watching. This quickly translated into a very queasy stomach and several fast trips into the bushes.

Suffice it to say at this pleasant juncture, the Birlader *kindelach* would sleep soundly on the warped wooden floors of the derelict, crop-drying warehouse just north of Rangsdorf, situated alongside the macadam Mariendorfer Damm. The signpost at the crossroads read "Berlin, 15km" in a northerly direction, and "Hamburg, 300km" westerly.

Zed-Zed's amended schedule called for the Wayfarers to stay over in Berlin from June 30th to July 10th, and cover the three hundred kilometers to Hamburg by July 21st, at the usual rate of thirty to thirty-five kilometers each daynever on the Sabbath. The port at Bremerhaven, the final land destination on the continent, was another eighty kilometers to the west and they planned to reach it by July 25th, providing an adequate five-day cushion before beginning the required quarantine period.

Mordecai agreed with this revised itinerary wholeheartedly, and before falling off to sleep, he haltingly indulged in a rare self-accolade. But as usual, he gave most of the credit to his God's guiding hand in helping him select such a competent cadre, so well seasoned now by three months of daily challenges. Every one of them passed in review, as his eyes fought off final closure for the night:

Zed-Zed, never failing to honor the marriage between forced flexibility and meticulous timing.

Branko, a diamond-in-the-rough, and ten times more valuable.

Sendehr, the walking map, whose precious mastery of the written word is detailing this event for posterity.

Menachem Berman, continually demonstrating that discretion is, indeed, the better part of valor; but always willing to look the other way when diplomacy and tact meet an immovable object.

Rivka, bless her, and her entertainment committee, contributing heavily to the ongoing morale, not to mention her unforgettable heroic role in the great escape.

Simmy, the Food Czar, like a mother with a huge family to feed. How does he do it day after day? Better we shouldn't ask too many questions!

Nuchim, who could have single-handedly raised and managed the funds for Columbus, with money left over for a voyage to India, which the Italian was trying to find in the first place.

Gershon and his klayneh *Maidele, Doctor Hippocrates and Nurse Nightingale, a most dedicated pair of caregivers.*

Everyone has complete confidence in them. So vitally important to our mission...and the health and well-being of all.

Mendel. Ah yes, Mendel. The intellect he adds to our combined ability to reason is beyond description. There is no doubt in anyone's mind that this group will be the most knowledgeable New Americans of 1904. They will speak more English than any other immigrants, excepting those who emigrate from Britain, of course. They will be familiar with more of the geography and history of their new land. They will, no doubt, thanks to our brilliant lehrer, *be among the best prepared citizens-to-be that America has ever welcomed. What more can be said about our lanky professor?*

Just short of lauding every individual Fusgeyer, Mordecai shifted his body on his bed roll one more time to quickly thank his God for the courageous point team of Sholem and Yaakov;the uplifting trumpeter and drummer and the melodious "four cantors; "the wonderful contributions of the feminine spirit from Chaike, Pessel, Esther and Tsippy; the Golub boys for their unyielding loyal support to Branko; and for all of the non-exempt cart *shleppers.* Now everyone was covered. This done, Reb Mordecai was about to issue one last heartfelt *omayn,* but certainly not before his nightly ritual of having a few choice words with *ribono shel olam:*

> *Dear God, you have protected us well. A few frightening moments but nevertheless we know that you are there for us. Would it be too much for this humble servant to ask you to remain close by at least as far as America? After all, who but you knows what we will encounter at the port and especially on the high seas? After that, I shall ask you no more. You have my solemn word on that. Just to Boston...and New York. Please!*

The resolute commander could now finally give himself permission to indulge in a long awaited, much needed, most deserving peaceful sleep.

§

Rabbi Nachman was showing no signs of fatigue after their afternoon *shpatzier* to Birlad's rustic, bench-filled, riverside park. He had been telling Nathan of the Finsterwalde incident and they enjoyed a good hearty laugh over it.

"That is some story. My, oh my! Branko is another one tailor-made for a Hollywood treatment. I'm thinking 'Rambo' Stallone, but I can't convince myself. Charlie Bronson in his younger days could have been the choice. Whoa! Sorry! My thoughts are wandering again, out loud as you know, but I'm sure they make little sense to you."

"On the contrary, 'Meester Hullyvood.' You're playing the popular game of casting a movie, I believe. Your Beely Creestel, is it, was planning to make a movie near Birlad two years ago. Everyone was excited to a peak. The government was ready to make all kinds of concessions since one of our Romanian basketball players, a giant named Muresan, playing as a professional in your country, was to be in it with Creestel. In fact, he's related to the Muresan family here in Birlad. For many years, while I was growing up, a Muresan owned one of the local pharmacies and Gershon, our Dr. Hippocrates, had worked for him in 1904. Do you remember when I mentioned this? It was our first day together."

"Yes, I do. The pharmacist defied the unwritten law by hiring a Jew to handle medicines...true?"

"That's right. Nevertheless, Creestel finally ended up making the film in the Czech Republic. A great disappointment for the whole district...including me, I might add."

"I remember seeing it advertised, yes; but Rabbi, now that we have Branko in the forefront, is there anything you can tell me about his life in America?"

"I still have much to share with you, dear friend. Branko? Very interesting, to say the least. A fascinating man. A life to match. My father's periodic letters from Mendel, Mordecai and Sendehr shed quite a bit of light on the continuing adventures of our Sergeant Horvitch...our big soldier, *der groisseh soldat*."

With this introduction, after returning to his home, Rabbi Nachman began to spin the intriguing story of Branko's life in America, to Nathan's delight. To no great surprise, it turned out that he became a policeman in New York. He had learned English quite rapidly with some intense tutoring from Mendel, and was assigned to the precinct covering Yorkville, which was predominantly German-speaking. Branko later married one of Rivka's actress friends and stayed with the Police Department, rising to the rank of Lieutenant of Detectives, solving some front-page cases along the way.

When the first war broke outeven though by then he was nearly forty years old, he volunteered for the United States Army—the soldier within him still fighting. His marriage was very shaky, he had no children, and perhaps these two circumstances drove him to enlist. He was assigned to a branch that specialized in training behind-the-lines spies. His knowledge of German was no doubt the reason for this assignment, and he became an expert at his job. When the United States entered the fray in 1917, Branko was sent to France where he served with distinction, going behind the lines himself on several occasions, winning medal after medal, including the prestigious French *Croix de Guerre* for rescuing three French spies from certain death. He also won a field promotion to Lieutenant. Nathan wondered aloud if his father had come across Branko in France. *If he had,* Nathan concluded, *he would never have said anything about it.*

Nathan was happy to see Rabbi Nachman's stack of letters from the New York trio, and he was glad that they would be able to shed further light on Branko, since they covered the better part of the '20s and '30s. By the time the war ended, Branko had become Captain Horvitch, but at age forty-three the army wanted to part company with him—

something about a severe decrease in funding.

Sendehr wrote that Branko did not take this standing still. With all the *chutzpah* he had so often demonstrated, he petitioned the General Staff in Washington to plead his case. They invited him to do so, and following this hearing they asked him to appear at the White House. President Woodrow Wilson was terminally incapacitated at the time, and the First Lady, Edith Wilson, took all appointments.

Sendehr noted that she had ordered the General Staff to send all visiting, highly decorated soldiers to her office to meet with her. Her noble purpose was to keep alive the patriotic spirit resulting from the victorious "war to end all wars," as well as to influence Congress to restore a sensible budget to the military forces. Any positive press conferences to this effect she saw could be influential. Her husband was barely alive, suffering from a series of strokes, but in one of his last lucid requests he insisted that Edith develop the foregoing projects. Never before was a First Lady thrust into such prominence.

Nathan, thinking of the legendary Eleanor Roosevelt, and Hilary Clinton's contributions to the Office, chuckled at the thought. In the meantime, he was engaged in the frustrating exercise of making sensible meaning out of lapses in the translation, from the letters, and Yossi Nachman's lack of familiarity regarding certain western terms and descriptions. This, of course, had been a continuing challenge throughout the past week, but somehow it was working out well...very well! Obviously, a goodly amount of poetic license filled the gaps.

Edith Wilson evidently was exceptionally impressed with Branko's encompassing presence, his pleasant demeanor and his never-before-heard Fusgeyer stories, in addition to his heroic exploits in France. Won over in this way, she personally called the Chief of Staff later that same day, who reinstated the rank of full Colonel to him and immediately installed him as White House Aide-de-Camp to replace Brigadier General Halstead who was retiring that month. Whether it was a whim, a case of being in the right place at the right time, or just our Branko's charismatic character that placed him with such good fortune, one will never know. Sendehr's letters included some of his own speculation, and that of Mordecai, Rivka and Mendel, but nothing definitive. The fact is, Branko somehow managed to retain this coveted position through the next three administrations—Harding, Coolidge and Hoover—before he retired at fifty-seven. He was besieged with intriguing job opportunities, none of which he accepted for some unknown reason. Sendehr seemed to think that the *soldat* wanted to be his "own man" again. Completely independent!

During the depression years everyone lost track of his wanderings, and when Mendel heard from him again he had divorced his wife, hastily married a spinster oil heiress from West Texas, and was off to travel the world. Mordecai received one last postcard with a picture of the Taj Mahal on it, in 1939. Sendehr and Mendel both received their final words from Branko the previous year...one got a postcard from Chile with a picture of a snowcapped volcano...the other received a picture of a Viennese street scene, sent less than a month after Hitler's *Anschluss*, with an ominous note:

> *Hi-ya Sendehr and Rivka! Remember this place? Nazis on every street corner. All hell's going to break loose in Europe. Here we go again! Fusgeyers forever, mates! Love, Big Soldier.*

As for photographs, Rabbi Nachman assured Nathan that he had some fading sepia tones of Branko in uniform, with Mendel and Esther, during their one visit to Washington in 1924. Sendehr and Rivka, the Anieloffs and the Buchmans spent an evening in New York with the visiting Colonel Horvitch that same year, and photographs were taken at that time also. Unfortunately, the infamous burning damaged most of them and the figures are barely recognizable now. Rabbi Nachman promised that he would show any and all remaining photos to Nathan when they returned to the house.

The entire matter of photographs had been broached a few times. First of all, there was only one group photo taken during the trek, from Vienna, aside from the Mendel-Esther wedding photos at the outset. This was understandable because in all likelihood no one owned one of those bulky box cameras of the time. *How sad*, thought Nathan. Once they reached America, a goodly number of pictures were frequently sent back to families and friends in Birlad. Eli Nachman was perhaps the most popular recipient, since he had placed many of them in a bound portfolio, which was, in turn, included with all of the papers given to the younger Nachman for safekeeping, before the Iashi troubles.

A teary-eyed Nathan was quite surprised that Sholem, too, had sent Eli Nachman two family photos, which included a five-year-old Nathan. Although badly singed around the edges, he recognized that they were taken at Nantasket Beach, near Quincy, on a family outing. Even after all his years in California, Sholem missed Quincy as his adopted home town, and was quick to compare Santa Monica and Venice Beaches unfavorably with Nantasket, Cape Cod and even the rocky strand of Quincy's River Street. Decidedly so.

Nathan declined the offer to take any of the photos back to California, feeling strongly that the mental images he had developed of all of the Fusgeyers would be sufficient. He had, however, taken two rolls of the *shul*, the cemetery, Rabbi Nachman, the Ushers and a few other townspeople. Herb and Rico had covered the rest of Birlad and vicinity, and the two very colorful side trips. The snaps of those topless beauties on the Black Sea beaches would take a heap of explaining by both dad and son...most especially the one showing Herb flanked and dwarfed by two dark-eyed, long-haired, long-legged Amazonians—honor graduates of the Sophia Loren School for Seaside Sexuality. Hmmm!

Nathan finally took his leave after two more hours of illuminating talk. Rabbi Nachman was ready for a good night's sleep prior to the next day's auto trip to Bucureshti, while Nathan wanted to have dinner with the boys before doing his packing. Both stood for a moment outside the glistening white home, remarking once more on the professional painting job. The place looked positively brand new and the boys had even replaced the *mezuzzah.* The Rabbi commented that his *rebbitzen* would be in for a most pleasant surprise when she returned from Israel. Importing house painters from Beverly Hills was not the usual practice in Birlad, or anywhere else on earth, for that matter!

The younger Friedmans had been waiting for Nathan in the hotel's empty dining room, and when he saw them Nathan decided that they should celebrate their last night in Romania at the Cafanea Popescu. The *saramura de peshte* had seduced his taste buds, and he found the *Feteasca* wine selections to be competitive with some of the best of Napa Valley. Rico could pack away a whole cheese pie, *placinta cu brinza,* by himself, while Herb referred to the cozy eatery as "Spago East...wa-yyyy East," knowing that a certain Wolfgang Puck back in L.A. wouldn't appreciate this humor one bit.

As had been the routine every evening, Nathan synopsized his day-long findings and discussions for an enthusiastic audience of two. The stimulating questions, particularly from Rico, and the pursuant discussions pushed these over-dinner sessions beyond midnight. This energized participation was a source of great satisfaction to the elder Friedman.

"Branko sure was a risk taker, and this time he got away with it. Good for him! Nice to hear something about his amazing life in America. Mordecai and Mendel, Zed-Zed— too bad he died so young—and Rivka. Sendehr. I could have guessed he would be into something literary; and she in the theater. Simmy. Nuchim. Menachem. How about some of the other guys? Where did they end up after arriving in America? Itzy and Mayer, and ..."

"As I told you, Rico, Rabbi Nachman has given me the list, in Yiddish, covering each Fusgeyer from information he has put together. I'll get some help reading it at the old Yiddishist hang out at The Workmen's Circle on Robertson. But, let's see, to answer your question, according to letters from Nuchim Krasnigor, the comedians first went to work at the Quincy shipyard. The supervisors simply couldn't handle them. They cracked everyone up too much! Rivet guns in the hands of uncontrollably hee-hawing co-workers could be lethal weapons—accidents waiting to happen—their bosses worried.

"The vaudeville theater in Quincy Square catered to the shipyard workers by offering half-price tickets every Wednesday night. Itzy and Mayer, who were doing reasonably well with their new language, auditioned for fill-in spots at one time, and their roles eventually became permanent. In attendance from time to time, of course, were Grandpa Sholem, 'the four cantors,' and Nuchim and Velvel Niedl's brother Melech, who had come to Quincy in '98. Nuchim's letters were keenly descriptive of their progress.

"Within a few months these hilarious kids became the headliners, murdering the English language, becoming the nouveau masters of malapropian satire, and their fans loved every minute of it. They soon quit their jobs at the yard, as their reputation spread to Boston and beyond. One night, a man sitting in the front row went back to their dressing rooms...turned out he was sent by Lazar Berel Mayer, the owner of 'The Gem,' a run-down vaudeville house in Haverhill, about thirty miles north of Boston.

"To make this long story a bit shorter, since I've got to pack and phone Grandma, I'll synopsize the synopsis. The comedy team was offered a starring spot with a new theater Mr. Mayer was opening in Boston. You may not know the name, but the Mayer were talking about here was later known as Louis B. Mayer, the Hollywood giant. Before he finally went to the coast and established Metro-Goldwyn-Mayer Studios, the laugh merchants were put under contract to appear in all of the Mayer-owned, combined vaudeville-movie palaces throughout New England and in and around New York; including the famed Catskill 'borscht belt' circuit upstate.

"As was to be expected, the many Birlad New Yorkers welcomed them with open arms when they appeared in any of several Manhattan and Brooklyn venues. Inevitably, many of them became unsuspecting targets of the duo's skits. A 1916 letter from Sendehr described a most irreverent rendition of the famous great escape, where Itzy plays the role of Avi as the estranged illegitimate son of Captain '*paskudnyak*' Ullbricht. Can you use your imagination on that one, boys? There should be further updates on their careers in the remaining letters when I have them translated."

And so it went. Since Nathan had mentioned Avi Semelweiss, to wrap up the last night in town he decided to let them in on Avi's remarkable career, which was the biggest surprise of all. He knew the boys would love this story, which he had planned to tell them on the long plane ride.

"Avi lived with an aunt and uncle in Brooklyn and played hooky from school more often than not. Instead of studying books, he was learning to play the great American pastime in a park near Coney Island with a gang of unemployed older kids, mostly Irish and Italian immigrants. Seems that Avi often visited Sendehr and Rivka and related the story to them as it progressed, which is how I can relate it now to you.

"The couple looked askance at his claims that he was developing into an honest-to-goodness baseball player; a shortstop with the speed to be an unstoppable base-stealer, and the hit-'em-where-they-ain't Wee Willie Keeler-type spray-hitter. In 1909, when he was nineteen and a ne'er-do-well at the countless menial jobs from which he was unceremoniously dumped, he was signed by a Brooklyn Dodger scout to play with a minor league team in Bluefield, West Virginia."

Sendehr, who evidently became a rabid baseball fan, had included a long series of sports page articles as he put together Avi's checkered career. These, in turn, were translated by a friend of Rabbi Eli's in Bucharest who was fluent in English, and the convoluted package was now in Nathan's hands...in Yiddish He could make out Sendehr's poetic description of Avi's insatiable 'capacity for mendacity, less the slightest veracity,' which he translated liberally now from a series of letters to Rabbi Eli, dated 1907-1930. Nathan went on, trying to remember the gist of Yossi Nachman's information, reading what Yiddish he could, and filling in the blanks for Herb and Rico. Whoever said any genealogical exercise would be easy? There had been times during the past nine days when Nathan envied those whose ancestral backgrounds sprouted forth from the British Isles. Nevertheless, he forged ahead with the unusual story of Avigdor Semelweiss with his audience's full and enthusiastic support.

"The scrappy ballplayer never did make it to the majors, but traveled the minor circuit for two decades, also playing with a U.S. Navy team in San Diego during the first war. In the early '20s Avi was traded to the New York Yankee organization and played an entire year with their Newark Bears, where his newly anglicized name appeared on the roster as 'Albie White.' Those Fusgeyers in the vicinty of New York and Newark made it a practice to watch him play, especially on Sundays, whenever possible. This occasion gave way to numerous Birlader reunion-picnics in the sunny bleachers of the Newark ballpark, families and all...at a quarter a head, babes-in-arms and toddlers free.

"The Anieloffs, the Buchmans and Rivka, not a died-in-the-wool baseball fan among them, vociferously cheered for the exciting, faster-than-lightning shortstop. Expert Sendehr spent the biggest part of each game explaining the intricacies to the others, with ten-year-old Alexander learning fast from his father.

"Much to everyone's disappointment, 'Albie White,' dubbed the 'Battling Bear from Birlad' by the Newark sportswriters, nearing thirty-five years of age, was reassigned to Columbus, Ohio, the next year.

"When Sendehr and Rivka last heard from him, he had tired of a long string of girlfriends, and finally married a teenage blonde-haired, blue-eyed Swedish immigrant in Northern Minnesota where he was playing for a St. Louis Brown's lowly Class C farm team in Duluth. They lost contact after that, as stated in that 1930 letter to Rabbi Eli, but rumor had it that Albie White wound up scouting for the Dodgers in the upper Midwest. As you can imagine, guys, Sendehr sure enjoyed telling this story!"

"Not as much as you, Grandpa!" Rico, especially, followed every word of the unusual story, and both he and Herb found it to be fascinating. It was. Somehow, one doesn't think of immigrants in the earlier years of the century playing serious baseball, but the fact is, there were more than most fans realized: Italians, Irish, Germans, Slavs, Scandinavians—and a rare handful of Jews, too. Former Fusgeyers? The one and only Avigdor Semelweiss; Birlad's contribution to America's national sport.

Walking back to their hotel, called "The Four Seasons...Not!" by the forever-nicknaming Herb, Nathan shook his head and sighed.

"I only heard Pop off-handedly mention the comics once to a crony of his at temple. Watching Sandy Koufax pitch one of his gems on TV, he casually said that he knew of an immigrant Jew from his hometown who played minor league ball. No details. Nothing further to say. Mr. Silence. Can you believe it? I remember him mentioning that so well, because that really surprised me—both that he knew a Jew in the minors, and that he almost seemed to be about to tell me something.

"It seems that some of the Fusgeyers did open up and talk of their experiences, although Sendehr wouldn't write about it for public consumption. Did Mendel talk of it in the classroom? Did Mordecai say anything of substance? Nuchim? Zed-Zed? Branko might have. Obviously, Itzy and Mayer did, but they're the only two I'm sure of. Strange, but I'm told, not unusual among those who emigrated. Thank God for Sendehr's letters and the journal. Thank God for Yossi Nachman!" Nathan looked heavenward, solidifying his gratitude with the Romanian night sky.

"Dad, that Louie B. must have been quite a piece of work. I once read where Bob Hope joked that the powerful producer came out to Hollywood with twenty-eight dollars, a box camera and an old lion. Then he built a monument to himself...the Bank of America!" The Friedman family laughter echoed off the lampposts and benches in the empty town square.

As he had expected, Nathan did not sleep well that night. His agile mind, reviewing the past nine days so full of Fusgeyer history, was racing as fast as Albie White running the ninety-foot base-paths of America.

§

Sendehr retrieved two letters, one from Eli Nachman and the other from Eliezer Viesl, that were waiting for him at the antiseptic Postal Office, only a short distance from the Labor Alliance dormitories where the Fusgeyers lodged. The obnoxiously officious postal "direktor" had informed Sendehr that an entire packet of letters were postmarked "Birlad, Romania," assuming that Sendehr was with a group of refugees who would be calling for their mail also. A turned up nose and a grimace that would stop Zed-Zed's watch accompanied his reference to "refugees." When Sendehr returned to the dormitory he would make the announcement so that those expecting mail from home knew that they should go to the Postal Office.

This had been the usual drill in Budapest, Vienna, Praha and Dresden. It bothered Sendehr that the same ten or twelve Fusgeyers got all the mail. He felt badly for those who hadn't had any contact since leaving home, but he was certain that they had neglected to stress to their loved ones that mail could be held for them at the various postal stations along the route. Well, there was little doubt that they would renew contact once they finally arrived in America. Sendehr's family had written in response to his letters and to the greetings he had sent with every letter to the Rabbi, and *der shreiber* was sure that they and the Rabbi were busily engaged in passing on news that all was well, to the entire community.

But now he couldn't wait to rip open the envelopes, and instead of going back to the others he walked to a miniature park on Oranienburgerstrasse, plunked himself down on a child-sized bench and read and re-read the two lengthy, wordy letters. Later he knew he would share their contents with Rivka, Mordecai and Mendel, and he was sure to read selected parts to the group at appropriate times, too.

Next, Sendehr went into the beautifully finished reading room of the Alliance headquarters. It was stacked with a wide array of German and Yiddish reading material— books; newspapers from all over Europe; periodicals; and even a few out-of-date English-language papers from London, Manchester, Liverpool, New York and Boston. Aside from Mendel, there probably wasn't another emigrant soul in the five-story building who could read or understand English, but Sendehr knew right off that his compatriots would certainly enjoy looking at the amazing picture-advertising for the latest in clothing fashions...especially Rivka and the girls. His sole purpose at this juncture, though, was to write letters back to his erstwhile correspondents in Sighet and Birlad. First of all, the good Rabbi.

> *Greetings Rabbi:*
>
> *So here we are in Berlin! I still find it hard to believe that we have covered such a long distance from home. I estimate 2,000 kilometers, more or less.*
>
> *I read your letter with great interest, especially your thoughtful comments regarding the Maharal and Rabbi Blankfort. Your reasoning and analysis make a great deal of sense. I most definitely agree that we must all adopt a calm wait-and-see attitude before we exercise any broad announcements in this regard. That certainly*

*would be a foolhardy and dangerous thing to do.
Interestingly, Eliezer Viesl's letter is almost a copy of
yours. It pleases me to know that you two think alike on
this provocative matter.*

*I must admit, and I said as much in so many words
in the weekly synopsis, that since entering this
foreboding country I have seen with my own eyes the
foundational xenophobia and Jew-hatred that could
someday escalate into a fulfillment of the so-called
Maharal-Golem-Blankfort prognostications. God forbid!
What we encountered in Franz Josef territory, in
Bohemia, in Moravia, Hungary and Austria, and even
back home did not adequately prepare us for the scene
here. The other situations were annoying and
harassing, but that was to be expected. Some serious,
some innocuous. One gets the intense ill feeling that
we're now playing much more than a name-calling
game. This is dark, fiercely dangerous prejudice, in the
realm of a militaristic, totalitarian, anti-Semitic,
xenophobic, venomous culture.*

*As we neared the outer city limits of this obviously
imperial city-state, after seeing some advertising
billboards (that I fully describe in the journal synopsis),
a sense that we were walking into a lion's den engulfed
me. This was much more than a passing thought or
petty paranoia. I discussed it quietly with Mordecai and
Rivka who admitted readily that they felt the same, in
different words, but the same uneasy sensations. I
suppose if I interviewed all of the others, there would
have been near-unanimity. Most of all, I was stunned by
their eerie silence. From our comedy team, not a joke, or
a pun, or an insult. Normally, there is great enthusiasm
when we approach a city or town, big or small. Velvel
Palastrant takes out the trumpet, Asher Leibovich his
drums, even the tone-deaf Kalman Fuchs squeezes and
caresses his concertina, everyone is singing, humming,
smiling, walking arm-in-arm, anticipating a rest, a hot*

meal, maybe a bed like the one we have tonight. Not today. Not walking into Berlin. No, not at all, Rabbi.

Please bear in mind that all of this was in the air long before we reached the central core of the city. Mordecai's unceasing pride, as well as our own, always has us marching in an organized manner, usually a column of twos or fours whenever we approach a densely populated area. Here, we all wanted our troop to look organized and determined. Our Mordecai instills in us a positive attitude, knowing that we represent not only our own purposeful mission, but that we are the ambassadors for every oppressed person throughout Romania and the Pale. That's a rather large order, but it puts a crisp spring in our step that serves as an effective internal morale booster as well—we must stand tall and proud, flags flying high for all to see.

All well and good, right? But here, our ragged clothes and crusty, mud-covered shoes were no match for the adversarial military we encountered everywhere we turned. The ground literally shakes from the high-stepping soldaten. Kaiser Willi has his troops, regiment by regiment, on what looks like perpetual display as they march in the most colorful uniforms imaginable; plumed hats, broad golden-tasseled epaulets, shiny knee-high boots, mirror-glazed swords and menacing rifles. Why? Was today some sort of local holiday, ceremony or festival? Maneuvers? Has a war been declared with the Hapsburgs? The Russians? The French again? It was almost as if Willi was giving us a military escort as we marched through the parks and avenues, all the way to the Labor Alliance building. It may have appeared as though we wereHerr Kaiser's guests of honor; only we were too terrorized to play the part. Of course, this was not the case, but Sholem and Yaakov kept retracing their steps to inform us that "Kaiser-troops up ahead," or "manned checkpoint around the corner," or "street blocked for a parade of some kind."

Berlin is a repulsive armed camp, quite unlike Budapest, Vienna and Praha, in every respect. Fortunately, only once did one of the commanders take time to notice us, spewing forth a nasty series of epithets, threatening to burn our "Jew rag-flag" and a few of us along with it, but nothing came of it. Neither did we hear much from the many people and police along the way, in the massive city park, or as we passed the zoo and the government buildings. It was almost like everyone had been ordered to ignore us, but we could feel the blood boiling under their white skins as we passed as silently as we could. We were far less than a mosquito bite threat to the security and well-being of any Berliner today, but they still detested the very sight of us.

We reached the Labor Alliance building at last. We were relieved when the entire staff greeted us on the street, as warmly as we had been received in Praha. We are staying as guests of the European Headquarters of the Alliance; their quarters are quite impressive, and should provide a comfortable stay for our most deserving contingent. I am sorry that I seem to have duplicated myself often between this letter and the synopsis, but I am unusually tense. I did, however, manage to pen a poetically structured piece, inspired by today's emotionally foreboding events:

BLACK BOOTS
(Shvarzeh Shtivln)

Black boots, jackboots, shiny black jackboots,
marching on the streets of Imperial Berlin,
tramp, tramp, tramping in the Tiergarten,
amid statuary of Hohenzollern lineal pride.
Black jackboots striking, as cadence counts,
sharply upon the Wilhelmstrasse, creating sparks

from Brandenburg Gate to
Alexanderplatz. Surely this nascent
state has issued a decree that Teutonic
manhood shall be redeemed by black
boots, jackboots, shiny black jackboots.

Is this a sign from our prescient Maharal,
or from his Golem's quivering sealed lips?
Black boots, jackboots, shiny black jackboots-
will their smashing leather heels never
stop?
Alas, when the precious flower of youth has
died, and all the blood soaked fields have
dried, will those black boots, shiny black
jackboots, pound the pavements of Europa
once again?

Sendehr Efraim
Berlin, Germany
June 30, 1904 (27 Sivan, 5664)
(translated from the Yiddish)

Mordecai guessed from the looks of things that well over
two hundred emigrating Yidden were staying in the impressive headquarters for varying lengths of time. Every floor
was full of cots, baggage, and people in a vast semblance of
outerwear. The third floor, assigned to the Birladers, had
nearly one hundred narrow cots, completely spoken-for.
Their roommates were families and individuals mostly from
the Pale, with the remainder hailing from Romania,
Transylvanian Hungary and Serbia. When the Fusgeyers
had arrived with their flags unfurled, it seemed to perk up
everyone in the room, quickly warming any suspicious reserve that they may have felt toward the newest visitors.

Mordecai took it upon himself to announce who they
were, where they had come from and where they were going. His introduction extended to a brief history of the trek

at the specific request of one of the onlookers, an emaciated man from Bialystok. The refugees gathered around Mordecai became wide-eyed in awe of the Fusgeyer adventure. They kept referring to the *Mogen Dovid*, whispering to one another—*narishkeit, mishigas, folg mikh a gang, a bubbeh meiseh*—of the sheer idiocy of flying it in the face of the Austrians and Germans.

Everyone on the dormitory floors was waiting for something; paperwork, extended transit visas, vouchers for ship tickets, railroad tickets for transportation to Hamburg or Bremerhaven, money from home, or from America, from London, or from who knows where? The Bialystoker, the pale man from the Pale, had been guaranteed passage from Rotterdam to New York, but ran out of money trying to get to the Dutch port. He confided in Mordecai that the Alliance, in conjunction with a contact for Holland-America lines, had assured him that they would make it possible by train passage...for over a month now!

That night's meal—barley soup, dumplings, roast meats, freshly baked rye breads and fruit from Germany's orchards—was pure manna from heaven as far as every Wayfarer was concerned. The Alliance staff informed Mordecai that this regal offering was a daily occurrence, thanks to the steady donations from Berlin's Jewish community.

One of the German communal organizations that assisted immigrants move to the west was solely responsible for the renovation of the eighteenth-century building ten years earlier. It wasn't as if the community ignored the plight of the shabby Pale or Romanian Jew. Not at all. But in the neighboring district of Scheunenviertel, the "barn quarter," the "notorious" *ostjuden* occupied overcrowded flats and tumble-down shanties. Within the power structure of the affluent,the long-assimilated members of the "Mosaic persuasion," so to speak, this was a major problem.

The feeling rampant among these old time residents was that just one more ill-clad, ill-fed *Poylisher* or *Russkie* or *Romanische Yid* could cause plague or a famine or a cosmic explosion or God knows what? Then their neighbors would subject the entire population of the "real" German Jews to ridicule, and possibly worse. How frightfully awful!

The *ostjuden* fear had taken hold among Berlin's Jews— far more so than in the other major cities of Germany and Austria—and the more influential elite put increasing pressure on the Managing Director of the Labor Alliance headquarters to get "those people" in fast and out faster. *They must move on to Holland, France, England and America!* Not so simple, since an increasing number of the immigrants had no means of going any further without substantial assistance. They were convinced that reaching Berlin even as a temporary destination was far better than remaining hopelessly mired in the morass of Eastern Europe.

Consequently, when the Birlader Fusgeyers first communicated with the Labor Alliance and actually pre-paid with hard money for the ship tickets, they received preferential treatment. *How unique! How refreshing!* In fact, the director of the Iashi office, "victim" of the humorously innocent "Branko caper," was still in awe of the bizarre circumstances that surrounded the transaction, and spoke of it at every opportunity. Embellished to the heights, one would imagine. Only the 1903 group visited Berlin for any length of time and were just as royally treated, but a few of the more loosely formed Fusgeyer bands from other towns in Romania had come without adequate funding or preparation or proper communication. Now, Mordecai felt it incumbent upon his troop to redeem the reputation of the Romanian Wayfarers, to set things right again—and they would, without a doubt in his mind.

Let the explorations begin! On their first full day in the city, everyone set out immediately following the morning meal of hot rolls and tea. But not before Mordecai and Menachem stressed, much heavier than ever before, the danger of *mashiganah masheen* traffic. Without a doubt, in this era of exceptional economic strength, Berlin vaulted to the vanguard of every new invention as each appeared on the world scene, especially the automobile. Berlin was first with a revolutionary new sewage system in 1876, had every one of its main streets sporting electric lamps by 1879, and boasted more telephones and motor cars per capita than any of its European rivals in 1904.

As for the aforementioned traffic headaches, the best Berlin could offer was a manually operated traffic lighting system with major flaws, supplemented by a police officer. Arms waving frantically, he takes his life into his own hands stepping in front of two moving lines; one with motorized vehicles, the other with horse-drawn contraptions. This recipe for disaster occurred at every major intersection in the city. The previous day, entering this maze for the first time, the Fusgeyers were caught in midstream numerous times, endearing themselves to the frustrated *polizei.* To have walked this far only to be crushed by one of these snorting, wheeled monsters was unthinkable. Hence the fair warning. Mordecai and Nuchim settled in the front office for their scheduled meeting with Franz Schechter, the Managing Director, to begin going over the final paperwork necessary for the port officials and for the Lloyd Line personnel upon their arrival in Bremerhaven. Newly stationed in Berlin, the HIAS (New York-based Hebrew Immigrant Aid Society) representative would meet with the assembled group the following Monday to offer them the latest information, including the job opportunities for new immigrants available in New York and Boston. Mordecai anxiously awaited that meeting.

Simmy, thankfully, had no worries about the cart. It was comfortably secured in a locked carriage house behind the building. He had taken all perishables and stored them in the kitchen, and now was free to roam at will with the others. Since the Alliance was meeting their every need— including, no doubt, a cart full of supplies when they departed for the port—the Food Czar happily foresaw the possibility of little or no begging required in the Jewish bakeries, butcheries and groceries of Berlin.

Branko's mini-arsenal remained with the cart, except for the hidden revolver he carried with Mordecai's tacit approval...or so *der groisseh soldat* led himself to believe.

"Mordecai, this call is for you," said the Managing Director, handing the oversized telephone to a very surprised young man with a creased brow.

Mordecai had only spoken through a telephone twice, back in Birlad. Once at Leventer's, and once at his father-in-law's glass-blowing shop. Awkwardly he placed the hearing instrument to his ear and spoke through the tall mouthpiece base, much too loudly.

"Yes, yes! I am Mordecai Anieloff! Please, who are you?"

He was pleasantly shocked to hear a familiar voice at the other end and whispered to Nuchim gleefully, "It's Nordau! Max Nordau!" Then to Nordau, "Max, where are you? How are you? How is Herr Herzl? How did you find me?"

Waiting to hear if these were the last of the questions, and deciding they were, for now, Max answered. "Mordecai, my dear fellow, I am here in Berlin attending a conference. Just on the off-chance that you and the Fusgeyers had arrived at the Labor Alliance I thought I would phone and ask if they knew anything of your schedule...and here you are! What good luck! Really, I had penned in my notebook that you would probably be arriving here around the first week of July. I hope everything has gone well for you and yours on the open road."

"Yes, fine thank you, sir! We are all together, just a few difficulties, but everyone is healthy and well. Morale is high. We intend to be in Berlin until the tenth and then we shall be off on the last land leg of our journey, to Bremerhaven. So very good to hear your welcome voice! It's been over a month since Vienna. Will we be seeing you?"

"Of course we shall see each other. I have so much to talk with you about. But you asked about Herzl, and I'm sad to say that he's not doing well, poor man. I'll tell you more in person. Please give my greetings to Sendehr and Mendel. You'll all be so pleased to know of the many newspapers and periodicals, world wide, that have carried my stories about your glorious mission. Viesl's as well! In fact, I'm here attending the International Congress of Newspaper Publishers and Journalists. An amazingly prestigious roster of attendees...Americans, too, including Joseph Pulitzer, Jacob Riis, Lincoln Steffens, and even the feisty Abe Cahan from the *Forvitz*. This is our first big international congress of the twentieth century. I'm quite overwhelmed to be part of it!"

"When can we meet, Max?"

"Tomorrow morning, at my hotel. Nine o'clock. I so look forward to seeing you!. We have a lot to catch up on. God bless you all! Herr Schechter will give you the directions. Put him back on, please."

Mordecai's thoughts raced between Herzl's ailing condition and to whether or not Elie Viesl was also at the conference, although there was no mention in his letter or by Max. As for the people Max mentioned, he knew only of Cahan. Who would he take along for the meeting? Certainly Mendel and Sendehr... maybe Nuchim and Zed-Zed. Menachem Berman? Branko? Just stay with the three? He'd give it some more thought before that evening.

When Mordecai and Nuchim finished their work-session with Herr Schechter, one of the staff people asked Mordecai to proceed to the reading room where three members of the Berlin Jewish community awaited him. He complied, reluctantly.

"A good morning to you, Herr Anieloff," offered Joachim Gruning. "May I introduce my wife, Frau Gruning, and my son-in-law, Albert Schine."

Obligatory salutations complete, the impeccably suited Herr Gruning continued.

"Herr Schechter has told me all about your grand adventure, my good man, and I read in our *Berlin Tageblatt* ..."

Mordecai was forced to interrupt at this point. "I'm afraid I shall have difficulty with your German. Do you by chance speak Yiddish?"

"You say Yiddish? If you're asking me to speak in your mother tongue, I cannot. My dear grandmama was from Galicia and spoke Yiddish, but we, as children, only conversed in German."

This meaningless small talk went on for less than a minute, and already Mordecai had become restless. Noticeably so. This prompted the son-in-law to fetch one of the female staff members who spoke Yiddish, though haltingly.

Gruning then continued: "We merely want to invite you to speak to our full committee session on Sunday evening. Our organization is committed to helping *ostjuden* as they pass through en route to the west and we feel that you are an excellent source of information and opinions in this regard. We are quite well known as the *Hilfsverein der Deutschen Juden* and we work closely with the Jewish Labor Alliance and occasionally the Alliance Israelite Universelle. Those French are so very difficult, don't you know. The J.C.A, the late Baron De Hirsch's colonization organization, continually implores us to send you people their way, and we do. Although Argentina is not very popular with the *ostjuden,* and Palestine less so.

"You people from the east have an incurably warped fixation on America, it seems. Believe me, *mein herr,* the streets of New York are covered with garbage and dung. Not a glitter of gold in sight. We have many good German families there—uptown of course—who have been able to lift themselves into astounding prominence during the past half-century. However, dear man, they spend half their fortunes now attempting to assist your people, the growing flotsam of *ostjuden* refugees in the teeming tenement blocks. *Ach,* good money after bad!

"But you organized Wayfarers seem to be of a different bent. Therefore, you people, particularly, must be sure that you not stay in New York. Go on to the west, young man. To Cincinnati, Chicago, or San Francisco. There you may have a chance. My uncle owns the biggest department store in Ohio and...I say, do you follow me, Herr Anieloff?"

With this monological lecture fast degenerating into an unacceptably insulting reprimand, the translator, a highly nervous, acne-faced teenager, struggled with each word.

Mordecai had to put an end to this, as he was blanching with each cumulatively degrading reference to "you people" and *ostjuden.*

"Thank you, young lady. I have been able to understand a goodly portion of Herr Gruning's words and I'll be able to cope with it from here on. Perhaps you will stay, please, in order to translate what he doesn't understand."

Turning to the three *Moishe Yidden* in their crisp "court-Jew" attire, Mordecai began to speak plainly in the melodious *mameloshen* of *his* grandmama:

"Thank you for your invitation. I do not accept. Good day, *meine tyreh baltoiwim.*"

With this, having obliquely, yet dutifully, recognized the good deeds of the *Hilfsverein* with his closing clause, Mordecai turned on his worn-down heels and headed quickly out of the building to join Nuchim and Zed-Zed for a long walk. What else would a Fusgeyer do on holiday? Not wishing to spoil even a minute of their outing, he didn't say a word to the others about the offensively boorish Herr Gruning.

Before the cooler-than-usual midsummer day was over, Berlin had been covered every which way by each group of four, five, six or ten Fusgeyers. They rubbed elbows with every conceivable type of *tureest*: the London family in all their finery; the Dutch businessman, somber and red-faced; the country Germans gawking at the Tiergarten statuary of grim-faced Kaiser Willi ancestry; and the first black-skinned people most of them had ever seen—Negro students from Windhoek in German Southwest Africa. It was no great surprise that the haughty locals were not at all impressed with the Birladers and their rather tattered marching ensembles; nor with anyone else encroaching upon their fair city.

As the champion long-distance walkers walked, they scanned the anarchic mix of architectural style that ranged from neo-classic to baroque to neo-baroque to Romanesque, to an unsightly hybrid to just plain, simple and boring. Many of the newer government buildings, such as the classic and grand 1894 Reichstag, and a few of the numerous museums were replete with filigreed historical and allegorical decoration at the service of imperial nationalism. Not that any of this made much of a difference, aesthetically or otherwise, to these small town, country youngsters. They had already spent time in equally modern and architecturally diverse cities, and were simply happy to have gotten this far alive, vertical and intact. Thank God and *omayn*, once again!

Rivka and Sendehr sought out the *Theater Unter den Linden*, one of Europe's most handsome venues, and easily found it on *Opernplatz*, just beyond the beautiful lime tree lined boulevard. Here again, there were two sets of troops drilling on this broad *platz*, the Kaiser's favorite parade grounds, just as there were when they had passed through the day before. The ticket office had posted the prices, but heavy red lines were drawn through the dates for every Bernhardt performance, and the words "Sold Out" were written in block letters. The German was close enough to the Yiddish phrase for them to understand completely, since the Romanized letters corresponded to those in the Romanian alphabet with which they were familiar. Sendehr was immediate in trying to soften Rivka's letdown, promising he would ask Herr Schechter that night to do everything possible to get a solo ticket for her. Mendel had told Rivka when he had translated the billboard, that the performances would be in French, with available abridged translations in German. Even Chinese or Latin wouldn't matter to her a bit! To see the great Bernhardt on stage would have been enough. *Dayenu!*

Everyone had been impressed with the beautifully designed and manicured grounds of the Tiergarten as they came through it the previous afternoon, the mass of marching troops notwithstanding. Many returned to stand in awe in front of the landmark giant needle, the *Siegessaule*, crowned by a golden, winged "Victory." Certain disenchanted Berliner critics took to proclaiming it *Siegesspargel*, "Victory Asparagus." Simmy Fieldelman smugly offered his anatomically explicit observation...best left to one's imagination.

The neighboring *zoologischer garten* was a highly popular attraction destined to draw the attention of most of the Birladers on their first full day in this renowned city of art, science, culture, and fifty-thousand jackboots. For some reason, none of them had visited the zoos of Budapest, Vienna and Praha,. In fact, aside from the more worldly Mendel and Branko, not a Fusgeyer had ever seen wild animals in captivity before this. Itzy's not unexpected comment, peering into the monkey cages: "*Nu,* which one is *der Kaiser?*"

Comfortably seated in one of the grand lobby's plush chairs at the fading, once-elegant Kaiserhof, Max Nordau sprang to his feet, enormous cigar in hand, to greet the familiar trio of Fusgeyers. It was a touching reunion as they all stood there for a moment; arms draped around one another. Mordecai was satisfied that he had made the proper decision not to add anyone else to the mix.

"I don't have a session until eleven. These wild writer-types stay out until all hours of the night, and would never make it to any earlier meeting anyway. So come, come, tell me everything."

"We shall, Max. But first, Herzl," requested Mordecai.

"His recuperation has not gone as we had hoped. A major setback last Sunday leaves his doctors in doubt of any recovery. I'll be wired or phoned with any change, better or worse. David Wolffsohn has been at his bedside since Tuesday."

"Yes, I remember. The man who will succeed him. Even though it is not quite unexpected, we are so sorry to hear this sad news, Max."

Mordecai asked Sendehr and Mendel to relate for Nordau their adventures from Vienna to Berlin.

He knew that Sendehr would elect to make some reference to the Maharal and Rabbi Blankfort, which he did. Max's immediate comments were much the same as Rabbi Nachman's and Eliezer Viesl's, and Sendehr knew enough not to belabor the point. There were others to make, and indeed, Mendel proceeded to tell of the great escape and entry into Germany, deferring to Sendehr for a description of their brief stay in Dresden, the Finsterwalde incident, and their initial reactions to Berlin. The highly respected man whose broad experiences with European society in general, and German history and culture, in particular, prepared him well for his response.

"So you think you are now in the one country where anti-Semitism romps even more unbridled than in Russia, your Romania, 'Dreyfus France,' and Congress Poland? Let us be honest, and throw jolly old England and your designated new home, the United States of America, into the nasty barrel, as well. They, too, belong there, you realize. Possibly, you are correct, my dear friends. Germany has a long unflattering history in this regard, recent emancipative lip service or not.

"As for the actions of some of our co-religionists that you find abhorring, I couldn't agree more. In their overeager attempts to be accepted by becoming more and more Germanic and less and less Judaic they have inadvertently placed themselves in the uneasy position that you have so quickly discovered. Dear me, 'geyers, your youthful journalistic powers of observation are truly impressive to this old war horse. And I mean that. So many other Easterners have passed through this intriguing city never once noticing this ever-widening schism between its Yidden.

"But as I say, the assimilated German Jew, embarrassed by the poverty-enveloped, terminally provincial *ostjuden,* has had to take on the burden of supporting them. The ulterior motive, as you have found, is totally self-serving on one hand, while quite vitally necessary on the other. This German Jew thinks he can eradicate the shame and eliminate the possibility of being painted with the same brush in two ways: help financially to send the Easterners to the ports as quickly as humanly possible; or, failing that, provide enough charitable assistance to elevate those who remain to worthy acceptability. The former being the option of choice, by far."

"One question comes to mind. How is it that so many destitute *ostjuden* can even enter Berlin, when billboards firmly state that unless they have transit visas or some proof of departure or job sponsors they are considered illegal aliens?" Mendel asked.

"Most Eastern European Jews, like your good selves, do have the proper documents and the required overland funding. For the others, as you can imagine, there is a preponderance of phony documents of every sort. Promises of work, a letter from a relative or friend, and even completely *ersatz* transit papers. A desperate émigré will find a way. *Unsereh Yidden*, surviving the Czars of Russia and the King Carols and the petty tyrants throughout Austria-Hungary, have proven to be extremely resourceful in this game of life. Many have stayed in the Scheunenviertel because they are simply out of funds to proceed to the ports, or because they don't wish to cross the ocean, or perhaps they are afraid of the unknown, or for reasons unfathomable to us. These are the adopted headaches for those Berliners of their so-called, what is it, uh, Mosaic persuasion..."

"We call them our *Moishe Yidden*, Max," interrupted Mordecai.

"Good, good! That's *perfect*. I shall always use that term from here on. *Moishe Yidden*. How wonderful!" the Zionist replied with glee, adding his hearty guffaw and saying, "However, the more serious situation in this country, in my humble opinion, gentlemen, is the endemically virulent anti-Jew fervor that permeates every pore of the *Deutsche volk*. Nothing new. Mendel, you're a student of history, and I'm sure you have shared some of this relevant knowledge with everyone."

"Indeed I have. I thought it important to brief the group. But if I hadn't said a word, they would have all seen it, heard it and felt it eventually. Not that we haven't experienced it in varying degrees since birth. Although, I might add, that my life in Salonika and Athens seemed relatively free of most forms of bigotry."

"Ah, yes. Classical Greece. Too wrapped up in complex

mythological history to worry about a few Yidden polluting the *plaka*. But, Sendehr, getting back to the Praha Rabbi and the Maharal, the enormous amount of anti-Jewish propaganda finding its way into every household and business throughout Germany increases by the minute. It's more than merely ubiquitous. One cannot walk down any street or alley of this city without running into that barrage of garbage. Why, it fills this very lobby every day. That table over there across the way, the entrance to the restaurant, in front of the door to each room. Of course, the perpetrators know that this hotel houses a few hundred attendees of the kind of conference that will provide some publicity for their trash, good or bad..."

"But where does the Maharal's or Blankfort's forecasting of world events come into this?"

"Aha, Mordecai—let's imagine for a moment that a highly impressionable young boy, in his teens—one of thousands who are exposed daily to some of the more convincing material floating about—begins to form a lifelong picture of the demonized Jew. Let us further imagine that he has all the attributes necessary to completely embrace, digest, embellish and, growing into manhood, achieve the power status to act upon this 'devilish menace to good Teutonic culture.' Given the proper set of circumstances, could he become the new Haman monster? In a far worse geometrically progressive scenario of death and destruction? I think so. I am certain, beyond a shadow of a doubt that this can happen sometime this century. Whoever is responsible for that frightening projection of Rabbi Blankfort's could very well be correct. Tragically so."

As Max Nordau spoke about these very real fears, at that precise moment, at a news kiosk in the centrum of the small Austrian town of Seyr, a fifteen-year-old is voraciously reading, studying, memorizing and saving the weekly notorious *Linzer Fliegenden* newpaper along with every piece of anti-Semitic literature available to him and the rest of the student body of the local Staatsrealschule. He will continue to do so when he's someday painting picture postcards, starving in Vienna. Is he the one? Is he the one? Possibly. Quite possibly.

"In the meantime, the world pays little or no attention. If these articles I had written about your mission had included anything remotely indicting this country, I guarantee you no American or British periodical would print it. They each look upon German culture and intellectual achievement with reverence—in awe of the Kaiser's benevolence in throwing open his universities to hundreds of their students, superior technical schools, its unmatchable conservatories, its superb museums and its meticulous well-stocked-stacked libraries. Germany is considered to be many other sovereign state's personal Herr Professor—the world's most prolific source of intellectual culture—and they all say, treat it as such for it can do no wrong."

At last, Max reached into his briefcase to pull out the fistful of newspaper and magazine clippings and handed them to Mendel.

"How much good these have done or will do, I have not the faintest idea. Look them over. Paris, London. Dublin. The *Berliner Tageblatt*. The *Zurich Press*. Both the *New York World* and the *New York Journal*. My Paris office wired out the story the day I wrote it, only two days after we met in Vienna. You see the group pictures? The text was written in French, German and English and all were printed by June 10th, with copies sent to Paris. Every editor agreed that your story is extraordinary, and historically significant besides. In fact I met with some of them at this conference. Pulitzer and Hearst papers both printed it verbatim, and Joe approached me at dinner last night. Fascinating comments. I'll tell you about them later. Suffice it to say that New York Congressman Hearst is seeking the nomination to run against Roosevelt, and he covets the Jewish vote. Meanwhile, Elie Viesl has thoroughly worked the Jewish newspapers all over the continent. Unfortunately, he couldn't be here because of an important story breaking in Brody, I'm told.

"But, my dear comrades, this much I do know. The Romanian Ambassador to Germany sent a messenger this morning with a rather terse invitation to meet with him Monday morning. A command performance. The poor boy is upset. I wonder why? Hah! Hah! He has no idea that you're in town now, nor does he know any family names or just where in Romania you've come from, per your instructions back in Vienna. I just wrote "Eastern Romania." Hundreds of towns with *Yidden!*"

"Good thinking, Max. We appreciate that. Our loved ones certainly do, also. Both you and Viesl seem to understand the necessity for these covert steps. Thank you, dear friend," offers Mordecai with outstretched hand.

"Now, the good part," instead of shaking Mordecai's hand, Max gripped it hard. "I want you three to come to that meeting. For good reason. This is a one-time opportunity for such an audience and it has the potential for a meaningful impact. This is the purpose of your mission, is it not?

An excited Mendel pitches in with, "Good God! This is more than we hoped for, ever! Precisely why we've walked across Europe with the *Mogen Dovid* flying high! I can't believe it! You've done it, Max ! You and your trusty pen!" With this, Mendel and Sendehr leaped up to embrace the man with the snow-white beard and giant handlebar mustache. His renowned trademark. Everybody's uncle!

A bit more subdued but just as appreciative, Mordecai finished the handshake and suggested that perhaps they adjourn to Max's room for more privacy. He wanted to discuss the logistics and strategy for such a historical session in full detail. Max agreed and they went up to the third floor room in the ornate caged elevator. The first such ride for Mordecai and Sendehr.

"I suggest that, if at all possible, we meet in a more neutral environment, gentlemen. Perhaps the American Embassy. I know the American ambassador and I'm sure I can talk him into acting as sort of a moderator, or mediator—or boxing referee as the case may turn out! We'll try to make it out as an invitation direct from the American to the

Romanian. That just might work. We may be bastardizing all the protocol for such things, but who cares, eh?"

"I agree, Max. This is a one-time opportunity that we mustn't botch. A forum, if you will. Right to the source where, hopefully, it will bear some edible fruit."

Max was impressed with the maturity and intelligence Mordecai continued to display. With all three, he felt that he was working with highly experienced intellect beyond their years, not just a small town *cheder* teacher, a glass blower and an aspiring journalist. He wondered what growing up in Birlad was like if it could produce this kind of individual in the midst of boycotts and pogroms, near-starvation and continuous poverty from the day each was born.

Just before eleven, the quartet had reached a full understanding, and each of the attendees had a critical task to accomplish before Monday's proposed meeting.

Max: the logistical arrangements. Beyond that, everything was preparatory, to be used at the appropriate time if the opportunity presented itself. Sendehr: a proclamation written in Romanian to present to the man from Bucureshti. Mendel: to copy it in English for the benefit of the American and prepare an introductory speech in English. Mordecai would follow in Romanian, although Max thought that the Ambassador could possibly be conversant in English. The truth of this matter was that a veritable international summit was about to take place somewhere in Berlin, with two twenty-four year-olds and a teenager at the center of it! The sheer drama of it all was nothing short of astounding. A drama of the absurd?

Three extremely happy and enthusiastic Fusgeyers bounced out of the old Kaiserhof that morning, waving their goodbyes to an equally ebullient Max Nordau standing at the enormous metal doors. Arm-in-arm they headed for the much-discussed "barn quarter," the Scheunenviertel, also called the "Jewish quarter," to observe the occupants and conditions firsthand before heading back to the Alliance.

They passed the imposing palace, der Stadtschloss, from which Kaiser Wilhelm II ruled an empire. Onward toward the classic Altes Museum and the multi-arched Bode' Bridge over the tranquil River Spree. Here, the narrowing, harrowing streets radiated to the north and northeast, into the tenderloin of the quarter so named because one of the Hohenzollern ancestors had highly flammable hay barns moved to it from the central city which had outgrown the need for such rural outbuildings. A few remained, hemmed in by the stench of rotting buildings and shanties and saloons and run-down shops and cafes. None of which any self-respecting Berliner would venture into, unless he was a landlord collecting rents. Good luck, *mein herr!*

Mordecai noted that there were sections of Iashi and Bucureshti and even Focshani and Bacau that had a similar appearance, except for the trash and garbage in the streets and the elbow-to-elbow masses of downtrodden scarecrows. If anything, the descriptions of the Scheunenviertel they had been given were adumbrated, at best. It just had to be seen to be understood. In a few words, the quarter was nothing less than Dante's inferno come to life—a Tartarean tableau covering entrance to exit. It was here where the poor souls of the Pale, Congress Poland and Romania were emptied onto German soil. The non-human *ostjuden*, the dross and the dregs.

As they were about to enter the sanitary-looking *Hilfsverein* kosher soup kitchen on the cobblestoned Sophienstrasse for a piece of *challah* and a bowl of mushroom-barley soup, they were accosted by six *ostjuden* teenagers; half-starved, pitiful rag dolls, begging for money. Two of the older-looking girls brazenly offered themselves to Mendel and Sendehr. The shocking disgust and rage and real horror the Birladers felt at such a gut-wrenching sight was something they would carry for the remainder of their lives. The six ragamuffins followed them into the dining hall, but now kept their distance and only seemed to concentrate on the available foodstuffs, which they proceeded to gobble up in a heartbreaking display of voracious hunger. Did their destitute parents send them out on the street to beg for money? This was a very common practice through-

out the quarter, as the three found out when they continued on their way through. Babies, four-year-olds, five-year-
olds, eight-year-olds, early teens, with sunken black sock-
ets for eyes and wrapped in filthy rags like mummies crawling out of an Egyptian tomb, all plead for *gelt, gelt, gelt.*

Mendel, Sendehr and Mordecai began to walk faster,
breaking into a trot until they neared the junction of
Auguststrasse and Hamburgstrasse, just a short block from
Oranienburgerstrasse. They were well distanced from the
"barn quarter" now. They had seen enough. Coming face to
face with hell on earth...a purely Jewish hell, hurt badly.
Oh, how it hurt! They wondered if any of their group had
already been to or planned to visit this epitome of squatter
squalor. Some, they thought, could cope with it and perhaps *should* experience it. Others, though, could easily get
discouraged by it, thinking that it was a frightening microcosm of what they would find in America.

For the first time, Mordecai could see things through
the eyes of the much-maligned German Jew. He could not
excuse any of their actions, but he would empathize more
and more with what they were trying to accomplish, regardless of their motives, ulterior or otherwise. He had come
to grips with the hard fact that all was not what it seemed;
that there was no right or wrong, nor black or white. In his
private thoughts, only one thing was certain. The ever-
present "Jewish problem/question," "*das Judefrage,*" was
owned by one and all: the German, the German Jew, the
ostjuden, the Czar, the Emperor, King Carol, Kaiser Wilhelm,
the Brits, the French, the Americans—yes, by most of the
civilized world. Each would eventually have to arrive at what
he perceived to be a viable solution. Mordecai reluctantly
concluded that there could be no winners, but there would
most definitely be a continuum of painful, tragic losses.

There wasn't a sad face among the rest of the Fusgeyers
on Friday afternoon, as they all sat around and compared
activities and adventures. Obviously none had yet seen the
Scheunenviertel. Without a doubt, the first three days of a
carefree Berlin romp were part and parcel of this highlight

tour of one of Europe's finer cities. Their leader was delighted with this pleasant gathering, as he stood alone off
to the side of the dormitory observing the myriad reactions. Just watching and listening. Sendehr and Rivka both
saw him standing there, and they understood.

None of the Fusgeyers went down the street for the brief
erev Shabbos service at the Neue *shul.* Some *dovened* in
the Alliance reading room, and all re-joined for the sumptuous Shabbat dinner in the dining hall. Mendel held a short
class after dinner, which an unexpectedly large number of
other guests who had no idea what was taking place also
attended. They sat on their cots, reverently, as the professor drilled his students on etiquette at the dinner table, in a
restaurant, on a subway train or trolley, using only English, of course...

> *Please pass the bread. May I please have another
> lemonade? I would prefer the white meat, if you please.
> Waiter, the menu please. Would you like to have my seat,
> madam? How much is the fare, conductor? How many
> stops is it to 33rd Street? What time does the last train
> leave? Timetable. Check. Change. Potato. Tomato. Cucum-
> ber. Butter. Cheese. Knife. Fork. Soup spoon. Dessert
> spoon?*

Time for Sholem's response:

> *Plizz, lady, seet nax to me. Dat's awright, I veel stend
> and rid the pepper. I like cucombehs, but not tamaytas. Di
> zoop spoon is not clean. Plizz tek it beck. Denks veddy
> motch. I vant crim chiz vit mein brad.*

Closing the rather brief session, Mendel reviewed the
oath of citizenship and started them on the first stanza of
The Star Spangled Banner, of which the "four cantors" gave
an unusual rendition, humming wherever they couldn't remember the words, which was often.

The Neue *shul* was far and away the most salient Jewish structure in all of Germany. It matched the Great Syna-

gogue of Budapest in size, with a seating capacity of three thousand. Its amalgam of architecture consisted of twin Moorish towers guarding the gold-encrusted cupola, turning the five-story building into a source of bursting pride for every Berlin Jew. The attending Prussian Prime Minister, Otto von Bismarck, at its widely heralded opening in 1866, praised the much-honored architect, Eduard Knoblauch. This one significant appearance preceding his Chancellorship of a newly united Germany five years later succeeded in boosting the morale of the German Jew to soaring heights never before achieved—only to be ignominiously dashed to the ground repeatedly, for many decades to come, and far beyond.

The magnificence of the domed sanctuary awed those Fusgeyers who attended on Saturday morning. This was sadly tempered when they were not allowed to sit anywhere but the last three rows—about 100 seats in all—which were reserved for any attendees in improper dress. Clearly conveyed by an usher in the traditional full dress and silk top hat, Mendel translated the guttural High German for those affected by the ruling. There could be little argument. The Birladers, at best, couldn't qualify for proper Sabbath dress anywhere on the planet other than some Beth Sahara in Timbuktu, if you will! This was the very first time that they were penalized for their lack of finery, not that sitting in the rear could be considered anything harsher than a teacher sending a child to the back of the room for impertinence.

Naturally, only Itzy Gelman took umbrage, telling the stiff-necked usher that he had left his top hat back in Birlad, but would send someone for it, and fully expected to seat himself in the front row for Rosh Hashonah. No translation necessary. Meanwhile, the "four cantors" were at their finest, projecting their voices above all others from the back of the enormous hall, despite an occasional sharp disapproving glance from the usher—not to mention the synagogue's paid cantorial artist's severe and steady glare from his podium on the *bimah*.

Sunday morning, at seven...an excitable night-robed

Herr Schechter literally ran up the three flights of stairs to announce to a groggy, arising Mordecai that Max Nordau was on the telephone for him. Schechter, a young bachelor from Heidelberg, had a one-room apartment adjacent to the office and the call had most likely awakened him. Mordecai hastily dressed as everyone around him wondered what in the world this was all about. Mendel and Sendehr, sensing it could be urgent, followed him down the stairs to the lone Alliance telephone.

"Mordecai, I'm sure you'll thank me for waking you at this hour when you hear what I have to say. No, it has nothing to do with our scheduled meeting tomorrow. Listen closely. I've managed to pull off a big one here! Last night, none other than the great buffalo hunter with some of his cast of feathered Indians and fully costumed cowboys came into the banquet hall where we were just finishing our after-dinner session. Imagine our great shock and surprise! For a brief moment I thought the Indians were there to scalp us...not that I have any worry there, heh-heh! Joe Pulitzer and a few of the other Americans had invited him, unbeknownst to any of the several hundred conference attendees. The man is an incurable publicity hound and probably leaped at the opportunity to appear before such an assemblage of ink jockeys."

Mordecai, looking at the concerned look on Mendel and Sendehr, interjected at this point: " Well, that must've been an exciting night for you..."

"Hold on...hold on, Mordecai. Patience. I'm coming to it. I'm coming to the best part. His show for this afternoon has been moved from the Kaiser Wilhelm II Stadium (Stadion) because of American Independence Day. Seems that the city ordnance prohibits the fireworks they've planned because of the close proximity of upper class residences. Therefore, The Wild West Buffalo Bill Extravaganza has been switched to the Mariendorf Horseracing Track for today only...and you are all going to be there!"

"W-H-A-T? What do you mean, Max?"

"You heard me, I'm sure. Since the race track spectator stands can hold half again as many as the Stadion, with plenty of standing room around the oval, the affable Buffalo Bill invited our entire congress as his seated guests and..."

"What does that have to do with our Fusgeyers..."

"You're old friend Max seized the opportunity. That's what! With everyone milling around, greeting the colorful entourage, including that pretty *pitzaleh* Annie Oakley, rifle and all, I sidled up to the big man of the American frontier and quickly told him about my fifty-seven Americans-in-waiting. Joe Pulitzer overheard and added his words of support, and before I knew it Cody—that's his name, William Frederick Cody, by God—put his hand on my shoulder and bellowed, 'Bring the kids along...I need all the Americans I can get...it's the Fourth of July, pod'nuh, don't y'know?'" Max's attempt at American English was close to indecipherable. Mordecai had handed over the phone to Mendel who immediately burst out laughing, not having heard any of the foregoing conversation, and translated, ever so loosely, for Sendehr and Mordecai.

"I say, are you still there, *kindelach?*"

"*Boruch Hashem,* Max. You've done it! By the grace of God you did it. How can we ever thank such consideration on your part?"

"Forgive the early call, but I didn't want to try a call at midnight. Now, Mordecai, you will have to meet me at the side gate entrance to Mariendorf by half after one this afternoon. Just have everyone board the 'Mariendorf' S-Bahn at the Alexanderplatz Station. They leave every half-hour. Suggest you catch the noon train. Cost only a few *pfennigs,* and I'm told it's only twenty minutes, but it's two kilometers more to the track. Can you manage such a long walk? Heh! Heh! It will be a show unlike anything you've ever imagined. The Kaiser, his children, his Chancellor von Bulow, everybody who's anybody will be there. And yes, it will give me the chance to corner the American ambassador about tomorrow's meeting. Getting him to clear his calendar won't be easy. Then I'll have to get the Romanian ambassador to agree. I'm assuming he'll be there kissing up to Willi, like they all do. *Oy vay,* it'll be a busy afternoon."

"Max, bless you, you can do anything you set your whirling mind to, it seems."

The out-of-the-galaxy announcement resulted in a whooping cheer that rattled the rafters of the building, waking any and all "sleep-ins." This was going to be a day of all days for the most appreciative "kids" of Birlad, to whom Max Nordau had just become as popular as Mendel's stories...Tom Sawyer, Rip van Winkle, Leatherstocking and Ichabod Crane all rolled into one. Or as Sholem would say, Tum Soyver, Reepvenvinkelman, Leydehseckalach and Eekabud Krenz. In fact, he had long ago tagged Mendel as "*unsereh ayn ayntsikeh Eekabud Krenz.*" He and many others adamantly insisted that Washington Irving's description of the country schoolteacher fit Mendel perfectly. Mendel, on the other hand, had given an English nickname to every one of his students, which he appended to the official roster of the 1904 Fusgeyer Contingent.

* * *

Engrossed, enthralled and completely mesmerized, seated in the high wooden stands, their hero Max among them, no one wanted the three-hour spectacular to end.

Spectacular? Why wouldn't it be so? With thirty thousand spectators crowding around the oval track and packed into every seat, bench and aisle in the rickety wooden stands, sixty thousand eyes riveted on the race track's infield so as not to miss a move, Buffalo Bill Cody was in his glorious element. The tall, quintessential westerner, wearing a ten-gallon Stetson, fringed deer-skin jacket, burnt-leather chaps and boots, and astride a white steed, was the center of all the action...and the action was nonstop, noisy, exciting, at times breathtaking. As his country's premium good will ambassador, all he may have lacked would have been the bespectacled American President riding alongside, "speaking softly, carrying a big stick." The "Rough-Riding" Colonel Teddy would have loved that, indeed; if he weren't in the difficult throes of playing the game of international statesmanship, delicately refereeing the Russo-Japanese naval debacle in the Pacific.

Arabs, gauchos, vaqueros, cossacks, cowboys and Indians went round and round the track, demonstrating the riding styles each was noted for. "A Congress of Rough-Riders of the World,"—from which the aforementioned T.R. had taken the heralded name for his San Juan Hill troops—thundered through the infield to the sounds of the brass band, trumpets blasting, bugles calling for a cavalry charge; a cast of hundreds, including a war party of Ogallala Sioux led by Louis Whirlwind Horse, Bill's trusted sidekick. Sioux, Shawnee and Apache pony soldiers attacked wagon trains of outnumbered settlers, and marksmanship contests featured little Annie Oakley with a wondrous display of accuracy on moving and stationary targets both. The "ooohs" and "ahhhs" and applause proved she was the darling of the show.

The German announcer—using a state-of-the-art locally invented megaphone, which under-amplified even as it made his voice seem a few octaves higher—took great pleasure as Master of Ceremonies. Each time Cody was involved in an act, the little pencil-mustachioed man with the oversized funnel dragged out the name for what seemed like minutes: *Herrrennnnn und Fraaauuuen und kinnnnderrrr, Bofffffffaaaaaallllo Beeeeeelll Coaaaaaaaaaaaaaddddeeee!* The enthusiastic German audience, the best and most appreciative in all the world according to Cody's publicity staff, cheered loudly from beginning to end with hardly a lull. Intermission? None. The momentum must go on!

If there was a highlight moment in Buffalo Bill's Wild West Show that stood above all others it would most certainly be the rescue scene that had been thrilling spectators from Buenos Aires to Paris to Stockholm to Milano since 1883. Marauding savages attack a stagecoach with eight or so passengers, and then shoot and kill the drivers. They "rough-up" the passengers and take them to the Sioux village as captives. Not to worry! Word gets to the United States Cavalry detachment and their Chief Scout. Aha! Buffalo Bill to the rescue! Usually, volunteers were taken from the audience to ride the coach and "suffer the indignities" of the ordeal. In England, back in the '90s, the venerable Queen Victoria herself watched on as her grandsons and son, now King Edward VII, were among the passengers. Later, in sending the hero a gift of a diamond brooch, she penned an accompanying note...*It was so exciting, I found it difficult to sit. I'm indebted to you for "saving" my family.* Royalty and the famous throughout the world clamored to participate in the traveling show, and did. It was to be no different on this beautiful summer's afternoon, July 4, 1904.

One of the more grizzled cowboys worked his way through the stands to find two more "victims" to join the other six who happened to be pre-selected. Never moving beyond the first few rows, the raw-boned wrangler asked for volunteers in English, a western drawl with appropriate explanatory gestures, from where he stood, right next to where Mendel, Max and Mordecai were sitting. Mendel stood up and faced the Fusgeyers, repeating the question in Yiddish for everyone to hear and understand what was going on. Lo and behold, the two hands to shoot up first were none other than those belonging to Yankel and Avi. For the next twenty minutes three rows of Fusgeyers sat on the edge of their excruciatingly uncomfortable wooden, attached chairs, watching intently and with some trepidation. Not for one moment did they believe that their comrades were in harm's way. Or were they?

The Deadwood Stagecoach's manifest consisted of the following:

Three of the Hohenzollern family children, two boys and a girl, Chancellor von Bulow and his son, and the three-hundred-pound Hapsburg Consul-General from Hamburg. Rounding out the list of intended "victims" were Yankel Golub and Avigdor Semelweiss, scions of the House of Golub and the notable Semelweiss dynasty in the far off, exotic, legendary "Kingdom of Birladomania!"

It all happened in a rush. When all the smoke and clouds of dust and pungent smells of gunpowder dissipated, there in the middle of the defeated Indians teepees stood a tall man in a white beard, waving his broad-brimmed, white Wyoming chapeau, bathed in the glory of stark gallantry. On each side of him, taking their bows as well, stood Yankel and Avi—the latter held the hands of two of the Hohenzollern heirs, and the former carried and soothed the half-dazed, little pig-tailed one with one strong arm while he held the hand of the von Bulow boy with the other. The usually somber Chancellor and the Consul-General stood smiling broadly off to the side with a group of their bare-chested, "mortally-wounded," former captors before coming over to shake the hands of their brave savior and his two Jewish "lieutenants." A sight to behold for the ages. An afternoon etched deeply into each Fusgeyer's memory.As a personal patriotic gesture, Buffalo Bill ended his show while the band played an uplifting rendition of John Philip Sousa's *Stars and Stripes Forever,* accompanied by a brief opening round of fireworks, and then followed by Francis Scott Key's *Star Spangled Banner.* This was in lieu of beginning the show this way, which he always respectfully reserved for the host nation's anthem. As the six cavalry held extra-large-sized "Old Glorys," which unfurled in the breeze, Mendel proudly and spontaneously led his students in the pledge, salute, and their heavily accented singing of the *Star Spangled Banner.* Just behind them, Abe Cahan, alongside Riis and Steffens, the notable social crusaders, and a small group of other American journalists, proudly observed this rare occasion. There wasn't a tearless eye among them.

On this American Independence Day, as advertised, all of this was immediately followed with a half-hour of continuous fireworks, engineered and orchestrated by German military munitions experts, painting the sky with every color in the spectrum, with exploding thunder that could be heard in London. Not a spectator left the grounds until Bill and his entire troupe rode out of the side gate heading for their custommade fifty-two-car train that was waiting for them at the Mariendorf station. On this day, the Kaiser, his military escort and all of the dignitaries whose vehicles, horse-drawn and motorized, awaited them.

The Fusgeyers were the very last to leave. They were as

good as glued to their seats, no matter how uncomfortable they were (after all, they'd been in less accommodating circumstances recently!). All profusely thanked their guardian angel before he, too, took leave. Max had noticed the two target ambassadors standing over at the side gate with a large group of his journalist cronies, and he wanted to press his case before their drivers showed up. He promised to telephone Mordecai as soon as everything fell into place for "the big meeting." Max Nordau, the alpha and the omega of the cocksure, personified.

As Max left the stands, Mordecai, Mendel and Sendehr peered over the diminishing crowds to catch a glimpse of tomorrow's unsuspecting prey. With everyone's adrenaline still gushing madly, and the afternoon sun starting to drop, they decided to forego the convenient S-Bahn and walk the estimated six or seven kilometers back to the Alliance instead. Since Mordecai carried the necessary papers with him at all times, they did not expect any problems as long as the entire contingent stayed together. During their meanders around the city each group had been instructed to carry one of the Alliance letterheads. In the event they were stopped and questioned, a phone call by the police to Schechter would suffice. In effect, the Alliance had long before worked all of this out with the Reichmarshal's office—with great difficulty, as expected.

On the walk back into the city, with everyone agog and abuzz with the happy events of the day, three distinct voices somehow managed to rise above it all.

Mayer: "It's good that we're walking back. I don't want my muscles to go soft."

Itzy: "Your only soft muscle is the big fat one wedged between your ears."

Yankel: "*Nu*, Mendele, I think maybe this Boffaleh Beel IS good for the Yidden!"

* * *

"Herzl is dead! My dearest friend Theo is gone...long live his idea!"

These were the grievous words that softly came through the telephone in Schechter's office to Mordecai upon his return from the jubilant day at Mariendorf.

Herzl had died just hours before and the funeral was to be Tuesday morning. Max Nordau planned to leave for Vienna on the overnight train the next day, Monday. Even in his sad state, he insisted on discussing the forthcoming meeting at the American Embassy.

"Mordecai, I was able to arrange everything to our advantage. We meet tomorrow at two. My train doesn't leave until eight. Plenty of time. Constantin Porumbescu, the monomaniac Romanian, is very upset with me, but I was able to get Charlie to agree to host the session and the man couldn't refuse. He knows very well that Charlie and Kaiser Bill are very close."

"Charlie?"

"Oh, say, I'm sorry. Charlemagne Tower[1], the American ambassador. Good old boy; terrible poker player. I'm the only person in Berlin who can get away with calling him Charlie. Charlemagne! God, can you imagine sticking someone with that name?"

Mordecai spoke privately for a bit with Mendel and Sendehr, and then announced Theodor Herzl's passing to everyone. During *mincha* the special prayer for the departed was invoked, followed by Mendel's brief talk about the man's fervent ideology, and his trials and many setbacks since establishing the World Zionist Organization eight years earlier. Rivka and Esther, knowing how much the Vienna meeting had meant to Sendehr, Mendel and Mordecai were especially affected by this enormous loss.

The man is dead, but the idea could live and possibly come to fruition, please God! The Maharal had predicted it. Mordecai had begun to believe it.

Charlemagne Tower, U.S. Ambassador to Germany, 1902-1908, is no relation of any kind to the author. It is merely a coincidence that both share the same surname. The Ambassador, appointed by Theodore Roosevelt to succeed Andrew Dickson White, was born in Pennsylvania in 1848 and came from a family of wealthy industrialists and landowners. The author is honorably descended from a family of 1890-1914 immigrants from the Russian Pale of Settlement.

The critical preparatory meeting, over tea and *strudel* at the kosher cafe near the Kaiserhof, went smoothly. Sendehr's simple but direct five-point proclamation, in Romanian and copied into English, took into damning account the major grievances:

1. The Government of Romania, while professing to endorse the basic idea that everyone within its borders deserves the right to practice any legal business in the pursuit of earning a living, promotes and recognizes boycotts of Jewish-owned businesses. At the same time, it penalizes to the point of legal indictment any Romanian who breaks the boycott for any reason. This practice alone would be enough to cause a mass exodus. *Dayenu! Destul!*

2. The professions practice a tacit agreement to bar Jews. Doctors, lawyers, teachers, engineers, scientists, chemists and pharmacists are restricted to working within the communities of fellow Jews. This practice alone would be enough. *Dayenu!*

3. The local school districts have banished Jewish students, as have all of the training colleges. This practice alone would be enough. *Dayenu!*

4. Anti-Semitic acts of violence have increased dangerously and dramatically since the Iashi pogrom of 1899, while the authorities choose to look the other way. This practice alone would be enough. *Dayenu!*

5. Parliamentary legislation for the past few years has singled out the Jew to be the unlucky victim of unfair, unfounded and unacceptable anti-Semitic laws and regulations. This practice alone

would be enough. *Dayenu,* Honorable Ambassador, enough, *destul!*

Signed: Sendehr Efraim Inkahss, Mordecai Inkahss, Mendel Inkahss

Max Nordau's summed up his reaction in one word: "Bravo!" He commended the use of *inkahss* (in anger) and *dayenu* (enough) as a stroke of sheer genius. Sendehr's mates, although this was the second time that they had heard the proclamation, proudly embraced him, kissing him on both cheeks, for a job so well done.

All four walked, no, strutted to the American Embassy in Pariser Platz with great anticipation of at least a small semblance of success. History held little hope.

* * *

Earlier that day, immediately after the typical morning meal, the HIAS representative, as scheduled, met with all of the two hundred who were heading for one of the ports. He suggested that the Fusgeyers meet with him separately, in the reading room, following this first general session, which delighted Mordecai.

Joseph Castleman, a first-generation American from Passaic, New Jersey, had been sent to Germany by the understaffed, overburdened and overwhelmed organization to help smooth the way for the continuing mass of Jewish immigrants. He was a pleasant young man of high intelligence whose position it was to cope with the seemingly insurmountable problems, without many of the means to do so. But he tried with all his heart and soul to be all things to all people. A thankless and formidable task, at best.

Castleman, in an acceptable *Rushiseh* Yiddish, outlined the procedures they would be subjected to during the required quarantine period in Bremerhaven. He also carefully reviewed the notorious medical exam dos and don'ts. Gershon and Maidele asked him many questions during this part of the instructions so that they could further prepare everyone. The HIAS man was astonished at such unusual organization, and answered each one of their questions to the best of his knowledge.

The most vitally interesting segment of his one-hour presentation involved the latest immigrant employment opportunities in New York and Boston. Most of the openings HIAS had been trying to fill were in the garment trades of New York. Castleman mentioned some newly discovered jobs in Newark and Philadelphia, and also stressed that the busy shipyards near Boston were still a viable option for those interested. He expected to stay at the Alliance for most of the day, talking with any of the individuals wanting more specific information up to and including actual commitments for some of the available openings.

"Reb Castleman, will you be available during this week, before we leave for Bremerhaven?" asked Mendel, in English.

"You can call me Joey or Yossel, if you wish. Your English is a surprise! By the way, my Yiddish is purely a hand-me-down. I have three older sisters!" he laughed. "Certainly, I'm at your service. My office is in the Community Building on the other side of the Neue *shul*. Just have Herr Schechter call in advance for anyone coming to see me."

"Yossel, you make the medical exam sound as frightening as we have always heard. Is it?" asks a genuinely concerned Doctor Hippocrates.

"It's only that thorough if there is any outward indication of a serious health problem—I was giving the worse case scenario. Other than that it's a superficial exam—eyes, teeth, visual abscesses, sores and so on. My guess is that none of you *shtarkeh menschen* have anything to worry about. Good God, you walked across the continent! *Oy, vay!* My whole body aches just thinking about it! Schechter tells me you all walked from the Buffalo Bill show in Mariendorf yesterday. *Darf zein mashigah!*" This set the whole group off with laughter, as a few began to leave the room while most of the others gathered around the HIAS man hoping that he might answer any personal questions they had or for any further job information.

Clearly, this was a new friend, Mordecai thought warmly. Here was a man of substance and good humor who had dedicated this young adult part of his life to help the emigrating Jew make the transition to America. Invariably, this priceless organization had become and would continue to be the principal link between one's former life in Jewish Europe, and that of a whole new world called America.

* * *

Max was pleased to see that the dapper and spirited Abe Cahan was already waiting for them in the Embassy's main lobby. He had asked the outspoken, controversial founder and editor of what was fast becoming the leading Jewish daily in North America to join in the meeting, and in fact he couldn't have been kept away with wild bulls. In fact, he had already spent Sunday evening cabling the Herzl story to his New York office and was to join Max on the overnight to Vienna. Max needed all the support he could get for this meeting. He was fully confident in the three young Fusgeyers, but a man with the credentials of Cahan would be invaluable.

The team of five huddled for a few short minutes, Cahan quickly perusing the English version of the proclamation, and enthusiastically proclaiming, "Great going, boys! Let's go get 'em!" The forty-four-year old Cahan had emigrated from the Pale in 1882 and had very little trace of an accent remaining in his nasal Americanized twang. He had authored some realistic novels of immigrant life, the most popular being *Yekl: A Tale of the New York Ghetto,* and when his paper "hit the streets" every day, growing masses of new Jewish-Americans snatched it up eagerly. After all, it was rightfully theirs.

Already seated around the solid teak conference table were:

Constantin Porumbescu, Romanian Ambassador to
Germany.
Nicolae Romanece, his senior aide.
Sergiu Barsescu, his personal secretary.
Robert Watchorn, U.S. Immigration Service, Special
Assignments.
Harold C. Wallace, Deputy U.S. Ambassador.
Cuthbert Breckenridge, personal secretary to the
U.S. Ambassador.
Charlemagne Tower, Jr., United States Ambassador
to Germany.

Five empty chairs were soon occupied by the newly arrived after they were escorted into the room. Wallace, the
Deputy, handled the introductions with impeccable diplomacy, and cross-table handshakes followed each one. Con-
dolences to Nordau on Herzl's passing were also forthcoming.

The American ambassador, as host, began by explaining to all in attendance exactly what the meeting was all
about. This was quickly supplemented by the Romanian
ambassador, speaking in a rather condescending, clipped
Oxford English.

"Mister Ambassador, thank you for hosting this meeting. Mister Nordau," he said, turning to the five who sat
side-by-side, "Why do you think you're here?" Porumbescu
obviously did not believe in beating around the bush.

"You, sir, can answer your own question." Max was no
wilting flower either. Porumbescu continued.

"Sir, you have insulted my government, the people of
the sovereign nation of Romania, and even the Jews you
say we have mistreated. Your article, appearing in newspapers and other periodicals the world over, is a preposterous, unadulterated falsehood, and I, sir, on behalf of all
Romanians and our good King Carol demand an unequivo-
cal apology, immediately followed by a printed retraction!"

Charlemagne Tower, a well-bred, sour-looking, rather
frail man in his forties, stood up at this point and asked

that both men try to set a more civil tone to these proceedings. A life-long student, lawyer, author, diplomat, and self-appointed cognoscente, Tower looked down the table and wondered, *why in hell did I agree to become involved with these ragged looking Yid revolutionaries and a crew of mad Romanians? This is something the boss* (who was glaring down on him from his ubiquitous "rough-rider" portrait above the fireplace) *would love to be in the middle of—it's really akin to his mixing it up with those Russkies and Japs fighting it out over in the Pacific. How de classé! Why it'll be a miracle if one of these commoners doesn't toss a hand-made bomb before this meeting is over.* He looked over to his deputy with a hangdog expression, as if to say, *get us out of this debacle, Hal!*

In a calculated move, with a dulcifying tone, Max now answered the Romanian's previous request: "These are three of the Jewish lads, Your Excellency. These are the people I wrote about. Wayfarers, Fusgeyers. I hardly think they would agree that my article in any way insulted them, as you say. On the contrary, I merely pointed out to the world that your government, despite warning upon warning—including one from the American Secretary of State two years ago—is undeniably guilty of denying these fine young men and their left-behind families and friends any semblance of civil or human rights, social dignity, or hope for the future."

With this he reached over to Sendehr's proclamation and asked Mendel to read it for the benefit of all. Since everyone in the room, aside from Sendehr and Mordecai, understood English perfectly well, there would be no need for the Romanian version.

Mendel was never more succinct. His " veddy British" speech easily overshadowed Porumbescu's. His delivery was beautifully and most effectively modulated, enunciated and punctuated. He spat out the *dayenus*, and followed each one with the Romanian companion word for "enough." When he finished, he walked around to the Romanian contingent, which now looked extremely uncomfortable, and crisply handed the proclaiming paper to Germany's ranking Romanian.

"There is not one shred of truth in this tendentious trash. There is no proof. Lies. All lies perpetrated by a Jewish conspiracy in league with the ongoing western efforts to discredit my country. We are being made the scapegoat for all of the crimes of neighboring Czar Nicolai's Russia. Not that Jews are handled with kindness in this cauldron of nationalism, either. Am I right, Ambassador Tower? You have eyes. I have eyes. You see and I see what is going on in the Scheunenviertel and beyond. I read the propaganda. The graffiti everywhere. The pamphlets. The newspaper editorials. There is more anti-Semitism in one square kilometer of Berlin than in my entire country. Don't you agree? And you, Mister Nordau, are being used as a vehicle for fabrication. You are being duped, sir. Duped. And in the process, your international reputation as a fair-minded journalist, at one time above reproach, or so I'm told, has been sullied beyond repair..."

Sendehr and Mordecai were not at all lost. Max and Mendel saw to it that they got the general meaning of the entire conversation. Not that the tone of voice alone didn't reveal what was being said, and how it was being said.

Heretofore Robert Watchorn, who sat next to Abe Cahan with whom he had been corresponding for nearly four years, had been silent, but he now felt that his time had come to speak up. Ambassador Tower had invited him to this meeting when he had met with him for an Embassy dinner that previous Saturday. Watchorn was a highly respected diplomat who served as the Immigration Service's Special Delegate to Romania in 1900: "To study the causes leading to the exodus of Romanian Jews, the number and character of those likely to emigrate to the United States, and the conditions which surround the people there generally, and which contribute to their leaving their native land." It just seemed natural to Tower that Mister Watchorn could be a meaningful presence at this meeting.

"We want to help my good friend Nordau, but we must be careful not to escalate the damn thing to an international pot-boiler, Watchorn," warned the politically correct statesman when he had telephoned him at his hotel that morning. Watchorn was only temporarily stationed in Berlin, working with two members of the House of Representatives—a Democrat from Massachusetts and a Republican from Texas—who were studying von Bulow's proposals for joint German-American intervention on the potentially explosive French-Moroccan situation.

"I'm sorry, sir, but I must categorically dispute your contentious remarks."

Porumbescu's jaw dropped precipitously at this statement, and a hush blanketed the uncomfortably warm room. *Careful, careful now, Watchorn,* silently prayed a cowering Tower. But the standing, Lincoln-esque figure, English born, and for many years a California oil man, pressed on.

"I spent nearly four months touring your fair nation in 1900. My commission was clear. You may or may not remember me, because if I'm to understand correctly, you were Ambassador to Norway at the time. However, your government has a dossier on me and my activities that would in all likelihood cover the surface of this entire table. My final report was decidedly not in the best interests of your country. It was, arguably, one of the most damaging documents adversely affecting any nation's reputation for human rights in modern times."

Porumbescu stared at Watchorn without interrupting. His aide repeatedly whispered into his ear and just as often was waved off. Once even physically pushed away. Porumbescu not only had heard of Watchorn's report, he had read it from cover to cover, discussed it, analyzed it, and like all other government officials, condemned it. To him, then, Watchorn was the enemy.

Tower gestured for Watchorn to continue, while Mendel quietly relayed the highlights of his opening remarks to Mordecai and Sendehr.

"Furthermore, Excellency, every intelligence report I have received since then has served to make the initial study a mild one by comparison. The simple and direct Fusgeyer document clearly and most eloquently sums up the case against your government. A practicing attorney-diplomat could not improve on it." With this he nodded approvingly toward the Boys from Birlad at the end of the long table.

For the next ten minutes the professorial statesman cited drastic cases of official anti-Semitism, constant agitation in the streets, demeaning textbook paragraphs presenting the Jew as a rabid animal, and the latest emigration statistics. He pointed out, with these as standing evidence, that Jewish emigrants from Romania who arrived in the United States had gone from a mere trickle in 1881 to an average of 7,000 each year since 1900. This number did not include those immigrating to Germany, France, England and other Western European nations, nor did it cite any figures to Canada, Australia, South America, or Palestine. It was an accepted estimate that more than thirty percent of the current 250,000 Jews in Romania would have left the country within the next five to six years. Without a doubt, pointed out the methodical Watchorn, massive Romanian Jewish emigration was increasing more rapidly than that of any other country in Europe.

"There must be a reason for this; and you, sir, know as well as any one exactly what that reason is. From the mounting display of indisputable data we all know that the human being leaves one place for another only if he has lost hope. The Jews of Romania have lived with hopelessness for decades. These young boys have ventured forth with more than fifty others in order to regain that hope. There are hundreds, perhaps thousands like them, groups of fifty, a hundred, marching through Europe protesting the conditions imposed by your government. And you can be as sure as there is a tomorrow that they will send for their loved ones as soon as finances permit...."

Could the cantankerous editor sit still any longer? Not beyond the point where the urgency to interrupt overtook him.

"Ambassador Porumbescu, I am Abraham Cahan, publisher and editor of the *Jewish Daily Forward* in New York.

I proudly, and also with deep sadness, printed every word of Max Nordau's article on the Fusgeyers and their forced purposes in my paper. I also printed the more public parts of Bob's report in 1900 because I strongly felt that my Yiddish readers should know the facts, just as I will immediately print the Fusgeyer proclamation. Even Joseph Pulitzer and William Randolph Hearst, those two disputatious contrarians, perennial battling foes, found space in their sensationalist fish-wraps to give Max a few paragraphs. In case you don't know, there are many others from Berlin to Buenos Aires who have done the same. There will be no let up, sir. Rare publicity had been given to the steady emigration of your Jewish non-citizens until now. But if you think Max's or Elie Viesl's stories of what's behind the Fusgeyer mission is putting pressure on your people in Bucharest, you ain't seen nuthin' yet. It's called freedom of the press, dear sir!"

By this time, Charlemagne Tower wished he could be transported to eighth-century France and become his namesake. If he had crept any lower his chin would rest on the over-glossed tabletop. He was forced to think the unthinkable...*my God, my God, is this the end of my career?*

Max saw the Romanian squirming, and seized the opportunity to regain the reins.

"Ambassador Porumbescu, none of us expects your government to buckle under the pressure Mister Cahan refers to. But we do hope that you will find it in your hearts to reevaluate your treatment of your minorities: Jews, gypsies, Greeks, Turks, and others. You are grossly neglecting some valuable national resources. And you do not stand alone, as I'm sure you realize. Franz-Josef, Czar Nicolai, and the Kaiser to one degree or another are guilty of this same xenophobic, totalitarian, nationalism; and their victim is always the already disenfranchised, the impoverished, and the boycotted. My more democratic fellow journalists have been targeting all of you for their entire professional lives, to little avail, or none."

With these words, the Romanian delegation, their initial intransigence now leaning more to the defiant side, arose in unmannerly unison, gathered its materials including the proclamation, and filed out the door. They had heard all they cared to hear. Tower was visibly upset with this immature exit. In his Harvardian circles one never, but never, compromised chivalrous manners.

The postmortem was animated, full of good fellowship, though; with even a politely tight laugh or two out of King Charlemagne. Nobody thought that anything material would ever materialize, if you will. The three Fusgeyers were pleased enough that they had received the opportunity to present their proclamation, and ecstatic with the growing amount of universal publicity for their mission. They were more than ready to be convinced when Max and Abe claimed a moral victory that would someday translate into full emancipation for the Romanian Jew. When? God only knows.

Robert Watchorn, a scarred veteran of these political donnybrooks vis-a-vis Romania and its exclusionary history, was sensibly skeptical, yet hopeful.

"There is no telling of the value of constant pressure by the press. It has unseated presidents, dethroned kings, it has toppled vast kingdoms, passed or defeated legislation and even more fundamentally, has changed people's opinions, directions, attitudes. Press pressure can destroy, it can build, it can remember, and it can forget. You gentlemen with your pens in hand know very well that it has been shown at times to be more powerful than the mightiest weapons. Let us hope and pray that this frustrating exercise eventually crystallizes into one of those victorious occasions."

The ambassador and his deputy walked their guests into the elegant lobby. Charlemagne Tower grasped each person's hand, ending with Mordecai, Mendel and Sendehr. "Welcome to America, gentlemen. We are delighted to have you."

Theodor Herzl's death received broad coverage in both the Jewish and German press of Greater Berlin. David Wolffsohn's name was prominently featured as his successor, particularly since he was a resident of the city. Max

Nordau was also honored as Herzl's closest friend, and as a key figure in the establishment and rise of the World Zionist Organization. In each article there were the usual comments on the discord between the eastern and western factions of the organization. This was a polite way of saying that the strong willed Russified Zionists and the immovable Western/Germanic Zionists continued to be immersed deeply within an inextricably polarized state. Inheriting this conundrum, Wolffsohn would have to cope with this unwelcome internal version of the eternally infernal *Judefrage.*

Kaiser Wilhelm II, to whom Herzl had twice made an impassioned plea for support of an independent Jewish State in Palestine, issued a formal statement of condolence to Berlin's Jewish community, in his customary paternalistic display of royal magnanimity.

After leaving the American Embassy, Max Nordau had told two Kaiser stories. The first was a popular anecdote involving his new bride, the Kaiserin Dona. It seems that when she first arrived in Berlin from Schleswig as the new Kaiserin in 1881 a typical Unter den Linden full dress military parade had been arranged, including horse-drawn floats representing various Berlin suburbs and nearby towns. All of a sudden, lumbering past the reviewing stand came an unauthorized entry brashly and unabashedly advertising "Singer Sewing Machines." On the flag-bedecked reviewing stand the twenty-two-year old Kaiser and his Kaiserin were mortified by this ultimate in low-class crassness. The European Managing Director publicly and severely reprimanded the highly imaginative, opportunistic local Singer representative on the spot, and fired him within days afterward. Thereafter, the Kaiserin refused to have any Singer product in the palace.

In the second story, Max told of his first meeting with the Kaiser and Kaiserin in Palestine, in 1898. When Herzl had heard that the Kaiser would be in the Holy Land to dedicate the German Protestant Church of the Redeemer in Jerusalem, he immediately concocted a quixotic plan and asked Max to join him. They traveled by train to Athens and by boat to Haifa, where the Kaiser was scheduled to address the large German colony. Herzl, who had been covering Europe for more than two years seeking support from every head of state including the Pope, had met with the Kaiser once before and found him to be one of the more receptive leaders. Now, in what had become an obsession by this time according to his many critics, Herzl would ask the Kaiser to intercede with Sultan Abdul-Hamid, giving his powerful support to Zionism's heretofore elusive objective: a legal charter from the Sultan for an independent Jewish State somewhere in Turkish Palestine. Even the far more pragmatic Max was impressed when they approached the Kaiser's aide, who warmly stated that he would arrange a meeting for the following evening. Herzl was encouraged as never before.

Neither Zionist was prepared for the shattering disappointment that befell they next. When arriving at the colony's villa for the scheduled meeting that next evening they were met by the same aide who curtly announced, "Not wanting to risk a disturbance in his current comfortable relations with the Sultan, His Excellency does not wish to pursue your noble request any further."

Max later learned from one of his fellow journalists that the Kaiser and Kaiserin had left for the Jerusalem church ceremony that morning as scheduled, never intending to keep the date with Herzl. He kept this from his already severely demoralized colleague and friend, who would not live to see his dream realized.

Mordecai and Mendel were mortified to hear of such deception. Sendehr merely shook his head, lips pursed, thinking that his outspoken negative reactions to Teutonic character and posture were well justified.

* * *

In somewhat of a plangent mood, given the mix of events

456

while in Berlin, Sendehr chastised himself for merely just going through the motions while writing in the daily journal. It was strange: he had so much to write about, and the prolific input from his best contributors kept pouring in, especially where everyone was off on their own during these ten days seeing and doing different things and participating in a variety of experiences. Tsippy and Chaike, Mottke Grunwald, Yaakov Nachman and Mayer Bernstein could always be counted on for some colorful bits and pieces of commentary, as could the "comedians" for their steady stream of clever humor. For the more prurient, there was always Simmy's ribaldry which begged for delicate surgical editing by Sendehr. All of this was more or less bordering on the mundane. Not to demean any word of it, but much in the way of the more provocative he saved for the supplemental, sometimes private, letters to Rabbi Nachman which he had written and sent at least once every week.

There were engrossing, stimulating subjects, always; but in Berlin, even more so. Sendehr, no doubt more deeply influenced by his Praha encounters than he had first realized, looked upon this past week as a message of deep foreboding. A time for looking at the past, tempering it with the present, in order to determine if and where there was a trend of some kind emerging. Was he overreacting to the Haman character? Or the possibilities of genocidal terror? The predicted decimation of European Jewry? The bloody transition from assimilation to God forbid, elimination?

Whatever was disturbing him from within, his nineteen-year-old sensitivities and sensibilities were in a furious fight to reject it. Sendehr found himself snapping at his friends and comrades, and yes, even at his Rivka. It had to stop.

He even likened this effect to the time when his father, Reb Moishe, had innocently told him the story of Vlad Dracula of Bran Castle. The episodes of the diabolical Count had frightened many a young one in Romania for centuries, not to mention the highly superstitious and impressionable peasant adult population. It upset him to the point of the constant dread that an army of bats would someday descend upon Birlad to suck the blood out of every little Jewish boy and girl. At the urging of Sendehr's loving mother, Channah, the gentle Reb Moishe thought the better of ever mentioning Dracula again; and as the boy grew older the fears and occasional nightmares completely subsided.

Nevertheless, in his current state of introspection the bats, the Golem, the Maharal, the Haman figure, Rabbi Blankfort and even the Romanian Ambassador Porumbescu, seemed intertwined in the raging fluids of his brain. They had to be flushed. He knew that.

At midnight, Sendehr was preparing to write Rabbi Nachman by the lamp light in the reading room. Everyone had long ago gone to sleep upstairs. Rivka had curled up in her cot next to his, but without him to hold her hand across the dormitory aisle as the two of them were prone to do before nodding off each night. There would be an early departure just hours from then...the Fusgeyers of Birlad would take to the road again in the morning on the last stretch of land before the long sea voyage.

Sendehr had concluded a few days back that coming closer and closer to the port, now less than four hundred kilometers due west, had a great deal to do with his own turmoil. This stark reality of the trek nearing its completion had evidently exacerbated the homesickness of a growing number of the wayfaring team.

As an obvious example, Heshy Rosen and Kalman Fuchs, to name just two, were becoming more outspoken of their trepidation and yearnings, up to but not quite including a return to Birlad. For the moment, Mordecai had succeeded in thwarting such an action, sincerely feeling that it was in their own and in their families' best interests to go on. And Sendehr was closer than ever to agreeing with his own self-analysis that to one degree or another, perhaps everyone was wrestling with similar feelings of permanent separation from everything and everyone that had molded their lives until now. The European continent itself was soon to be nothing more than a memory for them. The anxieties of meeting with and coping with an entirely new life in a strange land certainly had and would continue to have a turbulent effect on every and any nomadic soul...yesterday, today and forevermore.

Perhaps, he thought, he was just being overly analytical in internalizing these powerful emotions. *This, too, will pass,* he uttered with a doubting sigh and a wry smile, in his final attempt at calming before opening the inkwell and taking up the pen.

19

ENCOUNTERS: ROAD TO

BREMERHAVEN

*Each new wanderer...thought he was trying to
better his own condition only...but soon every
emigrating Jew moving westward realized he was
involved in something more than a personal
expedition...each came to feel he was part of an
historical event...*
From the Memoirs of Abraham Cahan, Editor, *The
Forward (Forvitz)*

*Dear Rabbi,
Everyone is asleep as I write this. Tomorrow we will
start on the last land leg of this great journey. The ten
days in Berlin, which I will synopsize for you in the next
few days, has my journal spilling over with
details...where do I begin?*

This would easily become the longest letter of the journey. Sendehr was becoming proficient in the art of select-
ing and detailing those items that he was certain the Rabbi
would want to know about: the Romanian Ambassador
meeting was at the top of the list, closely followed by the
Nordau and Viesl articles, the Buffalo Bill Wild West Show,
and conditions in the Scheunenviertel. Then he would need
to include something about the *Moishe Yidden*, the infernal
internal animosities, the mass conversions, the

assimilationism, the exclusionary politics of anti-Semitism, the inevitable comparisons to the situation at home, the homesick malady flurrying about, and, as always—a very personal comment concerning his rapidly maturing love for his *zeesa* Rivkeleh.

In this latter regard, Sendehr was pleased to inform Rabbi Nachman that Rivka finally saw the great Bernhardt perform thanks to the diligent efforts of the HIAS man, Joe Castleman. Alerted of the dilemma by Herr Schechter, he was able to *shnor* two tickets from none other than the Mosaically-persuaded Frau Gruning when he was the guest speaker at the Gruning's *Hilfsverein* meeting—as a substitute for the non-consenting Mordecai, no less! Sendehr insisted that Rivka take Esther along, allowing as how she would appreciate it more than he. Rivka was in full agreement.

Sendehr's description of the ambassador meeting included his proclamation, rewritten in its entirety. No doubt he was prouder of this than anything else he had done on the journey. Mordecai and Mendel could not stop praising the excellence of this work, and Max Nordau fully agreed. Even Charlemagne Tower had voiced his highly complimentary critique of the document. The young scribe's written words, along with Nordau, Watchorn and Cahan's powerful condemnations, was quite enough to render Porumbescu speechless, inducing his crassly taken "French leave." Strategic retreat, he would call it!

Rabbi, none of us knows where it will all lead.
Curing the accumulated ills that have been festering for
so many years is nothing that can be accomplished with
one meeting, or one piece of paper, or one speech. But
we can now sail off to America knowing that we gave it
our best efforts. Tikkun Olam *has to start somewhere!*
Our suggestion would be to have one of Iashi's
Jewish printers set it in type, print a goodly number of
copies, and distribute it to your colleagues throughout

Romania. In this way, maybe many of our landsmen can have the satisfaction knowing that a protest has been voiced, in writing, directly from their own kind of common folk. A note should be added stating that this was presented to the Romanian Ambassador to Germany on June 5, 1904, in the presence of the following: the American Ambassador Charlemagne Tower; Max Nordau, the Zionist journalist; Abraham Cahan, publisher of New York's Yiddish daily, The Forward; Robert Watchorn, United States Immigration Service, Special Delegate; and finally, three most humble Romanian Fusgeyers.

What do you think, Rabbi? Mendel and Mordecai both agree with me that this could be a powerful tool for boosting morale, which must be sagging to its lowest ebb with the newly imposed restrictions.

We further recommend that the mailings be dispersed from a number of different towns: from Iashi to Bacau to Piatra, to Vaslui, to Focshani, to Galatz, to Bucureshti and so on. These widely diverse posting marks will prevent the authorities from pinpointing any one location. You could mail as many as you wish from Iashi and on the way home. Whenever anyone from Birlad is going to any of the aforementioned towns, give him a stack to take along. As you can see, these necessary precautions are not to be taken lightly in these tempestuous times. We have been made acutely aware of these necessities during the journey and it has served us well to this point.

Knowing the character of his Rabbi and dear friend, Sendehr was certain that this would be done with great dispatch, and was already taking satisfaction as he wrote. Mendel had referred to the entire ambassador incident as our own "declaration of independence," something he had introduced to his English classes weeks before, with Sholem quickly fracturing the Preamble "Ve di pippuls...ve holt dese troots salf-hevydent."

There has been constant talk of the "Judefrage" here in Berlin, from Jew and German alike (and in many cases the line between the two is blurred beyond recognition). The Kaiser himself, statesmen, diplomats, government workers, teachers, college professors, the man on the street, the so-called "ordinary German"...all are asking for or suggesting a solution to this gnawing "Jewish Problem...Jewish Question." Germany is no different than Romania, France, England, or the Pale in that ugly respect. Even where there were no Jews there was still the infamous problem. Rabbi, it's not the problem, but the historic adopted solutions that forever concern us...slavery, the crusades; and now the pogroms, the boycotts, the trade restrictions—always something dreadful and discouraging. What next? Did Herzl, in fact, have the elusive solution? Here in Germany, I get the feeling that even our own people believe that THEY are really the problem that THEY themselves must solve. Do you see the universal negative attitude that has developed? Last night, Herr Schechter told us a joke on the subject, which, when one thinks about it, is just not so funny. On the contrary, critically enervating! Here it is!

At a Berlin educational institution attended by both German and foreign students, the professor asks for a paper to be written on the subject of "The Elephant." The British student entitles his paper, "The Elephant and British Colonialism in India," and goes on to write about the value of the beast in carrying supplies to remote outposts on the sub-continent. The German student entitles his paper, "Das Elephant und Military Campaigns," as to be expected. He refers to Hannibal the Carthaginian and the elephants he used in his successful mountain maneuvers...

The rare Jewish student simply entitles his paper "The Elephant, and the Jewish Problem"

THE WAYFARERS

How terribly sad, Rabbi. I can not help thinking the distasteful thought that the predicted new Haman will someday accomplish the most ghastly solution of all.

As more or less a mental exercise, Sendehr had opened the journal to Friday and began to flit back and forth between it and his letter to Rabbi Nachman, filling in events and notes and then continuing the letter. Perhaps he was using this as a punishing system for staying awake.

Theodor Herzl's death came as no great shock to the three of us who met with him in Vienna. May he rest with the peace he was not able to find on earth! The details are in the journal and will be synopsized. I'm sure you've heard the news.

We had a sad farewell with Max Nordau at the railroad station, but he assured us that he would be visiting New York in the spring. He invited us to be his guests at a fund-raising dinner at the big Waldorf-Astoria Hotel, kosher of course, with Rivka and Esther included. Probably wants to display us. You know, "the courageous youth of Romania, many of whom would have gone to Palestine if conditions were more conducive, blah, blah, blah..." As Mordecai says, we'll be worth a few million in pledges just by being there. The more shloompy our dress, the better!

Max is the quintessential Zionist, constantly driven by it. God Bless that man! He has done so much for our cause he certainly deserves what little help we can provide him.

Rabbi, on a more personal note, I want to know more details about the newly imposed trade restrictions. I'm worried about my family. Father must sell grain, thread, clothing—anything and everything—to keep his livelihood. I don't want to appear callously selfish, as I know everyone is adversely affected to one degree or another, but whatever you can do to move him in the right direction would be greatly appreciated. I know your

*own father must also be having a difficult time of it, but my
dearest Reb Moishe is so uncommonly stubborn and
proud! How about Mandelbaum? Can he be of help
under these impossible conditions, or not? I suppose
everyone is looking to him. Maybe the granary where
Nuchim's father is working. I'm upset as you can imagine, but then again, everyone here is worried, thinking of
family.*

*I'm truly sorry for the foregoing whining, Rabbi.
You, too, must be having a hard time making ends meet.
How can anyone give money to the shul under this
inhumanly repressive legislation? What does this do to
your marriage plans, or do I dare ask? Be sure to write
me as soon as you receive this, and send the letter to
the Bremerhaven Postal Station. I hope to fetch it before
we go into quarantine. At any rate, I will send you my
address just as soon as we settle in New York. I say
"we," because Rivka and I have begun "chuppa talk."*

Emes. The truth. The propinquity between them had
even developed into a sort of romantic idioglossia, where
only they knew the code words of the secret language that
sooner or later is incorporated into every love affair. More
than just the saccharine billing and cooing it makes sense
to the two lovebirds only, and is totally indecipherable by
even their closest confidants. If they wanted to go off alone
while in a crowd, for example, a prearranged word like "parasol," or "boots" or jokingly, "we're off to meet our *zaydeh* for
tea," or "Leml Leventer is waiting at the *tuchus* slide," and
off they would sashay, arms entwined.

*The Berlin visit was highly educational in every way,
Rabbi. We all learned a great deal of European life from
our dormitory mates representing all corners of the Pale,
Poland, Serbia, and even Croatia and Greece; from the
Moishe Yidden, bless them; from the ostjuden crammed
into the Scheunenvierte. Gevalt!; and from Max and Cahan,
Watchorn, Ambassador Tower, the Alliance people,*

Castleman, the HIAS man.

    *The ambassador even told us that his president,
Theodore Roosevelt (soon to be our president, and I
finally know how to spell out his name...may God watch
over him!), is fluent in German. Can you imagine? The
American President. Yes, Rabbi, he lived with a Doctor
Kitzwitz and family in Dresden for six months when he
was fifteen years old. He and his sisters were exposed
to only the German language during that stay.
According to Ambassador Tower, Kitzwitz was a
member of the Reichstag and a friend of the very rich
Roosevelt family. This came as quite a surprise to us,
but it was pleasant to know that our president is a man
of the world as we're beginning to find out: his sole
mission at this moment is to arrange a peace between
the Russians and the Japanese. In the long run, that
will be a good thing for* unsereh Yidden. *Strange, but
when the Czar takes a naval beating in Japanese
waters, ultimately a poor Jew in Odessa suffers the
pain.* Genug! Dayenu! *Pray for our Mister Roosevelt!*
Omayn.

    *Since we had more time here than anywhere else, I
learned to use a library for the very first time. A*
groisseh simcha fahr mir! *Berlin has many, but we
went to the central building and Mendel made it a point
to teach me exactly how to maneuver through the card
catalogs, the reference stacks, and the numbering
systems. It was nothing short of heavenly fascination
for me. His experiences in Athens and Salonika, finely
tutored by his "Brits," served this country cousin very
well indeed. Bless him! After two visits, I feel confident
to walk into New York's best. Of course, first I'll have to
gain a great deal of proficiency in English, although the
German books did not overwhelm me because there
were sizable English and Yiddish sections available.
Mendel says there will be much larger selections of
Yiddish books in New York's public libraries. He did,
however, warn me that the numbering systems might be*

different. But, Rabbi, at least I'm comfortable with the whole procedure and I feel very good about it. A writer should all but live in the libraries, I believe. As you can plainly see, my education continues every day, in every way.

I also learned something more about this Joseph Pulitzer who was attending the Publisher's Conference. Max spoke of him as a Hungarian half-Jew who immigrated to America before their Civil War. The poor man who owns one of the two biggest New York papers is virtually blind and actually came to Germany seeking help for other health problems. Unquestionably, we are greatly indebted to both him and his arch-rival Hearst for printing Max's article intact. Oddly, one wouldn't dare not to use it if the other one did. Abe Cahan told us that their fierce rivalry is unlike anything the American press has ever witnessed. He refers to both their papers as "fish-wraps," no less. He's obviously alluding to their papers' less than desirable tactics in reporting the news. Gott tsedanken, we got what we needed out of them, fish-wraps or not.

The highly regarded Berlin literati, both German and Jewish, seem to enjoy taking America to task. I read several articles, which Max showed us, that were most uncomplimentary. In a Jewish monthly magazine, our America is pictured as "a materialistic wasteland inhabited by Neanderthal automatons, where lynching, anti-Semitism, anti-immigration and ignoran , illiterate Philistines in positions of authority, are the rule of the land...completely foreign to the great works of art and music...a cultural desert surrounded by roaming anthropophagic Indians." This article is from a closed society whose landsleiter emigrated during the last century and now controls the vast financial empires throughout America, and especially New York, Nordau informed us. Unfathomable to me. Meanwhile, Max also pointed out one of the better German periodicals which unashamedly proclaims that "the collage of disparate

cultures promoted and welcomed by the Americans is
totally unacceptable to any good German. Our nation
thrives on Germany for Germans. That is our everlasting
goal!" This severe nationalistic dictum is nothing new to
us. It seems that we have heard and seen nothing else
since crossing the border into this warm and friendly
fairyland. As Itzy Gelman remarked at one time, "we're
about as welcome as Father Mihai at my Bar Mitzvah."
That neatly sums it all up.

When Rivka and Esther went off to the Bernhardt
performance, Mendel and I went back into the
Scheunenviertel. We found the cemetery where Moses
Mendelssohn's tomb is located, but in a walled-in,
nearly concealed courtyard nearby, the broken remains
of a much older burial ground exist. Hence, I give you
the following:

THE BURIAL GROUND
(Bais Oylem)
(On the discovery of an ancient cemetery in
Scheunenviertel)

Judischer friedhof, holy resting place of the
Jew, a forest of stones, on composted dry
bones overrun by the bulrush tangles of
centuries past, pillaged by the vandals of time.

1365

   1433

      1475

         1513

            1548

               1639

                  1711

moss covered tablets that speak the
unspeakable,a monument in solitary stance
cries out to be seen,its smoothness begging
to be touched by hand.
I hear ye, I heed ye, I am here!
ye are not forgotten, ye voices of martyrdom,
I embrace ye now, one and all.
'fore I depart, to scale the crumbling mortar,
I pause to reaffirm my faith, in ancient
prayer, for those once proud *minyans* of Old
Berlin, *a kaddish* for many millennia.
yisgadal
> *v'yiskadash*
>> *sh'may rabah*

Sendehr Efraim
Berlin, Germany
July 10, 1904 (7 Tammuz, 5664)

(Translated from the Yiddish)

*I am going to sleep. It's nearly two according to
the big clock in this room.
Best wishes to all in Birlad. A special greeting
with love to my parents.*

*Sendehr Efraim,
last letter from Berlin,
the early morning of July 11, 1904
(8 Tammuz, 5664)*

* * *

"I'm pleased that you've finally decided to go to Boston. Working in that boat-building yard may agree with you," said Yaakov, starting to take the point with Sholem.

"I hope so, Yak. I just like the idea of living in a town about the size of Birlad. Big city living is not my style, I'm sure. This *Kvinzee* sounds good to me."

"You'll have plenty of company. Nuchim, the four cantors, the comedians. *Gevalt!* Velvel's brother is there in *KvinCee*, I hear. Or is *KvinZee? Yes?*" asked Yak, looking back to see if the others had begun to step out yet.

"It will be very comforting to have them all with me, but not one is a runner like you, old friend," answered Sholem as he put an arm around his point partner.

The other Boston-bound 'geyers had family there but no prospects of decent employment. Since the HIAS man had told them about available jobs at the Fore River Ship and Engine Company yard, the pressure was off very early in the process. Joe Castleman was happy to give each of the interested parties until they arrive in Bremerhaven to decide, but they all signed up on the spot; not wishing to delay and possibly jeopardize their chances to fill the limited openings. Castleman was nice enough to give the Fusgeyers this first choice but he admitted to Nuchim that there could be many other Boston passengers in Bremerhaven who would compete for the jobs. He also confided to Nuchim that while all immigrant jobs at the yard were classified as "laborer," he knew that Nuchim's number-crunching prowess would eventually qualify him for "office status." Later that day, Mendel promised to tutor him in "office" vernacular while on board ship.

Velvel Niedl's older brother Melech had emigrated three years before and was working at a job with, of all things, a toy manufacturer, as a salesman. Velvel had thoroughly liked everything his brother had written about life in the smaller town of Quincy. It even had an active *shul,* which the successful merchant Leib Grossman had established. Coincidentally, Melech was living in a room on Stewart Street, just a few doors from the corner Grossman House, which generously provided temporary sanctuary for all Jewish immigrant workers under the HIAS provisioning contract with the shipyard. In Melech's last letter home he mentioned that there were openings available with the ship-builder, and now Castleman had offered the final confirmation. Velvel happily leaped up to snatch the opportunity. Said Velvel instructively, "Melech should know...Kwin-Zee, not Kvin-Zee or Kvin-Cee."

Nuchim, Menachem Katz, Mayer Bernstein and Yitzhok Myerz had quickly followed Velvel's lead. Sholem, observing these goings-on was moved into a snap decision also. Everything was working out quite well. *Beshert vet zein beshert!*

"Building boats, Yak. That sounds very exciting to me. I know exactly nothing about such things; but I think I will like it, the pay is substantial, and there will be Fusgeyer comrades standing beside me every day. I hope they will let the *chazzanim* sing while they work! Heh! Heh! What more can a poor Birlader *Yidl* ask?"

Aside from the speedster, though, no one else changed their destinations from New York to Boston to build boats in Quincy, although there were a few sign-ups for the new U.S. Naval Shipyard facility in Brooklyn.

Ready to march along the Oranienburgerstrasse to exit Berlin, only Franz Schechter and his Alliance office staff, and the affable HIAS man were standing by to see the Fusgeyers off. It was a far cry from the joyous turnouts in Praha, Budapest, Debrecen, Sighet, Znojmo, Bacau, and any number of the cities, towns and villages on the long trail, but they certainly didn't exactly expect the *Moishe Yidden*—the Grunings and their ilk—to pay any attention to their departure. In truth they were probably pleased to see more of the eastern rabble leaving Berlin. Maybe it was the brazen sight of the unfurled *Mogen Dovid* that kept them away, or the tooting Palastrant trumpet, or the drum beating of Asher Leibovich. Then again it could have been just plain apathy on the part of a Jewry that had sunk into the creature comforts of complete assimilation, and wanted to avoid any reminders of the *Judefrage*. After all, it didn't pertain to them personally. Even a child knows that if you don't look at something, don't touch it or let it touch you, it will go away. Someday, it will just go away.

None of this took away one iota of the sheer fun and joy for the Fusgeyers when Mordecai was about to give the signal to begin. Suddenly, an overly enthusiastic Alliance stenographer ran into the street to present him with a petite bouquet of purple pansies and a squeezing embrace. Giggling and squealing, the flaming redhead proceeded to spend the next few minutes hugging every one of the fifty-seven stalwarts, including the *shleppers*, rendering the likes of Simmy Fiedelman and the comic Mayer Kelemer uncharacteristically speechless...with mouths agape. Not so with the reliable Itzy who announced to all in his cackling stage voice, after the display of affection, which he had held closer and longer than anyone else, "Why should I leave Berlin! Tell me, please, why should I leave such delicious love behind?"

Sendehr and Zed-Zed had planned a route that would parallel the main road to Hamburg, rather than the highway itself. They would walk along the Spree Canal, through the city of Spandau, the marshlands of Mittelmark, and meet up with the River Elbe at Havelberg. There, they would opt for the south bank minor road. No foreseeable geographical barriers ahead. No major cities to cope with. Hopefully, nothing out of the ordinary.

One reality became abundantly clear as soon as they had marched out of Spandau, leaving its eerie looking castle behind them. They were not alone.

All along the road, swarms of immigrants headed west—families of five, groups of ten and more, individuals, pairs—and all noticeably in pathetic shape. In a series of conversations it turned out that they were Sheunenviertel refugees who had finally scored with one of the relief agencies and were now plodding onward to the port at Hamburg. A young couple told Sendehr that all of these walkers had taken money in lieu of railroad vouchers, preferring to walk so they could hear the additional coins jingling in their pockets. The particular aid agency, based in Amsterdam, had also arranged for each to have the required possession of $25 American (equivalent in German marks) waived at the ports. This had obviously taken a supreme effort in political gymnastics.

The mere sight of the freshly laundered *Mogen Dovid* flying in the soft summer breezes reduced many of them to tears of pride and joy...especially the few Romanians, who were from the Austro-Hungarian border town of Radautz. Most had heard Fusgeyer stories before, and now here they were in the flesh. One of the older women threw here arms around Zed-Zed, kissed him, thanking him profusely for being their guardian angel...a role that the schedule master vigorously denied, with a grin.

Mordecai's rigid policy of not taking on those with questionable papers would be difficult to enforce on this road where they expected to encounter hundreds of migrants walking to the ports. He gave the rare order to close ranks. It was necessary to do so, but he certainly didn't enjoy having to do it. It would be this way from here on. The fifty-seven Fusgeyers would weave in and out of long strings of refugees on the narrow road, in order to keep reasonably intact.

Branko and the Golubs periodically tried to do a bit of traffic control, but with little success. In a veridical sense, these gaunt scarecrows, who had suffered the harsh indignities of the Pale only to fall into yet another quagmire in the Scheunenviertel, just stared ahead. They paid little or no attention to orders, suggestions or admonishments, ignoring the lush beauty of the verdure—a unique marshland with a colorful variety of birds, grasses, ponds and streams—that filled both sides of the lane. One would be hard pressed to believe that just kilometers back they had left the outlying districts of one of the world's largest and most modern cities—but the sunken eyes of these self-exiles only looked dead ahead. They were going to the ports, at last. *Boruch Hashem! Omayn*, they would utter, again and again.

On the first night, near the picture-book town of Nauen on the Canal, Mordecai's resolve shattered completely. Yes, for good reason he had a firm policy regarding strangers joining the troop; but how could he ask the few pitiful stragglers to move away from the campsite? Two families from the Pale town of Domachevo on the River Bug (Boog), numbering eight adults with a combined brood of nine joined them that evening. They had little in the way of edibles or potables, and three of the older children were barefooted. Mordecai, everyone's eyes upon him, bade them an embarrassed welcome.

Maidele and Zed-Zed took the three children to see what they could put together for foot coverings. Gershon gestured to the other children, all under eleven or twelve years of age, and proceeded to do a cursory examination of each, dispensing medicines as required, before offering the same for the adults as well.

Rivka and Esther quickly made the rounds to gather up any spare clothing afforded by their comrades. They accumulated much in the way of trousers, shirts, skirts, jerkins, singlets, socks, shawls, and blouses, sweaters and coats, and gave them to the destitute recipients, with the help of Chaike, Tsippy and Pessel. As warm as it was, even the heavier items were tearfully appreciated.

Simmy graciously distributed a variety of food items for the evening meal to the heads of each family. They had not seen so much food since leaving Domachevo, aside from the soups of the *Hilfsverein* kitchen in Berlin.

Mendel gave the eldest, the *zaydeh* Reb Borochofsky, the honor of *davening mincha-maarev*. Later, by the glow of the campfires, the four *chazzanim* and the Fusgeyer instrumentalists provided some light musical entertainment, ending with the comedians and the somber guests of honor finally relaxed and laughed as they hadn't in a long, long time.

All of this occurred without so much as a word of suggestion between Mordecai and anyone else. While it all appeared as though they were quite used to the drill of accommodating others, it was entirely and utterly spontaneous. The deepest essence of brotherly love was at work on this midsummer's eve, in a tranquil grove of grayish spruce, by the levees of the Spree Canal.

A light rain had begun sometime during the early morning hours, sending those who had elected to sleep under the stars scurrying to the cart for a tent half. The better weather pundits slept on, dry and snug. Rivka and Esther gathered up the three youngest children, asleep with their parents under a torn umbrella, and placed them with the soundly sleeping Mendel under the Buchman tent covering. Esther moved in with Rivka and Pessel for what was left of sleep time.

At dawn, the July rain grew steadily heavier, the skies were a gloomy gray, and a creeping fog covered the canal. When it was time for the daily march to begin, the family Borochofsky, still in the midst of making preparations to leave, embraced Mordecai, Mendel, Zed-Zed and Sendehr, and reserved a special thanks for Rivka and Esther for their early morning kindness to their *kindelach.*

Though they were not expected to keep up with the much brisker 'geyer pace, Mordecai made it a point to announce that they would be most welcome to join up at the next projected stopover and break bread with them, no matter how late they arrived. Zed-Zed informed them that it would be about twenty-eight kilometers, just before the town of Friesack. Sendehr conferred with the men, explaining that when the railroad crossed the canal they should follow it just a few kilometers and keep an eye out for their encampment. He encouraged them by stating that with a late sun setting they could still arrive before dark at half the pace of the 'geyers.

It was at the exact moment when the grounds had been thoroughly cleaned and the group ready to embark that Rivka and Esther cornered Mordecai and his cadre. A hushed discussion went on for only a brief minute or two at most. Receiving unanimous nods of consent, the charming young femmes of Birlad walked over to the *shleppers* of the day, whispered their idea to them, and again, won nods of consent. From there, arm-in-arm they jauntily strode to the Borochofskys, chatted for a few seconds, and for the third time, nods of consent had seized the day. No need for the three undernourished ragamuffins to walk twenty-eight kilometers when transportation was available. Eh? Madamoiselle Bernhardt herself couldn't have topped this performance.

The good will quickly spread to the entire troop when they saw and heard what was taking place. First, Mordecai's invitation to the Borochofskys, and secondly, the temporary custody of the little ones, for the lack of a better term.

The resulting "feel good" mood fended off the encroaching fog, and a renewed bounce sharpened everyone's steps as the trekkers sloshed through the rain puddles, the little tykes squealing with joy as they rode atop the cart, at long last on their way to a future...where before, there had been none.

The corrugated metal-roofed, gingerbread Hansel and Gretel dollhouse that served as Friesack's railroad station was for some reason built more than a kilometer from the town itself, which the tracks noticeably bypassed. Perhaps the good citizens had rallied against the six or seven whistle-tooting Berlin-Hamburg trains, westbound and eastbound, that would have caused coal smoke and ear-splitting noise to annoy the residents, the merchants and the shoppers. This mirrored a rebellion that was in progress wherever the "iron horse" trod. By now, there were precious few regions anywhere in the world that didn't know of its many virtues, as well as its potential detriments.

A young man standing in front of the station where he had just alighted from the westbound hailed Sendehr, on his way from the campsite to Friesack to mail his weekly synopsis to Rabbi Nachman. He carried a tripod topped by a bulky camera-in-a-box, and what looked like a large pad of yellow paper tucked under his arm. He also handled a small gripsack, its leather strap slung over his shoulder.

In a decidedly Americanized "Yankee Yiddish" the stranger in the straw boater asked, "Say there, do you happen to be one of the Fusgeyers from Romania?" He was visibly relieved to hear Sendehr answering in Yiddish, rather than the more guttural German.

"Yes, we are camped beyond those hedgerows. And you are...?"

"Abe Cahan sent me from Berlin. I am one of his reporters back in New York and I've been attending the Publishers' Conference with him. Shmuel Cohn is the name. Shmuel Eli Cohn."

"Sendehr Efraim. Abe sent you? Way out here? For what, Shmuel?"

The two sat down on the lone wooden bench in front of the now empty station, and in minutes they were acting like old friends. Sendehr recalled Cahan off-handedly mentioning after their meeting at the American Embassy that he wanted to personalize the Fusgeyer story. Now he had sent this young reporter to interview some of the group in order to get the whys and wherefores of the mission. He was also prepared to take a series of photographs that would further enhance his personal narrative.

Cahan's *Forvitz* had, in just a few years, become the daily bread for the fast growing Jewish immigrant community in and around New York City. It was much more than a newspaper to every reader, his family and his neighbors. It was fodder for deep intellectual discussion, a veritable guidebook, a revered manual, and a holy catechism with unending debate material. While it was indeed used to wrap an occasional fish or *knish*, a *challah* or a pickle; one could also be sure that it was carefully read and re-read, and animatedly discussed and argued over by all parties before being relegated to this ignominious secondary use.

Abraham Cahan had phoned Schechter at the Alliance on Sunday, asking to speak with Mordecai, Mendel or Sendehr. Having been told that they had left earlier that same morning, the classic newspaperman was able to get their daily projected itinerary, which they had left with the Alliance office. From this, of course, Cahan was able to determine what their destination was each day and consequently felt comfortable in sending out young Cohn for some fieldwork.

Cohn, should the truth be known, was Cahan's sister's nephew, and he began his career as an errand runner for Cahan just five years back. His nose-for-news and winning personality made him an ideal candidate for the very low paying reporter's job within a few years. His challenging beat was Tammany Hall, where he served as Cahan's one and only newshound, and was by far the youngest on the block. Accordingly, everyone called him "The Kid," from the cigar-chomping Irish and Jewish politicians, to his many older colleagues, to the charwomen, porters and hackney drivers. "Well, well, here comes Abie's own, Shmuel Cohn," they would greet him in a singsong tone. But in the last few months before Abe thoroughly surprised him with an invitation to join him at the Berlin conference, "The Kid" scooped his fellow ink jockeys on three different occasions, beating out the sensationalist Pulitzer and Hearst papers, among others.

Although he was born in Lemberg/Lvov, and emigrated at the age of ten, his written Yiddish was excellent, if not a bit flowery, and highly favored by the readership. "Did you read Cohn today? Yeah, 'The Kid'—Cahan's Cohn. Great story!". Shmuel's English had developed nearly without a trace of Lemberg. He was of the rare bilingual breed at the time, comfortably conversant in either language. Additionally, he confessed to an elementary handle on "street Italian."

Abe Cahan knew his customers. Intimately well. They dearly loved the highly personal angle. Perhaps it was a folkloric *yenta* syndrome. His circulation increased dramatically when he began to cater to this hunger by soliciting personal correspondence which later became the *Bintel Briefs*, "The Bundle of Letters," in which readers contributed their heart-wrenching stories, problems, dilemmas of every variety, generating a published response from the busy Bundles' editor. Having already printed Max Nordau's story of the Fusgeyers, Cahan now wanted to continue it as sort of a symbolic immigration piece to answer the many questions.

Who are these kids? What kind of lives did they lead, and leave? Many say that they are mashiganahs, asking for trouble. Are they right? Why are they doing this? Things are takeh that bad? What can these pishers do about it?—and in a more personal, human interest approach—*Just what are they like? What are their hopes, their dreams, their innermost thoughts as they march across Europe? Do they write their families? Once a week maybe? Do they think about them? Are they homesick? What do they plan to do in America? How do they envision America, New York, Boston, etc.? What became of the Fusgeyers who already arrived? Have any gone back to Europe? How would they now advise other young people in the Pale, Romania, Poland?*

This, then, was young Shmuel Eli Cohn's assignment. From the editor himself.

"So you're the Sendehr Efraim the boss told me about. The writer who penned the notorious proclamation. I read Max Nordau's English version of it, which Abe had borrowed from him after Herzl's funeral. By the way, we were all saddened by that news. But, for what it's worth, I admire your technique. The *dayenu, Inkahss*. Great! I'm taken by it."

"Only if it gets results, Shmuel. Results!"

Shmuel Cohn's plan was to stay with the Fusgeyers for the next two or three days, interview a meaningful cross section of the group, take ample photographs, and catch a westbound at Dannenberg or Hitzacker, both of which were on the Fusgeyer route. He was on schedule to join Abe at Hamburg port where their Hamburg-America Line ship would leave for New York on the 20th. Most of the American conference attendees, including Riis and Steffens, were sailing with them. Meanwhile, Cohn verified Max's information that the long-suffering Pulitzer was going to remain in Germany, visiting three different health spas in Bavaria. He was desperate to find a cure for his chronic ear problem—not that it ever prevented him from engaging in royal battles with Bill Hearst!

"Are you sure that you want to walk more than a hundred kilometers with us?"

"When you work for Abe you're forced to do that every week. Too cheap to allow me a few cents to take a hack, or even the subway or trolley anywhere. Meanwhile, he drives one of those new motor machines." Both enjoyed a chuckle.

Shmuel walked with Sendehr to the postal building on the main street, chatting all the while. Here were two young men only a year apart, both incessant talkers and both incurable writers, both thirsting for knowledge, both building experiences, one a proud American Jew, the other about to be. No surprise there was instant kinship brewing here. Shmuel had even suggested that he introduce Sendehr to his vivacious eighteen-year-old sister, Dariel, but received an immediate wave off.

"Thank you, thank you, my dear Shmuel. But wait until you meet my Rivka and you'll soon see that I've spoken for and I'm spoken for, or whatever the terminology is in these serious matters of the heart. Heh! Heh!" And that, as they say, ended that.

On their way back to the campsite, Shmuel regaled Sendehr with story after story about the Kaiser. With a sharp eye and trained ear for such things, Shmuel had spent an exciting two weeks in Berlin, which included the satisfaction of just being at the Conference. The youngest attendee at that!

"You saw the atrocious *ahnenallee* at the Tiergarten, I'm sure. Kaiser Bill's cast of characters, Hohenzollern's all! Well, a *Tageblatt* writer showed me a copy of *Jugend*, one of the renegade anti-imperial magazines, full of humor, where an artist sketched the statues, replacing the heads with bottles of a popular mouth disinfectant. He told me that the magazine was forced to burrow underground deeper than ever before.

"Abe and I were invited to a dinner at the mansion of a wealthy Jewish industrialist, and Buffalo Bill was the guest of honor, along with three of his troupe including the Indian, Louis Whirlwind Horse—try that in proper Yiddish! Cody told us that the Kaiser is the best friend he has among all of the world's royalty he entertains. Said the cowboy,

'When I first met the Kaiser in the '80s he told me that his doctor once examined him and diagnosed a SMALL cold. The medical man was upbraided with the admonishment that it was a BIG cold, because anything about the Kaiser must be big.' Evidently the affinity between them, according to Cody, was largely due to the similarities of their first two names, which pleased them both. The Kaiser is Friedrich Wilhelm and the showman is William Frederick. Or as we would say in the States, Freddie William and William Freddie, or Fred Bill and Bill Fred. Take your pick, Sendehr. Or don't you care! You don't?"

With a smile, Sendehr responded with, "Speaking of names, Shmuel, how is it that you haven't Anglicized yours? Doesn't everyone? Even Abe, who no doubt was Avrum. Nearly every Birlader in America has a different name by now."

"Good question, friend. Deserves a good answer. I have been tempted during the ten years I've been there. Most Shmuels have become Sams or Samuels. The only Shmuels are to be found in the very orthodox, religious sects. When I got a little older and more comfortable with my Americanism, especially after Abe made me a reporter, I realized that there were numerous Sams working with *The Journal, The World, The Times* and even some of the Jewish papers, but there were absolutely no Shmuels. Why not be a little different? Unique. So I'm forever Shmuel. Shmuel Eli. Shmuel Eli Cohn. In English it's called, *what you sees is what you gets!*"

A pause followed, and then the reporter continued on with a question. "What about Sendehr? Do you have any thoughts?"

"I must say that we have all thought about such things. You'll soon meet a most extraordinary man who has been diligently teaching us English. In fact, I quite understood what you had just said about *'what I see I get'* thanks to this man. Well enough to know that there were grammatical mistakes in it. Heh! Heh! Mendel Buchman, our *lehrer*, has freely passed on so-called English 'nicknames' as well as English equivalents for all of our names. It has been a source of great fun and self-deprecating laughter. He tells me that Sendehr is of Russian derivation, a short name for Alexander, but is quick to admit he isn't exactly sure of it. So, at present I plan to go with Sender Efraim all the way. If I ever have a son, I'll name him Alexander. I like that name. Rivka does, too; but she has reservations because of the many Czars, *mumzerim*, by the same name. She, by the way, also plans to keep her name, as of now. On the other hand, Mendel is considering Melvin, Mordecai may go with Morton, Nuchim is leaning toward Nathan, Zed-Zed likes Sid, and our Velvels will probably become Williams, Bills, just like the great Cowboy Cody."

"Or the Kaiser, God forbid!"

With this last laugh, they walked into the encampment, and Sendehr began to put his new friend through the ritual of meeting the Birlader Fusgeyers. To begin with, they were all quizzically staring at them, wondering who the stranger in the straw hat, fashionable striped shirt and colorful red cravat might be. Before twilight set in many of them would be clamoring to be among the first interviewees...even some of the more religious who hadn't quite come to grips with picture taking yet, although none had refused the Max Nordau group photo request in Vienna. That age-old argument still required some hair splitting. Perhaps a *pilpul* session.

Shmuel Eli Cohn acquitted himself handsomely over the next three days. As Sendehr observed, the ingratiating manner of Mister Cohn could gain him entrance into any circle imaginable. He was one of those rare persons to whom one could not bring oneself to say "no." Abe Cahan had a prize package here, in Sendehr's humble estimation.

Shmuel was deeply touched by the Borochofsky children, taking an immediate liking to the youngest, five-year-old Yehuda Dov, lovingly labeled *der mazik* by Rivka. He used a goodly portion of film on the family and their little ones, and began writing a companion article about their plight and how ghastly their experiences on the road and in the infamous Scheunenviertel had been—until they met up with Mordecai and his Fusgeyers, that is.

By the time they reached the Hitzacker Depot, Cohn's sheets of yellow paper were filled from top to bottom, in the margins on each side. Of course, he couldn't get around to talking with everyone, and there were some who just didn't care to talk much. He had used all of his camera plates, and gave his home address and office telephone number to anyone who wanted it...and made doubly sure that Tsippy Eshman had it. It seemed to Sendehr that the reporter spent a rather inordinate amount of time "interviewing" the vivacious lassie. In return, she graciously gave the smitten one the address of her brother and sister-in-law in the Bronx where she would be staying, all the while successfully suppressing her little-girlish giggles.

Could it be that Shmuel had traveled over the Atlantic to find what he hadn't even been looking for? Rivka and Sendehr were as delighted as Tsippy. Tsippy from Mississippi. Or was it Tsippileh from Mississippileh? That night, don't think for a moment that the comedians didn't break into a rousing chorus of that little ditty!

Since it was only one o'clock when they had reached the Hitzacker Depot, Sendehr and Rivka decided to wait with Shmuel. His westbound was not due for two hours and there was so much more to talk over. The evening stopover for the contingent was less than three walking hours away, at Dahlenburg, so the couple could easily arrive there before dark. The depot was situated a short walk from the Elbe River where there was a beautifully manicured riverbank park—an idyllic spot to spend the afternoon.

Shmuel treated his two new friends to refreshments from the vendor's kiosk at the depot—frothy local lager for the boys and a fizzy cherry phosphate for Rivka. It could have been a park anywhere: three friends out for a stroll, a classic summer day, weeping willows, flowers everywhere in a riot of color, birds singing, the whitest of puffy clouds afloat in a God-painted azure sky. A picture of natural perfection in a land of programmed perfection, where all is not quite what it appeared to be.

Shmuel demonstrated an uncanny perceptiveness far beyond his few short years in the newspaper business whenever he forcefully articulated his broad knowledge, as he had done in many conversations during the three days prior. His comments to Sendehr, Mordecai and Mendel on the Maharal and Rabbi Blankfort mirrored Eli Nachman's response, chapter and verse. His opinions on Germany's *Judefrage*—while paralleling Sendehr's—also took into account the troubling similar situation to be found in New York with which he was all too familiar. He especially emphasized with the dichotomous actions of·the toplofty uptown German Jew perpetually looking down his nose in utter disgust at the Lower Eastside *ostjuden,* while contributing vast sums of money in a valiant effort to upgrade them; and the vocal and visible anti-immigrant, anti-Semitic attitudes of the average person on the streets of America, particularly where there was a large influx of ethnic cultures. All of this stood in stark contrast to the typically naive immigrant's view, which held a far more Pollyann-ish picture of a blissful life in America. Shmuel, not wanting to burst too many bubbles, thoughtfully tempered some of these statements during the interview process, but not for the more realistic Rivka and Sendehr.

Having listened intently to one of the conference's two keynote speakers, Jacob Riis, deliver "The American Press and the Problems of Integrating the Immigrant," Shmuel conveyed to his friends the thoughts of one of America's leading journalists and social reformers.

Matters that directly affected the Fusgeyers as they prepared to embark for life in America had been dealt with in a lengthy series of Riis articles in the *New York Sun,* and in more depth in his book *How The Other Half Lives,* published in 1890. It was a vividly visceral study of tenement living conditions, and for the decade following the prolific writing of the crusading Danish immigrant it managed to keep the horrors of New York's immigrant slums in middle-class America's line of sight. So much so, actually, that the

Police Commissioner of New York in the early '90s—none other than future President Theodore Roosevelt—profoundly influenced by the aforementioned book, led the way for tenement reform.

"Now here's the good news. I haven't wanted to say anything until it actually happens; but Riis promised Abe that he would personally send the English version of the Nordau article, along with a translation of the article I will have done by the time we get to New York, to his good friend Teddy at the White House. He told Abe to make sure I included your bombshell proclamation, Sendehr; and he reminded us that Roosevelt had already tried to intercede two years ago with a strong letter reprimanding the Romanians, sent by his Secretary of State—not much of a response then, but maybe he'll agree to light another fire under their *tuchuses* with these stories.

"Riis hinted to Abe that he would even consider suggesting that a special investigative commission be formed, consisting of the signatory nations of the Berlin Treaty, to be chaired by a Bob Watchorn, or someone of his ilk. Everyone knows Riis has been exceptionally close to the President since his days in New York City.

"You'll also be happy to know that the boss was able to convince Ambassador Tower to send a personal note to the President covering your now infamous meeting. What do you think of that?"

Sendehr and Rivka were pleased but speechless, and before either could offer their thanks, the loquacious one sped onward.

"Honestly, though, our President is so involved with both domestic and critical foreign affairs at this time that he may not respond. That Russkie thing again, you know.

"But back to what I was saying about the conference speakers. Lincoln Steffens, the co-keynoter, has spent so much time visiting the Lower Eastside many take him to be a convert, which he is not. Talking on the same subject as Riis, he projected more of a *Yiddishe tateh's* usual concern; stressing that those emigrating should begin thinking of intense, continuing self-education before they even board ship. He spoke as if personally addressing each of us, imploring the Europeans to counsel all those contemplating emigration to learn the language of their adopted country, read profusely, be prepared, never stop the learning process. Your Mendel is doing a remarkable job of this, all right! Steffen's book, *Shame of the Cities*, has recently been published, and he tells us it will be widely distributed in French, German and English throughout Western Europe. Another revealing condemnation of city blight."

Shmuel had also learned that Steffens, managing editor of *McClure's Magazine*, had previously edited a maverick paper, *The Commercial Advertiser*, and in the late 1890s numbered among his reporters one Abraham Cahan. Abe would often tell Shmuel that he "sharpened his trade at the hands of an expert like Lincoln Steffens," and that "five years of covering the Lower Eastside for his paper most likely fashioned me into a *flaneur par excellence.*"

"Whatever in God's name that is? Heh-heh! Fact is, Abe explained it to me at the time. It's fancy, shmantsy French for ' purposeful strolling.' Yeah! I suppose it could apply to a reporter appearing to be aimlessly strolling among the sea of pushcarts on Orchard Street, but in reality he's looking for something newsworthy to write. It could also refer to an artist walking in the same manner, but is actually looking for a certain subject to paint. So, there! We learn something every day, whether we need it or not!"

Listening to these eclectically illuminating reports from the field, Sendehr rekindled his hope of eventually working with a newspaper or magazine. He would do anything! Errand boy. Sweeper. Inkwell filler. Pencil sharpener! But first things first. He simply had to learn the language well enough to write. Then again, there was always the *Forvitz*, the *Tageblatt* and the few other Yiddish-language papers. He hesitated to ask Shmuel to intercede with Abe, deciding to leave that for his own personal visit once settled in New York. He was determined more than ever to build a career in the journalistic arena. Where and when were the only questions left to answer.

The subject of refugee conditions in Germany and in the border towns of Eastern Europe came up when Rivka asked Shmuel if he had been to the Sheunenviertel. "Friends, I, too, visited the worst parts of the Sheunenviertel last week and it was very disturbing. I rent a midget's room in the tenement district of the East Side and believe you me it is a cushy cloud in heaven compared to what I saw there. No matter where you end up in New York, as unacceptable as it might be, just compare it to the Scheunenviertel, or even to the temporary camps along the eastern borders we have all heard about."

"We'll try to remember that, Shmuel. But, tell me, now that you have completed the interviews and will probably write your story while bobbing about on the high seas, who gave you the most interesting comments of all? Aside from Tsippileh, of course!"

He paused for a moment, slightly off balance, and then expertly parried. "Good question, Rivkaleh! Not so easy to answer. I thoroughly enjoyed talking to each and every one I was able to find the time for. The cooperation was nothing short of excellent and I had the feeling that everyone enjoyed the experience—even you two. Right?"

"*Gott in himmel*, Cohn! You're more diplomatic than our own diplomat. You remember him—Menchem Berman! Get serious now, pretty boy, and answer my question, Mister New York Reporter of Shining Repute," thrusted the Queen of Retorts, with the flashing smile.

Listening to this repartee while lounging on the lush grass, hands behind his head, Sendehr was thoroughly enjoying this delightful interlude. O, how he wished it could last a while longer after the train departed, and perhaps drift into a delicious reverie, with his *zeesa* on the grass beside him. *If only we didn't have a three-hour hike ahead of us*, mused the dreamer.

"Okay, okay. I sincerely mean everything I said in answer to your highly provocative question. However, *der groisseh soldat* is positively captivating. He'll never get lost in America, or anywhere else for that matter. But there were so many in second place that…"

Both Sendehr and Rivka had privately guessed the answer. It was quite obvious to them. Young Mister Cohn went on, of course, to give high marks to each and every interviewee, placing Tsippy in a private category before delicately changing the subject.

"We have a dinner scheduled with Albert Ballin, the head of Hamburg-America Line, the night before we embark. He invited all of us Americans who are sailing on the 20th, about thirty in all, including a few fellows from Montreal, Winnipeg and Toronto, a Cuban journalist and two Mexican publishers. Fidel Mendez, the Cuban, is an interesting chap. Kind of a blowhard. Claims he fought alongside Roosevelt and his Rough Riders on San Juan Hill. I'll have to check that one out."

He described Ballin as a Jew who was a respected confidant of Kaiser Wilhelm and one of the present-day "court Jews" in every respect. His Hamburg-America Line had brought high honors to a nation that was fighting for that elusive acceptance among the world leaders. Courting the members of the Fourth Estate was obviously a propitiously correct move by the politically astute shipping magnate.

"That brings up a point, Shmuel. I've not asked you this before, but considering that the *Forvitz* is still a struggling business, according to your boss, how is it that he was able to spend so much money for two of you to attend the conference?" Rivka was most definitely in an interrogative posture, putting Shmuel to the test once again.

"Another good question from my inquisitor. Lady Torquemada, I presume? Sendehr, this *maidel* will no doubt be your eyes and ears when you are seeking leads for your stories. Your personal *flaneur*, old boy! There's an answer for everything, my dear Rivkeleh, and here it comes.

"Abe was having dinner with his former editor, Lincoln Steffens, who announced that he was one of the speakers at the conference. Abe mentioned that he would love to attend just to show that Yiddish newspapers were becoming a strong voice in America. He was certain that it would be a hardship for even the oldest and largest Anglo-Jewish papers from Boston, New York, Philadelphia and Cincinnati to afford to go, let alone the few struggling Yiddish-language representatives.

"Within a week, our office was visited by a person in a footman's uniform who delivered an envelope containing not one, but two round-trip steamship tickets, and a postal draft for one-thousand dollars. No name anywhere, just a typed note merely stating, *'The Yiddish language is drenched with tears, and it is too rich to be silenced. Please go to Berlin and make your presence known. May God be with you.'*

"When my flabbergasted boss telephoned Steffens to see if he knew anything about this gift from *Gan Eden*, he met with a stone wall. All Steffens would say was, 'I suppose I rang the right bells for you, Abe. See you on board, old friend.'"

"Did Abe ever figure it out?"

"He did, Sendehr. Almost immediately. Remember that we're talking about a newspaperman with damn few equals. He was aware that Lincoln Steffens enjoyed hobnobbing with the uptown Yidden—or as your Branko named them in Berlin, *Moishe Yidden*—from whom he had been singularly effective in soliciting significant donations for Lower Eastside charities. To them, Steffens was a rather nice *goy* who could be trusted—a real '*tikkun olam* believer.' To Abe, 'ringing the right bells' translated into the Fifth Avenue and Park Avenue mansions of the Warburgs, the Seligmans, the Loebs, the Kahns, the Lewisohns or the Schiffs. Unfamiliar names to you, I'm sure; but suffice it to say that these families historically referred to their coterie as "our crowd."

Young Mister Cohn, nose tilted up in the air, allowed the word picture to set in for a brief moment before continuing. Sendehr and Rivka grasped the graphic implication, and gave a knowing smile, as Shmuel continued.

"Carrying his deductive sleuthing one step further, Abe knew that only one of that crowd ever insisted on complete anonymity whenever giving a gift. The venerable Jacob Schiff.

Among all of the others, Schiff was a long-time favorite of Steffens, and Abe was convinced that this act of such superlative generosity came directly from the mahogany-paneled drawing room at 965 Fifth Avenue. It turned out he was right. How he verified it, I'm not at all sure, but you can bet that he did. That's my leader, bless the irascible Mr. Cahan!"

Time had just about run out; the usually on time westbound was due in five minutes, and final farewells were in order. Shmuel picked up his tripod, camera and gripsack, but the vocal chords didn't stop vibrating for a moment.

"Give my love to Tsipporah. I just know I will see her again. What do you think, Rivka?"

"Unless she meets someone better looking, richer and more intelligent on board ship, lover boy." For some reason this did not seem to resonate well with boy reporter.

Noticing, Sendehr quickly chimed in with, "*Daigeh nisht*, good friend. I know Tsippy cannot wait until she sees you in New York. I couldn't help notice the looks she gave you when she said goodbye a few hours ago. Otherwise, why did she march along mumbling, Tsippy Cohn, Tsippy Cohn, Tsippy Cohn?"

Shmuel's hearty laugh showed that Sendehr had erased his unwarranted doubts. Rivka's grin proved she was only joking. *My own personal female Itzy Gelman*, thought Sendehr.

Shmuel slipped in some parting words, "Remember my offer, *kindelach*. I know a fast-talking rabbi who will do your knot tying for a bottle of *schnapps*... the funeral home on my street doubles as a wedding palace!"

With this, and the ensuing laughs, hugs and kisses, the whistle tooting Berlin-Hamburg train could be heard and seen, steaming 'round the bend.

Knowing they would meet again soon, in America, painted the scene more on the sweet side, less on the sorrowful...a most welcome change.

20

ENCOUNTERS: THE PORT

The happy and the powerful do not go into exile.
from *Democracy in America.*
Alexis De Tocqueville, 1835

Give me your tired, your poor,
Your huddled masses yearning to breathe free,
Send these, the homeless, tempest-tost to me,
I lift my lamp beside the golden door!

Emblazoned on the base of The Statue of Liberty,

from a poem by Emma Lazarus

The original plan to bypass the city of Hamburg, en route to Bremerhaven, took the 'geyers away from another one of the main highways where throngs of refugees continued to head for Hamburg's port. More of the *Moishe Yidden's groisseh farlegenheit*, their big embarrassment, overfilled wagons, were scattered in walking groups, and supplemented periodic trainloads. Day in and day out. Much smaller numbers of them named Bremerhaven as their ultimate destination. When would this massive movement ever end? "When Czar Nicolai chants his *haftorah*, with King Carol and Father Mihai standing on the *bimah*," concluded one Itzeleh, the Jester.

It was here, just outside the substantial city of Luneburg, that they would wait for the Borochofskys in order to return the three "wards" who had enjoyed the comforts and fun of the cart for the better part of a week. Zed-Zed calculated that the family would probably be approximately two hours behind, so they would just have to stand by until they arrived. Mordecai planned to have them join in for a leisurely midday meal as a friendly parting gesture before they went their separate ways.

From this point, the family was only forty kilometers from Hamburg's port, and their quarantine period wasn't required to begin until the following Tuesday, July 27th. The relief agency had promised some shelter before they went to the dockside medical barracks for the required ten-day isolation period.

Everything was comfortably on schedule for both the Birladers and the most indebted Borochofsky family. While Sendehr laid out his maps to point out the evening stop to Mordecai, they calculated that Bremerhaven lay 130 kilometers to the northwest, and should be reached as planned on Thursday, July 29th. In Berlin, Joe Castleman had explained that the quarantine period at that port usually went into effect no less than ten days prior to anyone's sailing date. He had also verified their understanding that both Hamburg and Bremerhaven were not the safest places in the world to spend idle time. His warnings registered clearly with Mordecai and Branko, and they thought of them now as they reviewed important security measures. The cart would no longer be a factor. They had long ago agreed to dispose of it in Bremerhaven, either by sale or abandonment. It will have served an invaluable function and Mordecai had no qualms about recommending the practical use of a two-wheeled conveyance and the same *shlepping* pattern to any future Fusgeyers.

In the emerald green meadowland off to the side of the road, the Fusgeyers bid a fond farewell to the Family Borochofsky. Rivka, Esther, and in fact, the entire troop gathered round the three little ones who had been entrusted to their good care. The pet of the pack, Yehuda Dov, had charmed everyone, including some of the more somber, even

Heshy Rosen and Kalman Fuchs, who were still trying to cope with their acute longings for home. The *mazik* had a way of endearing himself to everyone in sight, and now with the benefit of nearly a week of improved nutrition, his piercing brown eyes sparkled and his cherubic little face shone brightly. He had become especially attached to Esther, and both had a difficult time in parting from one another.

Yehuda's frail mother fully understood, as did the parents of the other two children, and all were demonstratively appreciative for all the kind care and attention their children had received. Yehuda's father had stayed behind in Domachevo with his two older sons to keep his sporadic work as a wheelwright, until such time when he could save enough funds to join them in America. Meanwhile, the mother and her Yehuda Dov would live with the *zaydeh* and *bubbeh* wherever they settled. This story line was the norm, the rule, not the exception, among the hundreds of thousands of those who had emigrated from Europe. Someone stayed behind. Always someone. Did all of these stories end happily-ever-after in joyful reunions? Fairy tales had no place in the tumultuous Europe of 1904.

* * *

That night, Sunday, July 25, 1904 (22 Tamuz, 5664), camped next to a bubbling rock-bedded brook on the far side of the spire-dotted town of Brackel, Esther and Mendel announced that they were going to be parents. When? January. *Siman tov un mazel tov* reverberated through the warm night air. They were too close to town for any loud music noise, but there was immediate embracing, kissing, backslapping, and *l'chaim* toasts all around. This precious unborn child had found fifty uncles and five aunties in one fell swoop.

The teacher beamed from ear to ear, and the pregnant mama blushed and never looked more radiant. The unborn would be born in America, and for that everyone gave thanks to God, with a thunderous *omayn!*

Over the next few days, since most of the wagon and walking groups headed for Hamburg, emigrant traffic all but disappeared from the country road Zed-Zed and Sendehr had carefully mapped out. Those people of "great embarrassment" to the *Moishe Yidden* of Germany had appreciably thinned out for the time being. There would be more. In time, many more, for years to come.

The voice of the locals in all of the small towns and villages had noticeably changed since leaving Berlin. The sight of the Fusgeyers and their Star of David flag flying, weaving among the long streams of refugees en route to the ports, elicited very few nationalistic shouts of "Germany for Germans" and the like. Instead, there came the more personalized, farewell taunts of "Goodbye Jews," "America can have you!", "The Indians are waiting for your scalps, Jews!", "We hope your goddamn ship sinks!", "Keep going Jew bastards, A-mer-ika is that way!" These comments were hurled at them from the usual perpetrators: the tavern dwellers, the brat-pack children, the factory workers on their way to and from work, the draymen, and the unemployed.

These disparaging exclamations meant little to the *ostjuden*, and less to the Fusgeyers. Inured since early childhood, by now they took it all in stride. Literally. Not missing a step in their gait. Every now and then, some of the younger Birladers, led by their hypersensitive ringleader, Avi the Actor, would heckle back with some choice scatology accompanied by anatomically obscene gestures. As expected, Simmy and Itzy were also known to join in the bravado. In general, the cadre frowned upon this, mostly looking the other way, but Shmuel Cohn had made it quite clear to them that America offered more of the same. Perhaps a bit more subtle. Perhaps again, not.

Crossing the narrow bridge spanning the muddy Hamme-Oste Canal, the first road sign the trekkers had seen in two days announced *Bremerhaven, 35km.* The next encampment, scheduled for the village of Beverstedt on a tributary of the River Weser, meant that the last segment of their ambulant journey would take them into the port by that next afternoon. That night, following Mendel's English class, Mordecai thought it was a good time to address the full gathering. He filled his pipe with good Dutch tobacco, his one luxury, and began:

"*Kindelach*, as you all know and must feel, the end of our long trek is within sight tonight. Here in the quiet of this beautiful summer's evening, I, as your proud and humble leader, want to express my deepest thanks to each and every one of you from the depths of my heart. For what, you may ask? For you, and who you have proven to be these last four months—my most courageous and loyal comrades—fulfilling our common and noble purpose.

"We have come across Europe together, friends. It has at times been difficult, but, in truth, it has been much easier and more pleasant than I ever imagined. And that's because of all of you. You've teamed up to make it that way."

At this juncture, Mordecai Anieloff repeated the question he had asked whimsically during one of the evening entertainments, "What will each of you be doing a year from now?" For the next half-hour not a Fusgeyer was omitted as Mordecai, in a humorous, yet serious and personalized commentary spilled forth his predictions for their lives in America. And, he wasn't very far off.

* * *

He was done. This had been Mordecai's way of acknowledging everyone. He saved Branko for last, for good reason, which became obvious when he was invited to say a few well chosen words after receiving the praise heaped upon his broad shoulders by his commander. The *soldat* was clearly ill-at-ease, but his vital message came through as intended.

"This is not the time for complacency. We cannot afford to drop our vigilance in any way, comrades. Tomorrow, we will be entering a world into which none of you has ever ventured forth. The iniquitous world of the port city. It is different than most anything we have encountered thus far. To illustrate, allow me to share some of my very own experiences while in the Emperor's army..."

Mordecai had been planning this presentation since the day that Castleman and the Alliance director Franz Schechter had warned he and Menachem Berman of certain ugly conditions at the German ports. Nothing very new, because of the past worrisome reports from the other Birlad contingents, but Hamburg and Bremerhaven were consistently labeled as chaotic, alarmingly fraught with serious and potentially dangerous scenarios. He had decided to postpone it until they were nearing Bremerhaven, not wanting to alarm his people too far in advance.

"It is only a matter of being forewarned, and therefore, forearmed," assured the ex-soldier, using his most confident tones. " I want every one of you to know that Trieste and Fiume on the Adriatic coast had very dark reputations when I was on temporary duty at these ports. Mendel can tell you that he saw with his own eyes what I am about to discuss with you in detail, and he constantly heard all of the warnings when he was a student in Salonika and a teacher in Athens.

"But, here is the difference, and the reason why we are bringing this to your attention here and now. Listen closely, please. Bremerhaven and Hamburg are far worse than all of the others. Why? Because the German police and military seem conveniently to abdicate when unpleasant things are flourishing in their very midst. Emigrant trash is fair game. Whether we want to acknowledge this or not, we are included."

A steady buzz had begun by this time. The tension was obvious, but no word of disarming humor was forthcoming from Simmy, Itzy, Mayer Kelemer or anyone else. They knew when Mordecai was serious. Branko always was, for the most part.

"So, *nu*, what exactly is it we're facing, *soldat*? You're keeping us in suspense, y'know."

Bezalel Udler's question was a fair one, and it was also most likely what everyone else was thinking by this time.

"Bez, I'm getting to it. Hold on there."

Branko took a long drink from his canteen and continued, fifty-six comrades rapt in close attention.

"When we enter the city of Bremerhaven, according to all reports, it will be swarming with every kind of thief, thug, scam artist, degenerate, *zhoolik un farbrekher*...all scum. It has been reported for years now that the two main German ports have attracted more concentrated crime than all of the rest of the country combined. Why? The destitute emigrant, even if he has only a scant amount of money, is easy prey. Thousands pour into the ports every month from all over Europe, as you will soon see for yourselves. And, as I've said, there is virtually no conscientious law enforcement to deal with any criminal activity. Anarchy reigns unchallenged.

"Bremerhaven, and more specifically in and around its dock area, is utterly lawless territory for these consummately impudent scofflaws. They are quite free to roam around and commit any and all types of crime, and none of the naive victims know how or where to file a complaint, and even if they wanted to, there is no place there that can or would help them. The situation in Hamburg is the same, where even larger numbers of emigrants wait for a ship.

"But there is a far more egregious movement afoot that demands our undivided attention, our wits and our foresight, and this is the most important of all. Mordecai and I are very concerned, but we can deal with it effectively if we follow strict orders."

It was there and then that the Fusgeyers of Birlad first heard a word that was heretofore distinctly foreign to them: "shanghai." This universal seaman's term signified the kidnapping and impressing of itinerants, drunks, sojourners, wayfarers, *luftmenschen*, and most commonly these days, naïve emigrants awaiting passage. This onerous activity had long been the scourge of port cities throughout the world. Branko again mentioned those ports wherein he had personal experience, and added those he had heard about: Marseille, Livorno (Leghorn, Italy), Constantinople, and most notably Tangiers, which was reputed to be among the most dangerous of them all in this regard. Only since the unprecedented enormous increases in emigration from all European countries had it become a problem of such magnitude in the German port cities.

Relief and assistance organizations such as HIAS, the *Hilfsverein*, the Labor Alliances, the Alliance Universelle and various Western European human rights groups had estimated unofficially that more than 1,000 separately recorded "shanghai" incidents had occurred in the years since the century began. More than four hundred in 1903 alone.

In only a very few cases had the subjects eventually returned from their shipboard "imprisonment." The female traveler was not at all immune to these and other incidents of outright unlawful detention. Castleman had told Mordecai and Menachem heart-wrenching stories of several who had been kidnapped and sold into some sort of "white slavery," and he had hastened to add that these were not at all rare, either. In fact, some of the wealthier members of the teeming Moroccan Jewish communities in the *mellahs* of Tangiers, Mogador, Casablanca, Fes and Marrakech were unwittingly drawn into a web of deceit.

Lied to by the diabolical purveyors of human flesh that these were orphans of the Czar's pogroms, who needed employment as maidservants, the Moroccan Jews honestly thought that they were doing a *mitzvah*, by "purchasing" the girls for inordinate sums. Faced with an insurmountable language barrier, since their new "employers" only spoke Arabic or French, the poor innocents had little alternative but to stay on. Again, very few if any ever found their way back to their families, which by then would have been in America, mourning their terrible loss, not ever knowing the fate of their daughters. This tragic tale struck a most powerful blow, even as Branko synoptically diluted it in order to soften its effect on the distaff side of the Fusgeyer family.

Meanwhile, Branko continued, it was important for everyone to know exactly what the dangers ahead would mean to their well being. The Bremerhaven and Hamburg City Police completely ignored the social agencies' "shanghai" reports, while the assigned port security staff passed off the phenomenon by classifying each incident as "probably voluntary," or saying that "there is no acceptable evidence," or "without written family complaints there is nothing we can do about such allegations." The family was usually too intimidated to put anything in writing for fear that authorities would strip them of their passage documents and lower their priority ranking. The relief agencies suspected that in many of these tragic cases, sacrifice of the one daughter for the safety and America-bound transportation of the entire family could have tragically been the prevailing rationale.

Mordecai stepped in at the appropriate time to address the solutions to these very real potential problems.

"It is quite simple, friends. I have made a unilateral decision based on everything Menachem Berman and I heard direct from HIAS and the Labor Alliance. I have combined this information with all that Branko just shared with you, and also reports that Sendehr analyzed from past Fusgeyer groups, on the pitfalls of Bremerhaven and Hamburg.

"Firstly, from the minute we enter the town of Bremerhaven until the time we board ship, no one is ever to be alone anywhere. Is that clear to every one of you?"

All heads nodded in solemn agreement. Those who waited for a flippant remark from the usual suspects heard none.

"Secondly, we will isolate ourselves even before our quarantine period begins. The only other Birlad group to embark from Bremerhaven was last year's, and Shmulkeh Tomashevsky had written of a bluff overlooking the River Weser on the northside of the docks, where they, too, had remained until going into quarantine. Sounds good to me. We don't want to be lost among the masses strewn all over the port. That's only asking for trouble.

"Thirdly, no one will leave that area, except for Simmy,

who will have to shop and *shnorr,* in order to supplement our current non-perishable food supplies to take on board. We must be self-sufficient, especially after some of the reports we have had concerning the shipboard food, or lack thereof. Simmy, are you listening? Good. Branko and two of the Golubs will escort you at all times during these missions. They have my permission to take the three pistols and carry them, concealed, on these occasions, with Branko in absolute charge. We cannot afford even the slightest indiscretion, *soldat.* I hope you hear me well, Brothers Karamazov!"

This last quip lightened some of the faces before him. Mordecai had begun to feel that he and Branko had been messengers of such gloom and doom that it would be wise to soften the proceedings, though only a few had understood the Dostoyevsky reference.

"Fourth point; ladies; attention, please. Rivka, Pessel, Tsippy, Chaike, Maidel and Esther will not leave the campsite for any reason, nor shall any of the others, and the six of you are to remain within the campsite perimeter, never on the edges. I know I'm sounding like a *yenteh,* but I am determined to walk on board with fifty-six of my Fusgeyers all in good health. Do not deny me my mission. Please."The young women returned in kind their leader's wide, assuring smile.

"And finally, the town of Bremerhaven, except for our walking through it tomorrow afternoon to get to our bivouac site, is entirely off limits. Only our Defense Committee and Simmy, as I mentioned before, will be allowed to go back into town. How many times? We'll see how great a bounty the King of the *Shnorrers* finds on his final assignment!

"Branko, Zed-Zed and I have already laid out a solid around-the-clock guard schedule. All along the way, Branko has personally trained Yankel, Yoni and Yossi in weaponry procedures for this eventuality, so one of them will always be standing, armed, alongside those of you who will be assigned to sentinel duties.

"I know I'm moving away from my more passive policy that has gotten us this far, but for the two weeks we're in Bremerhaven we will diligently pursue the most vigilant security. Do we think anything untoward will beset us? No. Will we be ready if it should? Yes, you can count on that. Are we being slightly paranoid because of the information at hand? Yes, we are. Is that necessary? Definitely!"

The leader had spoken, perhaps more forcefully than ever before. He wore his mantle of command comfortably, although he heavily favored the diplomatic avoidance of conflict. The effect he had on the Fusgeyers, every last one of them, was never less than positive, and they did not disappoint him now.

Their reactions, as they stood around the dying campfire discussing what lay ahead in Bremerhaven, convinced Mordecai and a few of the cadre that the troop would follow these necessary orders to the letter. Yes, there were a few scattered mumbles of an "overreaction," "*narishkeit*," a chauvinistic "who would dare cause us any trouble," and so on. But Mordecai was certain that none of this would equate to anyone's ignoring the very real threat.

The loss of the Singermans and Yehuda Gelman to the Argentine lure of the Baron De Hirsch organization still distressed Mordecai. It was as if he were responsible, which he certainly was not. That Mordecai Anieloff was the shepherd of his flock, as protective as a nervous father, was never in doubt by anyone. It had become sort of a Biblical scene during these many months of togetherness, and in a way, he dreaded the separation that would inevitably occur when they reached America. Until that time, he would go to the greatest lengths to honor the tacit contract he had made with mothers and fathers, sisters and brothers, grandparents and Rabbi Nachman, for the safe deliverance of their loved ones under his wing. And thus far, he had kept that faith.

The stench became palpable as the broad River Weser came into view. It would stay in place relentlessly until they were ready to board the *Cincinnatus* and sail for the open sea. Was it the reeking mass of thousands of bathless, perspiring emigrant bodies crowded into spaces for hundreds? Was it the smelting plant and the noxious fumes that spewed forth from its 50-meter chimneys across the river? Was it the oceans of disinfectant splashed about the red brick quarantine barracks by the barrel-full? Or was it the dye vats at the tannery downstream near the city of Bremen? Possibly the sickening sweet aroma drifting in from the pulp mill in adjoining Lehe? The answer was an inexhaustible blending of all of these.

"Dante's inferno" was the curt description to which Mendel wryly attached the Bremerhaven scene as the Fusgeyers plodded through on the only avenue leading to the docks. They would have to go this route to reach the campsite destination, and it began to look like an endless Machiavellian gauntlet the moment they entered the town's chock-a-block purlieu precincts.

It was proving even more difficult to keep everyone together than Mordecai or Branko imagined. For the first time since leaving Birlad, Sholem and Yaakov had been discharged from their point duties and were marching alongside the contingent as an additional security measure. The cart, its final *shleppers,* and the six women were placed in the middle of the line-up, and an armed Golub took up the rear, with Branko alternating between the middle and the rear.

It is doubtful whether any of the Birladers were able to process the sights and sounds they were thrust into at this juncture. What they had envisioned did not match what they were seeing. Shouting, screaming, screeching. Placards protesting, contesting or detesting, every conceivable person, monarchy, movement, idea, religion, race, country. Languages? Another babbling Tower of Babel.

Sendehr summed it all up in one of his daily journal entries, as only he could do so well, and yet it was a remarkable feat since he had to wait to record the details with pen and ink until after they had arrived at the blufftop campsite. In addition, he tediously copied it verbatim so it could serve as a letter to Rabbi Nachman in lieu of his usual weekly synopsis. It was that important to him to do it this way. Sendehr's power of observation, ably supplemented by colorful inputs from his trusty "reporters," enabled him to paint an accurate and complete picture of this purgatorial port of last resort.

Journal Entry, Number 120
July 29, 1904 (26 Tammuz, 5664)

This day, above all others, shall remain lodged in my tightly packed memory as long as my good God allows me to live and breathe. Have we all died suddenly and arrived in these bowels of hell? Was it something we ate last night, or this morning? Is it God punishing us for our ego-driven selfishness in leaving our parents and families in Birlad? Is this just a bad, a terribly bad nightmare?

We literally and physically had to force our way, meter by meter, to navigate through the hordes, and all the while we were herded together like wild ponies by Branko, the Golubs and Mordecai. Sholem and Yaakov, no longer on "point," helped out. We just had to maintain our formation as true as humanly possible, not allowing ourselves to split up until we could re-form after reaching some open space. There was no way to avoid this. In order to get to our bivouac site, according to the sparse '03 notes from Shmulkeh Tomashevsky, we had to follow the approach to the docks. They didn't have a cart or wagon to consider, but access to the bluff, which is an amazingly tranquil spot— close as it is to what I'm going to describe in detail—is limited to a rocky, narrow uphill path along the river side of the karst outcropping. One way in, one way out. Today's shlepping crew had rough going for what has been the last pull of the trek. Gott tsedanken! We owe many thanks to our benefactor, Avrum Leventer.

THE WAYFARERS

People were pulling us, yelling at us, pushing us, jostling—no, actually accosting us. Every vendor we saw was hawking inedible looking food, selling every scheme, dream and product one can possibly imagine— some of which defy description. I will try.

The Medieval Age still lives in today's Bremerhaven. One could conjure up visions of the Black Death, burning-at-the-stake, arrows and spears hurtling through the air. Gevalt! If I appear to be overstating, please forgive my Yiddishe imagery. These are my true and honest thoughts. In all due respect to Shmulkeh, his journal notes did not adequately describe the port. I am merely attempting to rectify that by including everything in a copy of this entry for Rabbi Nachman, for the benefit of future Fusgeyer contingents. I am certain that Hamburg is every bit as chaotic so this will apply to either German port...

Insurance policies seem to be the most popular product. At least there were more of these salesmen warning about the dangers at sea than any other scare- mongers...

"Icebergs, boys and girls! Death-dealing, giant icebergs all over the North Atlantic. Many a ship has met its fate by smashing into one of these white mountains in the middle of the night! Colliding with another ship coming from the other side is even worse! Big storms have been known to capsize these flimsy, floating coffins! Waves the size of the horizon can crush your boat like a matchbox! Get your insurance policies here! See to it that your loved ones in Bialystok, Minsk or Vilna cash in on your untimely deaths. Peace of mind! Big returns on small investments. Make mama and papa rich and they will light a candle for you every week. What are you? Jews? Your Talmud tells you to care for your loved ones even after your death. Guaranteed by the honorable Deutsche Bank and the venerable Allianz Insurance Companies. They paid out

billions last year alone. Don't be left out! Come, come, now. Be wise. Be smart. Be benevolent."

Vay iz mir! To say that these peddlers of fear, and there were countless numbers of these mongering ghouls blocking our way, frightened the intestines out of me...and all of us...would be the awful truth. I don't think even one of our 'geyers ever thought for a moment of the dangers of collision with icebergs, a giant whale, or another vessel. Now we will! They've sowed the seeds in all of our minds.

Even the practical, sensible Nuchim, who was marching beside Rivka and me, began to mumble about buying policies for everyone with money from our well-funded "bank." Rivka, with her iron-bound nerves, laughed at this. I did not. Mordecai, when he heard, failed to register any emotion. He was too busy trying to keep everyone reasonably together, preventing any breach in the formation. Most everyone was visibly upset. Not only with the unsettling insurance warnings, but also with the unfolding of such a God-less scene all about them.

Seasick medications of every variety, tea leaves, rock candy, raw beets with cooked onions, hog-stomach pepsin, belladonna the panacea, unknown powders and tinctures with mysterious ingredients, weird gypsy preparations, glass evil-eyes for rubbing, giant crucifixes with or without Yeseleh, Stars of Dovid, miniature mezuzzahs, rosaries and "worry" beads—all promised to ward off the dreaded "mal de mer." To quell the fears this hawking caused many among us, Gershon and Maidele insisted that from their supplies they would work up both an effective preventive and an equally effective antidote over the next two weeks. We trust them implicitly.

The twin scourges of dreaded medical inspection—trachoma and tuberculosis—the next oft-mentioned cures, were addressed by white-coated pseudo-physicians and nurses. They went one large step

beyond the seasickness charlatans. Seated at small
tables, with visible diplomas from Europe's leading
universities, each with an impressive imprimatur, they
offered numerous highly suspect concoctions in vials,
with eye-droppers, bottles, jars and powder packets,
each sporting verbosely worded labels. Large signs
behind and above the tables proclaimed: "Rid yourself
of that nasty, bloody cough! Try our cough-stopper now!
Do not take the chance of being rejected by the Doctors
or Immigration Officials. TB cured in two days or your
money back! Eyes tearing with pus? Apply eye-bright
drops and clear sight will be miraculously yours again."
One of the more enterprising "doctors" addressed the
favus problems, which we know as ringworm, by
presenting the pine tar shampoo "guaranteed to kill the
highly contagious culprits, your hair will grow back
within six months, and this certificate so signifies." He
was as bald as a cannonball!

Oddly enough, most signs were printed in German,
Polish, Russian, Romanian, certain Slavic dialects, and
Yiddish. The Hebrew lettering was crude, with
laughable errors, but it showed that a significant
number of emigrants flowing through here are unsereh
Yidden. Max Nordau claimed that percentage to be as
high as one-quarter. Makes sense.

Foodstuffs of every sort are hawked along the way,
too; but Simmy will take care of that end with his usual
methods. Of course, he'll be under guard, as Mordecai
and Branko decreed sensibly last night. I, too, was
allowed to quickly stop in at the postal office on our way
in, where everyone waited outside while I picked up all
Fusgeyer mail, including letters from Rabbi Nachman,
Max and a surprise note from Shmuel Cohn. As always,
every letter I've received on the trek will be included
within the journal. I plan to send only one more
synopsis to Rabbi Nachman, which will cover the
remainder of our stay in Bremerhaven. That will be
Number 16 in the series and I will ask HIAS to mail it

for me. This journal will be kept until the day we arrive in New York, at which time I will send my last synopsis, covering the ocean voyage and disembarkment. Back to the horrors, now...

Throngs of heavily made-up prostitutes, all ages, all sizes, all colors, nearly outnumbered the vast number of obnoxious mongers. They were brazenly strutting everywhere in broad daylight. You would think that the comedians and Simmy would have mouthed some choice remarks, but the sheer gravity of the crushing mob reality seemed to stifle their potent, combined chutzpah. *However, Avi and his little* banditten *more than made up for the silence. Then again, there have been times when this mission has been a game for the* yinglach. *Maybe it's better that way. In all honesty, aside from some harmless scattered mischievousness, they have all participated with honor, never having shirked their duties. There will plenty of time for them to grow up in America, please God! Avi's heroics during the great escape will always be an integral part of Fusgeyer history. Rightfully so.*

There were cameras and film plates, picture postal cards galore the latest American clothing styles—hats, straw and felt, vests, trousers, skirts, dresses, blouses, shirts, sweaters, jerkins and jackets lined both sides of the street on metal racks. A very small number of emigrants with money to spare were stripping to their underwear, trying on clothes right out in the open— boldly unashamed (yes, women as well!)—shoes and boots of all types, socks, rainwear slickers, umbrellas, and undergarments. I heard a peddler selling neckties and gloves shout, "You must have a tie on or you won't be allowed to enter America! Ladies, you must wear gloves at all times in New York. It's a law!" Another opportunist was vociferously selling the virtues of American red, white and blue-striped flags. "Be a patriotic Amerikaner!" this man cried, "Wave the flag of your new country and good things will happen for you!

*Long live Boffallo Beeel Cody and Teddy Rosebelt!" This
from an elderly German national, resplendent in what
Branko pointed out to be a much too tight, old Prussian
army uniform.*

*Eyeglasses, dentures; one size fits all. Water
purification powders: "the public water in America is
foul-tasting." Prayer books for all religions. Photographs
of "your ship" were ringing up brisk sales: the*
Staatendam, *the* Carmania, *the* Darmstadt, *the* Furst
Bismarck *and our own* Cincinnatus. *Photographers
also were in abundance all along the avenue, and many
of these falsely promised to send the picture to a loved
one—for a fee, of course. Astrologers, tarot readers,
illegal(?) gypsy fortunetellers, crystal ball and all—
phony lawyers drawing up phony wills.*

*Zed-Zed called it the "circus of the damned"—a
jungle of gehackteh fleysh boiling over, day and night,
seven days a week. The unsophisticated emigrant is the
prey, and all of the aforementioned, the happy hunters.
The Postal Director told me it has been this way ever
since emigration began to increase dramatically when
the new century began. There is no end in sight.*

*Only when we finally found the obscure path along
the limestone cliffs—which ultimately led us to this
beautiful bluff overlooking the entire harbor, the town
and the river—did we feel we had left the last nudniks
behind. None tried to follow us, and for this we are most
grateful. Upon arrival, intact, we immediately collapsed
with a collective sigh of great relief, offering our thanks
to God.* Omayn!

Sendehr afforded a good deal of ink to the most disturbing elements of the port scene: the notorious criminal
element, including the infamous evil white-slavers, who
stood out in the crowd with their visible side-arms; and the
sanguineous "shanghai-ers," who operated only in the last
hour or two prior to sailing. Diabolically, their tramp freight-
ers and their "new non-paying passengers" were usually

into the North Sea before family or friends would discover the victim's disappearance. To all of this, the port authorities and the thinly deployed uniformed police turned their backs, as usual.

The peripatetic missionaries and politicos appeared on every street corner. The socialists, the anarchists and the trade unionists were all looking to convince the emigrants that once they arrived in America there were political options for them. Ironically, where they would be *shnorring* to raise money for their cause, they actually gave out free gifts: pencils, pens, ink in tiny bottles, paper, note pads, propaganda brochures, and even cheap cravats, kerchiefs, and pins with the name of the organization printed thereon.

Certain refugees trotting alongside the Birladers were spreading the rumor that the Marxist-Socialist revolutionary Rosa Luxemburg, known by most Europeans as "Bloody Rosa," *Blutige Rosa,* was coming to town that week. The native of Polish Zamosc in the Pale was scheduled to give her fiery speeches to every emigrant group that deigned to stand still long enough (and not get trampled) to hear her combustible words. Her aim, like that of most other radicals at the port, was to imbed her arguments (in both Yiddish and German) into the receptive emigrant minds. Who knew? There might be hundreds of gullible recruits here, having the potential to become good American socialist allies some day.

During the past three years, in every speech, the educated and brilliant theorist stressed, in not too subtle a manner, the viability of socialist internationalism. As a Jew living in Germany, Luxemburg strongly felt that her adopted country would be the center of a world socialist revolution. Within the year she would be proven wrong, as even with a failed revolt Russia caught fire with anti-Czarist actions, destined to explode into worldwide communism.

Sendehr dryly noted in the journal that there weren't enough soapboxes to go around for all of these firebrands flooding into Bremerhaven, already bursting with divergent views on every issue known to humankind. As Mendel was quick to point out and explain, their greatest asset was their "lie-ability."

The over-zealous missionary corps was another story altogether. What better audience than confused, desperate, downtrodden refugees about to board ships that would take them to certain oblivion? Here in German Bremerhaven, the Lutherans were by far the most active and most evident. They seemed to be everywhere one looked, and never in groups of less than three or four or more. Remember the good Pastor Hof?

Other Protestant sects, particularly those more fundamental in creed, were also very much in view. The guttural rhetoric never seemed to vary by more than an "amen" or a "praise God" or "Jesus loves you." The target was the Jew, the typically papist Pole and Slav, and the occasional gone-to-seed quondam Protestant. How many heavenly citations the most ardent missionary received for each act of "spreading the good news," as commanded in their New Testament, who knows? It may have been weighted thusly: ten for every Jew, eight for the papists and a mere three for offering salvation to a fellow Lutheran or Presbyterian gone astray.

"Repent now, accept Jesus as your Lord and Savior...if you're ship goes under, your soul will go to heaven...do not embark without accepting the Lord!...America has no place for non-believers...we have three churches in Bremerhaven, all ready to accept your conversion. Catholics, what has your allegiance to the Vatican done for your wretched lives? They hate the Irish and the Italians in America because they're chattels of the Pope. Become a real Christian Lutheran today."

For the Jew, however, it was an approach of love and false respect—he was special—a lost child of God. "Jesus forgives you, my child. If you will open up your heart to one of your own, He will listen. You give up nothing, my dear son of Abraham, sweet daughter of Sarah, and you gain the love of Jesus, *Yeshua hamashiach,* the true Messiah. Remember, you can still be a Jew...one who accepts Jesus into his life to make it complete..."

This incessant badgering went forth from every corner in Bremerhaven. Outside the wire fence enclosing the quarantine barracks each denomination stationed one of its missionaries daily. They just never ceased spreading the "good news."

There were those of weak character—so homesick, so caught up in the pandemonium, so hungry, so exhausted from the overland journey, so addled by hellish lodgings— that they capitulated...to a degree, that is. Enticed by the offer of a hot meal—kosher if required, faux as it may be— and a place to bathe, a few from each faith did succumb. However, in most cases, these new allegiances were rendered null and void with the first belch.

The Birladers were not in the least vulnerable to these proselytizers and their ilk, as demonstrated by their unanimous repellent reaction to Pastor Hof and his sincerely emotional appeal, which fell flat on fifty-seven pairs of deaf ears. Later that night, though, Mordecai voiced his concern that other young people traveling alone could easily be persuaded to take the bait. Considering the lower literacy level of those not having had the advantage of a Rabbi Holtzer or Eli Nachman, or a *lehrer* the stature of a Mendel Buchman, it is small wonder that they could fall into the clutches of a well-meaning, well-practiced servant of Jesus Christ. There were all too many recorded incidents proving this to be true, both at the European ports and later in America.

No other individuals or groups had yet discovered the bluff-top, covered with lush grass and stately alder trees, when the Fusgeyers arrived there at last. Mordecai, seeing that the cliffs on three sides were much too steep for any intruders to climb, relaxed his orders slightly. The girls were no longer restricted to the center of the camp, and instead were allowed to roam all over the grounds. Branko figured that one guard at the head of the only path would be sufficient. Mordecai agreed. All other orders issued the previous night would stand firm Many of the Wayfarers still felt the stress of their journey through Bremerhaven, and were just as happy to stay in the close company of the others anyway.

The docks were far below and the nearest sign of life was at a 300-meter distance. One could be sure that the festivities that evening, following the evening meal and Mendel's classes, would include the entire entertainment menu: music, dancing, the comics, the cantors and any impromptu improvisations. Mordecai asked Rivka to go all out since he wanted to get his comrades' minds far away from the gnawing and annoying scare tactics to which they had been subjected coming through town. That was a tall order, to say the least. Thoughts and dreams (nightmares!) and discussions concerning the apparent dangers of sailing on the high seas would vex them from this point onward. Icebergs, collisions, storms, seasickness—and of course the concern about the medical examinations, trachoma, tuberculosis, and fauvus—serious uncertainties all.

If there were three common Yiddishe pastimes during twenty-five years of Czar Alexander III and the Romanoffs, and the King Carols, and the Father Mihais—pogroms, boycotts and forced impoverishment—they would be worry, worry and again, worry. After this unforgettable day all three would have a healthy workout.

Near midnight, Rivka and Sendehr sat on the grass, bare feet dangling over the bluff's edge, the moonlit river glistening below them.

"Just think, Rivkeleh, on this very spot, Johann Smidt, the far-sighted mayor of Bremen in 1827, surveyed the possibility of developing a deep-water harbor. You see, the river had silted up fifty kilometers to the south and Bremen could no longer handle the larger ships of the time. That is exactly how Bremerhaven became a major port."

"Where in the world did you learn that?"

"When Mendel introduced me to the Berlin Library's cataloguing system he looked for a book on the ports of Europe, and found one written by a retired British Naval officer, in English and German. He read the brief Bremen-Bremerhaven story to me. I could have spent days in that library. Most intriguing!"

"It would have helped if you could better understand German, love!"

"*Nu*, Sendehr, you wanted to talk about Rabbi Nachman's letter?" It was Mordecai; his aromatic pipe smoke would have given him away, even if the night had been pitch black.

"I was going to wait until tomorrow. I'm afraid the news is no better. Actually much worse. Sit down here with us. Rivka hasn't heard the details, either. As I told you before, Mordecai, I don't know how much we should reveal to everyone, but you'll be the judge."

"That bad?"

"It's the boycott. The government has assigned a special prosecutor to every district, for the express purpose of strictly administering the boycott laws for complete adherence. Remember how loose it had been before we left? Rabbi Nachman even listed those who are teetering on the edge of losing their jobs or their businesses. It isn't pretty. Here." Sendehr handed the six pages of grim news over to Mordecai. By the light of a moon full of promise, he proceeded to read the Nachman letter.

> *Birlad, July 20, 1904*
> *(17 Tammuz, 5664)*
>
> *Dear Sendehr,*
> *I read your letter over and over again...the*
> *Proclamation, the meetings, and Herzl's death, which by*
> *the way was widely reported here in Romania. Your*
> *poetic piece on the cemetery was very moving, and*
> *when I read it to the congregation I could see that it*
> *moved them as well. Reb Mandelbaum was particularly*
> *receptive of the news of your eloquent proclamation and*
> *eagerly supports your suggestion to disseminate it all*
> *over Romania. His sponsorship is more than adequate*
> *and I will get to it in a few days. All of our Jews in the*
> *country must read it, I agree! We're so very proud of all*
> *of you! However, thus far we haven't noticed anything*
> *positive coming out of Bucureshti.*

THE WAYFARERS

If anything, Romania's resolve in crippling its Jews is stronger than ever before. The old timers who go back to the middle of last century, like my father, yours and Sholem's and many others, unanimously shake their heads, agreeing that the government has never before been so vehement in their restrictive efforts. It has reached the ugly stage, Sendehr. Take this, for example:

Three local Romanian school children stopped in at the Fiedelman bakery last week to buy some sweets. One of the special prosecutor's team of spies reported them and the little ones were expelled from school for a month. The parents blamed it on the Fiedelmans, not knowing of the spy involvement, and as a result a gang of unemployed shikorim smashed their plate-glass window into shards. Father Mihai, as to be expected, lashed out at the Fiedelmans in a public harangue aimed at our entire "blood-drinking" community at last Sunday's mass. The dear priest also succeeded in interceding with the new official to return the boys to school, on the grounds that the Fieldelmans had lured them into the shop in order to cheat them out of their few coins.

I wish that were the sum and substance of our recent troubles, but I must be honest with you, and you can then be as selective as you wish in passing on this news. Mordecai has to know, of course. The very distraught Fiedelmans asked me to have you break the news to Simmy, also. But, as I began to say, the list of travesties has gotten longer with each passing day. When hunger hovers over a community, violence is never far behind.

A roving band trashed Avrum's smithy while he was in shul just last Saturday. They set six shoeless horses loose, and it took him two days to recover them. One was badly gouged in one eye.

Reb Berman's glass business, which depended heavily on the goyishe trade, is on the brink of disaster. He's thinking of moving away to Bucureshti to work for

another glass blowing shop. He wants Mordecai and
Menachem to know and he will write to them after you
arrive in America. His morale is surprisingly good
regardless of his current situation.

Not so with so many of the others. Hoodlums have
damaged three of the shtieblach to varying degrees.
Thanks to God, our shul has been so far untouched. I
don't know for how long.

Rosen the tailor, also heretofore very popular with
the Romanians, has seen his trade drop off nearly fifty
percent! He's hanging on by a thread, and I don't mean
to be funny. This is no laughing matter. Sholem
Friedman's father dealt with many boycott breakers, but
that has come to a sudden stop. The same story applies
to my father and to many others.

In another vein, I'm happy to report that your dear
father is among six men hired by Moishe Mandelbaum
on a "temporary" basis, to improve all of his properties:
the one remaining chicken farm, the orchards, three
small houses in the outskirts of town, and the proposed
extension to Avrum Leventer's barn, which he recently
purchased. He plans to prepare it for one of his future
enterprises—the motor carriage mishigas.
Conservatively, I see at least a few months of work for
your father and the others. In reality, everyone knows
that Mandelbaum can do the jobs with half the men.
The man is a princely tzaddik above all others. Truly
one who is God-sent.

Reb Mandelbaum has also approached Captain
Polinou to discuss the boycott situation, but to little or
no avail. Not even a bribe would help. Our "ally," at
times now shrugs his shoulders with the arrival of the
special prosecutor. He claims that his hands are all but
tied, and he must defer to the new man while he, the
grob Polinou, has been assigned to normal day-to-day
police duties only. Bucureshti's sanctimonious satraps
have warned him a few times to stay out of the "boycott
business."

Some more good news: the boys from Galatz were, indeed, imprisoned at Theresienstadt as you predicted. I warned Rabbi Leibsohn in Galatz that this could happen, and he wrote to the Labor Alliance office in Prague for help in investigating the matter. Shortly thereafter he received a "ransom" cable. Rabbi Leibsohn petitioned the Galatz Benevolent Society and they, in turn, quickly sent a sizable bank draft to the extortionists at the prison, for "expenses incurred by your young vagrant troublemakers," and they were released. The Prague community, through the efforts of the Alliance, agreed to fund their railroad tickets to Bucureshti. The entire Galatz community owes you great thanks, as Rabbi Leibsohn duly noted in his conversations with me. A mitzvah, Sendehr. A mitzvah. *A blessing on your* keppeleh!

Meanwhile, Shlomoh Marcovici tells me our own Benevolent Society is out of funds for the first time since 1881, so those of the most desperate families requiring help now have to apply to Bucureshti's Yiddishe Workmen's Aid Association. Like all relief organizations throughout the continent, they, too, are feeling the pinch just as badly, so all hope for the worst cases is running out like sand in an hourglass.

Nachman's letter went on to address the rest of the contents of Sendehr's most recent letter from Berlin, and Mordecai read through it slowly, methodically, reading certain passages aloud for Rivka's benefit, before quietly and neatly folding it, and handing it back again to its addressee. The three of them sat in a cocoon of silence, bombarded by the disparate emotions of utter sadness on one hand, and a thin smattering glimmer of joy on the other.

Under a clear sky full of brilliant stars, with a new moon bathing the entire camp in its light, very few Fusgeyers succumbed to sleep. Each one was tightly tensed up after the day's events—full of satisfaction at having safely arrived at the port, and full of apprehension so thoroughly belabored.

The future that had seemed so far away in April was here and now.

The well-traveled *Mogen Dovid*, pole planted on the harbor side of the hill, handsomely unfurled in the gentle night breezes. In the spirit of continuing trouble avoidance, Mordecai asked for the Kaiser's multicolored banner to be flown, too. With the usual reluctance, the order was honored. At first light, these two symbols of distinctly divergent peoples would be viewed by the unbelieving eyes of dock workers, ship crews, the patchwork quilt of emigrant refugees from all corners of the central and eastern regions of the continent, the port and town authorities, those already in quarantine, those ready to board one of the two ships embarking that next day, the hustlers, the *hondlers*, the mongers and the swindlers—all would look up at an anomalistic pairing they had never before witnessed in their lives. To all of them, it seemed a *fata morgana*—a mirage within a mirage that defied the eyes.

Herzl's flag had reached an acme; though shared, it was nevertheless a lofty peak. Although Bremerhaven was hardly Haifa, Mordecai was sure that he would have been very pleased.

* * *

The vote was a unanimous 56-0, Mordecai rightfully abstaining. He had decided, along with the entire cadre, that Sendehr should read the Rabbi's letter to the entire assemblage right after breakfast and morning prayer. Nuchim followed, confirming that the "bank" was once again very fluid with far more than enough for everyone's $25 (American) proof of temporary subsistence to be shown when required, still leaving a sizable surplus. These positive statements from the frugal and fiscally responsible Reb Nuchim had paved the way for Mordecai to make the impassioned *tzedakah* plea, and rarely had he been more eloquent.

"There is no need to go over anything Sendehr or Nuchim just shared with you. The Rabbi's letter tells all as it is, today and tomorrow, in our Birlad. It will always be our Birlad, even years from now when you're all flag waving, *reicheh Americaneh*, sitting in manor houses on the Hottson Reevah. Yes, of course, we all will be sending money to our loved ones just as soon as we settle; but our families are suffering, the community needs what little help we can afford right now, today. Nuchim tells me that we can send a substantial postal draft to Rabbi Nachman for delivery to Shlomoh Marcovici, the president of the nearly bankrupt Benevolent Society. This will provide vital emergency relief to those hundreds of families on the brink of disaster. Reb Mandelbaum can't do it alone, friends."

After the affirming vote, a beaming Leibel Marcovici approached Mordecai and Sendehr.

"Thank you both, on behalf of my father and the growing number in need. His heart must be broken, not to be able to help, even in a small way. He's been involved with the charity ever since I can recall, but now with this frustrating crisis, thank God we can send something."

"I wish we could do more, Leibel. Our community needs us immediately, and they'll be counting on us in the years to come. *Unsereh tsudreyter shlemiel* and his parliament of *mumzerim* leave us no choice but to become successful in America. All those who went before us are doing their part, I've been pleased to see, and now we must do ours...repeatedly." Mordecai's assuring words, distinctly heard by those gathered around him after the meeting, lingered in their minds for days to come.

There was much ahead to be done before the quarantine period arrived. At the top of the list, Mordecai and Nuchim, escorted by Branko, had to complete final arrangements with the Lloyd Line office situated at the entrance to the harbor. Following this meeting, Nuchim would be escorted to the postal office in order to purchase the postal draft to send to Rabbi Nachman. Simmy, with his Golubguard, was scheduled to go on one of his last two scavenging ventures. The last would be on the day before isolation began. At that time, he would attempt to sell the cart and all of the tent halves. What he couldn't sell, he was to abandon on the streets.

Whoever still wished to talk with HIAS concerning employment opportunities could do so in the quarantine blocks. Joe Castleman's assistant, Shammai Kurtzman, was permanently assigned to both the Hamburg and Bremerhaven ports, dividing his time between the two. Additionally, he tried to spend one day a month in Rotterdam, followed by a day in Antwerp, dependent upon ship schedules. The budget, strained beyond reality, was nevertheless used frugally and adroitly by the vital agency. HIAS was able to accomplish most of its primary mission goals in New York, and in its newly opened sub-office in Boston, and by making periodic visits to Philadelphia. Hardly a Jewish emigrant from Eastern Europe had anything to give but praise and thanks for the nurturing organization. The century ahead would severely test HIAS to the breaking point, under the onslaught of nightmarish conditions once envisioned by the Maharal, through his Golem, and channeled forward to old Rabbi Blankfort of Praha.

In the late afternoon, Mordecai returned with welcome news from the Lloyd Line office. The Passage Master had told the Fusgeyer leader that their quarantine period had been reduced to seven days due to the heavy summer sailing schedule. There was only so much room for passengers in the red brick quarantine barracks, which had been built during the sweep of cholera epidemics in the '90s. Additionally, Mordecai announced that the final schedule for the *Cincinnatus* included a refueling stop in Cobh, Ireland, and a two-day layover in Halifax, Nova Scotia. There, some specially suited, Polish, coal-mining equipment would be off-loaded, along with a large group of veteran Polish and Czech miners en route to the burgeoning mines at Sydney, near Cape Breton. For Mordecai and the others this explained why the voyage would take an unusually long twenty-three days.

All other arrangements had been confirmed and Mordecai showed off fifty-seven identification tags, each with a Fusgeyer's name imprinted thereon. These would serve as the passage coupons, to be surrendered to the purser at sailing time. Sensibly, Mordecai announced that they would all be kept in one secure place until that time to prevent the possibility of any individual losing his or her tag.

Perhaps it was actually viewing these one-way tickets to America that sobered those gathered atop of the bluff. The sole occupants of the hill became unusually introspective, and only a few talked in muted tones for the next few hours, prior to ushering in the Sabbath eve. Once again, the stark and naked reality that began to show itself during the Berlin hiatus crept into the scene. This was the beginning of the end of the journey. Once the gangplank was removed two weeks hence, there would be no turning back from this juggernaut hegira.

The impact of Rabbi Nachman's letter had so affected Sendehr that he had opened both the Shmuel Cohn and Max Nordau letters, gave each a cursory glance, placed them in the side pocket of his badly frayed campaign jacket, and all but forgot about them. This quiet period of reflection now reminded him of their existence, and he took them out again. Rivka came to join him, and together they began to read. Shmuel's letter, mailed from Hamburg the day he sailed, was written in his breezy, signature style. He had some very positive thoughts on both Sendehr and Rivka's chosen career paths, noting that Abe Cahan was outspokenly impressed with Sendehr, and wanted to talk with him once he was settled in New York. But Shmuel was adamant in insisting that he not consider working for the *Forvitz*:

> *You're far more suited to be a strictly independent, what we call 'freelance,' writer. Even Abe will tell you that the smaller periodicals, weekly newspapers, newsletters and such have been proliferating in the exploding Yiddish-speaking community, and the one thing they all lack are intelligent, well written articles by independent contributors. Even Congressman William Randolph Hearst, who fancies himself as a possible*

Democratic candidate to run against Roosevelt, has gotten into the Yiddish-language newspaper game with The Yiddishe Amerikaner, *as a supplement to his* Morning Journal. *I'll wager that his arch-rival Joe Pulitzer has voiced some choice unprintable remarks on that one! But believe me, Sendehr, you don't want to end up as a puppet, jumping at Abe's whim, writing about only that which he has assigned. There's just too much restriction for a person with your talents. Don't think for one minute that I won't be out of here as soon as I build an impressive portfolio of my own writing.*

As for you, Rivkaleh, one of my older colleagues who is a drama columnist at the Times, *and was also attending the conference, thinks he can get you a job working with his bethrothed. She happens to be a seamstress-costume designer for Sammy Desmond's "Famous Stage Artists" troupe, whatever in hell that may be. It's a start,* maidel! *Better famous than infamous! At least you'll be in the right circles.*

It was clear that Shmuel's goal was to help his new friends avoid the typical immigrant's lot—working in one of the hundred's of unventilated, poorly lit eastside "sweat shops;" or peddling some unexciting product tenement-to-tenement; or anything classified as a domestic, a common laborer or worse. Historically and unfortunately, most of the Fusgeyers, especially at the outset of their new lives in America's vast land of opportunity, had found themselves thusly immersed. To escape this, or sidestep it altogether, was certainly the more attractive route. In Shmuel Cohn, Sendehr and Rivka had a valuable and street-smart friend, indeed.

He went on to describe colorfully the Albert Ballin baroque mansion in Hamburg and the gala evening he attended therein:

THE WAYFARERS

Ballin is your typical German-Jew who considers himself much more the former and a lot less of the latter. What you call a Moishe Yid. (I favor that deprecating term and you can be sure I'll use it often in my writing. The uptown crowd will love that!) In my questionable opinion, Herr Ballin is an insufferable ass who does nothing but try to capitalize on his connections in high places. I'll say! None other than Kaiser Willi is his best friend. Or so he thinks. My guess is that being the owner of Hamburg-America Line and a multimillionaire on top of that would qualify him for certain upper-echelon circles of friends and acquaintances. His castle ranks with anything I've seen on Fifth Avenue or those in Newport, of which I've seen photographs. (That's in the little state of Rhode Island where the Vanderbilt crowd spends each summer in the most ostentatious mausoleums known to modern man.) In conversation, with a giant cigar stuck in his face, Herr Ballin clearly made it known to everyone in the drawing room that the Second Reich had no room for revolutionaries, socialists, communists, anarchists, gypsies, chassids, papists, Turks, Asians...did he leave anyone out? I wonder who?

This stunned the few Irish-Catholic newspapermen in our group, and lit a roaring fire under my boss whose socialist philosophy is chiseled into every editorial he has ever written. In fact, Abe and I had just yesterday interviewed "Bloody Rosa" Luxemburg down at the Hamburg harbor where she was spouting her revolutionary doctrine to a large group of emigrants from your Romania. I think my hard-nosed mentor fell in love with the fire-breathing dragon. It would serve them both right. Ay,yi,yi! I sure do have strong opinions for such a yingel. This one I kept to myself, not wanting to be stranded in Germany with no way to get home. If you don't know, she's a rabid Polish socialist. Maybe you'll see her in Bremerhaven, as she seems to gravitate toward the emigrant masses, expounding her theories so that her comrades in New York can gain some new recruits. Give her my love. No, make that Abe's!

But back to Abe's reaction to his host's ugly remarks. He went jaw to jaw with the shipping magnate in front of the whole dinner crowd, as only Abe Cahan can do so well. With his mouth and his pen the man has no peers and no limits. He spoke—no, ranted is more like it—in Yiddish knowing full well that Ballin with his stratified Prussian-class German understood everything. Although born in Germany, Ballin's entire family were Yiddish-speaking immigrants from Kovno, something that Cahan had discovered from a Hamburg newspaper publisher. I just sat back, relaxed and thoroughly enjoyed the whole match. Gentleman Jim Corbett, Abe was not! Pardon my reference to someone with whom you're not familiar, but Corbett is an American boxer, fighter, who acts like a gentleman even when demolishing his opponent. Abe's rhetoric simply pulverized the target. No gentlemanly finesse about it. When Ballin could stand no more, he merely signaled for the string quartet to commence playing.

On leaving, Abe and I were the only guests who refused to shake hands with the mumzer. I think I did it out of respect for Abe rather than any personal animosity for Herr Hamburg-America Line, although the man is most demonstrably a Kaiser-loving, self-hating member of that "Mosaic persuasion." I hope he hasn't given his ship captain orders to fling us overboard. Heh-heh!

By the way, the food was awful. Much too Deutsche-heavy for my simple tastes! Well, next I guess I'll see you two in the "Big City." Phone me when you escape from Ellis Island. Remember, it's a long swim to Manhattan Island!

Wedding date yet? Please, please give my best regards to Tsippy!

Bon Voyage to all of the Fusgeyers!
Your friend, Shmuel,
Hamburg, July 20, 1904

Shmuel had scripted the last six lines in English, but Rivka and Sendehr were able to make out more than just a few of the words, and were very proud of that. Mendel helped with the rest.

Upon his return from Vienna, Max Nordau had written his letter in German rather than his highly error-prone Yiddish, and included a clipped copy of a short but shocking article from the leading Berlin daily:

You "rabble rousing" Fusgeyers continue to receive extensive worldwide press coverage. This should serve to make your upcoming voyage a satisfying one:

Tension between Romanian and U.S.

Ambassadors

Berlin, July 22 – His Excellency, Constantine Porumbescu, Romania's ambassador to Germany since 1902, has filed a formal complaint with the American Embassy, charging that Ambassador Charlemagne Tower, Jr. knowingly caused him and his sovereign nation "irreconcilable embarrassments" during a meeting held at the American's office two weeks ago. Without going into detail, and refusing to answer direct questions from the reporters, the obviously distraught veteran of six ambassadorial posts prior to 1902 used a long string of profanities. In the end he managed to state that his colleague in Washington has been sent a cable so that he could make a personal call to the Secretary of State and possibly President Roosevelt. Ambassador Tower refrained from specifics, emphatically stating that Porumbescu was "over-reacting" to the incident. The American, given to lavish parties sometimes attended by Kaiser Wilhelm, has become very popular in the Berlin diplomatic community since he was assigned here last year. Tower would only say that the Romanian ambassador was invited to the meeting which included the noted Paris journalist and Zionist Max Nordau, one Abraham Cahan, an American Jewish newspaper editor, a United States Immigration Department official, and three young unidentified Romanian Jews. The purpose of the meeting was not revealed by either embassy. (Further news of the affair will appear in this paper as it happens.)

Branko translated the letter and enclosed article for the benefit of Sendehr, Mordecai and Mendel. Rivka eagerly listened, particularly enjoying a hearty laugh over the article. Branko would read the article to the entire assemblage after the Sabbath eve service, for a bit of choice evening entertainment. It wasn't exactly the result that the "three young unidentified Romanian Jews" had hoped for, but they all agreed that it was an auspicious start. As Mendel explained in between chuckles, considering the ultimate goals they had set, any "press" was "good press." As difficult as it was to come to terms with that, Sendehr, for one, simply shrugged it off as another one of the *lehrer's* many folksy adages.

The remainder of Max's letter reported on the massive outpouring of worldwide friends and Zionist sympathizers at Theodor Herzl's burial in Vienna. He also voiced some private thoughts not to be repeated, concerning David Wolffsohn's abilities, or lack thereof, to take over the reins. The Russian faction simply did not respect him; and in Max's opinion, they would ride roughshod over him, quickly usurping uncontested control of the movement from the Westerners. As much as he disagreed with their methods and ultimate aims, Max's words sounded every bit as though he had given up the fight to preserve the status quo of Herzl's policies. *So be it,* thought Sendehr.

The next few days seemed to drift along slowly. For the first time, the Wayfarers of Birlad were thrown into various stages of an annoying state of ennui, though liberally laced with anxiety over the voyage yet to come. The surrealistic bluff-top, sort of an eagle's aerie under Jewish and German flags, looking down on a berserk Biblical Sodom below, became something that each one would find difficult to expunge from his or her mind in the years to come. Oh, it was pleasant enough. Mendel held more than the allotted English classes, and rounds of laughter abounded, especially with Sholem's increasingly dramatic renditions of *gehackteh Yinglish.* Sendehr and Rivka related much of what they learned from Shmuel Cohn, followed by provocative discussions on every known and rumored aspect of life in urban America, holding everyone's interest and undivided attention each evening. Mealtime was better than ever. Simmy's highly successful foraging expeditions into the den of iniquity had handsomely enhanced the food supplies, and it he had even "found" kosher items in a little grocery store in the sparsely populated Jewish section of the port city. Furthermore, he returned with every bit of Deutsche currency expense money that Nuchim had given to him. Yossi Golub, one of his armed bodyguards, revealed the mystery of how the food czar accomplished his feat, as so often he had.

"The baker-boy is a genius. No one can refuse him, I swear. He could *shnorr* the last drop of water from a man crawling in the desert! He could beg the gloves off a freezing Eskimo! Can you believe me when I say he actually embarrassed me a few times? I couldn't watch. But when this little woman in the Jewish grocery actually grabbed his hand and kissed it, thanking him for coming to her store—that was too much! This, after she had given us two large boxes filled with some of the very *geshmuckteh* things we have enjoyed these last few days. A genius, no! A *teivl*, yes. Yes. Yes. A *teivl!* "

With this, and a big smile, the burly Yossi rushed over to an unsuspecting Simmy, and gave him a crushing "bear-hug" as the whole camp applauded and cheered. No one even dared to think how the group would've done without a Simmy on this great trek. Mordecai, looking on, could have added numerous names to that thought. In turn, all would have added his.

There were visitors, of course, as expected. Mordecai didn't think for one minute that fifty-seven people camping on a hill with flags flying would remain unnoticed from below. The harbor security police, *Der Haven Polizei*, climbed the hill, but surprisingly not until they had already occupied the bluff for six days. Distinctly out of Prussian martinet character, the *Leutnant* seemed to enjoy his talk with Branko, was full of smiles, and told his underling to check the still-filled cart for any contraband. He suggested, mind you, that they were sure to clean the area when leaving, and then simply saluted Mordecai, Menachem and Branko and took his leave. Stunned, all three stood there for a full minute, totally numb. Obviously, what the officer saw satisfied the innate Prussian mindset that respected the Fusgeyers' self-sufficiency and martial-like organization, rare among departing emigrants.

Other visitors included two *Lubavitcher chassids*, who also broke the mold so firmly etched in their minds since the Szatmar confrontation. These two young men, in full regalia, were actually quite charming and soft-spoken. Coming from the core of their dynasty, the Pale town of Lubavitch near Minsk, their Rebbe, Sholom Dov Ber, was sending them to America to establish a *Chabad* school in Boston. They were also booked for passage on the *Cincinnatus*, and since it was Friday, they asked if they could stay to usher in the Sabbath. A bit reluctant to do so, Menachem Berman who had been carrying on most of the conversation, saw no great harm in agreeing to something that in reality could not be refused.

"We have nothing but kosher food here, so you will join us for a Sabbath dinner also."

"Thank you, thank you, Reb Menachem. It is so difficult to find kosher food here in Bremerhaven. We replenished our supply between trains in Hamburg where we spent last Sabbath. There, Jewish stores are plentiful. But by now we have quite run out again"

"Where are you staying?" asked Menachem.

"Another problem here. *Vay iz mir*, we didn't know a place like this town existed anywhere in Europe. We found some lodgings near that steeple down there. Full of Yidden, maybe thirty or a little more, in five small rooms. One toilet in the back of the place. Mats thrown on the floor. Quite filthy. But we understand that the town has no better to offer the streams of people waiting for their ships. We just arrived Sunday, and that was all that we could find. The quarantine can't begin soon enough for us. *Omayn.*"

While so many pairs of suspicious eyes looked on, Mordecai asked, "Why did you decide to climb up here, dear sirs?"

"*Oy, oy, oy!* You are on everyone's tongues down below. The stories, I'm sure, are so embellished by now, that they have you elevated to a 'Maccabean army sent by G-d to protect everyone' during their miserable days in Bremerhaven." This unexpected remark broke down the reserve of the onlookers and a bit of warmth surged through the Birladers as the taller of the two *chassids* went on. "We learned the truth from some Romanians staying in our hovel. They are from Iashi and they related the exciting, though brief, Fusgeyer history to us. In fact, one family had a son who went to America with an Iashi group in 1900. In Lubavitch we knew nothing of this. Now we are truly in awe of your remarkable mission and wish you well in America."

Rather than have them walk down the dangerous path after dark, Menachem convinced the two to stay and pray with them the next morning, too. This did much to erase the memories of that upsetting Sabbath morning in faraway Szatmar.

A few peddlers came also, to hawk their wares. Each was not too politely rebuffed by a menacing Golub as they tried to maneuver the obstacle course strewn with boulders and rocks.

And at precisely the time when morning Sabbath

prayers were finishing, *Blutige Rosa*, the self-crowned princess of the socialist movement made her less-than-grand entrance. She and her entourage of three collegiate Germans had gotten past the guard once they convinced him that they were not selling anything. Little did young Yoni know how far from the truth this was!

Projecting herself to the center of the arena, she mistook one of the Lubavitchers, who had been leading the prayer service, as the Fusgeyer commander. She brazenly grabbed his hand in order to shake it. When the shocked Rabbi Azriel Feinberg recoiled as if he were an asp ready to strike, his *tallis* flew off, fluttering to the grass like a magic carpet landing. At that point, Mordecai, wishing to avoid any further miscalculations by the visitor, quickly stepped forth, folding his own *tallis* and extending his hand to the wide-eyed young revolutionary.

"Mordecai Anieloff, Birlad, Romania. And you are?"

"Rosa Luxemburg, once of Zamosc in Russian-occupied Poland. More recently, a resident of Berlin. Perhaps you have heard of me?"

Now regaining her full composure, the dark-haired, striking woman continued on, not waiting for any response from Mordecai.

"You are the talk of the town, y'know. Everyone points to this hilltop, each with a tale of what they imagine to be going on here. By the way, I didn't mean to upset your comrade. He wouldn't be a *chassid* by any chance?"

"Correct."

"*Oy vay, mein Gott, entshuldig mir!* I know! I know! They are not to be touched by a female hand, other than those of their wives or daughters. I've made that mistake countless times since my childhood in the Pale. When I was a teenager, we girls made an adventure out of grabbing the hands of unsuspecting *chassid bochers*, giggling mightily and running away, hoping our parents wouldn't be told. Nasty little brats, no?" Mordecai had warmed to this woman since her initial intrusion. He smiled with closed lips, as he was wont to do in this type of rather disarming circumstance. He knew very well what Rosa's political goals were and he was interested in hearing what she had to say, certain that all of his Fusgeyers were also as open-minded. *Blutige Rosa* with all of her demonstrated *chutzpah* had earned herself a captive forum on this Sabbath afternoon, overlooking the hustle and bustle of one of Europe's busiest ports of embarkation.

Shabbosdickeh kiddush was especially sumptuous on this fortuitous occasion, the amazing Fiedelman having outdone himself once again. Delicious mounds of *shmaltz-herring, shnapps,* bottles of sweet kosher wine, sweet little egg *kichlach* and honey *lekach,* and other *milchadickeh moychels* had come from the very "generous" *shnorring* victims. One last "raid" was scheduled that evening, with quarantine looming for Monday, the 9th of August. Simmy's goal was to supplement any edible, *pareveh* shipboard victuals. The contingent not only counted on him, but also would heavily bet on his ability to come through in flamboyant style.

That Sunday evening, Sendehr wrote in his daily journal with his usual aplomb.

Journal Entry No. 130
August 8, 1904 (7 Av, 5664)

This is my last entry before we march into the isolation barracks early tomorrow morning. There is a feeling of certain serenity at this point, knowing that this will be the last step before we take to the open sea. There is a degree of trepidation concerning the qualifying physical examinations we face next week, but Doctor Hippocrates has been very assuring in his initial preliminary findings for each of us. He feels that there is nothing for anyone to be overly concerned about. He was mainly looking for signs of tuberculosis, favus (scalp infection) and trachoma. I never before heard of any of these terms back in Birlad. Gershon, and possibly Maidele, are the only ones that have even the slightest information as to the questionable symptoms. Branko had come across tuberculosis in his army days, and Mendel saw a trachoma case in Salonika. The rest of us are completely naïve. We've come this far, and maybe God will help us the rest of the way.

Adding to my coverage in yesterday's journal, of Blutige Rosa, *I think she found us, as a group marching across a hostile Europe, a lot more fascinating and interesting than we did her and her* farbrenteh *political theories. Having briefly met Abe Cahan in Berlin, I found that his stance was very similar to hers, as further verified by Shmuel Cohn's letter. The man feels strongly that socialism is the inevitable cure for everything that may be wrong with America, and indeed, the entire world. His* Forvitz *blares this forth in every editorial, on every page.*

Shmuel told us that the movement is especially strong with the Jewish working class in New York. May I ask, what other class is there? Oh, yes, the so-called "uptown Deutsche Yidden," of course. Outnumbered by much more than a thousand to one, I would safely say. Perhaps the Zionists, who Nordau claims have only 20,000 adherents in America, lean toward this socialism. Stop! Forgive me for going off on this point. I agree with anyone who is reading this journal that it is of little bearing on our journey and its goals. Our chassidishe *friends, Rabbi's Azriel Feinberg and Fischl Breslauer, stayed until this morning. This was a very good thing, as I alluded to in yesterday's journal also. They proved to be most mannerly, of good humor, and were most pleasant and respectful of our individual religious views. Their vigorous, highly spiritual dancing last night, loudly and sweetly singing their melodious* nigunim, *was wonderful to experience. Some of the tunes were hauntingly beautiful, and Rivka and I hummed them late into the night. Velvel Palastrant's accompaniment, largely improvised, was remarkable, and the four cantors'*

531

background harmonizing was never better. None of us had ever quite seen a mix the likes of this, and when Azriel did the "bottle dance" with an opened wine bottle balanced on his head, the applause was deafening. To see the muscular Golub brothers do their version of the kosatzke, partnering with the more gentle chassids was the closing highlight of the evening.

I was so tired after the festivities that I left out these colorful reports in the journal, which I'm now bringing to light. My general feelings for the ultra-orthodox received a big boost toward more tolerance. I feel very good about this. I venture to say that most everyone on this hill would agree. I would only hope that there are many more Lubavitcher Feinbergs and Breslauers than there are Szatmar Gelbfeders. Someday, perhaps, I'll find out. New York should have the answers.

Rosa and her three blond henchmen also stayed the night and thoroughly enjoyed our lively brand of entertainment. They must think that we did nothing but sing, dance and laugh our way across Europe all the way from Birlad. Ha! They should only know! Rosa never did get to speak to a gathered assembly here on the hill; instead she and her boys managed to corner almost everyone at one time or another during the evening. Rivka, Tsippy and Mayer Bernstein separately reported some of these revealing conversations to me, and I won't try to bore the reader with every bit of information.

To sum it up, rather, Madam Luxemburg has been merely taking opportunities to prepare as many emigrants as she can to open up their minds for the socialist point of view when they arrive in America. She and her party felt strongly that this was well worth the effort, and the receptive, ready-made audiences of the past year, in Hamburg, Bremerhaven, Rotterdam and Antwerp have already given them a heady feeling and a good start. In my opinion, the woman is a tigress, and will make many more enemies than friends before she goes silent. Although she prefers to have Germany lead the way in revolutionary social change, she reluctantly admits that the Russian proletariat is closer to exploding into revolt.

Inasmuch as that corresponds to the Maharal's vision of massive 1905 pogroms in the Czardom, it is frightening. In a connected way this could be the first legitimate test of the Prague forecasts. I'll be sure to note this in my synopsis. Why must every one with a prediction come to me with it?

I haven't talked much about today's events, mainly because it has been a busy day, and like the others I have been nervously preparing for tomorrow's move into the barracks. We have distributed about half of the tent halves to take along primarily for anyone wanting to use these as covers on deck during the voyage. Last year's reports referred to this possibility, especially during the warm nights we may or may not have at sea. The cramped, close quarters we expect make this alternative a viable one. We also distributed all of the foodstuffs to carry into quarantine and onto the ship a week from now.

Branko and the Golubs will carry the weaponry, and the tools went along with the remaining tent halves and the cart. I am pleased to report that Simmy and the three Golubs took the cart into town this afternoon and while unable to find a buyer, they met a group of Polish Yidden just disembarking from a ship in the harbor who were, believe it or not, coming back from America!

Their three destitute families totaled eighteen people, three of whom were under twelve years of age. According to the story they told, they had given the new world a noble try for over a year, but met with one setback after another, detested the tenement and sweatshop conditions, and pooled their money to return home to Lodz, which is about eight hundred kilometers from here. Not so far! Heh-heh!

They wanted to purchase the cart in order to transport all of their belongings and to conserve their shrinking funds by walking home. Simmy, seeing their ragged clothing, gaunt faces and bony bodies, simply turned it over to the patriarch of the group, wished him luck and walked away. The poor bewildered elder called after him, insisting that they wanted to pay something, but Yankel told us that Simmy wouldn't even turn around to listen.

All of us are as proud as proud can be of our shnorring czar. "He may be tart, but he has a heart!" as Mendel said in English, with explanation.

The toasts during our evening meal, our last on this lovely bluff top, were all to Simmy and his great mitzvah. His long lost humility returned to outshine the moon tonight.

On the other hand, this poignant story has caused a wave of distress amongst us. This is the first time we'd heard of Yidden returning from America. Mordecai and Mendel were quick to point out that this was an isolated case, and that obviously there have been and will continue to be those who, for some reason, failed to find their lost hopes in di goldeneh medina. Yet, the level of concern has risen perceptibly, while the great unknown still lurks beyond the horizon.

Tomorrow's entry will include a detailed description of what the isolation quarters are all about. I am most anxious to find that out. We all are.

After setting aside the journal, Sendehr asked Rivka to walk with him to their favorite spot, at the base of a low hanging alder tree on the most remote, isolated edge of the bluff. It overlooked the river and rolling farmlands of the Bremerhaven basin. The pair had spent many an hour here during the past week. It had become, by possession, their very own private sanctuary, duly honored by everyone in camp. Mendel and Esther, the new parents-to-be, had one of their own at the harbor-side. All other view points, and there were many of them on the broad mesa, were fair game for anyone, groups or individuals, to sit and contemplate their future quietly, enjoy the panorama, to talk, to brood about conditions back in Birlad, or just to laze about.

"Sendehr, please don't. Not here. Not now."

"Why not, my *zeesa* one? We're quite alone."

"*Mir tor nit*, Sendehrel. You know my feelings. *Mir tor nit.*"

"It doesn't get any easier. I love you with all my heart."

"And I love you, sweetheart, with all my soul. Remember, we'll be married soon. We'll both be thankful that we waited."

"November 16th. Your birthday. It seems like such a long way off...can't I just..."

"No. Please, dear. We can wait. We'll get settled. Find work. And before we know it, we'll be man and wife. It will be so very beautiful, my dear little boy."

"And in the meantime...yes, yes, I know, *mir tor nit, mir tor nit.*"

The kiss that followed this frequent tete-a-tete between these incurable lovebirds was simply delicious. It always was. And so it was to be...for the time being.

Henry Diedrich, the United States consul for Bremen and its port city, had been under extreme pressure. All of the German steamship lines, Hamburg-America and Lloyd included, insisted that the American doctors were far too strict in their immigrant admittance procedures. When passengers were denied entry at Ellis Island or East Boston for serious reasons, medical, criminal, or psychological, the steamship companies were obligated to return them to Germany, which was becoming increasingly costly. As many as ten percent were turned away, which amounted to fifty to a hundred passengers per shipload.

However, Consul Diedrich, with the full support of Ambassador Tower in Berlin, deftly turned the tables by ordering the Germans to do a more complete job of examining emigrants before they are allowed to board their

America-bound vessels. This had been an ongoing point of mutual contention for more than a decade, and the on-again, off-again quarantine requirements first introduced during the cholera epidemics of the '90s were once again tightened up in early 1903.

The barracks, their entire perimeter enclosed by a flimsy wire mesh fence, were relatively clean and Spartan. Each room held eight adults, and there were forty tightly packed rooms in each of two buildings. Toilets? Two at each end of each building. Baths? One in each building. Dining hall and kitchen? One, for all. It must be noted that the quarantine only applied to steerage and second-class passengers. First-class passengers, whoever they may have been, were exempt.

The Birladers were assigned to eight adjacent rooms on the second floor of one of the two barracks. It was here that they would honor Tisha b'Av, the ninth day of the month of Av, the most mournful of fasting days. It had often been called "the blackest day in the Jewish calendar," commemorating the destruction of both Temples: the First by Nebuchadnezzar in 586 B.C.E. and the Second by Titus the Roman in the year 70 C.E.

Fasting started at sundown on their first day in isolation, and would continue until sunset on Tuesday, August 10th, the Ninth Day of Av. During the afternoon hours of Tuesday, all of the Fusgeyers and more than two hundred of the Jewish barrack-dwellers gathered in the dining hall for special Tisha b'Av services, which were conducted admirably by the Lubavitchers, Rabbis Feinberg and Breslauer. They called upon the four Fusgeyer cantors to chant the Prophet Jeremiah's song of grief at the destruction of the First Temple, from the Book of Lamentations. It was a most moving, tear-filled ceremony, particularly in light of all of these Children of Israel having left their homes, families and friends for the great unknown.

Looking on in awe of this dramatic expression of grief for events that occurred so many centuries in the past were two respectfully quiet groups of fellow emigrants. One, the twenty-man Pole/Czech mining crew headed for Nova Scotia's coal fields; and the second, as it exceptionally coincidentally turned out, a four-man contingent of light-skinned, blond-haired Finns whose ultimate destination was Quincy, Massachusetts, U.S.A., and its renowned granite quarries where jobs awaited them.

That evening, after the fast, the major gulf in language notwithstanding, one of the Finns who was proficient in German chatted with Branko, and was told of the eight Fusgeyers also immigrating to Quincy. An almost immediate kinship developed as Nuchim, the four cantors, Itzy, Mayer and Sholem spoke with the amiable young men through Branko's interpretations. They valiantly tried to learn the proper pronunciation of the strange Finnish names of Eero Ruuttila, Oswald Honkalehto, Hugo Laukkanen and Eino Kauranen, who in turn struggled mightily with the guttural "ch" of Nuchim, Menachem and Yitzchok. With this auspicious beginning, it seemed conceivable to Sholem Friedman, resident "language maven," that the future Quincy-ites could very well be trading Finnish and Yiddish words and phrases long before they would arrive in Boston.

All would soon find Quincy to be a model microcosm of the much larger American melting pots, where one would ask the question:

> Could this New England town,
>
> that spawned rebellious
> Adams and John Hancock,
> be home to homeless,
> haven for hounded,
> Finn and Italian,
> Syrian and Jew?
>
> From "1913," by the author,
>
> *Hear O Israel,* 1983

Happily for all, the answer would turn out to be a resounding "yes," in the shipyards or deep in the quarries,

537

and in every part of town.

Sendehr wanted to finish writing his letter to Rabbi Nachman, combined with the synopsis covering the quarantine week, so that the HIAS representative could mail it for him. This would be his very last communiqué from the continent of Europe. The next would have the postmark of New York City, New York, U.S.A.

Dear Rabbi,

I've decided to combine my synopsis with this letter. A few things of major significance have occurred during our week of quarantine, even though I haven't filled many journal pages.

First, and most importantly, we have all passed the final physical examinations, with one exception, it grieves me to say. You will have to tell his family, but Asher Leibovich, our drummer boy who we all love dearly, has a contagious eye infection. No, it is not trachoma, as we all feared. The doctors gave him ample medication and they think it will clear up in thirty days or less, but they would not pass him through for tomorrow.

You'll be relieved to know that we came up with a viable solution. Chaike "with a heart of pure gold" Traubman insisted on staying with Asher in Bremerhaven until he's well enough to pass inspection. She is a good friend of Asher's sister Leah in Birlad, and just couldn't let him stay here alone.

Our HIAS man, Shammai Kurtzman, was successful in arranging to exchange Asher and Chaike's passage certificates for a ship leaving on October 2nd, arriving in New York on the 17th. He delivered the necessary papers to them this morning and Nuchim provided them with adequate funds to cover their expenses. To make matters even more assuring, Shammai has placed them with a Jewish family in Bremen and they'll be taking the wagon transit there tomorrow afternoon. The address you can give to the Leibovich and Traubman families is:

Herr Felix Goldmann

Klausenstrasse 6

Bremen

Note: Bremen, not Bremerhaven

Gershon was able to get a complete diagnostic report from the doctor and had Branko and Mendel translate it into Yiddish, and then Mordecai translated it into Romanian. Some team! Vay iz mir! We will have HIAS mail it to pharmacist Muresan, asking him to contact the Leiboviches and explain it in layman's terms. "Conjunctivitis," I believe it is called. Again I say, God Bless HIAS. Although sadly disappointed, Asher is taking it very well. Rivka and I will be sure to meet them when they arrive in October. Chaike is, indeed, an angel! Please tell her family and the entire congregation, Rabbi.

The shipping lines employ all the doctors and nurses and they have been pleasant and seemingly efficient. The two that conduct the examinations in our building, Doctors Brinkenhoff and Schlessinger are Jewish, and both have relatives in America. Brinkenhoff, the eye specialist, was quite apologetic when he gave his decision on Asher, and was overly generous in the medication he dispensed. We were all quite impressed yesterday when the doctor gave his home address in Bremen to Chaike and Asher. Frau Goldmann is one of his patients, and he suggested that if the infection was not clearing in a week they should ask her to telephone him. Knowing that Asher is in such good and caring hands has taken the sting out of the whole incident.

Bloody Rosa doesn't give up easily. She and her lieutenants were standing by the enclosing fence chatting with thirty or forty of the quarantined yesterday, drumming up interest in her socialist revolution. Mendel, during English class tonight, issued a sensible warning to our people that I hope everyone will heed. It went like this:

"It's all well and good to listen to a Rosa Luxemburg or anyone else with a definitive political philosophy, but you are about to become guests, and eventually citizens, of a country that doesn't look kindly on people who propose the violent overthrow of the existing government. Be careful. Please be careful. If socialist philosophy is something that you feel is supportive of the worker, then by all means follow it, always keeping in mind that the United States of America is a nation of laws that everyone must follow, day in and day out."

Not these exact words, Rabbi, but I'm sure you understand what Mendel is concerned about. So am I. There are those among us who are naive and susceptible to the Rosa Luxemburgs of the world. It seems to me that Abe Cahan has learned exactly where to draw the line in his thinking, his editorials, and his books and articles. I'm sure that a goodly number of our Fusgeyers are not nearly sophisticated enough to understand these complex political theories. I know I'm not, even with my voracious reading and constant discussions. We all have a great deal to learn and experience, which should prove to be both challenging and rewarding.

As for job placements, in addition to all of those who signed for openings while in Berlin, six more were assisted by Shammai. Velvel Palastrant will be working in a brass musical instrument factory in Paterson, New Jersey, just across the Hudson River. Doesn't that fit him well? Zed-Zed found something in Brooklyn with a jeweler who needs a watch repairman. Mendel Paretsky will be a tailor in a men's department store. Knowing him, he'll own the store in a month! Mottke Grunwald, his brother Hershel and Pini Kantorovitz took the openings for laborers that HIAS had listed for the construction of various subway extensions.

Most everyone else either has something waiting with relatives, or they will wait to see HIAS in New York. For example, you may remember that the Golubs are going on to work in their uncle's brewery in Scranton, Pennsylvania. According to a map I saw here, that appears to be more than one hundred miles from New York, but at least they'll be with family. The Udler boys are joining their father at his dry goods store in the Bronx. Shmuel Cohn passed on some good ideas for me, and a possible job for Rivka. I'll tell you more about it when we get there.

Aside from the three physical examinations there was little or nothing to do during the past week. We met Yidden from every part of the Pale, central and eastern Europe...goyishe Romanians from Bucureshti, Ploeshti, and Tulcea...Poles, Lithuanians, Latvians, Ukrainians, White Russians, Bulgarians, Bosnians, Serbians, Macedonians. Everyone going to America. More than I expected are heading for Canadian cities, too; and, in fact, three Jewish families from Warsaw are going to New York, then on to Mexico City by train. Gevalt!

We are stopping in Ireland to take on fuel before going on to Halifax, Nova Scotia, in Canada, to deliver some Polish and Czech coal-miners. Met some friendly German-speaking Finns, surprisingly destined for Quincy, with our people.

We are allowed out on the grounds as long as we stay a few meters from the fence if there are any people on the other side. This doesn't stop the vendors or the army of proselytizers. They smell blood whenever we venture out, but we were getting soft with this inactivity, so Nurse Nightingale insisted that we walk or trot around the buildings every now and then. That's all Sholem had to hear! He, Yaakov and Avi began holding informal races to the delight of hundreds of the idle detainees.

Friday morning, the four Finns, dressed in the strangest-looking short gatkes, challenged them to a longer than usual run, ten times around both buildings. Our indefatigable Sholem, barefoot as always, beat the pack by at least twenty meters, followed by two of the Finns and Yaakov, with little Avi close on their heels. It was thrilling to watch, and we especially enjoyed the display of good fellowship as they all shook hands and hugged. Through Branko's interpreting they made a date to race the decks on board ship if allowed, but barring that, Sholem called for a re-match once he and the quarry workers were settled in Quincy. They all agreed, "We'll find each other. The town can't be that big." We all wish we could see that race.

The cast voted unanimously to hold a farewell performance of "Dos Vinshfingerl." It was announced as "free of charge" for anyone in either barracks. The Yidden attended en masse, and oddly, even many goyim stayed through the entire performance in the dining hall. The applause was thunderously enthusiastic; many attendees had never seen a stage play. All of us put our last surge of energy into it, and everyone had a most rewarding evening. Numerous people asked Rivka if we would do it again during the voyage. Each member of the cast endorsed her answer..."Why not?"

With the strict quarantine measures, there also seems to be a bit of laxity. Clergy, HIAS and other relief organizations set one small room aside for use. For example, Shammai Kurtzman can only enter the room through a restricted corridor, and he can talk with anyone through a specially constructed inside window, passing papers through a slit in the paper-thin wall. A richtigeh mishigas, although it certainly has not hampered his effectiveness in any way. From time to time, there has been a Catholic priest in that office, a Lutheran and other Protestant ministers, an insurance salesman, Hilfsverein and Alliance Israelite representatives, each announced by a schedule posted on a board. The Jewish Labor Alliance only visits

Hamburg, I was told, since most people requiring their assistance stop in at their Berlin offices as we did.

There is still an uneasy feeling permeating our group. Yes, the fear of seasickness and the accompanying fear of the sea. The Poles, the Czechs, the Finns, and in fact, everyone in the barracks has a certain amount of both. The rumor mongers don't help one bit. The insurance salesman who has access to the "office" here is not much better than his obnoxious counterparts who waylaid us on the way into town. He has blatantly quoted statistics on ship disasters that have since been whispered about in every European language, Yiddish no exception. He has been here every day and is selling policies that cover the voyage, port to port, for Deutsche money only, at the equivalent of about five American dollars. In the event of the insured's death due to the ship sinking, one thousand dollars will be paid to a beneficiary, to whom the policy must be mailed before we sail tomorrow, of course. Yes, I've seen a few of our people looking over the sample document which is printed in four languages including Yiddish. Buyers? I can't say for sure. Shammai does not in any way endorse this, and is quick to state it's as good as *aroysgevarfen di gelt*.

Meanwhile, whenever the priest or ministers are here, the area adjacent to the "office" is full of frightened goyim, most praying, some prostrate, others weeping, rosary beads and crucifixes flashing everywhere. There is, of course, no need for a visiting rabbi. There must be at least eight among the Jews here. Aside from our two Lubavitchers, there are two yeshiva bochers from Lublin, an eighty-year-old rabbi and his two sons, also rabbis, from Vitebsk and Karlin, and a rabbi with his wife and seven yinglach from a shtetl near Vilna. There may be others, but we are already well covered with holiness. Our crossing is fully insured.

THE WAYFARERS

What more can I say at this point, Rabbi Nachman? Shammai Kurtzman will mail this on Monday. By that time we'll be within sight of England's southern coastline. Aside from the nervousness, most of our Birladers have spent a quiet, almost inert-like Sabbath day. The calm before the storm? Oy, God forbid! Wrong choice of words. In contrast, the final realization that our walking is finished has not yet set in among a few of us, namely the yinglach. The sight of the ship at eight o'clock tomorrow morning will fix that, no doubt.

Steerage quarters, according to what the Passage Master told Mordecai last week, have been upgraded from open dormitory to curtained quarters for eight. He also promised that both Hamburg-America and Lloyd had given in to the many petitions from relief agencies for better bathing and toilet facilities. Very promising, indeed. The officer even apologized for the lack of kosher food, which was still something being seriously considered. Even that is a victory of a kind.

Rabbi, I've never put this in writing before, but just being able to be in such close contact with you all these months, coupled with your most informative letters, has given me, and through me each of us, a strong link to everyone and everything we have left behind. Birlad will always be our home, no matter where we live or what we do in life. And you are Birlad, Rabbi. You represent who we were and who we are, and this we should never allow ourselves to forget or regret.

For your support and your love, for your sage counsel and your warm friendship, for your knowledge so generously shared, and for your patient listening, I thank you. We all thank you. May God shine His countenance upon you, your wife-to-be, your many kindelach to come, and upon all of our loved ones. Omayn, omayn!

Yours, in correspondence and friendship,
Sendehr Efraim

Bremerhaven,Germany,
five after midnight,
August 15, 1904 (14 Av, 5664)

§

"Not an RRB in sight." Rico was surprised and disappointed. He had hoped to encounter the melodramatic pretense offered by the infamous Romanian Road Blocks, the RRBs, one more time before leaving this intriguingly exasperating country. The ten fascinating days of intensive discovery had blown by like a hurricane, a weather phenomenon from which this part of the European landmass had total immunity.

Herb at the wheel of the trusty Fiat, which had taken the Friedmans through a goodly portion of Romanian territory, was just as happy that the unpredictable army appeared to have pulled in its horns. Nathan Friedman and Rabbi Yossi Nachman in the back seat, heavily into final storytelling and discussion since leaving Birlad, paid little or no attention.

"We have come a long way together, Rabbi. I can never thank you enough for marching me 1,500 miles in my father's century-old footsteps. You have given me an invaluably precious gift to take home."

"No, no, my dear Naftali. I should thank you for giving me the rewarding opportunity of once more telling the entire story, from beginning to beginning. Yes, from the beginning in Birlad, to a new beginning in your America.

"Now that we have walked together, we must from here both go on alone. I still have my *shul* and my diminishing flock to care for, and you have your own interesting life in which to do good deeds, one of which is to repeat the story you have just heard. You must do this, Naftali. Please, my son, please tell the story over and over again. I know you will."

Entering the outlying rundown districts of the capital, Herb estimated that they would deliver the supreme storyteller to his brother's apartment shortly after noon, giving the Californians ample time to arrive at the airport, deposit the rental car and board the Delta flight to LAX.

Going home!

Galaxies away!

La revedere Romania!

* * *

Gazing out of his window, seven miles above the same ocean Sholem had once crossed by ship, Nathan had become somewhat morosely pensive. He had decided at the outset not to use a tape recorder while conversing with the Rabbi. Too impersonal and uncomfortably intrusive. Therefore, the storage portions of his keen mind were filled with the vast amounts of historical data he had accumulated. It was all there—to massage, to contemplate, to remember, to later record, and above all else, to relate to others for posterity—the glory and the story of the Fusgeyers...they who went by foot.

Epilogue

Bremerhaven, August 15, 1904.

The gangplank swayed ever so slightly, as both the eager and the reluctant boarded the *Cincinnatus*. Waiting on the dock for the signal to proceed from the Passage Master, were the very last of the morning's emigrants...fifty-five patient Wayfarers, the dauntless Fusgeyers of Birlad. The moment the Passage Master raised his hand and nodded to them, they began to walk up the ramp single file as he checked the name on their passage coupon against the manifest held in his hands.

Once on deck, none of the Birladers went below to inspect their assigned quarters as directed by two ship's officers. Rather, they defiantly lined the rail waiting until every last one of their comrades stepped foot on the ship. The officers seemed to understand, and finally turned away to other duties.

Mordecai and Branko, satisfied that everyone was on board and awaiting them, then briskly walked the remainder of the gangplank, knowing that Mendel and Yankel were just a few steps ahead. In fact, the teacher and his pupil had stopped, facing each other on the narrow incline, with all eyes from above and behind fixed on them.

Putting his hand on Yankel's broad shoulder, Mendel sighed deeply:

"Can you believe it, good friend? We are going to America!"

Yankel, for the first time tried to please the *lehrer,* speaking in a slow, stammering, deliberate English, weeping all the while:

"*Nu,* Mendeleh...vill eet be goot fur di Yidden?"

Smiling broadly through his own tears, Mendel squeezed Yankel a bit closer, and issued forth in choked-tone English:

"It will be good, Yankeleh. It will be very good!"

APPENDIX

CHAPTER NOTES

Author's afterthoughts, observations and clarifications.

Historic figures with speaking roles appearing in *The Wayfarers*:

> Abraham Cahan
> William Frederick Cody (Buffalo Bill)
> Theodor Herzl
> Franz Kafka
> Rosa Luxemburg
> Max Nordau
> Charlemagne Tower, Jr.
> Robert Watchorn

Prologue

Ask a class of history students what they think their study of history is all about, and invariably the majority will answer in one word...dates. Conscious of this prevailing opinion, I encountered an annoying dilemma while researching the material for the prologue. According to a number of history texts and encyclopedias, Alexander II was assassinated on March 1st (1881); however, there were two exceptions to this date which I found in two very trustworthy sources: *A History of the Modern World- 8th Edition*, by R.R. Palmer and Joel Colton, (McGraw Hill, NY, 1995) and *Dictionary of World Biography*, Frank N. Magill, Editor, (Fitzroy Dearborn Publishers, Chicago and London, 1999). Both proclaimed that the assassination occurred on March

13th (1881). I opted to go with these two. The one thing that impressed me above all else was the fact that the Palmer-Colton tome is in its EIGHTH edition. Surely someone would have caught any glaring error. So March 13, 1881 it is.

Chapter 1

Quincy 1904

*The Thomas Jefferson quote was selected as it seemed to fit the mindset of young Sholem Friedman when he arrived in Boston, walking on to Quincy.

- The description of the road Sholem walked from Boston's North End to Quincy Point is based on research and associated information so ably provided by the Research Departments of libraries in Boston and Quincy, as acknowledged.
- All other references are also historically accrate. The fictional exception is as follows: There was a Leib Grossman, with many descendants still living in the area, but there was no Grossman House *per se* that provided board and room for Quincy's immigrant shipyard workers, as far as any research was able to determine.
- Ships carrying immigrants did, indeed, dock at East Boston's Immigration Station. My father at the age of 13, and his oldest sister, 19, arrived on July 5, 1913, after making the overland journey by foot, horse drawn wagon and train from Ignatovka in the Russian Ukraine, to the port at Hamburg. My grandmother and her five younger children arrived in East Boston on May 14, 1914, one month before the entire European

continent exploded in warfare. My grandfather, Samuel Tower (*pronounced Tuvehr in Russia, but automatically transposed to Tower on the ship's manifest. "V's" became "W's" for many immigrants from that part of Europe*) had earlier paved the way, arriving at Ellis Island in December, 1912, and making his way to Quincy, working as a riveter in the shipyard, not to his liking, and later opening a small dry goods store. Their journeys are featured in the piece entitled "1913," in my book *Hear O Israel*, (Paideia House, 1983).

- The Hebrew Immigrant Aid Society (HIAS) was the key support organization for the millions of Jewish immigrants arriving in America, especially during the years 1890-1914, and into the decades following the First World War. Words of praise for their vital contributions can be found in many his stories covering the era, as well as within the chapters of this novel. They were perhaps the first immigrant aid organization to identify themselves with a distinctive blue cap, with white Hebrew letters for HIAS embroidered on it. It would be lost in a sea of identifying baseball logo caps today, but a hundred years ago they stood out as beacons of light for the confused immigrant coming off the ship.

Chapter 2

Beverly Hills 2000

- Genealogical research has become a universally exciting adventure for millions. One of the main protagonists in this story, Nathan Friedman, is just one of those who carry out the study to its logical extreme. The resurgence in genealogically driven pursuits seems to reach into every ethnic corner, and the age of the computer is in no small way responsible. The fact that travel to all parts of the world is within the grasp of most anyone who wishes to do so plays a major role in this exciting family sport. "Lets find out where Grandpa played as a boy, where he had his first kiss, his school, his place of worship, where he worked, where he met Grandma..." The genealogical sleuth has entered the scene with a vengeance, and more and more people are taking the younger generations along with them, as Nathan does in this chapter...going there to visit the towns and villages, the cemeteries, the churches, the town halls, the synagogues, if they're still standing, and perhaps discovering someone locally who still remembers.

Chapter 3

Romania   2000

- The military road blocks (RRB's) were in common usage, especially during the Ceausescu regime. I was subjected to many of these during my travels through the country. Recently, two good friends on a trip from Hungary through Romania were stopped, not by the military, but by armed men in civilian clothes. It turned out that these distressing checks are now conducted by "contrac tors." Homeland Security?
- During the severe food and fuel shortages that have plagued the country, it was at times a nightmare for even the hardiest of visitors. Just finding food and fuel was a daily chore, ending up in wild frustration or complete failure. The restaurant scene is one that was endlessly repeated everywhere in Romania during the

Ceausescu period, now carrying over somewhat into current times. On several occasions I experienced a ten-page menu, with only one or two available items! Twice, my gasoline-driven rental car was incorrectly half-filled with diesel by a seemingly innocent attendant! There were no visible markings on the pumps, of course, but petrol stations were fifty to a hundred miles apart, with no guarantee that the product would be available. Long lines for bread, meat, milk and other staples were common throughout Romania, as well as the neighboring Soviet Union...much more likely in the cities.

Chapter 4

Birlad 2000

- This chapter, highlighting the first meeting between Nathan Friedman and the Birlader Rabbi, sets the stage for the Fusgeyer story. In my travels throughout Romania in the recent 80's, I found among the remnant Jews occasional references to the revered Fusgeyers. This triggered a deepening interest and eventual further research into this fascinating, history-making period of massive emigration. Hence, *The Wayfarers*.
- The Jewish Labor Alliance, headquartered in Berlin, is purely fictitious. There were numerous Jewish refugee relief organizations throughout Europe and America during these migrationary decades, and the Jewish Labor Alliance is more or less a composite of those. *Alliance Israleite Universelle* (Paris) and *Hilfsverein DerDeutschen Juden* (Berlin) are two of the actual agencies, mentioned herein.

Chapter 5

Birlad 1904

- The scenes herein are composites of those that took place in numerous villages, towns and cities during the Fusgeyer movement, 1899-1914. Although the vast majority of Fusgeyer contingents emanated from Romania, there is verifiable evidence of a minimal number that started out from within the Russian Pale (including Poland) and also from the eastern regions of the Hapsburg Empire (Transylvania/ Erdely, Galicia and Slovakia).

Chapter 6

Goodbye Birlad, Forever

(See note on Chapter Five above)

Chapter 7

The Trek Begins

- Once a Fusgeyer contingent reached America and sent back reports to their home town or village, it was possible for each succeeding group to chart the stopover locations. This valuable information made each day's goal realistically reachable, and it took away a certain amount of anxiety regarding the safety of the surroundings, especially when in open country as described on this first day, and those yet to come.
- Historically, those on the farms were much less apprehensive about the Jew. In the villages, towns and cities, there was a gnawing fear that

the stranger, Jew or any other, if he were to settle in the area, represented serious competition for jobs. Emotions ran high, and frequently amok. The Fusgeyers encountered this situation constantly, from Birlad to Bremerhaven.

Chapter 8

Prislop Pass

- Prislop is the major mountain pass separating the eastern and western slopes of the Carpathian mountain range in the vicinity of northern Romania, and the eastern extension of the former Austro-Hungarian Empire. Though it is not nearly as high and dangerous as, say, Donner Pass in the Sierras, it nevertheless posed serious problems for any travelers during a snowstorm. Timing was a major dilemma for all walking emigrants...start out in spring, run into a late snow storm and suffer the oppressive heat of summer...leave in summer, face the heat and tempt an early fall snow somewhere in Germany or a winter storm at sea. Generally, all Fusgeyer contingents left in early spring, and those who opted for the northern route through the Carpathians had Prislop Pass to contend with. There were no known disasters of the infamous Donner variety.

Chapter 9

Pesach - Sighet

- Sighet is the birthplace of the great writer, Nobel Peace Prize recipient Elie Wiesel. The fifteen-year-old and his family were rounded up by the Nazis and their Hungarian *hilfswilige* (generically known as "hiwi's"), willing helpers, in the spring of 1944, along with all of the town's Jews. Ultimately, they were transported to the death camp at Auschwitz. I feel comfortable that my vision of an earlier version of Elie Wiesel (Eliezer Viesl) living in Sighet c.1904 is a reasonably credible one. I have featured references to Elie in two previous books. One piece is entitled *The Conscience (Hamatzpun-*Heb.*)*, and the other, simply *Sighet.*

• Chasia Zitovitz is a purely fictitious character, based on the real Chasia Helfman, a cell mem ber of the People's Will who participated in the assassination. Pregnant, she was captured and died of miscarriage complications in a hospital, under guard. The information on the planning and execution of the plot is factual, as is the name of the bomber.

Chapter 10

Encounters: Road to Budapest

• The confrontation with the Szatmar Rebbe merely mirrors the continuing, seemingly unbridgeable chasm between various elements of Judaism...the ultra-orthodox, the more modern orthodox, the traditional or conservative and the liberal or reform. The same can be said for any of the world's religions.

• Those espousing extreme nationalistic ideals throughout the Europe of 1904 had nothing but animosity toward large groups "invading" their turf. The horsemen of the Hungarian plains, the *csikosh*, were especially adept at harassing Jewish emigrants ...threatening, robbing and occasionally causing injuries and even death to those who were in the smaller, more vulnerable contingents. The Hungarian military units of the Austro-Hungarian Empire tended to be a bit more restrained, but did nothing to stop the hard riding "cowboys of the Hortobagy."

Chapter 11

Encounters: Budapest

- Agents/recruiters of the JCA (Jewish Colonization Association) fanned out throughout Europe during this period of mass migration. They were less than successful in trying to convince significant numbers of Jewish emigrants to take advantage of Baron De Hirsch's exceptional generosity. A relative handful ended up in rather remote regions of the United States or Canada, or on the pampas of Argentina and Southern Brazil, where many eventually moved on to the big cities of Buenos Aires, Sao Paulo and Rio de Janeiro.
- The first modernized metropolis that most Fusgeyer contingents encountered was Budapest. I tried to imagine the awestruck country cousins as they observed "life in the big city" with it's innovations, crowds of citizens and "city ways." The scenes could have easily been c.1904 small town Missourians, Ohioans, Georgians or Texans the first time they arrived in Kansas City, St. Louis, Cleveland, Cincinnati, Atlanta, Houston or Dallas. Budapestians had the deserved reputation of being most hospitable to emigrating Jews from the east, and a substantial number stayed on. References to Hungarian Jews who reached the heights of success in business industry and government are actual names.

Chapter 12

Encounters: Road to Vienna

- The wanton destruction of the gypsy camp near Budapest was a typical military act of the times. They were rarely granted more than a modicum of freedom and were subjected to the same ceaseless harassment as Jews and other minorities. It was certainly no surprise later in the century when Hitler labeled the gypsies subhuman and summarily targeted them for extinction.
- Fusgeyer contingents, and indeed many other transient individuals and small groups en route to the ports, had been warned of the frigid welcome they would receive in Vienna. Nevertheless, the Romanian Fusgeyers had pledged to carry their protest into every village, town and city en route. Most of them opted not to give up an opportunity to see the fabled, cultured city of music and the arts ...its infamous, acutely xenophobic Mayor Karl Lueger and his ilk, be damned!

Chapter 13

Encounters: Vienna

- The information in the paragraph concerning Doctor Freud was gleaned from numerous references to his years in Vienna.
- Fervent Zionists all along the path of the Fusgeyers (or for that matter, any westward emigrating Jewish group) gave it their best efforts to deter them, trying to convince them to reverse their steps, to head eastward to the Holy Land. The not-too-encouraging reports coming

back from Palestine seemed to heavily outweigh
the dreamy visions offered by Theodor Herzl's
supporters, most of whom still hadn't been
there. After all, especially for those going to
America, a waterless, desert wasteland sur
rounded by armed and angry Arabs, the occu-
pying Turkish military and swamps laden with
swarms of infectious malaria-carrying
mosquitoes, could never compare to streets
paved with gold in a Golden Land
(*goldeneh medina*).

- Max Nordau, the popular European journalist,
  was, indeed, a source of great compassion and
  unswerving support during Herzl's last days.
  His continuing public lectures, provocative
  essays and feature articles contributed
  significantly to the excruciatingly slow but
  certain rise in Zionist recognition the world
  over. I tried to paint a portrait of the two
  vision aries, imagining their deportment in the
  event they had an opportunity to personally
  meet with young America-bound Jews in the
  intrepid Fusgeyer mold.

Chapter 14

Encounters: Road to Prague

- Entering the Moravian and Bohemian provinces
  of the Empire during this period, the cry for
  independence was building to a crescendo that
  could not be silenced. Thomas (Tomash)
  Masaryk and his growing ranks of supporters
  were under constant surveillance by the
  Emperor's operatives. This, and the fact that
  Germany's saber rattling to the north was a
  factor to be wary of, made it consistently uneasy for the transients. At worst, the constant

threat of incarceration or forced deportation, proper papers notwithstanding, with trigger-happy elements on all sides, was very real and carried out frequently. There were routes that could have bypassed this region, but by this point most groups were determined to make the shortest beeline for the port.

Chapter 15

Encounters : Prague

- Blending the young "Kafka-esque Kafka," if you will, with the provocative tales of the Golem, a rabbi prone to hallucinatory episodes, and the legendary mysterious aura of Praha (Prague), has in all likelihood been mined over at onetime or another by writers with richer imaginations than my own. If not, why not? At any rate, introducing the courageous Fusgeyers into this mystical mix is uniquely of my own doing, and I'm fully prepared to suffer any critical consequences of such audacity, if need be.
- The mammoth makeover project of decaying Prague was taking place at the beginning of the 20th century. Those who have recently visited have seen the attractive results of the most ambitious municipal facelift in all of Europe at that time.*
- Fusgeyer lodgings in all of the bigger cities ran from comfortable to rustic to Dickensian squalor. Prague and Budapest were the favorites, but many contingents rather favored camping under the stars, as did thousands of smaller independent groups.

*(Another strange coincidence occurs in this chapter... this time involving the full name of my

559

late wife Judy. When approaching Prague from the south, the Vltava can be crossed on the Karluv Most (Charles Bridge). At that point the ancient span is guarded by both a large and a smaller tower. As the text describes, the latter is named for the beloved 8th century Bohemian Queen Judith, and is popularly referred to as "the Judith Tower." On earlier visits to the city I hadn't heard any mention of this ... but in the '90's I read the story in an obscure guidebook, and later at my request, my friends Shirley and Nathan Krasnigor (Nuchim) came across postcards verifying this while visiting Prague)

Chapter 16

Encounters: The Great Escape

- By far, the greatest source of unskilled labor for the Hapsburg military building projects came from the hapless emigrants transiting the Empire en route to the North Sea ports. In most cases, even the most minimal infraction was all the excuse needed to exploit the bewildered refugee. Roads had to be constructed and improved, barracks and forts had to be built or repaired. Dams and levees, bridges and tunnels, walls and whatnot... all awaited the plentiful, cheap labor. And who was there who could and would intercede on behalf of the hapless foreigner?
- Theresienstadt/Terezin served as the main fort between Prague and the German border during this time. A half century later, the fortress became Hitler's sham concentration camp, presented to the International Red Cross inspectors as a model of "German compassion" for its unfortunate prisoners. Most faced certain death after they were finally transported to one of the more "real" camps.

Chapter 17

Encounters: Road to Berlin

- The condescending mindset of the German-Jew became evident to the millions of *ostjuden* as they entered the relatively newly unified nation. Dresden, with its proximity to the Austro-Hungarian borders, served to introduce this heretofore unknown phenomenon to the "inferior" Jew of the east. The less-than-welcoming attitude became more pronounced as the emigrant went further into the heart of Germany, especially in Berlin.
- The likes of Pastor Hof were to be found throughout Germany, especially at the ports (Chapter 20). The massive movement of poor, Jewish underclass emigrants crossing Germany translated into heaps of fodder for conversion. Research shows that scant few succumbed. Rabbi Nachman's letter to Sendehr and the Fusgeyers, addressing the unsettling predictions of Prague's Rabbi Blankfort, would have been a likely response from younger members of the rabbinate. Predicting the future seems to be a pastime, almost like a grand sporting event, throughout history ...but when it was coupled with tales of the Golem from medieval times to the early 20th century, even some of the most persistent doubters listened more intently. Rationale flourished profusely... still does, whenever and wherever forecasts of any kind are offered.

Chapter 18

Encounters: Berlin-a foreboding

- The intense militaristic demonstrations in and around Berlin alarmed many foreign visitors from the 1870s to the eve of WW I, and later during the decade preceding WW II. One can imagine transitory individuals and groups, being at first impressed and soon disturbed, as were the Birladers. Sendehr's piece on the "black boots, jack boots" paints the foreboding picture with frightening clarity.

- Buffalo Bill Cody, very much the great American icon to the crowned heads of Europe during this period, was a most significant influence on particularly the younger generations throughout the central and western parts of the continent. His appearances, along with the proliferation of the Western Dime Novel, in translation, gave added impetus to those who dreamed of immigrating to the land of the cowboy and the Indian.

- It was the primary mission of the Fusgeyer contingents to have their protests heard by people of influence. To meet with the Romanian ambassador to Berlin, in the office of the Ameri can ambassador, in the presence of distinguished members of the press, would have been an impossible dream. This writer chose to make it possible, albeit in retrospective fiction. Robert Watchorn, a special envoy from the U.S. Immigration Service, was widely known for his investigative work throughout Eastern Europe, in determining the political reasons behind such massive migrations to the west. He later became President Roosevelt's appointee to head the Immigration Service.

Chapter 19

Encounters:Road to Bremerhaven

- Abraham Cahan's quote heading this chapter was especially true in the Fusgeyer mentality. Theirs was not at all a personal expedition, but was driven by a burning desire to be part of an historical event, telling the world of the motivating forces behind their march to freedom.

Chapter 20

Encounters: The Port

- The last exceptionally unsavory emigrant experience before leaving the shores of Europe was at the port... Rotterdam, Antwerp, Hamburg, Bremerhaven or any others. All references, letters, interviews and memoirs uncovered by my research pointed in some way to the inherent unwanted influences and constant dangers to be found therein. Today, some of these scenes can be revisited anywhere in the world where large groups of refugees await transportation to a new life... and eventual freedom from want and fear.

Note: Throughout the book, the letter-writing between Sendehr and Rabbi Eli Nachman, and the letter from Shmuel Cohn, where script-handwriting fonts are used, actually represent the Hebrew-lettered Yiddish which would have served as the common communication link between these characters.

ACKNOWLEDGMENTS

Writing historical novels requires help. Lots of it. I discovered that early in the project-planning phase and took bold advantage of family, friends, research specialists, bookstores, libraries, editors, overseas contacts, literary agents, publishers, The Library of Congress, The United States State Department...and of course, the all-encompassing Internet.

It all starts at home, where else, for the most direct and honest criticism, most painfully so at times. My indefatigable critic is a stickler for detail and nit-picking...but oh, so vitally necessary. My dearest Roz seemed to relish putting me on the defensive, chapter by chapter, if not line by line and word by word...but whenever she conceded full approval I knew I could go on with the story in good conscience. Our discussions over correct Yiddish dialect are classic. I am, therefore, enraptured by a resident, handy-dandy editor-critic-analyst-wife-lover-friend-alter ego of the most invaluable variety. A mere "thank you" is not nearly enough. I'll work on it.

My dad, Maurice Tower (Moishe Leib), a 1913 immigrant who my American-born mother, Ann (Channah), could goad into telling me all that he could remember of his journey to America, provided illuminating input over the years that eventually found its way into my prior books and this novel. Both passed on in 1985, but I was fortunate enough to salvage even a few of the many ideals and values that they so graciously demonstrated during my storybook childhood ...one that was aglow with unconditional love, mutual respect, and above all, laughter and fun. I know that this is contrary to the popular notion that abuse, alcohol, hard drugs, dark skies and abject poverty are the prerequisites for any writer worth his pen. But, so be it, and you dear reader, are the ultimate judge.

Judith Tova Tower, my beloved departed first wife, to whom my most recent book was proudly dedicated, provided a long-continuing source of the aforementioned bliss-ful home and family environment for forty fulfilling, blessed years. I like to think that Judy would have loved this story.

Where do I begin to acknowledge all of the others who were so important to the development of this novel, begin-ning to end? A good start would be with Eric Scott Gould, a Yale Drama School graduate, a fine aspiring actor and my good, young friend, who was so intrigued with the story he immediately saw a film-in-the-making. As you know, Los Angeles is "Script City, USA." If you're not writing one, sell-ing one, reading one, rejecting one or planning one, you must live in Bakersfield. The project was soon abandoned in favor of publishing the book first, and so I continued on with *The Wayfarers*, Eric occasionally acting as a welcome cheerleader *cum* critic.

The Research Department of the Thomas Crane Public Library in Quincy, Massachusetts, especially Linda Beeler, Mary Clark and Jeanine Thubauville, had always been most attentive and rapidly responsive in answering my e-mail lists of questions concerning turn-of-the-century Quincy. During my childhood, high school and college years I spent countless fulfilling hours in the reading rooms of this ven-erable institution. My previous books reside in its "Quincy Author's Room." A most grateful thanks to all of you from one of the "home boys"...also a tip of the hat to the library staff of the University of Massachusetts, South Boston cam-pus, for being most helpful concerning the Boston of 1904...its place names, street names maps and neighbor-hoods, etc.

By the same token, the Beverly Hills Public Library, heavily endowed by its generous, celebrated citizenry, be-came a most prolific resource for me. It's reference rooms stack up to those in any major city. Los Angeles Public Li-brary branches, all over this wide spread metropolis, of-fered excellent reference services on a number of occasions.

Dr. Paul Claussen, the U.S. State Department's Chief Historian, generously provided some very meaningful as-sistance by phone and fax, as did Mary Wolfskill at The

Library of Congress. Thank you both. For example, Dr. Claussen stunned me when he came back with information that the ambassador to Germany in 1904 was a man named Tower...Charlemagne Tower, Jr. As the footnote in Chapter 18 emphatically states, absolutely no relation! Allen J. Petersen of Tower City and Fargo, North Dakota was also helpful in this regard, and provided a rare photograph of the ambassador.

A sincere thank you to Rita Krakower Margolis and Sol Margolis, of Rockville, Maryland. Sol is the grandson of Shlomoh Margolis , an actual Fusgeyer who appears in the story...Mihaela Barba, a young lady engineer from Iashi in Romania, graciously shed some important e-mail light on my research concerning old Iashi and Birlad...Paul Pascal and Gertrude Ogushwitz, both former editors of the Internet ROM-SIG News covering genealogical search in Romania, were most cooperative in their e-mail and telephone correspondence. Based on his interesting supplemental information, two of Paul's ancestors are also mentioned herein.

The Romanian Consulate in Los Angeles, although not treated very kindly in Chapter 2, was truthfully an effective source of solid informative material on the Romania of 1904. In my travels to their country, during the less-than-welcoming Ceausescu regime, they eliminated as much red tape as possible for me. *Va multzumesc foarte mult!*

I'd be remiss in not mentioning the gigantic book emporia, Barnes and Noble, Brentanos, Rand McNally, and Borders, for "allowing" me to browse, shmooze and take notes...without buying. I feel just a tinge of guilt, but I'll get over it. After all, it is certainly the collective sort shared by millions.

During a visit to Vancouver, Brendan Moss of "Le Magazin" turned out to be a hospitable source of four hard-to-find 1902 color maps of Central and Eastern Europe. This was a welcome surprise to me and I'm forever appreciative. With the American dollar so strong in Canada, this time I bought.

Is there a writer anywhere who hasn't spent an enormous amount of time and money copying drafts and final manuscripts in a Kinko's... that den of ubiquity? I did better than that, at half the price and twice the personalized service. I was blessed to have Tip-Top Printers nearby, straight down the hill, owned and operated by the exceptionally accommodating and pleasant Mizrahie family, and the affably competent Nichie Ricardo. Thank you, *chaverim! Todah rabah!*

In this Windows-Microsoft age, he who doesn't have a computer "guru" close by will eventually throw his shoe at the garbled screen. Fortunately, friend and former colleague Stewart Margolis served this role far beyond the normal call of duty. Heartfelt kudos from Stu to Stew!

Along the way, I sincerely appreciated a variety of other sounding-boards which gave me the added assurance that my storytelling was on the right track ...my hundreds of keenly perceptive Elderhostel students who have given such enthusiastic receptions to my numerous history courses and the preview presentations of *The Wayfarers,* arranged by Marcia Rhodes, the Elderhostel administrator of the Center for Studies of the Future, in Ventura, California...the students of Julie Thoma's Advanced Placement European and American History classes, and Glen Hirshberg's Creative Writing seminars at Campbell Hall School: rather captive, but most critical audiences of exceptionally bright college-bound young adults...Gayle Brinkenhoff's esteemed book club consisting of twenty-five exceptionally literary women in the Santa Barbara-Ventura area...dear old friends Judy and David Sanders who graciously invited me to tell the Fusgeyer story to their Palos Verdes "lunch bunch" of fifty men and women, voracious readers all...likewise, the charming Nancy Lander and her astute book club members in Tustin, California...and David Epstein, Isaac Nathan Publishing and editor/publisher of *The American Rabbi,* for his most helpful guidance as the publisher of my most recent book, *Withered Roots.*

What kind of a doting grandpa would I be if I didn't include my joy-giving grandchildren by freely using their names and personalities for certain characters: Shane ("Shmuel Cohn"), Eric ("Rico"), Dariel , Cayla and Jesse ("Yehuda Dov"). They're all in the story, somewhere. Find them!

* * *

"Poetic license" is a keen tool to use when writing a piece of fiction, even though I've blended in numerous actual historical figures, places and events. In so doing, I borrowed freely when using names, particularly where they could be somewhat disguised in most cases, with the Yiddish-ized Hebraic equivalent. For this, I fraternally give a wink-of-the-eye salute to the following old-time friends, good sports all (I hope!)...the "Quincy Boys:" Nathan Krasnigor (Nuchim), Bill Needel (Velvel Niedl), Mel Needel (Melech Niedl), Menachem Mendel Katz, Mort Bernstein(Mayer), Mel Bookman(Mendel Buchman), Richard Weiner (Ruvain Veiner), Gene Myers (Yitzhok Myerz), Bob Kurtzman (Rabbi Yaakov), and Bob Adler (Zacharya Udler). Others from around the USA are Bernie (Berel) and Don (Dov) Singerman, Mitch Silver (Menachem Mendel Zilber), Sanford Schulhofer (Rabbi Shmuel), Gary Jacobs, Milt Weiss (Gershon), old army sidekick Bill Palastrant (Velvel), Dr. Michael Brinkenhoff and Dr. Gregory Schlessinger... and the following, all deceased, may God rest their good souls: Shammai Kurtzman, Barney/Bernie Adler (Bezalel Udler), my uncle Joe Castleman (Yossel), after whom the amiable Berlin HIAS man was modeled, Dr. Allan Warmbrand (Eliyosef)... and my colorful late colleague, buddy and mentor, Harold C. "Hacker" Wallace, the Squire of Cornish, New Hampshire, "just up the road a piece" from the reclusive J.D. Salinger. Remember *Catcher in the Rye?*

It is with humble respect that I offer a very special embrace to the small and highly selective group of previewers whose comments can be read within this book ... Doctor Eliahu Yehuda Schochet, widely revered professor, rabbi and prolific author, who not only served as the model for the Birlader Rabbi of 1904, but who also poured a steady stream of encouraging commentary my way... Colonel Robert A. Stein of the universally respected University of Iowa Writer's Workshop and a prolific writer of several novels... Doctor John K. Roth, noted scholar, author, expert analyst of the works of Elie Wiesel, Pitzer Professor of Philosophy, and Chair of the Philosophy and Religious Studies Department at Claremont McKenna College... Rabbi David Baron, author of the unique book, *Moses on Management,* and spiritual leader of the exceptionally novel Temple Shalom for the Arts... and two big thumbs up for Steven Spielberg, an aspiring up-and-coming filmmaker (!), who graciously took time from his day job to review the manuscript and issue a laudatory comment, as he also did with one of my previous books, *Withered Roots.*

And finally, but without which none of this would have been in print, a sincere bow to my publisher, R.J. "Ron" Richard of The Lighthouse Press, who saw something of significant value in this story that he wanted to share with the vast book reading public. His continuing farsighted leadership, along with the meticulous, highly competent editing of the caring, persistent, patient and witty Molly Kalkstein, and Mel Savoie's dedicated formatting, has resulted in *The Wayfarers* now being held in your hands. Tell your friends.

Stuart Tower, Los Angeles, 2003

ROSTER: 1904 BIRLAD FUSGEYER
CONTINGENT #4

Name and Age	Occupation
Cadre:	
Mordecai Anieloff, 24	glass-blower
Menachem Berman, 23	glass designer
Mendel Buchman, 26	cheder teacher
Rivka Demkin, 21,	seamstress
Sendehr Efraim. 19,	unemployed
Simmy Fiedelman, 18	baker
Branko Horvitch, 29	ex-soldier, blacksmith
Nuchim Krasnigor, 23	bookkeeper
Gershon Maibaum, 22	pharmacist's apprentice
Zacharya Zelman, 21	watch repairer
Fusgeyers:	
Avrum Avramovici, 14	student and messenger
Mottke Bercovici, 22	roofer, laborer
Pincus Bercovici, 15	student
Mayer Bernstein, 21	granary, bag sorter
Esther Buchman, 19	seamstress
Tsipporah Eshman,18	dairy-maid
Menashe Federman,16	candlemaker
Dov Feinstein, 26	baker
Sholem Friedman,17	grain merchant's helper
Kalman Fuchs, 17	shoemaker's apprentice
Itzy Gelman, 20	rope-maker
Yehudaman,25*	chicken farm hand
YehudaGelman, 25*	chicken farm hand
Yankel Golub, 21	brick factory worker
Yossi Golub, 20	laborer
Hershel Grunwald, 21	farm hand
Mottke Grunwald, 23	painter
Naftali Grushkin, 15	student, inn worker
Leib Kalisher, 15	student, laborer
Pini Kantorovitz, 25	winery worker
Yankel Kantorovitz, 16	candlemaker

Destination	Mendel's English Nicknames
New York	Commander
New York	Diplomat
New York	Professor
New York	Bernhardt
New York	The Writer
New York	Food Czar
New York	Big Soldier
Boston,Quincy	Red Hill
NewYork	Hippocrates
New York	Zed-Zed
Newark	School Boy
New York	Nails
New York	Pin Cushion
Boston,Quincy	Crusher
New York	Blondie
New York	Mrs. Tsippy
New York	Feathe Man
New York	BagelMaker
Boston, Quincy	Speedy
New York, Philadelphia	Squeaky
Boston,Quincy	Comedian
New York	Farmer
New York	Farmer
Scranton	Muscle Man
Scranton	Mad Man
New York	Smokey
New York	Rembrandt
New York	Bell Boy
Cleveland	Kid Kalish
New York	Big Bee
New York	Little Wick

THE WAYFARERS

Name and Age	Occupation
Menachem Katz, 21	tailor
Maidel Kaufman, 18	housekeeper
Meyer Kelemer, 17	cobbler
Asher Leibovich, 15**	student, musician
Yehuda Livadaru, 27	tailor
Leibel Marcovici, 21	grocery clerk
Moishe Meiervici, 19	dairy hand
Yitzchok Myerz, 20	farm worker
Yaakov Nachman, 17	grain helper
Velvel Niedl, 22	town worker
Velvel Palastrant, 16	student, musician
Mendel Paretsky, 19	tailor's apprentice
Dov Posner, 24	grain merchant
Benyumin Rabinovici, 21	upholsterer
Heshy Rosen, 16	student, house painter
Avigdor Semelweiss, 14	student
Dovid Shapira, 24	taylor
Ruvain Shapira, 20	tailor's apprentice
Berel Singerman, 20*	chicken farmer
Dov Singerman, 21*	chicken farmer
Avrum Tishkoff, 21	laborer
Chaike Traubman, 17**	housekeeper
Bentzion Tuvehr, 23	silversmith
Moishe Leib Tuvehr, 21	bookkeeper
Bezalel Udler, 24	blacksmith
Zacharya Udler, 19	cobbler
Velvel Varshavsky, 18	shochet's helper
Pessel Vinocur, 19	housekeeper
Menachem Mendel Zilber, 17	carpenter

Berel and Dov Singerman, and Yehuda Gelman, left the group in Budapest to join the Jewish Colonization Association colonies in Argentina. The Singerman brothers eventually went to California to buy a chicken ranch in Petaluma. Gelman remained in Moisesville, Argentina where he and his family prospered.

Destination	Mendel's English Nicknames
Boston, Quincy	The Tenor
New York	Nightingale
Boston. Quincy	Straight Man
New York	Drummer Boy
Chicago	Man
Bridgeport(CT)	Slim
New York	Milkman
Boston, Quincy	Farmer Isaac
Boston, Montreal	Scout
Boston, Quincy	Bidgie
Paterson (NJ)	Billy Bugle
New York	Beau Brummel
New York	Brains
Philadelphia(PA)	B.R.
Boston, Montreal	Artiste
New York	Peanut
New York	Big Brother
New York	Kid Brother
New York	Rooster
New York	Hay Seed
Fort Wayne (IN)	Abe
New Haven (CT)	Mother Hen
Passaic (NJ)	B.Z
Passaic (NJ)	Gentleman Jim
New York	The Hammer
New York	Little Hammer
Philadelphia(PA)	Cut-throat
New York	Little Mama
Rochester (NY)	Moneybags

**Asher Leibovich was rejected at the port in Bremerhaven due to a conjunctivitis condition. Chaike Traubman decided to stay with him while he was being treated. Both were able to board a ship in October, sailing to New York where they were greeted by Sendehr Efraim and Rivka Demkin.*

Fusgeyer Itinerary, April 1, 1904–August 15, 1904
Romania and Austro-Hungarian Transylvania (Erdely)

April	1	Fusgeyer Contingent marches out of Birlad at 9:00 am, arrive Vlad Murescu farm for first overnight encampment
	2	Bacau
	3	en route (Buhushi, Roznov, Savineshti)
	4	Piatra (School kids yell, "Go to Palestine!")
	5	en route (Tarcau, Bicaz, Borca)
	6	Vatra Dornei ("Freilacher Berel", the "egg man")
	7	Cirlibaba
	8	en route (difficult steep incline to the pass)
	9	Prislop Pass (heavy snowstorm, first major test)
	10	Prislop Pass (downhill rough going...snow, rain and quagmires)
	11	Borsha (Hungarian military post, Captain Sandor incident)
	12	en route (Viseu De Sus, Viseu River Valley)
	13	Cuhea (the beautiful Tisza Valley...Ieud, Rozavlea, Vad (Izei)
	14	en route (through the fruit orchards of the valley)
	15	Vadu Izei (farm town close to Sighet)
	16	Sighet (Sighetul, Sziget...meet Rabbi Kurtzman and their hosts)
	17	Sighet (Pesach seders, meet Eliezer Viesl the journalist)
	18	Sighet (Second night of seders...for most, their first seders away from home...all made to feel exceptionally welcome by the Sighet folk
	19	en route (Sapintsa, Negreshti-Oash, northwestern Maramuresh)

20	en route (Orashu Nou, Livoda, the valley of the River Szamos)
21	Szatmar (Szatmarnemeshti, Satu-Mare)
22	en route (*Shabbos* ... after highly vociferous, challenging encounter with the Szatmar
23	en route (via Carei, Valea-lui Mihai)

Hungary and Austria

24	Debrecen (large, rare Protestant city in Catholic Hungary ...over night in a barn next to the beautiful classic synagogue. (Debrecen community overly generous with supplies...wagon loaded to a peak!)
25	en route (the broad grasslands of Hungary, the Hortobagy)
26	en route (the famous old inn, site of Branko's lost love)
27	en route (frightening *csikosh* encounters near the town of Hortobagy, and later at the Tisza River ferry-crossing in Tiszafured)
28	en route (harassment continues by the hardriding *csikosh*)
29	en route (Tiszafured, Poroszlo in the vast grasslands)
30	Jaszapati

May	1	Jaszbereny
	2	en route (via Nagykata)
	3	en route (via Tapioszecso)
	4	Sulysap (slowed by driving rainstorm)
	5	en route (via Gyomro, heavier rains grind the march to a halt)
	6	Budapest (Mordecai has trepidations about big city influences)
	7	Budapest (*Shabbos*...all enjoy the city's many attractions)
	8	Budapest (new shoes for all! The fund-raising

play is per formed for the first time, with great success. Eliezer Viesl's article be comes the first Birlad Fusgeyer notice in print. This becomes the most significantly satisfying day of the journey to this point)

9 Aquincum (the Roman Ruins just north of Budapest, the tense "wounded Sholem" inci dent and the brutal gypsy round up and deportation perpetrated by the callous Hun- garian military)

10 en route

11 Esztergom (Mordecai refuses to take on other emigrants)

12 en route (along the Danube

13 Szony (via Labatlan and a series of riverbank villages.

14 Komarom (for the Sabbath)

15 Komarom

16 Raab/Gyor (upsetting incident with the Austrian military, and Mordecai wisely de cides to leave and to make camp at Ottoveny)

17 Mosonmagyarovar

18 Rosovce (via Hegyeshalom and Rajka...in Slovak region)

19 Petrszalka (outskirts of Poszony/Pressburg)

20 Poszony/Pressburg (another of the double and triple-named cities in the Austro-Hun- garian Empire)

21 Poszony (now named Bratislava, capital of today's Slovakia)

22 Poszony (Shabbos, and once again, the play is a big success in the Saturday evening performance)

23 en route (another heavy rainstorm, camp in Fischamend on the banks of the Danube/ Donau)

24 en route (arrested by an Austrian cavalry troop, escorted to the holding-pen outside of the town of Schwechat)

25   Schwechat (detained by the Austrians)

26   Schwechat (still held, along with many others seeking entrance into a Vienna/Wien made in hospitable by its xenophobic mayor)

27   Vienna (finally admitted with a pass expiring four days later on the last day of the month, approached by Max Nordau who invites Mordecai to meet with his colleague, Theodor Herzl)

28   Vienna (Mordecai takes Mendel and Sendehr along for the historic and illuminating meeting with the Zionist leader)

29   Vienna (Sabbath day)

30   en route (after photo-taking session arranged by popular journalist Nordau who plans to write articles of the Fusgeyer mission ... camp in pine grove near Stockerau)

31   en route (via Hollabrunn, overnight in Haugsdorf)

Moravia and Bohemia

June 1   Znojmo/Znaim (*Shavuos* celebration at Znojmo *shul*)

2   en route (vineyards of Moravia, rolling hills)

3   en route (passing through Stitary and Desov)

4   en route (via Jemnice, in the Bohemian high lands)

5   Telc (encamped for *Shabbos* just west of Teltsch/Telc)

6   en route (via Jindrichuv Hradec, steady rainf all, very muddy going for trekkers and cart-shleppers)

7   en route (Sobeslau/Sobeslav, encountering Austrian cavlary commanded by Captain Ullbricht, the notorious *paskudnyak* who tears up their transit documents, exacts an enormous tribute payment and gives them ten days to

exit the Empire or else!)

9   en route (via Tabor, small, welcoming Jewish community)

10   en route (via Konopiste Castle, home of Arch duke Franz Ferdinand, continuing on to an en campment twenty kilometers southeast of Praguee/Praha)

11   Prague/Praha (for a two day Sabbath rest ... Alliance staff provides adequate lodgings, hot meals and they meet the venerable Rabbi Moshe Blankfort.Walking along the river at night, Sendehr and Rivka meet young Franz Kafka and his cousin Fegeh who invite them for a picnic hike on *Shabbos* afternoon)

12   Prague (the Golem, Maharal story is alluded to by the ninety-three-year-old Blankfort, piquing Sendehr's interest. That night, he is granted a meeting in the Rabbi's quarters, and is presented the unimaginable, highly provocative predictions)

13   en route (the Fusgeyers march out of Prague after a most eventful stay, camping on the banks of the Vltava/Moldau that night. Sendehr relates the entire Blankfort discussion to both Mordecai and Mendel that night)

14   en route (passing beyond Melnik, at a bend in the River Labe, near-tragedy strikes as the army abducts nine Fusgeyers, impressing them into the Emperor's road building brigade. Rescue plans are immediately developed and the "great escape" is underway. Successfully!)

15   en route (secreted in a vast forest ten kilome ters north of Terezin/Theresienstadt the fifty-seven members of the BirladerFusgeyer contingent wait for nightfall and march through out the night to reach the relative safety of Germany)

Germany

16   Breitnau Barracks, Imperial Germany Army
      border post.
17   en route (via Dippoldiswalde, meet the
      stragglers from Galatz Fusgeyer contingent,
      in total disarray)
18   Dresden
19   Dresden (*Shabbos* , and a less than warm
      welcome from the community. The play is not
      received in the manner the cast had been
      accustomed to in other cities. First contact
      with the German Jew, those of the so-called
      "Mosaic Persuasion", later dubbed *"Moishe
      Yidden"* by a knowing Branko)
20   en route (via Moritzburg and Radeburg, heavy
      rains)
21   Grossenhain (rains make the roadways
      impossible to negotiate as Shalom and
      Yaakov discover empty barn...the only
      available shelter since leaving Dresden)
22   Grossenhain (unable to move on, as streams
      in the vicinity overrun their banks, washing
      out two nearby bridges)
23   Grossenhain (fourth day of an incessant
      deluge)
24   Elsterwerda (break in the weather,
      finally...the Pastor Hof meeting just north of
      Grossenhain, camped in Elsterwerda, and an
      evening performance of the improvised
      "Theater of the Absurd")
25   Munchhausen (dangerous stone-throwing
      incident in the town of Finsterwalde ... move
      on to Munchhausen for the Sabbath rest day,
      weather turns sunny and very warm1)
26   Munchhausen (*Shabbos*...rest day)
      en route (via Luckau and Golssen

27 en route (via Baruth and Neuhof, closing in on Berlin and three billboards announcing Buffalo Bill, Sarah Bernhardt and Berlin's visitor restrictions)

28 en route (via Zossen and Mittenwalde)

29 Rangsdorf (last encampment before Berlin, in another derelict barn...and the very welcome announcement for the happy troop that Berlinwould be a ten day stopover, for the very practical reasons listed in Chapter 18)

30 Berlin (the march into Berlin is one none will forget...Sendehr's "Black Boots" found in Chapter 18 describes the aura in full)

July 1 Berlin (Fusgeyers "tour" the city)

2 Berlin (meeting with Max Nordau)

3 Berlin (*Shabbos*)

4 Berlin (Theodor Herzl dies the evening before...Buffalo Bill's Wild West Show on American Independence Day)

5 Berlin (The meeting with the Romanian Ambassador)

6 Berlin (the next five days are spent in visiting the sights and sounds of the city, the notoriously impoverished Jewish quarter, the Scheunenviertel, Berlin, a hotbed of anti-Semitic literature, everywhere)

7 Berlin

8 Berlin

9 Berlin

10 Berlin (farewell to Berlin ... *Shabbos* at the Oranienburg *shul*)

11 en route (out of Berlin, overnight at Nauen where they meet a destitute family of emigrants from the Pale...they give shelter, clothing and food to the children and the family)

12	Friesack (Shmuel Cohn, Abe Cahan's reporter, joins the Contingent, on assignment from the "boss")
13	en route (via Rhinow, to Havelberg)
14	Domitz (via Werben, entering the River Elbe Valley)
15	en route (via Hitzacker, where Shmuel leaves for Hamburg ...and on to Dahlenburg ...daily incidents of anti-migrant emotions)
16	Lunenburg (fewer groups on road going to Bremerhaven, many more heading for the nearby Hamburg port)
17	Lunenburg (*Shabbos*, warm welcome by the Jewish community)
18	Lunenburg (parting of the ways with the Borochofsky family)
19	en route (decide to do less kilometers, not wanting to get to the port at Bremerhaven any sooner than the 28th)
20	Hanstedt (via Garlstorf, just south of Hamburg)
21	en route (via Welle, with a major heat wave making noontime walking very uncomfortable, decide to wait it out near Tostedt)
22	Tostedt (violent thuderstorms break the heat wave)
23	Zeven (taunting by locals more vociferous than ever, the closer to the port they get, some isolated incidents of rock-throwing)
24	Zeven (*Shabbos* ...German military unit checks transit papers)
25	Brackel (Mendel, Esther announce that a child will be born!)
26	Brackel
27	Kuhstedt
28	Beverstedt

29   Bremerhaven (arrive amid extremely chaotic
     conditions)
29   to August 15th (in Bremerhaven, until their
     ship sails)
(August 8–15, quarantine period)

Cincinnatus leaves port at 8:33 am, according to Zed-Zed's
watch, on August 15, 1904, with fifty-seven Birlader
Fusgeyers on board.

GLOSSARY

Most of the conversations in *The Wayfarers* are in the Yiddish language, albeit "translated" and printed in English. Accordingly, I have liberally sprinkled in Yiddish words and phrases, perhaps in defiance of those eschatological naysayers who have pronounced the language dead and forgotten. Think of it as a small contribution to what growing numbers of contraposers see as a rebirth of the *mamaloshen*. To quote the anonymous benefactor for Abe Cahan's 1904 trip to Berlin (Chapter 19):

"The Yiddish language is drenched with tears, and it's much too rich to be silenced ..."

The alphabetical glossary that follows mainly includes words in the European Yiddish of the 19th and 20th centuries as used in the book, as well as those in the Hebrew, Romanian, German, Hungarian and Russian languages ...indicated by (Heb), (Rom), (G), (Hu) and (R), respectively. Because Yiddish has drawn freely from numerous other languages, ancient and modern, please excuse what you may inevitably find to be slightly different spellings and translations. Some of the words, although they are in the original Hebrew, have been so long associated with Yiddish speech I have not classified them as Hebrew.

(Note: "ch" and "kh" sounds are mostly guttural, coming from the back of the throat, vibrating the uvula. Try it. It's not so difficult.)

A

abi gezunt zoll er zein	as long as he will be well
ahl chait (Heb)	forgive me
ahleh (alle)	all
ahneevesdik	humble

583

alef, bais (Heb)	a, b (as in a,b,c,d, etc.)
alivai (halevai)	it should only be so (hopefully)
aliyah (Heb)	to go up (to emigrate to Israel)
alte (alteh,alta)	old
aroysgevarfen di gelt	thrown away money
auf riffen	call up (to the synagogue's dais)
auf wiedersehen (G)	good-bye, see you again
ayn ayntsikeh	one and only
ayn calohenu (Heb)	prayer service closing hymn
aynekel (ayneklach)	grandchild (grandchildren)
azeh geht dos	that's the way it is

B

balabusteh	a praiseworthy housewife, hostess
balagan	bedlam, noise
balagooleh	wagonmaster, teamster
baltoivim (Heb)	benefactor(s)
banditten	bandits
beshert (beshairt)	meant to be (*kismet,* master plan)
bimah	pulpit
bissel (zu essen) (bisl)	a little bit (to eat)
blozehr (bluzehr)	blower (glass blower, trumpet blower)
bocher	young man, bachelor
Boruch Hashem (Heb)	blessed be the Lord
boychick(lach)	young lad(s)
bubbeh (bubbe)	grandma
bubbeh meiseh (mayser)	grandma's tale (old wives' tale)
bulvan	a blockhead (in a nice way, usually a big strong man)
buna evrey (Rom)	good Jew
buna ziua, vorbesc Romaneshti? (Rom)	good day, do you speak Romanian?

C (now you can give the uvula a workout!)

calleh	bride
Chabad (Heb)	Acronym for wisdom, understanding and knowledge
challah	Sabbath bread
chaseneh	wedding
chazzan(hazzan)(im) (Heb)	cantor (s)
cheder	Hebrew school
chinek (tchinek..no uvula!)	tea kettle
chuppa(h)	wedding canopy
chutzpah	a lot of nerve, brazenness

D

da, da, va multzumesc foarte (Rom)	yes, yes, thank you very much
daigeh nisht	don't worry
darf zein (mashigah)	you have to be (crazy)
daven	pray
dayenu (Heb)	enough
der alte iz farfallen	the old man is finished, washed-up
der Rebbe geht redn	the Rabbi is going to speak
destul (Rom)	enough (as in *dayenu*)
Deutschland uber alles (G)	Germany over all else (national anthem)
dornishtag	Thursday
dos shtetl un dos dorf	town and village
dreck	excrement
dred erein (in der erd)	go under the earth (go to hell)
dritte	third

E

einglaybenish	superstition
emes (Heb)	(that's) the truth
entshuldig mir	forgive me
eppes essen	something to eat
erev Shabbos(Shabbat) (Heb)	Sabbath eve

ess	eat
evresc,evriesc (Rom)	Jew, Jewish, or Hebrew

F

famisht	mixed up
fantazyeh	fantasy
farbrecher	criminal, law breaker
farbrenteh(r)	someone who is "on fire" (with an idea)
farfallen	gone, finished, it's all over
farshtayst	I understand, do you understand?
feigeleh	little bird
fendl	little pan
Feteasca (Rom)	brand of Romanian wine
folg mir	believe me, listen to my advice
folg mich(mikh) a gang	believe me, that's a long way
foon (fon)	from
freilach(er)	happy, a happy one
fress	eat (a lot)
fuhrt gezunt (gesunt)	go in health, travel in health

G

gantzer velt	the whole world
Gan Eden (Heb)	Garden of Eden, paradise
Gaon (Heb)	a genius
gatkes	underpants
gehenna	hell
gehuckteh yinglish (fleish)	chopped-up English language, chopped meat
genug	enough already!
geshmuck(teh)	healthy, well
gevalt (oy gevalt!)	a cry of fear, or amazement, wonderment
gluhz(glohz)(glezzaleh)	glass (small glass)
goldeneh medina	the golden land
golem	a robotic, lifeless figure
goniff	thief

586

goy, goyim	Gentile(s)
gott tsedanken	thanks to God
grob	uncouth, ill-mannered, low class
groisseh (soldat,bochers)	big (soldier, young man)
gulyash (Hu)	Hungarian stew
guten abend (G)	good evening
guten Shabbos	good Sabbath (greeting)

H

Haman	Minister of ancient Persia, particularly cruel to the Jews in his realm (synonym for anti-Semite)
heimish(e) (haimishe)	informal, comfortable, welcoming
ha melech (Heb)	the king
ha tikvah (Heb)	the hope (Israel's national anthem)
havdalah (Heb)	service for ending the Sabbath day
hawt zein eigeneh mishigas	has his own irrational ways
heilige (G)	holy
hondler	a slick salesman, negotiator

I

imu vorbitzi pare rau (Rom)	I'm sorry, I don't speak......
indicatzi mi mi va rog (Rom)	please show me
in gantzen(gantsen)	total, everything
intratzi va rog (Rom)	come in, please

K

kaddish (Heb)	mourner's prayer, giving glory to God
kashruth (Heb)	the Jewish dietary laws (in observance of)

587

kayn eyn oreh	no evil eye (phrase to ward off a curse)
ken gehen	can go
khaverim (chaverim) (Heb)	friends, comrades
kichlach	egg pastries
kiddush (Heb)	sanctification
kinder, kindeh (kindelach)	children, little children
kishke	intestine
klayneh (kleine)	small
klezmer (klezmorim)	musical group, musicians
knaker	big shot
kopp(keppeleh)	one's head, brain, little boys head (term of endearment)
kosatske (R)	wild Russian dance
kosher (Heb)	appropriate, permissible, in full compliance with Biblical dietary laws
krank, krankshvester	sick, nurse
kugel (lokshn)	pudding (noodle pudding)
kvittlech	notes (on little pieces of paper)
kvell(n)	to burst with pride, bursting with pride
L	
landsman,	a person from your district or town, people
landsleiter	from your hometown or district
lang leben	a long life, long live (so and so)
la revedere (Rom)	goodbye
l'chaim (chayim) (Heb)	to life (a toast)
lekach	cake
lokshen	noodles
luftmensch	one who makes a living from thin air
l'shana haba'ah b'America	next year in America

(Yerushalayim) (Heb)	(Jerusalem)

M

ma'arev (Heb)	in the evening (evening prayer)
macher (groisseh macher)	one who has made things happen (a successful person)
mach(t)	make (makes)
mach nisht kein tumul	don't make noise
maidel(e), maidelach	girl (young woman), little girl(s)
mamaliga (Rom)	corn mush (Romanian staple dish)
mamaloshen(mamaloshn)	the Yiddish language, mother tongue
mandelbroit	almond bread (Jewish biscotti!)
marea Britanie (Rom)	Great Britain
masheen (mashine)	a machine, usually an automobile
mashgiach (Heb)	kashruth inspector
mashiach (Heb)	messiah (an anointed one)
mashiganah	crazy person (are you crazy, mad, nuts?)
mashigah(meshugah)	crazy (you'd have to be crazy, mad, nuts!)
maven	expert
mayshescaynem	old age home (retirement home)
mazel (tov) (Heb)	luck (good luck)
mazik	mischievous child, an imp
mechitza	curtain separating men and women in an orthodox synagogue
Mein Kampf (G)	*My Struggle* (Adolf Hitler's infamous book)
mensch	a fine human being

mezuzzah (Heb)	doorpost scroll, holding Deuteronomy, Chap.6
milchadickeh	dairy foods (non-meat)
mincha	daily late afternoon prayer
minyan	ten men (minimum required for prayer service, but women are now accepted in all but the orthodox synagogues)
mishnah torah (Heb)	a review of oral law, a codified core of the laws
mitnagdim (Heb)	religious leaders opposed to the Chassidic movement of the 18th and 19th centuries
mir tor nit	we must not (do it)
mishigas, mishigus	irrationality, madness, crazy idea
mittvoch	Wednesday (middle of the week)
Mogen Dovid (Heb)	shield (or star) of King David, (the flag containins the star)
Moishe Kapoyr	one who is upside down, a contrarian
moychel,meichel (fur di boychel)	a tasty mouthful for the stomach
mumzer(h) (mumzerim) (Heb)	bastard(s)
musaf (Heb)	prayer service

N

nar (mit a loch im kopp)	a fool (with a hole in his head)
narish(keit) (kayt)	foolish(ness)
nigun(im) (Heb)	melody, tune(s)
nisht (nit)	not
nu	well?(go on!)
nu (Rom)	no

nudnik (nudzh)	a pest (to badger someone)
noch (a mohl)	yet once more

O

omayn	amen!
ostjuden)	Jews from Eastern Europe
oy (vay)(iz mir)	Oh! Woe is me!

P

paintner	painter (of houses)
pareveh(parve) (Heb)	neutral food, not dairy nor meat
paskudnyak (R) (also Polish)	scoundrel, nasty person
passaportul varog (Rom)	passport, please
payos(t), payotim (Heb)	side curls (on a boy or man)
pesachdickeh	acceptable for Passover food
pferd	horse
piatsa (Rom)	plaza, town square
pisher, pitzaleh	a nobody, a little squirt
polizei (G)	police
preevaht	private, for your eyes only
punim	one's face
puszta (Hu)	the grassy prairie of Hungary
putz (potz)	penis, a derogatory term used for "fool"

R

rabbi (Heb)	Jewish religious leader, teacher
reb	term of respect, mister, sir
rebbe	a chassidic rabbi
rebbitzen	wife of a rabbi
reicheh	a rich, wealthy person
restaurantul (Rom)	restaurant
ribono shel olam (Heb)	Lord of the Universe
richtigeh	the real thing, a real one

ruggelach	rolled pastry
Rushiseh	Russian, a person from Russia

S

saramura de peshte (Rom)	Romanian grilled fish dish
savarina (Rom)	rum-soaked cake (savarine, French)
sehr (gut)	very (good)
scrietzi va rog (Rom)	write it out, please
scuzatzi ma (Rom)	excuse me
Shabbos (Shabbat- Heb)	Sabbath
shadchan	matchmaker (marriage broker)
shah (shtill)	quiet! be still!
shamus	janitor, beadle, sexton
shayn(eh)	beautiful
shema (sh'ma) (Heb)	hear ("Hear O Israel" prayer)
shiddach	a marriage match
shicker (shikorim)	a drunk (drunks)
shicksie, shicksa	a non-Jewish woman, girl
shiva (Heb)	mourning period of seven days
shlemiel	a social misfit
shlemazel	a chronically unlucky person
shlepper	someone who pulls a conveyance (a cart, a sled), or a nee'er-do-well
shloomp (y)	unkempt person, raggedly clothed
shmateh	rag
shnor(r)(er)	to beg, one who begs, a moocher
shochet	one who kills chickens ritually
shpatzier	walk

shtarkeh	strong
shtetl	small town, townlet (not a village)
shtiebel (shtieblach)	small place(s) of worship
shtimme	voice
shul	synagogue
shundeh	shame
shweig (nisht fur die kinder!)	be quiet! (not for the children to hear!)
shver (zu zayn a Yid)	difficult (to be a Jew)
siman tov (Heb)	a good sign (along with good luck)
simcha(h) (Heb)	joyous celebration

T

taiglach	honey-dipped pastry
takeh	really? for sure?
tallis (tallit- Heb)	prayer shawl
takeh	really, indeed?
tateh	father, dad, papa
teffilin (Heb)	phylacteries
teivl (tayvul)	devil, in a playful sense
tikkun olam (Heb)	the responsibility to repair the world
tomovateh	an intellectually-challenged person
tor nit	must not
trayf (eh)	non-kosher
tsatskeh, tsatski	a little toy, plaything (loose woman)
tsimus	stewed fruits, a mess, a mix-up
tsitter	shake, as if afraid
tsudreyter	one who is confused, demented
tuchus (tuches)	buttocks, rear end
tumul	commotion, ado

tyereh,tyer	dear(s), dear (as in expensive)
tzadik (Heb)	a righteous man
tzedakah (Heb)	charity

U

umgepahtchkit	without form or sense, hap-hazard
umgeveyntlekh oder gevyntlekh	unusual or usual
unde esta sinagoga (Rom)	where is the synagogue?
unser(eh)	our(s)
utca (Hu)	street, avenue

V

vayter, veiter	further(more)
velt	world
vershluganeh(masheens)	annoying machines, damned automobiles
vershtehen(zie)(farshtayst)	understand, do you understand?
ver vaist	who knows?
vier(chazzanim)	four (cantors)
vilde (banditten)	wild (bandits)
viszont latashro (Hu)	goodbye
voch	week
vorbitz engleza (Rom)	do you speak English?
vos vet zayn (zein), vet zayn	what will be, will be (i.e. que sera, sera)
vunderlech	wonderful

Y

yarmulkeh	skull cap
yenims velt	the world of the others, underworld
yenteh, yenta	busybody, gossip (female)
yeshiva bocher	young student (at religious school)

Yid(den), Yidl, Yiddlach	Jew(s), little Jew(s)
Yiddish	Jewish, the language
Yiddishe nishomer	Jewish soul
Yiddishe nomen	Jewish name
Yiddishkayt(keit)	Jewishness, Jewish feeling
yingel, yinglach	young boy(s)
Yinglish	fractured Yiddish, mixed with English, or vice versa
yontifdickeh	special for the holiday

Z

zaydeh	grandfather
zayt ges(z)unt (gezint)	be well
zeesa	sweet one
zhid (R)	Jew (in a derogatory sense)
zhido, zheedo (Hu)	Jew (in the same sense)
zhoolik (farbrecher)	hooligan, unsavory one (criminal)
zvei(zwei) mohl, dritte mohl	second time, third time

Note: Yiddish was the language of the Fusgeyers and millions of others who came to America seeking freedom in the latter half of the 19th century and during the 20th century. The majority of Holocaust survivors in the world today also claim Yiddish as their primary language. Just prior to World War II, it is estimated that there were over 12,000,000 Yiddish-speakers in the world...a number which has been drastically reduced.

If you enjoyed the audacious character of Branko Horvitch, you will be pleased to know that there is much more to come

BRANKO

A Novel

In praise of a good man's journey through life's adventure

(Coming in 2004, the 100th anniversary of The Fusgeyer Trek)